JUBILEE TRAIL

Jubilee Trail

GWEN BRISTOW

CHICAGO
REVIEW
PRESS

Cover design: Joan Sommers Design
Cover image: Digital illustration by T. J. Romero. Original images of c. 1866
wagon train and mid-1800 daguerreotype of unknown woman courtesy of the
Library of Congress.

Copyright © 1950 by Gwen Bristow
Copyright © renewed 1978 by Gwen Bristow
Foreword by Nancy E. Turner copyright © 2006 by Nancy E. Turner
Foreword by Sandra Dallas copyright © 2006 by Sandra Dallas
All rights reserved
This edition published by Chicago Review Press, Incorporated
814 North Franklin Street
Chicago Illinois 60610
ISBN-13: 978-1-55652-601-5
ISBN-10: 1-55652-601-6
Printed in the United States of America
5 4 3 2 1

FOR BRUCE

FOREWORD
by Nancy E. Turner

To PICK UP a copy of *Jubilee Trail* is to step back in time to an era of high social polish and a certain sense of security—the conviction that the settling of the United States of America was the best opportunity the world had to offer. This feeling adds emphasis to Gwen Bristow's charming and disarming narrative style. *Jubilee Trail* is a classic Western, a lush romance, an action adventure, and a survivor story, told with 1950s sensibilities. It rings with truths—about right and wrong, good people in hard circumstances, and perseverance against adversity—that deserve to be reckoned with.

Complexities of character abound, and the depth with which each character is depicted makes the reader's trek across the early frontier as intriguing as the protagonist's—Garnet, a young woman who comes of age as we travel with her. Bristow's words go down like a drink of cool water on a dusty Western day as they draw portrait after portrait, every scene filled with action, until the reader closes the final cover and recognizes how skillfully the author has suspended our disbelief. This romantic depiction of the American West sets itself up simply as a memorable framing of a period of time, a coup d'oeil of a moment gone by, but it has become, in retrospect, a part of our history.

FOREWORD
by Sandra Dallas

WHEN I WAS fifteen, I spent a week at my grandparents' house in Moline, Illinois. Granddad was a railroad man, operating a switch engine in the Rock Island yards, but he had a romantic streak, and his bookshelves were filled with historic novels. That was where I discovered *Jubilee Trail*, and in just a few days I devoured Gwen Bristow's story of two women who go west in the mid-1840s. *Jubilee Trail* was the first epic novel about the West I'd ever read, and I loved the majesty of the western trail as well as the self-reliance of the two heroines, Garnet and Florinda. After all, this was 1954, and independent women in fiction were a scarce lot.

Already aspiring to be a writer, I promised myself that one day I would write my own novel about the West. Although over forty-five years passed before that book, *The Chili Queen*, was published, I never forgot the richness of Gwen Bristow's story. *Jubilee Trail* was in the back of my mind as I wrote *The Chili Queen*, and I hoped some impressionable young girl might read it and discover for herself the grandeur of the West and its tradition of strong women.

A half-century has gone by since I read *Jubilee Trail*, and I picked up the book again with trepidation. How many times have we returned to a favorite book of our youth, only to find it is really pulp? Would *Jubilee Trail* be such a disappointment? That original cover was not encouraging. The painting of Garnet, with her bright red lips and black curls, made her look less like a pioneer in 1845 than a model of 1950, the year the book was published. The book's heft—564 pages—warned me it might be just another of those overwritten epics so popular in the 1950s. Moreover, the *New York Times* review of February 5, 1950, called it "ponderous" and pointed out that Bristow took six pages to tell how a wound made by a poisoned arrow is cauterized with a hot iron. But then, who would expect the *Times* to like such a full-blown Western saga? Despite my misgivings, I plunged ahead, and I discovered after a few pages that I was as captivated with *Jubilee Trail* now as I had been as a teenager.

Jubilee Trail is the story of Garnet, a proper young New Yorker, who marries Oliver Hale, a fur trader, and sets out with him for California. In New Orleans, the couple meets Florinda, a "variety actress." (In 1950s novels, heroines were never called *hookers*.) The three are reunited in Santa Fe and travel the treacherous Jubilee Trail to California. Once there, Garnet discovers that neither California nor her husband is what she expected. Oliver's brother, the tyrannical Charles, controls the family *rancho* and Oliver as well, to Garnet's disgust. Moreover, Oliver has kept a secret from Garnet that threatens to destroy them all. As her life falls apart, Garnet turns to Florinda and to John Ives, her husband's closest friend, for support. This is not just a Western epic, it is also a romance, and by page 564 Garnet has discovered a great deal about love and about herself. Little wonder the book became a bestseller and Bristow a celebrated author.

Naturally, Bristow was proud of the book and its popularity. In a December 3, 1950, *New York Times* interview, she told a reporter, "Did I wonder about having written a poor book because it was popular? No, not at all. I wrote the best book I could, and I was mighty happy that so many people liked it." Success didn't alter her life, she said, although she did go out and buy a new car.

Even without *Jubilee Trail*, Bristow (1903–1980) was a celebrated writer. She began her career by collaborating on mysteries with her husband, Bruce Manning. Later she branched out on her own with what she called her "Plantation Trilogy"—*Deep Summer*, *The Handsome Road*, and *This Side of Glory*. Those books, like *Jubilee Trail*, were prized by readers for their rich historical settings, finely drawn characters, and tidy endings.

Of course, *Jubilee Trail* is a novel of the era in which it was published. The dialogue smacks of 1940s expressions. There are pages filled with adoring glances and no sex. And the book *is* just a little bit ponderous. But those flaws don't interfere with the narrative. In fact, some fifty-five years after *Jubilee Trail* was first published, such idiosyncrasies actually add to the book's charm; they let us view 1840s California through 1950 eyes.

Then, of course, there's something to be said for a novel that makes you feel fifteen again.

JUBILEE TRAIL

ONE

IN THE SUMMER of 1844, Garnet Cameron graduated from Miss Wayne's Select Academy for Young Ladies. This was a boarding-school on a country estate in upper Manhattan, and Garnet had been a pupil there for four years. On graduation day she was awarded three medals: for music, horsemanship, and politeness.

Garnet was halfway between her eighteenth and nineteenth birthdays. She had black hair, so smooth and shiny that it had blue lights in the sun. Her eyes were gray, fringed with heavy black lashes, and her cheeks were so red that she had sometimes been accused of painting them. In spite of her rich coloring she was not beautiful. Her face was too rugged to meet any ideal of beauty; her forehead was too square and her jaw was too strong and her lips were too full and red. But she had a firm slim body, her waistline was a mere trifle, and the clothes they were wearing just now were admirably designed to show a well-set figure like hers. A daytime dress covered a girl from throat to instep, but the bodice fitted almost as if it had been pasted on, and the skirt flared just enough to emphasize a tiny waistline without being too full for graceful movement. Garnet was very graceful. At Miss Wayne's Academy part of her daily routine had consisted of walking up and down a circular staircase with a book balanced on her head.

She was perfectly healthy, and looked it, and she took a great interest in living. Garnet would have liked to know all about everything. Her main complaint about the world was that it had given her so little chance to know anything at all. She seldom said any such thing out loud. After years of good breeding, Garnet knew that nobody wanted to hear a young lady speak her opinions.

Garnet lived in Union Square in the city of New York. In Union Square the houses stood around a park, where in summer a foun-tain played all day. Children rolled their hoops under the trees, and ladies and gentlemen strolled along the gravel walks. Whether in the green of summer, or in winter when the trees were bare and the windows around the park were rosy with firelight, Union Square had an air of well-being. Anybody could have seen that this was a nice neighborhood and the families who lived here were nice people. Garnet's father was Mr. Horace Cameron, vice-president of a bank in Wall Street. Her mother was a charming woman who had found life agreeable so far and expected it to remain so. Garnet had two younger brothers, named Horace, Jr., and Malcolm, who went to the grammar school that prepared boys for Columbia College. They were a pleasant family, well-bred and well-behaved. On graduation day at Miss Wayne's, when Garnet received her medals and made a curtsy of respect, her mother's friends said she looked like an ideal of proper young ladyhood. Or she would have, if only she had not had such violent red-and-black coloring. And it was a pity her features were not more delicate. But at any rate, she was a nice girl and no doubt she would make a good marriage.

When Garnet got home that evening she put the medals into her bureau drawer. As she shut the drawer she gave a sigh of relief. Her schooldays were over. In a few weeks more, as soon as she could get some clothes, she was going to take a holiday with her mother at Rockaway Beach. They were going to stay at a fashionable hotel and meet a lot of people, and she would never have to think about Miss Wayne's Select Academy any more. Now at last she was grown up, and she had a right to expect that something exciting was going to happen to her.

But at first, nothing happened.

She received two proposals of marriage, both of which she declined as fast as possible. The first offer came from a young gentleman she met that summer, while she and her mother were at Rockaway Beach. He belonged to a good family, but Garnet thought he was so stupid that he ought to be charitably locked up somewhere. As usual she did not say what she thought. Her mother had taught her so well how to do these things that when she refused him the young man got the impression that Garnet was going to remember him wistfully as long as she lived.

The second proposal came in September, after she had come back to New York. The young man's name was Henry Trellen. Garnet's parents were disappointed that she would not have him, for he would have been a brilliant match. Henry Trellen was enormously rich, and an only child. He lived with his widowed mother in a darkly magnificent house on Bleecker Street. The house reminded Garnet of a mausoleum, and Henry's mother reminded her of a marble angel on a tombstone, and Henry himself bored her to the yawning point. She thought she would as soon be locked up in a cemetery for the rest of her life as be married to him.

2

She did not say this. She said that after careful study of her heart, she was sure she did not love him.

Her parents did not insist. They had married for love and they wanted her to do the same. She had plenty of time, and her mother saw to it that she had ample chances to meet eligible young gentlemen.

Garnet loved her parents, for they were sweet and lovable people. She would have liked to please them. But she detested the eligible young gentlemen. They were often handsome and sometimes rich, but they were always dull. They were so stuffy with good manners that they acted as if young ladies were not quite human. To hear them talk, you would have thought there must always be a haze of make-believe between the two sexes, through which men and women must never see each other plainly. Garnet danced with them and flirted with them, and did it rather well, but she could not get excited about it. For Garnet found no relish in saying one thing and meaning another; by nature she was as simple and direct as a shower of rain. The system of whispers and head-tossings and fluttering lashes by which young ladies were supposed to get husbands, seemed to her just plain silly. She could do it, but her heart was not in it and it made her tired.

A girl must have beaus, of course, but Garnet wondered if there was not, anywhere on earth, a young man who would talk to her as if he and she were two reasonable people living in the same world. She told herself there must be such a man. There might even be one in New York.

But though she had lived there all her life, she did not know much about New York. Garnet thought about it often that fall, as she stood at her window and watched the trees of Union Square, red in the crackling October wind. New York, New York—such a gay, thrilling town, and she could have so little of it! There were so many places in New York where she was not allowed to go, so many streets that she had never even walked on.

New York was growing like a morning-glory vine. Now in 1844 it was a town of nearly four hundred thousand people, a hundred thousand more than had lived here ten years ago. They had a railroad to Philadelphia and another to White Plains; they had ferryboats that went every five minutes to Brooklyn; and they had steamcars that left the City Hall Depot every fifteen minutes for Harlem. They had splendid public baths, where for twenty-five cents you could stand under a shower or lie in a marble bathtub. At Castle

Garden, across the bridge from the Battery, they had two swimming pools, one for gentlemen and one for ladies. They had fountains in the parks and fire-hydrants on the streets, for New York had the finest waterworks in the world.

Broadway started at the Battery and ended at Fourteenth Street. If you walked these two brilliant miles you could see all the most famous places in New York. The gayest part of town was City Hall Park. If you were walking up Broadway toward the park, you would pass the Astor House on your left, at the corner of Broadway and Vesey Street. The Astor House was the finest hotel in America. It was five stories high, with white steps leading to an entrance between white columns. Facing it across Broadway you saw Barnum's Museum. The museum had a big sign showing you mermaids and sea-serpents, to hint at what you could see inside. Just above the museum you came to the park.

Around the park you passed restaurants and theaters, saloons and gambling palaces. If you were rich enough you could dine at John Florence's, at Broadway and Park Place. Or you could go to the Park Theater and see the greatest stars in the world. If your taste was less refined, you could risk your money in the gambling rooms, or you could see a show offering music and lovely girls. If you were a lovely girl yourself, you could visit the studios of fashionable artists, who would paint your face on ivory and frame it in gold. It would cost you a hundred dollars, but if you were pretty enough it was worth it. Here you also saw Plumbe's Galleries, where for five dollars they would clamp your head in an iron thing and take your picture. It was great fun, but the pictures always had a scared look; for as soon as they clamped your head in the iron thing you began to wonder what would become of you if the place caught fire.

But there was not much danger of fire. A man was always on duty in the cupola on top of the City Hall, to look for fires. The City Hall was fifty feet high, so the man could see over the whole town. If he saw a fire he rang a bell, the number of strokes telling where it was, and the wagons rushed forth to put it out.

Around the park, Broadway roared and clattered. But as you crossed Chambers Street on your way uptown, you noticed that things were getting less noisy. For here you were passing the great stores of fashion, the greatest of which was the store of Mr. Alexander Stewart. As you went by Stewart's you heard the clop-clop of highbred horses and the voices of ladies; you passed windows full of cut glass and silver, furs and velvets and silks, fine gauzes

4

that tumbled in the sunshine like waterfalls. As you went on uptown, Broadway grew shy and respectful, minding its manners. By the time you reached Union Square you could hardly hear the downtown noise at all.

Garnet had shopped on Broadway with her mother, she had been to concerts and to plays that were suitable for young ladies. But she knew this was only a fraction of New York. She would have loved to investigate those exciting places around City Hall Park, and those streets that led mysteriously away from it. Of course she never said so. Her parents would have been amazed, and hurt. Even if she said yes to one of the eligible young gentlemen and became a married woman, she was sure she would never go inside a gambling palace or a naughty theater. The whole town was full of things that ladies were not supposed to be interested in. Well-bred young men took it for granted that Garnet was not interested in things like that. They took it for granted that she was not interested in anything except getting one of them for a husband. Good manners kept Garnet from telling them she had turned down Henry Trellen, who was the greatest catch of them all. But she often wished she could.

From June to October, Garnet wondered if nothing was ever going to happen to her. And then, one day in October, something happened. A young man named Oliver Hale came to town. And though neither her father nor her mother knew it, Oliver started the most enchanting ripples on the smooth white surface of her life.

Things took place so strangely. It was very odd to think that if there hadn't been that scandalous murder last summer she never would have met Oliver at all.

The murder had occurred in August, while Garnet and her mother were at Rockaway Beach. Two men were shot in a brawl at a gambling palace in New York. One of the men was an ex-convict of uncertain origin; his death had interested nobody. At least, it had not interested any of Garnet's friends. If the other victim had been like him she would never have heard of the murder.

But the other victim was Mr. Francis Selkirk, aged forty-six, a wealthy man who had lived in Washington Square. Mr. Selkirk was a gentleman of imprudent habits, used to frequenting haunts of sin.

5

But he was also rich and well connected, and he had recently married a high-born lady about half his age. His death in a gambling-house brawl started a buzz of talk at the summer hotel. Garnet was immensely interested, but nobody would tell her anything about it. The older ladies stopped whispering as soon as she came near, and her mother told her positively that she must not show indecent curiosity by asking questions. So Garnet knew almost nothing about the Selkirk murder, except that it had happened, and that the police seemed unable to fix upon the guilty person.

Mr. Selkirk's relatives made angry demands that his murderer be brought to justice. But this was very difficult. There were many witnesses, for the gambling house had been full of people that evening. But most of them had been patronizing the bar, and their stories were not to be trusted. The weeks went by, nobody was put on trial for the Selkirk murder, and people began to talk of other things.

This was all Garnet knew. Except that she always had an unbecoming curiosity about things that did not concern young ladies, she did not dream that the Selkirk scandal was of any importance to her.

But it happened that Mr. Selkirk had died without making a will. His estate was put into the hands of his bank. Garnet's father was Mr. Horace Cameron, vice-president of the bank, in charge of settling estates. One item of the Selkirk property was a store dealing in cloth and household goods. Mr. Cameron sold the building, and since Mr. Selkirk's widow was willing to take a loss in order to have the business done quickly, he advertised the merchandise for sale at a low price.

This was the reason Oliver Hale came to the bank one day in October, and asked for Mr. Cameron. Oliver had just arrived in New York. He had never heard of Mr. Selkirk and was not interested in the manner of that gentleman's death; but he had seen the advertisement of cloth and household goods at a bargain. Since these were the staples of his trade, he told Mr. Cameron he would be glad to have a look at the lot.

Oliver was a prairie trader. He had come to New York to buy merchandise, which he would pack into covered wagons and take to the Mexican provinces that lay west of the United States. He was twenty-six years old. That was young for such an arduous enterprise, Mr. Cameron said. Oliver laughed and replied that he had been in the prairie trade since he was eighteen. Most of the

6

men in the trade were under thirty, he added; when they got older, they usually settled down to an easier way of living.

Oliver was a genial young fellow, his talk of frontier commerce was interesting, and one day Mr. Cameron brought him home to dinner. Mrs. Cameron, who had rather expected anybody from the frontier to be uncertain about forks, was agreeably surprised at Oliver's polished manners. To her adroit questions, Oliver replied that he had grown up in Boston. He laughed as he told them how he had left Harvard in the middle of his college course, because frontier adventures were more to his liking than Latin and Greek.

Garnet listened with interest, but she was not at all sure that she liked this Mr. Hale. She thought he was the oddest-looking man she had ever seen. He gave her such an impression of size and strength that she was surprised to notice that his height was only average. He had big thick muscles, knotty under his clothes. And though he was well dressed, in a black broadcloth suit and a brocaded vest and a linen shirt with a high stock about his neck, he wore his clothes as though he felt silly in them. He made her think of an actor dressed up in a fancy costume and trying to pretend he was used to it.

Oliver's hands were quite clean, but they were rough and horny like the hands of a day-laborer, and they looked as if he had had to do some furious scrubbing to get out the dirt. He had thick sandy curls, neatly cut but unruly; and his face was extremely puzzling. It was a rather handsome face, with merry brown eyes and a humorous mouth, but it looked as if it had been put together from two faces that did not match. The upper half was deeply tanned and weathered, and the laughter-crinkles around his eyes were white in the tan, as though he had spent months laughing at an almost unbearable glory of sun. But his cheeks and chin were as white as those of a lady who never went outdoors without a veil to shield her complexion. Garnet tried not to stare at him, but to save her life she could not help giving a quizzical glance now and then at that face of his. Once Oliver caught her eye as she looked at him across the table. He gave her a little private smile, and she blushed.

After dinner they were alone for a few minutes. The boys had been sent upstairs to do their lessons, Mrs. Cameron stopped to speak to the servants, and Mr. Cameron went to get the brandy for his guest. Garnet led Oliver into the parlor. As he drew a chair to

7

the fire for her, he smiled at her again, as though they had a secret agreement about something, and the crinkles around his eyes quivered with amusement as he said,

"I had it shaved off ten days ago, in the barber shop at the Astor House."

"Oh!" Garnet exclaimed. She put her hand to her lips, embarrassed that he had noticed her attention. But she was glad to have the matter explained. "So that's it," she went on. "You've been wearing a beard!"

He nodded. "There's no chance to shave on the trail. I looked like Robinson Crusoe when I got here. In fact, I still do." As he spoke he turned over his great laboring hands. "I got these," he said, "from dragging pack-mules over the mountains."

"Tell me about it sometime," she begged eagerly.

"I'd like to. If I asked you to go riding with me, would you say yes?"

"I—I don't think my mother would let me," Garnet answered, embarrassed again when she heard how regretful her voice sounded. "She doesn't know you well enough."

"I'll take care of that," Oliver said. He was about to say more, but just then her mother came into the parlor.

Instantly, Oliver's manner changed. He became gracious and deferential, as a gentleman should be in the presence of ladies. Though he was quite formal, he managed to be so engaging that Mrs. Cameron began to think his unusual appearance was very interesting. A man who had traveled in strange countries would be sure to enliven a dinner-party. She was giving a dinner next week, for which she needed an extra man. Just then Oliver asked her casually if she knew his aunt, Mrs. William Fortescue of Bleecker Street. Of course Mrs. Cameron knew the Fortescues; her family had lived in New York since colonial times, and she knew everybody. Before he left, Oliver had been invited to the dinner.

When he came to dinner the next week, Oliver did not get, nor even seem to want, a chance to be alone with Garnet. He made himself charming to everybody, especially the older ladies. The next morning he sent flowers to his hostess.

Garnet saw him again, at a very dull party given by that very proper aunt of his, and at other parties given by other hostesses who were glad to find so courtly a bachelor. He paid Garnet no special attention, until one day when she received a note from

8

him, asking if she would do him the honor of riding with him the next morning.

Garnet asked her mother. By this time Mrs. Cameron had no objection. She said she wished every man were as well-bred as Oliver Hale.

They mounted their horses in front of the house, and set out for the bridle-paths uptown. As they rode away, the wind spanked Garnet's red cheeks and blew her hair in little black locks across her forehead. With a grin of admiration, Oliver exclaimed,

"Now at last we can say something to each other. I like you. I like you very much."

It was so different from the way other men spoke to her that she did not know what to say. Oliver laughed mischievously and added,

"Let's be honest. You hate those damn parties as much as I do. Don't you?"

Nobody had ever said "damn" in her presence before. Garnet began a dignified rebuke, but Oliver laughed at her, and in another minute she was astonished to find herself laughing too. She asked, "Why have you been going to those parties if you didn't like them?"

"You know as well as I do," said Oliver. "I had to make a good impression on your mother before she'd have let me go out with you. Couldn't you see how hard I was working?"

Garnet was not used to such candor. She said, "Why—thank you!"

"You're welcome," said Oliver. He laughed and sighed together. "You know, Miss Cameron, I've been out of the United States for eight years. I'd forgotten American girls were brought up to be such fools. But you didn't look like a fool, even the first time I saw you."

Much as she liked his frankness, she had no idea how to answer it. So instead of trying to answer, she asked,

"Where have you been all this time?"

"Mostly in California," said Oliver.

Garnet frowned slightly. "Where?"

"California." Oliver smiled with a trace of mischief.

Garnet searched her knowledge of the world. "You're going to think I'm very ignorant, Mr. Hale," she said after a moment. "But I never heard of that country."

Oliver drew a long breath of relief. "Thank you," he said.

"For what?" asked Garnet.

"For being honest enough to say you never heard of it. Most of

9

them pretend they have. Then they call it something wrong and prove they haven't. Don't apologize. California is one of the most remote and least-known spots on earth. Very few people on this side ever heard of it."

"Where is it?" she asked with interest.

"On the Pacific Ocean."

Garnet puckered her lips, thinking. "You mean in Asia? Near China?"

"No, the Pacific Coast of North America. I'll tell you about it some day. But not now. Let's talk about you."

The next thing she knew she was telling him about Miss Wayne's Select Academy. She told him how they had taught her to stand and walk and curtsy, and how many times she had trudged up that circular staircase with a book balanced on her head. Oliver laughed and laughed, and asked how she had survived it with such a rosy healthy look about her. Garnet told him how often her red cheeks had embarrassed her. She told him about the time a new teacher had ordered her to go upstairs and wash her face, scandalized to think that a young lady should be painting herself like an actress; and how she had pressed her fingers to her cheeks and made white marks, which immediately turned red again, thus proving that no amount of soap would give her a ladylike pallor of complexion. She told him how the other girls had teased her about it. And how she had tried to drink vinegar to get pale, but the stuff made her sick. And how the teachers were always saying, "Miss Cameron, you must not walk so fast. It really does not look well. And Miss Cameron, *please* try not to laugh so much!"

Oliver was amused and sympathetic by turns. He told her he had a pretty good idea of what she was talking about. Young men at Harvard were not forbidden to laugh or to walk fast, but they were stuffed as full of nonsense as a Christmas turkey with chestnuts, and he hated it, and that was why he had gone out to the West.

Garnet had a sense of exhilaration. This was the sort of man she had been wanting to meet. They talked and talked, and by the time they came home—reluctantly, but she had to be prompt or her mother would have been concerned—she felt more at ease with him than she had ever felt with Henry Trellen or any of her other beaus.

She saw him again, at the opening of a new play at the Park Theater. They went riding together several times more. Garnet did not tell her mother how frankly they talked to each other. Mrs.

Cameron had seen Oliver's company manners, and liked them; Garnet did not want her to get the idea that he was not a proper escort.

Besides their formal meetings, Oliver often had to call at her home. Outfitting a wagon train for the prairies was no simple matter. Her father was handling a good deal of Oliver's business for him. If Oliver happened to call when her parents were not at home, naturally the servant would bring him in to be received by the young lady of the house. It was only courteous for Garnet to say, "Won't you sit down for a few minutes, Mr. Hale, and get warm by the fire?"

He had been dropping in for several weeks before she realized that he had a mysterious genius for knowing when everybody would be out but herself. By this time she was enjoying his visits too much to comment on this to her parents. She would say, "Oh by the way, father, Mr. Hale came by today with a note for you. I put it on your desk." She felt guilty, but not guilty enough to say that instead of stopping for five minutes Oliver had stayed an hour.

One morning in January, 1845, Garnet was at home practicing her music. It was a cold, bright day, and when she glanced up from the piano she could see ice flashing on the trees outside. As the sun struck the ice it sent little rainbows skittering among the branches. Garnet enjoyed watching it. She loved exciting weather, and she loved sun and rain and crackly trees and the way things grew.

Garnet's piano was in the small parlor. This was the room they used every day, to spare the big formal parlor on the other side of the hall. The small parlor was not a luxurious room, but it was a very pleasant one, with bookcases and good pictures, and deep cushioned chairs. On the table lay this morning's New York *Herald* and New York *Sun*, and the January issues of *Graham's Magazine* and *Godey's Lady's Book*. After a walk the other day, Garnet's father had brought in some pine-twigs with cones, which he had arranged on the mantel over the fireplace. He liked having green things indoors in bitter weather. Like every other room in the house, the small parlor had a look of good taste and simple comfort.

As Garnet played the piano, the light struck blue flashes from her black hair and danced up and down the folds of her dress. It was a charming dress, made of sheer white wool printed with little sprigs of red flowers. The bodice was closed in front with a row of red silk buttons, and the skirt spread from her slim waist-line and rippled on the floor around her. Her fingers were busy on the keys. Nobody would have guessed that she had declined her mother's invitation to go shopping because she had a secret hope in her mind.

She was hoping Oliver would call again this morning. The excuse she had given her mother was that she had such a lot of practicing to do. Her nineteenth birthday had occurred this month—such a little while after Christmas—and on Christmas and her birthday both she had received a lot of new music among her presents. It was important to learn the pieces, so when her friends called she would be ready to entertain them with the music they had given her. Mrs. Cameron was upstairs now, putting on her bonnet and shawl. She approved of Garnet's decision to stay at home. She was glad Garnet was so careful about showing appreciation for gifts.

Garnet's conscience pinched her slightly. It had not been really a lie, for she did have to practice. But though her mother was a darling, much more reasonable than most people, she certainly would not have approved of Garnet's being alone with any young man as much as she had been alone with Oliver this winter. She would have thought it forward and unladylike, and dangerous. And while Mrs. Cameron would have begged mercy for a forger or a thief, she had no patience with girls who were forward and un-ladylike.

Garnet finished the waltz she was playing, and put a new qua-drille in its place. As she began to play the quadrille she heard the door open. Glancing around, she saw her mother in the doorway.

Mrs. Cameron was thirty-eight years old. She was not a beauty and never had been, but she was a striking woman, tall and dark, with a figure nearly as slim as Garnet's. Ready now for the street in a costume of blending shades of green, with a camel's hair shawl and a bonnet with a sweeping plume, she was smiling hap-pily. She loved shopping, and meeting her friends among the gorgeous displays at Stewart's.

As she saw her mother, Garnet turned on the piano-stool and stood up. Mrs. Cameron smiled. She was proud of Garnet's beauti-ful manners.

"I'm going now, my dear," said Mrs. Cameron. "Is there any-thing I can get for you?"

12

"Could I have some new pink ribbon for my white cashmere?" asked Garnet. "The old ribbon got streaked. I think the iron was too hot."

"Why yes, I'll look for some. Good heavens," Mrs. Cameron exclaimed, coming toward the fireplace, "have the boys scratched up that easy-chair again?" She bent to look at some unmistakable scuffs on the mahogany, shook her head and sighed. "The way those little Hessians tumble about, you'd think we ran a gymnasium." She slapped the chair playfully, as though annoyed with it for being unable to resist the games of her two healthy young sons. "Well, it's got to be revarnished. I'll stop in at Osgood's this morning and tell them to send for it."

She started for the door, but turned around.

"Oh dear, I'm almost forgetting what I came to tell you." Quite unaware that she was bringing great news, she took a thick folded sheaf of paper from her muff. "Here's a list of goods your father left for Mr. Hale. He'll call for it some time this morning."

Garnet felt a tingle down her backbone. As she took the papers she tried to look politely interested, as though this was no more important than a scuffed chair. "Yes, Mother," she said, "I'll give it to Mr. Hale when he comes by."

"And do keep up the fires, Garnet. It's very cold." Mrs. Cameron kissed her prettily gloved fingertips and went out.

Left alone, Garnet laid the folded sheaf of paper on the table. She went to the piano and played through a few more bars of music. When she heard the front door close, her hands dropped into her lap. She went back to the table, unfolded the papers, and looked at the writing.

It was a list of merchandise, of the sort Oliver was buying from the estate of the late Mr. Selkirk. Two thousand bolts of calico, six hundred bolts of white muslin, four hundred frying pans, one thousand packages of needles, and so forth. Garnet put the list back on the table. Cloth and frying pans and needles she could understand. But there was a great deal about Oliver's trade that she did not understand.

She had asked him a lot of questions, and he had done his best to answer them. But she knew so little about the prairie country that she could hardly follow him. She had studied geography at school. Her teachers had taught her about the states along the Atlantic Ocean, and a few important places on the Mississippi River, such as New Orleans and St. Louis. But about what lay

13

west of the Mississippi River they had told her nothing at all.

But now, Garnet reflected eagerly, she had a chance to understand. Her father had just ordered a globe of the world for her little brothers to use when they studied their lessons. The globe had arrived yesterday. It was now up in the boys' room.

The boys were at school. Garnet went up to their room and got the globe. It was heavier than she had thought, but she lugged it downstairs to the small parlor. Bending over the globe, she turned it and then held it still.

Her right hand lay on the Atlantic Ocean and her left on the Pacific. Between her hands was the continent of North America. Garnet studied the map, a frown of concentration between her black eyebrows.

On the east side of the continent were the twenty-five states of the Union, and several territories. Beyond them was the heavy black line of the Mississippi River. West of the Mississippi she saw the Missouri River, and south of that was another river, the Arkansas. Both of these flowed into the Mississippi. The river-lines were clear on the map.

Garnet knew the settled part of the United States ended at the Missouri River. She had heard Oliver say that the little towns on the Missouri marked the American frontier. Beyond this river was still some United States territory, but no white people lived in that region. On the map, she found that it was labeled only with the names of the Indian tribes who hunted there.

South of the Missouri, the Arkansas River flowed east. The land belonging to the United States ended finally at a line drawn from the Arkansas. Beyond this line, everything was foreign. Down to the south lay the Republic of Texas. Below Texas was Mexico. Mexico was a big country; on the map the name started south of Texas and stretched all the way up the Pacific Coast till it reached a big square in the northwest, which was called the Oregon Territory.

The map gave her plenty of information about the eastern half of the continent. But it told her very little about the rest. Except for the letters along the Pacific Coast saying "Mexico," and the other letters higher up saying "Oregon Territory," the whole western half of the continent was nothing but a big ivory space. The space was blank but for capital letters spread out to say, "GREAT AMERICAN DESERT."

At school, they had not taught her anything about the western

14

half of North America. Until Oliver came to town, she had never thought about it. Everybody knew, or thought they knew, that there was nothing out there but a lot of useless plains with some buffaloes and Indians rambling around.

But Oliver said there was a great deal more than this. Oliver said that this ivory space, trackless on the map, was not really trackless. Across it lay a long thin line, the mark made by the turning of wagon-wheels. Every spring, as soon as the snow had melted on the prairies, merchant caravans went winding into the West.

Until Oliver told her about them, Garnet had never heard of those intrepid men who carried their goods out beyond the American frontier. But Oliver knew, because Oliver was himself a prairie trader. Oliver had been out there. Oliver had been to that country with the strange beautiful name, California.

Garnet scowled at the globe. This was the best globe that could be bought. It was new and up-to-date for the study of geography in this year 1845. But she could not find a country called California.

She looked along the Missouri River, along the Arkansas, and through Mexico and the Republic of Texas. She looked at the Great American Desert. She looked all the way up into western Canada. She could not find it.

Oliver said he had been living in California for eight years. He was going back there this summer. She could not believe he would have made it up to tease her.

But one thing she was sure of. California was not on the map.

T W O

OLIVER STOOD by the fireplace, his elbow on the mantel. He had arrived twenty minutes before. Garnet was bending over the globe again.

For several minutes now, they had not said anything. Oliver was quite content not to talk. He enjoyed watching her, as the light flashed on her blue-black hair and her rosy cheeks.

But Garnet wanted to talk. She looked up from the globe.

"I want to ask you something, Mr. Hale," she said.

Oliver grinned at her. His thick sandy curls were tumbling over his forehead, in the way of curls that would not obey a hairbrush.

Though he had been in New York three months, his prairie tan had been so deep that his forehead was still darker than his chin. He was regarding her with the gay irreverence that he still never showed when her parents were around.

"Go ahead, Miss Cameron," he said to her.

"Were you teasing me," asked Garnet, "when you told me there was a far country called California?"

"Teasing you?" he exclaimed with a start. "Of course not. Why Miss Cameron, I live there!"

"Yes, that's what you said. But if there is such a country, why isn't it on the map?"

Oliver began to laugh. "I told you," he answered, "California is one of the least-known spots on earth."

"But where is it?" she asked.

Oliver came over to her. He put his big hard fingers on the coast that lay along the Pacific Ocean.

"It's here," he said. "California isn't a separate nation. It's the northernmost province of Mexico." Looking down at the map, he shook his head. "But the coastline doesn't look like that. They've put the harbor of San Diego too far north, and they've made just the merest dent for San Francisco Bay. In fact, it's *all* wrong."

"But why don't they get it right?" she asked impatiently.

"I suppose they don't know any better. So few Americans have ever been to California."

"I see," said Garnet, nodding thoughtfully. She reminded him, "You've been promising to tell me about the prairie trade. Maybe the globe won't be much help, but I'll try to keep up with you. Please tell me."

"What do you want to know?"

Garnet drew up a chair before the globe and sat down. "Everything. How long have the traders been crossing the prairies?"

"I'm not sure. Twenty or thirty years."

"Always by the same road?"

Oliver sat down on the arm of a big chair near her. He smiled as he looked at her. Oliver's mind was not on his business at the moment, but he answered readily.

"It's not a road, Miss Cameron. It's just the mark of the wheels. The wagons have cut deep ruts in the earth, and the ruts are hardened as though they'd been cut in stone. You can see the track for miles ahead of you. In the distance it's like a long blue line."

Garnet drew in her breath eagerly. She looked at the globe,

wishing she could see that long blue line. Oliver's smile widened as he watched her.

"Do you know," he said, "your hair flashes like a blackbird's wing?"

Garnet was looking at the globe. Without raising her eyes, she said,

"Please don't be like everybody else! Saying silly things about how I look. I know I'm not beautiful."

"Aren't you?" asked Oliver.

She did not answer. Oliver got up from the arm of the chair and sat on the floor, linking his big rough hands around his knees. From where he sat, he could look up at her lowered face. His lips quivered with amusement.

"Why no," he said, "now that you remind me, you're not beautiful." He chuckled softly. "My dear girl, you don't need to be."

Garnet's red cheeks got redder. "I don't know what you're talking about," she said shortly.

"Then maybe you wouldn't understand," said Oliver, "if I told you that's the greatest compliment I ever paid a girl in my life."

As so often before with him, Garnet did not know what to say. She was not looking at him, but she could feel his eyes stroking her. Instead of answering, she said,

"I thought you were going to tell me about the trading caravans."

"Oh yes, so I was," Oliver said promptly. But though she still could not look at him she could feel him looking at her. "Where was I?" he asked.

"You hadn't begun," said Garnet. "Where do the wagons start?"

"From Independence. That's a town in Missouri. It's the last town on the American frontier."

Garnet felt relieved to have the conversation become impersonal. Besides, she really did want to know. "And the traders go all the way to California every year?" she asked.

"Oh no. Not the traders who start from Independence. They don't go all the way to California. They can't. It's too far."

"But you've been there!" Garnet objected.

"Yes. But you can't make the journey both ways in the same year. There are two groups of Western traders, you see. Every spring they start from opposite sides of the continent. They meet in the middle, and exchange goods. Then each party turns around and goes back where it came from." Oliver bit his lip. "Miss

Cameron," he exclaimed, "are you really interested in all this?"

"Of course I am!" she returned, and for the first time since he had sat on the floor by her chair, she looked at him. Oliver was amused and a trifle incredulous. "I'm interested in anything I don't know about," said Garnet.

"Even in dirt and sand and swearing bullwhackers?"

"What's a bullwhacker?"

"A man who drives ox-teams on the Santa Fe Trail."

"All my life," said Garnet, "they've been telling me I had too much curiosity. But I like to know things. And you—" she stopped.

"Yes?" he prodded her. "And me?"

"You're the first gentleman that ever talked to me like a human being!" she burst out, and blushed to have said it.

"There are so few people in New York," said Oliver, "that I can talk to like a human being."

They both laughed. Oliver was thinking that those black-fringed gray eyes of hers were quite enchantingly wicked. She'd be a lot of fun if a man could get her out of this hothouse before they smothered her spirit entirely.

"Please go on," begged Garnet. Oliver looked as though he had forgotten his subject, so she prompted him. "The traders start from opposite sides of the continent," she said, "and meet in the middle."

"Oh yes." Oliver picked up his narrative. "Well, every year in April, the traders from the United States take their goods to Independence. At Independence, they load the goods into covered wagons. Each trader has his own wagons, and his own crew, packers and muleteers and ox-drivers and cooks. He takes his train to a meeting-place on the prairie called Council Grove. At Council Grove they organize the big caravans."

"And after Council Grove, do they all travel together?"

"No, the traders are very free souls. They make up parties, but they don't all travel in one party. Those who get to Council Grove first, join and leave first. Sometimes they catch up with each other out on the prairie, and go on together."

"Where do they go?"

"To Santa Fe. That's a town in a Mexican province called New Mexico. It's about eight hundred miles west of Independence."

Garnet nodded. "I understand so far. Go on."

"Well, in the meantime, while those traders are on their way from Independence to Santa Fe, another caravan is coming to Santa Fe to meet them."

"Where does this other caravan come from?"

"From California. That's the group I've been working with. Every year, in April, while the Missouri traders are packing their wagons, our party is meeting in California. We start from a little village called Los Angeles. We use pack-mules instead of covered wagons, because we have to cross some very steep mountains. We come east while the men from Missouri are going west. And in midsummer, about the first of July, the two caravans meet in Santa Fe."

"I know what you're taking to Santa Fe from New York," said Garnet. "Cloth and household goods. But when you come the other way, from California to Santa Fe, what sort of merchandise do you bring?"

"Mules. Thousands of mules. The California mules are the best on earth. The Missouri traders buy them and drive them back home. And we bring silks and jade from China, and spices from the islands in the South Sea."

Garnet looked at the map, and the big space on which the map-makers could only write "Great American Desert." She thought of silks and jade and spices from the islands. Raising her eyes again, she asked, "How far is it from California to Santa Fe?"

"About nine hundred miles."

"Mr. Hale, you mean that you men ride nine hundred miles and back, every year, on mules?"

Oliver laughed. "Actually, we ride about twelve hundred miles each way. Los Angeles and Santa Fe are nine hundred miles apart as a bird would fly it, but traveling on land we have to make a long detour around a canyon."

"What's a canyon?"

"A crack in the earth. Some of them are very small. But the one I'm talking about is the great canyon of the Colorado River. We have to go around it."

"Is there a road from Los Angeles to Santa Fe?" she asked.

"No road at all. Not even a track. Just the trail as we know it in our heads."

"Then it hasn't a name?"

"Why yes, properly it's called the Great Spanish Trail, because the journey was first made by Spanish explorers. But we call it Jubilee Trail."

19

"I like that," said Garnet. "Why do you call it Jubilee Trail?"

"Well, it's pretty hard going. We feel like shouting such a jubilee when we get to the end of it."

Garnet looked again at the long hard miles on the map. "Did you mean to live out there," she asked, "when you left Boston?"

"No, we didn't mean to go to California at all. We meant to go as far as Santa Fe, and then come back with the men from Missouri."

"We? You and who else?"

"My brother Charles. It was his idea to go West in the first place."

"Charles?" Garnet repeated. She thought a moment, and said, "I don't think you've ever told me you had a brother."

"Haven't I?" For the first time since he began answering her questions, Oliver's eyes left her. He looked across at the fire. "Why yes," he said slowly, "of course I have a brother. Funny I never mentioned him. Charles is ten years older than I am."

Garnet smiled questioningly. "Why don't you call him Charlie?"

"Who, Charles? I never thought of it." He was still looking at the fire. "Charles isn't exactly the sort of man who'd be called by a nickname."

"Dignified, you mean?"

"Why yes, that's it. Dignified."

"How did he happen to know about California?" she asked.

Oliver turned back to her. "Oh, we'd always heard of California. Our parents died when I was a child, and we lived with our uncle. He had a shipping company. The shipping companies in Boston pack a lot of goods for the Western trade—for the overland wagons to Santa Fe, and the ships that go to California around Cape Horn. Charles was working in the shipping company, but Charles is ambitious. So while I was studying at Harvard, he came to me with the idea that I quit college and go into the Santa Fe trade with him."

"So you quit?"

"At once," said Oliver, "with a yelp of joy. I'm not very intellectual. We used Charles' savings to outfit some wagons. Charles is the sort that always has savings. When we got to Santa Fe, we met the traders who had come from California. They said the trade on that side was very profitable, so we decided to go on to California and see for ourselves."

"And when you got there," said Garnet, "you liked it, and stayed?"

"That's right. I'm still trading—I'm a restless soul, and I don't like settling down in one place. But Charles has settled down. We have a rancho near Los Angeles, and he takes care of it."

"What's a rancho?"

"It's something like a farm. Only they don't plant things much, they raise cattle. That's for the hide trade. They ship thousands of hides from California every year."

"What are they for?"

"Leather." Oliver made a gesture toward his shoes. "Nearly all the shoes in the United States are made of leather from California."

Astonished, Garnet pulled her skirt back from her feet. She had on black kid slippers, with silk lacings crossed and recrossed around her ankles. "Why Mr. Hale, you mean these shoes of mine came from California?"

Oliver grinned and nodded, glad of the chance she had given him to admire her ankles.

Garnet saw his glance and dropped her skirt, but she was too much interested to feel more than a flash of genteel embarrassment. "Do you bring the hides by the overland trail?" she asked.

"No, they're too bulky to be packed on mules. The Yankee ships get the hides. The ships come out from Boston, and trade all over the Pacific—that's how we get the Chinese silks we take to Santa Fe."

Garnet felt a sense of enchantment. It glowed between them like a radiance, and through it she saw Oliver, as though he had gathered to himself all the wonder of the dim far places. The coals in the fireplace settled with a little soft noise like a sigh. Garnet remembered that her mother had told her to keep up the fires. But she couldn't stop now to see to fires. She asked,

"What sort of people live in California?"

Oliver had been watching the blue lights in her black hair. He was still watching them as he answered,

"Mexicans. Only they don't like to be called Mexicans. They like to be called Californios. And a few hundred foreigners like me, mostly Americans."

"Are there any Indians?"

Oliver shrugged. "There are some two-legged animals, but calling them Indians is rather an insult to tribes like the Navajos and the Sioux. We usually call them Diggers."

21

"And the Californios—how did they get there?"

"They're descendants of some colonists the Spanish government sent up from Mexico about eighty years ago. But the Spanish empire was dying. They sent up the colonists, and a few priests to do missionary work among the Diggers, and then forgot about them. Later, when Mexico won its independence from Spain, the Mexicans sent governors up to California. But California is so far from everywhere, and so hard to get to, that Mexico pays it very little attention. The people have just kept on living there because they're there. The fact is, California is nearly empty. It's a tremendous country, bigger than New York and New England and Ohio combined, and from end to end of it there are only five or six thousand people who are white or partly white. The Diggers—I don't know how many of them there are, but they're dying out. You can ride from dawn till dark without meeting a soul."

Garnet had always lived in a crowded spot. She could hardly imagine such emptiness. "And the country—what is it like?"

Oliver turned his head toward the window, and looked out at the sun flashing on the icy trees in Union Square. He brought his mind back from New York to California, and spoke slowly.

"It's a magnificent country, Miss Cameron. It's beautiful, in a strange way that's hard to describe to people who haven't seen it— mountains and canyons and deserts, and miles of wild flowers, and thousands of cattle grazing on the slopes; and great ranchos, and a few scattered villages, and distance, and emptiness, and bigness. Everything is big. The mountains in California make the Adirondacks look like pimples on the face of the earth."

Garnet glanced around the room. Its simple comfort looked very dull. "What is New York like, after you've seen California?" she asked softly.

Oliver gave an apologetic laugh, as though he felt almost embarrassed. "It looks *little*, Miss Cameron. I know that sounds foolish, but it's true. You feel like a man blundering around in a toy village made for children to play with in a nursery." He ran his hand back over his rough curly hair. "Everything here is jammed so close together," he went on. "There doesn't seem to be room enough. You feel smothered. You're always scared you're going to run into something."

The coals in the fireplace sighed again. Garnet got up and walked over to the hearth. Looking down at the grate, she asked,

"When are you going back?"

"I'm leaving New York in about six weeks."

"That will be March," said Garnet.

"Yes, March. I'll pack the goods I've bought here, and take them down to New Orleans. From New Orleans, I'll take them up the river to Independence."

"And then to Santa Fe?"

"That's right. I have a partner in Los Angeles, an American named John Ives. He'll bring our goods from California to Santa Fe, and we'll go on to California with the mule-train."

Garnet picked up the tongs and reached toward the coal-scuttle.

"Let me do that," said Oliver. Scrambling to his feet, he came over and took the tongs from her hand.

"Isn't it a mighty dangerous journey?" Garnet asked. "Aren't there Indians out there on the plains, and cannibals, and—all sorts of things?"

"There are Indians, of course. I don't think any of them are cannibals. It's dangerous, but we're very well armed. The caravans always get through."

Garnet's throat felt suddenly tight. As Oliver set down the tongs, she exclaimed,

"Oh, I do envy you so!"

"Do you, Garnet?" he asked. He was looking at her intently. It was the first time he had ever called her by her first name, but she hardly noticed it.

"Why shouldn't I?" she answered. "You go to those gorgeous places, so beautiful and so full of adventure, and I just do the same things everybody else does. I practice my music and buy dress-patterns at Stewart's and go to plays at the Park Theater. In the summer, while you're on the trails West, I'm at Rockaway Beach!"

"Do you always go there in the summer?"

"No, we go to different places, but they're all pretty much alike. My mother says we may go to Europe next year."

"But that doesn't interest you?" Oliver asked.

"Why yes, it does, in a way—I've never been to Europe—but—" She stopped, and he said,

"Go on, Garnet. Tell me."

The thoughts she had been thinking so long came tumbling out over her lips.

"I've never said this before, but I think you'll know what I mean. There won't be anything different about going to Europe. We're the sort of people who take our own world with us wherever we go.

23

The best hotel in one city is very much like the best hotel in another city. Nice people are just nice people, no matter where you meet them. Oh, *do* you understand what I mean?"

Oliver took both her hands in his. "What do you want to do, Garnet?"

Garnet looked up at him. She was thinking that she really should not allow a man to hold her hands like this. But he was not flirting. His smile was very gentle. She answered,

"I want to find out what goes on in the world! I want to know what people are like who are not like me. There are so many kinds of people I don't know anything about. I pass them on the street. I wonder what they do, how they live, what they think about. I want to go to the places I'm not allowed to go to. I'm tired of the Park Theater. I want to go to the Jewel Box."

She caught her lip between her teeth, as though she had accidentally spoken a word that should not be used in nice conversation. But Oliver was not shocked. He only looked puzzled.

"The Jewel Box?" he repeated. "What's that?"

"It's a variety theater on Broadway, near the park. You mean you've never been there?"

He shook his head. "But now that you remind me, I believe I've seen it. There's a big sign, with flowers and Cupids all over it—is that the place?"

Garnet laughed regretfully. "There's the difference between us. You could have gone there any time you pleased, so you've hardly noticed it the whole time you've been in New York. And I can't go there, so I'm dying of curiosity about it."

"But what's wrong with it?" asked Oliver. "Why can't you go there?"

"I don't know!" she returned with exasperation. "It's there, and when we drive past it in the evenings I see crowds of people going in. Well-dressed people, too. But nobody ever mentions the Jewel Box. Not around me, anyway."

"Oh Lord," said Oliver. "What do they want to do with you? Wrap you up in pink tissue paper and put you in the closet?"

"Yes!" exclaimed Garnet. "Sometimes it does seem like that."

"Why don't you ask about the Jewel Box?" he suggested with a grin. "Just to hear what your proper friends would say?"

Garnet glanced down, smothering a little laugh. "I did."

"What happened?"

"You won't tell on me?"

24

"Certainly not."

She looked up. "Well, there was a young gentleman named Henry Trellen. He and I were walking up Broadway one day, and as we were about to pass the Jewel Box I thought I'd speak of it, very innocently, you know, as if I'd never thought about it before. So I glanced up at the sign, and remarked that I'd never been there."

"What did he say?"

"He said—" Garnet became very pompous as she quoted—"He said, 'I am sure, Miss Cameron, that the type of entertainment presented at the Jewel Box would neither amuse nor instruct you.' "

"Oh my dear grandmother," said Oliver. "Did you slap his silly face?"

"I felt like it. I really did. But I can't do things like that. So I just dropped my eyes and said, 'Pray forgive me, Mr. Trellen. I had not been told that the Jewel Box was an improper resort.' And he said, very sweetly, 'I am sure you had not. I cannot imagine any deliberate suggestion of indelicacy coming from you, Miss Cameron.' "

Oliver laughed, half in derision and half in sympathy. Garnet did not add that soon after this conversation she had received a very formal letter from Henry Trellen, laying his heart, hand, and fortune at her feet. A lady never mentioned her proposals, but she said to Oliver,

"That's the sort of gentlemen I'm used to. Now maybe you know why I was so glad when I met you."

"Do you want me to take you to the Jewel Box?" Oliver offered.

"They wouldn't let you."

"We could say we were going to a concert."

"I wouldn't do that. No, it's not important." She tried to explain. "I mean, the Jewel Box itself isn't important. It's just that every time I pass the Jewel Box I'm reminded of all the things I can't do. The things people keep away from young ladies. They might not even be interesting things. Maybe if I went to the Jewel Box I wouldn't like it, and wouldn't want to go there again. But I want to know, so I can make up my own mind—do you understand? I mean, if they would just say to me, You can go to the Jewel Box any time you want to—I'd feel—well, I'd feel unwrapped from that pink tissue paper and taken out of the closet."

Oliver was laughing softly. But he was not making fun of her.

Garnet had never talked to anybody so frankly before. She felt as though a knot inside her had been untied. Suddenly she realized that Oliver had been holding her hands all this time. But it seemed all right for him to do so. She did not try to take her hands away.

There was a silence. Their eyes met. Oliver was not laughing any more. His eyes were no longer mischievous, but earnest, and his big hands were holding hers so hard that he hurt her. He said, very softly,

"Why don't you come with me, Garnet?"

Garnet felt a quiver run through her, like a tingle of fire. Oliver said,

"You dear girl, come with me."

Garnet's lips parted. The tingle had come up into her throat, and she could hardly push her voice past it. She gasped,

"Oliver—are you—"

"Yes," said Oliver, "I'm asking you to marry me. I've never wanted to marry anybody before. I never thought I'd want to. But I want you."

All the brightness in the world exploded in front of her. Through the brightness she saw Oliver, with his big shoulders and his sunburnt forehead and his rumpled curls, and beyond him the trail into the far golden promises. She said, still almost unbelieving,

"You want to marry me? You want to take me to California?"

"Would you go to California with me? Do you mean you would?"

"Would I go to—" Garnet could not say any more. Her breaths were all confused. Oliver went on, talking fast.

"It's a hard journey, Garnet. I've got no right to ask you to take it. I ought to say I'd quit the trail now, and settle down in a civilized place like New York or Boston. But I can't quit now. I've got to go back this year. My brother's expecting me, and my partner John Ives; and there aren't any mails. I can't wind up the business unless I'm there to do it. But we can go to California this summer, and next summer we can come back for good. We can live in New York or Boston or anywhere you please."

Garnet tried to make her breaths behave. She could not answer. Oliver thought she was hesitating, and he drew her closer to him.

"I'm such a fool, Garnet. You haven't said you'd marry me at all."

When she did manage to speak, her voice was low and tense with wonder.

"But Oliver, of course I will!"

"Now?" he pled. "Before I go to California? You'll come with me?" His voice was shaky with eagerness. "I ought to ask you to wait for me. But I can't ask you to wait! It will be nearly two years before I can possibly get back to the States—and my dearest darling girl, now that I've found you, I can't do without you for two years!"

Garnet shook her head violently. "No, no, don't ask me to wait! Please take me with you!"

"It's a terrible journey," he warned again. "From here to Santa Fe it's easy, but beyond Santa Fe—we go through deserts and wild bare mountains, we sleep on buffalo robes, you'll travel with strange hard men and the sort of women you've never seen before, we live outdoors, we eat strange food, we—Garnet, it's not like anything you've ever done, if you weren't blooming with health I'd never dare ask you to do it—but will you? Will you, Garnet?"

His words were like jewels in the air between them. Garnet began to laugh.

"Oh, Oliver, won't you ever understand what it's like to be me? Don't you know every word you say makes me want to go? Don't you know you're telling me what I dreamed about every day at that Academy for Young Ladies? Yes, I'll go with you. I'll eat strange food and I'll sleep on a buffalo robe, and I'll love it. Oh, Oliver, take me to California!"

Oliver swept her into his arms and kissed her. He held her so close to him that she thought he must be crushing her ribs. It was wonderful. Oliver was splendid and the whole world was suddenly as glorious as she had always dreamed it might be. She was going over the Jubilee Trail to California.

THREE

GARNET AND OLIVER were married in March.

Her mother had shed tears, and her father was graver than Garnet had ever seen him. They liked Oliver. But they said to Garnet that they hadn't known him long enough, and neither had she. Garnet exclaimed,

"I know him perfectly well! And I love him. He loves me. Don't you understand? Didn't you two love each other when you got married?"

That was a strong argument. They had loved each other very

much, and they still did. But everybody had said her mother was throwing herself away.

Mrs. Cameron's name had been Pauline Delacroix. Her father's ancestors were French Huguenots, her mother's were English adventurers. She belonged to a family as old and proud as any in New York. Horace Cameron was the son of an obscure Presbyterian minister from a small town upstate. He had come to New York with no fortune but his head and his hands, and when Pauline met him he was only a minor clerk in the bank.

Pauline had a number of suitors. From everybody's viewpoint but her own, she could have made a far more promising marriage.

But Pauline loved him. To get her parents' consent to the marriage, she and Horace had to fight a battle that lasted a year. Her parents finally yielded, though her mother wept through the ceremony and her father was so angry he could hardly be polite to the wedding guests.

They began their married life in a tiny little house,.with only one servant. But Pauline had fun being thrifty with Horace's pay. She produced her first baby without making any fuss about it. Altogether, she was so delighted that her parents had to forgive Horace, whose only crime was that of making Pauline happier than she had ever been in her life before. As the baby was a girl, and as she was born in January, Pauline's father proved his change of heart by ordering a set of garnets, the January birthstone, for his granddaughter to wear when she grew up. Pauline named the baby Garnet for the jewels, because she was so glad to have her father's favor again. Both she and Horace were essentially conservative, and except for marrying each other they had never done anything that other people did not approve of.

Everybody approved of them now. Horace had risen in business, they had their three children and their home in Union Square. Nothing had happened to shock them, until Garnet said she was going out to the end of the world with this strange young man.

They were frightened. But Garnet said she loved him. Her mind was made up. And they remembered, quite well, what it was like to have your mind made up when you were in love.

Very well, her father said finally, if she loved him she could marry him. But did she have to take that dreadful journey? If Oliver had to make one more trip to California, he could make it without Garnet.

Garnet protested violently. Oliver laughed at her father's fears.

Oliver pointed out that Garnet was quite healthy. He wanted to take her with him, and she wanted to go. If she hadn't wanted to go—but she did want to, that was the sort of girl she was and that was why he loved her.

At last, one day, Garnet's father led her off alone. He stood with his hand on her shoulder, looking down at her bright cheeks and her zestful eyes. He asked, slowly,

"Do you love him so much, Garnet?"

"Yes, father," she said.

"You're quite sure, daughter?"

"Of course I'm sure! What are you thinking of?"

He smiled faintly. "I'm wondering," he said, "if you're in love with Oliver, or in love with California."

"Father, don't be silly! I'd marry him if he wanted to take me to Smolensk!"

"I think you would," her father said gravely. "But would you marry him if he only wanted to move into the house next door?"

"I don't know what you're talking about," Garnet pled. "I love him, father! I know what I mean. I've had chances to get married before. I didn't love those men, I didn't have to think two minutes to be sure about it. But I love Oliver." She begged, with tears in her eyes, "Don't you know what I'm trying to say?"

He did know. He knew very well. But he asked,

"You don't want to wait until he comes back next year?"

Garnet shook her head vehemently.

Horace Cameron drew a long hard breath. He had never wanted to go out to the end of the world. He had what he wanted: his charming wife and his home and his position in the bank, and the pleasant security of his well-ordered days. Pauline had what she wanted too; he had heard her say a hundred times that she thought herself a very fortunate woman. But Garnet wanted something else. He did not understand it, he thought; and then he reminded himself that he understood it very well.

He was thinking. Not about himself and Pauline, two quiet happy people who would not have liked to travel beyond the range of clean sheets and safety. But about the people who had come before them. He seldom thought about those people. They were just names in yellowing family Bibles, or mossy epitaphs in the cemeteries. But they had been real and alive, once. They were the Huguenots, the Scottish Dissenters, the English pirates who had stormed up and down the coasts of the American colonies until they got old and virtuous and finally settled down on shore. Those people had come into the wilderness for the glory of God and the chance to have their own way. They were heroes now. Horace had thought sometimes that a good many of the people who were heroes after they were dead must have been great nuisances while they were alive.

But they had had a quality in them, a quality of strength and daring and defiance. And this was something you could never quite breed out. Sometimes, after many comfortable generations, it quieted down, as it had quieted in himself and Pauline. But it was there. Americans had it, or they wouldn't be Americans; their ancestors would have stayed at home. So he and Pauline had passed on something they did not even know they had, and here it was, blazing up at him in their daughter.

Garnet did not know why he had been so silent. He looked at her long and thoughtfully. She asked,

"Will you let me go, father?"

"Yes," he said gently. "I'll let you go."

All of a sudden, though she did not know why, she burst into tears. He put his arm around her, and she buried her face on his shoulder. He led her to a chair and she sat down, and he sat on the arm of it with his hand holding hers, while he told her what he had been thinking about. Garnet listened wonderingly. At last she said,

"Is that what I've got? I never thought about it. But you have it too."

"I'm afraid not, Garnet," he said.

"Yes you have. Because if you hadn't, you wouldn't understand it. And you're wonderful, and I love you very much."

There was a long pause.

"You'd better go to your room now, Garnet," he said, "while I talk to your mother."

Garnet had shed tears, but as she went upstairs she could feel her heart beating fast, as though keeping time to a dance-tune. Her father had said yes.

Her room was warm and cheerful. It had two windows hung with flowered curtains, overlooking the little square of garden between this house and the next. The bed had twisting mahogany posts holding up curtains that matched the window draperies. On the wall were flower prints in oval frames. There was a bureau with a tall mirror, and on the wall above the washstand was a white linen splasher to keep soapsuds from spattering the wall.

There was always a fire here in winter. Some people thought a bedroom fire was a foolish extravagance, but Pauline did not. Garnet's great-grandfather had shivered nobly at Valley Forge, but Pauline said this was no reason why Garnet should shiver in New York when her father was perfectly well able to buy coal.

Garnet sat down on a hassock by the fireplace. She wondered how it would be to live outdoors for weeks and weeks, and what sort of men the other traders were. She and Oliver would go to California this summer, and spend the winter on the rancho with Oliver's brother Charles; then next summer they would come back. They would reach New York in October or November of next year. By that time she would have been away a year and eight months. Some of her friends would have been to Europe, but anybody could go to ordinary places like that. She alone would have been out to the end of the world.

There was a tap on the door, and her mother came in. Garnet stood up.

Pauline came over to her and took her hands. She did not say anything. She stood looking into Garnet's eyes, long and searchingly. At last Garnet said,

"Mother—did father tell you?"

"Yes, dear, he told me." Pauline's teeth closed hard on her lower lip for an instant, but when she went on her voice was steady. "Garnet, my darling, do you love him very, very much?"

Garnet nodded. She smiled dreamily.

"And you're sure you want to go to California with him?" Pauline asked.

"Oh yes! Mother, he's wonderful."

"Yes, I know," said Pauline. "Sit down here by me, Garnet."

She drew up a chair, and Garnet sat down on the hassock again. Pauline held her hand.

"I want you to be happy, Garnet," Pauline said softly. "I want you to be happy always."

This time her voice had a little quiver. Garnet looked up in astonishment. Her mother was always so busy and cheerful. But now, in spite of her efforts, there were tears in her eyes.

"Mother," Garnet exclaimed, "are you—are you crying?"

"I'm afraid I am." The tears trembled on Pauline's eyelids. She took out her handkerchief and wiped them away. "I'm sorry," she said, and managed to smile. "I thought I'd done all the crying I was going to do. But—it's so far away, Garnet!"

Garnet threw her arms around her mother's waist. "Mother, you're so good! I don't know how to say this—but so many girls' mothers would be pacing the floor and carrying on—but you don't."

"No, Garnet, I don't and I never will," Pauline said firmly. "You've heard your father and me talk about the trouble we had getting married. We laugh about it now. But it wasn't funny then. I loved my parents. I remember it—the nights I lay awake and sobbed till morning, the days I was so nervous I couldn't hold a fork at table. And all because he hadn't a dollar and they didn't know who his grandfather was." She stroked Garnet's black hair. "And I remember too, when they told me my baby was a girl, I thought: whatever happens, she's not going through what I did to get the man she wants. Unless he's an utter reprobate, she can have him."

Pauline was not crying any more. But Garnet was.

As soon as she could speak, Garnet promised that she would be very, very good. She would write home every chance she got. She would write from New Orleans, from Independence, and again from Santa Fe. One of the returning traders would bring her letter while she went on to California. And if there was a Yankee ship in port at San Diego, she would send a letter by the captain.

Next year, Oliver would bring her back to New York. Then they would live just like other people. Oliver would manage the New York office of his uncle's shipping company. They would have a house like this one, and a carriage. She would do everything right. Her mother and father would never, never have any reason to be sorry they had let her marry Oliver. And she would always love them, better than she loved anybody in the world but Oliver, because they were so good and wise.

Garnet and Oliver were married in the parlor of her home in Union Square. His uncle came down from Boston for the ceremony. The elder Mr. Hale was a ruddy, jovial man, and Garnet liked him. He told her how glad he was that she was going to bring Oliver back home. He had no sons of his own, and he had always wanted one of his nephews to take over the business when he got old.

The other guests were astounded, or doubtful, or puzzled, or— Garnet caught it here and there—envious. These last ones shook hands with Oliver, and made the proper remarks of congratulation, and added, almost bashfully, "You know, I used to think when I was younger—those ships that go out to Asia around Cape Horn—what is this country again, Mr. Hale?"

"California," Oliver said politely.

"Yes, yes. Is that near India? Well, well. Good luck, young man."

Garnet began to understand what her father had said about Americans. She wondered why more of them hadn't had the nerve to do what they wanted to do.

Three hours after the wedding reception, Garnet and Oliver took the coastwise boat for New Orleans. The boat left from the end of Wall Street. There was a bitter wind blowing, and the fog on the East River made it hard to see the outlines of the city. Garnet and Oliver stood on deck, watching through the gathering gloom.

"I can't believe it," said Garnet. "I'm on my way to California. Before I see New York again—"

The wind blew the rest of her words down her throat. Oliver smiled at her. She was wrapped in a heavy fur-trimmed mantle, and her hands were tucked into a muff. Little tendrils of black hair were blowing out from the edge of her bonnet. The wind had made her cheeks red as apples. Oliver put his head down close to hers so she could hear what he was saying.

"Garnet, darling, I haven't got the faintest idea what sort of husband I'll make. I didn't hear half the minister said. So I suppose I've promised a lot that I don't even know about. But I love you."

"I love you too," she said.

She looked up at him. Oliver's face was aglow with teasing mischief.

"And by the way," he continued.

"Yes?"

"There's a variety theater in New Orleans, something like the Jewel Box. Probably even naughtier, if I know anything about New Orleans. I've never been to this theater, but I'm told it's quite spectacular. We'll go to see the show as soon as we get to town."

"Oliver!" She gasped with delight that he should have remembered. "You mean really?"

"Yes, I mean really. I mean—" Oliver laughed softly. "I mean, darling, you're finally unwrapped from the pink tissue paper and out of the closet."

33

FOUR

THE JOURNEY to New Orleans took two weeks. Garnet had never been so far from New York before.

New Orleans was strange and enchanting. The air was like silk, and the noises were not quite there, like music played in a room with damp walls. Garnet and Oliver stayed at a hotel several blocks above Canal Street, where Oliver extravagantly took a suite of two rooms.

As for Oliver, he was simply wonderful. Garnet had loved him very much when she married him, but she hadn't been able to imagine how much fun it was going to be to have him with her all the time. Oliver was an ardent but considerate lover. He liked her the way she was, and had not the faintest wish for her to pretend to be anything she wasn't. He answered all her questions, he took her everywhere she wanted to go, whether it was proper or not. She saw the docks, the warehouses, the dark narrow streets; and he took her to dine in funny little restaurants where the tables were covered with red-checked tablecloths and nobody spoke English but themselves. And one morning, when they had been there a week, he told her that this evening they would go to see the show he had promised her. The theater was in the old part of town, below Canal Street. It was called the Flower Garden.

Oliver was very busy that day, getting his goods unloaded and repacked. But she was not lonely. She went shopping, and bought a lot of things she didn't need, just for the fun of prowling around the stores.

He came back at dark and took her to dinner, but she was too excited to eat. And then they got dressed, and Oliver went down to order a carriage, and she waited for him, looking at herself in the mirror. And then at last, the door opened and Oliver came in, saying,

"Ready?"

Garnet turned around from the mirror. The lamplight danced over her as she turned. She had on a white satin evening dress and white gloves, and the garnet necklace her grandfather had given her when she was born. The blue lights flashed in her black hair, and her cheeks were rosier than ever, for she was so thrilled that she could feel her heart bouncing in her chest. Oliver smiled and made a bow.

"The carriage waits, madame."

Little ripples of anticipation ran up and down her back like merry teasing fingers. She tucked her hand into the bend of his arm and they went downstairs.

The carriage stood in front of the hotel entrance. They climbed in, and as the hackman shut the door Oliver said to Garnet,

"Stay close to me when we get there."

She promised. Oliver chuckled and explained,

"I'm not trying to keep you from seeing everything. But New Orleans is the wickedest port this side of Marseille. It's just not safe for you to be alone."

Garnet tingled with adventure. He went on,

"And if anybody speaks to you, don't answer. Just give him a withering look. You know how to do that."

"Yes, I know how to do that," Garnet said, laughing under her breath. "That's one thing they did teach me at Miss Wayne's Select Academy."

The carriage crossed Canal Street and turned down into the area near the docks. The streets in this part of town were dim. The air was heavy with strange odors from the shipping in the river. The carriage went slowly, bumping over cobbled pavements too old for comfort.

Oliver said teasingly, "It's a good thing you've never been in New Orleans before. If you lived here, you might embarrass some of your most gallant dancing partners this evening."

"How?" she asked.

"By recognizing them," he said, "in company with girls who aren't at all like you."

Garnet was not sure what he meant. He explained that a great many wealthy men kept lodgings in this part of town for women of the sort that ladies like herself were not supposed to think about. Garnet was thrilled. She had never seen any women like that.

"And by the way," Oliver continued, "when we get to the theater, you'll notice that half the women in the audience aren't white. Don't show any surprise."

"You mean there'll be Negro slaves at the theater?" she asked, puzzled.

35

"No, free quadroons. They're the most expensive mistresses in New Orleans. Some of them are very beautiful."

Garnet gave a little excited shiver. This was really what it meant to be a woman of the world. She glanced at Oliver. Here inside the carriage there was very little light, but she could see his merry eyes and his look of amused sophistication. She was proud to have such an escort.

The carriage came to a halt. They got out, and Garnet looked around.

They were in front of a large brick building, with a wide entrance through which she could see brilliant lights. Over the entrance were two wrought-iron lamps. Between the lamps was a sign bearing the words, "Le Jardin des Fleurs," and underneath, "Flower Garden."

Other carriages were driving up, leaving gentlemen in black capes, and women who looked very graceful in the semi-darkness. There was a jumble of voices, some speaking in English and some in French, and others in languages Garnet had never heard before. Several groups of sailors were approaching on foot. With them were girls, and these girls were not attractive at all. They laughed and talked in loud raucous voices, and as they came nearer Garnet's nostrils caught the smell of stale whiskey. Oliver wiggled his nose derisively, and led her inside.

While he paused to get the tickets, she looked around again.

It was the most splendid theater lobby she had ever seen. The carpet was soft and deep, and the light came from three cut-glass chandeliers with crystal droplets. On the walls she saw two life-size paintings of women in very scanty gauze draperies. One of them was lying on a scarlet rug; the other was picking flowers in a remarkable meadow where asters, poppies, daisies, and peach blossoms were all in their prime together. Garnet looked at the pictures, and looked away. She hoped nobody had noticed the start she had given at the sight of so much nakedness right out in public.

The lobby was full of people. Evidently those who were going to the cheaper seats had to use another door, for everyone here was well dressed. They all seemed to know one another. The men were greeting their friends, the women were laughing and tapping each other's shoulders with their fans. Except that they were making more noise, Garnet thought at first that they were not much different from an audience at the Park Theater in New York. But then she noticed that there were many more men than women.

And Oliver had been right about the women. They were graceful and they were gorgeously dressed, but at least half of them were not white.

So these were the quadroons. Though Oliver had warned her, Garnet watched them in amazement. Some of them were beautiful indeed. They had skin like coffee with lots of cream, large dark eyes, black hair piled up with flowers and jewels. Many of them had such clear Caucasian features that they looked like white beauties who had darkened their skins for theatricals.

Garnet felt suddenly shy. She wondered if anybody who looked at her couldn't tell right away that she didn't belong in this array of expensive sin. Just then a handsome young fellow caught sight of her, and paused. He smiled at her, asking,

"Alone this evening?"

She started, and froze him with her eyes. Oliver turned from the ticket-window.

"She's not alone," he said sternly.

"Oh, sorry, my error," said the young stranger. He went on inside. Garnet drew closer to Oliver.

Oliver took her arm, smiling. "You did that very well," he said.

"Did I?" She laughed delightedly. Oliver gave her arm a squeeze as he looked over the lobby.

"What do you bet," he whispered, "that the star of this show is a dazzling blond?"

"Why?"

"Rarity," said Oliver. "Come on in. I've taken a table right under the stage."

Garnet did not understand what he meant by a table. In the theaters she had visited, the audience had sat in rows of seats. But when they went in she saw that the main floor of this theater was provided with rows of tables, each with its own group of chairs. Girls were walking among them selling drinks. The men already seated fondled the girls' arms and slapped at their skirts, and the girls didn't mind. Sometimes they laughed and sometimes they paid no attention. Above the main floor was a balcony, but evidently the more expensive seats were around the tables, for it was here that the best-dressed spectators were taking their places.

A young man, who looked bored with the whole business, took their tickets. He led them to a table for two, just in front of the stage as Oliver had promised. Garnet sat down, holding the printed program he had given her.

She looked up at the scarlet curtains hiding the stage. The foot-lights flickered behind metal reflectors, throwing lights and shadows over the curtains. The orchestra began a lively tune. Garnet spread out her program on the table before her. By the light from the stage she read that the first performers would be the Barotti Brothers, Jugglers of International Renown. After this would come An Array of Famous Beauties Never Equaled on This Continent. Below these words, in a line of fancy capitals reaching across the page, was the single name JULIETTE LA TOUR.

Garnet wondered if Juliette La Tour was the dazzling blond Oliver had prophesied. Before she could read any farther, Oliver's voice interrupted,

"She wants to know what we're drinking."

Garnet looked up. A waitress was standing by their table. On one arm she carried a basket of bottles, and with the other arm she held a tray of glasses balanced against her hip. She was not as young or as pretty as Garnet thought she should be: she had a hard face with a line between the eyebrows, and her voice was raspy as she announced,

"Sauterne, burgundy, claret, champagne, cognac, whiskey, ice two dollars extra, or est-ce que vous parlez français, monsieur?"

"No, English," said Oliver. "Shall it be champagne, Garnet?"

Garnet nodded happily. The girl whisked two hollow-stemmed glasses from her tray and set them on the table. "I'll be right back," she promised.

A couple of other corks popped behind them. A moment later their waitress returned with the bottle in its bucket of ice. She released the cork, while Garnet watched, wondering if she could ever learn to do it so expertly. The cork popped, and shot up toward the ceiling. Garnet caught it as it fell.

"I'm going to keep this," she exclaimed.

The cynical lips of the waitress parted in a smile. "First time here, sweetheart?" she asked.

"Why yes. And it's lovely."

The girl poured the champagne. Her eyes gave Garnet a humor-ous challenge. "Haven't seen Juliette, then?"

"Juliette? Oh, the one whose name is in big letters on the pro-gram? No, I've never seen her."

"Nor you either, mister?" she asked. Oliver shook his head, and the waitress glanced back at Garnet. "Look out, dearie," she warned.

Oliver handed her a bill and told her to keep the change.

"Thanks," said the girl, and she smiled at Garnet. "Bon soir, mademoiselle," she said as she went off.

Garnet stared after her. "Oliver! She called me mademoiselle!"

"Naturally," said Oliver, with a grin.

Garnet's wedding ring was hidden by her glove, but she demanded, "Do I look like a girl who—who'd be in a place like this with a man she wasn't married to?"

"Do you want me to take you home?"

"Of course not!"

"Then shut up," Oliver said merrily.

Garnet felt a delicious naughty excitement. They raised their glasses. The champagne tingled against the excited quivers in her throat. "Suppose I get tipsy?" she asked.

"I'll take care of you. Go ahead."

"Imagine," said Garnet, "just imagine, *me* being married to a man who'll say that."

The orchestra changed to a louder tune and the curtains began to part. Garnet turned toward the stage. She saw a flowered backdrop, before which the renowned Barotti Brothers, in tights of red and yellow, were bowing to the audience.

The Barotti Brothers tossed plates around and caught them on sticks, and balanced sticks and plates on their noses. They did it with great skill, but few of the spectators paid them much attention. People were still coming in, and the buzz of voices was loud in spite of the music. The Barottis were just here to get the show started. Garnet liked them, but as she had seen acts like this before she was not greatly impressed. The audience was not impressed either, but it was a good-humored gathering, and the jugglers got a good round of applause when they were done.

By this time most of the chairs were occupied. The customers were settling down to sip their drinks and enjoy the show. The next number was the Array of Famous Beauties, a dozen chorus girls all dressed alike in green. They whirled up their skirts to show a greater display of legs than Garnet had ever seen before in a public place, while they sang a song about being in love with several men at once and finding it very confusing. A man in the balcony shouted, "Pick 'em up, sisters!" Everybody thought this was very funny, and a lot of others began to chant with the music, "Pick 'em up, sisters, pick 'em up, sisters!" Garnet thought the dance was quite revealing enough without any extra picking up of skirts.

They got a good deal more applause than the jugglers, and came back, this time to do a dance with male partners. Somebody called, "Redhead, third from the end, you're losing your underwear!" She wasn't, but she gave a start, and for an instant interrupted her dancing before she caught herself. Everybody shouted with glee. They applauded more loudly than before when the girls and their partners danced off.

Garnet felt her cheeks burning. Leaning over, Oliver asked in an undertone, "Are you shocked?"

"I—I guess I am," she confessed. "I've never seen anything like this before."

"Want to go?" he asked mischievously.

"Oh no!" Garnet exclaimed. She sternly gave herself orders not to blush any more.

The stage was empty now. Two men came out from the sides, carrying more lights. As they went off, the music changed. It became slower, and the drums began to roll as though to herald an event of importance. Though the stage was still empty, a stirring of applause began in the audience.

This, evidently, was what they had come for. The earlier part had been merely a preface, entertaining enough but not worth any further attention. Garnet glanced down at her program, at the name JULIETTE LA TOUR in big letters across the page.

The roll of drums rose to a thunder. The musicians accompanied it with all they had. As the music increased the applause increased with it. The whole audience sat forward.

The curtains at the center back parted slightly. In the opening they saw a tall, laughing young woman with hair like ivory and blue eyes that were nearly as big as dimes. She was wearing a wickedly-cut dress of black velvet shot with silver.

The applause crashed a welcome. Garnet leaned nearer, looking. She had never, never seen anybody like this.

The girl on the stage was beautiful, but she was more than merely beautiful; she had a radiant vitality that made you want to stand up and cheer. Her figure was superb, and the black and silver dress left no doubt about it. Her hair was so pale that it had a white sheen, like moonbeams. Everything about her was shining: her hair, and her healthy skin, and the long silver gloves that beckoned your eyes upward to her white shoulders. At her throat she wore a diamond pendant. There were more diamonds in her hair, and bracelets outside her gloves. The stones were so small that they had to be real. She looked humorous, and tempting; and with it all she had a certain teasing innocence, as though she knew she had been born to give pleasure and she simply loved doing what she was born for.

At first she stood where she was, laughing, while she let them look at her. After a moment she came toward them, her arms held out to them and her whole being as joyful as if she were going to meet a lover she had been waiting for all day. They clapped and shouted and stamped their feet; they could not have heard her if she had tried to say anything, and she did not try to. She kissed her hands to them over and over, her silver gloves twinkling and her fair hair shimmering in the light, and it was as though she were exclaiming to them, "Oh, I love you, I love you, and we're going to have such a grand time!"

The orchestra went into the opening bars of a quick tripping melody. The girl on the stage made a gesture of restraint toward her admirers. Ready now to hear her, they began to get quiet, and she broke into a song that seemed to bubble up spontaneously from her own merriment.

> *Oh I do love living and I have such fun!*
> *And I'll have a whole lot more before I'm through—*

There was nothing remarkable about her voice except that she easily filled the theater with it. She had a decidedly medium range, and had sense enough not to try to go beyond it. But she sang with laughter under the notes, and so clearly that they could understand every word. They loved it.

> *For I never have been sorry for the things I've done,*
> *I'm just sorry for the things I didn't do.*

Garnet reflected that she couldn't have very much to be sorry for. But with twinkling self-reproach the girl explained,

> *The balls I never danced at,*
> *The men I never glanced at,*
> * The evenings I would sit at home and sew,*
> *The drinks I never tasted,*
> *And all the time I've wasted—*
> * My God, the time I've wasted saying no!*

Garnet began to laugh. She had been shocked by the chorus girls. But somehow this singer did not shock her at all. This girl was so full of mirth and joy; she looked like an embodiment of

41

pleasure, doing what she wanted to do and having a wonderful time. The rhythm of the music changed again. The singer swished her skirts enough to let them see that she had legs, but not enough to take their minds off the song as she continued,

> My mother used to say to me that men were most unpleasant,
> And I believed her—yes I did, for that was long ago—
> So this is why you find that I'm so busy just at present,
> I'm making up for all the time I've wasted saying no.

She went on to tell them what a shy maiden she used to be. Then she told them about her adventures, gaily spinning her tuneful yarn. Some of her phrases were quite new to Garnet, but she used her eyes and hips so expertly that a Chinaman could have guessed what she was talking about. Her hearers shouted with laughter. Many of them had evidently heard her sing the song before, for when she came to the choruses they sang with her, tapping their feet and clinking their glasses until the newcomers shouted to them to be quiet. They verged on rowdiness, but this singer did not get rattled like the chorus girl. With no appearance of effort, she kept her audience under control. She was a radiant temptation, but she was also a highly finished artist who knew exactly what she was doing, and she did it so well that Garnet laughed and laughed. When at last the singer ended her audacious performance and tripped off the stage, Garnet clapped her hands until the palms felt scorched.

Oliver was laughing too. Leaning across the table again, he asked,

"Is that what you wanted?"

The singer had come back to take her bows. Turning her eyes from the stage, Garnet looked up at him in delight.

"Oh yes, yes, yes! Only I didn't know—Oliver, I just didn't know variety actresses were as good as that!"

"Most of them aren't," said Oliver.

The girl went off and came back several times, but at length it was obvious that the audience was not going to get quiet without another morsel. She paused, just beyond the wings. The orchestra repeated the tune, and she added,

> So when the preachers scowl at me and say, "What are you doin'?"
> I tell them they should really see the folks who watch my show—

She kissed her hands to them, merrily exclaiming,

42

You meet the nicest people when you're on the road to ruin!

Turning, and waving goodby, she finished over her shoulder,

I'll never, never waste another evening saying no!

Then at last she flashed off into the wings. Garnet turned to Oliver again. She beckoned him to bend his head nearer hers.

"Oliver," she whispered, "that actress—is she a—is she a fallen woman?"

It was the only term she knew for what she was thinking of. Oliver replied with smothered laughter.

"Yes."

"How do you know?"

"Because she looks like it, for one thing. And she didn't buy those jewels out of her salary. Besides, what would she be doing here if she wasn't?"

Oliver was having the time of his life. Garnet knew he was having it because she amused him so much, but she did not mind that. She plucked at his sleeve and whispered again.

"Oliver, tell me a word for it. I mean, tell me the words you thought of when you saw her."

Bringing a pencil from his pocket, Oliver tore a strip from the margin of the printed program. His eyes teased her as he scribbled on it and pushed the bit of paper across the table. On it Garnet read, "Splendid strumpet."

Garnet nodded thoughtfully. She crumpled up the paper with a vague feeling of astonishment. She didn't know just what she had expected, but she had not known that when she saw a strumpet she would see a person of such rare quality. Looking down at her program, she said,

"Juliette La Tour—the name sounds French. There aren't many Frenchwomen as fair as that."

"I don't think she's French. Nearly all performers in this sort of show take highflown names. She's probably called Bessie Jones back where she comes from."

"Oh, stop being so matter-of-fact. It's a lovely name anyway."

There was a male quartet, then a troupe of acrobats, then Juliette or whatever her name was came back. She was more provocative than before in a princess gown of blue velvet, with a gold chain around her neck and gold bracelets outside her gloves. This time she was accompanied by several men, and she exchanged a musical

43

argument with them, beginning, "What do you expect of a girl who looks like me?"

When the curtains closed for the intermission Oliver asked Garnet if she would like more champagne. She shook her head. She was too excited to want anything.

The curtains opened again. The star displayed her charms in a series of breathtaking gowns, then there were several numbers without her. Then at last, she climaxed the show with an exhibition that was announced on the printed program as a dance.

She appeared in a dress of filmy black over pink, and long black lace gloves. The music began slowly, and she kept time to it with a graceful swaying that showed them a lot of gauzy pink petticoats frothing around her black satin slippers.

As the music gradually became faster she raised her arms and began to move her hips. At first it was a slow, seductive twirling that still only fluttered her skirts. But as the tempo of the music increased, her whole body began to turn and twist and ripple. Her skirts lifted and swirled around her, showing them her long slim legs glistening through tights of black lace. She moved faster and faster; the pink skirts rose about her shoulders and drifted down and whirled up again and spun outward. By now they saw that most of her bodice was gone, leaving nothing but two semicircles of black lace to tease them with her breasts, as the gloves and tights of black lace were teasing them with her arms and legs. Swift waves of movement went through her, up and down and back again. The skirts were like a rosy cloud blown around her, never letting them see everything at once nor anything for more than an instant at a time, and never quite revealing as much as she kept on promising.

It was a brilliant performance, and outrageously beautiful. They began to applaud long before she had finished. As she went on they applauded louder, adding shouts and whistles of admiration. In her chair before the stage, Garnet sat bewitched.

She knew she ought to be scandalized. But she just couldn't be. Oliver had no doubt used the right noun to describe that woman, but he had also used the right adjective. She was splendid.

The dance went on and on. If the spectators had had their way it would have gone on indefinitely. But at last the dancer whisked out of sight. If their enthusiasm had been noisy before, it burst like an explosion when she had finished. Garnet sighed in rapture.

That wicked, wonderful dancer, these shouting people, everything—this was *life*.

The dancer came back several times to curtsy. But though they
were clamoring for more, she only laughed and shook her head.
Her laughter was gay and teasing, as though she were telling them
they had had their money's worth, and if they wanted more they
could come back tomorrow night.

The curtains closed. The show at the Flower Garden was over.

F I V E

BEFORE THE SHOW, Garnet had been too excited to eat. But now
she said she was hungry. Oliver told her there was a room at the
hotel open for late suppers.

When they went through the lobby, a clerk handed Garnet a
package that had been delivered for her that afternoon. "What
have you been buying?" Oliver asked as they sat down at table.

"A book of engravings."

"And what," he inquired, "are you going to do with a book of
engravings on the California trail?"

"Don't be so practical. It was such a dear old shop, and the sales-
man was so nice to me, I just had to buy something. I want a crab,"
she announced as the Negro waiter came over to them.

Oliver ordered a crab for her and a cup of coffee for himself. But
just as she began to eat, Oliver sprang up. He had caught sight of
two of his employees, passing the door that was open between this
room and the lobby. He wanted to tell them the salt meat had
arrived this afternoon and could be packed first thing in the morning. They had to carry salt meat for the first part of the trail, for
they would not run into buffalo until they had passed Council
Grove. If he could speak to his men now, he wouldn't have to go
out so early tomorrow. Would Garnet mind eating alone while
he talked to them?

She did not mind, so Oliver went outside. Garnet ate the rest of
her crab. Several other customers, having finished their suppers,
left the room, and she was alone with the waiter. To have something to do while she waited for Oliver, she began to look at the
book of engravings.

45

The pictures were of beautiful girls, one to a page. Under each picture was a fanciful name—Veronica, Esmeralda, Melisande, Mignonette, Florinda. Garnet smiled as she read them, wondering if there were any real women with such names.

A step sounded in the doorway. Garnet half closed the book, thinking it was Oliver coming back. But she heard a swish of silken skirts, and as she looked around she caught her breath. The person coming into the room was the silver-blond actress from the Flower Garden.

The actress was alone. Her clothes were showy and expensive—a plaid silk dress and a mantle of squirrel fur, and a fashionable dark blue bonnet with a plume.

Garnet felt the ripples running up her spine again. The fabulous creature was passing right by her own table; Garnet could have reached out and touched her if she had not been too well-bred to do so. And evidently the actress was going to sit down and eat her supper here, for the waiter was coming forward to meet her. He was bowing in pleased welcome. She must be a favored customer. Garnet hoped Oliver would be a long time coming back.

"Good evening, Cicero," the girl was saying to the waiter. They appeared to be very good friends. "What have you got for me tonight?"

Her enunciation was very distinct, and she had a trained stage-voice, clear as music. The waiter rubbed his hands.

"Something mighty fine, ma'am, mighty fine. They call it étuvée de viandes, it's got chicken in it, and ham and beef, and lots of vegetables and bay leaf and seasonings, oh, it's mighty fine."

"It sounds like it. Lord, I'm hungry. Bring me the stew, lots of it, and some rice with cream gravy, and a big pitcher of milk. And some biscuits and strawberry jam."

"Yes ma'am, I sure will. And what about some oysters first, while they're steaming up the stew in the kitchen?"

She gave an undignified but appreciative whistle, and kissed her fingertips in the air. "Yes, of course, oysters. With horseradish. You're a wonder, Cicero, I don't know how I lived so long without you." Then she began to speak more seriously. "Tell me, Cicero, how's Larry been today?"

He shook his head. "Still right poorly, ma'am. He gets stronger, I think, but it takes a long time."

"Yes, I know it does," she said with sympathy. "Here." Taking a bill out of her purse she slipped it into his hand. "Get him something real pretty to play with. That'll make him feel better."

"Thank you, ma'am, thank you. He sure will appreciate it, ma'am. You're mighty nice to us."

"Oh, shut up. Go crack those oysters before I starve to death."

"Yes ma'am," Cicero agreed. "Now you sit right over here, ma'am, side table away from the draft."

He drew out the chair for her before going off to crack the oysters.

The actress sat down and proceeded to make herself comfortable. She threw back her shawl, took off her bonnet, and put up her hands to loosen her hair. She had on dark blue kid gloves that matched her bonnet.

Garnet felt ashamed of herself for staring. She tried to pretend she was interested in her book. Turning the pages, she looked at the pictured faces with their fantastic names: Veronica, Esmeralda, Melisande, Mignonette, Florinda.

Somebody opened a door in front of her. This door, which was opposite her own table, led directly from the street. Two men came in from outside. The door banged behind them, and they called, "Hey, waiter!"

Garnet started in alarm. The men were well dressed, but they were unsteady on their feet. They looked around, demanding of the air, "Where's the waiter? Can't a man get a drink?"

As the waiter had gone out, the room was empty but for Garnet and the actress and the two strange men. The actress sat at a side table and they did not see her, but Garnet was directly in front of them and they saw her at once. One of them pointed at her, exclaiming joyously, "Hi there, sweetheart!" They started toward her.

She sprang up in fright. But before she could push back her chair they had reached her. One of them caught her wrist and gave her what he thought was an inviting smile as he exclaimed,

"Good evening, pretty thing! What you doing all by yourself?"

"All by yourself," the other repeated. "That's too bad, now we'll take care of that."

"I'm not alone!" she cried, trying to jerk herself away. "I'm waiting for my husband!"

They appeared not to hear her. By this time the second man had caught her other hand. They both flopped into chairs, talking together.

47

Garnet looked around wildly for Oliver. But he was gone, and the door to the lobby was closed. She tried to pull her hands free, but they were holding her, and talking with all their might.

"Now now, you don't want to run off, do you? Pretty girl, stay with us, buy you a drink—"

Then, suddenly, Garnet saw the fair-haired actress in the showy plaid dress. She appeared behind the two men, and slipped her arms around their shoulders. Leaning down between them, she began to whisper in a voice of friendly warning.

"I wouldn't, boys, honestly I wouldn't."

They turned in astonishment. "And who do you think—" one of them began indignantly. But as he saw the tempting vision before him his hand loosened on Garnet's wrist. The actress slipped past him, placing herself against the table so that she stood in front of Garnet.

"I hate to tell you, boys," she advised them, "but you're playing with fire." She bent her head close to theirs and went on, her voice still a chummy half-whisper. "Her husband's a steamboat pilot with a gun on each hip. He's here with her, just stepped out and due back any minute, and only this afternoon he busted a fellow's jaw for getting too close to her. I saw him do it, right in front of this very hotel."

The two men were regarding her with interest. They had both let go of Garnet. "Say, I've seen you somewhere," one of them was saying.

With a swish of skirts the actress lifted herself to sit on the table, pushing the book away to give her room. She was not looking at Garnet. Her attention was all on the two foggy-eyed men.

"Of course you've seen me," she answered teasingly. "Can't you think where it was?" She leaned sideways, supporting herself with one hand, and crossed her knees at the edge of the table with a movement that uncovered several inches of black silk stockings with white clocks.

"What you doing all by yourself?" the other man asked. It seemed to be the only greeting his fuddled head could think of.

"Well, I *was* looking for somebody to keep me company. Only I don't know why I should want to pay attention to a couple of gents who never have noticed me enough to remember me, after all the time I've been around."

"Say, I know!" He slapped her knee, laughing as though the recollection were a great achievement. "Down at the Flower

Garden—" He began to sing, decidedly off key, several bars of her song about "The time I've wasted saying no."

"Now then, that's better." She smiled upon him in congratulation, and the other fellow, not wanting to be outdone, began to whistle in some slight relation to the same tune. The actress laughed intimately. "Well, it sure is nice to run into a couple of my friends, unexpected like this. And just when I was feeling kind of lonesome, too. Maybe we could all have a drink together, what do you say?"

They said that was fine. They said it in a great many bumbling words. Garnet huddled back in her chair, keeping very quiet. She was not frightened any longer. She almost forgot she had ever been frightened. She looked and listened, while the men chattered and the actress went on with her inviting lines and gestures, and all Garnet's thoughts concentrated into one big awesome phrase: "So *that's* how they do it!"

She was so fascinated that she was almost sorry when she heard the actress say,

"They lock up the bar in this married women's hotel at ten o'clock, but there's a nice place down the street where we can get anything we want. You know, Tony's."

They wanted to go to Tony's, they must go to Tony's right away, and they made a great noise about it. None of the three paid any more attention to Garnet. The men got up. Their girl-friend steadied the shakier of the two with a hand on his elbow. As they passed her table she picked up her shawl, and they all three went out through the doorway by which the men had entered.

Garnet stared after them. She had a feeling that she ought to go now, and look for Oliver. But the actress had left her bonnet, so she must have meant to return, and Garnet wanted to thank her. How nice she was, how very kind—Garnet hardly knew how to express the idea of protection offered in such a way, but it was very kind all the same.

The waiter came in carrying a platter on which some raw oysters were arranged around a jar of horseradish. He looked around for his customer, but noticing her bonnet still there he set the platter on the table. A moment later the street door opened and the actress came in alone. She closed the door and slid a bolt into place, and came over to Garnet.

"It's all right, dearie," she said with a reassuring smile. "They won't bother you any more."

She was about to go back to her own table, but Garnet had sprung to her feet.

"Wait a minute. I—I don't know how to thank you, but I'm very grateful." She hesitated an instant, then rushed on. "I didn't know what to do."

"I know you didn't, sweetheart. It's all right."

Garnet fumbled for words. She did not want to comment on the fact that while she hadn't known what to do, the other girl so obviously had. But the actress was not at a loss. She patted Garnet's arm, saying,

"You saw me bolt the door, didn't you? They can't get back in. So don't worry."

"I'm not worrying. I'm just so glad you happened to be here."

"Why, I live in this hotel, dearie. I come in for supper lots of evenings after the show."

"Tell me how you got rid of them," Garnet begged.

"Oh, I lost 'em at Tony's. Said I didn't like what the bartender was showing us, and went around to see what was on the shelf." She shrugged. "End of act."

She had a gay voice and a friendly spontaneous smile. Garnet smiled back at her, shyly. The actress lost no beauty on close inspection. She had classic features and a skin like milk and roses, and her blue eyes did look as big as dimes.

"Please don't go yet!" Garnet exclaimed. As she spoke she took a step nearer, and her hand brushed the edge of the table, knocking off the book of engravings. It fell on the floor, open. Before Garnet could bend to get it her companion was picking it up for her.

"What pretty pictures," she said, straightening a crumpled page. "There now, keep it shut and the wrinkles will smooth out." She smiled comfortingly. "You aren't still scared, are you, dearie?"

"No indeed, I'm not scared any longer. That's not why I asked you to stay. I wanted to tell you—I saw you tonight at the Flower Garden. You were wonderful!"

"Why, thank you. Mighty sweet of you to say so. I saw you there too, down in front with a gent." She added, with a friendly amusement, "You hadn't been there before, had you?"

"Why no. I've never been in New Orleans before. I've always lived in New York. This is my honeymoon trip."

"And your husband's showing you the town?"

Garnet nodded. "And I'm so glad to see you again now, so I can tell you how much I enjoyed your entertainment, Miss—why, I don't know what to call you. There was a name on the program, Juliette something, but do I call you that?"

The actress looked at her with a sudden intensity that made Garnet uncomfortable. "Why don't you want to call me that?"

"Why—my husband said it probably wasn't your real name. He said most ladies in the theater took stage names. You see," Garnet apologized, "you're the first actress I've ever met. I didn't mean to be rude."

The other girl was laughing now, softly and kindly. "You're not rude, darling. I don't believe you could be rude if you tried. Your husband was perfectly right. Juliette is just a fancy tag, they like everything French in New Orleans. My name is Florinda."

"Why—thank you, Miss Florinda," Garnet said. She spoke slowly. Her mind had skipped back to the book of engravings. When the actress had picked up the book from the floor, she had smoothed out a page, and the picture on that page was labeled Florinda. But maybe it was just a coincidence. Garnet caught at her manners and added, "But I am being discourteous, asking your name before I told you mine. I'm Garnet Hale. Mrs. Oliver Hale."

"And I'm pleased to meet you, Mrs. Hale, and you're a dear, and I'm glad you had fun at the show. Come back next week. I've got a couple of new songs, and a dress that's going to take the roof off." She kissed her fingertips in the air again. "Black satin. Fits like an onion-skin."

She was so gay and unaffected that Garnet began to laugh. Maybe her name really was Florinda. Anyway, she was a darling person and Garnet felt quite at ease with her now. Just then they heard the opening of the door that led from the lobby. Oliver came in, turning on the threshold to call to his men,

"And box it tight. There's plenty of bumps on the way to Council Grove."

Garnet spoke to Florinda. "That's my husband. I want to tell him how kind you were to me."

Oliver had a momentary look of surprise as he recognized Garnet's companion, but he smiled and bowed as Garnet said, "May I present my husband?" That was all she could say, as she did not know Florinda's last name. She went on to explain that two drunken men had been annoying her and Florinda had made them leave. Oliver started with indignation.

"How did they get in?" he demanded. "I thought that outside door was supposed to be locked at night!"

"Well, it wasn't locked," said Garnet. "They came right in from the street."

Oliver spoke to Florinda gratefully. "Thank you very much. It was extremely kind of you, Miss—Miss La Tour, isn't it?"

"No, it isn't," Florinda returned smiling. "As I was just saying before you came in, that's a stage tag. My name is Grove, Florinda Grove."

"I don't know how to express my gratitude, Miss Grove."

Garnet did not hear what they said next. She was thinking. The book of engravings, Florinda. And when Oliver came in, he was saying, "—on the way to Council Grove." It was very odd for anybody to snatch a name out of the air like that.

The waiter came in with a tray holding the rest of Florinda's supper. He paused in surprise as he saw the oysters still untouched. Florinda called to him,

"Hold it, Cicero. I met these friends of mine and started talking." Turning back to Oliver, she dropped her voice confidentially. "Do me a favor, will you, Mr. Hale?"

"Certainly. What is it?"

"Don't say anything about that door not being locked. The waiter there, he's supposed to lock it every night at ten. But his little boy's been awfully sick and he's worried about him all the time, and when you've got worries on your mind you just can't help forgetting things. You know how it is, don't you? He'll get in trouble if they find out."

Oliver nodded understandingly. "Of course. I won't tell on him."

"Thanks. That's mighty nice of you. Well, I guess I'll say good night now and get my supper. I've got an early rehearsal tomorrow. Pleased to have made your acquaintance, I'm sure."

She waved at them and went to her own table. Garnet looked back at her as they went out. She was thinking that she ought to be angry with Oliver for his carelessness in leaving her alone, after warning her that New Orleans was the wickedest port this side of Marseille. But she couldn't feel angry, for if he hadn't left her she would not have met Florinda. And while Florinda was a strumpet who danced in black lace tights, all the same Garnet thought she was one of the nicest people she had ever seen.

SIX

OLIVER WAS NOT SURPRISED when Garnet told him how Florinda had picked up the name she gave them. He laughed, and said it was time she learned not to ask people what their real names were. When she got into the wild spaces west of Santa Fe, she would meet a good many men who had left their names behind them.

Garnet was astonished. She hadn't known about that. But she promised to remember.

They slept late the next morning, and it was nearly eleven o'clock when they went down to breakfast. One of Oliver's clerks was waiting to speak to him, so after breakfast he gave Garnet the key and she started upstairs.

When she reached the second floor, she saw two men walking along the hall toward the head of the staircase. One of them was a big common-looking fellow with a red face; the other was more slender and more neatly dressed. They were talking heatedly. Evidently they were angry about something. As she approached them, Garnet heard the big red-faced man saying,

"—ain't left the hotel, I'll swear to that, the damn slippery—"

She did not hear the rest, for they went past her. Garnet glanced after them distastefully as she went on toward her own door.

Her rooms were near a turn in the hall. In the corner made by the turn was a big cabinet with glass doors, higher than her head. The cabinet held sea-shells and wax flowers and a lot of other souvenirs, with a sign saying you could buy them downstairs. Garnet paused to look up at the exhibit, wondering why tourists were always supposed to waste their money on trash they would never dream of buying at home.

A breeze from an open window blew her skirts around the corner of the cabinet. She took a step closer and drew the skirts away, handling them carefully to prevent a snag. Lifting her head again, she gave a start.

She was looking into the shadowy space between the wall and the cabinet. Huddled back into the space was the blond actress who had said last night that her name was Florinda Grove.

Florinda was bending forward, listening. The voices of the two

53

angry men could still be heard, though their words were indistinct. Looking over her shoulder, Garnet saw them reach the head of the stairs and start down. She looked back at Florinda.

Florinda had not moved. She must have seen Garnet, but she gave no sign of it. Garnet saw now that she was sumptuously arrayed, in a green-striped taffeta dress and a cape of marten fur and a bonnet with green ribbons. Even in the shadows she was flashing with jewels. As she looked, Garnet was suddenly conscious of her own dress, a plain navy blue silk with white collar and cuffs. She wondered if Florinda had really meant to wear that outfit on the street. But she forgot Florinda's clothes as she looked again at Florinda's face.

By now her eyes were more used to the dimness. She could see that Florinda's fine skin was chalky, and her features were stiff like those of a plaster cast. Florinda's eyes were staring blankly at nothing. She looked like a woman scared out of her wits.

All of a sudden Garnet remembered the words of the big beefy man. "—ain't left the hotel, the damn slippery—"

Good heavens, those men must have been talking about Florinda. They were looking for her, and she had rushed behind the cabinet to hide from them. Garnet could not imagine why they wanted her, but it must be for no good reason or Florinda would not be so terrified.

She thought quickly. Her own room was not twenty steps away. Nobody would think of Florinda's being there.

Holding her skirts carefully, so that no rustle should attract attention, she walked into the narrow space. "Come with me," she said sharply under her breath.

Florinda gave her a look of cold suspicion. "What do you want?" she demanded in a frightened whisper.

"Be quick, Florinda!" Garnet urged. "Come to my room."

"*Your* room?" Florinda's eyes went fearfully over her. From the hall came another sound of footsteps. Florinda's hand closed tensely around Garnet's wrist. A Negro maid went past, carrying a broom and dustcloth. Luckily she did not turn her head. They heard her knock at a nearby door and go in to do her daily cleaning. Garnet exclaimed, as vehemently as she could in a whisper,

"Don't just stand here! Somebody else will see you the same as I did."

Florinda gave a slow, doubtful shake of her head. "I don't get it, dearie. What's the idea?"

"Don't you know me?" Garnet demanded.

"Sure, I know you. You're the kid I talked to last night in the supper-room."

"And now you're in trouble, aren't you?"

Florinda shrugged bitterly. She did not answer.

"There were two men bothering me last night," said Garnet, "and you took care of me. Now there are two other men bothering you and I'm going to take care of you. Come to my room. Nobody's going to look for you there."

Florinda's blue eyes widened. "Hell for breakfast," she said earnestly.

Repressing a start at her shameless language, Garnet said,

"My room is just down the hall. I'll stand at the door so you can tell which one it is."

Without further argument she hurried to her bedroom door and unlocked it, noticing thankfully that the room had been made up while she was at breakfast, so there would be no risk of intrusion.

Florinda came out from behind the cabinet. She gave a quick glance at both ends of the hall, picked up her skirts, and ran like a scared rabbit to where Garnet was standing. Drawing her inside the room, Garnet locked the door.

"Now then," she said with determination, "you can wait here till they've gone."

Florinda dropped into a chair. For a moment she sat up straight, looking around to make sure there was nobody else in the room. Then at length she leaned back, closing her eyes and taking deep slow breaths. The color began to come back into her face. Garnet waited, giving her time to recover.

After a minute or two Florinda opened her eyes. She turned her head with a smile of deep wondering gratitude.

"You are an angel," she said. "You are a complete, unbelievable angel."

Garnet did not feel angelic. She felt scared at this impulsive adventure and she was wondering where it was going to take her, but she did not want Florinda to know this. So she smiled back, asking, "Can't I get you something to make you feel better?"

Florinda put her hand up and stroked her lips. She had on green kid gloves that matched the green stripes of her dress. "Could I have a drink of water? My mouth feels all dried up."

"Why of course." Garnet filled a glass at the washstand and brought it to her. "Wouldn't you like a glass of wine?"

"No thanks, darling. I haven't got wits enough right now to want to addle 'em."

Garnet brought smelling-salts and a flask of lavender water from the bureau. "Take off your bonnet," she said, "and I'll bathe your forehead."

"I'm not the fainting sort, Mrs. Hale," Florinda protested in some surprise. But she obeyed, holding her bonnet in her lap and leaning back with her eyes closed while she whiffed at the smelling-salts and Garnet patted her temples with lavender water. Florinda's white-gold hair was parted in the center and drawn back to show the tips of her ears, and in her ears was a magnificent pair of square-cut emeralds. Garnet gave an exclamation when she saw them.

"What beautiful earrings!"

Florinda smiled. "Nice, aren't they? Gent gave them to me." She opened her blue eyes again. "Gee, that lavender water feels good. You're terribly sweet, Mrs. Hale."

"My first name is Garnet. Why don't you call me that?"

"I didn't think I knew you well enough. But thanks, I will."

Garnet put the stopper back into the flask. Florinda sat up and looked around at the two windows overlooking the street. She walked over to one of the windows, and sheltered by the curtain, she looked down. After studying the street she came back.

"Look, Garnet," she said seriously. "I don't want to start any trouble for you."

"You're not going to. This is my room and my husband's, and we know our rights. Nobody can come into a private room without being invited. Nobody's coming in here. So you can stay with me, just as I told you, until those men go away."

"They're not going away, sweetheart," said Florinda. She took off her fur cape and hung it over her arm. "And there's another angel-face down there by the front door. I think he's waiting for me to come out."

"Well, he can't stay there forever," Garnet insisted. "We have the parlor next door, and if you have to spend the night with us you can sleep on the sofa. Anyway, wherever it was you were going, you can't go now, so just stay here."

"Good Lord," Florinda said softly, still incredulous. "I was going to rehearsal," she added. She turned up the face of a little jeweled watch pinned to her bosom. "They'll be wondering what's become of me."

"They'll have to rehearse without you," said Garnet, sitting down on the edge of the bed. "So forget about it."

"Look here, baby," Florinda said sharply. "Why are you hiding me? You don't know me."

"You didn't know me either when you made those drunkards let me alone. And lots of people wouldn't have been interested in that Negro waiter enough to care whether his little boy got well, or whether he got scolded for leaving the door unlocked. You're in trouble, Florinda, and I don't know why, but I don't think you deserve it. You're too kind and thoughtful."

"You sweet kid," Florinda said tenderly.

Garnet repeated, "You can stay here, Florinda."

Florinda gave her a puzzled glance. "What's that you keep calling me?"

"You told me last night your name was Florinda Grove," said Garnet. She glanced down, running her finger along a crease in the counterpane. She half expected Florinda to tell her another name now, but Florinda only laughed a little, saying,

"Why yes, so I did." Without more comment, she added, "Well, you're wonderful to let me stay. I don't know if we can hold 'em off forever, but at least it's a break between acts. Gee, I'm still shaking. I was never so scared in my—"

There was a knock on the door. Florinda stiffened. Garnet opened the door to the parlor and gestured toward it. Snatching up her bonnet, Florinda slipped past her. The knock turned into an impatient pounding, and Oliver's voice called,

"Garnet, it's me! Let me in!"

"It's my husband, but you'd better stay where you are," Garnet whispered. She closed the parlor door and called back, "Yes, Oliver, I'll be right there."

She thanked heaven that it was only Oliver at the door, for she was panting so hard that anybody could have seen she was up to something. Grabbing his hand, she pulled him inside and locked the door after him.

"What's the matter?" he exclaimed in alarm.

"I've got something to tell you. Sit down."

To Oliver's astonished questions, she answered, "No, nothing has happened to me. But do you remember the actress from the Flower Garden?"

Oliver laughed. "Oh Lord. I might have known you'd pick up that moonshine blond again. What is it now?"

She told him about finding Florinda hidden behind the cabinet, and about her coming here to hide in the parlor. Oliver was dubious. He was still more dubious when she admitted that she had no idea what the strange men wanted. But he shook his head with affectionate resignation. "All right, all right. If she can get away I'm not going to stop her. But that's all I'm going to promise till I find out more about it."

He went across the room and opened the parlor door. Florinda was standing just beyond it.

"Come in here," said Oliver.

Florinda came back into the bedroom. She stood holding her bonnet and wrap, waiting as though ready to go away if he should tell her to. But though Oliver was not as readily moved by other people's concerns as Garnet, he was not heartless. Besides, Florinda was exceedingly fair to look upon. He demanded,

"Now tell me what this is all about."

Florinda lifted her shoulders and lowered them in a graceful shrug. "Well, to be brief, sir, I need to get out of here. I need to get out of town. If I don't get out of town without being seen by certain people, I'll go to New York in a pair of handcuffs."

Garnet winced at the words "handcuffs." Oliver stood looking thoughtfully at his unexpected guest. Florinda bore his scrutiny without flinching.

"You're taking it very calmly," Oliver commented at length. Garnet could tell by the way he spoke that Florinda had begun to win his liking. Oliver was used to danger, and he liked people who kept their heads. He would have had no patience with tears and fainting fits.

"I'm pretty scared," Florinda said frankly. "But I don't get hysterics, Mr. Hale."

Oliver nodded with approval.

Florinda spoke again. "By the way, I might tell you that if you do help me get out of town, it's not going to cost you anything. I've got money, and I've got it where I can get it."

"We weren't thinking of that!" Garnet protested.

Florinda smiled at her. "Maybe not, dearie. But I'm used to paying my way."

Oliver was considering. "Candidly, Miss Grove," he said, "I'd like more details."

Florinda gave him an ironic little smile.

"Of course," she reminded him, "you've got no reason on God's earth to believe me."

There was another sound of knocking on the door.

SEVEN

THIS WAS NOT the tap of a caller requesting friendly admission. It was a series of whacks that shook the door on its hinges.

Garnet felt her pulses jump. Florinda jammed her fist against her mouth. Oliver jerked around toward the door.

At that instant, somebody outside tried the doorknob, rattling it as though he had a right to be angry because the door was locked. He began to pound again, shouting, "Open in the name of the law!"

The parlor was no safe hiding-place this time. Garnet sprang over and flung open the door of the wardrobe, pointing violently toward the inside. Florinda was trembling, but she scrambled in, pulling her skirts after her. Oliver exclaimed toward the racket outside,

"You needn't break down the door. I'll let you in."

By this time he was angry. If Florinda's pursuers had wanted to turn him into her champion, they could have chosen no better way to do it. Oliver had spent eight years leading pack-trains, and he was not impressed by yells and bluster. He flung open the door.

"What is the meaning of this?" he inquired.

A couple of men stood there. One of them was the big red-faced fellow Garnet had passed in the hall. The other was not his former companion, but Mr. Maury, the hotel manager. The ruddy stranger was pompous; evidently he was the one who had been pounding. But Mr. Maury was unhappy and apologetic.

"I'm sorry this intrusion has been necessary, Mr. Hale!" the hotel manager exclaimed wretchedly. "But this officer is looking for an escaped criminal—he has a warrant."

Poor Mr. Maury spoke as if he were in pain. He was not accustomed to disturbing his guests with warrants.

Oliver gave him no help. He stood there like a man secure in his own righteousness, who was indignant at not being also secure in his own bedroom. Mr. Maury floundered in misery.

"He thought—I assured him he must be mistaken—but he was sure—"

"You better let me handle this," cut in Mr. Maury's ruddy companion, giving him a shove with his elbow. He was not miserable at all. On the contrary, he seemed to be enjoying himself. "My name is Kimball," he announced. "I seen her come in here. Room 23, ain't it?" Mr. Kimball satisfied himself with a significant look at the number on the door. "Room 23 it is, I seen her with my own eyes. Now you," he demanded, glaring at Oliver, "you got a woman in here with you?"

"Certainly I have," Oliver returned. He made a gesture toward Garnet, who was standing at one side. "This lady," Oliver continued, "is my wife. Have you something to say to her?"

The two visitors looked at Garnet. Mr. Maury was suffering agonies. But Mr. Kimball gazed unabashed, his eyes going up and down her figure with a fleshly interest that would have roused her fury even if Florinda had not been hiding in the wardrobe. With Oliver at her side, she was not frightened as she had been in the supper-room last night. She gave him the stare Miss Wayne had taught her. It was a gaze of insulted dignity, calculated to reduce its victim to ashes.

The man was used to out-yelling opponents, but he had never tried to out-stare the graduate of a young ladies' academy. He bore Garnet's eyes a moment, then he began to get even redder than he naturally was. He cleared his throat, looked down at his shoes, flicked his toe at a speck of dust on the carpet, and looked up again.

"Well, I seen skirts!" he declared defiantly.

Oliver did not reply. Garnet did not shift her eyes.

But as though the sound of his own voice had given him courage, Mr. Kimball went on. "I seen skirts, and I seen 'em come in here. And I seen 'em to be green skirts." He nodded solemnly. "Green they was."

Oliver glanced around at Garnet's plain navy blue dress. He smiled slightly.

"I hardly think," he said, "that we men can be blamed for making mistakes about ladies' apparel. If you have passed this door during the morning, you may have seen Mrs. Hale entering the room."

"There now," exclaimed Mr. Maury, "I told you! Mrs. Hale, I do beg your pardon."

"There ain't nobody else in here, is there?" demanded Mr. Kimball, stepping across the threshold and peering around.

Her success with her eyes gave Garnet courage to use her voice. "Will you kindly get out of my bedroom?" she requested coldly.

"He's not going to trouble you, my dear," Oliver assured her. He came over and put his arm around her shoulders. Standing thus he turned his head toward the red-faced man. "Step back to the other side of that door," he ordered.

Oliver was used to dealing with men of tougher makeup than this. The intruder obeyed him.

"Come on away!" Mr. Maury begged. "That woman's not here. She can't be. I told you!"

The burly man did not obey Mr. Maury. Standing just beyond the doorway, hands in his pockets, he surveyed the room. Garnet moved to sit down in a chair facing the door. Her teachers had prepared her for parlors and ballrooms; they had not dreamed, nor had she, how useful this same preparation would be in outwitting the law. She leaned back, drooping gracefully, like a helpless female trembling before big rude men.

Mr. Kimball began to speak to Oliver, uncomfortably.

"Well, maybe I'm wrong, sir. But we're on the track of a desperate character. She lives in this here hotel, and I sure thought I seen her going in here." He shuffled his feet. "Must have been one of the other rooms along here, likely."

"Would you care to look in the other room of this suite?" Oliver asked. He brought the key from the bureau.

They waited while Mr. Kimball unlocked the hall door of the parlor. After a minute or two he came back.

"Ain't nobody in there. Thank you, sir. Mighty good of you, co-operating like this. Sorry to have troubled you. But we got to do our duty, you understand."

"Are you sure this woman is still in the building?" Oliver asked.

"Oh, she's here, sir, no mistake. She came in last night, and she ain't been out this morning. We've got men at all the doors. And one of our men's gone into her room to wait, in case she should come back in there. She can't get away," he assured them. "Don't you worry about that."

Oliver addressed Mr. Maury. "Would you mind telling me," he asked with dignity, "how this respectable hotel happens to be harboring a criminal?"

Mr. Maury wrung his hands. "Now Mr. Hale, how could I know who she was? She came and went like anybody else and paid her rent on time. How could I tell she was wanted for murder?"

61

"Murder!" gasped Garnet. This time she was not acting. She sat forward, wide-eyed with horror.

Mr. Kimball nodded solemnly. "Yes ma'am, murder." He went on, to let them know he was only acting like a good citizen when he came to their room. "You can see that in a case like this we got to look out for everything. Desperate character she is," he repeated.

Garnet had never seen a desperate character. But she remembered Florinda's gaiety, her easy friendliness; the description simply did not fit. "Are you sure?" she begged.

"Yes ma'am," the big man returned with emphasis. "Shot up a gambling house right in the middle of New York city, she did, shot it all to pieces, killed two men, two of them."

Garnet gave a little gasp. Of course. The Selkirk murder. Somebody had shot Mr. Selkirk and another man in a gambling house. But not Florinda! No, no, no. She heard Oliver ask,

"But who on earth is this woman?"

"If you mean what's her name, sir, I can't say I rightly know. Don't guess anybody knows for sure. She changes her name every year or two, and with good reason, no doubt about it. Past few months she's been performing at a place downtown called the Jardeen dess Flowers, under the name of Juliette La Tour." He took a notebook from his pocket and began turning the leaves importantly. "Before that, she was doing her stuff at the Jewel Box in New York."

"The Jewel Box!" Garnet echoed.

"Yes ma'am. Not a place you'd ever go to if you was in New York. At that time she was calling herself Charline Evans."

"And her crimes have been so dangerous," said Oliver, "that the New York police had to send a small army after her?"

"Oh, we ain't the regular police, sir. Wouldn't trust the police for this," he boasted. "You know how stupid them fellows are, can't see what's in the same room with them." Enjoying his spot as the center of attention, he elaborated with gusto. "Truth is, we was hired private."

"Private?" Oliver repeated with a puzzled frown.

"Yes sir. You see, one of these men she killed was a fine gentleman, yes indeed, had a beautiful home and just the sweetest young wife you ever saw, heartbroken the poor lady is. Name of Selkirk."

Garnet did not hear Oliver's answer. The big man's words had scalded her mind. It wasn't true. It couldn't be true.

The big man was still talking. "Yes sir, I'll tell you how it was.

She shot Mr. Selkirk because, well, to be frank, he'd been keeping her when he was a bachelor. You know how some of them rich men are with actresses. But when he got married, he told this fancy woman he was done with her, just like a high-minded man ought to do. But she wouldn't let him go. He was her last chance, you see. She was through at the Jewel Box. Not that them girls at the Jewel Box are supposed to be angels, but she'd got too drunk and disorderly even for them."

Garnet felt a stab of wrath. Florinda was *not* drunk and disorderly. Last night she had ordered milk with her supper, and this morning she had refused a glass of wine. Garnet looked anxiously at Oliver. He was not looking at her, but she saw a tiny crinkling at the corner of his eye. She had seen it before. It meant that Oliver was being very polite, but that he was faintly, privately amused.

The big man went on. "She pestered poor Mr. Selkirk and pestered him, but he told her as plain as he could that he was through. So finally, when she found out he meant what he said, she followed him to the Alhambra Gambling Palace one night. The Alhambra Gambling Palace on Park Row. She followed him there, and shot him dead." Mr. Kimball gave a slow nod. "Now ain't that a terrible thing?"

"Terrible," Oliver agreed virtuously. The little crinkles were fairly quivering now. "But you said she shot two men. Who was the other one?"

"Name of Mallory, sir. He was another fellow happened to be gambling there that night, sort of bum. I guess one of her shots went wild." Mr. Kimball shook his untidy head regretfully. "Well now, after all this, would you believe it, the police let this woman get away. Yes sir, she got right out of town. She disappeared. I guess she thought she was safe." He paused for his climax. "But guess what happened then."

"I can't imagine," Oliver said dryly.

"Well sir, poor Mr. Selkirk had a friend. Fine gentleman named Mr. Reese. And this friend, he couldn't stand the idea of this disgraceful woman going free. So he hired us to look her up. And finally we traced her to New Orleans. It took quite a while, New Orleans being two weeks from New York and it taking such a long time for letters to go back and forth. But we found her," he assured them complacently. "And when we found her, here was this shameless creature, flaunting herself right out on a public stage

63

just like she didn't have a thing on her conscience." He shook his head again, saddened by the thought of such depravity. "Ain't it dreadful what a woman can do? Yes sir, sometimes I think when they're thoroughly abandoned, they can carry on worse than us men."

But now that he had heard the story, Oliver was not interested in Mr. Kimball's philosophy. As though he had just remembered Garnet, he said,

"Thank you for your explanation, Mr. Kimball. But frankly, sir, I must ask you to withdraw. I believe my wife has heard about all she cares to."

"I'm sure of it," Mr. Maury urged. "My good man, you should not have gone into those sordid details in the presence of a lady. I hope, Mrs. Hale, that you suffer no ill effects from this experience!"

"Don't you worry, ma'am," Mr. Kimball said to Garnet soothingly. "We'll get that woman before the day's out. By night we'll have her safe in handcuffs."

The word "handcuffs" ran over Garnet's nerves like a rat. She stood up and faced her visitors.

"Don't worry, Mrs. Hale!" Mr. Maury begged her miserably.

Garnet looked him over disdainfully. "I am not worried about anything," she said with frozen composure, "except having my name on the register of a hotel that is patronized by such people. I assure you, gentlemen, that I am not used to living under the same roof with murderers and—and strumpets!"

Mr. Maury was wringing his hands again. "But Mrs. Hale, how could I know?"

"This is my honeymoon trip," said Garnet. "I thought it was going to be a beautiful time that I could remember as the beginning of my life's happiness. And here my room is broken into, I am accused of harboring a—a woman of ill repute—"

"Mrs. Hale!" groaned Mr. Maury.

She drew herself up. "I don't think you knew who she was, Mr. Maury. But if you want respectable people to stay here, I certainly think you'd better be more careful." She turned to Oliver, though she did not dare to meet his eyes lest they both start giggling. "I feel quite faint," she murmured.

Oliver responded nobly. He gave her his arm, and she leaned against him.

The manager and Mr. Kimball bowed themselves away with

64

more apologies. Oliver closed the door behind them. Turning the key, he said clearly,

"My dearest, I can't tell you how sorry I am that you were disturbed like this! Lie down and try to compose yourself. Would you like a glass of sherry?"

His lips were trembling with mirth, but his voice was tender. Garnet answered plaintively.

"Why yes, thank you, that might be refreshing. You are always so considerate of me."

"I'll pour it at once," said Oliver. He brought the sherry, letting the bottle clink noisily against the glass as he poured.

But when she had taken a sip of sherry, Garnet could hold herself in no longer. She whispered,

"Can't we let her out, Oliver? She must be about to smother!"

"I'll draw the curtains," said Oliver, with a glance at the door. "Perhaps darkness will help relieve that headache."

Garnet nodded. He drew the curtains and lit a lamp. As he approached the wardrobe, Garnet felt a tremor. She was wondering how Florinda was reacting to what that awful man had said about her. He had such a strident voice that she must have heard every word.

The wardrobe door swung open. Oliver said in a low voice,

"All right, Florinda, the coast is clear."

But for a moment Florinda did not move.

She was shaking with laughter. To keep silent she had gagged herself with one of Garnet's petticoats, stuffing the cloth into her mouth and clamping her teeth on it. At the sight of Garnet and Oliver a fresh gust of merriment swept through her, and she continued to hold the petticoat to her face, helplessly. They waited, laughing too.

At last Florinda pulled the ruffles out of her mouth. She took Oliver's hand and stepped down.

Garnet held out her handkerchief. Florinda took it and began to wipe away the tears her laughter had brought to her eyes. She sank into a chair.

"I'm sorry," she gasped. "But I couldn't help it. You were so funny, both of you. I never heard such an act." She blew her nose joyously.

Garnet was reflecting that it was odd about people. Some of them reveled in trouble, rolling over in it and wrapping it around them, never talking about anything but what they had been through and demanding respect for still going through it. One would think, to hear them, that it was a virtue to pinch a wound every morning to make sure it would not get well.

But others, like Florinda, simply rejected trouble. They pushed it away as soon as they could. They laughed at it.

Florinda had leaned her head against the back of her chair and was stretching herself from head to foot like a cat.

"Gee, it's good to get unwound again," she said to them. "Garnet, that last bit from you nearly put me in chains. One more line about insulted virtue, and I'd have laughed out loud and they'd have heard me."

Oliver pulled up a chair and sat down. "Well, that settles it," he said with finality. "I'm on your side."

"I got that by the way you talked to them," said Florinda. She laid a finger along a stripe of her taffeta skirt, as though to be sure her glove matched the stripe in color. Without looking up, she asked, "But why, Mr. Hale?"

"I don't know anything about the Selkirk murder," said Oliver. "I've heard of it—in fact, I bought some goods from the Selkirk estate for my Western trade. But I don't believe that tale about somebody's disinterested friendship."

Florinda gave him a sardonic smile, sideways. Oliver continued, "It costs a lot of money to search the country. And after all, Selkirk is dead. It's not doing *him* any good."

Florinda had listened with shrewd admiration. "You figured that out all by yourself, didn't you? You're a bright young man, Mr. Hale."

"I'm bright enough, but I think even a blockhead could see through that. One might almost get the idea," Oliver concluded, "that Selkirk's friend had a strong personal reason for wanting you hanged."

Garnet went cold. "*Hanged?*" she echoed.

"That's what happens when you're convicted of murder," Oliver reminded her.

Florinda shrugged. "Well, frankly, Mr. Hale," she said, "I don't think any jury would hang a girl with a face like mine. But I could get a term in the New York state prison. And I probably would."

"That's awful enough!" cried Garnet.

"And when I came out of there," Florinda said, "I wouldn't have a face like this." She said it so bitterly and knowingly that Garnet exclaimed,

66

"Florinda! You've never been to *jail*, have you?"

"No, darling. But I've known some women who have. I know what they do to you there."

"What, Florinda?" Garnet demanded. She felt slightly sick. She had never thought about jails before.

Florinda spoke tersely. "You work fourteen hours a day making bags and blankets. The food they give you is swarming. If you break the rules they beat you with a leather strap on your bare back." Her hand went out, almost unconsciously, to stroke her fur cape as it lay on the chair beside her. "I've seen them when they come out," she added. "All they want is a bottle of gin and a hole to crawl into."

Garnet's lips were drawn back from her teeth. "I never heard of anything like that!" she cried. "I've lived in New York all my life!"

Florinda smiled at her briefly. "I guess we didn't grow up in the same part of town, dearie."

Garnet thought of the stately quiet of Union Square. She thought of all those streets in New York that she had never been allowed to walk on.

"You're not going to prison," she said firmly. "Florinda, you didn't do what that dreadful man said, did you?"

Florinda stood up. With both hands she pushed back her silver-blond hair. Her back to the curtained window, she faced them both.

"No," she answered.

"I knew it," said Garnet.

Oliver spoke practically. "Who did kill Selkirk, Florinda?"

"That—'disinterested friend.' His name is Reese. I think you've guessed that already."

"All right," said Oliver. "Go on."

Florinda put her hands on the back of the chair in front of her and held it tight while she answered.

"I did work at the Jewel Box. I was the top star there. The stage name I used was Charline Evans."

Oliver nodded. Florinda continued,

"But it's not true about Selkirk. Oh, I'm no angel with a halo on my head, I guess you know that. But it just happens I never had anything to do with Selkirk. I never even spoke to him in my life. And I didn't kill him."

Oliver said, "Were you accused of killing him when it happened?"

"Yes. Reese killed him. Then he told the police that yarn about my being Selkirk's girl-friend and said I'd killed him in a rage because I couldn't get him back. Reese is a rich man, old family and all that sort of thing, I knew the police would believe him before they'd believe me. So I got out of town. My friends helped me get away. I came down here. It's a two weeks' journey, it seemed like coming to the end of the world. For a while I kept out of sight. But I didn't hear a whisper from New York. There were at least fifty people who saw Reese take out his gun and shoot—the police would have to believe some of them. So finally I thought the whole thing had blown over as far as I was concerned. And I was dying of lonesomeness, I'm a sociable creature. Besides, I can't live forever without working. So I went down and got a job."

"How do you get a job in a place like the Flower Garden?" Garnet asked eagerly.

Florinda smiled. "Why dearie, it's not hard, not if you know your trade. I went to see the manager and told him a yarn about London and Paris, which he didn't believe, and then he said, 'Why did you quit?' and I said, 'I had a little trouble about a man.' He believed that, so he said, 'What can you do?' I said, 'Give me some music and I'll show you.' So he called a fellow who played the piano. He said I could do a number in the show he was opening for Christmas. I did the number, and stopped the show."

"I don't wonder," Garnet said softly.

"Yes, dear, you saw me last night. I'm the greatest entertainer in the country."

"And you still heard nothing from New York?" asked Oliver.

"Not a thing. I didn't get a hint that anybody wanted me until this morning. I came out of my room on the way to rehearsal, and saw Reese and that beefy gent at the end of the hall. I'd never seen the beefy one before, but I knew Reese right away. I ducked behind that cabinet before they saw me. It didn't take me two seconds to figure out what had been going on. I think Selkirk's family has been after the police to put somebody on trial for shooting him, and Reese hired that crew to bring me back so I could take it instead of him."

"And you think you could be convicted?" Oliver said.

Florinda shrugged wisely. "Reese can bribe witnesses and scare the police, Mr. Hale. I can't."

Oliver nodded slowly. He asked, "Were you there the night of the shooting?"

Florinda made a grim little movement of her lips. It could hardly be called a smile. "Yes," she answered, "I was there."

She said nothing else. Oliver considered. Florinda had been speaking in a steady voice. But Garnet saw that her hands in their fancy green gloves were holding the chair rigidly, as though she needed support, and her eyes were narrow and tense. Garnet could see by Oliver's thoughtful face that he was still not content. She demanded in alarm,

"Oliver, don't you believe her?"

"Why yes," said Oliver, "I believe her." But he was regarding Florinda shrewdly. "You haven't told us very much, you know," he said.

"Haven't I?" she asked quietly.

"Why no," said Oliver. "You said there were at least fifty people in the gambling house that night. There must be some reason why Reese thinks that you, and not one of the others, could be convicted for the murder."

Florinda shut her eyes for an instant, and took a quick breath, as though she were in pain and trying not to cry out. Garnet walked over and put her arm around Florinda and stood by her defiantly.

"Oliver Hale," she said, "you let her alone."

Florinda turned her head. Her blue eyes were so soft and tender that Garnet felt tears very close to her own.

"Thank you, dear," Florinda said in a low voice.

She went back to the chair she had occupied earlier and sat down, resting her arm along the back of it. Garnet stood by her. Florinda took Garnet's hand in hers, and held it while she spoke to Oliver.

"Mr. Hale," she pled, "suppose I talked till day after tomorrow? What good would it do? For all you know, I might just be spinning a yarn to make you sorry for me. And besides—" She stopped, and Garnet felt the hand holding hers give a little shiver. Florinda could defy trouble, but she could not defy tenderness. Garnet had a feeling that maybe Florinda had not had very much tenderness in her life. Florinda said, "And besides, I can't talk about it."

She put her forehead down on her arm. Her gay taffeta dress rustled as she moved, and the light danced over her jewels as though everything she had on was laughing at her as she begged,

"Don't make me tell you any more." She drew a short shuddering breath. "Mr. Hale, did something ever happen to you that you just *couldn't* talk about? Something that you had to push down deep inside of you and forget, because if you didn't forget it you'd go perfectly mad?"

Oliver moved uncomfortably. He did not answer. He could not; nothing of that sort had ever happened to him. Garnet caught herself wondering if Oliver had ever had a profound experience of any sort. Well, she hadn't either, now that she thought about it, but she did feel a strange sense of understanding.

Still without lifting her head, Florinda pled,

"Please help me get out of here! I can pay for it. I don't care where I go. I'll go to Europe, I'll go to South America, I'll go to some quiet little village up the river and take in sewing. I'll never make any trouble for anybody as long as I live. But don't send me back to New York!"

Oliver stood up. "Good Lord, Florinda," he exclaimed, "I'm sorry!"

He put his hand on her shoulder.

"It seems pretty obvious," he added, "that you don't deserve the New York state prison. I guess the rest is none of my business."

Florinda raised her head. "Thank you," she said softly. "Thank you. And please—" she smiled contritely—"forgive me for carrying on like that. I won't go to pieces again."

Oliver smiled too. "Oh, stop being sentimental." He glanced at Garnet. His face was humorous again. "And now that the hotel is surrounded like a fortress under siege," he said, "and there's a man in Florinda's room so we can't go in there to get any of her belongings—well, now I suppose we'd better start thinking up a way to get Florinda out of town."

EIGHT

They discussed the problem. Florinda did not know what men might be on guard at the doors, but she said Reese had probably taken care to hire men who could recognize her. She had been on the stage all her life, so thousands of people knew what she looked like.

Oliver agreed. "I don't think there'll be any trouble putting you on a boat," he added, "if we can get you past the doors and into a closed carriage. But getting you out of the hotel—that's going to be difficult."

Florinda put her chin on her hand. "Isn't there any way," she asked, "to make me inconspicuous?"

Garnet burst out laughing. She hadn't meant to. It just happened. "Inconspicuous?" she repeated. "You?"

Florinda looked across the room at her bejeweled reflection in the mirror. "Yes, dear, I see what you mean. But another costume might help."

Oliver shook his head. "We could get you a quiet dress, of course." But his eyes went over her silvery hair and her resplendent figure. "That's not enough."

"Oh, hell for breakfast," said Florinda.

They were silent. Then Garnet gave a sudden little gasp. She had an idea.

"I know!" she cried. "Oh, I know! Florinda, will you do exactly what I say?"

"Why yes, darling!" Florinda exclaimed. "What?"

"All right, listen to me. If you'll keep your mouth shut and not talk about damn and hell and bottles of gin—"

"Oh dear. I'll keep my talk nice, really I will. What else?"

"There's just one sort of woman," said Garnet, "who can go about with her face covered, in clothes that hide her figure, and have everybody step aside respectfully to let her pass."

"What sort, for heaven's sake?" Oliver demanded.

"A widow," said Garnet. "A newly made widow, in a heavy black veil that comes down to her knees."

"You're right," Oliver exclaimed with admiration.

"You're a genius," said Florinda. "Can we get the costume?"

"Oh yes. That's one dress you can always be sure of finding in any town. Widows are being made every day, some of them most unexpectedly. There's always a shop with funeral weeds made up. That's something I *know* about," she insisted.

Florinda was delighted. After a little discussion, Oliver began to outline a plan. By this time Oliver was enjoying himself very much. He liked intrigue.

"I'll go down and tell the clerk at the desk that a relation of mine has just come in from a plantation down the river. She is taking a boat for—for wherever there's a boat going tonight, I'll ask about that first. I don't suppose it makes any difference where you go, does it?"

71

"No difference at all. I'll take any boat I can get."

"My dear cousin is in great affliction," Oliver continued, "for her husband was buried only last week."

"She came South with her husband," Garnet contributed, "in the hope that the mild winter would restore his health. Now she's going home."

"Yes, excellent, that will account for her traveling so soon after her bereavement. She wishes to seek consolation in the bosom of her family. While she's here waiting for the boat, my wife is taking care of her. She wishes on no account to be disturbed."

"Nobody's going to remark that they didn't see your afflicted cousin come in?" Florinda suggested.

"If they do, I'll say I brought her in by a side entrance out of respect for her natural wish to have privacy in her grief. However, I don't think Mr. Maury is going to trouble us with any more questions about anything." He picked up his hat. "Now I'll go ask about boats."

"I'll buy the clothes," said Garnet. "I seem to remember a shop on Royal Street that had widow's weeds on display."

Oliver said he would be back in a few minutes, and told Garnet to wait for him. She began making a list of the things Florinda would need. A mourning costume, toilet articles, black cotton stockings. Florinda had on black shoes, which would do, but her stockings were silk, and Garnet had to explain that ladies in deep mourning did not adorn their ankles with silk stockings. "And some baggage," she added, "Oliver can get that. What are you laughing at?"

"You," said Florinda. "Me. All this."

She linked her hands behind her head and stretched out. Garnet's gaze went admiringly along her perfect profile. Florinda said,

"Garnet, there are some nice folks down at the Flower Garden and I don't guess I'll ever see them again. I'd like to tell them goodby. If I write a letter, will you keep it and drop it in the post office after I'm gone?"

"Why yes, I'll be glad to."

"Thanks." Florinda bit her lip regretfully. "I wonder what they're going to do without me tonight. I never walked out of a show before. I feel like a traitor."

"But it's not your fault!"

"It is too, in a way. I should have kept out of trouble."

She looked so remorseful that Garnet searched for something

to catch her interest. "Now don't sit here worrying while we're out," she said briskly. "You can write your letter—here's a pen, and there's some paper and sealing-wax in the table drawer. And I have several good books." She picked up a copy of *Two Years Before the Mast*, which she had bought because it told about a voyage to California.

Florinda took the book and turned it over in her hands, examining the cover and opening it tentatively in the middle. She handled it with such artless unfamiliarity that Garnet exclaimed,

"Florinda, didn't you ever read a book?"

Florinda tried to remember. "You mean, start at page one and read every page right through to the end?" She shook her head. "Why no, I don't believe I ever did."

Garnet could not think of anything tactful to say. She changed the subject by telling Florinda that if she got hungry, there was a bowl of fruit in the other room. Fortunately, just then Oliver came in.

"There's a boat leaving tonight for St. Louis," he said. "It stops at Natchez, Vicksburg, and several other towns on the way."

"Just what I need. Get a stateroom all the way to St. Louis. I can leave the boat sooner if I need to."

"In the name of Mrs. Florinda Grove?"

Florinda agreed. Oliver did not comment that this name was safe because she had never used it till last night. He had meant what he said when he told Garnet that people's names were their own business. He said he had a carriage waiting to take Garnet and himself on their various errands, but before he could open the door again Florinda interposed.

"Just a minute, dear people." She was gathering up her skirts. "Oliver, take a look out of the window."

"What are you doing?" he demanded.

"I told you this wasn't going to cost you anything. When I said I had money where I could get it, I meant I had it under my petticoats."

"That's not necessary. You'll need whatever you've got. I'm not very much attached to money," he answered smiling. "I'll take care of this."

"Oh, stop going on like a charity worker. I've got lots of money. Look at the scenery, Oliver."

As she evidently had her mind made up, he yielded and looked

73

out of the window. Beckoning to Garnet, Florinda rested her foot on a chair and raised her skirts.

Her stockings were held by pink ribbon garters embroidered with rosebuds and fastened with gold clasps. Her drawers and petticoats were made of such excellent muslin that Garnet felt a pang of regret for the other clothes she would have to leave in her room. Stitched to the lower edge of her corset was a strong fat canvas purse.

Taking out a roll of banknotes, Florinda put her foot back on the floor and shook her skirts into place. "Here, Garnet," she said. "If it's not enough, let me know."

Garnet took the bills. Oliver turned around. Florinda added, "You're the nicest people I ever knew. I love you both."

She kissed her hand to them as they went out.

Florinda's roll of bills amounted to a hundred and ten dollars. Oliver said this would not be enough, but they agreed to tell her it was. He told Garnet to buy the clothes, while he got the steamboat ticket and a couple of carpetbags. He would leave those with Florinda. Then he had to go down to the warehouse, but he would be back at six o'clock to escort his afflicted cousin to the boat.

Garnet told the dressmaker she was buying an outfit for a friend whose husband had been killed that morning in an accident. The good lady did not think of doubting the story. Her business was run for just such emergencies.

It was all very exciting. When she came back to the hotel, laden with bundles and boxes, Garnet looked like a bride glowing with the joy of a shopping spree. Florinda said Oliver had already brought the bags and steamboat ticket. "Now show me what you've got," she added eagerly.

Gathering up her skirts, she sat on the floor before the pile of bundles. Garnet stirred up nests of tissue paper and brought out the sad black garments. Florinda went off into gales of laughter at the sight of them. While Garnet spread the dress on the bed, Florinda rummaged in the other boxes, delighted to find that Garnet had provided her with a hairbrush and a looking-glass and some clean towels.

"You darling. I'll travel in luxury. Oh my soul, look at all these black cotton stockings."

"Well, you can't wear the same pair all the way to St. Louis," said Garnet. She opened a bureau drawer. "I couldn't find any

74

readymade underclothes, so I'm going to give you a nightgown—"

"Oh Garnet, I couldn't!"

"Yes you can, so be quiet. And some chemises and drawers."
Garnet smiled over her shoulder. "When you picked up your skirts,
I noticed that everything you had on was perfectly immaculate. So
you're not going on a long journey with no change."

"Imagine," said Florinda softly, "you thinking about my pants.
Thanks, angel."

"Don't you want me to help you pack?"

"Oh no. When you've been on the stage, you get so used to
packing you can do it with no trouble at all." She was taking
handfuls of tissue paper out of the boxes. "This will be fine to
keep the clothes from rumpling. I'll put in the marten cape first.
Lucky I was wearing it today."

"When you change your dress," said Garnet, "you'd better take
off some of your petticoats. A widow's dress isn't very full. How
many petticoats are you wearing?"

"Seven."

"Put four of them into the bags."

"All right, I'll leave room for them."

Florinda began folding the fur over her knees. Garnet noticed
that she was still wearing her gloves. She wondered if all actresses
took such care of their hands. It must be awkward to work with
gloves on, she thought, but Florinda did not seem to find it so.
Garnet curled up on the bed and gave her some instructions about
the journey.

"If you stay in your cabin most of the time," she concluded,
"nobody will think anything of it. But it's all right to sit on deck
when you need fresh air."

"Yes. I understand." Florinda curled up a corner of the tissue
paper between her thumb and forefinger. "Garnet," she said gently,
"aren't you going to give me a chance to tell you how I feel? I
don't know just how to say it, but all this—it makes me so warm
and lovely inside."

For a moment Garnet did not answer. Then she said, "You don't
need to thank me."

"Why not, baby?"

"Because I've had such a wonderful time doing it. I guess you
wouldn't have thought of that," Garnet said shyly. "You've had
such a sparkling sort of life. Theaters, and the way you look, and
everybody cheering."

Florinda tucked the fur into the carpetbag, and paused to reflect on what Garnet had said. She looked around. "What are you used to doing, Garnet?" she asked.

"Why, the usual things girls do. You know."

"But I don't know. Sometimes I've wondered."

"Wondered? What do you mean?"

"About girls like you. Girls who live on Bleecker Street and Union Square. I've seen them shopping in Stewart's, and walking on the street with their mothers. I wondered what they did all day."

Garnet heard her with astonishment. She had not dreamed that Florinda might be as curious about her as she was about Florinda. "Haven't you ever known anybody from my part of town?" she asked.

Florinda was folding her supply of clean towels. "Gents," she answered. "Lots of gents. But not ladies. You're the first one I ever talked to. Tell me about you."

So Garnet told her about day school and dancing school, and Miss Wayne's Select Academy, and then how she had met Oliver when he came to New York to buy merchandise for the California trade. Florinda put her head down on her hand, laughing.

"Oh dear, it does sound so sweet. And you're really going to take a trip to that strange country?"

Garnet nodded.

"Gee, it sounds like a long way. You're awfully brave."

"I'm not as brave as you are," said Garnet.

"Me? I'm not going out to the last end of nothing."

"No," said Garnet, "but you don't even know where you're going. And you're all alone."

"Oh, that doesn't matter," Florinda said as she folded up Garnet's nightgown. "I'll be in a civilized country, at least. And I won't be alone long. I'll get settled somewhere, and I'll make friends."

She put in the nightgown and began folding the extra chemises. Garnet clasped her hands around her knees and watched.

In spite of that casual answer, she thought Florinda was very brave indeed. Only yesterday she had been the star of a brilliant show. And today she was leaving all that, and leaving everything she owned except what she had happened to have with her when she started for rehearsal this morning. But she was doing it so cheerfully, as though it were no more difficult than memorizing a new song. Garnet looked over Florinda's gaudy dress and her emerald earrings and her jeweled watch, and wondered where she had learned such courage.

"How were you brought up, Florinda?" she asked abruptly.

Florinda put the chemises into the bag. She replied good-humoredly.

"Well, dear, I can't say I *was* brought up, not if that means select academies and medals for politeness. I guess I just raised myself."

"But—" Garnet began, and hesitated. She did not want to be prying. But she did want very much to know what Florinda meant.

"I don't mean my mother wasn't good to me," Florinda amended, as though she thought she had sounded disloyal. "But she had to work, you see, and then she was sick a long time. She fell off a scaffolding backstage, and she couldn't work after that. She died when I was thirteen."

"You mean she had to work all the time you were a little girl? What a shame. Didn't she have any people to help her?"

"No, she'd been raised by an uncle, but he was dead. She sang in theaters. She had a nice voice, and she was quite pretty. We got along all right when I was a child. I could work too, you see."

"You could work? But not when you were a little girl!"

"Oh yes I could, dearie. They used me in some baby scenes before I could talk. And when I was eight years old I got a part with lines. I never had any trouble getting parts in those days, I was a beautiful child." Florinda began to laugh. "Really, Garnet, you needn't sit there with your mouth open like it was something awful! I never minded."

"Then you've been working all your life, literally."

"Why yes, dear. If you're too polite to ask how long that's been, I'm twenty-three."

"I've seen plays with child actors in them," Garnet said slowly. "But I never thought the children were supporting their parents."

"Most of 'em are, dearie," Florinda said dryly. She began putting away the extra pairs of black cotton stockings.

"But your father!" Garnet exclaimed. "Why didn't he make a living for you? Or did he die early?"

Florinda was wrapping up her looking-glass so it would not be broken in travel. "I never laid eyes on my father," she answered without raising her head. "He went off before I was born."

Garnet clapped her hand to her mouth. "Please forgive me! It's none of my business. I'm so sorry I asked."

"Oh for pity's sake," Florinda said. "You're such a nice girl." She laughed shortly, and explained. "My father was a Norwegian sailor. One night when he had shore leave he came to the theater where my mother was singing. He liked her, and not long afterward they were married. She was madly in love with him. But he turned out to be a gilt-edged weasel. He went to sea again, and she never saw him any more."

Garnet heard her with dismay. "But Florinda," she protested, "maybe he didn't mean to desert her. Maybe the ship was lost. Didn't she try to find out if the ship was lost?"

Florinda smiled ironically over her shoulder. "You'd have found out, Garnet, and I would. But she didn't. She was one of those trusting helpless people who wouldn't know how to go about it." Florinda tucked the looking-glass into place, and after a moment she added, "To tell you the truth, she didn't want to find out. She kept trying to believe he was going to come back."

"Then—she never knew?"

"Oh yes, she knew at last. An old actor in a show she was working in got sorry for her. I suppose he thought it would be easier on her to hear the truth, whatever it was. So he went down to the shipping company and inquired. The ship wasn't lost. Nice safe voyage to Brazil, and then back to the home port in Norway. Town called Trondheim, or some such name."

"But—" Garnet was thinking hard. She had just been married herself, and she wanted to dissent. "Maybe something happened to him in Trondheim. Maybe he wanted to come back to her, and couldn't."

"No, dear, he didn't want to come back," Florinda said coolly. "His ship had touched at New York on the way home from Brazil. He was in port for two weeks. But he didn't come near my mother. She didn't know he'd been in New York again until that actor found out about the voyage."

"Oh Florinda, how could he!"

"I don't know, dearie. I don't know how any man could leave anybody sweet and helpless like her with a baby coming. But he did."

She picked up a pile of black-bordered handkerchiefs, laid aside one to be carried this evening, and put the others into the bag. Garnet asked,

"What did she do, when she really couldn't doubt the truth any longer?"

78

Florinda picked up a box of toilet soap. Her answer was simple. "She fell off the scaffolding."

"She—you mean she did it on purpose?"

Florinda paused, holding the box of soap. "No, I don't think she did it on purpose," she answered slowly. "I think, when she found out what sort of man she'd been loving all those years, she just didn't care what became of her. She wasn't interested enough to be careful."

Garnet felt a pain all over. "And you were only thirteen?"

"I was twelve. It took her a year to die." Florinda was looking down. Her eyes followed the design printed on the box.

"And you went on working in theaters, all the time she was dying?" Garnet asked.

Florinda was still examining the box. But she did not seem to be looking at it; she seemed to be looking through it, toward something a long way off.

"Not all the time. I couldn't get parts. I'd always had parts when I was a little girl, because I was so pretty, and I knew how to act. But when my mother had her fall, I was getting too big for child parts and not grown up enough to play ladies. The gawky age, you know, when your hands and feet get too big and you're out of balance all over and nobody wants to look at you. I worked, of course, I had to work. I got a job sweeping out a saloon. I served drinks too, and sang for the customers, but I couldn't earn very much. It wouldn't have been too bad, though, except for seeing my mother. She suffered so much pain."

Florinda was briefly silent, remembering. Without lifting her eyes, she went on.

"Sometimes I thought I couldn't stand watching her. I can take what happens to me, but I can't stand seeing other people suffer. I used to hope, every time I went out to work, that she'd be dead when I got back."

Garnet saw her give a strange little smile, sideways.

"There was a horrible old man who peddled dope around the saloon. He had the jerks and I was scared of him. But he was very kind to me. He gave me some stuff to give her sometimes. It looked like a white powder. I don't know what it was. But it put her to sleep. He never charged me anything for it, he just gave it to me. Sometimes the strangest people are so good. Later on, when I was working at the Jewel Box and had lots of money, I went back down there and found him. I thought maybe he'd want to go to an old

79

folks' home and be comfortable, but he didn't want to. So I gave him three hundred dollars so he could get as coked up as he pleased."

Garnet swallowed hard. A sad story usually brought tears to her eyes. But this did not make her feel like tears; this was deeper than sadness. She asked,

"And you've never heard anything of your father?"

Florinda shook her head.

"Do you suppose he's dead now?"

"I hope he is," said Florinda. She spoke with a quiet rage. "I hope he died screaming, like my mother died. I hope he died in a tenement four flights up, with no water except what you could lug up in a bucket, and rags stuffed in the window to keep out the snow."

She gave a low, bitter little laugh. "Funny, you making me remember all that. I don't like to remember it. It makes me ashamed of myself."

"Oh Florinda, not ashamed! You were just a child! You did the best you could."

"Yes, I did the best I could. But I mean, I'm related to him. I hate to think I'm related to a man like that. And I look like him."

She was sitting very still on the floor, among the bags and boxes and the litter of paper. There was a silence. Garnet looked at her beautiful profile and her great blue eyes and her silvery hair. She wondered how it would feel to see such a reflection in the glass, and to remember that what you were seeing was your legacy from such a father. She said suddenly,

"You're not helpless like your mother."

"No, dear, I'm not." Florinda laughed tersely. She roused herself, and turned the carpetbag around to go on with her packing. "I always get along," she added.

"Yes," said Garnet, "and I think you always will."

"Oh, I will. You're mighty right. Nobody's going to kill me the way that man killed my mother."

She picked up the box of soap, and glanced over her shoulder at Garnet.

"I'll die of something one of these days, no doubt," she ended coolly, "but I'll be damned if I die of a broken heart."

She said it with a half-humorous energy. Garnet had no doubt that she was right.

NINE

Florinda gave a short little laugh. "Look, Garnet. Let's stop talking about that cockroach I'm descended from. It's no fun."

"Why of course. We'll stop right now," Garnet agreed. She changed the subject. "You've just about finished packing, haven't you?"

"You're a sweetheart," Florinda said gratefully. "Yes, I believe this is everything, except for the clothes I've got on. I'll put them in later, when I've changed."

Garnet looked at the black clothes on the bed, and then at Florinda again.

"What are you thinking about?" Florinda asked.

"Your disguise. You know, your hair is so unusual, it might be noticed. When you dress up, brush it tight under your bonnet."

"That's an idea. My hair's a dead giveaway." Florinda stood up, and glanced at herself in the mirror over the bureau. "But Garnet, won't I look kind of suspicious with not a lock showing?"

"No, I've got an idea." Garnet was taking out her own hairpins. "Bring me the sealing-wax, and light the candle."

"Garnet, what are you doing? My dear child, you're not cutting off your hair!"

"Just a little bit, I'll never miss it. Give me the black bonnet. Now look."

Using the sealing-wax, Garnet stuck two loops of her own black hair under the front edge of the bonnet, so it would look as if the wearer's hair were parted in the middle and drooping over her forehead. Florinda whistled with reverence as she helped her.

"This is great. I wish I had your head, dearie. I could use it."

"You can take out the black hair as soon as you get on the boat," said Garnet, "unless you see somebody you've known before." She shook her hair and put a comb into it to hold it back from her forehead.

Florinda was stroking her green-ribboned bonnet with affection. "I do hate to throw this away. It was very expensive. Could I put it into the bandbox the black bonnet came in? Would it be all right for a widow to carry an extra bonnet?"

81

"Why of course, that's quite all right." Garnet picked up a bandbox, labeled "Mme. Sidonie Drouet, Finest Widow's Weeds, Bonnets, Veils," and the same words repeated in French. "I had to have this wrapped in brown paper," she said, "so the label wouldn't show. You won't need to wrap the outside, but your green bonnet should have lots of tissue around it so nobody could see the color if the box-top should slip. I'll wrap it while you're taking off your dress."

She knelt on the floor and began to smooth out the bonnet-ribbons.

"Thanks," said Florinda. "I'll be mighty glad to have it. Well, I'll get undressed now."

Turning to the mirror, she took off her bracelets and began to unbutton her gloves. Garnet wondered again why she had been wearing gloves all this time. Thinking back, she remembered that in the restaurant last night, though Florinda had taken off her bonnet and shawl, she had not taken off her gloves. And in the theater, she had worn gloves with every change of costume. Garnet wondered if the gloves were merely a fancy, or if Florinda had some reason for wearing them all the time.

She reached for a sheet of tissue to be wrapped around the bonnet. Just then she heard Florinda's taffeta dress rustle, slipping over her petticoats to the floor. Garnet glanced up.

She caught her underlip between her teeth and bit hard. She had not gasped aloud, but she had nearly done so. Without looking around, Florinda bent to gather up her dress. Garnet bit her lip as hard as she could.

Florinda's hands and arms were covered with scars. The scars were big shiny red patches that crinkled like paper as she moved, and between the patches was a network of skin drawn this way and that, like cloth that had been torn and badly mended.

Garnet looked down again and pretended to be very busy wrapping the bonnet. She heard Florinda pick up her dress. The rustling of taffeta and tissue paper sounded loud in the room.

Garnet knew what made scars like that. They were burns. A girl at school had had one on her arm, caused by an overturned lamp. But that had been a small burn received in childhood, barely noticeable now. These marks of Florinda's were new, and they were not small. The scars seared her hands and crisscrossed her arms above the wrists. Even above her elbows were several little pinched-looking places, as though sparks had fallen there.

Garnet tried to think of some ordinary remark about something else, but for the moment she could not. She could not think of anything, except that at some fairly recent date Florinda had fought a battle with fire. It had not crippled her, and time would probably make the scars less glaring than they were now. But part of her beauty was gone forever. Garnet felt revolted, as though she had been looking at a work of art made ugly by vandals.

She remembered. "Did something ever happen to you that you just *couldn't* talk about?"

So that was it. Garnet was very glad she had not given an audible start when she saw Florinda's tortured hands. She would go on, not noticing them. She thought that if she were to see Florinda every day for the rest of her life, no power on earth would ever drag out of her a word to show that she had ever noticed them.

There were some things you could not talk about. Garnet did not know what they were. But she had learned today that they did happen.

She had finished wrapping the green bonnet. She put it into the box and glanced up again.

Still facing the mirror, Florinda was untying the strings of her petticoats. She was doing it as serenely as though her hands were normal. But they were not normal. Besides the twisted skin, her fingers were not as flexible as they should have been. Garnet felt an impulse to say, "Let me help you," but she smothered it with a feeling of shame that she had even thought of saying it. Florinda had learned, no doubt with grim determination, to make her damaged hands do the work of good ones. An offer of help would be cruelty beyond what Garnet could bear to think of.

Florinda had on seven petticoats. Without turning her head, she asked,

"Take off four, you said, didn't you?"

"Yes," Garnet answered, "four." She felt glad to have the conversation started again. Tucking some loose paper around the bonnet, she heard the starched petticoats rattling down.

Florinda stepped out of her skirts and gathered them into her arms. "Why Garnet," she said, "how nicely you've packed that bonnet. Now I'll get these things put away, then I'll climb into that funeral rig. My dear, how do widows ever get married again, if the gents can't see them except in scary outfits like that?"

Garnet looked up. Florinda was half laughing, half scowling at the funeral dress, and as Garnet raised her eyes Florinda stuck out her tongue at it like a bad child making a face at the teacher's back. Garnet began to laugh. She laughed and laughed, and Florinda laughed too. The tension was broken, and Garnet felt as relieved as if the tension had been a string around her neck.

"They don't wear black all their lives," she answered. "After six months they lighten it up with touches of white. Sometimes second mourning is very becoming, especially to young widows with fair hair like yours."

Florinda piled the petticoats on a chair, and kneeling on the floor again she began folding her taffeta dress. The scars were red as flames beside the whiteness of her shoulders. "I look divine in black," she was saying. "But not all covered up in it like something out of a haunted house. Throw me that nice big piece of paper, will you?"

Garnet obeyed. "How well you do that!" she exclaimed, watching Florinda tuck paper into the sleeves and smooth it between the folds of the skirt.

"I'm used to it, dearie. There now, pretty thing," she said to the dress, "in you go." She scrambled up and set to work on the petticoats.

Garnet felt as if something else had been spoken. It had passed between them clearly. Florinda had kept the scars hidden as long as she could. But she had to reveal them when she changed her dress. So she had done so, giving Garnet a chance to see the scars, and to be shocked by them, and to ask about them if she wanted to ask. But Garnet had not asked, and by now Florinda knew she was not going to. Through her chatter, she had said plainly, Thank you.

"Now then," Florinda went on, "I'll turn myself into a weeping widow."

She changed her silk stockings for the respectable cotton ones. Her pink silk garters looked very odd around the sober cotton tops. This done, she took out her hairpins. Her hair tumbled below her waist in a rippling silver-gilt sheet.

"What marvelous hair you have!" Garnet exclaimed.

Florinda was not modest about her looks. "It is nice, isn't it?" she agreed. "When I was a little girl in shows I always wore it down, with a blue ribbon. The audiences loved it. They said I looked like a little angel. Where's my new hairbrush?"

"Here it is."

Garnet brought the hairbrush to the bureau. She had not put up her hair after taking it down to cut off the locks she had stuck under the bonnet-brim, and as Florinda saw their reflections side by side in the glass she gasped with delight.

"Garnet, *look* at us! Aren't we gorgeous together?"

Garnet smiled at the contrast—her own blue-black hair and rosy cheeks, beside Florinda's porcelain fairness. "We do look pretty, don't we?"

"Pretty? Hell for breakfast, we're a sensation! I wish we could do a sister act. We'd bring down the house. I'd dress us—oh, Garnet!" She sighed with ecstasy. "You'd wear white and gold to show off your coloring, and I'd wear black and silver to show off mine. Think of it. Can you sing?"

Garnet laughed and shook her head. "No. I can carry a tune, but my voice is so little you can hardly hear it across a room. Anyway, I'm not an actress."

"Oh well, it was just a vision."

Florinda sighed again, letting it go the way of all visions. She screwed up her hair and pinned it tight. Garnet brought her the black petticoat. Florinda giggled as she slipped it over her head.

"Garnet, this thing is simply enormous in the waist. If you ask me, I think it was designed for a woman who was expecting a great blessing. I'll cross the drawstrings in back and tie them in front, that's the only way to keep it on. Now help me get into this dress. How do you open it?"

"It opens down the front, stupid, can't you see? Hold up your arms and let me pull it down over your head."

Still giggling, Florinda complied. The thin red skin of her scars flashed as she held up her arms. Garnet hated having to look at them.

"Hell for breakfast," Florinda remarked, as with one hand she gathered the dress at her narrow waist and with the other she began to button it up the front. "Even a most respectable lady doesn't have to pretend she's shaped like a watermelon. Why Garnet, it's nearly the same size all the way up. I can hardly make it meet across the bosom."

Garnet was looking with dismay at the tightness of the black cloth across Florinda's breasts. "That's not decent," she protested.

Florinda looked at herself with great amusement. "Well, dear, that's the way God made me, and this is the first time I've ever had cause to regret it. I look damned awful, don't I?"

"While you're pretending to be an elegant widow," Garnet ordered sternly, "*don't* swear."

85

"I won't, sweetheart, honestly. I'm going to be so good you wouldn't know me."

"And unless you can alter the fit of that dress," Garnet advised, "keep your shawl around you whenever you leave your stateroom. Now here's a wedding ring in this little box."

Florinda slipped the ring over her scarred finger. She picked up the bonnet, tried to put it on, and laughed helplessly as she tangled herself in the veil.

"Please, Garnet!" she begged.

Garnet helped her arrange the long heavy folds. Florinda was choking with merriment. The veil covered her nearly to her knees. Garnet helped her put on the shawl, and arranged the veil outside it.

"Now the rest," said Florinda. "Black gloves, black-edged handkerchief, black purse. I'm all ready." She turned back to the mirror, and gasped. "Garnet, you are a wonder. *Look* at me."

Garnet looked. As she looked, a pain came up and pressed hard on her throat.

Florinda was gone. There was nothing left of her but a cloud of blackness. Every inch of her was covered. Behind the heavy black veil was a face, but it was shrouded, indefinite, just a ghost of a face. Florinda stared through the veil, laughing at the black bundle of herself in the mirror.

Garnet realized suddenly that the day was nearly over. In a few minutes more, Oliver would be here, and Florinda would go with him to the wharf. How strange it was, she thought. This time yesterday she had not known there was such a person as Florinda on earth. But today she knew her so well. She knew that Florinda had fought a battle with life, and had fought it with a splendid gallantry. And now Florinda was about to set out on a journey with no idea how it was going to end, and she was laughing as though she thought it was funny.

Garnet had heard a great deal of laughter in her life. She wondered now how much of it had been merriment, and how much of it had been a clear shining courage.

Florinda turned from the mirror, exclaiming,

"Say, I'd better start getting used to my costume. Watch me, Garnet. Am I right, the way I do this?"

Florinda knew her trade too well to try to play a scene without rehearsal. She walked around the room, picking up her skirts modestly as she came to imaginary stairs. She raised and lowered the veil several times.

"You're doing it very well," Garnet said at length.

"Yes, I think I can manage. The main difficulty is seeing through this black fog. But if I can get away, I won't mind a stumble or two."

Garnet looked around. The empty boxes on the floor had an air of grim finality about them. "Is there anything else we should do?" she asked.

"Oh yes, that reminds me—the letter I wrote is in the table drawer. It's addressed to one of the girls at the theater. Thanks for taking care of it."

"I'll mail it after four days," said Garnet. "By that time you'll be a long way off."

"Yes, a long way off." Florinda paused. She threw back her veil again. "Garnet," she said, "before I go—I just want to tell you I'll remember you as long as I live."

Garnet felt her throat getting choked up again. "I'll remember you too, Florinda," she said in a low voice.

"You're so good," said Florinda. "I—well, I guess if I was the weeping sort I'd be shedding tears about now."

Garnet put her hand to her eyes. "I am shedding some. I'm sorry. But I—I don't want you to go like this!" She pulled out her hand-kerchief and dried her eyes. "I don't know where you're going," she said brokenly.

"I don't either, Garnet. But wherever it is, I'll be thanking you for it when I get there."

Garnet swallowed hard.

"I didn't mean to make you cry, dear," Florinda said gently. "I just wanted you to know."

"I'm not crying any more," Garnet said. She twisted the damp handkerchief between her fingers. "Florinda, will I ever see you again?"

"I don't know, dearie."

"You can look me up if you ever come back to New York. My father is Mr. Horace Cameron. He lives in Union Square. And Oliver and I will be there again next year. You can find us in the city directory."

"I don't think I'm ever going back to New York, Garnet."

Garnet clenched her black eyebrows and thought hard. "I might see you in St. Louis," she suggested hopefully. "We're going through St. Louis on our way to Independence."

"I won't be in St. Louis when you get there," Florinda answered. "I might get off at one of the towns lower down. And even if I go all the way to St. Louis, I won't stay there. With things the way they are, I wouldn't feel safe in a river port."

"No, I suppose you're right. There are too many people going through St. Louis this time of year."

There was a long silence. Florinda stood turning her black purse over and over between her black-gloved hands. "Well, anyway," she said finally, "I'll never forget you. Any time you happen to be lonesome you can think about me and know I'm thinking about you. Because I will be thinking about you, every day I live."

They heard a knock at the door. Garnet opened it a crack and saw Oliver.

"Is she ready to go?" he asked.

"Yes, she's ready. Come in."

Oliver burst out laughing as he saw the dismal figure in black. Taking Florinda by the shoulders, he turned her around and around, laughing at the way the baglike dress hid her curves. He said a boy was waiting to carry her bags. He'd go and bring him in.

As he went out, Garnet crossed the room quickly. "Goodby, Florinda," she said.

Florinda threw back her veil again. "Goodby, darling." She put her hands on Garnet's shoulders and kissed her. "You're the nicest girl I ever knew," she said.

There were footsteps in the hall outside. Florinda lowered her veil. When Oliver came in with the boy, she was standing by her bags, slumped like a lady weighed down by sorrow.

The boy picked up the bags. For his benefit, Oliver gave Garnet a brief husbandly kiss, saying, "I shan't be long, my dear." He turned to Florinda, offering his arm with respectful affection.

Standing in the doorway, Garnet watched them go off together down the hall. They were doing it well. Florinda walked with dragging steps, and Oliver patted her hand comfortingly as it lay on his arm. Garnet watched until they disappeared around the turn, past the cabinet where Florinda had been hiding this morning.

She went back inside and closed the door. Going to the window, she pushed back the curtain. The dark had come down, but there was a street-light near by. A line of hacks waited by the curb. Several people were coming and going through the entrance. Garnet waited tensely.

It seemed like a long time, though it was only three or four minutes before she saw them. She might have missed Oliver in the dim light, but there was no mistaking the shrouded figure at his side. Garnet held the curtain so hard that her fingers hurt. A hackman opened the door of a closed carriage. Oliver assisted Florinda inside, and the boy handed him the bags. The carriage drove away.

Garnet realized that she had been holding her breath. She let it out, and her hand, suddenly limp, released the curtain. This was all. Florinda was gone. Florinda was safe. There would be little if any risk among the crowds at the wharf.

She was very glad. But she had a big sense of lonesomeness.

To give herself something to do, she went to the table and looked for Florinda's letter in the drawer. She found the letter, addressed in the scrawly uneven hand of one not much used to writing. But there was something else beside it, a little parcel wrapped in a sheet of writing-paper, addressed simply "Garnet."

Garnet picked it up. Something fell out with a clatter, catching the lamplight like a little shower of stars. Almost unbelieving, she recognized the two splendid square-cut emeralds Florinda had worn in her ears.

Florinda had folded the sheet of paper around them. On the reverse side of the paper she had written a note.

Dear Garnet these are for you they are reall. I want you to have them because I am so greatfull you will never know how much. And please do not worrey about me dear I alwas get along fine. I am not going to worrey about you ether because you will get along fine too. You are the sort that does.

Look dear I know you were bothered about my name. Well my right name is Emma Norquist but now really can you imadgine a girl who looks like me going around with a tag like that. When I was a little girl they billed me as Little Miss Geraldine Montgomery but I have thought of a lot of better names since then. More romantick I mean. When you asked me about my name last night I remembered Florinda out of your book of pictures. And then Oliver said something about a counsell grove and that seemed to fit just fine. I did not think I woud ever see you again so I forgot about it before this morning. But now that I am using it I like it very

*much. In fact I think Florinda is the most ellegant name I ever
had.*

*Well dear goodby thank you for everrything. I will remember
you and love you if I live a hundred years.*

Your true frend,

Florinda Grove.

T E N

THOUGH THEY had said goodby with such finality, Garnet still
hoped she would find Florinda when she got to St. Louis. But she
did not.

St. Louis was the busiest town she had ever seen. The population had tripled in the past five years, and was now close to fifty
thousand people. It was a town being made while you looked at
it. They were putting up new houses as fast as they could. Every
morning Garnet was waked up by the racket of saws and hammers.
The streets were packed with carriages, drays, ox-carts, and covered wagons; she had never seen such a jam of traffic, not even in
downtown New York. The sidewalks were full of people. There
were traders making ready for Santa Fe, clerks and bullwhackers
looking for jobs with the wagon trains, merchants loading their
goods on the Missouri River boats that would take them to Independence. Everybody in town seemed to be on the way to
Independence.

The hotel where Garnet and Oliver stayed had gaudy red plush
furniture, and mirrors with gilded frames. Every room was occupied. Sometimes they had to stand in line at the dining-room door
before they could get in for a meal. But it was a comfortable place
and the food was good. These busy people got hungry, and they
had plenty of money to pay for what they ate. The waiters brought
them big thick plates piled with beef and ham and venison, and
hot cornbread dripping with butter, and rich deep fruit pies; and
they set out mugs of coffee and bottles of whiskey and wine. The
tablecloth was usually splashed with coffee and pie-juice, for there
was no time to change the cloths between the relays of diners.

It did not matter. The whole town was young and noisy and

Garnet loved it. This was life, not life thin with watery grace, but life rich with people doing things and making a big lusty noise about it.

But nowhere did she see Florinda.

Of course, Garnet reflected, there was no reason why she should. Florinda had taken a boat that was ultimately bound for St. Louis, but she need not have come all the way. She could have left the boat at any town above New Orleans. Or if she had come all the way to St. Louis, she could have boarded one of the stagecoaches that left every day for inland towns. For all Garnet knew, Florinda might have friends anywhere who would give her shelter until that wretched Mr. Reese had been convicted for killing Mr. Selkirk.

Garnet could only hope, with passionate sympathy, that Florinda had not met anybody on the boat who knew her. And she hoped that some day they would see each other again. Maybe, next year or the year after, Florinda would send a gallant misspelled note addressed to Mrs. Oliver Hale, in care of Mr. Horace Cameron in Union Square.

Garnet and Oliver left St. Louis in April. They took a boat up the Missouri River, and traveled two hundred and fifty miles west to Independence. Here they stayed at the famous hotel run by Mr. Smallwood Noland. Oliver told her this was the last hotel in North America. There was a hotel out on a Pacific island in a town called Honolulu; but between Independence and Honolulu there was not a single place of public lodging. From here to Santa Fe, and from Santa Fe to California, they would have to take care of themselves. In Santa Fe the traders lodged with private families. In California she and Oliver would stay at the rancho with his brother.

Independence was not as big a town as St. Louis, but it was even noisier, and more crowded, and it was all a-bubble with business. The streets were full of signs saying, "Goods for the Santa Fe trade! All new, all cheap!" Everybody in town had something to sell. The traders were buying mules and oxen, and hiring drivers, and picking up last-minute bargains. They were taking to Santa Fe all the manufactured goods the people of New Mexico would use for a year. The traders bought and bought, and their men packed the goods into the wagons.

While his men packed, Oliver took Garnet with him every morning to watch them. Oliver had fourteen wagons. Garnet was amazed at the size of them. Oliver told her these covered wagons of the

Santa Fe Trail were the biggest wagons in the world. Loaded, they weighed five tons each. The contents of one wagon, if spread out, would cover an acre of ground. To move one wagon over flat ground required ten yoke of oxen, and if the going was rough the men had to double and triple the teams.

She asked him if it would not be easier to pack smaller wagons and take more of them. Oliver laughed mischievously, and said yes, of course it would. These great lumbering prairie schooners were the Yankees' way of thumbing their noses at the governor of Santa Fe.

Santa Fe, he told her, was part of Mexico; and Mexico was one of the worst-governed countries in the world. The governor of Santa Fe was a great big globe of sin named Armijo. The people of the town despised him. They said he had got his start in life by stealing sheep and then selling them back to their owners.

Señor Armijo had the power to lay customs duties on goods brought in from the United States. Most of the money went to his own pockets. The Yankees knew this, and the native customs clerks knew it too. The Yankees had always bribed the clerks to overlook half the goods they brought in.

Armijo knew the clerks cheated, and it made him furious, but he could not examine every bale of goods himself. So one summer he angrily put a tax of five hundred dollars on each wagon, besides the tax on the goods inside it. Anybody, even lazy Armijo himself, could count the wagons as they came through the pass. Nobody could rob him of this.

Since the new tax took no account of size, the traders promptly got rid of their small wagons and began to bring these big ones. They stuffed the big wagons with more goods than they had ever carried before, winked at the clerks, and let fat Armijo rage.

That wasn't very honest, Garnet observed. Of course it wasn't, Oliver retorted, but what were they going to do? If they paid Armijo's taxes, they would have to charge two dollars a yard for the cheapest cotton cloth, and a dollar for a package of needles worth ten cents. Nobody could pay such prices. After a season of that, there would be no more traders coming to Santa Fe, and fat Armijo might even have to go to work for a living.

The wagons had great canvas covers, thick enough to shield the goods from storms. At front and back the men spread heavy osnabrig sheets with blankets between them, to keep out dust and rain. When they got to Santa Fe the blankets would be taken down and sold. American blankets were contraband in Santa Fe, because the governor had ordered the people to use only local wool. But the traders had been bringing in blankets this way for years. It was part of the game. They sold the blankets more to annoy Armijo than to make any profit, for by the time they got there the blankets were too battered to be worth much.

To load the wagons took a week. Garnet enjoyed watching the men at work. They were tough and unshaven, and their speech was dreadful, full of words she had never heard before. But the men were strong and healthy and gloriously competent, and she liked them.

At length they began their journey. Garnet climbed into the big mule-drawn carriage in which she would ride and sleep until she reached Santa Fe. They rode to Fort Leavenworth, the military post that guarded the frontier from Indians. Passing Fort Leavenworth, for nine days they rode across a fair green prairie starred with flowers. Then they came to Council Grove, a hundred and forty-five miles west of Independence.

The going was easy. Even when a heavy rainstorm came up one night, Garnet was snug and dry inside her closed carriage. The men cooked outdoors. The meals were good, for besides the flour and salt meat, they had brought carrots and potatoes and onions, and dried apples, and cheese, and a lot of other delicacies she had not thought she would have on the trail. These would give out soon, but by that time they would be seeing the buffalo herds, and there would be fresh meat in plenty.

Council Grove was a beautiful wood about half a mile wide. The trees were thick—oaks, walnuts, hickories, and elms, lovely with their new spring leaves. Here they found other traders who had left Independence ahead of them. During the four days they camped at Council Grove more wagon trains kept coming up. Still other traders, Garnet was told, had already gone on ahead of them. They would probably catch up with these early starters, out on the prairie ahead.

While they camped at Council Grove the men cut down trees, and slung the logs under the wagons. They would need these for repairs on the journey. After Council Grove the trees gave out. Garnet found it hard to imagine a treeless landscape, but Oliver told her that from here on they would see only prairie grass, and a few leafy but useless cottonwoods. The men elected captains of the caravan, and chose scouts to ride ahead of the train. From here to

Santa Fe, they would live like an army. The trail was hard. But these men knew it by heart. They knew every mountain, every creek, every sign of weather. They were not adventurers and they had no notions of romance. It was their job to get the wagons to Santa Fe. They always got there.

Oliver taught Garnet how to use a rifle. She would probably not need it, he said, but it was foolish to cross the prairies without knowing how to shoot. Trying not to sound scared, Garnet asked him about Indians. Oliver laughed and said very few of the Indians between here and Santa Fe would be troublesome. He told her how to read Indian tracks. You got down on the ground and looked carefully. If you saw tracks of colts and children, and prints of lodge-poles, you knew this meant a whole tribe out together, hunting and curing meat for the winter. They wanted to be let alone, and would not shoot unless they were shot at first. But if all the tracks were those of men and full-grown horses, this meant a party on the warpath. If you found tracks of a war-party you noted which way they were headed, and you turned and went the other way to avoid them if you could. But there were not many war-parties. This time of year, most Indians had nothing on their minds but hunting.

"You're a greenhorn," Oliver said to her. "The greenhorns always think that when you sight Indians, shooting's the first thing you do. It's not. That's the last thing you do."

So Garnet was not afraid any more. But she practiced and practiced with her rifle, and learned to hit a tree at ten yards. The men laughed at her indulgently, but they said she was going to make a good frontiersman. They were a tough lot, and their profanity blistered her ears, but they knew their trade. Garnet liked them more and more.

Everything was strange, and everything was fascinating. Oliver adored her, and the other men said he was lucky to have her. Garnet had never been so excited. Life was opening up before her like a great big shining morning.

On the tenth day of May, just as the rising sun was making red streaks above the prairie grass, the wagon train rode out into the great emptiness. They were on the trail to Santa Fe.

ELEVEN

GARNET REACHED for the leather water-bottle that hung by a strap from her waist. Pulling out the stopper, she took a drink. The water was warm; but she had been forty-one days on the trail, and by this time she did not mind warm water. The water washed the dust out of her throat, and the wetness was delicious.

She and Oliver were riding in the carriage. It was an odd vehicle, not like any carriage Garnet had ever seen before she took the trail, but it was strong and comfortable. The carriage had a leather seat in front, and an oblong body with a flat canvas cover, held up by metal rods at the corners. In the daytime the four sides could be rolled up like window-shades, and fastened to the top so air could blow through. At night the sides were lowered. This made the carriage like a little house, and they unrolled their bedding and slept there.

Oliver was driving the mules. As Garnet put the stopper back into her bottle he smiled at her.

"Tired?" he asked.

"Yes," Garnet said frankly, "and I'm about roasted, and terribly hungry. What time is it?"

Oliver glanced at the sun, and back at her. "See if you can tell."

Garnet squinted toward the sun. She had on green goggles, bought in Independence, to protect her eyes from the glare and dust. The sun was over on her left, very high.

"Ten o'clock?" she ventured.

"Very good," said Oliver. "It's nearer half-past ten, but you're learning."

"Half-past ten," said Garnet. "That's better. It's closer to dinner. I'm so hungry I could eat half a buffalo."

"So could I," he agreed fervently. Taking one hand from the reins, Oliver lifted his own water-bottle. He pulled out the stopper with his teeth and held it in his hand as he drank. When he had drained the bottle he held it out to her. "Empty. Fill it up for me, will you?"

Garnet unfastened the strap from Oliver's waist. Balancing herself carefully, she climbed out of the carriage. She walked around to the back, and went on walking to match the pace of the mules while she uncovered the barrel of water that swung between the two rear wheels. When she had refilled Oliver's bottle and her own, she scrambled back into the carriage and fastened the strap again at Oliver's waist. He took another drink, gratefully. Getting up on her knees, Garnet pulled a big blue handkerchief out of her pocket and wiped the streaks of sweat off his forehead, holding her handkerchief carefully so no flutter of cloth should blur his vision.

When she had sat down again she turned over the handkerchief to wipe her own face, and looked sadly at the brown smear on the blue cloth. She was covered with dust. She could see the dust in the folds of her printed cotton dress, and feel it scratching her skin inside her clothes. It even sifted through her sunbonnet, and when she brushed her hair it would rise in little swirls. There were two thousand animals in the caravan, and every one of them kicked up its own small cloud of dust. The small clouds whirled up to make a big cloud that hung nearly motionless in the air and trailed behind the caravan for miles.

Garnet thought longingly of buffalo meat and dried beans. The caravan always started at dawn, without pausing for breakfast, and by noon she was so hungry she gobbled like a pig.

"Oliver," she asked, "where will we camp for the nooning?"

"Rabbit Ear Creek. It ought to be pretty close by now. Go limp, Garnet. We're coming to a wallow."

Garnet held to the seat with both hands, set her feet firmly against the footboard, and let go all the rest of her muscles. The first few days she had sat here as primly as though she were riding on a city street, and the jogging of the trail had bruised her black and blue. But now she knew how to make herself limp as a rag, and the jolts did not hurt her. The wheels bumped into the buffalo-wallow, with a creak and rattle that made it sound as if the carriage were coming apart. Garnet heard Oliver swearing at the mules as they pulled out. The carriage settled again into its normal swinging rhythm, and she looked up.

"All right now?"

"All right," said Oliver.

Garnet moved back into place on the seat. The wallows were an awful nuisance. She wondered why buffaloes always had to roll over in the same place. They were the stupidest animals on earth. She had seen them, in long lines that blackened the whole horizon, marching across the prairie to a waterhole. They swayed along sedately until some old brute at the head of the line took a notion to roll over on the ground to scratch his back. He rolled over, got up, and ambled on. But as though he had given an unquestionable command, the buffalo behind him immediately rolled over in the same spot. When the third buffalo reached that spot he rolled over too, and so did the fourth and fifth and sixth and every one of the rest, until by the time the thousandth buffalo had paused to wallow in the same spot they had worn a great big hole. Oliver tried to avoid the wallows, but he seldom could; by the time he saw one it was usually too late to turn aside.

Oliver's forehead was brown with dust. He had not shaved since they began the journey, and by now he had a big shaggy beard. The dust had settled on it so thickly that his beard looked as if it was covered with cobwebs. He had on an old hat, to protect his head from the sun, and the hat too was thick with dust. He wore a plaid shirt, the colors of which had long since faded to shadows, and heavy homespun trousers of no color at all. His sleeves were rolled back, and his arms were so sunburnt that the light brown hairs looked almost white. Oliver's muscles were like ropes under his skin. The men on the trail did the hardest kind of work. No wonder Oliver had surprised her in New York with his great rough hands.

Garnet glanced down to where a seam in the upper part of her sleeve was beginning to strain. Her clothes had fitted her in New York. But here on the trail she worked too. Her muscles were getting strong and unladylike.

She felt the new hardness in her arm. "I hope," she said to Oliver, "when we get to California, your brother won't be disappointed if I don't look like a delicate lady. I'm getting so tough and brown!"

Oliver glanced at her sideways. "Charles isn't expecting anything. He doesn't know about you."

"Oh, of course he doesn't. I keep forgetting that. Do you think he'll like me?"

"Don't worry about Charles." Oliver spoke so shortly that he surprised her.

Garnet turned on the seat. "Why, what do you mean? Are you worried about him?"

"He might be—a bit difficult at first," said Oliver.

"But why?"

"He'll be surprised to find I'm married, that's all. Good Lord,

97

Garnet, we won't get to California for another four or five months. Don't start worrying about Charles."

Garnet frowned, thinking. Oliver was looking straight ahead at the mules, guiding them carefully over the rough ground. A wave of dust blew into her face. She coughed, and Oliver smiled as he said,

"Try not to cough. It makes your throat raw. Swallow."

Garnet swallowed. "I know. I'll try to remember."

The dust had made the mules restless. Oliver was having a hard time with them. But though he could not turn his head, he spoke to her understandingly.

"The going does get tough sometimes, doesn't it? Ten thousand things to remember, and nothing to do tomorrow but remember them all over again."

Garnet held to the seat, admiring the expertness with which he handled the mules. But she wondered why he had said just now that she was not to worry about Charles. She had not thought of worrying about anything.

Oliver had never talked to her much about Charles. He seemed not to want to talk about him.

Well, she would ask him about it later. If there was anything she ought to know about Charles before she met him, Oliver would certainly tell her.

She listened to the rumbling of the caravan. The wagon-wheels creaked as they turned. The oxen bellowed in wrath at the men who made them work in this dusty heat. The bullwhackers, walking beside the teams, yelled and swore at the oxen, and cracked their whips in the air as they strode along. Garnet listened to the noise, and though she was so tired that her bones ached, she smiled at it proudly. No matter how you felt, there *was* something about the Santa Fe train, this brave sweating challenge to the emptiness.

The caravan was a mile long. It moved fifteen miles a day. There were a hundred merchandise wagons, besides the carriages and baggage-drays. The wagons moved in four lines, with the carriages among them, so each trader could keep in charge of his own crew. Ahead of the train rode the scouts, and behind the wagons plodded the extra mules and oxen. When they left Council Grove there had been only forty wagons in their company. By this time most of the traders had joined the big train, but here and there along the trail they could see the remains of campfires, showing that there were still more wagons ahead.

They had come six hundred miles from Independence, and they had two hundred miles still to go before they reached Santa Fe. For six hundred miles they had not seen a single human dwelling. But across this empty space the traders were carrying a million dollars' worth of goods. The men had packed the wagons so tight that when they got to Santa Fe the bolts of cloth would hardly be wrinkled, and it was a rare pot or pan that would have even a dent. It was a great job. Garnet was proud to be part of it.

She could feel the sweat trickling down between her shoulder-blades.

"Oliver," she asked, "what comes after Rabbit Ear Creek?"

"Round Mound."

"And after that?"

"The rocks. Then the mountains."

Garnet looked back, at the dust hanging like a thundercloud on the sky. The sky itself was bright blue, with little fleecy clouds. It had been bright like this for days now, pouring down a pitiless heat. The country was baked dry. Nothing grew here but buffalo-grass, coarse hard tufts that even oxen hated to eat.

In a day or two they would come into the land of the great rocks. But here there were no great rocks. Here, there was nothing. Nothing but dust and flatness.

The ground did not feel flat under you. It was full of bumps and wallows. But out there it looked flat, smooth as a sheet of paper. Far, far ahead, Garnet could see the mountains. At this distance they looked like strips of gray muslin waving against the sky.

The country was silent, empty, motionless. Even on the farthest horizon Garnet could not see a moving speck that might be a buffalo, nor a fixed dot that might be a tree. She could not see anything but the shimmering light and the buffalo-grass, and the white bones of buffaloes, and the distance. The caravan was a mile long, but when you looked out there it seemed no bigger than a worm, creeping through the great loneliness.

When you looked out there, you forgot the creaking and shouting around you. You seemed to be living in the midst of a great silence. The silence rose over you. It threatened and scared you. It reminded you that this was a journey across eight hundred empty miles, and you were here in the midst of it. You could not go back. No matter what happened, you had to go on. If you were ill, if you were dying, the wagons could not stop to let you die in peace. They had to go on. Even if you died, they would pause only a few minutes to bury you, and then go on. They had to get to Santa Fe.

"Garnet," Oliver said suddenly.

She started, and turned her head. "Yes? What is it? Do you want more water?"

"No, I still have some. But Garnet, don't look out there too much."

"Why not?" she asked in surprise. "What is there to look at?"

"Nothing. That's what I mean," Oliver said. "It gets you."

"I don't understand."

"The silence," said Oliver. "The loneliness. I can't explain just what it does. But you know how you jumped when I spoke to you."

She nodded. "Yes, I did. I wasn't thinking about you. I was thinking about the silence."

"Well, don't think about it. Think about Santa Fe. We're going to have a great time when we get there." Oliver gave his attention to the mules for a moment, and then went on. "When we get into the rocks," he said, "we'll send runners ahead to Santa Fe to find out what new taxes Armijo has thought up to bedevil us, so we can figure out ways of getting around them. And Santa Fe's going to be fun. By this time, every other building in town is turning into a saloon or a gambling house."

"Will you take me to those places?"

"Of course, I'll show you everything. We're going to stay with a family named Silva. They're fine people. I've had lodgings with them every year I've been there."

The going was fairly smooth now, and the mules were quiet. Garnet resolutely kept her eyes off the great loneliness. Oliver went on.

"And pretty soon, the California traders will be coming in. They're an odd lot, but I think you'll enjoy them. John Ives, for instance—that's my partner—he'd be at home in your mother's parlor. But some of the others are backwoodsmen who think New York is a place where everybody has strawberries and champagne for breakfast, and the women all dress like Florinda."

As he mentioned Florinda, Garnet felt a stab of wistfulness. Oliver was not much concerned about Florinda. Garnet had told him about her mother and father, and about the scars on her hands. Oliver was interested, but not deeply so. He had met a lot of unusual people in the course of his Western adventures, and

Florinda was only another one. So when he mentioned Florinda now, Garnet did not confess that she still felt sentimental about her. She only laughed at his description of New York as imagined by some of the traders, and Oliver added,

"When you meet the men from Los Angeles, don't ask them any questions and you'll get along very well."

"You mean they've all got shady pasts?" she asked doubtfully.

"Well, not all. But it's an unwritten law that when you meet a man who prefers to stay west of Santa Fe, you don't ask him why. If he wants you to know, he'll tell you."

A horseman came riding back from the head of the train. He reined his horse as he reached their carriage. Oliver spoke to him.

"Yes, Reynolds?"

"How're you, Mrs. Hale?" the horseman said cordially. "Rabbit Ear Creek," he said to Oliver. "We're about to corral."

"Good. Water in the creek?"

"So-so. Brush. We'll have to hack."

"Thanks, Reynolds," said Oliver. Garnet sighed rapturously. Mr. Reynolds grinned at her.

"Yes ma'am, I feel like that too. I could eat an ox."

He hurried on to tell the next man. The shouts began to go up from end to end of the train.

"Rabbit Ear Creek! Corral!"

Garnet scrambled over the back of the seat, into the body of the carriage. She began letting down the four canvas sides. This meant the nooning, three blessed hours for rest and food. Having closed the carriage for privacy, she took off her sunbonnet and shook down her hair, and got her wash-basin out of the chest. She waited for the carriage to stop before filling it. As long as the carriage was moving, water would splash out of the basin and be wasted. While the carriage jogged, she occupied the time by brushing her hair.

She felt the carriage stop. Drawing the front curtain aside she spoke to Oliver.

"All right, Oliver?"

"All right. Save some water for me."

Garnet made her way through the dim body of the carriage to the back, where she dipped a bucket into the water-barrel. The men were rushing about and shouting as though they had never lined the wagons for a nooning before. Mr. Reynolds, riding past her, waved and called a greeting.

She waved back at him. Lowering the curtain again, she took off her dress and did as much washing as she could with her ration of water. She pinned her hair in two tight braids across her head. Here on the trail it was foolish to leave any ringlets blowing to catch the dust. When she had buttoned her dress she rolled up the sides of the carriage and got out to empty the soiled water. Her elbow resting on a carriage-wheel, she watched the men make corral.

The great wagons lumbered up in four lines, as they had been moving all day. When they came in sight of the creek, the heavy wagons waited until the light vehicles had drawn into a group, close together. Then the bullwhackers maneuvered the four lines of merchandise wagons so that they formed the four sides of a square around the drays and carriages. The men unhitched the oxen, and bound the wagons together with chains. This formed the corral. The big hollow square was like a fortress. Inside it the baggage, the men, and the animals were safe from attack.

They had had no Indian trouble. When they sighted parties of Indians, scouts would go out from the caravan with presents in one hand and guns in the other, and when they had all glub-glubbed eternal friendship the scouts came back to the train.

Garnet had found that Oliver was right about Indians. They did not often attack a Santa Fe caravan. They looked wistfully at the fine mules and horses, and would steal any of them that wandered from the line of march. But few Indians had guns. They were no match for the well-armed traders, and they knew it. She had not seen an Indian closer than a hundred yards off.

The men had left the corral open at one corner, through which the bullwhackers were leading the animals outside to graze. The men whose turn it was for guard duty took up their posts around the corral. The cooks went outside too, and began digging holes for their fires.

Garnet walked outside. Twenty men were hacking at the brush in the creek, to open a place where they could cross. As they hacked, other men laid the branches in the creek-bed, to make a road, so the wagons could get over without sticking in the mud. Still others were on their knees filling the water-barrels. The bullwhackers brought the oxen down to drink, shouting ear-scorching oaths while they herded the oxen downstream, so they would not wander up and pollute the water that was needed for human use. Garnet watched them all with admiration. The routine of the trail had a hard, strong beauty. Everybody knew what to do and how to do it. No wonder these men could laugh at fat Armijo's tricks with the customs.

As she watched, the fragrance of coffee came up to her nostrils. It reminded her that she had had nothing to eat since last night. She had brought her bowl and cup from the carriage, so now she looked around for Oliver's cook.

She saw him, squatting on the ground before a shallow hole in which he had made a fire of buffalo dung. There were no trees hereabouts, and therefore no wood. For weeks now, their only fuel had been buffalo chips. The brush of the creeks was no good. It blazed up quickly, but died down before it had done more than warm the outside of the pots. Buffalo chips did not blaze much, but they smoldered with a slow, steady heat, and the pile of them in the fire-hole looked like a heap of glowing coals.

Oliver's cook was a lean young fellow from Missouri, named Luke. Luke had set up two stout iron rods at either end of the fire, with a bar across them, from which hung a big pot of buffalo-meat and another of coffee. Besides the pots, Luke had set up several pairs of long thin sticks for cooking bread. The bread-sticks were stuck into the ground on either side of the fire-hole, and leaned against each other over the fire. Around the sticks Luke had wrapped long strips of dough, and he sat turning the sticks carefully so the dough would be baked on all sides.

Half a dozen of Oliver's men were already lined up before the fire, waiting to be fed. They grinned at Garnet as she approached. She smiled back at them, asking if Rabbit Ear Creek was going to be a hard crossing.

No ma'am it wasn't, they told her; they'd have been glad if it was harder, because that would have meant more water in the creek. It was tough giving the oxen enough to drink, when you had such a stingy little creek to do it with.

While they talked they kept looking at her, as though she were the most beautiful object on earth. Before she left New York, Garnet had never dreamed that there were any circumstances in which men would show such frank consciousness of her sex. At first it had shocked and humiliated her. By this time she knew she had to put up with it, and her best defense was to ignore it. The men were not going to bother her, some of them because they were decent fellows and others because they knew Oliver would shoot them if they did. But though she had been very innocent about these things when she took the trail, it had not taken her long to find out that she could easily have been a disturbing element among them.

She was the only American woman in the train. There were four Mexican women, wives of bullwhackers, who went back and forth every year to take care of their husbands. When Garnet passed their cooking-fire they always smiled politely and said, "Buenos días, señora." But they made no attempt to be friendly, because their husbands were bullwhackers and her husband was a trader, and the lines of caste on the trail were strict.

Garnet tried to meet all the men in a pleasant but impersonal manner. But not all of them met her like this. Some of the men avoided her; some of them never missed a chance to speak to her; others gave her an exaggerated courtesy. Only a few of them, like Mr. Reynolds, had enough self-possession to treat her in an ordinary friendly way. She had noticed that when they stopped for the night the other carriages always left a space around the carriage that she and Oliver occupied. The bullwhackers, who rolled up in their blankets and slept on the ground, never went to sleep close to her carriage. It was not as if the men had any particular delicacy of feeling. It was simply as if they wanted to keep away from something they would rather not be reminded of until they got to Santa Fe. Oliver had never said anything about this to her. She wondered if he thought she had not observed it.

But not even Oliver, dear and adoring as he was, knew how much this journey was teaching her. In her six weeks on the trail Garnet had learned more than in all her years at school. Along with the hardening of her body had come a wise hardening of her mind. She was not sure she could have put it into words. Even if she could have done so, she had no other woman to talk to and she did not think any man would understand it.

She did wish there was another American woman along. A woman friend would have eased the strain of so much new knowledge. They would probably have talked about it, but even if they had not, there was so much else they would have talked about. They could have told each other how hard it was to wash their long hair when they had to be so careful of water, and they could have wondered how the styles in clothes were changing while they were away. Things like that, woman-talk. Men did not understand woman-talk and they could not be expected to. But when women shared confidences about any of their own feminine concerns they had an understanding of the rest. She supposed it was the same way with men. Men probably had things in common that they could not share with even the wisest and most beloved women. Garnet wondered how Oliver would have liked spending weeks and weeks in a company of women without a single man to speak to. She had never thought about this before, the curious lonesomeness it gave you to be cut off from your own sex. As she stood among the men of Oliver's crew, waiting for Luke to cook the buffalo-meat, Garnet reflected that she was really growing up.

"Yes ma'am," Luke said to her heartily. "Here you are, straight from the hump-ribs."

Garnet started, and her reflections vanished in the reminder of how hungry she was. "Oh, thank you, Luke!" she exclaimed. She watched him scoop up the stew with his big ladle. Luke filled her bowl, and the odor of the rich meat stew was so exquisite that it made her shiver.

Luke poured coffee into her cup, and took up a bread-stick that had been set to cool across his basket of dried buffalo-meat. He touched the bread to make sure it was cool enough to handle, and slipped it off the stick. Garnet broke off a big piece and hurried off to eat.

She sat down on the ground, leaning her back against a wheel of one of Oliver's wagons. The meat was steaming hot and it had a thick gravy with beans floating in it. The coffee was hot, and the bread was hot too, crusty on the outside and soft in the middle. In place of butter, she spread her bread with marrow from the thigh-bone of a buffalo, and sprinkled it with salt.

It was all so good! Garnet thought about the meals at home, served on white tablecloths with china and silver and crystal. They had been pretty, but they had never tasted as good as this. She ate every morsel, scraped out the bowl with a piece of bread, and went back to the cooking-fire.

"Luke, I'm ashamed of myself," she said as she held out her bowl.

"Now, Mrs. Hale," he objected, "buffaloes is meant to be et." He filled her bowl again, and grinned as he poured out the coffee. "Eat it all up, I wouldn't have no job if you folks didn't like my cooking."

Garnet laughed and went off to gobble some more. As she sat down by the wagon she saw Oliver coming up from the creek and going over to Luke to get his dinner. On his way he passed the fire where the four Mexican women were cooking. They glanced with approval at his long strides and his big muscular body and ex-claimed together, "¡Buenos días, Don Olivero!" Hungry as he was, Oliver paused long enough to smile back at them and say, "¡Buenos días, señoras! ¿Cómo están ustedes?" Oliver liked being noticed by women. But he had given Garnet no reason to be jealous. He was passionately in love with her, and so she had been glad to see how much other women admired him. She was proud that such an attractive man had chosen her. But she did suspect that he had made a good many conquests before he chose her. She did not know much about these things, but she had sense enough to guess that no man could be as expert a lover as he was unless he had already had abundant experience.

Oliver brought his bowl over and grinned at her as he sat down. He liked seeing her enjoyment of the buffalo-meat, as he had liked watching her excitement in the theater where she had first seen Florinda. He was showing her his part of the world, and as he did it he had the frank pleasure of a boy showing his playthings to his chum.

For a while he was too busy with his dinner to talk. But when he had finished, and they sat sipping still more coffee, Garnet asked,

"Can I wash any clothes today?"

"I'll bring you some water." He gave her a smile of apology. "I'm afraid it won't be very much."

"Oh dear," said Garnet. "When I get to Santa Fe I'm going to soak in soapsuds for a whole day, and scrub my clothes till I make holes in them."

"You can soak all you please, but you won't need to scrub your clothes," Oliver promised her. "Señora Silva will do your laundry."

"Just think," said Garnet, "having clothes ironed again!"

Oliver smiled at her affectionately. His cheeks crinkled above his beard. "Is it very hard on you, all this?"

"No, really it isn't. Everything is such fun, and I feel so well all the time." Oliver was about to get to his feet to bring the water, but she stopped him. "Wait a minute. I want to ask you something."

"Go ahead. To you, my life is an open book."

"Oliver—you said awhile ago that I wasn't to worry about Charles. Will he be very much upset to find you're married?"

"Oh Garnet," Oliver exclaimed, "don't bother about him. Charles will be surprised to find I'm married to an American girl, that's all. He's been hoping I'd marry a California girl from one of the big rancho families. Charles is ambitious."

"But haven't you got a right to marry anybody you please? What business is it of his?"

"No business at all, you're right," Oliver said. He got up. "Don't bother about Charles," he repeated. "Please don't."

He spoke lightly, but she could not help feeling that his lightness was not quite sincere. She looked up at him keenly. "I wouldn't—but aren't you bothered about him? Just a little bit?"

Oliver did not seem to hear her. He said, "I'll meet you at the carriage," and went off.

Garnet looked after him. Funny, the way Oliver tightened up whenever Charles was mentioned. But he was right about one thing: this was no time to bother about it. She had work to do.

Oliver had left his eating utensils with her. She carried them down to the clear place in the creek, and scrubbed them with sand before going back inside the corral. Already some of the men were stretching out on the ground for their midday nap. Garnet picked her way among them. Mr. Reynolds, who sat on the ground by his own carriage, sewing a button on his shirt, called to her merrily.

"You needn't be so careful, Mrs. Hale. They wouldn't wake up if an ox stepped on them."

Garnet laughed and untied her sunbonnet.

"Mighty pretty hair you've got," said Mr. Reynolds.

Garnet thanked him and climbed into the carriage. As she let fall the curtain Oliver came up with two pails of water.

"Best I could do," he said, smiling regretfully. "Use one pail for washing and save the other for us to drink. Hand me out a blanket, will you?"

She obeyed. Oliver spread the blanket on the ground, lay down on it, and went to sleep with his next breath.

The curtains of the carriage were still closed. Garnet took off her dress and opened the chest in the corner. A pile of soiled clothes lay crumpled in the chest. She washed a pair of stockings for herself and a pair for Oliver, and a pair of drawers for each of them, and hung the clothes on a line stretched inside the back curtain. This was all she could do with her ration of water.

She took down her hair. Unrolling the mattress, she spread it on the floor of the carriage and tumbled down upon it. She was so sleepy. It was good to shake her hair loose. She wondered if Charles would like her hair as much as Mr. Reynolds liked it. Maybe if

Charles liked her looks, he would more easily forgive Oliver for marrying an American instead of a Californian. But it was none of his business. She went to sleep.

At three o'clock the men hitched again. In the afternoons Luke drove the carriage, so Garnet and Oliver could ride horseback.

They rode to the head of the caravan to escape the dust. Now that the view ahead was no longer blocked by the great wagons, she could see Round Mound. It was like a cone with a rounded top, rising abruptly from the plain.

"It's not as big as I thought it would be," she remarked to Oliver.

He answered with amusement. "Yes it is. It's a thousand feet high."

"Why Oliver, it's not!"

"How far away do you think it is?" he asked.

"About half a mile."

"It's eight miles away," said Oliver. "That's the air in these parts. It's so thin that as soon as you get out of the dust-clouds everything looks right next to you."

Garnet stared at the mound, almost unbelieving. It looked so close. She could see the bushes nestling in the splits of the rocks along its sides.

Now that the dust was behind them, the landscape had a curious look of unreality. The sun glittered through the thin air and made ripples on the ground ahead. The ripples looked like ponds of water. Garnet knew they were false ponds. But though her mind told her they were not there, her eyes kept on seeing them. They looked real. She saw trees bending over the ponds, reflected upside down in the water. As soon as she came close, the ponds disappeared. The trees were only stones or tufts of grass, and where the water had been there was nothing but dry ground. But as soon as she looked up she saw another pond ahead. She blinked and looked aside, trying to get the mirages out of her eyes, but they were still there.

She asked Oliver if veteran travelers saw the pools too. He said yes, everybody saw them, and you got so used to knowing they weren't there that sometimes men in dire need of water ignored a genuine pool only a mile to the right or left of them.

The looks of things got stranger and stranger. Everything seemed to move in the wavering light. You couldn't tell what anything was. When you got your mind adjusted to the idea that everything was farther away than you thought, you kept mistaking near objects for distant ones. A tuft of grass looked like a buffalo, bones of animals looked like roving Indians. The scouts knew this, and they rode grimly, very alert, speaking to nobody. The landscape was so full of false alarms that they had to keep tensely watchful. After seeing a hundred Indians that weren't there, they were in danger of mistaking a real Indian party for another clump of grass.

The false ponds wriggled ahead. Garnet asked Oliver, "When do we reach water again? Water we can be sure of?"

The next water, Oliver said, was at Rock Creek, eight miles past Round Mound. They could not reach Rock Creek till tomorrow. But she was not to worry; they had filled the barrels with enough to provide for cooking and drinking tonight.

He lapsed into silence. Garnet wondered what on earth was the matter with him. This sudden urge to tell her not to worry—she had not thought of worrying. Oliver was bothered about something, but it was nothing as plain as the chance of a water shortage.

Two of the guards rushed away from the line, shouting that they had sighted buffalo. Garnet reined her horse quickly. The buffalo were moving in a slow swaying line, against the horizon to her right. Oliver snatched up his rifle.

"Fresh ribs tonight!" he exclaimed, and dashed off.

The wagons did not stop. The horsemen could easily catch up with them when they came back. Garnet stayed by the wagons, watching the men ride away. In a moment they were almost lost in the dust raised by their horses' hoofs. She could hear them shouting, and their rifles cracking in the air.

Twenty minutes later the hunters came back, blushing into their beards. The buffalo had been nothing but a line of brush. Oliver rested his rifle, saying, "Damn fool I am."

"Oh Oliver," she protested, "don't be so silly! How could you tell the difference? I thought it was buffalo."

"You're a greenhorn. I ought to know better."

"I don't know how. You certainly weren't the only one."

But Oliver was ashamed of himself. He shouldn't have been. The other men were laughing about their mistake. Nobody could blame them, and nobody did. The most seasoned veteran of the trail couldn't tell what he was seeing in this shaky light. Any other day, Garnet thought, Oliver would have laughed too. But today he was in a bad mood. She wished he would talk to her about it.

But he did not. The sun moved westward, and hung glaring into their eyes with such force that they could see even less than before. Mr. Reynolds rode back from the head of the train with orders to make corral. They had come five miles since the nooning. Round Mound was still ahead of them, looking no farther away than the length of a city block.

The men made corral. There was no water here for the animals, but the bullwhackers led them outside the corral to graze until dark.

At sunset there was another cry of buffalo, and this time the buffalo were real. It was not a large herd. They had come so far West that most of the great herds lay behind them. But the men were good hunters, and they led in a line of mules laden with chunks of meat. The bullwhackers worked outside the corral, cutting the meat into long strips to be hung on ropes stretched along the wagon-sides. What they did not eat at once they would dry in the sun, to be used later.

Luke was making a soup from the ribs. He grinned at Garnet as she passed the fire.

"Fine meat tonight, Mrs. Hale," he said. "Fat young cows."

Garnet heard him thoughtfully. When she and Oliver sat eating supper, she asked,

"Oliver, why do the men always aim at female buffalo?"

"Because they give the best meat. And male hides are rough. They don't make good robes. What are you scowling about?"

"I was just thinking. If we always kill the young females, who's going to produce the calves?"

"Oh, we leave plenty of cows. Indians aren't as choosy as white men, and there aren't enough white men on the prairies to make any difference to the buffalo herds."

"I still think it's foolish," said Garnet. "Because we've killed hundreds and hundreds of cows, just this summer. And one male buffalo can have a harem, but one female can't have any more calves by a dozen husbands than she could have by one."

"Oh Lord," Oliver exclaimed, "haven't you got anything to think about but the loves of the buffaloes?"

"Oliver," she demanded, "what's the matter with you?"

"Why, nothing. What makes you think there is?"

"You've been so silent all afternoon, and now when you do say something you sound as if you're mad with me. Is something not going right in the train?"

"No, no, everything's fine. I didn't mean to be cross." He

squeezed her hand penitently. "But I'm tired, dear, and this thin dry air is hard on everybody's temper."

Garnet did not answer. She washed the bowls and spoons, and took them back to the carriage. It was getting dark. She lowered the sides of the carriage, laid the bedding in place, and put on her nightgown.

There was a lot of noise outside. The oxen wanted water. They howled and bellowed for it. The mules wanted water too, and they kicked angrily at the wagon-chains. Oliver put his head into the carriage and asked for a wash-basin.

A few minutes later he came in. He undressed, but he did not lie down. He pulled a blanket around him, for though the days were so hot, the air cooled quickly when the sun went down. Wrapping his arms around his knees, he sat where he was, thinking.

Garnet raised herself on her elbow.

"Oliver, I don't want to pester you. But if you're worried about something, I wish you'd tell me."

It was pitch-dark in the carriage and she could not see his face. Oliver felt along the mattress till he had found her hand. "I suppose I ought to," he said. "I don't want you to think I'm mad with you."

"Then you are troubled," said Garnet.

"Yes, I am," said Oliver. He picked up her hand and kissed it. His rough whiskers pressed on her skin. "Garnet, you know I love you very much, don't you?"

Garnet laughed a little. "Of course I know you love me, Oliver."

There was a pause, Oliver drew her close to him and kissed the hairline on her temple. She waited. At length Oliver said,

"I've got to tell you about Charles."

Garnet sighed with relief. She sat up. "That's it. I thought so."

"I've been thinking about him," said Oliver. "I couldn't get him off my mind all day."

"What is it about Charles?" she begged. "Is he a wicked man, Oliver?"

"He's one of the finest men on earth," Oliver said with emphasis.

She had no answer to that. So she waited again. Oliver took a deep breath and went on.

"Garnet, Charles has been my father, my mother, everything. I don't remember my father at all. My mother died when I was seven years old. Charles was almost a man then. He was seventeen, and old for his age."

"Yes, Oliver. Go on."

"He's not like you and me," said Oliver. "We make friends easily, and get along with pretty nearly everybody. Charles doesn't. I think I'm the only person on earth Charles really loves."

He paused. The racket of the animals seemed a long way off. She hardly heard it any more. "I don't quite understand, Oliver," she said. "Do you mean Charles can't bear the thought of your loving anybody but him? He doesn't even want you to get married?"

"No, he wants me to get married," said Oliver. She felt him move uneasily beside her. "But Garnet—Charles is a fine man, but he has one fault. A lot of men wouldn't call it a fault. It's the fault of Caesar, the fault of the fallen angels. Charles is ambitious."

T W E L V E

There was a long silence. At length Garnet said,

"You've told me that before. It must be important. But I don't quite see why. I thought ambition was supposed to be an excellent trait."

"Oh, I'm sure it is. I don't understand it very well, I haven't got it myself."

"Tell me about Charles," she said.

Oliver answered slowly. "Charles should have been born a king. But he was simply the son of an honest businessman in Boston. After our father died we lived with our uncle. He had no children of his own, and he wanted us to go into his shipping business. In fact, Charles did go into the business for a while. But Charles can't stand taking orders from anybody. He wanted to try the Western trade."

"Yes, you told me that," said Garnet. "You liked the idea of the trail for fun and freedom. But Charles liked the thought of money."

"Not money exactly. Of course that was part of it." Oliver pushed his curly hair off his forehead. "When Charles saw California, he knew this was what he wanted. As soon as he could, he asked for a rancho."

"How does a foreigner get a rancho?"

"It's very easy. All he has to do is live in the country two years, become a citizen, and get baptized a Catholic. He signs a few papers and asks for a grant of land. There's so much land, they're glad to give it to him. After that, he buys a few cattle, sits down to wait for the natural increase, and sells the hides."

A little dry wind rattled the carriage-side. Oliver reached up to make sure it was fastened, and went on.

"The rancho was granted to both of us jointly, but I've never paid much attention to it. I like the trail. But Charles spends all his time on the rancho. There are forty thousand acres and ten thousand head of cattle, and I don't know how many native retainers running around and getting in each other's way. He lives in a wild sort of feudal magnificence. The great native rancheros bow to him when they pass, and ask his advice about getting credit for their hides with the Yankee ships that come around the Horn. Charles is a great man in California."

"But what's wrong with that?" asked Garnet. "Forty thousand acres, feudal magnificence—it sounds grand to me."

Oliver took another long breath. "We have forty thousand acres, Charles wants eighty. We have ten thousand head of cattle, Charles wants twenty. When we get all that, Charles will want to double again."

"But what does he *want*, Oliver?"

Oliver answered simply, "Power."

Garnet frowned, trying to comprehend. Oliver turned around, as though he wished he could see her face in the dark.

"I'm putting this as plainly as I can," he said. "You see, California is like Europe in the Middle Ages. There are a few great families who own everything. The rest of the people work for them on the ranchos, or live in scattered little villages along the coast."

He moved restlessly. She could barely make out the shape of his big shoulders.

"I've used the word 'work,'" he said. "I shouldn't have. The native Californios don't know what work means. Life is too easy. The country is so vast, land is so cheap, and the cattle take care of themselves. There's nothing to do except round up the cattle once a year and slaughter them for their hides. The Yankee ships buy all the hides they can get. They'd buy more if they could get them, but the natives won't work hard enough to increase the yield."

"Oh, I see," Garnet said slowly. "Charles isn't a native."

"Charles is a Yankee," said Oliver. "He likes to work. He likes to organize, to rule. And California—very few people outside California ever heard of it. But the imperial governments know it's there. And they know also that Mexico can't defend it. The United States already has a consul in Monterey—that's the capital. The British government has sent out several ships to explore the coast. The Russians have fur stations along the northern borders."

"Oh!" she exclaimed. "You mean somebody is going to come in and conquer it?"

"I mean," said Oliver, "California is going to drop like a ripe apple into somebody's lap. When it does, the native lords are going to be utterly bewildered. They've spent their lives in a fairy-tale Arcadia. They've never seen a bank or a newspaper or a voting-booth. But a great landowner, a man who has influence with the natives and who also knows business and politics as they're run in the modern countries—he can have plenty to say about what goes on."

Garnet tried to get this straightened out in her mind. She said, "I understand. California is going to be taken over by one of the great countries. And before that happens, Charles wants to be the biggest man in the province. So that when it does happen, he can step into the new government, as a sort of assistant king."

"Exactly. Don't ask me why he wants it. I'm not made like that. But Charles is."

Garnet pulled her knees up under her chin and looked into the blackness around her. "But Oliver, I don't see what all this has to do with me. If Charles wants to be king of California, I'm not going to stop him."

"This is going to be hard," said Oliver. He moved uncomfortably. "All right, Garnet, here it is. There's a kind of power that comes with property, and another kind that comes with prestige. The great native rancheros respect Charles and stand considerably in awe of him. But still, he's a foreigner. He wants to be one of them."

Oliver stopped. He felt for her hand again under the blankets.

"What does he mean by that?" Garnet asked.

She felt Oliver bracing himself to answer. "Charles has set his heart on being allied by marriage with great Californios."

"But why should I care?" she asked. Then the idea dawned upon her, and she stiffened. "Why Oliver—he means you too?"

Oliver squeezed her hand. "I had to tell you sometime. I've blasted Charles' hopes of me. I've gone and married an American girl. And now, because of you, I'm going to leave California next year, and live in the United States again."

114

"Good heavens above me!" said Garnet. She jerked her hand away from him and sat up straight. "Do you mean Charles wants you to marry some girl because she's got a rancho, whether you're in love with her or not?"

"You don't know Charles. He'll never understand why I couldn't fall in love with a rancho instead of a girl."

Garnet shook her head. "Why doesn't he marry one of those California girls himself?" she demanded.

"He probably will. Or when California changes hands, Charles will marry some rich woman of the conquering country. Anyway, when he does get married it will be a mighty good alliance. You can be sure of that."

"But why doesn't he let you alone?"

For a moment Oliver said nothing. Then he answered dryly, "Two good alliances are better than one."

But Garnet had noticed his hesitation. She began to laugh. "Oh Oliver, I understand! You'd choke before you'd say it. But what you mean is, girls don't fall in love with Charles, they fall in love with you. Darling, I've seen how women look at you. I bet they don't look at Charles like that. I bet you could have married half a dozen rich girls in California before now. Couldn't you?"

Oliver laughed a little too. "Why Garnet, I don't know. I never asked them." He put his big warm arm around her.

Garnet leaned against him. "Oliver, you don't have to be so modest. I fell in love with you. I don't have any trouble understanding how other girls could fall in love with you too. I'm just so glad you didn't want to marry them."

"You're mighty right I didn't want to marry them," said Oliver. He gave a sigh of relief, as though glad to be getting this off his mind at last.

"But did you think you might marry one of them eventually," she asked, "to please Charles?"

"Well, I suppose I did. Charles has been so good to me. But I didn't think about it very much."

Garnet laughed again, softly. "Oliver, have you had a lot of trouble with girls?"

"Oh Lord, yes." Oliver braced himself to go on. "I might as well tell you. I've always been in trouble with girls. Charles has spent half his life getting me out of scrapes. Oh my darling, you've married a wretch, but honestly, I'm an innocent wretch. I never did set out to break any girl's heart. But I guess I haven't always been a model of good behavior." His arm tightened around her. "Garnet, do you mind hearing all this?"

"No, not a bit. I want to hear it."

"Well, there it is," said Oliver. "Women do seem to find me a likable fellow. Charles has set his heart on my marrying the daughter of some great native family. And now when I come home with you—Garnet, Charles isn't going to see you as the girl I love. He's going to see you as a block to his plans. He's not going to welcome you. There. I've told you."

For a little while Garnet was silent. At length she said, "Oliver, you do love me."

"I love you more than anything else on earth."

"You love Charles too, don't you?"

"Yes. But that's different."

"I know it's different. But you're sorry you've had to disappoint him, aren't you?"

Oliver found this hard to answer. But finally he said, "Yes, now that I'm being perfectly frank, I am sorry. The only thing I could have done for Charles, after all he's done for me, would have been to marry as he wanted me to. But after I saw you, I couldn't."

"Oliver," she asked after a pause, "why didn't you tell me all this before?"

"I've wanted to. But I dreaded it."

"You shouldn't have dreaded it. I'm so glad you finally told me."

"Are you, sweetheart? I thought it was going to hurt you."

"I'm not hurt," said Garnet. "Don't you understand? Charles can't hurt me. The only person who can hurt me is you."

"I'm never going to hurt you, dearest."

"You never will," said Garnet, "if you'll just love me and trust me. I don't care about Charles. I'm not married to him. I'm married to you. I think Charles' idea of marriage is stupid. It's worse than stupid. It's revolting."

"Don't blame him too much, Garnet. A great many people think of marriage as he does."

"A great many people," said Garnet, "haven't any respect for things they ought to have respect for. Charles isn't going to worry me." She pulled his rough head down to her and kissed him where his hair grew down into his beard. "I'm going to say something that would put my mother to bed with shock if she could hear me. I'm going to say it because it's exactly what I mean. To hell with Charles."

Oliver burst out laughing. He put both arms around her and kissed her so hard that his beard nearly scratched the skin off her face. She did not care. She loved him. Oliver was wonderful. To hell with Charles.

But in the middle of the night Garnet woke up. She woke with a sense that something had been pestering her mind. The camp was quiet except for an occasional kick or bray of a restless animal. Beside her she could hear Oliver's deep regular breaths, so evidently he was still asleep. With this thought of him she realized what had waked her. She had been troubled about Oliver.

It seemed to her that Oliver was overly concerned about Charles. She raised herself, and felt his powerful arm, and moved her hand up to his hair. The curls were tossed about like the unruly hair of a child. His forehead was warm and faintly damp, like the forehead of a sleeping child. Why did he, right now, remind her so much of a child? She knew before she had asked herself the question. It was because Oliver had been talking like a child. He had sounded like a little boy who was afraid he was going to be punished for being naughty.

Garnet had thought she knew Oliver so well. She had had a much better chance to know her husband than most women had after so brief a period of marriage. Most wives and husbands led such separate lives, the woman spending the day at home while the man went to business. But since they left New Orleans she and Oliver had been together day and night. She shared his work and helped him do it, and she had seen him among the men who worked with him. The men liked Oliver. Everybody liked him, wherever he was, because he had a rare talent for adapting himself to all sorts of people. Oh, Oliver was easy to live with. If he had had any sulkiness or bad temper she would have known it by now. And he was handsome and loving and strong—never until tonight had she felt a suspicion that there were any flaws in his strength. But tonight he had sounded afraid.

Maybe, Garnet thought, I'm imagining things. I was such a baby when I left New York, and since then everything has been so new and surprising. Or maybe Oliver had that frightened manner because he didn't realize how much I've grown up and he thought I was going to be worried. Well, we aren't anywhere near California yet. There's plenty of time for us to talk about Charles.

A gust of wind flapped the carriage-curtains. Garnet drew the blankets about her shoulders and snuggled down. She thought of the vast windy prairie outside, and how safe and warm she was in the carriage with Oliver beside her. She went to sleep again.

But they did not talk much about Charles after that night. Oliver had very little time or energy to talk about anything. The trail was getting harder, and he had all he could do to take care of his wagons.

They passed Round Mound and came into the land of the great rocks. Here the trail began to climb. They had to jerk around sharp corners, and the going was rough. Sometimes it took them hours to make a mile. There were streams among the rocks, but the air was so dry that the spokes of the wheels got loose in their sockets; the rims shrank away from the heavy metal tires around them, and the wheels screeched wildly on their shrunken axles. The wagons cracked at the joints, and they had to stop a dozen times a day for repairs.

The men mended the wagons with wood they had cut at Council Grove seven weeks ago. They bound the wheels with strips of dried buffalo hide saved from their hunts. As they went upward the air got drier and thinner. The oxen were nervous, hard to manage; the men were nervous too, and quarreled all day long. As their tempers got shorter the work got harder. The number of miles they could go in a day grew less and less, and to rest both men and beasts they had to take longer noonings.

There were no buffalo among the rocks. But they had brought dried meat, and there was plenty of game—wild turkeys, hares, an odd bird that the men called a prairie chicken, and sometimes fish from the streams. They had no bread, for up here there was not fuel enough for baking it. They roasted the meat and ate it with dishes of dried beans.

Oliver had one of his men drive the carriage while he rode up and down the line of his wagons, giving orders and working as hard as any of his crew. Garnet walked most of the time. Now and then she tried riding horseback, but walking was easier than guiding a horse along these dizzying climbs. By the time the wagons stopped she was so, tired that it took all her will-power to wash even a pair of stockings before she went to sleep.

They went up into a fierce land of red and gold, where every noise brought an echo, and the mountains loomed into radiant distances. Garnet had never imagined such heights as these. No wonder so few people had ever crossed this continent, she thought. There

118

were only a few people in any generation who were strong enough to conquer such mountains, and she had a sense of glory to be one of them.

The trail began to descend, as they made a detour around the highest peaks. They went by several squalid little settlements, mud hovels inhabited by people whose main occupation seemed to consist of dozing in the sun. The people were so dirty that Garnet demanded of Oliver,

"Why didn't you bring a wagonload of soap?"

He laughed at her. "My dear, I'm a merchant, not a missionary."

"Are the people in Santa Fe as dirty as this?"

"Of course not. Do you think I'd have brought you if they were?"

Now and then some of the villagers had an attack of wakefulness, and came out to the camp offering bread and cheese for sale, and a fiery drink called aguardiente. Several of the men got blissful on the aguardiente, and others welcomed the bread and cheese as a variation of their meat diet, but Garnet declined. She was not as fastidious as she used to be, but she could not eat anything that came out of those pigsties.

The trail climbed again, through more mountain passes, and at last they went up a ridge that Oliver told her was called the Glorieta Range. A thrill of excitement began to run through the line. They were nearly there.

All of a sudden there was a great bustle. The men scrubbed their clothes, and patched them and sewed on buttons. Mirrors appeared from mysterious hiding-places. Whenever they could spare time from work the men clustered about the mirrors, preening. Not a man in the train had used a razor since they left Independence, but now they shaved off their beards, and cut their hair, and combed and scoured till the whole camp smelt like soapsuds. A few of them, who had especially magnificent whiskers, did not shave, but instead waxed and curled their beards with foppish elegance. They took out cherished articles of adornment—fancy belts and sashes, new shoes, shirts of red and blue calico or plaid flannel, or even white shirts still crackling from the starch they had received back in Missouri. For as Oliver explained to Garnet, Santa Fe was full of girls, and the girls were—well, very kind. Every man in the train wanted to ride into town in splendor.

Oliver became splendid too. He called Luke, who helped him get rid of his beard. When Garnet saw him she could not help laughing. Oliver's face was half brown and half white, as it had been the first time she saw him in New York. When she looked around, she saw that all the men had that funny two-faced appearance, and she wondered if the girls of Santa Fe thought Yankees just naturally looked like that.

Then at last, one morning, Garnet looked down from the ridge, and below her in the valley to the north she saw Santa Fe.

The town was a mile away. She saw a river, overgrown with bushes and cottonwood trees; and an open square. Around the square was a cluster of white shoe-boxes, shining in the sun. These shoe-boxes were the homes of the people. Oliver told her they were built of adobe, which meant bricks made of the local earth. The houses were naturally brown, but Santa Fe spruced up to meet the traders as much as the traders spruced up to meet Santa Fe, so every summer, before the arrival of the caravans, the houses were freshly white-washed in honor of the foreign guests.

Among the houses, facing the square, was a church with a fat bell-tower, and on the north side of the square was a long low building with arches supported by columns all along the front. This was the governor's palace, where fat Armijo dwelt. Around the town, scattering into the country fields, were brown shoe-boxes. These were the homes of people too poor or too lazy to whitewash. Beyond them were farms, and flocks of sheep and goats. The fields stretched northward, laced with irrigation ditches that sparkled in the sun like silver threads, and beyond the plain the mountains rose again.

Luke dragged over a chest from their baggage-wagon. Oliver put on a white shirt and a black suit, and a tall silk hat, and shiny shoes and a pair of black kid gloves. Garnet took out a dress of printed muslin, and a straw bonnet with flowers and pink ribbons, and white stockings, and black kid slippers with silk lacings. They got back into the carriage, where Luke had dusted off the seat and polished the metal rods that held up the top, and they rode down into Santa Fe.

The people had sighted the caravan hours ago. Now they were all in the street, thousands of them, and they were dressed in all they owned—men in embroidered coats and boots with silver spurs, girls in silks and satins and fine lawns, Indians who had come to town for the trading, in full glory of paint and blankets. The Indians stood back, watching in silence, but everybody else cheered and shouted as the caravan came in. The traders waved their tall hats and bowed like leaders of a conquering army. Behind them, the great wagons came creaking through the pass.

The home of Señor Silva was just off the plaza. There were four rooms, with a passage dividing them two and two. Every summer the family withdrew into two of the rooms, leaving the other two for Oliver's use. The family consisted of Señor and Señora Silva and their two youngest children, girls of thirteen and fourteen. The older children were married and gone, and this left room for the Silvas to add to their income by taking a trader to lodge.

The man of the house was very grand in his best red coat and blue trousers, and the ladies wore dresses of flowered calico, with low necks, and full skirts short enough to show their ankles. They all bowed and curtsied and smiled, babbling in soft musical voices, and Garnet stood smiling back at them while Oliver translated what they said. They were delighted that Don Olivero had brought a wife this year. They regarded her with infinite curiosity, the girls and their mother reaching shy eager hands to stroke her strange clothes. Oliver answered what seemed like hundreds of questions, and Garnet felt almost ashamed of herself for not being able to understand what they were about. She saw Oliver laugh and shake his head as he answered something Señora Silva asked, and she turned to him.

"What is she saying, Oliver?"

"She wants to know if you're going to have a baby."

Garnet gasped at such candor. "Good heavens!—Oliver, do they understand what I'm saying?"

"Not a word."

"Then—what makes her so rude?"

"She's not rude, my dear. That's the first thing they always ask a young married woman. She wouldn't be polite if she didn't ask."

The señora was patting Garnet's arm and saying something else. Oliver translated.

"She says you're not to worry. You are young and you look quite healthy, so no doubt you will soon find yourself expecting one."

Garnet hoped she was not blushing, but she was afraid she was. She expected to have children, but she had been very glad to find that she was not complicating the hardships of the trail by having a baby right away. That had been one reason for her mother's tears at the wedding, she knew; Pauline had been dreadfully apprehensive lest Garnet find herself with child somewhere on this wild journey. But so far, she had not. She gave her attention back to Oliver, who was translating again.

"Señora Silva says she did not know she was to have the honor of receiving a lady, but she hopes the rooms are quite as luxurious as those you're used to. They're not, but they're clean and comfortable. Now she's asking if you're hungry."

"I can answer that!" Garnet exclaimed gratefully, and turning back to Señora Silva she said with emphasis, "¡Sí, sí señora! Tengo hambre—¡gracias!"

All four Silvas laughed and babbled, and Garnet inquired of Oliver,

"How do I say I'd like a bath?"

"You ask for agua caliente. That means hot water. I'll tell them."

The señora nodded, and gave orders to her daughters. The girls ran off, and Oliver led Garnet into the rooms that he and she would live in.

The rooms had whitewashed walls. Around the walls, to the height of a man's shoulder, hung curtains of bright figured calico. Oliver said this was so the whitewash would not rub off on your clothes. There were no chairs, but along two sides of each room was an adobe bench built along the wall, with cushions scattered upon it. In one room was a table and in the other a bed. In the bedroom a basin and a pottery jug of water stood at one end of the wall-bench, and in both rooms there were mirrors hanging on the wall. The floor was of clay, packed almost as hard as stone, and on the floor were rugs of black-and-white woven figures. The bed was covered with a blanket that looked like the rugs. Garnet went over and felt the blanket. It was beautifully light and soft.

"Think you'll like it?" Oliver asked.

"Oh yes! Just think, tonight we'll sleep in a real bed, and before that we'll wash in hot water! I've almost forgotten what hot water feels like. Oliver, it *is* luxury. Tell them I said so." But she looked around, puzzled, and he asked,

"What are you looking for?"

"Furniture. Don't the people here use chairs, or wardrobes, or extra tables, or anything?"

"Not unless they're very rich. Wood is too scarce."

"There are lots of trees."

"Cottonwoods. Pretty, but no earthly use. Too soft."

"Oh, I see." Garnet took off her bonnet. "It's wonderfully cool in here."

Oliver led her to the window, and she saw that the outside wall of the house was three feet thick. He explained that this kept the houses cool in summer and warm in winter. Both the rooms had little egg-shaped fireplaces, built in corners. But fuel was costly. Cottonwoods were no better for burning than for building. Wood had to be cut in the mountains, and brought down on the backs of little donkeys called burros. The houses were built thick and tight, so the people would not need fires except in bitter weather. .The windows had heavy wooden shutters instead of glass. In warm weather like this, you could leave them open all the time, because they did not face the street, but opened on a little courtyard at the back of the house. The room with the table—which Garnet supposed you would call a parlor to distinguish it from the bedroom—had an outside door of its own, opening on a passage that ran from the street between this house and the next. They could receive their own visitors without disturbing the Silva family.

Assisted by Señor Silva, Oliver dragged in the chests that held their clothes. The girls brought in jugs of hot water. They left reluctantly, with many backward glances, and Oliver warned Garnet,

"You'd better get up the laundry this afternoon, and don't be surprised if you see them examining every garment stitch by stitch. You aren't the first American woman they've seen—every now and then a trader brings his wife with him—but you're the first they've had living with them, and they're bursting with curiosity to know what you wear under that peculiar-looking dress."

Garnet laughed and said she didn't mind.

When they were dressed again, they went out to the room with the table. Señora Silva and her daughters were setting out dishes of red and blue pottery, piled with strange-looking food that had a spicy smell. Garnet sat down on the bench and Oliver passed her a plate piled up with flat round things that looked like pancakes. She picked up her fork.

"No, no," said Oliver. "Look."

He picked up a pancake with his fingers and rolled it like a lamplighter.

"What are they?" she asked.

"Tortillas. The local bread. Made of corn, and very good."

She tried to roll one like his. The tortilla was hot, and very good indeed. Señora Silva filled her plate with a stew made of mutton and onions and beans and chili-peppers. She poured bright red wine out of a bottle. The stew was highly spiced, and at first it burnt Garnet's tongue, but she was so hungry that she did not mind. The wine was delicious. Oliver told her everybody drank wine with

123

every meal, even children. And by the way, she must never ask for water until she had finished a meal. It was very discourteous. Señora Silva would think her guest didn't like her cooking, and wanted to wash out the taste of it.

They finished the stew, and Señora Silva brought them cheese made of goat's milk, and a platter heaped with grapes. The cheese was very rich, and it had an odd taste, but after a nibble or two Garnet decided that she liked it. The grapes were the most delicious she had ever eaten. "Is this a banquet?" she asked Oliver. "Or do we eat like this every day?"

"We eat like this every day. And for breakfast there'll be hot chocolate, very thick and rich, brought to the bedroom."

Garnet sighed with rapture. "Breakfast in bed! After all these weeks of jumping up at daybreak with no breakfast at all. Oliver, tell her the dinner was very good, and I'm so wrapped in luxury I don't know myself, and I hope I can learn some more Spanish so I can tell her how nice she is."

Oliver translated. Señora Silva smiled and curtsied and told him his bride was charming and she wished them long life and many children. When they left the table, Oliver took Garnet for a walk around the plaza.

The streets were full of people—traders and bullwhackers, most of them with a girl on each arm; and groups of Mexicans who lounged against the buildings, watching the foreigners. They stared when they saw Garnet, and chattered. Oliver told her not to mind, but she clung to his arm, feeling as strange as they thought she was. Oliver pointed out the public buildings and residences of the leading citizens. At the southeast corner of the plaza they came to the principal inn of Santa Fe, the Fonda. While the Yankees were in town the Fonda never closed its doors. Oliver told her nice ladies did not often go there, but he would take her if she wanted to see it. Garnet said of course she wanted to see it. She wanted to see everything.

As they strolled toward the Fonda, they saw a man in American clothes, very drunk and merry, being helped out of the doorway by two laughing Mexican youths. "Oh dear," said Garnet, "let's wait a minute for him to go by."

Oliver drew back with her against the wall. The Mexican boys were highly amused by the antics of the American. He was singing, but neither words nor music made any sense.

Oliver got a good look at him, and laughed. "Oh Lord, it's Deacon Bartlett. I might have known it."

"Deacon? He's not acting like a deacon."

"The pride of St. Louis," Oliver assured her. "He got here with his wagons last week."

Deacon Bartlett had stopped singing, and was trying to tell the Mexicans something they could not understand.

"I'd better help him," said Oliver.

"You're not going to speak to him, in his condition!"

"Why yes, why not? He's forgotten all the Spanish he ever knew, which never was much. Señores!" Oliver called. He went up to the two Mexicans, who were trying to keep the deacon from stumbling into a near-by irrigation ditch.

There was a rapid conversation in Spanish, and Oliver turned back to Garnet.

"The deacon offered to pay them to see him home," he explained, "but they couldn't make out where he lived, so I told them. It's a house just down a side street here. He always takes lodgings with a couple named Moro, because they live so close to the Fonda. Let's make sure he gets there."

Keeping a little distance, they followed Bartlett and his escorts down a street lined with small adobe houses. "These aren't nearly as nice as ours," Garnet said.

"No, a nice family like the Silvas wouldn't have Bartlett. The Moros are willing to put up with his goings-on because they need the rent."

The Mexican youths were standing in front of one of the houses. They had thrust Bartlett inside, and were now grinning and chattering at someone within. As Garnet and Oliver approached, they heard a feminine voice from just beyond the doorway.

"Gracias, señores, el señor es—es—oh damn, no hablo español, no comprendo español either—quit giggling and go on home! No tengo mas dinero—don't you understand that? Hell for breakfast, go away, won't you?"

Garnet stopped short and gasped. She knew that voice. She knew it so well that she hardly heard Oliver as he exclaimed,

"My God, Garnet, don't tell me that's the moonshine blond!"

Garnet broke away from him. She ran to where the two Mexicans were standing, and halted by them. For an instant amazement made her speechless. In the doorway of the little dark house stood Florinda.

Florinda had on a blue cotton dress, and over her head was a black shawl, which she was holding tight under her chin while she laughed helplessly and struggled with the language. Oliver had followed Garnet, and as she caught sight of them Florinda held out her free hand. She had on black silk mitts that covered most of the hand but left her fingers free.

"Oh, you darlings!" she cried. "I was never so glad to see anybody in my life. Come on in."

Garnet had already scrambled up the low step. Florinda put an arm around her waist and hugged her. Florinda was not surprised to see them, for she had known they were coming to Santa Fe, but Garnet was so astonished that her head felt jumbled. Oliver stood by the step, where the Mexican boys were still lingering. Florinda whisked her attention to the immediate problem.

"Oliver, you speak Spanish, don't you?"

From somewhere in the dimness of the little room beyond, Garnet heard a snore. She looked past Florinda's shoulder. Deacon Bartlett sat on the wall-bench, his head down on the table. He was quite comfortable.

THIRTEEN

"Do GET RID of these boys," Florinda was begging Oliver. "Tell them Mr. Bartlett is all right now and I'll take care of him and I've given them all the money I'm going to."

As Oliver spoke to the boys, Garnet demanded,

"Florinda, how did you get here?"

"Over the plains, darling, about a week ahead of you. Yes, Oliver, what do they want?"

Oliver was laughing. "They say you paid them well, they weren't asking for more money. They want to see your hair."

"Oh, rats," said Florinda. She had evidently heard this before.

"They heard you had long hair the color of cornsilk," said Oliver. "They won't go away until they see for themselves."

"All right, but tell them they can't touch it. They all want to make sure it really grows on my head."

Oliver warned the boys. They promised, and watched with interest while Florinda threw back her shawl, yanked out her hairpins, and shook her hair down. The boys exclaimed. When they had had a good look, Florinda grabbed Garnet's hand and ducked inside.

The room was small and rather dark, for it had only one window in the thick adobe wall. Mr. Bartlett sprawled on the wall-bench, his head on the table, peacefully snoring. Paying no attention to him, Florinda tossed her shawl on the table, and laughing sadly, she began to pin up her hair.

"Is that why you wear a shawl over your head?" Garnet asked.

"I don't dare open the door without it. And on the street— the way they follow me around, you'd think I had three legs and a tail. Thanks, Oliver," she added as he came in and shut the door behind him. "Are they gone?"

He nodded. "Don't be too hard on them. They've seen tow-headed men, but men have their hair cut. They never saw billows of flaxen hair like yours."

Florinda sighed. "All my life," she said, "I've been a ravishing beauty. I had to come to *this* jumping-off place of creation to find I'm just a freak." She tucked in a last hairpin.

Garnet was biting her thumb, looking apprehensively at Mr. Bartlett. Except for the two men who had annoyed her in New Orleans, she had never been so close to a drunken man before. "Florinda," she whispered, "is he—is he all right?"

Florinda gave him a gentle poke with her finger, as though he were dough and she wanted to see if it had risen enough. Mr. Bartlett made no response.

"Are you going to leave him there?" Garnet asked doubtfully. Mr. Bartlett might be unconscious, but she was still afraid of him.

"I'll drag him out of the way if Oliver will help me. I can't lift him by myself."

Oliver said he would be glad to help. Florinda opened a side door leading to a bedroom, and they dragged Mr. Bartlett up and got him inside. From the next room, Garnet heard Florinda giggling as she commented on Mr. Bartlett's sad state. Florinda didn't seem to be scared of him at all. She just thought he was funny.

Garnet sat down on the wall-bench and looked around.

The room was empty of furniture, except for the wall-bench and the table, and a chest that probably held clothes. There was an array of bottles in one corner. Everything was orderly, as though somebody had done her best to be a good housekeeper with what she had. On the table were red and blue pottery dishes, the cups neatly turned down; and at the end of the table was a tray of grapes and apples, and a red jar holding some branches with unfamiliar yellow flowers.

Yes, Garnet reflected, Florinda must live here. She could not imagine Mr. Bartlett gathering flowers, or keeping his bottles in such neat rows by the wall.

Oliver was coming back. He closed the bedroom door behind him.

"Where's Florinda?" Garnet asked.

"Soothing her friend back to sleep. She'll be here in a minute."

"But Oliver, why did she come to Santa Fe?"

"I don't know any more about it than you do. She said we were to wait, and she'd tell us." Oliver sat down on the bench by Garnet, and stretched his legs under the table. "Well, well," he said, "think of the deacon. I never thought he could make a conquest like this."

"You mean she's too good for him?"

"I mean, my dear, you saw the furs and jewels she was wearing in New Orleans. Her lovers haven't been yokels like Bartlett."

"But who is he, Oliver?"

Oliver grinned and helped himself to a sprig of grapes from the dish on the table. "Did you ever see a pious hypocrite?"

"Why yes, I think so."

"I bet you've never seen one like Bartlett." Oliver shook his head wisely. "Bartlett is one of the leading merchants of St. Louis. His store gets the trade of all the best people, because he's such an uplifting influence in the community. He's a pillar of the church, doesn't drink or gamble, leads crusades against saloons and dance-halls and other dens of vice. He stands it from September to April. Then in April he leaves St. Louis for Santa Fe. He stays fairly sober on the trail, has to, you can't lead a wagon train if you're in a drunken daze, but at least out in the open he can forget his piety and use language that would send him into a coma if he heard it at home. And when he gets to Santa Fe, he really lets go and raises cain."

Garnet was amazed. "He drinks like this all the time he's here? But how does he do any trading?"

"He has a partner. An American named Wimberly, who lives in Santa Fe all the year round. As soon as Bartlett gets his wagons through the pass, he's done. Wimberly does the selling, while the holiest deacon of St. Louis swaggers around the plaza with a girl on each arm, singing songs and pouring down aguardiente until he falls on his face and somebody gets him home."

Garnet could not help laughing, though she was still puzzled. "But don't a lot of the traders go through St. Louis?" she asked. "Don't they burst out laughing when they see him poking around with a Bible and a temperance tract and a sanctimonious look?"

"They burst out laughing," said Oliver, "but they don't tell the local worthies what they're laughing at. It would spoil the fun. And don't you tell on him either, if you should run into anybody who knows him when we go back through St. Louis next year."

"But where did he meet Florinda? In St. Louis?"

"I've no idea. Here's Florinda. She'll tell us."

Florinda opened the bedroom door noiselessly, and gave them a mischievous smile as she closed it behind her. Oliver went to meet her.

"How's Bartlett?"

"Safe in dreamland. I don't know how long it'll last. Thank you both for waiting. Don't you want something to drink?" She made a gesture toward the bottles. "Red wine, white wine, aguardiente— he's got everything."

Oliver declined, saying they had just finished dinner. "Can I pour some for you?" he asked.

"No thanks. I don't like any of it." Florinda sat down, past the corner of the wall so she could look diagonally across the table at them. She glanced down, running her finger along the joining of two boards in the table. "Look, dear people," she began, "you're not annoyed with me for coming to Santa Fe, are you?"

"Of course not," Oliver answered in surprise, and Garnet added, "I'm nearly speechless with being so glad to see you. Why did you think we'd be annoyed?"

"Well, you might have been. And I did want to explain. I wouldn't like to have you get the idea that I was hanging on to your coat-tails, expecting you to take care of me."

"I never thought of it," said Oliver.

"I'm so glad," said Florinda. She went on earnestly. "You see, I haven't told Mr. Bartlett I knew you. He won't remember how I spoke to you today, so if you want to have it that you never laid eyes on me before you got here, that's all right. I won't bother you at all."

"Oh for pity's sake, Florinda," said Oliver, "tell Bartlett anything you please. I don't mind his knowing about New Orleans. And I'm sure Garnet doesn't."

Garnet agreed, and Oliver asked,

"Did you come with Bartlett all the way from St. Louis?"

She nodded. "He asked me to come out here, and go back with him this fall."

"You didn't tell me you knew any of the Santa Fe traders," said Garnet.

"I didn't. I'd never heard of Santa Fe before you told me. I met him on the boat." Florinda gave them a humorously intimate smile. "There's something else I want to tell you. Oliver, is Mr. Bartlett a very good friend of yours?"

"Why no. I've met him here every summer for several years past, when I came to Santa Fe from Los Angeles. That's all."

Florinda adjusted one of the flowers in the red jar. "Then—if he didn't know quite as much about me as you do, you wouldn't think it was your duty to tell him?"

Oliver chuckled. "My dear Florinda, I've no sense of duty toward Deacon Bartlett. I'm not going to tell him anything."

"Thank you so much. I didn't think you would, but it's good to be sure."

"What don't you want me to tell him?" Oliver asked.

"Well—" Florinda was laughing silently. "Well, you see, Mr. Bartlett doesn't know I've ever done anything like this before."

"Oh," Oliver said with amusement.

"But really," Florinda urged, "I haven't hurt him. I kept him entertained on the trail, and I mended his clothes and washed them whenever there was water enough, and since we've been in Santa Fe I've put him to bed when he was drunk and made cold packs for his head and waited on him the morning after. He's just as happy as he can be. I haven't done him any harm."

"My dear girl, it never occurred to me that you had. If you're asking me, I think he's very lucky."

Garnet was laughing. She hadn't meant to laugh. But when she was with Florinda, it seemed she was always laughing about things that had seemed serious before.

"Maybe I'd better tell you how it happened," Florinda continued. "Oliver, do you mind if I say all this in front of Garnet?"

Oliver said no, and Garnet exclaimed,

"If you don't tell me what happened I'm going to die. He doesn't know you were the star of the Jewel Box?"

Florinda shook her head. She glanced around at the bedroom door. A heavy snore reassured her. She turned back to them.

"Well, it was like this. Here I was on the boat, all dressed up in those black clothes. And they did the job, Garnet, just like you said they would. Everybody was so nice to me. The gents bowed, and the ladies smiled at me with such sweet sympathy, and everything was just lovely. There wasn't a soul who gave a sign of knowing me. So the second day I went up on deck for some air, like you said I could. There was a gent who had just got on that morning. He was traveling alone. He drew up a chair for me, and picked up my handkerchief, and offered me a magazine to read. All in the most respectful manner. I thought he must be a preacher, or maybe a college professor." Her lips trembled merrily as she added, "You'd never think it to see him here, but Mr. Bartlett can be as dignified as a tree full of owls."

"Yes, I know," said Oliver. "Then what happened?"

Florinda gave them a wide-eyed look. "Now really," she said, "I've been around quite a lot in my time, but for the first day or two he had me fooled completely. It didn't occur to me that this noble gent was putting on an act the same as I was. He kept doing little things for me, like moving my chair out of the wind and bringing me a rug to put over my knees. I thanked him as nicely as I could. To show appreciation I even read some in his magazine. It was just awful, something about how it was everybody's duty to set a good example for everybody else. I didn't understand it very well. Then after a while he sat down and talked, and I'm always glad to have somebody to talk to. I don't like sitting around by myself. He said what a pity it was for me to be left a widow so young, and to have to travel without a protector, and so forth. I told him what you had told me to say, that I had brought my husband South for his health and he had died there."

Garnet was holding her fist to her upper lip, so she would not laugh out loud and interrupt the story. Florinda went on.

"The next time I saw him on deck he asked me to tell him some more about myself. And you know how it is—when a gent asks you to talk to him about yourself, what he means is he wants you to listen while he talks to you about himself. I tell you, that man talked for three days without stopping for breath."

Florinda laughed as she remembered it.

"I didn't mind listening. I like to hear people talk. He told me he was a Santa Fe trader. He said he had been down the river to buy some goods, and now he was on his way back home to St. Louis. What he said about the trail was like what Garnet had told me, so I knew that much was true. But then he started in like most gents do, telling yarns. You know what I mean—here was a good-looking woman, and he had to impress her with what a big hero he was. Lord have mercy, how that man can talk! He told me how many Indians he had killed, and every time he got into an Indian fight it seemed like he was doing it single-handed, with a whole war-party after him and stampeding buffaloes ahead of him and his wagons on fire. And he was never afraid because he knew God was going to preserve him."

Florinda whistled softly. "Honestly, Oliver, I don't know how he fools them so in Missouri. The men might believe that holy act he puts on, but I should think any girl who knows anything at all about gents could see through him like glass. Sometimes gents just talk like that for the fun of talking. They don't really expect you to believe them. But Mr. Bartlett—why, he thinks you believe every word of it. And—oh dear, maybe I shouldn't say this, but when a gent thinks you're believing every word he says—" She paused, looking from one of them to the other.

"I think I know what you mean," said Oliver. "He starts to believe it himself. Then he's helpless."

"That's it. You can make him do anything you please."

"So—?" Oliver prompted.

"So all of a sudden," said Florinda, "it occurred to me that I might like to go to Santa Fe. I'd been practically cracking my head with trying to figure out what I was going to do when I got off that boat. I don't know how to be anything but an actress, and I didn't dare show my face in public again. I might have got a place pulling bastings for a dressmaker, but as long as that man Reese was combing the country for me I wouldn't have felt comfortable even in the back room of a dressmaker's shop. In fact, I was in boiling water up to my neck and I had to get out of it. I thought it would be a fine idea just to disappear for a while. Nobody would think of looking for me eight hundred miles beyond the frontier. Besides, it wasn't like anything I'd ever done before, it would be a real adventure and it might be fun. And Mr. Bartlett was sitting there so pleased with himself. He was—well, excuse me, Garnet, but he was trying to seduce this simple-minded young widow, and with his great opinion of himself, it wouldn't be any surprise to him to find that he'd succeeded." She smoothed back a lock of her hair and fixed it in place with a hairpin. "So I let him persuade me to—Oliver, how do you say it in front of a nice girl?"

Oliver suggested, "To leave the narrow path for the primrose path?"

"That's it. The primrose path in this case being the Santa Fe Trail."

"Was it hard?" he asked.

"He thought it was," said Florinda.

"I mean, was it hard for you?"

"For me?" Florinda said, with such innocent astonishment that Oliver put his head down on his hand and shook with mirth. Garnet laughed too, but at the same time she gazed upon Florinda respectfully. She did think, however, that Mr. Bartlett should have been ashamed of himself.

Florinda waited for Oliver's laughter to subside enough for him to hear her again. Then she went on.

"Don't you see how it was? I never meant to start anything with that widow's costume. But the way things happened, I couldn't explain it. And as I told you, I haven't done him any harm."

"And as I told you," said Oliver, "I think he's very lucky." He glanced around the room. "I've seen these lodgings of Bartlett's before. They never looked like this. Orderly, dusted, flowers on the table."

"He loves it. And don't you see, if you told him the truth, it would spoil everything for him. He feels so proud every time he looks at me. He thinks he's made such a conquest."

"I understand," said Oliver. "You can trust us both."

"Thank you so much," said Florinda. "Nothing about the Jewel Box, or the Flower Garden—"

From the room behind her Mr. Bartlett called her name. Garnet started. But Florinda made a good-natured gesture. She began to get up.

"Well, dear people, I'll see you later. That's my cue to go soothe his fevered brow."

Garnet stood up too. As Florinda started toward the bedroom door Garnet put a restraining hand on her arm.

"Wait a minute. I haven't thanked you for those emeralds."

"Sh, darling!" Florinda glanced at the door, and dropped her voice to a whisper. "Don't mention emeralds. He doesn't know I ever had any." She opened the door. "Yes, Mr. Bartlett, here I am."

Oliver set up shop in a building that he rented every summer, not far from the Silvas' house. Customers streamed in all day long. He was very busy, and Garnet did not see much of him between breakfast and dark. But she was not lonely. For now that Florinda had made sure her presence would not be unwelcome, she came to see Garnet nearly every day.

Garnet seldom saw Mr. Bartlett at all. Florinda said he usually woke up with a heavy head, and required cold packs and firewater before he could get up. But once on his feet, he went off to the Fonda or the gambling houses, and Florinda had plenty of leisure. She spoke of Mr. Bartlett with a humorous tolerance, as though he were a child she had promised to take care of. But Garnet could not help asking if life with him didn't get to be an awful nuisance.

Florinda shrugged. "It's better than the New York state prison," she answered, good-humoredly.

She was always good-humored. She expressed no regrets for her brilliant life on the stage, and when Garnet asked her what she expected to do after this summer, she returned, "Why, I don't know, dearie. I'll get along somehow. I always do."

Garnet smiled admiringly. By this time she had no doubt that Florinda would always get along somehow.

Florinda usually came with a basket of sewing on her arm. She had had a few clothes made in St. Louis, she said, but there had not been time to get many. Mr. Bartlett had told his partner that she was to take anything she wanted from his store, so she had plenty of material. She cut and fitted her dresses with a good deal of skill. When Garnet commented on her expertness, Florinda said that in the early days of her career she had made most of her own costumes. "You can't afford dressmakers when you're in the chorus," she added.

But her stitches were sometimes straggly. She did her best, but her fingers were not pliable enough for really fine sewing. Garnet pretended not to notice this, but one day she suggested,

"Don't you want me to help with your dresses? I've got nothing to do."

"Can you sew?" Florinda asked in surprise. "I didn't know fine ladies like you were taught anything useful."

"You do have the silliest ideas," Garnet retorted. "Girls' schools always have sewing classes. Let me hem the collar while you're doing that skirt seam."

"You're a sweetheart," said Florinda, and a few minutes later she exclaimed, "Why Garnet, you do beautiful work!"

"I ought to. I must have spent a thousand hours stitching and then having to rip it out and do it over."

After that Garnet always helped with the sewing. She picked out bits of the garment that would show, like collars and buttonholes, so Florinda's uneven stitches would be set into the less noticeable places. She wondered if Florinda was aware of this. If she was, she never said so. She gave lavish thanks for Garnet's help, but neither of them ever said anything to suggest that Florinda's hands were imperfect.

While they worked, Señora Silva came in often, bringing them a plate of fruit or a bottle of wine. She took it for granted that Florinda was married to Mr. Bartlett, and Garnet did not enlighten her. Florinda enjoyed the grapes and apples, but she would not touch wine of any sort. To avoid hurting the señora's feelings, she would accept the wine with thanks, but when Señora Silva had left she would fill a cup and then empty it out of the window. Garnet thought maybe Mr. Bartlett's antics had scared her, and tried to tell her that this wine was so very light that a cup of it was no more harmful than a cup of tea. But Florinda shook her head smiling. "It's all right for everybody else, dearie. But you know how some people can't eat strawberries without breaking out in a rash? That's me and Demon Rum."

She made no further explanation, and Garnet did not ask for one. Stern abstinence did not seem to be in tune with the rest of Florinda's behavior, but it was, after all, her own business.

Garnet was glad to have Florinda there. On the trail she had been so lonesome for feminine companionship, and Florinda was always good company. They talked about clothes, and their experiences on the trail, and their impressions of Santa Fe. Sometimes they talked about New York. They had never seen each other in New York. Their two worlds had been split as though by a wall. But they had walked on the same streets and shopped at the same stores, they might even have brushed elbows on a crowded sidewalk and said, "I'm sorry," without glancing under each other's bonnet-brims. They had a lot to say to each other.

When Oliver came in he took her sightseeing. The streets were dirty and picturesque, and always full of people—traders and bullwhackers, blanketed Indians, little girls selling vegetables from baskets, big girls carrying jars of water and glancing temptingly at the Yankees, men leading tiny burros laden with wood, fine gentlemen in embroidered coats and trousers. They visited the gambling houses, where she saw more fine gentlemen, and fine ladies too, for in Santa Fe the gambling houses were the centers of social life. One evening she went with him to the Fonda.

It was early, but the place was full of Yankees, and their Mexican girl-friends, and a few Mexican men sipping wine or strumming guitars. Florinda was there, at a table with Mr. Bartlett and several other traders. She was pouring drinks for them and keeping them entertained, but as usual she was not taking anything herself. When Garnet and Oliver stopped by the table to speak to the group, she asked plaintively, "What do you have to do to get a drink of water in Mexico?"

Oliver got her a pitcher of water, though with some difficulty. The waiters at the Fonda were not used to serving it. He and Garnet found places to sit, and Mr. Bartlett, only slightly tipsy, rambled over and joined them.

His main topic of conversation was Florinda. She was a fine woman, he told them, finest woman he'd ever known. They mustn't think anything wrong of her because she was here with him. Young widow, came of a very good family in New York, just having a little adventure. Her relatives would be furious if they knew.

They listened gravely, and Oliver agreed with him that Florinda was a very fine woman indeed, and anybody could see that she had a most elegant background.

"She had a bad accident," continued Mr. Bartlett. "Nursed her late husband through his last illness. Making hot packs for him, boiling water splashed all over her hands. She has to wear gloves. Guess you've noticed. Poor woman. Self-sacrificing. Fine woman. Noble woman."

When they left the Fonda, Oliver remarked, "I observe that our friend Florinda is a very expert liar."

"I suppose he asked about her hands," said Garnet. "She had to tell him something. And whatever the real reason is, she just won't talk about it."

"She certainly knows her trade," Oliver added with amusement. "She's got Bartlett dancing on a string."

The next day, when Florinda brought her sewing over, Garnet kept her eyes on the buttonhole she was making as she said,

"Mr. Bartlett thinks very highly of you, doesn't he?"

"Why yes, dear, he does."

136

Florinda had been basting the hem of a skirt. She snipped the thread and put her needle back into its case.

"Would he be very angry if he knew—" Garnet hesitated, not sure how to finish the rest of it. Florinda answered with a knowing smile.

"He'd throw me right out on my ear, sweetheart. I've known gents like Mr. Bartlett before." She stood up, and coming around to Garnet she bent and dropped a kiss on her head. "Don't worry about me, angel. I've been in tight places before. I never worry unless something happens."

As she straightened up she caught sight of her reflection in the mirror, and paused to smooth her hair. Her hair was not rumpled, but Florinda never ignored a looking-glass. When she saw one, she looked at herself with a rapture that Garnet could only liken to the rapture with which some other people read great poetry or heard great music. Florinda smiled happily at the glass, and picked up her work again.

"Does this hem look straight to you, Garnet?"

"Yes, but you'd better try it on before you stitch it."

"All right. You can see if it hangs even. Then I'll have to go. It's about time for me to get home and make a cold pack for Mr. Bartlett's head."

"Does he always come in like that?" Garnet exclaimed.

"More or less. Anyway, he likes me to be there."

She tried on the skirt, folded it up, and said goodby.

A few minutes after she had left, Oliver came in. He said he had passed Florinda on the street, with half a dozen traders gallantly and tipsily seeing her home. Oliver poured out a cupful of wine for himself, and sat on the edge of the table, swinging his legs.

"Garnet," he began, "there's something I've been wanting to say to you about Florinda."

"You don't mind her coming to see me, do you?" Garnet asked in alarm. She knew some of the other traders were surprised that she and Florinda were friends.

"Oh no, I don't mind that. I like her myself. But when we get to the rancho, don't say anything about her to Charles."

Garnet was picking up some scraps of thread from the floor. She raised herself on her knees. "Oliver, what is it now about Charles?"

"Why, nothing. Except that Charles is descended from the old Boston Puritans."

"Then so are you."

Oliver grinned at her over the rim of his cup. "Yes, but Charles is just like them."

The room had begun to get dark. Señora Silva brought a candle to the door, and Garnet lit the blue pottery lamp on the table. She sat down on the wall-bench.

"Do you mean," she asked, "that Charles is like what Mr. Bartlett is like at home?"

"Something of the sort. Only Charles is like that all the time." Oliver turned toward her, like a grown man explaining something to a child. "Listen, Garnet. There's no reason to bother Charles with things he wouldn't understand. And he wouldn't understand why you like Florinda."

"Why?" she asked.

"Because, you big-eyed innocent, you're a virtuous woman. Women like you ought to want women like Florinda locked up. If you can't lock them up you should certainly ignore them with lofty scorn. You know what I'm talking about."

"Yes, of course, that's what I was always told. But when I got to know Florinda, my ideas did a lot of changing."

"That's the difference between you and Charles," Oliver explained patiently. "You can change your ideas. Charles can't. He's like that, Garnet. You'll get used to him."

Garnet reflected. "Oliver," she said, and her own voice sounded strange to her, "are you *scared* of Charles?"

"Oh, for pity's sake," Oliver said with a touch of exasperation. He went on, persuasively. "Look here, Garnet. When you get back to New York, are you going to tell your mother that when you were in Santa Fe your most frequent visitor was a variety actress who was living in sin with a trader?"

Garnet stroked the side of the blue pottery lamp. "No, I suppose not. But—"

She hesitated. It seemed to her that there was a lot after that *but*. Oliver might deny it forever, but he *was* scared of Charles. Even here, nearly a thousand miles from California, Oliver was as conscious of Charles' disapproval as if he himself were a little boy and Charles a schoolmaster in the next room. She did not understand it, and she did not like it.

When Oliver went into the bedroom to get ready for supper, Garnet curled up on the wall-bench and thought hard. That strange unpleasant idea she had had on the trail was creeping back into her mind. She tried to push it away. But there it was, real and ugly. It was the idea that Oliver was not as strong and fearless as she had thought he was when she married him. She still did not want to admit that there was anything Oliver was afraid of. Garnet told herself not to think about it.

FOURTEEN

They had been in Santa Fe two weeks now, and it was time for the mule-train from California to be coming in. Before it arrived, Oliver said he wanted to take some goods up to Taos, sixty miles north of Santa Fe. With several other traders, he loaded a string of pack-mules and set out, promising to be back in a few days.

The California train arrived before he returned. Garnet was sitting up in bed one morning, drinking the chocolate brought to her by one of the Silva girls, when she heard a great commotion outside. Exclaiming, "¡La caravana de California!" the girl ran out into the passage.

Garnet got dressed as fast as she could. She was eager to see the men she would be with for the rest of her journey.

The plaza was full of people, waving and shouting to the men, and dodging the vast throng of mules. Garnet had never seen so many mules in her life. There were thousands of them, pouring down through the pass. Some of the mules were laden with packs and others were unloaded. Drivers were herding the unloaded mules into open spaces on the slopes above the town, while those with packs were plodding about the plaza. There were a lot of men keeping them in line, though Garnet could not count them in the confusion.

Some of the traders were native Californios and some were Yankees, but she could not tell which was which, for they all looked like savages. Copper-colored with sunburn, they had tousled hair and ferocious beards; they wore torn dirty shirts and trousers, flapping as they rode, and great boots fuzzy with the mountain dust. They had murderous-looking guns in their belts. Garnet saw one or two men with light hair and rust-colored beards, and these she judged must be Yankees, but she could make no distinctions among the others. They were all shouting—at the mules, at each other, at the people in the street—and they were laughing, and flexing their great muscles, and leaning from their mules to grab the hands of pretty girls. Some of them were singing, and though they were so dirty and so bearded and so fierce-looking, they were radiant with triumph, and whatever they were shouting or singing, it all sounded like one great splendid hurrah. "Here we are! We've done it again!"

Pressing against the wall to keep out of their way, Garnet felt the little tingles that rippled through her whenever something really thrilling took place. The California traders gave her a feeling deep down inside her that she could not have expressed. It was a feeling that these men were strong and right and splendid, the sort who rode proudly over the earth and built empires in the waste places. She was proud to be going with them to California.

She caught sight of Florinda, not far away in the crowd. Florinda was holding her shawl over her hair, but for once she did not need it, for the people were too much interested in the traders to notice anybody else. Garnet edged her way along the wall and spoke to her.

"Morning!" said Florinda. "Isn't this a circus?"

They heard a string of angry Spanish as one of the traders shouted to a muleteer. Garnet smiled. "They're grand, aren't they?"

"Grand? Hell for breakfast, I never saw such a bunch of horrors in my life. Maybe they'll look human when they've washed and combed, if they ever do anything like that." But Florinda smiled too as she added, "Still, they might be fun to know."

"Why don't you come and have breakfast with me?" Garnet invited. "Señora Silva went out to see the traders come in, but she'll be back soon."

"I'd love to, but I don't dare. Mr. Bartlett's not up yet. I've got to get back to take care of him. He was gorgeously drunk last night, he's going to have a head like a watermelon. But will you be at home later?"

"Oh yes. Oliver's in Taos, you know. I don't often go out without him."

"I'll drop around." Florinda twisted the fringe of her shawl around her finger. "There's something I want to say to you."

"You can't say it here?"

"No, I haven't got time." Florinda looked serious, but she did

140

not explain. "I've got to get back now, before he wakes up. See you later."

They said goodby, and Garnet went home. After breakfast she got out her sewing—she was embroidering a collar for Florinda—and it kept her busy for the rest of the morning. The town was very noisy. She guessed that the California traders were celebrating their arrival.

Early in the afternoon, Señora Silva came in with a pile of laundry. Garnet put the clothes away, and changed her dress for a printed muslin with a pink bow at the throat. After those weeks of rough-dried clothes, she loved the feel of crisp dresses fresh from the iron. As Florinda might be here any minute, when she was dressed Garnet began arranging some fruit on a platter. She wondered what Florinda wanted to talk to her about.

There was a knock on the door. Garnet set down the bunch of grapes she was holding and went to open it. But instead of Florinda, the caller was a man she had never seen before.

The stranger was dressed in the brilliant clothes of a Mexican aristocrat. He stood on the ground below the step, splendid in the sun: he wore a scarlet jacket trimmed with black silk braid, and blue trousers laced up the sides with silver cords, and boots of embossed leather with silver spurs. His hat was black felt, broadbrimmed, with a silver cord around the crown. As Garnet opened the door he took off his hat and bowed to her. The sun glittered on his dark hair.

"Buenos días, señorita," he said to her. "Perdone usted esta intrusión."

He spoke with formal courtesy. He was standing with his back to the light, but now that he had taken off his hat she could see that his hair grew into a point on his forehead, and he had a long face, scooped at the temples. His mouth was straight, almost grim, and he did not smile as he spoke. He did not look as if he ever smiled very much.

Garnet answered him politely. "Buenos días, señor," and her mind hurriedly went looking for words that would tell him Oliver was not at home. The stranger said,

"Tengo una carta para Don Olivero."

Garnet hesitated a moment, silently translating. Tengo, I have; una carta, a letter—oh yes, the man had a letter for Oliver. "Gracias, señor," she said, and tried to apologize for her slowness. "Perdoneme, señor. No hablo español bien. Soy americana."

A frown of astonishment appeared between his black eyebrows. "You are an American?" he asked.

"Why yes!" she exclaimed, glad to find that he spoke English. "I speak very little Spanish—I got here only two weeks ago."

"You will forgive me," he said, still with grave courtesy. "I mistook you for one of Señora Silva's daughters. I had not been told that there were any American ladies visiting in Santa Fe at present."

Garnet wondered where he could have been. With all the attention she and Florinda had received, she had thought nobody in town could have been unaware of them. But probably he did not live in Santa Fe; he must be a rich ranchero who had come to town to buy goods for his household. He was so grave he was rather forbidding, very different from other Mexicans she had seen. Rich or poor, they were the cheerfullest people on earth. But she tried to be cordial.

"I'll be glad to give Mr. Hale a message," she offered.

"Then I was correct in assuming," said the visitor, "that Mr. Hale has his lodgings here, as usual?"

"Oh yes. Won't you come in, sir?"

"Thank you." He came up the low step, and a ray of sunlight streamed through the doorway after him.

Garnet indicated the wall-bench. "Please sit down. Mr. Hale isn't at home, but I'll tell him anything you want me to. How fortunate that you speak English!"

She had taken a step to one side, to give him room to pass her. He turned toward her, so that now the sun fell full on his face as he said,

"I am not a Mexican. Permit me to introduce myself. My name is John Ives. I am Oliver Hale's trading partner."

"Why—" Garnet looked up at him, and began to laugh at herself. "How foolish of me, Mr. Ives! Of course you are not a Mexican. I was deceived by your clothes."

She felt a bit ashamed, and surprised that she could have been mistaken. While he stood outside, below the step, she had not realized how tall he was. He was a good deal taller than most natives of Santa Fe, and very lean and hard. Now that the sun shone on his face she saw that it had the same half-and-half look of tan and whiteness that the other traders had had when they first shaved off their beards, and his features were no more Mexican than her own. She saw too that though his hair was dark, his eyes were a light blue-green, the color of ice on a winter lake, and just as cold. His face had a granite grimness. Garnet was reminded of those stern fathers of their country who had been cut in stone for the museums. But she tried not to let her thoughts get into her voice as she went on,

"And of course I recognize your name, Mr. Ives. Oliver has spoken to me often of his partner from Los Angeles. I'm glad to see you. I am Mrs. Hale."

His green eyes narrowed involuntarily. His thin lips parted in astonishment. "You are Mrs. Hale?" he repeated. He said again, as though to make sure he had really heard her, "Mrs. Oliver Hale?"

"Why yes," said Garnet. She wet her lips. She had expected that Oliver's California friends would be mildly surprised to hear that he was married, but she had not expected them to be shocked. Most men got married in the course of their lives. As he said nothing, but seemed to be trying to get used to the news, she continued, "Oliver and I were married in New York last March."

By this time John Ives was himself again, formal and sternly controlled. "Permit me, Mrs. Hale, to wish you every happiness. When I see Oliver, I shall congratulate him on his good fortune. But I believe you said he was not at home? Will you be good enough to tell me where I can find him?"

Garnet felt a twinge of puzzled irritation. She had thought she was going to like the California traders, but she did not like this one. Talking to him was about as cheerful as talking to a snowball. But she tried to be polite.

"I'm sorry, Mr. Ives, but my husband has taken some goods up to Taos. I'm expecting him back in a day or two."

"I see," said John Ives. "In that case, I shall not trouble you further. Please tell Oliver that I am lodging with Señor Ramos. It's where I usually stay. He'll know how to find me."

He made a movement toward the door. Garnet held out her hand. "Don't you want to leave the letter you brought for him?"

"Letter?" He took a step backward, and frowned. "What letter?"

"Didn't you say you had a letter for Oliver?"

John shook his head gravely. "I don't recall mentioning a letter, Mrs. Hale."

"But you did!" Garnet protested. This was getting stranger and stranger. "I don't understand much Spanish, but I understood that. You said 'Tengo una carta para Don Olivero.' You said it quite clearly."

His lips parted in what she supposed she would have to consider

143

a smile. It was not a friendly smile, nor even an unfriendly one; it was simply the courteous movement of the lips that a man might make if he picked up a strange woman's handkerchief in the street and returned it to her. "Excuse me, Mrs. Hale," he said, "but I am afraid you must blame your imperfect knowledge of the language. I said nothing about a letter."

Garnet felt her irritation rising. He did have a letter; he had said so when he thought she was Señorita Silva and he was about to ask her to bring Oliver out to receive it. But now that he had discovered she was Oliver's wife and Oliver was out of town, he was not going to trust her with it. She tried to hold on to her temper, but she could not help showing her annoyance as she said,

"You needn't be afraid to leave it, Mr. Ives. I don't read letters that aren't addressed to me."

"I have no letter for Oliver, Mrs. Hale," he answered curtly. "Good evening."

He turned again toward the door. Garnet bit her lip. She thought he was the most insolent man she had ever seen. John was about to go out when another shadow fell across the threshold and Florinda's voice called,

"Garnet! Shall I come on in?" She stopped as she saw a stranger. "Oh, excuse me. I didn't know you had company."

Florinda looked very lovely in a blue dress with yellow gloves and ribbons, and a blue scarf over her hair. For an instant neither John nor Garnet said anything. Garnet was struggling to swallow her wrath. John was not moved by Florinda's beauty; he only looked mildly surprised to see another woman who was obviously not a native. Florinda glanced from one of them to the other.

"I guess you're busy," she said cheerfully. "I'll come back later."

"Oh no, please!" Garnet exclaimed. She was glad to see Florinda. Maybe Florinda's easy humor would loosen up this tight knot of humanity before them. "Mrs. Grove," she said courteously, "may I present Mr. Ives?"

John bowed. "How do you do, Mrs. Grove," he said, and Florinda smiled brightly, saying,

"Pleased to meet you, I'm sure."

"Mr. Ives is Oliver's partner from California," Garnet explained. "He arrived with the Los Angeles traders this morning."

"Not really!" Florinda said. She came inside. Setting her sewing-basket on the table, she looked him over. "Gee, mister, you sure made a quick change! I can't believe it—the shave, the haircut, the fine raiment! Did you bring all those clothes with you?"

John gave her his chilly smile. "No. Some of the women in Santa Fe spend the winter sewing for us. If you saw us as we rode in this morning, you will understand that we are glad to have new clothes when we get here."

He was no more cordial with her than he had been with Garnet, but Florinda was never abashed when there was a man around. She stroked the black braid on his scarlet sleeve.

"They do a mighty fine job of it. Do you live in California?"

"Yes, I live there."

"But you're an American, aren't you? Where'd you come from, back in the States?"

"I was born in Virginia, Mrs. Grove."

"Virginia. Pretty place, I've heard. Never been there myself." But even she could not help feeling his chill. She looked up at him inquiringly. "Say, really, are you sure I'm not in the way? I can come back to see Garnet any time. I live just around the—"

From outside they heard footsteps, and men's voices raised in song.

> Oh, the dust it blows and it tickles your nose,
> And it lasts a long, long way,
> But the girls and the wine are mighty fine
> When you get to Santa Fe!

With the last word came a noisy pounding on the wall beside the door.

"Hey, Oliver! Anybody home?"

John shrugged slightly, evidently not surprised, as three men burst in through the open doorway. They were all talking at once.

"Hi there, John! Well, and two beautiful ladies already! How'd you get so lucky? Introduce us. Where's Oliver?"

They were California traders, splendid now in clothes of blue and scarlet, and they were all somewhat the worse for the wine they had been singing about. John took a step forward.

"Just a minute, boys," he said firmly.

They paused, looking from him to Garnet and Florinda with grins of anticipation. John said,

"If the ladies will permit me, I will present three of Oliver's friends from Los Angeles." He spoke as though they stood in a Virginia drawing-room. "Elijah Penrose, Silky Van Dorn, and Texas."

The men bumbled delightedly. So far, Garnet distinguished them by noticing that Elijah Penrose was clean-shaven, Silky Van Dorn wore a mustache, and Texas had a beard.

"How do you do," she said.

"Pleased to meet you, I'm sure," said Florinda.

By this time the men had had a good look at them. They broke into exclamations.

"God love us all! Yankees! Now would you believe it?"

They would have embraced both the girls, but John made a restraining gesture and they obeyed him.

"Please, gentlemen, stay where you are." He indicated Florinda. "Mrs. Grove."

Silky Van Dorn, the man with the mustache, grabbed Florinda's hand and bent over to plant a kiss on her yellow glove. She laughed.

"Don't mind him, Mr. Ives. I like it."

"And the other lady, John?" asked Texas, the bearded one.

"If you will give me a chance," said John, "I'll tell you. The other lady—" He paused to make his words emphatic. John might be an iceberg, but he was no fool. He was used to drawing-rooms, but he was used to less elegant places as well, and it had taken him only a second to grasp that there was a difference between Florinda's breeding and Garnet's. "The other lady," John told them clearly, "is Mrs. Oliver Hale."

Again they all burst out talking at once. Garnet could not tell which of them was saying what.

"Mrs. Oliver Hale! Hear that, boys? Now what do you think! Oliver's gone and got himself a beautiful wife! Where'd you come from, Mrs. Hale?"

They were surprised, but they were not, as John had been, shocked. They laughed, they thought it was great, they were just plain delighted about it. They said they knew Oliver had some good reason for going home last year. They wanted to know if he had been secretly engaged all this time or if he had just found her by lucky chance after he got there. Garnet tried to answer, but they weren't listening. They were so happy to see two American women that they were bubbling over, and they wanted to do the talking themselves. Garnet laughed too. They were merry with liquor, but she liked them. This was what she had expected the California traders to be. Letting them talk, she tried to straighten them out in her mind.

146

Silky Van Dorn was bowing to her, his hand over his heart. She received his homage and nearly burst out laughing at him. No wonder his friends had nicknamed him Silky. He had a most elegant mustache, waxed and curled up at the ends; he had wise dark eyes, and a hooked nose, and a general air of cool, calculating shrewdness. Silky looked like the city villain in a melodrama, the one who was going to woo and then abandon the country maiden. To complete the picture, Silky should have had a black cloak and a jeweled dagger. Actually, he had on a bright-colored Mexican suit, and instead of a dagger he had a pistol in a holster at his belt, but she would not have been surprised if any minute now he had stepped back, twirling his black mustache and hissing, "Now, me proud beauty, you're in me power-r-r!"

But it was too early in the play for that. Hand on his heart, like the villain in the first act, Silky was purring, "Ah, madame, you cannot know what pleasure your presence gives to an exile from home! Oliver is a fortunate man, one chosen of the gods indeed!"

Garnet bit back her giggle and tried to offer him the platter of fruit. But Florinda, wiser in these matters, had already picked up two bottles of Oliver's best wine, and was saying,

"Here, gents, have a drink on Oliver, why don't you? If you'll just reach me those cups from the end of the table—that's it, Mr. Penrose, thank you. No, don't try to hold them all at once. Just set them down—there, that's right, and I'll pour."

"Charming," murmured Silky Van Dorn.

Mr. Penrose was not murmuring anything. His eyes glassy with liquor and adoration, he was gazing at Florinda. Garnet guessed that he was not used to women of easy sophistication like hers. Penrose was a strong square block of a man, whose Mexican clothes made him look like a boy absurdly dressed up for a school pageant. He would have looked perfectly right if he had been wearing overalls and pushing a plow along the furrows of a farm. You would have glanced at him from a stagecoach window, saying, "Backbone of the nation," or some such words. Florinda poured the wine into the pottery cups. Penrose picked up his cup, his eyes blissfully on her, and gathered up his courage to speak.

"Thank you, ma'am, and here's to you, Mrs. Grove."

"Florinda," she invited him. "That's my name, you might as well use it if we're going to be friends."

Penrose beamed at the honor. "Why yes ma'am, Miss Florinda,

147

thank you ma'am. Where'd you come from, Miss Florinda, if I ain't making too bold to ask?"

"New York. Ever been there?"

"New York!" Penrose echoed with awe. "Why no ma'am, I ain't been there. Ain't never been east of Missouri. New York, fine place, I bet."

"Why yes, Mr. Penrose, it's all right if you like big cities. Myself, now, I think I like the country best. I certainly did like Missouri when I came through."

"Did you honest, Miss Florinda?"

Florinda was sitting on the table, and Penrose raised himself up to sit there by her. He began telling her that she sure did remind him of his sister Kate.

Silky was lifting his cup of wine and offering a toast to the fairest ladies this side of heaven. John had taken a cup, and was holding its thick pottery handle as he stood in the background, watching the scene but not taking part in it. The other newcomer, Texas, was also holding a cup. He took a long drink from it, and came over to Garnet. She was sitting on the wall-bench, watching the others with amusement, but as Texas approached her his eyes caught hers and held them. Texas was looking at her with the wistful tenderness she had sometimes seen in the eyes of the men on the trail.

"Can't I pour you some wine, Mrs. Hale?" he asked.

Garnet did not want any, but he so evidently wanted to do something for her that she said yes. He brought her a cup.

"It's mighty nice to see an American lady again," Texas said softly.

Unlike the others, who had shaved since this morning, Texas had kept his beard, but he had trimmed it neatly. His hair had been trimmed too, and his voice was as gentle as his eyes. Texas was nice.

Garnet smiled at him. "We'll have plenty of time to get acquainted," she said.

"Not near enough," Texas said regretfully. "We'll be heading back to California in three weeks. And Oliver will be taking you home, I guess, won't he?"

"Now, Texas!" Silky rebuked him, theatrically. "Don't remind us that we must leave these lovely ladies so soon. Let us bask in their beauty while we can."

Garnet shook her head. "But gentlemen, we won't have to say goodby. I'm going with you to California."

148

"Are you, now!" Texas exclaimed in delight.

Silky flourished his cup, and finding it empty, filled it again. "Now that," he cried, "is good news indeed. A joyful journey, Mrs. Hale!"

Penrose did not hear them. He was prattling to Florinda. But John heard them, and he crossed the room to where Garnet sat. Ignoring Silky and Texas, he looked down at her, and his eyes reminded her of lumps of green ice.

"Did I hear you correctly, Mrs. Hale?" he asked in a low voice. "Did you say Oliver was taking you to California?"

"Why yes," said Garnet. She felt uncomfortable again. "We're going to spend this winter on the rancho with his brother Charles."

"Indeed," said John. That was all he said.

But Texas smiled happily, stroking his beard. "You just looked so sweet and pretty, Mrs. Hale, I figured Oliver would want to take you back to civilization. But I'm mighty glad you'll be with us. We'll do all we can to make the going easy for you. Won't we, boys?"

"Ah, yes!" Silky promised. "You have no idea, gracious lady, how glad we are that you're going."

John Ives, however, was not glad. His icy eyes went over her. He looked like a man thinking of things he did not wish to discuss. The others were exuberant; they were all talking again, so that she could not make much sense out of what they were saying, but they were having a good time. John was not having a good time. She asked him in an undertone,

"Why shouldn't I go to California, Mr. Ives?"

"You heard what Texas said, Mrs. Hale. It's a hard journey."

But that was not the reason he did not want her to go, and she knew it. Whatever John was thinking of, it was something the others were not thinking of, and very likely something they did not even know about. She stood up slowly.

"Why don't you want me to go to California, Mr. Ives?"

Her voice was not loud, but it was clear to him under the racket in the room. John answered,

"I haven't said I didn't want you to go. Believe me, Mrs. Hale, I have no wish to interfere with your plans."

He turned aside again, and went over to where the wine-bottles were standing. Garnet's eyes followed him. In this atmosphere of easy mirth, John was like an icicle on a summer day. He glanced back at her.

149

"May I fill your cup, Mrs. Hale?"

"No, thank you," said Garnet.

He said nothing else. The others were paying no attention to him. Penrose was trying to hold all Florinda's attention, but Silky had claimed a part of it. Silky was asking,

"Tell me your name again, fair lady."

"Florinda. Florinda Grove." She smiled at him. Florinda was as faithful to Mr. Bartlett as if she had been married to him twenty years, but when there were men in the room she could no more help flirting than she could help seeing them.

"Florinda Grove," repeated Silky. With thumb and forefinger, he twirled the end of his black mustache. "I don't remember the name. But it does seem to me I've had the honor of your acquaintance."

Garnet started. But Florinda laughed and shook her head.

"You've got me there, Mr. Van Dorn. Can't imagine where we could have known each other. I've never been to California."

Silky frowned, still stroking his black mustache, and he looked so much like the villain flattering the simple maiden that Garnet nearly laughed again. For Florinda was no simple maiden; she could parry as long as he could.

"But in New York, possibly?" suggested Silky. "Didn't I hear you mention New York?"

"Sure, born there," said Florinda. "But I haven't been there for quite a while."

"I haven't either," said Silky. "But I was born there too. It must have been in New York that I knew you."

Florinda's blue eyes rebuked him. "Can't say I'm very much flattered, being forgotten so soon."

"Ah, it is not you I have forgotten," he assured her grandly. "What man could forget such charm as yours? But a man might well look at you, and be too enchanted to note the time and place."

"Now really, I couldn't forget a man who said lovely things like that. So it must have been somebody else you said it to the first time." With a teasing lift of her eyebrow, Florinda switched her attention from Silky to the adoring Mr. Penrose, who was attempting to slip his arm around her. She gave him a slap on the wrist. "Behave yourself, Mr. Penrose. I don't know you well enough."

Silky chuckled at Penrose's simple evidence of affection, but he was still perplexed. "Did you ever, by any chance, deal the cards in a gambling palace?"

"No, I never did. Here, Mr. Penrose, hold that cup with both hands and I'll pour you a drink. I said *both* hands, Mr. Penrose."

John glanced at her, frankly puzzled at her presence in Garnet's lodgings. Garnet felt like telling him to mind his own business. John crossed the room to Garnet, and bent his head.

"I'll get rid of these men, Mrs. Hale. I'm sure they are annoying you."

"I don't mind them at all," said Garnet, but he had already turned on his heel. His voice cut through the babble.

"This is enough, boys. Let's go."

They protested. They didn't want to go. Mr. Penrose was now begging Florinda to give him just one little kiss. John said curtly, "That will do, Penrose. We're going now."

Florinda gave Mr. Penrose a little push away from her. She slid down from the table. "Run along, fellow. We're just friends, you know. Not kissing-kin."

"Get out, all of you," said John.

They began to obey, reluctantly. Evidently he spoke with an authority that they respected. John continued,

"I can assure you that Mrs. Hale is not accustomed to receiving prolonged visits from gentlemen in her husband's absence. So say goodby now, and clear out."

They backed toward the doorway. Having reached it, they made elaborate bows and farewells. Silky Van Dorn said sadly, "You're sending out three broken hearts, ladies."

Garnet laughed, and Florinda waved goodby. Out in the alleyway that led to the street, the three callers burst into song again.

FIFTEEN

JOHN DID NOT LEAVE at once. He shut the door behind the others.

"I hope, Mrs. Hale," he said, "that you were not too greatly disturbed. I'll see that they get to the Fonda. If I were you, I should bolt the door for the rest of the day."

He was about to go out after them, but Florinda detained him. "Is your name John?" she asked.

"Yes, Mrs. Grove."

"Well, Johnny, since Santa Fe seems to be bulging at the seams today, will you see me home from here?"

"Certainly, Mrs. Grove. I'll go with these men to the Fonda, and return for you. Good evening, Mrs. Hale."

"Good evening," said Garnet.

He went out. Taking his advice, Florinda slipped the bolt. She turned around with a long expressive whistle.

"Whew! That seemed like old times, it really did. Say, Garnet, who's your happy boy-friend?"

Garnet sat down slowly on the wall-bench. "John Ives? I don't know anything about him but what I told you. He's Oliver's trading partner."

"He looks like his mother rocked him in a coffin instead of a cradle. But the others are fun, aren't they?"

"Yes, I liked them." Garnet dropped her voice. "Florinda, that man—John Ives—he doesn't want me to go to California."

"Why not?"

"I don't know. But he doesn't want me to go." Garnet began to pick up the cups and put them at one side of the table, so Señora Silva could take them when she brought in the supper. She changed the subject. "Did Mr. Van Dorn frighten you?"

"Who, him?" Florinda twirled an imaginary mustache. "Not overmuch."

"Where has he seen you?"

"Dancing at the Jewel Box, I suppose. He said New York."

"What are you going to tell him?"

"You heard me, didn't you?"

"You aren't worried?"

"I was for a minute, when he said something about a gambling palace. But later I asked him how long since he'd been in New York, and he said four years. So he couldn't have been in the Alhambra the night I was thinking of. That was last August, not quite a year ago." Florinda helped herself to an apple.

"He kept looking at your face," said Garnet, "and trying to remember it."

"If he saw me at the Jewel Box, dear, he wasn't looking at my face." Florinda stretched out on the wall-bench. She put her arm under her head and leaned back against the cushions. For a few moments she munched the apple. At length, without turning her head, she said, "Garnet, I'm bothered about something else right now."

"What? Can I help you?"

"No, you can't, and I don't know whether I ought to say any-thing about it. But I'd sort of like to get it off my chest."

Garnet felt a tremor. "Don't tell me Mr. Bartlett is getting tired of you!"

"Oh no. Quite the contrary." Florinda put the core of the apple back on the dish. She examined a spot of dampness the apple had left on her yellow glove as she said, "He's addled for love of me. He wants to marry me."

"No!"

Before she knew what she was doing, Garnet had begun to laugh. Florinda turned her head on the cushion with a faint smile.

"It *is* kind of ridiculous, isn't it?"

"I never heard of anything so absurd. That silly bumpkin, think-ing he's so smart and sophisticated, and you!"

Florinda examined her glove again. "Yes, dear," she said dryly. "Me. The greatest entertainer that ever stopped a show."

"Does he know who you are?"

"Of course not. He wants to marry that high-minded lady who was knocked off her pedestal by the big hero. He says we'll be mar-ried as soon as we cross the frontier, before we get to St. Louis, and nobody will ever know we weren't married before we went West together. We'll live happily ever after, in a white house with ginger-bread trimmings and wax flowers under a glass bell on the mantel-piece and a crayon portrait of grandpa on the wall. He says he'll quit the trail and settle down as a sober merchant all the year round. I'll belong to the Ladies' Aid Society and have social afternoons invit-ing the other ladies over to stitch garments for the orphan asylum. And you're right, of course it's funny. But I don't know whether to laugh or not. I feel like a wretch."

Florinda had spoken in a dry monotone. At her last lines Garnet made herself choke back her laughter. She asked,

"But why do you feel like that, Florinda? You didn't mean for him to fall in love with you."

"Good Lord, no." Florinda sat up. "But it's my own doing, Garnet, don't you understand? Oh, hell for breakfast, I've had gents act sentimental about me before. It didn't bother me. I laughed at them and said, 'If you can't be your age you'd better go home to mamma.' Because they knew what they were getting, and it was their own fault if they didn't take me the way I was. But this time— oh, you know how it started, that black dress and all. He wanted to think he'd made a great conquest. So I played up to it. I let him

153

think he'd mended my broken heart and all that sort of nonsense. And now it's blown back and hit me in the face. He's in love like a kid on a white lace valentine. And what am I going to do?"

"Can't you tell him you're not in love with him?"

"Oh Garnet, you're so innocent!"

"Yes," said Garnet, "I guess I am."

"He's sure I'm in love with him," said Florinda. "I'm so in love with him that I threw away the scruples of a lifetime. And if I'm in love with him, and if I'm really a nice lady at heart, why shouldn't I be joyful that he wants to make me a nice lady again?"

"You couldn't possibly tell him the truth?"

Florinda gave a low eloquent whistle. "What? Tell that conceited hero that I made a fool of him? And me eight hundred miles from the American frontier?"

"Good heavens above, Florinda! He wouldn't *leave* you here!"

Florinda gave her a slow smile of wisdom. "Listen, dearie. I'm not educated like you. But I know men. And I know men like Mr. Bartlett."

She got up and walked over to the mirror. Standing there, she untied the bow of ribbon at her throat and tied it again.

"Mr. Bartlett takes himself seriously, my dear. He thinks it's been just too, too clever of him to keep up that righteous reputation in St. Louis while he came out here and acted up to his idea of cosmopolitan sin. And if he found I'd been making fun of him all this time—no, thank you."

"So what can you do?" asked Garnet.

Florinda drummed her fingers on the edge of the mirror. "I wish I could go to California," she said.

"I wish you could too. I'm going to miss you dreadfully."

"I might manage it. If I can't, I'll just have to pray that Silky Van Dorn won't remember me, and I'll have to go back to Missouri with Mr. Bartlett, and him all shiny-eyed and planning to marry me." Florinda gave a long guilty sigh. "But whatever I do, Garnet, I'm going to have to tell Mr. Bartlett sooner or later that I made a fool of him. And I don't know how I'm going to stand it. Because I tell you, he's walking around in a bright pink haze. And I'm a cockroach."

"No you're not," Garnet said quietly.

Florinda shook her head. "Maybe you still don't understand, dearie," she said in a low regretful voice.

"Yes I do. Come back here, Florinda."

Florinda came back to the wall-bench. She sat down.

"Florinda Grove," said Garnet, "why don't you be your age too?" Florinda gave her a puzzled look. Garnet went on.

"Mr. Bartlett didn't have any pity for that innocent young widow he was seducing."

"My God," said Florinda. She stared at Garnet blankly. "I never thought of that."

"Well, I thought of it," said Garnet. "I thought of it the first day when you were telling us how you met him on the boat. I guess," she said with a touch of shyness, "I thought of it because I'm the sort of woman you were pretending to be just then. I thought you had been terribly clever to do what you did, but I thought—well, I thought if Mr. Bartlett had had a shred of decency in him you couldn't have done it."

Florinda was leaning forward, her elbows on the table. She pushed her sewing-basket aside without looking at it.

"Garnet, I don't quite understand. Tell me some more."

"Well, I do understand!" Garnet exclaimed. "As far as he was concerned, Mr. Bartlett was taking a lady away from her home and her friends. Very likely he was ruining her life. He was planning to abandon her as soon as they got back from the journey, and if her friends had found out what she'd been doing they'd never have received her again. I know about things like that, Florinda! Now and then I've heard nice people talk about a girl who's been—well, they call it 'unfortunate.' They say they're sorry for her, because the poor young thing was too innocent to know what she was getting into, but they don't speak to her. A girl like that is disgraced. Sometimes she's so desperate she kills herself."

Garnet stopped, out of breath. She had spoken so vehemently that she had had no time to breathe. Florinda was still staring at her, speechless.

Garnet caught her breath and went on. "If Mr. Bartlett wanted a pretty girl to amuse him this summer, why didn't he make sure before he started that she knew what she was doing and would have some place to go when she got back? He didn't do that. He took what he thought was a sheltered lily who loved him so much that she didn't realize what it was going to cost her."

Florinda's eyes were wide with horror. "Why—that insect!" she gasped slowly.

She said it with such astounded innocence that Garnet nearly burst out laughing again. "It never occurred to you?" she asked.

Florinda shook her head. "No, it didn't. I've seen plays where a village girl drowned herself in the river because she'd been done wrong by a gent from the big city. But I never thought of it being real, I guess. My God. That pig. That psalm-singing villain."

"Yes," Garnet agreed with emphasis. "And if he's fallen in love with you, and if you laugh at him, it serves him right. He's just being hanged with his own rope."

Florinda stood up again. She walked to the end of the table, and turned around. Her beautiful lips were suddenly tight and hard. She looked so coldly angry that Garnet was surprised. Florinda said in a low voice,

"He's no better than that scoundrel who pretended to marry my mother."

Garnet looked down. She had not meant to remind Florinda of that.

"Garnet," said Florinda, "I like men. I like 'em fine. But I don't like that kind of men. Oh, Lord," she broke off, "don't let me get started on that again." She pushed her father aside and began to laugh. "Just you wait. You wait till I get through with that sanctified lout. Oh, Garnet, darling, how did I ever live without you? When I think how wicked and bothered I've been feeling! Thank you, darling, thank you!" she exclaimed.

Taking the edge of the table with both hands, she lifted herself to sit on it, and drew her sewing-basket toward her.

"Too late to do any work now, I guess. John Ives will be here any minute to see me home. Garnet, I think I'll put some fancy metal buttons down the front of this dress."

"I saw some the other day," said Garnet. "At Mr. Reynolds' store, I think."

"But I'd have to pay for them there. Mr. Bartlett has some too. I saw them, but that was when my conscience was hurting me and I didn't take them."

Garnet bit back a smile. By this time she had discovered what a noble gesture Florinda had made when she insisted on paying her way out of New Orleans and left her emeralds besides. Florinda hated to spend money.

"Are you going to take them now?" Garnet asked.

"Why yes, why not? Mr. Bartlett said I was to have anything I wanted. My conscience isn't bothering me any more, so I think I'll go get those buttons in the morning. Is that John?" she asked, as they heard a knock at the door.

156

Garnet went to answer the knock. The caller was John. He asked gravely if Mrs. Grove was ready to go home now. Florinda picked up her basket and sprang down from the table. John bowed to Garnet, and they went out.

Garnet shut the door after them. For a few minutes, talking about Mr. Bartlett had made her forget John Ives. But now her earlier uneasiness came back to plague her. John had been shocked to hear of Oliver's marriage, she was sure of it; and he wished she was not going to California. She did not understand it. She wished Oliver would hurry back from Taos.

Outside, John and Florinda were walking along the rackety street. The plaza was crowded with traders and girls, making a great deal of merry noise. Several men called to her, but they did not try to stop her. Evidently they respected John's presence. Neither she nor John said anything until they were passing the Fonda, when John asked,

"Where do you live, Mrs. Grove?"

"Right down this side street. I'm here with Mr. Bartlett. I guess you know Mr. Bartlett, don't you?"

"Bartlett from St. Louis? Why yes, I know him. I saw him at the Fonda a few minutes ago."

"That's where you'll usually see him. Two more houses. Here, this is it."

John touched his silver-corded hat. He was about to leave her, but she put her hand on his arm to detain him. This little side street was almost deserted.

"Wait a minute, Johnny. I'd like to say something, if you don't mind."

"Not at all," said John.

"Your friend Silky Van Dorn. Who is he?"

"He used to be a professional gambler in New York. When he left there, I believe he played for a while on the Mississippi steamboats. Now he gambles in mules."

"I see." Florinda smiled thoughtfully. "A professional gambler. I'm not surprised. I know the type. Did you hear him say he thought he'd seen me somewhere?"

"Yes, I heard him." There was a glimmer of amusement on John's thin lips. "Shall I drop him a hint that he's not to say it again? Is that what you wanted to tell me?"

"I did want to. That's why I asked you to bring me home. But—" Florinda smiled mischievously. "But since then, it's occurred to me

157

I might want to change my mind. There's an idea scratching at the back of my head like a hairpin." Florinda considered, making a mark on the ground with the toe of her slipper. She looked up. "I believe I'll think it over. Don't say anything to Silky."

"Very well."

"Thanks."

"Is that all you wanted to say to me?" John asked.

"Not quite. I'd like to say something else. This doesn't happen to be any of my business, but I'd like to say it anyway."

"Go ahead."

"You said something to Garnet."

"Garnet?"

"Mrs. Hale."

"Oh yes."

Florinda glanced down the street. There was nobody near. She looked back at John.

"You gave her the impression that you didn't think much of her going to California."

"Did I?"

"Yes, you did. She told me so." Florinda paused, but as he did not answer she went on. "Is there any reason why she shouldn't go?"

"I know of no reason," said John, "why Mrs. Hale should not do anything she pleases."

"Is that all you're going to say?"

His ice-green eyes met hers. "Yes," he returned, "it is."

"All right. Don't talk if you'd rather not. But look, Johnny. If there's any trouble ahead for Garnet, give her a hand, will you? She's a grand person. She's the grandest person I've ever known. And she's married to a man who somehow impresses me as not being quite good enough for her. Maybe I'm wrong and I hope I am. Still, I've been around a good deal and I size up people pretty fast. And I've sized you up too, and I think you'd be cool in a hurricane, and if Garnet ever needs a friend you might be a good one to have."

John smiled at her faintly. "If you have sized me up, Mrs. Grove, you may have noticed also that I like to mind my own business."

"Do you really? I don't. Not all the time. Well, I guess I'll see you again, so goodby for now." She smiled at him. "Thanks for bringing me home."

"You're quite welcome. Goodby."

Florinda went indoors. John put on his hat and started back through the noisy street to his own lodgings.

SIXTEEN

SILKY AND PENROSE called to see Garnet again the next day. Sober now, and penitent, they wanted to apologize for having come to see her while under the influence of liquor. They assured her that they had the greatest respect for ladies, and would not have dreamed of popping in like that if they had known they were to meet, not Oliver, but Oliver's charming wife. And they hoped they hadn't said anything offensive, and if they had, would she please, please forgive them?

Silky did most of the talking. Penrose was not so glib with words, but he beamed and agreed. They brought her presents. Penrose gave her a jade necklace and Silky begged her to honor him by accepting a length of flowered satin. They had bought these from Yankee ships at San Diego, they told her, and the necklace and the satin had both come all the way from China.

Garnet thanked them, and said they had not offended her at all yesterday. She thought they were funny.

She saw no more of John, or of Texas either, and to her surprise Florinda did not come over. Several times in the next few days she saw Florinda on the street, the center of a group of men on their way to the Fonda or one of the gambling houses. Mr. Bartlett was always with her. He would hold her arm possessively, beaming proudly at the others, evidently delighted to have them see him holding such a treasure. The gentlemen swept off their hats and bowed to Garnet as they passed, and Florinda waved blithely. Whatever her plans for the future, she did not seem to be worried about them.

A week after the arrival of the California men, Oliver returned from Taos. Oliver was in high spirits. They had made a good trip, and now he was eager to see the mules John had brought. He went by his store, leaving a message that John was to meet him there, and came home again to change his clothes. Garnet asked him,

"Oliver, how did you ever happen to go into partnership with that man? He's so different from you!"

Oliver was lacing his shoes. "My dear," he said, "John is an ideal foil for me. I enjoy life too much to be a really tight-fisted businessman. John never thinks about anything but money."

"He was shocked when he learned you were married," said Garnet. "And he was simply appalled when I said you were taking me to California."

"It's a hard journey," said Oliver, "and you look as if you ought to be sitting in a garden under a parasol. John doesn't know how much nerve you've got."

"Do you think that's the only reason?" she asked doubtfully. "He thought I'd crumple up on the way?"

"Why yes, of course that's what he thought, and you can't blame him for thinking so." Oliver tied his shoestrings, and looked up seriously. "We aren't going through any land of enchantment and roses, you know. You'll live rough and you'll eat disagreeable foods, and sometimes water will be doled out by cupfuls. I know you can stand it. In fact, with your liking for new adventures, you'll probably even enjoy it. But you can't expect John to know that."

"I think he brought you a letter," said Garnet.

"Did he? From Charles?"

"I don't know. He wouldn't leave it with me." She told him how John had addressed her in Spanish, and then had denied having a letter.

Oliver laughed as he heard her. "That sounds like John. He doesn't trust anybody. It's probably a letter from Charles, telling me what's been going on at the rancho this past year. Of course I know you wouldn't read it. But John would figure you couldn't resist the temptation to find out whether or not it came from a girl." He ruffled her hair and kissed her. "I'll go on back to the store now. Home before dark."

Garnet walked with him down the passage that led to the street. He went off, and she stood watching the people go by. The street was always interesting. Everything went on under a faint haze of tobacco smoke. The natives of Santa Fe, men and women and sometimes even children, smoked all the time. They carried bags of tobacco and packets of thin brown paper, from which they rolled little tubes they called cigaritos. Ladies of the upper classes held the cigaritos with little gold pincers, so the smoke would not stain their fingers. The smoke curled about their heads as they stood

160

in the street talking, and made fragrant blue patterns over their bright clothes.

Garnet saw Florinda, coming down the street with Bartlett, Silky, Penrose, and several others. They were all laughing and talking, in great spirits. As the men bowed to Garnet, Florinda paused.

"Oh Mr. Bartlett, do you mind if I run in and show Garnet these beautiful silver buttons you gave me? Wait here, I won't be a minute."

"Sure, sure, my sweet, go right in."

Mr. Bartlett, scented with liquor as usual, smiled upon Garnet happily. He was proud that Mrs. Hale had recognized Florinda's noble qualities, in spite of the fact that her morals had need of repair. Florinda slipped into the passage, and chattered as she drew Garnet back inside the house.

"Look, Garnet, real silver! Mr. Bartlett said if I was going to use metal buttons I might as well have good ones. He's so generous all the time."

"Shall I keep them for you?" Garnet asked. "You might lose them on the street."

"Why yes, you take them. I'll get them later." She closed the door, and lowered her voice. "Why don't you drop around to the Fonda tonight, Garnet? It might be fun."

"Florinda, what have you got in your head now? You haven't spoken to me for a week!"

"I've been busy, dear, helping to give Santa Fe its reputation. Well, I'd better run along. The gents want to play monte." She opened the door and started out. "Thanks for taking care of the buttons. Well, let's go, Mr. Bartlett."

Garnet had walked back into the passage with her. Florinda went off with her friends. Garnet heard them say, "Hi there, John," and a moment later she saw John Ives on his way to meet Oliver at the store. Garnet had an uncomfortable feeling that John and Oliver were going to talk about her.

She went back into the house, and told herself that she was simply being foolish. Oliver wasn't uneasy, and certainly Oliver knew more about John than she did. Out here on the trail, she was meeting with so many new experiences that it was no wonder she was getting jittery. She resolutely got out the collar she was making for Florinda, and set to work.

When she saw Oliver that evening, he did not seem to be

troubled. He told her John had brought a fine lot of mules and other goods to be sold to the Missouri men. With the blankets Oliver had bought in Taos, and the others they would get from the Indian weavers around Santa Fe, they would make a profitable trip to Los Angeles. They had a lot of work ahead of them, but everything looked fine so far, and now he was as hungry as a coyote.

"Did he bring you a letter?" asked Garnet.

"Why no," said Oliver, "he didn't." Oliver was pouring water into the wash-basin.

"I wonder what he said to me, then?" she asked.

Oliver began to scrub his face. "I asked him, but he doesn't remember exactly the words he used—'I came to see Oliver,' or something like that. Stop making me talk, Garnet, now I've got soap in my mouth."

Garnet felt better. It was a relief to find that she had really misunderstood what John said.

While Señora Silva served their supper, Oliver told Garnet about the mountain of supplies he would have to get for the journey to California. "You won't be seeing much of me from now on, I'm afraid," he said, "but I hope you'll understand."

"Oh yes. That's all right."

Oliver smiled at her affectionately. As Señora Silva understood no English, they talked as freely at meals as if she had not been there. "Garnet," he said, "are you as fond of me as I am of you?"

She nodded. "I love you enormously."

Señora Silva took away their plates and brought the goat's milk cheese that usually ended their meals. Oliver said nothing for a moment, then as he picked up his cheese he added thoughtfully, "You know I'm not good enough for you, don't you, Garnet? Because I'm not."

"No, I don't know anything of the sort. I've had more fun since I've been married to you than I ever had in my life before. That reminds me, can we go to the Fonda this evening?"

She briefly told him that Mr. Bartlett had asked Florinda to marry him. She did not know what was going to happen at the Fonda, but she wanted to be there. Oliver was amused, but he said, "She'd better be careful about telling him the truth. Bartlett won't think it's funny."

Garnet had no time to repeat what she had said to Florinda about Mr. Bartlett's being a wicked deceiver at heart. They had finished supper, so she put on her bonnet and shawl and they went out.

The Fonda was full of noise and people and tobacco smoke. Florinda was there, surrounded by Mr. Bartlett and a dozen other Americans. She was merrily entertaining them, as though she had nothing on her mind but her present occupation of pouring drinks. As Garnet and Oliver came in she waved to them gaily. The men gave Garnet exaggerated bows. Oliver found a place to sit, and the waiter brought them a bottle of wine.

Florinda's group was not far away. Mr. Penrose sat on the table, strumming a guitar and singing snatches of song. He played very well, though he was slightly drunk and kept having to ask for help. Florinda was chattering.

"No, really, Mr. Van Dorn, you drink that yourself. I don't like it. Go on playing, Mr. Penrose, I like to hear you. Why yes, of course I remember that song. I heard it in my cradle."

She lifted herself to sit on the table by him, and sang to guide him.

> "Oh maybe you think
> That my cheeks are so pink
> Because I've been dreaming of you—

That's how it goes. Everybody knows it, it's a thousand years old. But go on playing it. Right now I've got to see how Mr. Bartlett's getting along. He needs a drink. Yes, Mr. Bartlett, here it is. Brand-new bottle, all for you."

Mr. Bartlett was staggering and happy. She filled his cup and laughed appreciatively at something he said to her.

Garnet looked around. She saw Texas, apart from the others, sitting with a cup and bottle in front of him. He was drinking quietly, as though it were a matter of business. John Ives approached through the crowd. He had a cup, but he was carrying it sideways, his finger through the handle. The cup was empty, and John appeared quite sober. He paused on the other side of the table and greeted her. Garnet returned his greeting, and John continued,

"May I interrupt you?" he took a paper from his pocket and offered it to Oliver. "Here's a list of the prices we're offered for the mules."

"Good work," Oliver said as he glanced over it. "Sit down."

He moved nearer to Garnet, and John sat down on his other side. In a moment they were deep in conversation. Oliver was here only to humor Garnet; he thought Florinda was an entertaining minx, but he was not much interested in her ultimate destiny. He was asking John about the growth of mesquite on the desert. The height of the mesquite had something to do with indicating the water supply, but Garnet did not understand it, so she looked back to where Florinda was busy with her admirers. Penrose was trying to find his way through another tune. Florinda prompted him, but she added laughing,

"Say, Mr. Penrose, you sound like you came over with Columbus, singing all those old songs. You've been away too long. I'll sing you some new ones. But first get me a drink of water. My throat's as dry as a bone."

"Florinda knows all the songs," Mr. Bartlett boasted unsteadily. "She remembers all the words, too. Fine woman, Florinda."

"Come over here, Mr. Bartlett, and let me straighten your collar. You look like a bum. I can't have the whole town talking about how badly I keep you."

Mr. Bartlett approached and let her straighten his collar. He loved it. Silky Van Dorn came nearer, gazing up at Florinda with foggy-eyed curiosity.

"Now where did I see you? Such a ravishing woman, how did I ever forget?"

Florinda swept her blue eyes over him, teasingly.

"You still don't remember?" she asked.

"Not yet. But I will. So fair a face, such golden hair!"

"It's not golden. It's flaxen. It's nearly white."

"But so beautiful! I'll remember, I know I will."

She gave him a tantalizing smile. "Some day I'll tell you."

"You know where it was?" he exclaimed.

"Why certainly. Only you've hurt my feelings by not remembering, so I'm going to let you worry about it a while. No, don't take that bottle, Mr. Van Dorn, that one belongs to Mr. Penrose. I'm keeping it for him while he finds me a drink of water. This one's yours."

Oliver turned from John, and spoke to Garnet. "Florinda's not going to give herself away, is she?"

"I don't know. A lot happened that I haven't had time to tell you about. Mr. Van Dorn thinks he remembers her from New York."

"She'd better be careful," Oliver remarked again.

Garnet looked at Florinda uneasily. Florinda was listening with a show of fascinated attention to something Mr. Bartlett was mumbling to her. Just then Texas, in his corner of the room, half raised himself from his bench and shouted, "I've never been to New York. I came from Texas. Republic of Texas." He sat down again, and rested his chin morosely on his hand.

Oliver laughed and shook his head, and John glanced across him to say to Garnet, "Don't be afraid of Texas, Mrs. Hale. He's quite harmless."

Mr. Penrose was passing their table. He had stuck his guitar under his arm, and he was carrying a pitcher of water with both hands. He paused by Garnet.

"Now Mrs. Hale, please don't you mind Texas," he urged. "Texas is all right."

"Why yes," said Garnet, somewhat puzzled. "I'm sure he's all right."

Mr. Penrose's square flat face was very earnest.

"You see, ma'am, Texas can't take a drink like other folks. He don't touch a drop for weeks and weeks, but when he does it's like he'd been struck by lightning. But he don't bother nobody while he's drinking. He just wants to sit by himself and get it over with."

"Yes, I see," said Garnet, though she did not see at all. She had thought that when men got drunk they did it for fun. She had never heard of anybody who wanted to sit by himself and get it over with.

Mr. Penrose went on past her and delivered the pitcher. Florinda thanked him with an enchanting smile, and accepting the pitcher she took a long drink. Mr. Penrose sat by her on the table again and went back to strumming his guitar.

Florinda leaned nearer him. "Now stop playing those old tunes. I'll teach you some new songs, straight from New York. Listen." She began to hum a tune, without words. Mr. Penrose gazed up in adoration, delighted by all the attention from this beautiful lady straight from New York. But though he tried, he couldn't get the tune right.

"That's a hard one, Miss Florinda!"

"Yes, I know it is. It's hard to play, and hard to sing too. There aren't many people who can sing it."

"I bet you can sing it," said Mr. Penrose.

"Why of course I can. I can sing it without music. Want to hear how it goes?"

"Yes ma'am! You sing it. I bet it's beautiful when you sing it."

"It sure is. Come over here, Mr. Van Dorn. I don't believe you've ever heard me sing."

"Florinda sings fine," boasted Mr. Bartlett. "When she sings, it's beautiful."

Silky Van Dorn poured himself another drink. "She's beautiful doing anything."

"Now then, Mr. Van Dorn, that's the way I like to hear a gent talk. It sure is nice to have friends who say such things. Now you try to follow me on the guitar, Mr. Penrose."

Florinda flashed her eyes over the assembly. She looked very lovely through the swirls of tobacco smoke, with the light of the lamps flaring on her hair. The men began to draw nearer to her. Looking straight at Silky, Florinda started to sing. Her voice was very gay and clear, and her tongue rippled over the syllables with a brilliant speed.

This unspeakable commotion on the border of the ocean
Is all caused by my devotion to a sailor from the sea,
Oh my sailor man's the skipper of a great big Salem clipper,
She is called the Flying Shipper and she's flying him to me!
He's bringing me some silver shoes, he's bringing me a shawl,
He's bringing me a necklace and an Oriental fan,
You never would believe me if I tried to tell you all
The presents I am getting from my loving sailor man—

The noise in the room had begun to quiet down as the men stopped talking and listened. Silky Van Dorn took a step closer. Florinda went on singing. She sang faster and faster, but with every syllable still clear, and her voice went skipping up and down the music with never a false note. It was a hard song to sing, a trick song; no amateur could have managed it. But Florinda, though she had no great voice, was expert at using the voice she had. She babbled on with delicious enjoyment of her own skill.

Garnet heard Oliver say, "Why that little fool—she's telling him!" There were other exclamations all around her, but Florinda did not pause.

Oh, sailor men go sailing and they do forget you fast,
But sailor men are mighty good providers while they last—

"My God!" shouted Silky Van Dorn. He gave a thump to the table with his fist. The wine splashed out of his cup. Florinda broke off in the middle of a note, and pulled her dress aside. The other men were demanding to know what he was so excited about. Silky was shouting in tipsy delight.

"Bartlett, you fool, why didn't you tell me? How did you do it? And me forgetting—how did I ever do that? Me forgetting the greatest singer that ever knocked 'em over in New York! And you—" he pointed his finger at Florinda—"oh you beautiful deceiving woman, what made you keep teasing me? Teasing me and making fun of me—"

The other men were making so much noise that Garnet lost the rest of what he said. She heard Oliver ask,

"Does she know what she's started?"

"Yes, she knows," said Garnet. She could not take her eyes off Florinda, who was laughing at the excitement she had provoked. "Let her alone. She's making trouble and she wants to make it."

Florinda was not trying to say anything. But everybody else was. The men wanted to know what Silky was talking about, and he was trying to tell them. Forgetting his lordly poses of speech, he was prattling with all his might. Mr. Bartlett was trying to understand, turning his head unsteadily from Silky to Florinda and back again. Florinda still sat on the edge of the table, her ankles crossed gracefully, laughing to herself.

"Look here," Silky was demanding, "is this a joke on me? Did everybody but me know who she was? Am I the only damn fool in Santa Fe who didn't know? Say, sweetheart, what made you change your name?"

In the hubbub Mr. Bartlett protested, "Changed her name when she got married. Widow lady. Lost her husband last winter—"

"Trouble with you, Bartlett, is that you've been drinking. Her a widow lady? Don't make me laugh any more than I'm laughing."

"You're drunk!" announced Mr. Bartlett.

"Me drunk? No, no. Just had enough to make me sharp. Why didn't you tell me, you fellows?"

Florinda reached out and put her hand on his elbow. When Florinda had something to say, she could say it so it could be heard. "Nobody knew, Silky. It was a secret."

"What? You mean—Bartlett, you mean you've been keeping it to yourself all this time? Believe me, if I'd had Charline of the Jewel Box—but you brought her all the way out here and told nobody? You're a selfish pig, Bartlett, that's what you are." Silky looked him up and down, and laughed uproariously. "But you're better than I thought you were! How'd you do it? Her with every masher from the Battery to Washington Square at the stage door, and you—" Silky swallowed his drink at a gulp. "*You!*"

The other men stared at Bartlett with new respect. Bartlett blinked. The men were crowding around Silky and Florinda, begging to know more. Oliver and John had both stood up. John was asking, "What on earth is this about?" Even Texas was sitting up straight, saying something incoherent to the air. Oliver took Garnet's arm.

"You'd better let me get you out of here, Garnet."

"No, no! We're not going yet! She might need some help."

Silky was talking. Bartlett, still bewildered, was making some drunken protests. Florinda took Silky's arm again, and he looked up at her. Florinda laughed, and in a clear voice that could have been heard in the back of a theater balcony, she said to him,

"He didn't know either, Silky. He was such a country bumpkin, I thought it would be fun to see how long I could keep him fooled."

Silky burst out into mocking laughter. The other men began to laugh too. They looked at Florinda, and they looked at Bartlett, and as the idea dawned on more and more of them, their merriment got louder. Florinda said,

"Go on, Silky. Tell them."

Silky needed no permission. He was already telling them.

"—and there I was, just a common card-player from Park Row, saying, 'I've got to meet that girl, what do you have to do to get acquainted?' And they said to me, they said, 'You have to have a diamond necklace and your arms full of sables, no less, why man, she's got Bleecker Street on its knees, what would she be doing with a bum from Park Row? What can you give her that she wants, you—' "

Garnet saw Mr. Bartlett. He was drunk. But he was not too drunk to understand that everybody was laughing at him now. His face turned white, and slowly began turning red again. Garnet closed her hand on Oliver's elbow. "Oliver! Go out there near her! She's going to need you!"

Oliver was half amused and half exasperated. Florinda had started this herself and he thought she should have known better. But he said, "All right. Come on, John. You stay here, Garnet."

She stood up and they pushed past her between the bench and the table, and got free. They began making slow headway through the mob packed around Florinda. Silky was still talking.

"But I was clean knocked over, flat as a pancake I was, and boys, you'd have been there with me if you'd seen her do that dance in the black lace! So I went around to the stage door, heart pounding like a kid's in the springtime, and boys, they were right in all they'd said. Men six deep on all sides. And out she comes, wrapped up in ten thousand dollars' worth of furs, and on each elbow a gent, a real gent in a silk hat, and another gent making way for her like they would for a queen. I couldn't get near. She never even saw me. And there stands a carriage with purple curtains and matched black horses, and in she goes, and as she gets in I catch the sparkle of a bracelet that must have sent one of those gents howling from his bank, but that's what she cost and I guess she was worth it, and they all—"

The other voices drowned his again. The men were full of awe at Florinda, and vastly amused at Bartlett's sputtering embarrassment. In his far corner of the room, Texas was blinking and trying to stand up. He was very drunk. Florinda sat quietly on the table, watching Silky as though she were the audience and he the show. She was smiling a little, as though enjoying the performance.

"Of course you never saw anybody like her!" Silky shouted in derision. "Where'd a bunch of yokels like you ever expect to see anything like the star of the Jewel Box? You've never been to New York. You nor Bartlett either. Think of her pulling a joke like that on Deacon Bartlett. What she'll have to tell them when she gets back to St. Louis, about the holiest hell-chaser in town!"

Bartlett had elbowed his way to stand in front of Florinda. He stood there, swaying on his feet. Florinda laughed at him softly. Bartlett was blind with rage. John and Oliver were trying to shove through the mob toward him, but before they could reach him Bartlett made an inarticulate noise in his throat. Having found his voice, he let go a string of sizzling words, and gave Florinda a blow on the side of her head that sent her toppling sideways.

It almost knocked her to the floor. But Mr. Penrose, with a roar of wrath, caught her with one arm and with the other aimed a blow at Bartlett's head. The blow glanced off the side of his cheek, but by this time John and Oliver had reached him. Oliver grabbed one of Bartlett's arms and John the other. The rest of the men surged between him and Florinda. They were all yelling at once. Florinda was an American woman, rare and precious in this foreign land, and they would have been glad to tear Bartlett to pieces for striking her. Bartlett staggered between John and Oliver, struggling to get free and swearing in wild anger. Texas was on his feet now, swearing by various gods that he'd kill that brute Bartlett if he dared hit that lady again. Above the pandemonium Silky was exclaiming,

"What did I do? Wasn't I supposed to tell them? Charline—Florinda—I didn't mean to start anything!"

Florinda had straightened up. Penrose had his arm around her. She smiled her thanks to him, while she pushed back the hair that Bartlett's blow had sent falling around her face. Her gloves were blue silk; they glimmered against her bright hair. Her clear warm voice answered,

"It's all right, Silky. He hasn't hurt me."

Garnet stood pressed back against the wall. John and Oliver did not need to protect Florinda now, they had to protect Bartlett. In this gathering, Florinda's sex and her beauty and her nationality were all the protection she needed, but Bartlett had to have help if he was going to get out alive. John and Oliver were dragging him out of the crowd. Bartlett was kicking. John used his fist to give him a well-aimed crack on the head. Bartlett crumpled up like a doll.

Garnet had never seen a riot before. She was frightened. But she saw Florinda turn her head, looking for her. Their eyes met, and Florinda gave her a cool private smile.

Garnet lowered her head and bit her lips to keep from laughing. All of a sudden, that little smile had told her why Florinda had wanted her to be here tonight. Florinda had meant this to happen, just as it had happened, but nobody knew this except the two of them. And Florinda was an actress. When she did a scene, she needed an audience who could appreciate it.

Without any visible excitement, John said to the man next to him,

"Here, Reynolds, give me a hand. Oliver, we'll get Bartlett out of here. You'd better take care of Mrs. Hale."

Garnet had been so quiet the others had forgotten she was there. But hearing her name, two men moved over to stand on either side of her. Oliver handed his side of Bartlett to Reynolds, and began to make his way back to her. John and Reynolds dragged Bartlett toward the door.

Dismay had shocked Silky into something like sobriety. He moved over to Florinda again. Mr. Penrose still had a sheltering arm around her. Silky, almost in tears, was pleading with her to forgive him. Florinda tweaked Silky's mustache, forgivingly.

Her eyes followed John and Reynolds as they dragged Bartlett to the door. John called over his shoulder,

"He's out, boys. We'll take him home and lock him in."

The door banged shut behind them. There was a sudden uncomfortable silence. Nobody knew how to go on from here. The men's heads turned back to Florinda questioningly.

Florinda smiled at them, a brilliant smile, warm and friendly. She reached up to feel her cheek, still red from Bartlett's blow. She shrugged, and her clear voice spoke to them all.

"I wonder," she said, "who's going to make a cold pack for his head in the morning."

All of a sudden, from the corner of the room, they heard applause. It was Texas. Drunk as he was, Texas knew triumph when he saw it.

He clapped his hands. As though it had been a signal, the others joined him. They clapped, they shouted, one or two of them began to cheer. It was as though Florinda had appeared on the stage.

Florinda began to laugh. This was a noise she was used to.

In another minute she had got out of Mr. Penrose's sheltering arm and was standing on the table. She laughed, and kissed her hands to them, over and over, as she had laughed and kissed her hands to hundreds of other audiences before them. She was simply dressed, in a printed muslin gown she and Garnet had stitched in Señora Silva's parlor, but her vigor and richness needed no special costume to make it real. Her vitality flashed through the dingy room as it had flashed through the Jewel Box.

She was back where she belonged. She was a great entertainer and she knew it, and in a dozen seconds they knew it too. They shouted and applauded; even the few Mexicans in the room, who had not understood a word of what had been said, grinned and drew nearer.

For a moment she stayed like that, letting them look at her. Then she raised her hands and swept out the racket. Her voice went out to them, not loud, but so perfectly placed that every man in the Fonda could hear what she said.

"Well, boys, this is the first time in three months I've had a chance to act natural. And oh, what a pleasure it is!"

Pulling a handkerchief out of her bosom, Florinda waved to them as if she were greeting her friends after a journey.

"Tell me—have any of you besides Silky Van Dorn ever been to the Jewel Box? Then you don't know what you've been missing and it's time you found out. Mr. Penrose, have you got that guitar?

Give us some music. Take your seats, gents, take your seats. We're going to put on a show!"

SEVENTEEN

OLIVER INSISTED that Garnet go home now. It was some time before she heard what happened after she left.

Florinda gave them a show that lasted till past midnight. By this time most of the traders were drunk, and several were blissfully unconscious. They noisily agreed that it was the greatest evening they had ever spent in Santa Fe. And Bartlett was not only a fool, he was also a brute, and what was more, he was ridiculous.

Silky was having a bad attack of conscience. He had started all this, he said over and over as he stared into his drink. It was his fault that Bartlett had tried to beat her up. That so beautiful and so defenseless lady, and it was all his fault.

When at last Florinda said this was all for tonight, the men were still not satisfied. Florinda answered their protests by saying she was hoarse now, but would sing for them again whenever they wanted her to. She slipped down from the table and started across the room. Silky caught her wrist as she passed him.

"Charline," he mumbled—"Florinda—which do I call you?"

"Call me Florinda. I'm so used to it now."

"Are you ever going to forgive me, Florinda?"

"Why of course. It's perfectly all right. I've been having a grand time amusing the gentlemen."

He sighed guiltily, shaking his head at a splash of liquor on the table. Silky's eyes were like pieces of glass. His mustache was limp and drooping. He was about to burst into tears.

"But what can you do now?" he exclaimed. "You haven't got any place to spend the night."

Florinda smiled, without answering. Her eyes were glassy too. She had not been drinking, but her performance had been hard work and she was tired.

"You can have my room," Silky offered in a burst of stricken generosity. "I don't mean what you think. I'll go bunk with Penrose."

"Why Silky, that's mighty nice of you. But I wouldn't think of putting you to such inconvenience. I'll be all right."

Silky smiled with the gratitude of one who has made a worthy gesture and does not have to live up to it. Florinda walked over to where John was sitting quietly by himself. John had returned to the Fonda after delivering Bartlett to his lodgings at the house of Señor Moro. He had been here ever since, drinking very little, and watching her with ironic admiration.

"You are very good," John said as she paused in front of him.

"Thanks," said Florinda.

"What are you going to do now?" he asked.

"Don't worry, John. I wouldn't let anything like this happen unless I was ready for it." Florinda reached into the pocket of her dress. She held out her hand, and showed him a key on the palm of her blue silk glove. "I got a room yesterday while Mr. Bartlett was sleeping off some firewater. One of the Missouri gents helped me, since my Spanish is so rocky. I told him Mr. Bartlett and I were tired of living at the Moros' and wanted to move."

"I see. But what do you want me to do about it?"

Florinda glanced eloquently around them. The Fonda was hot and airless and full of drunken chatter. From the plaza outside they could hear the voices of other traders as they emerged from the gambling houses.

"I don't quite like the idea," said Florinda, "of going out by myself right now. Since you're the only sober man in sight, I thought maybe you'd go with me. It's not far."

"All right," said John. He stood up.

"Is Mr. Bartlett still unconscious?" she asked.

"I'm sure he is."

"Then if you don't mind, I'd like to get my things. I'm all packed, and it's only six steps to the Moros'."

John enlisted the aid of a fairly sober Mexican boy. They went down the dark little street that led from the Fonda to Bartlett's lodgings. Bartlett was still lost in a drunken slumber. Florinda showed them two stout boxes. John shouldered one and the boy the other, while she picked up the carpetbags she had brought from New Orleans. They went back across the plaza, past the gambling houses, to a small residence where Florinda had managed to get a room. John and the boy set down the boxes. Florinda had brought a candle with her, and lit it at a lantern hanging at the door of a saloon as they passed. Now she used it to light the pottery lamp on the table in her room. John turned to the boy, his hand in his pocket, but Florinda stopped him.

"Here, John." She held out a piece of silver. "Give him this. When people are nice to me, it doesn't cost them anything."

With a faint smile, John took her money and paid the boy. As the boy went out, Florinda sat down on the edge of the bed. John stood by the door.

"Is there anything else?" he asked her.

"No. Thanks for coming with me. Oh yes, one thing more. Tell me, are those men as drunk and silly on the trail as they are in Santa Fe?"

"No, they're very different on the trail. This is a reaction from three months of strain."

"Is it a terribly hard journey to California?" she asked thoughtfully.

"Yes. Very hard." John had put his hand on the latch, but he turned around. "Why do you ask? Are you planning to come with us?"

"I was thinking of it."

"It's none of my business," John said gravely, "but you won't like that trail."

"Why not? Do you think I'm a city softie?"

"No, I think you have a great deal of courage. But it takes more than courage to get across the Mojave Desert."

"I guess it is pretty tough. But other people stand it. What makes you think I couldn't?"

"The heat," said John. "You're too pale for it."

Florinda glanced at herself in the mirror on the wall. The lamplight danced over her fair cheeks and her hair. She smiled.

"Ever been in New York in summer?" she asked.

"Yes, and New York is frigid compared to that desert. I wouldn't want to be responsible for getting you across it."

Florinda turned her eyes from the mirror and looked directly at him. "I'll be responsible, Johnny."

"All right," he answered quietly.

Florinda yawned. "Well, I can't think about it now. I'm so tired I hurt all over. That's the first time I ever held the stage all evening without a break. Good night, John."

"Good night, Mrs. Grove."

"Look, Johnny, you can stop that courteous flubdub now. 'Mrs.' is a handle that doesn't fit me very well."

Again he smiled faintly. "As you prefer. Good night, Florinda."
He went out. Florinda bolted the door after him. She got out a
nightgown and began to undress. As she took off her clothes she sang
a snatch of song.

> *My grandma used to say, boys,*
> *That I must be modest and nice,*
> *But where would I be today, boys,*
> *If I'd taken my grandma's advice?*

For several days, Garnet hardly saw Florinda. She caught sight
of her on the street, with Penrose and Silky and other California
traders, but Florinda only waved and did not pause. Garnet did
not see Mr. Bartlett at all. The men who came to call on Oliver
said Bartlett hardly put his nose out of doors. They prophesied
that this was his last journey to Santa Fe; after this he would prefer to stay in St. Louis where everybody looked up to him.

They laughed at Bartlett and laughed at him. Because, they said,
Florinda couldn't have fooled *them*, not a bit of it. In fact, every
man who spoke of Florinda dropped a hint that he had suspected
the truth all along. He hadn't wanted to say anything, of course,
but the first time he saw her he had guessed that she wasn't an
artless young lady who had been lured into an escapade. Why, anybody could have seen that, except a chump like Bartlett.

Hearing them, Garnet went off into the bedroom and smothered
her face in a towel and laughed till she nearly choked. Until now,
she had never realized that when men had lived a long time without
women enough to go around, they could be just as catty as girls
in the manless confines of a boarding school.

John came to see Oliver often, but John did not talk about Florinda. John seldom talked about anything but business.

Ten days after Florinda's show at the Fonda, Oliver came in one
afternoon to get the list of supplies he had stocked for the trail.
"I hear Florinda's going to California," he said to Garnet.

Garnet was not surprised, but she asked, "How is she getting
there?"

"They say she's going with Penrose."

"Penrose? But why on earth did she choose him?"

"I don't know. I don't even know why she wants to go at all."
Oliver picked up a ledger and started out. "Maybe she'll tell you.
I'll be back for supper."

Oliver went to the store again, and Garnet sat down by the table. She had to finish the letter she was writing to her parents. Mr. Reynolds was going to take it back for her, and drop it into a post office when he got to Missouri.

But it was hard to concentrate on the letter. Garnet cut a fresh quill, and looked down at the paper. Her parents were the most lovable people on earth, but there was so much she couldn't write to them. She had described the scenery, and the buffalo hunts, and the quaint adobe houses of Santa Fe; but she was sure they wouldn't understand about Florinda, or about the sort of men she was meeting here. She had begun to have a troublesome feeling that it was going to be harder than ever for her to behave like a perfect lady when she got home next year.

She was glad to hear a knock at the door, and sprang up in welcome when she saw Florinda come in. Florinda said she would like to have the silver buttons Mr. Bartlett had given her.

Garnet was not interested in silver buttons. She demanded, "Florinda, is it true you're going to California?"

"Why yes, dearie, I am." Florinda sat down on the wall-bench. "Are you glad?"

"Of course I'm glad! Tell me about it. Did Mr. Penrose ask you to go with him?"

Florinda smiled serenely. "He thinks he did."

"What do you mean?"

"Well, dear, he's been gazing at me starry-eyed ever since the first time he saw me, right here in this room. So when I got rid of Mr. Bartlett, I started to gaze starry-eyed back at him. That's all."

"Do—do you like him?" Garnet ventured.

"Why yes, I like him well enough. He's such a muttonhead that he's very easy to get along with, and he thinks I'm wonderful. He's never been off the farm, except out here, and he's so excited to have a New York actress for his girl-friend that he can hardly keep count of his mules."

Her eyes, very wise and naughty, met Garnet's as she added, "Silky Van Dorn is so relieved, dear."

"Relieved? About what?"

"Well, you see, he thinks he gave away the whole show by talking too much. So he was afraid I was going to come rushing up to him and say, 'You got me into this, now you've got to take care of me.' Silky likes me fine, but he doesn't want to take care of anybody but himself. But oh, he felt so guilty. He came over to see me the next day, all bleary from last night's liquor, and told me if I didn't have any way to get back to Missouri he'd see that I got safely to California. I said everything was all right, I was managing myself just beautifully. He was so joyful he started admiring me right away for my stalwart character. It's much better that way. He's smart, and when they're smart I'd rather have them admire me for my character than adore me for my big blue eyes."

Garnet had no idea how to answer such remarks, so she did not try. She was thinking of the future. "What are you going to do in California?" she asked.

"I've no idea. If I don't like it, I guess I can manage to come back to the States next year. But I hope I can get along there." She picked up the quill Garnet had been writing with, and stroked her own cheek with the feather end. "I don't want to go back to the States, Garnet," she added seriously.

"Are you still scared of Mr. Reese?" Garnet asked.

"Not exactly. That witch-hunt can't last forever." Florinda was looking down as she played with the pen. "But—I guess I can say it to you. When I left the States, I meant to go back. It didn't occur to me there was any chance of my going on to California. But the more I thought of going back, the less I liked it."

She spoke slowly, in a low voice. Garnet did not interrupt her. Florinda went on.

"You remember, in New Orleans I told you something had happened that I didn't want to think about. I wanted to get a long way from it. New Orleans was better than New York. But it wasn't far enough. It was still American. Away out in California, everything will be different. There'll be nothing to remind me of anything that happened before I got there. I can start over." She smiled intimately. "Understand, darling?"

"Yes," said Garnet, "I think I do."

She remembered Oliver's telling her that most of the Americans in California had gone there because there was something in their own country that they wanted to get away from. She thought of John, who was so silent about his past life; even Oliver, who had known him for five years, did not know why John had left Virginia. She thought of Texas, who had never even told his friends what his name was, and who periodically went off by himself to get drunk. And now Florinda was joining their company, hiding her scars under her fancy gloves, and hiding her secret wound under her frivolous laughter.

177

They were both silent for some time. After a while Garnet asked, "Have you seen Mr. Bartlett?"

"No, dear, and I don't expect to. He's getting out of town as fast as he can. He's not waiting for the big train back. He doesn't want to see anybody."

"You know, Florinda," said Garnet, "you weren't very nice to Mr. Bartlett."

"Did you expect me to be?"

"I didn't think you were going to make him the laughing-stock of the whole train."

"Hell for breakfast," said Florinda, "if he'd had sense enough to laugh at himself instead of nearly breaking my jaw, nobody would have laughed at him. I was mighty pleased when he hit me. I thought for a minute he wasn't going to do it. But as soon as he did, all the rest of them felt noble because they hadn't hit me, so then they were all on my side. The gents sure do like a girl who makes them feel gallant without making them do anything to prove it." She stood up. "Say, Garnet, it's getting late. I've got to go and fascinate Mr. Penrose. Can I have the silver buttons?"

Garnet took the buttons out of her sewing-basket. "Are you going to give these back to Mr. Bartlett?"

"Give them back? Why no, I'm going to sew them on my dress. Why should I give them back?"

"Why—I just thought—"

"My God, don't be so childish," said Florinda. "They're real silver."

She took the buttons and said goodby. Left alone, Garnet went back to her letter.

". . . In two or three days we will leave here for California. Oliver says we should reach his rancho about the first of November. My health is excellent. Oliver is the most devoted husband any girl could ask for, and I am very happy. Give my love to the boys . . ."

She shook her head. It was a long letter. But it seemed to her she had not written any of the really important things that had happened since she left New York.

She wished she could talk to her parents instead of writing them. She wished she could tell them about Oliver's odd shyness on the subject of Charles, and ask if they understood it any better than she did. But no! she said to herself with a start. That would be shamefully disloyal. If she suspected that Oliver had any weakness, it was her business to be quiet about it. She signed the letter and folded it, and got out a stick of sealing-wax.

On the tenth day of August, 1845, they left Santa Fe and rode westward to the Rio Grande del Norte. They were on their way to California.

EIGHTEEN

THE LOS ANGELES TRADERS did not use wagons. When you rode to California, you did it in a saddle.

The men rode mules, since mules stood the journey better than horses, but as a tribute to their city breeding Garnet and Florinda each had three sturdy little mares. Garnet called hers Daisy, Sunny, and Kate. Florinda called hers Amaryllis, Gloriana, and Celestine. "I like great big beautiful names," she said.

There were two hundred persons in the train, and a thousand mules, besides a flock of sheep that they drove for fresh meat. There were no buffalo ahead of them. The pack-mules were loaded with blankets, silver, and American goods the traders had bought in Santa Fe. There were eighteen traders, six of them native Californios and the others Yankees. There was also a troop of muleteers and servants, mostly Mexicans, and ten women.

Garnet and Florinda were the only Americans among the women. Two of the Californio traders had brought their wives, and two Yankee traders were accompanied by Mexican girls who were not their wives. There were also four camp-followers. They were half-breed girls, born of white fathers and Indian mothers in the trapping country north of Santa Fe. They had blank, stolid faces, and they took care of themselves with easy skill. Garnet was glad they were there. All the training of her lifetime rose up reproachfully and told her she ought to be shocked at their presence. But she was not shocked. She knew that because of these girls, the journey to California would be easier on her than the journey to Santa Fe had been. There was no sense in pretending to feel a virtuous indignation when she did not feel any such thing. The half-breed girls never spoke to her, or as far as she could see, to anybody else. They were simply there.

Unlike the men on the Santa Fe Trail, the California traders had a lot of personal servants. Every trader had at least one boy who had nothing to do but wait on him; most of the traders had two or three. These men knew how to put up with hard times when they had to. But they saw no reason why they should not enjoy as much comfort as they could get. With no resources except what they could pack on the mules, Garnet was surprised at how comfortable they were.

They started at dawn, and rode till word came back to make camp for the nooning. By this time she would be very hot and tired, but as soon as she slipped out of her saddle one of Oliver's boys would take her horse, while another boy ran to fill her water-bottle. To stretch her cramped muscles, Garnet walked over and watched the muleteers unloading the mules. They took off the packs, and tethered the mules with long leather thongs, called reatas, which they tied to picket-pins driven into the ground. Here along the Rio Grande there was plenty of grass.

While she walked around, the boys built her a house. They piled up saddles and mule-packs to make four walls, and over the walls they spread a blanket for a roof. When the house was ready, one of the boys brought her a pail of water so she could wash in privacy while the cooks made up the fires.

By the time she came outside dinner was ready. The food was good. There were chunks of fresh mutton stewed with peppers and dried onions, and slabs of goat's milk cheese, and fat red Mexican beans. Sometimes there were birds the men had shot. In place of bread there was atole, a cornmeal from which they cooked hot mush; or pinole, a mixture of parched corn flavored with sugar and cinnamon. Mixed with hot water, atole and pinole made good porridges.

After dinner everybody went to sleep except the men whose turn it was for guard duty. Garnet slept in her little house, or on a blanket outside if the day was too hot. The men slept around the central pile of packs and saddles, so they could spring up and use them for breastworks in case of attack.

At the nooning, only Garnet and Florinda had shelters. The rest of the company were used to living outdoors and felt no need of privacy in the daytime. But when they stopped for the night, the camp was a village of little houses. Each one had packs and saddles for walls and a blanket for a roof, and inside it a warm pile of blankets and buffalo robes for a bed. Though the days were hot, the nights were surprisingly cool. The houses were set close together for safety. At a signal of alarm, the men could snatch off the blanket-roofs and shoot from behind the walls. These walls were snug and tight, for the boys who built them were clever youngsters, proud of their jobs. The California trade was dangerous, and the traders were looked upon with respect in the country around Los Angeles. The boys who served the traders, like the pages who waited on the knights of old, enjoyed a good deal of social prestige at home.

When they came to the Rio Grande they turned north, and followed the river up to where it met a little stream called the Chama. Here they crossed the Rio Grande, and they followed the Chama northwest to a sleepy little adobe village called Abiquíu. Past the village, they rode along the Chama into a wild, Indian-ridden country of hills and shrubs and colored rocks.

The Indians along here were Apaches and Comanches, the fiercest tribes of the West. They lurked on the high rocks, ready to swoop and attack at the slightest sign of carelessness in the train. But there was no carelessness. These men knew their business. They went about it with such competence that though Oliver had to warn her about the Comanches, Garnet was not much afraid.

The Comanches, he told her, were the world's most accomplished torturers. They took a horrid pleasure in slowly dismembering their captives. Oliver handed her a pistol, and told her to carry it in a holster strapped to her waist. Back among the trees of Council Grove he had taught her how to use a rifle, and now, early in this new trail, he made her fire at targets he pointed out, to be sure she could still use it.

"Now remember," he said to her, "a good frontiersman is one who knows about the dangers, and is ready for them, but doesn't worry about them. Understand?"

Garnet nodded grimly. She was thinking of what she had been doing this time last summer. She had been at Rockaway Beach, sipping lemonade on a cool corner of the hotel veranda. Oliver went on.

"We're very well armed, and we know how to take care of ourselves. But I had to warn you. Now if you're as smart as I think you are, you'll carry that gun but you won't lose any sleep over thinking about why you're carrying it."

Garnet promised. And she found, as they traveled among the rocky hills, that it was quite impossible for her to lose any sleep for any reason. Whenever they stopped, she was so tired that she fell asleep as soon as she lay down, and her sleep was like black velvet.

She saw that Florinda was also carrying a gun, and as they rode along the Chama River Garnet asked if Mr. Penrose had told her about the Comanches.

"Why yes, he told me," said Florinda. "He made them sound quite unpleasant. It seems that if they catch you alive they have a social party and amuse the guests by taking you apart."

"You weren't scared?"

"Sure I was scared. But then it occurred to me that these mule-trains have been going through here ever since about the time I was born. So I figured they could get through one more time."

"That's what I was thinking," said Garnet. "Nothing has happened so far."

"No, and I don't think anything's going to. These chaps know what they're about."

Garnet looked with admiration at these watchful silent men who had been carousing in Santa Fe only last week. Here they never relaxed their vigilance. Most of them started the day with a drink of whiskey, saying it warmed them in the chill of the early morning, but they knew too much to get drunk on the trail. Garnet noticed that Texas, who had spent his time in Santa Fe sitting alone and getting it over with, had evidently got it over with. Here on the trail he never touched a bottle.

They were riding through a country of such wild splendor that Garnet gasped with wonder at every turn. The trail was climbing among great rocks, not dull-colored rocks like others she had seen, but vast tumbled formations of black and red and copper, a hundred shades of color lying in vivid layers against a vivid blue sky. Among the rocks grew trees that looked something like pines; and bushes with rough gray leaves, on which yellow flowers were beginning to bloom.

The rocks near the stream were flat-topped, and their colors lay in gaudy slanting stripes. Farther away, brilliant against the sky, were great red rocks like castles. They had square walls and round towers, like the fortresses of medieval Europe. But they did not look like the pictures of real castles. They looked as those castles might have looked if they had been made larger and more splendid by the fancy of an artist, with towers and turrets and battlements built for the warriors of dreams. There were hundreds of them, miles and miles of red grandeur. As she watched them Garnet drew in her breath with a little sound of ecstasy, and Florinda asked,

"What's the matter, dearie?"

"All this," Garnet said softly. "The rocks—Florinda, what do they look like to you?"

Florinda glanced around. "Well, those big flat ones look like layer-cakes. Those big red blobs, they don't look like anything."

Garnet turned her head slowly and stared at her. Florinda, slapping a gnat that had lit on her nose, remarked that this blamed country sure did get as hot as the inside of a cow. Garnet reluctantly understood that Florinda was one of the people who could ride through a land full of glory and never see it. To Florinda, beauty meant clothes and jewels and her own self in the glass. She had never noticed a mountain or a sunset in her life.

So Garnet did not talk any more about the spectacle around them. But that evening, while the cooks were making the supper-fires, she walked past the grazing-space and stopped to look out at the rocks. The declining sun was sending long blades of light among them, striking fantastic colors from the piles, and the shadows lay purple on the ground, like goblins. Behind her Garnet heard the shouts of the men and the braying of the mules. Ahead of her she could see a guard, crouched on his haunches, motionless. One hand shielded his eyes, the other lay ready on his gun. Garnet stood very still. Oliver had warned her never to make any sudden motion behind a guard.

The sun slipped behind one of the far red castles, and the light among them was suddenly a thicker purple, though there were still crowns of gold on the towers. Garnet turned her head to follow the stretching shadows. A few feet to the right of her she saw John Ives, standing beside a rock. Garnet thought she was being very quiet, but John must have heard the rustle of her skirt on the ground, for he turned toward her.

"Good evening, Mrs. Hale," he said.

Garnet bit her lip, embarrassed to have disturbed him.

"I'm sorry, Mr. Ives. I didn't see you on duty here. I was trying not to get too close to the other guard."

"I am not on duty." He glanced at the splendor ahead. "I was looking at the rocks."

Garnet took a step nearer him. "Do you think they're beautiful too?"

John nodded. With a six days' growth of black beard he had begun to look very unlike the immaculate gentleman she had known in Santa Fe.

"Beautiful isn't exactly the word, is it?" he said. "But I suppose it has to do. I don't know any words for it."

Garnet glanced uneasily at the guard. John said,

"We aren't disturbing him. He's used to the ordinary camp talk."

John seldom spoke to anybody unless it was necessary, and she wondered if she was in his way now. But she did want to know about the rocks. So she asked,

"What are they? Why do they look like that?"

"I don't know. I've wondered too."

"What are these odd trees that look like pines?" asked Garnet.

"Piñons. They are a kind of pine."

"And these gray bushes with the yellow blooms?"

"Chamisa. They're just beginning to bloom now. In another month they'll be covered with yellow flowers." His eyes went over her with a faint surprise, and like Oliver last winter, he asked her, "Are you interested in all this?"

As she had answered Oliver then, she said to John, laughing a little,

"I'm interested in anything I don't know about." He did not reply, and she asked, "Is that so surprising?"

"Why yes," said John. "So few people are."

Garnet looked up at him. It was hard to see a man's expression when his face was all rough with a week's beard. "I don't believe you like people very much," she said.

He laughed tersely. "Do you?"

"Of course I do. Most people seem to me to be all right. And the ones who aren't—lots of the time it's not their fault."

"Possibly not. But don't you find it restful to get away from them, now and then, into a great emptiness like this?"

"Restful? Why no, I hadn't thought of that." She looked out at the goblin shadows. "Some day, you know, this may not be empty. People might come to live here."

"I don't think they can improve it much," John said dryly. He glanced over his shoulder. "I think I hear the spoons jingling. Come on, nobody's going to feed us if we don't go ask for it."

They started to walk back toward the campfires. "I think you're rather horrid," said Garnet.

184

"Do you? I think you're rather funny." He touched his hatless forehead, and walked off to speak to one of his muleteers.

A boy filled her bowl with meat from one of the big kettles. Garnet sat down on the ground and ate her supper. When she had washed the bowl, she sat by the entrance of her saddle-house and watched the men hurrying around to make camp for the night. The shadows had drawn in thickly now, and the evening was chilly. She would have liked to sit by the fire, but Oliver had warned her never to sit by the fire after sunset. Silhouetted against the flames, she would make a perfect target for a roaming Comanche. Garnet looked out at the great rocks, wild black shadows now against the gray-blue twilight sky, and wondered if there would ever be towns among them. She remembered the day she had seen the California traders ride into Santa Fe, dirty and fierce and tired, when she had thought they looked like the sort of men who crossed all boundaries and set up empires in the waste places.

Oliver came over to her. "It's getting dark," he said, "and the mules are all picketed. Shall we go to bed?"

He pushed aside the blanket that hung down over the entrance to their shelter. Garnet went inside and began to take off her clothes. She slipped in between the buffalo robes and stretched out.

"Oliver," she said as he came to lie down by her, "why didn't you tell me how gorgeous this scenery was?"

In the darkness she heard him laugh. "My darling girl, in another month you're going to be so sick of scenery that you'd give your thumbs for the sight of a blank brick wall."

"John Ives isn't tired of it."

"John's an odd creature. I suppose he likes rocks and mountains because they can't talk."

"Who is he, Oliver?" she asked.

"I don't know," said Oliver. "John came to San Diego on one of the Yankee clipper ships. He walked up to Los Angeles and presented himself at Mr. Abbott's store, asking for work."

"Who's Mr. Abbott?"

"He's a fat jolly Yankee from Maine. He has a big store in Los Angeles, where he trades in hides from the ranchos. All the Yankees who come to buy hides know about him. I suppose John had heard of him on the ship. Mr. Abbott put him to work stacking hides and keeping credit records—they don't handle much money, you know. It's all done on paper. Very few people in Los Angeles know how to read and write, so John made himself very useful as soon as he'd learned Spanish. I met him at the store. John had saved some money, and when he found out I traded with Santa Fe he asked me about it, saying he wanted to go into the trade himself. I know a smart man when I see one, so it wasn't long before we were working together. He's a mighty good trader."

"And that's all you know about him?"

"Yes, it is. When he got off the ship he had nothing but a bundle of clothes, but he's obviously a man of education."

"Hasn't he any friends at all?"

"Well, there's a half-civilized Russian who rambled down from one of the fur stations up north. John picked him up and taught him a little English. They seem to like each other."

Oliver laughed to himself again.

"Garnet," he added, "I'm not jealous. But don't get the idea that John admires you for your beautiful black hair and rosy cheeks. He'll notice you today, and tomorrow he'll pass you by as if you were invisible."

"Yes, I think he'll do just that," she said thoughtfully. "I wish I understood him. I like to understand people."

"Your boundless curiosity," said Oliver, "is going to get you in trouble one of these days. Speaking practically, where's your rifle?"

"Right here by me. Is anything happening?"

"No, but I've got a shift of guard duty at midnight. John's on guard till then and he'll wake me. You'll have to be alone for a couple of hours. But you'll be all right. I'll be back before daybreak. I won't ever take the dawn shift if I can help it."

"What is it about the dawn shift?" asked Garnet.

"Organized raids nearly always happen at daybreak. If there should be anything like that, I want to be with you."

Garnet smiled happily as she felt Oliver slip his arm around her. She remembered her own dismay when she had suspected that Oliver was not entirely brave. Now she wondered why she had thought of that at all. Oliver was not afraid of anything, except the chance that she might be hurt.

NINETEEN

THEY WENT up the Chama to its source. As the stream dwindled they had less and less water to use. The air was so dry that Garnet was thirsty all the time, and the dust blew into her nose and mouth, and made her teeth feel gritty. When they stopped to make camp the boys built her house as snugly as ever, but they could bring her only half a pail of water for washing.

Then the Chama gave out completely. The next creek, which was called the Rio Piedra, was thirty-five miles away. The dry stretch took them only two days' riding, but they were the longest days Garnet had ever lived through.

The boys had filled the bottles before they left the Chama, but the water was so precious that she could take only a sip at a time, and Oliver warned her not to waste any on washing. The heat was violent, and the sun glared on the bare rocks around them. Most of the men wore goggles, and thick leather gloves to shield their hands from sunburn. They protected their heads with high-crowned Mexican hats. Since Garnet and Florinda could not grow beards, they wrapped their faces in veils. Garnet looked enviously at the Mexican women and the half-Indian prostitutes. They did not seem to mind the sun at all.

She and Florinda rode side by side, but they talked very little. Talking made your throat feel crustier than it did already. When they did speak, they talked about the river ahead, and how good it would be to drink cool water and get clean again.

But when they came to the Rio Piedra, at the end of a long morning's ride, she found that it was not a river at all.

It was a shallow ditch with a bottom of sand. There was no water in it except a few mud-puddles. The mules rushed for the mud-puddles and drank them up immediately.

The cooks cut down some dry bushes that grew in the ditch, and managed to roast some mutton. Garnet's mouth was so dry that she could hardly eat it. There was only a little water left in her bottle, and though she drank it all she felt as if she had not had any. But Oliver told her to go to sleep, everything was going to be all right. She was so tired that she lay down on her blanket and obeyed him.

When she woke up that afternoon, she saw with amazement that now there was water in the ditch. The men had dug holes in the sandy bottom, and the holes had filled with water and were spilling over. These creeks, Oliver told her, sank underground in summer. You had to dig for water as though it were gold.

The water had a funny taste, but she did not mind a bit. She drank and drank, and she even had a basin-full for bathing purposes. They filled the leather bottles and crossed the ditch, and set out again over another stretch of dryness.

The landscape was still full of splendid colors, and there were great cactus growths like writhing arms. But in spite of her goggles the light hurt her eyes, and she did not look around as eagerly as she had at first. "What are you thinking about?" Florinda asked her as they rode.

"A green hill," said Garnet, "with a brook tinkling down the side of it."

"I wish I hadn't asked you," said Florinda. She pushed down her wrappings of veil and took a sip from her bottle. "My hair is turning the color of an old brick," she added, "from all this dust."

Mr. Penrose, who rode up just then, hastened to reassure her. "We've only got about ten more miles of this stretch, Florinda. Then we hit the Rio Dolores. It always has water in it."

"Gee, that's fine, Mr. Penrose," Florinda exclaimed. She gave him a winning smile before she began to pull up her veil. "It's really fun, seeing all this new country. And I've been in the habit of washing my hair too much anyway."

"This hot weather doesn't bother you, does it?" Mr. Penrose asked.

"Not a bit," Florinda lied brightly.

Mr. Penrose smiled at her with worshipful admiration, and rode off to pick up the leather thong that was dragging from one of his mules. Garnet reflected that sometimes it must be very inconvenient to be a strumpet. She was bearing the dry stretches grimly, but she didn't have to pretend to Oliver that she liked them.

Florinda never complained about anything to Mr. Penrose. She took care of him as she had taken care of Mr. Bartlett, performing all sorts of small feminine services that the boys would never have thought of. Mr. Penrose would never have thought of them either, but he loved receiving them. When he napped at the nooning

Florinda folded a blanket to put under his head; when he broke his boot-lacings she put in new ones, so he would not have to tie knots in the old lacings as he had always done before; and she was always telling him to stay right here and rest while she brought him another cup of coffee. She treated him with sprightly good-humor, and gave him no excuse to be jealous. If any of the other men made advances to her, she let them know, with steel-edged pleasantness, that it was no use.

They climbed for a day and a half, till they were so high that they could see for miles over ranges of blue mountains. At last they came to the Rio Dolores. It was a small thin stream, but it was water, cool and wet and delicious. Along the bank there were cottonwood trees, and in the creek there was even a bed of watercress.

After dinner Garnet went down to the creek to wash some clothes. She was hanging them on the bushes to dry when she saw John coming toward her. Taking up an armful of garments she had wrung out, he helped her spread them on the bushes. Garnet felt a moment's embarrassment at having a man who was almost a stranger handle her drawers and stockings, but he did it indifferently, and when they had finished he said,

"Come up here a little farther. I'll show you something you might find interesting."

She followed him, past the guard, up toward the place where the stream came bubbling out of the rocks.

"Here," John said, and they paused. He pointed down at the water. "Take a look at that."

"But what is it?" she asked. "It's just the source of the creek, isn't it?"

He smiled. "This is the first river you've ever seen flowing west."

"Why—" Garnet hesitated, and tried to think back. The Hudson, the Mississippi—they flowed south; the Arkansas flowed east and southeast; the Rio Grande went south and then east; but she could not remember all the smaller streams she had ever seen. She looked up at him. "Why yes, it's flowing west, but is that important?"

"It's important if you're interested," said John. "Right here, we're standing on top of the North American continent. This is the Great Divide."

Garnet looked wonderingly at the spring, and back at John's face with its thick black beard and his green eyes under their black eyebrows. He looked more friendly than she had ever seen him. "What is the Great Divide?" she asked. "I never heard of it."

John told her about the rib that divided all the rivers of North America. Garnet sat on a rock, looking with astonishment at the great harsh mountains around them. "This is an amazing country," she said at length. "You were right—beautiful isn't the word for it. What would you call it? Spectacular?"

John had picked up a handful of pebbles and was throwing them one by one into the water. "I don't think there are any words for it, Mrs. Hale. The civilized languages were made by people who'd never seen it. Maybe we'll have to wait another thousand years for the words."

"It's so *big*," said Garnet. "I don't think I ever knew what bigness meant till I came out here. Oliver told me that when he came back to New York everything looked so little, and jammed so close together. Now I know what he meant."

John picked up more pebbles and threw them in, one by one, as though he enjoyed the clink they made when they hit the water. Garnet said,

"Of course, I haven't seen California."

Without turning around, John said, "You're going to like California."

"I'm sure I will," she answered. "Oliver says it's a glorious country."

"It's more glorious," said John, "than Oliver or anybody else can tell you." He spoke in a low voice. He was half turned away from her and she could not see his face, but she thought he sounded like a man talking about a beloved woman.

"You like it very much, don't you?" she said.

"Yes," said John, "I like it very much."

She wished he would go on. From the way he spoke, she thought his description would be more exciting than Oliver's. "What do you like best about it?" she asked.

"The bigness," said John, "and the emptiness, and the flowers. But it's hard to talk about it to someone who hasn't been there."

"Why?"

"Because—" He turned his head to smile at her over his shoulder. "Because you won't believe California till you see it. Nobody does."

"Yes I will. And I wish you'd tell me about it. Because, don't you understand, these dry stretches are so hard. You've crossed here before. You know what you're going to have at the end of the crossing, but I don't. If you'll tell me about it, the way you see it, I'll have it to think about when I get so thirsty and tired."

"Yes, I do understand that. When we're on the dry stretches, I always think about California. The snow on the mountains, and the miles of flowers."

He looked out over the barren rocks, as though he could see the flowers of California beyond them. He spoke slowly.

"The flowers don't just bloom here and there. They grow in solid sheets, acres and acres of wild yellow poppies like a cloth of gold. Beyond them are acres of blue lupin, and then sheets of pink sand-verbena and purple sage—it's like a great patchwork quilt spread over the world. Up on the slopes is the dark green chaparral, and in the chaparral there's the yucca, like white candles twenty feet tall, and higher up you see more acres of flowers edging against the snowline. All around you there's the scent of the sage. It's a hard spicy fragrance that blows over you all the time. You stop your horse on a hill, you sit and look because it hurts you down in your chest and you can't go on. The mountain peaks are white, and the sky is so blue it's almost purple, and there's the endless distance of mountain ranges around you and those miles of flowers below, and you want to burst into tears. You're ashamed of yourself, and you turn your horse around to go on about your business, and just then you catch sight of some horny old rascal who left the States just in time to escape being hanged, and he's looking at it and you hear him say 'God Almighty!' and by the way he says it you know he's not swearing."

There was a silence. Garnet looked around at the hard bare rocks, and at the thin little stream that was leading them to California. From below them the noise of the camp sounded faint and far away.

"Thank you," she said softly. "Thank you very much."

John was still looking out at the distance. As she spoke he turned sharply, as though he had forgotten she was there. He gave a short grim little laugh.

"If you ever tell anybody I talked like that," he said, "I'll swear the sun is afflicting your head. Come on, let's go down. I've got a shift of guard duty pretty soon, and I want to get some sleep."

He took her arm and helped her scramble down the rocks. When they had passed the guard, John said goodby and walked away. A few minutes later she saw him stretched on the ground alongside several other men, sound asleep.

Garnet reflected that he was a very puzzling person. He liked the earth he lived on. But he did not like the people who lived on it with him. The other men, whatever their backgrounds, merged into a neighborly unit; their common undertaking and their common peril drew them together. But though John did his part of camp duty so well that they all respected him, he shared nothing of himself.

Yet he did talk to her, and she wondered why. Maybe it was because she liked the earth as much as he did. She also liked John, in an odd way that she did not understand.

For six days they followed the Rio Dolores. The river led them west and then northwest among the mountains. The going was tiresome, but they had water and good food—fresh mutton and wild birds, besides the salt meat they had brought, and the cornmeal porridges. The days were blazing hot, the nights were colder and colder. One afternoon they ran into a shower of rain, but they rode through it gratefully, and Garnet found to her surprise that nobody caught cold.

The Comanches were behind them now. They had had no Indian trouble. Now and then they saw a few stray Indians, but the men sent scouts to meet them, carrying presents of beads and ribbons and bright cloth. Sometimes they traded with the Indians for game or fresh fish.

When they left the Dolores they turned due west, and for forty miles they went panting through a stretch of bare purple mountains, without water. Garnet rode until she ached with weariness, then both she and Florinda got off their horses and walked. Florinda looked very tired. There were dark rings under her eyes, made darker by the dust that had settled there. "This is one hell of a country, isn't it?" she remarked as they toiled upward. Her voice was husky with dust.

"It's awful," said Garnet. She paused to take a sip from the bottle that hung at her belt.

Florinda pulled down the veil that covered her mouth, and took a sip too. In spite of the heavy folds of veiling, her face was flushed with sunburn. Garnet was tanned like an Indian, but Florinda was already paying the price of her complexion. Her pearly skin simply would not turn brown. She wrapped the veil about her face again, and from under its covering she asked,

"Do you know what we see after this?"

"Oliver says we're going toward the Grand River."

"What's grand about it?"

"Well, it's a river."

"Yes, that's grand. Water."

Garnet spoke to her with sympathy. "I believe you feel this heat even more than I do."

Florinda shrugged. "John warned me. But don't worry. I can stand it."

They fell into silence again. The hoofs of the mules clattered on the rocks. The few sheep that were left bleated for water and grass. There was none of either.

It was only about nine in the morning, but already the sun was a torture. Garnet's throat felt like a nutmeg grater. She fingered her water-bottle yearningly. Oliver caught up with her. He was walking too, half leading and half dragging a loaded mule. With his free hand he held out some smooth pebbles.

"Put one of these in your mouth," he said, "and suck it like a candy drop. It keeps your mouth wet and you can swallow oftener."

Garnet took the pebbles and gave one to Florinda. They did help. Oliver was doing everything he could to make the dry stretches bearable for her. It was not his fault that it was forty miles between rivers. Garnet thought about the shining sheets of flowers in California, and the snow on the peaks. She was glad John had told her about that, and told it as he had. Now among these baking rocks she could tell it to herself, over and over again.

Then at last they came to the Grand River, singing over the stones with a sound like music. On its banks there was fresh grass for the animals, so the train paused here a day to rest. They got themselves clean, and washed their clothes, and the boys cooked big delicious meals. They killed the last of the sheep they had driven from Santa Fe. It was no use to try to take them further, for the sheep could not climb the rocks ahead. From now on, the train would have to depend on salt meat and such game as they could get in the mountains.

Oliver told Garnet they were getting into the country of the Utah Indians. The Utahs were not cruel like the Comanches behind them, nor stupid like the Diggers ahead. They were an intelligent tribe, and white men could trade with them. But the caravan did not relax its guard, for the Utahs were accomplished thieves.

193

Garnet had hoped they would follow the Grand River, but they did not. They rode across it, Garnet clinging fearfully to the pommel as her little mare Sunny picked her way among the stones of the river-bed. But Sunny was strong and sure, and Garnet came up on the other bank with nothing worse than a splashing. They went on, west-northwest, toward another stream called the Green River. Some miles to the south, Oliver said, the Grand and Green Rivers joined to form the Colorado, but they could not go down there, for the Colorado was too big to be crossed. They had to go around it. This added to the journey, but there was no other way.

They were up in dizzying mountains. The scenery was majestic, but Garnet was so tired of scenery that she hardly looked at it any more. The noons were fiery, and the nights were so cold that sometimes there was frost on the ground when they woke up. The water of the mountain brooks was almost icy. Garnet's teeth chattered as she washed in the pails the boys brought her.

One afternoon, when they were finishing their dinner, a guard came in with news that a dozen Utahs were approaching the camp. Garnet saw the other women, Mexicans and half-breeds alike, fall on their faces and cover themselves with blankets. She and Florinda were sitting together. Oliver came quickly over to them with blankets in his arms. He told them to lie down, and he piled the blankets on top of them and threw saddles and packs around the blankets, helter-skelter so it would all look like a pile tossed there for the nooning.

"Oliver!" Garnet cried from under the heap. "What's going to happen to us?"

She heard him laugh regretfully. "Nothing. You won't be comfortable, but you'll be safe. The Utahs just want a free meal. But if they see women, sometimes they want to buy them and it makes for arguments. Be very still."

They heard the grunts of the Indians, and white interpreters talking to them. There was a clatter of pans. Garnet remembered Oliver's telling her that Indians were always hungry. She felt for her gun. She had been warned never to use the gun unless she absolutely had to. It was better to pretend you loved the Indians, and treat them like honored guests, than to get into a fight. Still, it was a comfort to feel the gun there.

She and Florinda lay very still. Their muscles began to feel cramped. It was intensely hot under the blankets. They heard sounds of gobbling and grunts of pleasure. After awhile Florinda whispered,

"Do you think we dare peek?"

"I'd like to," said Garnet. "I've never seen an Indian close up. I think maybe—wait a minute."

Careful not to stir their covering, she inched her hand toward the edge of the blanket and raised it a very little. The sudden light from outside dazzled her for a moment, and she could not see anything. Then as her eyes got used to the glare, she saw the Indians.

They were squatting in a ring about twenty feet away, gobbling so fast that they were not paying attention to anything beyond them. Garnet could smell the food, and with it a nasty odor of unwashed bodies. She felt her nose wrinkling with disgust.

The Indians were big strong dark men, nearly naked. They might have been good-looking if they had been washed, but evidently they considered water only good for drinking. Their greasy black hair was twisted up with ribbons and feathers. They wore dirty finery consisting of fur and beads and loin-cloths of bright fabrics they had got from earlier trading caravans. Their bodies were crusted with dirt and sweat. They held the bowls up to their faces and ate like dogs, chewing noisily, and as they ate they scratched, in a businesslike manner suggesting that they had good reason for it. When a bowl was empty its user turned it upside down, holding it with one hand while he rubbed his belly with the other, croaking for more food.

Garnet heard Florinda whisper, "That's enough. Drop the blanket before I throw up. Hell for breakfast!"

Garnet dropped the blanket. "Don't mention breakfast," she whispered back. It seemed to her now that the odor of the Indians was everywhere. She felt sick.

"They say those creatures can smell game like a dog," whispered Florinda. "I don't know how they ever smell anything but each other."

"We'd better be quiet," Garnet warned.

They lay still. It seemed to her that they lay there almost forever. They dropped off to sleep, but the aches in their muscles woke them up again in a few minutes. The air under the blankets got hotter and stuffier. When they finally felt the blankets being pulled off them, they were both in an agony of cramp.

Silky Van Dorn was uncovering them. They heard him say,

"All right, ladies. You can stand up now."

He gave them each a hand. Garnet tried to stand up. But her legs had no feeling in them. She fell down again, and looked up at him helplessly. "I'm numb all over, Mr. Van Dorn!"

"I know, I know, it must be terrible," said Silky. His fine mustache was lost now in a wild growth of whiskers, but he smiled as grandly as ever. "This is what you ladies get for being so young and beautiful. Just move a little bit at a time. Here, take a drink, it helps."

He pulled a bottle from his pocket. Garnet took a sip to be polite. The whiskey burned her tongue, but even that was welcome because it was a fresh sensation. Florinda shook her head and Silky offered her his water-bottle. Garnet saw Oliver coming toward them, with Texas and Penrose. Oliver put his hands under her armpits and dragged her to her feet. She held to him, for she could not stand up alone.

Texas asked courteously, "Are your lower limbs beginning to feel prickly, Mrs. Hale?"

"Why yes, they are," said Garnet.

Florinda, holding Penrose's shoulder as she struggled to stand up, said grimly, "I feel like I've got ants all over me."

"That's fine," said Texas. "It means the blood's flowing back. Now I'll make you both some good hot coffee."

Garnet's house had been built before dinner, so now Oliver helped her get inside it. Dropping the blanket across the entrance, he slapped her thighs and rubbed them to bring back the circulation.

"You stood that very well," he said.

"How did you get rid of the Indians?"

"Oh, we finally shook our heads, smiling brightly and stroking our guns. Then we gave them some beads and other stuff. They're gone."

"I hope I never have to look at another Indian," said Garnet. "I never knew anything alive could be so repulsive."

Oliver rubbed her legs and laughed. "Wait till you see a Digger."

"They aren't worse than these!"

"My dear, compared to the Diggers, the Utahs are models of fastidious elegance. Utahs are human. Diggers—" He shrugged, unable to think of a suitable word.

Texas brought a pot of coffee. It was hot and strong. When

she had drunk it, Garnet went outside, to move around a little before lying down for her afternoon sleep. But the men were re-packing. They had meant to rest here, but now they said they had better move on. There might be more Utahs in the neighborhood, and they couldn't feed them all.

So they went on. The next day they reached the Green River, which was so turbulent that the mules could not cross it until they had been unloaded. The men cut down trees and made rafts, and took the goods over on the rafts, and loaded the mules again on the other side. Garnet had to plunge into the river on horseback and trust Sunny to swim across. Twenty times she thought she was going to fall off and be drowned, but Sunny was a tough swimmer and got her safely over.

They went on again, through mountains ever higher and harder to climb, through stingy little streams flowing between high cliffs of rock. West, northwest, west again, then southwest through a break called Wasatch Pass. Garnet was so tired that she slept as if she had been drugged, but she was never rested when she woke up. She was tanned dark brown, but the sun still scorched her skin and made her eyes drip with tears.

She and Florinda usually rode together, but they seldom talked. Florinda kept her face so wrapped that she found it hard to speak. She was suffering acutely from the sun. But she rarely said so, and she still managed to keep cheerful when Mr. Penrose was around.

They came to the Sevier River, which was shaped like a horse-shoe, and followed the eastern arm of it. Then they went through the mountains to a rocky depression called Bear Valley, then southwest through more mountains. And then, suddenly, they came to a high green paradise called Las Vegas de Santa Clara. When she saw Santa Clara, Garnet put her hands to her aching head and burst into tears.

She had not meant to do anything so childish. But she was so tired! And here before her was a spring, a bright spring that leaped out of the rocks and flowed through a field of grass and wild flowers. The air was damp, and the ground was soft, and the flowers were blue and yellow in the grass. In the stream were great beds of watercress, and along its bank were trees, and in the trees there was the sound of birds.

All around the meadow were miles of mountains, but she did not look at them. She wished she would never have to see a mountain again.

They had come six hundred miles from Santa Fe, though it would not have been so far if they had not had to loop and turn as they followed the streams. The journey had taken them thirty-four days. It was now September. In the air of this high plateau there was a tingle of autumn, and the smoke of the campfire had a scent like the smoke of burning leaves. Oliver told her they would rest here for two days. The men hunted and fished, and bathed joyously, shouting and laughing as they scrubbed, and the water of the stream was all bubbly with soapsuds. Garnet and Florinda washed their hair and their clothes, and when they had hung their clothes on the bushes they spread blankets on the ground and went to sleep, rapturous with cleanliness.

They woke up ravenous, and ate a huge meal of birds and fresh venison, and bowls of atole with gravy, and a salad of watercress from the stream. When the night came down it was very cold, but Garnet and Oliver wrapped up warmly in the buffalo robes, and Garnet thought that never had she lain in such a comfortable bed. Remembering the soft mattresses and white sheets of home, she thought pityingly that right now there were people tossing upon them, unable to sleep. She stretched out in the buffalo robes, and though she had already had a nap during the day, she slept for twelve hours.

In the morning there was even breakfast, for the first time since they left Santa Fe. Oliver's boy Manuel brought her a bowl of atole and a piece of fresh broiled fish, and he grinned at her exclamations of delight. Oliver brought his bowl over and sat on the grass by her. "How do you feel?" he asked.

"Marvelous. Simply marvelous."

"You've been great," said Oliver.

"Have I really stood it well?"

"Magnificently. The men were doubtful about you at first. But they aren't any more."

Garnet smiled, glad she had done well, and more glad that those awful dry stretches lay behind her. "It'll be easier going back next spring, won't it?" she asked.

"Oh yes. There's always more grass and water in the spring. Besides, on the spring journey it's easier to keep cheerful. When you're headed east you know the road is getting easier all the time. But when you're headed west you know it's going to keep on getting harder."

Garnet set down her bowl abruptly. Oliver was eating, too much interested in his food to notice that he had frightened her.

"Is the trail ahead much worse than what we've already been through?" she asked. She tried not to sound scared.

Oliver did not look up. "Why yes, some of it is pretty bad. But you're used to it now."

Garnet felt the way she thought a turtle must feel when it was drawing itself into its shell. She did not want to go on. She looked around. The mules were peacefully cropping the grass. The men were playing cards, or mending their clothes, or cutting each other's hair. They did not seem to be frightened. They knew what lay ahead, and they weren't scared of it. She must be very childish to feel scared. It was only because this was her first crossing. She stood up, saying she would get the clothes she had washed yesterday and start mending them. She went down to the stream.

The Mexican women were there, scrubbing their own clothes against the rocks. They spoke to her cordially. They had crossed before, and they didn't seem to be frightened either. Florinda came down to the bushes and began gathering up her laundry. Florinda had evidently had a good sleep too. She looked better than she had looked for days.

John Ives walked toward them, and asked if he could help them carry the clothes. Filling his arms, he walked with them to the shadow of a big rock where they were going to do their mending. "You're very industrious," he said to them.

"We're not nearly as industrious as you are," said Garnet. "You men never stop working."

"We're used to it," said John.

"How long have you been on this trail, John?" asked Florinda.

"Five years."

"Gee, you must like it."

"No, I don't," he said. "This is my last crossing. I've just received a land-grant in California."

"And you're going to live on it?"

"Yes. Shall I put these clothes here on the grass, Mrs. Hale?"

"Yes, thank you."

John put down the clothes, and left them. Garnet and Florinda sat down on the grass and opened their sewing-baskets.

"Nice friendly chap, isn't he?" Florinda observed.

"He's all right. He just prefers his own company."

"He likes you," said Florinda. "But he sure doesn't like people in general."

Garnet began to sew on a button. "Florinda, why do you suppose he doesn't like people?"

"I think he's scared of them," said Florinda.

"Scared? John isn't scared of anything!"

"Not anything he can shoot," Florinda said coolly.

"What do you mean?"

"Well, a man can't shoot his friends. So he doesn't want any friends. I think he's been hurt. Hurt bad."

"Hurt? John?" Garnet said, and frowned. "You mean a girl broke his heart?"

"Maybe, but I don't think so. There's other ways to be hurt, dearie. I don't know what it was." Florinda dropped the subject of John. She looked around, listening to the chirping of the birds, and gave a long happy sigh. "Garnet, isn't it wonderful just to sit here, and know we won't be moving all day long?"

Garnet agreed. She was puzzled by John, but this day was too precious to be wasted on puzzling about anything. They stretched on the grass, sewing, and watching the men hang up strips of meat from their hunting to be dried for the journey. It was lovely, like an outdoor picnic.

TWENTY

FROM THE SANTA CLARA meadows they rode south to the Virgin River. The riding was hard, but there was water enough, and along the Virgin River the days were not so hot as they had been. Oliver said they were now out of the Utah country. Any Indians they met hereafter would be Diggers.

Once or twice the guards found Digger tracks around the picket-ground. Scouts went out, well armed, to frighten the thieves away. It was no use to try to trade with Diggers. They wanted mules, and would go to any lengths to get them.

"What on earth do they want with them?" Garnet exclaimed to Oliver.

"Why, to eat," he answered in some surprise.

"Do they eat *mules?*" she asked in disgust.

"Of course. They'll eat anything. If they can get a mule, they stick an arrow into it and go off to call their friends. By the time they get back the mule is dead and they have a party."

"You make me sick!" she cried.

"Well," said Oliver, "you asked me."

When they left the Virgin River they went through a dry, ugly country to another stream suitably called Muddy Creek. They were going downhill, and the days were getting fiercely hot again. They started before daybreak, took long noonings, and rode till late at night. Garnet began to dread seeing the sun come up. Even early in the morning it beat furiously on their heads, and though they rested during the worst heat the days were dreadful. The only growth was cactus and low dry shrubs, and there was no shade but that of the rocks. Even on their shady sides the rocks flung out waves of heat.

The men wrapped their heads with strips of cloth, like turbans, and over the turbans they wore their high-crowned Mexican hats. Garnet and Florinda wrapped their veils close about their necks and faces. Sometimes it was hard to tell who was who, because they were all so covered against the sun.

The mules were so wretched that they gave endless trouble. Garnet suggested that to save the boys work, Florinda could share her saddle-house at the noonings. Instead of eating outdoors they carried their bowls of atole into the shelter to escape the sun, raising the blanket over the entrance to give them air. They were lying down in the shelter, trying to get comfortable for their noon sleep, the day the Diggers came to dinner.

They heard one of the men shouting words in a strange language, and Garnet looked outside. She saw Oliver and Penrose running toward the shelter. "You stay there, ladies!" Penrose called before he reached it.

Oliver pulled the blanket down over the entrance and flung himself on the ground before it. He held up the blanket a few inches from the ground, speaking to them through the crack.

"An old Digger yelled to us from a rock. We had to yell back that we were friends, so now there's a pack of them coming into camp. We'll feed them. Stay here, and you'll be all right."

As they had done when the Utahs called, Oliver and Penrose hurried to pile packs and saddles around the shelter so it would look like a stack of goods. "This," said Florinda, "is getting monotonous."

But it was better than being covered by the blankets. The shelter was too low for them to stand up in it, but at least they could sit up and move a little. They sat there, baking like muffins in the airless heat. Pretty soon Florinda made a wry face.

"Do you smell what I smell?"

"Yes," said Garnet. "They're worse than the Utahs."

"I didn't think anything could be worse. But they are. Let's peek."

They crawled forward and raised the blanket an inch or two from the ground. A Digger was sitting only a few feet away. He smelt like a privy. He was quite naked. His skin was nearly black, what they could see of it, for he was caked with dirt. His hair, straight and coarse as a horse's tail, hung wildly over his face and his back. Caught in it here and there were leaves and burrs and bits of twigs, and crawling through his hair were colonies of vermin. As they looked, he glanced at the ground and picked up a lizard that was running alongside him. He pulled off the lizard's tail and thrust the squirming rest of it into his mouth. As his teeth crunched on it he grunted with satisfaction.

From where they lay, Garnet and Florinda could partly see nine or ten others. Most of them were stark naked. The rest were draped with bits of cloth or strings of beads. Their filthy hair streamed over their faces, and behind their hair they had nasty little eyes and big drooling mouths. Their bodies were squat and pot-bellied. As they waited for the white men's food they kept picking up creeping things from the ground and eating them. They gave forth a nauseating stink.

Garnet felt goose-flesh rising all over her. She could not look any more. She let the blanket fall, and in the dark little shelter she and Florinda waited, trying not to get sick from the odor. When she thought about why she was hiding from them, Garnet felt her flesh crawl.

She remembered the Utahs. They had at least been healthy-looking; all they needed was soap and water. But those things out there—she hated to call them men. She wished she had not looked. She hoped she would never have to see a Digger again.

But she did have to, not long afterward.

They crossed Muddy Creek, and for five days they rode across a vast plain of sand ringed with mountains. The heat was fearful. To spare themselves and their mules they traveled at night, riding under a sky set with enormous white stars. Though the days were so hot, the nights were cold. The men wrapped blankets around their shoulders, and shivered in the hard dry chill. Hot or cold, they were always thirsty. There were depressions in the sand called waterholes, but there was seldom any water in them. The men dug, and waited till water seeped into the holes, but there was never enough. They rationed the water by cupfuls.

The plain was littered with the white bones of mules, left from the feasts of Diggers who had raided earlier caravans. Among the mule-bones were human skeletons, broken and tossed about in the sand. These were the bones of traders who had not evaded the Digger arrows, and bones of Diggers who had been killed in their fights for mules. The skulls grinned blankly at the sky.

The men paid very little attention to the bones. They were so used to the sight of death in the desert that they simply kicked a skull aside if it got in their way. But Garnet and Florinda shivered at the sight of them.

The train started every evening at sunset. At midnight they paused for a rest and supper. The mules gnawed at the dry desert brush; the men's food was pinole mixed with cold water. Even if they could have gathered enough brush for a fire, they would not have dared to make a fire at night. Diggers might be lurking anywhere among the mountains, and the light of a fire could be seen for miles. If Diggers saw the camp they would come swarming down, panting for a mule-feast. As the pinole was made of corn that had been parched before the grinding, it was a wholesome food, but a cold soggy mush was not tempting.

After the midnight rest, they mounted again and rode to the next waterhole. Sometimes they reached it at sunrise, sometimes they had to plod for hours after the sun came up and turned the sky white with heat. When they came to the waterhole they stopped again, and after another bowl of pinole they tumbled down exhausted on the sand, pulling blankets over their heads to shut out the glare. It was like trying to sleep in an oven.

Garnet was so scorched and tired that she could hardly move. Her throat burned and the whites of her eyes were red with the glare. She knew now what Oliver had meant when he told her, on the heights of Santa Clara, that the worst part of the journey was still ahead.

Oliver tried to make the going endurable. He told her this stretch of desert was brief and there was a good camping ground ahead, with a fine fresh spring called the Archillette. Garnet set her sand-crusted teeth and went on. She watched Florinda with awesome admiration. Florinda was suffering tortures from the heat and dryness, but she almost never said anything about it. She was evidently doing her cynical best to give Mr. Penrose no trouble. Penrose liked Florinda very much, and was proud to be the recipient of her favors. But his attitude toward her was about like the attitude of a child toward a doll. When he wanted her, he took it for granted that she would be available. But when he had something else to do, he took it for granted that she was getting along all right by herself.

Florinda had expected this sort of arrangement, and did not protest it. Her white skin blistered and her eyes were nearly blind with the harsh light; sometimes Garnet saw her put both hands to her head as though she thought it would burst open if she did not hold it together. But she did not complain. Though Garnet was herself aching with weariness, she knew Florinda was suffering more than she was. Her own hair was black and her skin could turn brown to protect itself. But Florinda had received her pale beauty from a race bred among the icy fiords and cold green mountains of the North. She was a healthy woman, but her constitution had never been meant to bear the baking of a desert sun. Garnet spoke to her with sympathy. Florinda gave a tired sigh, but all she said was, "Yes, dearie, it's pretty awful. But I'll get there. See if I don't."

As they rode under the big white stars, Garnet tried to tell her about the flowery shores of California. Out here in this place of sand and bones, it was hard to remember what flowers looked like.

And then at last, three wretched weeks after they had left the meadows of Santa Clara, they reached the oasis of the Archillette.

Maybe, Garnet thought, the Archillette did not really look like a bit of paradise. Maybe it was not as beautiful as the most beautiful park in the world. But here, after that stretch of sand, it was the most beautiful place she had ever seen, and she went up to the spring and knelt down on the grass and let the tears pour out of her burning eyes.

The Archillette was green. It was threaded by a clear cool stream that gushed out of the rocks and went chattering between two lines of willows and cottonwood trees. The time was October, and the leaves of the cottonwoods were yellow as butter. They blew over the grass like flakes of gold. Kneeling on the stones, Garnet cupped her hands and dipped them into the water and drank and drank, and she washed her face and threw handfuls of water into her hair to cool her aching head. Oliver came over and knelt by her and put his arm around her shoulders.

"Great, isn't it?" he said. "And you've been great. Now you can rest. We're going to camp here three days."

"Can I drink all I want, Oliver?"

"Yes."

"And have a real bath?"

"Several baths, if you like. And we'll have something fit to eat. The boys are gathering sticks right now. There'll be a hot meat stew and hot porridge and coffee. We might even bring down a bird or two."

They had a royal supper, and that night Garnet slept as long and as peacefully as she had slept on the Santa Clara heights three weeks ago. But the next morning, she found that the Archillette was not quite the haven she had thought it was.

She was walking around, enjoying the miracle of the bright green coolness. Downstream, near the place where they had picketed the mules, she saw some green sprigs that looked like watercress. As she walked over to gather it, she stopped in horror.

In front of her was a field of human bones. In the early sun the bones were white and shining. They were scattered aimlessly, as though the place were a dreadful dump-heap, skulls and ribs, arms and legs and pelvic bones. Garnet turned her head, toward the men who were busy with the mules.

The men were working calmly. They were filling the pails, attending to mules that had bad legs or shoulders, mending the thongs that held the mules to the picket-pins, as though a field of bones was no more remarkable than a field of grass. As she looked, one of the boys found something in the way of a picket-pin he was driving into the ground. He picked up a thigh-bone, and without a second glance at it he tossed it over to the main dump before going on with his work. Garnet turned around and ran back the way she had come.

At the edge of the picket-ground she found Oliver directing his muleteers. He saw that she was distressed, and walked a little way off with her, asking what the trouble was. Who, Garnet demanded shakily, had those people been?

Oliver led her to a flat stone by the side of the stream and they sat down. He said he had not wanted to frighten her yesterday. But the Archillette was a famous camping ground. It was as well known to the Diggers as to the white people. Diggers often prowled about the Archillette, hoping to spy travelers with fine mules and horses that could be stolen for their feasts. These bones, like the bones in the desert, were the remains of people who had been killed here in years past. She probably had not noticed, but they had put on a double guard last night.

There had been some bad attacks here. Only last year, the Diggers had massacred a group of Mexicans from Los Angeles who were trying to catch up with the main caravan. The Diggers had murdered the men, carried off the women, and were feasting on the horses in a cave when a party of white scouts had found the bodies. The white men had pursued the Diggers and killed most of them at their feast, and they had managed to rescue one of the Mexicans alive.

Garnet was shuddering. Oliver smiled at her gently.

"Yes, Garnet, they're loathsome creatures. Try not to notice the bones. Keep busy, and don't walk beyond the guards for any reason. If you hear a long low whistle, grab your gun."

Garnet tried to take his advice and keep busy. She had plenty to do. Since they left Santa Clara there had been very little chance for washing clothes. Already, all the other women and a good many of the men were doing their laundry in the stream. She brought a pile of clothes and a cake of soap, and got to work.

Florinda was scrubbing briskly. She looked fairly well, and was in good spirits. Yes, she said, she had seen the bones. "But I guess," she added, "when you get used to this desert, you forget they were ever human."

Garnet bent her head and rubbed a dress of hers against a rock in the water. "Yes," she agreed grimly, "that's how we've got to think of them. They're just *things*. Like old clothes."

They heard laughter and the sound of shots. The men were setting up the skulls and using them for target practice. They were having a contest, to see which one could put a bullet through an eye-socket at the greatest distance. Garnet felt her skin crawling. She kept her eyes on the soapy water. "They're just *things*," she repeated under her breath.

Beside her she heard Florinda's voice. "Honestly, Garnet, do the fellows have to be *that* gruesome?"

"Nobody thinks it's gruesome but us," said Garnet. "This is our first crossing."

The rifles cracked over the bone-field. Somebody shouted that Texas was a great shot. Texas said why, that was nothing, he could put a bullet through an eye from farther than that and he'd prove it if they'd move back a bit. All of a sudden, as she wrung out the dress, Garnet found that she was not shocked any more. She looked up at Florinda, and they both began to laugh.

"It's just plain ridiculous," said Florinda.

"They're like children," said Garnet.

"Like kids who've got nothing to play with, so they make toys out of whatever they can find."

"After all," said Garnet, "those skulls aren't people any more. These traders will do anything for living people. When those Mexicans were attacked here last year, the other white men chased the Diggers at risk of their own lives—they'll do that without a minute's hesitation. But once you're dead, you're dead. They can't do anything, so they just don't pretend."

Mr. Penrose strolled up to them, carrying his rifle. "Say, Florinda, that's fine, all that washing. I haven't had a clean shirt in so long—say, do I smell cooking?"

"I believe you do, Mr. Penrose. I can finish these later. Let's go over and see how dinner's coming along."

Garnet spread her clothes to dry. The rest of the day she lay dreamily on a blanket, dozing and enjoying the rare luxury of idleness. At dark she watched the men change guard before she went into her saddle-house to sleep.

She slept soundly, but she had rested so much in the afternoon that she woke up while it was still dark. Oliver had had a shift of night guard duty, and he was still asleep. Moving carefully so as not to wake him, Garnet lifted the flap in front of the entrance. The stars were shining and the camp was quiet but for the occasional bray of a mule. There was a pail in one corner of the shelter. It was only half full, but that was enough. She made her toilet and softly began to get dressed. Any minute now the camp would come to life and there would be a smell of coffee. She was hungry.

She had put on her dress and was tying her second shoe when she heard a long sharp whistle. Oliver sat up.

"What's that? My God, it's the signal!"

Before she could answer they heard a shot, then another shot, then rifles began to crack all over the camp. Oliver had pulled down the blanket that covered the saddle-house. He was on his knees, holding his gun over the wall, sighting. She heard him say,

"Your gun, Garnet! It's a Digger raid."

Garnet had grabbed her gun. She knelt by him, holding it. She

207

could hear the other shots, and the voices of the men; she saw the dawn like a gray streak among the stars; she saw figures, and among the shots she heard cries. She set her teeth hard, and felt sweat creeping down from her armpits, and heard what was like a voice speaking to her from inside her head.

"Here it is, Garnet. This is what you expected so long that you stopped expecting it. This is an Indian fight. And you are going to shoot. You are not going to scream or shiver or act like a lady. You are going to shoot."

The noise around her was tremendous. From all the saddle-houses, the men were shooting. They were pushing down the back walls of the houses and shoving the saddles forward to give themselves a solid line of breastworks. Keeping his gun in his right hand, with his left Oliver broke down the back wall of his shelter to give himself room to move. Holding his gun over the side wall, he fired twice and reloaded.

Sighting again, he moved away from her, past the place where the back wall had been. He fired again. The animals were kicking and howling in terror. There was more light now. Garnet saw figures crawling on their bellies, black against the sky like great worms. She took aim, but she had never fired at a moving target, and as soon as she took aim at a figure it was not there. The voice inside her head ordered her, "Shoot!" Another weak little voice protested in sudden horror, "I can't! I can't kill a human being! I can't!"

She bit her lip so hard she thought she was going to bite it in two. She took aim, and the figure moved; she aimed again, and fired. Nothing happened. The figure came on.

There were other figures, not human, mules that had broken from their picket-thongs in a surge of fright. The light was clearer. There was a red streak in the sky. She saw an animal running. It was not a mule. It was Sunny, her brave little mare, Sunny who had carried her so many tiresome hot miles and had swum her safely over the rivers. "Don't run away, Sunny!" the little voice in her tried to cry out. "Don't run away. This is where you belong—not with them—they'll eat you!"

She felt hot with anger. They were not going to eat Sunny! She fired at another wormy black figure. She heard a yelp. Maybe she had hit him, maybe it was a yelp from another shot. A mule gave a howl and rolled over. She saw the arrow sticking out of his side. She loaded her gun again.

She remembered her instructions. Keep low. Don't show anything over the wall but your eyes. Don't give them any more of a target than you absolutely have to. As she peered over the saddle-wall she heard a dreadful animal-howl of pain very close to her, and in the dawning light she saw Sunny drop and roll over. There was an arrow in Sunny's flanks. Garnet heard herself cry out. It was not a loud cry; probably nobody else heard it in the general noise. But she had heard it, because she had given it. It was a cry of wild rage. They had put an arrow into Sunny, into her brave strong little Sunny, and she was going to kill them for it. She was going to kill them all. There was a wormy figure that looked very close. He had a bow in his hand. Lying belly down, he was fitting an arrow into the bow. Garnet took aim. She felt quite cold and careful. She fired. He dropped his bow and flung up his arms with a yell, and then he collapsed and rolled over, and lay very quiet.

Beside her she heard Oliver's voice say, "Good work! I knew you could!" He fired again.

Garnet stared at the motionless figure. It was not more than twenty feet away. She knelt by the saddle-wall, only her eyes and forehead above it, but she could see clearly. Around her the shots were peppering the air, and the arrows were singing. Her gun slipped out of her hand. Her mouth fell open. She said, though her words did not make any sound,

"I've killed a man."

There was a strange dampness on her forehead. The sweat was rolling down her sides, and it felt cold. Her hands felt cold too. Her lips were dry. They made words, without any voice.

"This is what it's like. They've all done it. I had to do it. I've killed a man."

The stern strong voice inside her head exclaimed impatiently, "He'd have killed you, wouldn't he? Don't be such a delicate little blossom!"

She picked up the gun and loaded it again. She tried to take aim. But her hands were not steady. She raised herself, trying to brace her body against the saddles. Just then she heard a singing, very close, and she felt a stroke of pain that was like a fire and a blow at once. She tumbled down backwards, just as she remembered that she had been told never, never to raise herself above the saddle-wall where she could be seen.

But she had done it. She had done a stupid, foolish, greenhorn's trick. She hated herself as she lay back, too dizzy to get up, and felt the pain like a fire in her left side.

Her legs were doubled up under her, her head touched the ground. She turned her head, and tried to see what had happened. The daylight was full now and she could see. The upper part of her left sleeve had been cut open as though with a knife, and in her arm, just below the shoulder, was a big red gash. Blood was spurting out of the gash like a fountain. She could see the blood seeping into the blanket she had slept on last night. Beside her, on the blanket, was an arrow with a stone head. The head was stained red with her blood.

She raised herself a little, and the pain shot through her arm like a blade as she tried to straighten out her legs. She looked around for Oliver. But Oliver was not there. Fright gave her a rush of strength. She sat up, and over the saddle-wall she saw now that the Diggers were running, and the white men were giving chase. Just after she had killed the Digger, while she was half paralyzed with horror at what she had done, Oliver had leaped up and gone to drive out the enemy. He did not know she had been hurt.

She felt dizzy and terribly weak, and before she knew it she was flat on her back again, trying to breathe while she bit her lips against the hot pain that was coming in bigger and bigger gusts with the beating of her heart. The blood was spouting out of her wound. It was bright red, and it felt warm as it ran down her chilly skin.

Garnet put her uninjured right hand to her forehead, and said aloud, "I've got to do something about this."

But as she said it, and realized that she had only the scantiest notion of what to do, she saw somebody creeping toward her among the lines of saddle-walls. Garnet started with fright. Then she saw that the person approaching her was not a Digger thief, but a woman. She was one of the half-breed prostitutes who had followed the train from Santa Fe. The girl was drawing herself forward on her elbows, expertly avoiding any move that would lift a part of her body above the breastworks.

She reached Garnet, and sat by her crosslegged. She did not say a word. As matter-of-factly as though this were part of the usual day's routine, she took up the hem of Garnet's skirt, held the edge between her teeth while she tore off a strip of cloth, and picked up Garnet's arm.

Garnet winced at the movement. The girl did not notice her. She took a competent look at the wound, and tied the strip of cloth tightly above it. The bleeding stopped.

Garnet said, "Why, thank you," and then remembering that the girl did not understand English, she said, "Gracias, señorita."

The girl paid no attention. Dropping to her elbows again, she calmly pushed herself over the robes that had formed the bed. Garnet watched her wriggling down between the saddle-walls, looking for somebody else who might need help.

TWENTY-ONE

OLIVER SAID, "You tell her, Texas. I haven't got the nerve."

He walked away and began helping his men round up the mules that had broken their picket-thongs during the daybreak attack. Garnet lay on a blanket he had spread for her in the shade of a big rock. Oliver had taken off the half-breed girl's tourniquet, and had washed the wound, telling her that Texas would give her a bandage later. Texas was the one who always attended to wounds.

Garnet wondered what he wanted Texas to tell her. She raised herself on her good elbow. Her left arm was throbbing, but she tried not to mind it. The camp looked like a field of battle. The Diggers were gone, but there were some of them who would never go anywhere again; their corpses lay here and there on the grass, crumpled black things that she hated to look at. She had read in sentimental books about dead people who looked peacefully asleep, but now that she had seen dead bodies she knew that they did not look asleep at all. They just looked *dead*. There was no other word for it.

Some of the Diggers had only been wounded, and had lain howling themselves to death. When the white men came back from the chase they had mercifully put bullets into their heads. Sunny was dead too. Oliver had shot her himself. She lay over there, dear little Sunny, with several mules they had had to kill. Garnet had heard Mr. Penrose remark that when the white people had gone, the Diggers would come back to the Archillette. They would not bother with the human corpses, but they would gather up the animals' bodies and eat them. When she heard him say that, she could not feel sorry any more that she had killed a Digger. She wished she could kill them all before they could eat Sunny.

Penrose had not been hurt, and he had said Florinda was all right too. But several of the men had been wounded. They lay on blankets, waiting for Texas to help them. One Mexican boy had been killed. Later on they would give him burial. They would scatter stones on his grave and try to make it look as if there was no grave there, for if the Diggers noticed a place where the ground had been disturbed they would dig it up, thinking maybe somebody had buried a favorite horse to keep it from being added to their dinner.

But before they buried the boy they had to round up the mules. About a hundred mules had managed to break their thongs, and of these several had run away beyond catching. But it was vital to save as many as possible, for without mules to carry their supplies they would starve a long way this side of California.

There was a lot of shouting and rushing about, but there was very little confusion. Though she still felt sick and dizzy, Garnet could not help admiring the skill of these men. With wild yells of profanity, they captured the mules, untangled the thongs, and got the camp in order again. In a dry place away from the creek several boys were already building a fire.

Garnet glanced up at Texas, who had come to sit on the ground by her blanket. With such examples of courage around her, she reminded herself that she must not wince at whatever it was that he had to say. Under the dust and sweat, Texas' face was grave. She asked,

"Is it going to hurt when you bind up my arm, Texas? That's all right. I'll try not to make any fuss."

Texas shifted his position uneasily. He sat crosslegged, his big knotty hands between his knees. He looked at his hands as he answered,

"Well ma'am, not exactly that. It's going to hurt, of course, but I've got to tell you about it. You see, these wounds made by Digger arrows, we have to give them a little treatment before we tie them up." He pulled his big leather gloves out of his pocket and began to stretch their fingers.

"Why Texas, you don't have to apologize. It's my own fault that I got hurt. I raised up too far over the barricade."

"Now, now, Miss Garnet, you mustn't say that. You mustn't even think it. No ma'am, you're a soldier that got wounded in battle, and that's an honorable wound in anybody's country. There's not a man in this outfit that don't respect you for it, and if there was one of 'em that wouldn't help you all he could, he'd be a son of a bitch and we'd—excuse me, Miss Garnet. Now here's a drink of water. Drink a lot. You've lost blood and when you've lost blood you need water. Now lie down again flat. That's right. I'll tell you what the treatment is."

Texas put his hand under her head and settled her as comfortably as he could. Garnet passed her tongue over her lips. Though he had just given her a drink, her mouth still felt dry.

"Why yes, Texas," she said, "tell me. What do you want to do?"

She heard Texas draw a deep hard breath. He put his rough hand over hers. "I want to burn your arm with a red-hot iron, Miss Garnet."

"No!" She jerked up, and at the movement her arm gave her a thrust of pain. She grabbed her elbow just below the wound. "Texas! It's raw! The flesh is gaping open—you can't!"

"I guess. I've got to, Miss Garnet," he said.

Garnet stared up at him. Every nerve in her body was rolling up into a knot of horror. She felt her mouth opening like a square, the lips drawn back from her teeth. Her skin felt wet and crawly under her clothes. Texas made a pointing gesture. Her eyes followed his hand, to where the boys had made the fire. She thought they had made it for cooking, but now she saw that they had taken three of the iron rods from which they usually hung the pots, and had thrust the rods deep into the pile of wood under the flame. The six men who had been wounded lay on blankets together. One of them was groaning audibly. Garnet gasped,

"Are you going to burn them too?"

"Yes ma'am. They know I've got to. They've been here before."

"Ah!" Garnet heard herself make a deep shuddering noise. Texas put his arm around her and gave her another drink.

"Now, now, Miss Garnet. You've been mighty brave. Try to be brave just a few minutes longer."

Garnet tried to be brave. "But why do you have to do it, Texas?"

"You lie down, ma'am. I'll explain everything."

Garnet lay down. Every muscle she had was stiff with fear. She heard the mules braying angrily, and the men swearing at the Diggers who had caused all this trouble. One of the boys, who was a good friend of the boy who had been killed, was crying as he worked.

"It's like this, ma'am," Texas was saying. "Those Digger arrows are dangerous. Some folks say they're poisoned. Other folks say it's just that the Diggers are so damn filthy that everything they handle is poisoned. But anyway, if a Digger arrow cuts your skin, even a little scratch, it's liable to make trouble. And I mean trouble, Miss

Garnet. I've seen men who were scared of the burning, men who had just a little cut that they thought would heal up without it, and I've seen those little cuts swell and turn purple and send out shoots of poison till the men died howling, begging us to shoot them. Sometimes we do have to shoot them, because they're so wild with the fever they might kill us if we didn't. I'm sorry, Miss Garnet, but I had to say it."

Garnet's tongue felt too big to be kept inside her mouth. "Does that—always happen?" she asked thickly.

"No ma'am, not always. Sometimes the wound heals up fine. But you never can tell at the start. And by the time you can tell, it's too late. You'd better let me burn that cut, Miss Garnet."

Garnet swallowed, but there was nothing to swallow. Her mouth was dry again. "All right, Texas," she said. "You can burn it."

"There now, that's fine," Texas said heartily.

Garnet shut her eyes and put her good arm over them. She wondered if she could keep her teeth clenched and not scream when he did it. In front of all these people she must not scream. She must not let them think she was a delicate lady who couldn't stand the trail. She must not let Oliver be sorry he had brought her along. "I chose this myself," she said fiercely in her mind. "I wanted to come to California. Maybe if I have something to bite on I won't scream. I'll bite on something, very hard."

Through the turmoil of the camp she heard footsteps on the ground close by her. John's voice asked, "How is she, Texas?" and Oliver asked, "Did you tell her?"

Texas answered them. "Sure, I told her. She's fine. Taking it like a veteran."

Garnet opened her eyes. Oliver was kneeling by her. His hair and beard were so shaggy that she could not see much but his eyes, but he was looking at her tenderly.

"I'll give you a big drink of whiskey first if you want it," he said to her.

She shook her head. "I'd rather not. It would go right to my head. I might scream or something."

John bent and took a look at her wound. "It's an ugly gash, but not too deep," he said. He gave Garnet his brief grim smile. "Scream all you feel like, Mrs. Hale. Nobody will mind." He picked up the water-bottle. "Nearly empty."

"I'll fill it," said Oliver. As he went down toward the creek,

Florinda came and knelt by John. She had not heard what Texas said, and she was smiling at Garnet cheerfully.

"I've been wanting to see you. But I had to get my clothes on first. You did get a bad cut, didn't you?"

"You're all right?" Garnet asked.

"Yes, by the merest luck. I was never so scared in my life. I was sound asleep when it started. Gee, I must have looked funny, kneeling there in my little white unspeakable shooting over a pile of saddles."

"I hear from Penrose that you got two of them," said John.

"He's flattering me. I don't think I got but one. But I'm all right. Garnet's the wounded soldier. Can't we do something to help her?" Florinda bent and looked at the wound with concern. "Say, John, shouldn't we tie that up? Won't it get full of dust?"

"Texas will wrap it later," said John. One of his muleteers called him, and he stood up. "You stay with her, Florinda," he said as he turned to answer the muleteer.

Florinda tore a piece from the end of her petticoat, and dampening it with water from her bottle she began to bathe Garnet's hot forehead. "Does it hurt very much, darling?"

"Not too much. But—" Garnet shivered, and the fear she had been ashamed to show the others burst out of her. "But Florinda, do you know what they're going to do to me? Texas is going to burn this gash with a red-hot iron."

"Oh, Garnet!" Florinda cried. She dropped the bottle, and the water ran out on the earth. "Not that raw wound!"

"Yes. And I'm scared. I don't want them to know how scared I am. Florinda, when he comes over here with that iron—I don't know how long it'll be, it's got to get red-hot first—when he comes over here, hold my hand tight and don't let me start yelling like a baby."

Florinda made an inarticulate noise of dread. She squeezed the wet cloth. The water ran down the fingers of her leather glove and dripped on the ground. Oliver came back with the bottle he had gone to fill. He sat by Garnet, telling her to lie still and try to relax. She was very thirsty, and though she lay in the shade of the rock she was very hot. Her arm was throbbing. Oliver held the bottle to her lips and told her to drink all she could. Florinda got up and walked away.

John gave directions to his muleteer. He glanced at Garnet, where she lay on the blanket with Oliver sitting by her. Turning on his

heel, he walked rapidly over to the stream and made his way along
to a pile of rocks overgrown with bushes. At the edge of the stream,
where the rocks shielded her from sight of the camp, he saw Florinda. She was sitting in a huddle on the grass. As she heard him
approach she turned her head.

John stopped. He looked her up and down.

"Go on back," he said.

"Go on back yourself," she returned shortly.

"What made you run away?" John asked.

"None of your damn business."

"Stop acting like a rabbit," said John. "Go back and hold that
kid's hand."

She said nothing.

"For God's sake, Florinda," he demanded, "what's the matter
with you?"

"I'm not going to sit there," she said through her teeth, "and
watch them brand her like a cow. And you can't make me. I won't
do her any good by being there."

"Yes you will. She asked you to stay. I heard her."

"She doesn't need me."

"I think she does. You're her friend, and you're somebody of her
own sex, and she wants you. It's not a pleasant operation, you know.
I had it done once; I've still got the mark on my leg. It's no fun to
feel that iron going into your flesh. You hear it sizzle, and you smell
yourself cooking, and besides, it hurts."

She flashed him a look of disgust. "If you don't mind, I'd just as
soon not hear any more charming details. And I'm not going to be
there to see it or hear it or smell it. I'm staying here."

"Very well," said John. "But I own I'm surprised. I didn't know
you had such dainty sensibilities."

"Sure, dainty sensibilities, that's me. I'm a fine lady who faints
at the sight of blood. Get the hell away from here and let me alone,
won't you?"

John shrugged contemptuously. "Funny, isn't it? When I
watched you on the dry stretches, I thought you had plenty of
nerve. But some people are like that. When it's taking care of
themselves, nothing is too much. But when it's giving a lift to
somebody else, they act like sick chickens. I'm sorry I troubled you."

Florinda turned her head and looked straight at him. She smiled
at him sweetly. In her low, clear voice, using words Garnet would

216

not have understood, she told him what she thought of his ancestors, his anatomy, and his probable destiny.

John smiled with appreciation. "What a magnificent vocabulary. It's a pity you haven't got the guts to live up to it. Right now I shan't try to match it, because if you won't give Garnet a friendly hand I'm going to. But we must really have a name-calling contest, one of these days." He paused. She said nothing. In a different voice, John asked, "You won't stand by her, Florinda?"

Florinda drew in her breath sharply. "John, I—I can't."

"Why not?"

"Because you were right when you said I hadn't any guts. I haven't. I'd just shake and get sick."

"You told me once in Santa Fe that you thought very highly of Garnet. I got the idea that you meant it."

Florinda looked down. He saw her chest move quickly with her short hard breaths. John broke a stick off an overhanging bush and scratched it along the side of the rock. Without looking up, Florinda said,

"Garnet has done more for me that you'll ever guess. If it hadn't been for her God knows where I'd be now."

"If Garnet ever did you a kindness," John said shortly, "I'm sure she never thought of being paid for it. That was not what I meant. But I think she's your friend and I think you want to be a friend to her. Don't you?"

Florinda swallowed hard. "John, do you really think it'll be easier for her if I'm there?"

"Yes, I do."

"All right," said Florinda.

She shuddered. John stepped forward quickly and helped her to her feet.

"Good," he said. "Thanks."

Florinda did not answer. They walked up from the stream, past the men who were profanely picketing the mules, to where Garnet lay on the blanket. Her eyes were closed. Florinda knelt down by her and stroked her forehead. Without looking up at John, she said, "Here I am, Garnet."

Garnet opened her eyes. "Oh Florinda, I'm so glad you came back! Where'd you go?"

"Why, I just went for more water. I had upset my bottle, you know." Florinda wet the cloth again. "Now I'll keep your head cool."

"You're going to stay with me?" Garnet asked softly.

"Of course." Still without looking up, Florinda spoke to John and Oliver. "Say, boys, the sun's moved since she lay down here. Would it hurt her if you dragged the blanket to follow the shade? That's it, fine. Now I'll wash her face again."

As the cool cloth touched her forehead Garnet heard Texas call from the fire. "Ready?" he shouted.

"Right away," John called back. "Mrs. Hale?"

"Yes," Garnet said breathlessly.

"We'll have to hold you," John said, "so you won't jerk by accident and get an extra burn. Put your head on my knee. That's right, turn your face over so you won't have to see it."

Garnet hid her face against John's strong hard thigh. Oliver lay down beside her and put his arm across her body to hold it still. Florinda took her right hand and held it, while she stroked Garnet's hair tenderly. Garnet heard her say, "It'll be over in a minute, darling. Make all the noise you please."

"Lord, yes," said John's voice above her head. "When I had this done I let out a yell they could hear in Los Angeles."

Garnet shut her eyes tight. She felt Texas pick up her wounded left arm. The movement gave her a twinge of pain. She thought, I must not scream. I don't believe John yelled and I won't either. I've got to bite on something. Why didn't I ask them for something to bite on? I'll bite John's trousers.

She closed her right hand and gripped Florinda's hand as hard as she could. Florinda's glove was sticky with sweat; it made for easier holding. The hand inside the glove gave her a comforting pressure in reply. Garnet opened her teeth and clamped them on the cloth of John's trousers. The cloth was rough and gritty. She could feel the sand on her teeth. She thought, Now, any minute, it's coming. I'll bite hard and I won't scream.

She felt Texas tearing her torn sleeve all the way down. She clenched her teeth on John's trouser-leg with all her strength. Then she felt the iron.

She felt a blaze like an exploding volcano in her arm. The fire rushed all over her, into her neck and across her back and down to the tips of her toes. Her muscles jerked; she could feel John's hands and Oliver's, holding her, not letting her jerk. There was a hissing noise as the iron went into her flesh, and a sickening smell, and a bitter salty taste in her mouth as she clenched her teeth, harder and harder and harder. She felt tears starting out of her

218

eyes and sweat pouring out of her whole body, and a thick nasty choking stuff in her throat, and she gripped Florinda's hand till she thought she must be breaking the bones of it. The fire shot through her and she heard her flesh sizzle like a steak. She could *not* shut her teeth any harder, and she could not breathe and if this lasted any longer she was going to choke. And then Texas said, "That's all, Miss Garnet, that's all," and Oliver loosened his arm around her and took her shoulder and tried to lift her up, saying, "It's over, Garnet! Can't you hear me? You can move now, sweetheart," and above her John was exclaiming, "Now, you damned little cannibal, take your teeth out of my leg!"

Garnet felt herself loosening. She let Oliver raise her up. Oliver had both arms around her. He and Texas were saying how brave she was. She had stood it without making a sound. There was a fiery pain in her arm, but it was not as bad as it had been.

She had let go of Florinda's hand. Florinda was tearing a piece out of her own petticoat to make a handkerchief. Garnet saw vaguely that Florinda's face was a strange greenish color and there were big beads of sweat running down her cheeks. Florinda wiped off the sweat with the cloth.

Garnet felt something wet run down her chin. She put up her right hand, wonderingly, to wipe if off, and stared when she saw that she was wiping off streaks of blood.

Everything was still a little bit confused. She had made such a violent effort that she could not get her senses in order all at once. But she stared at her hand, and she stared at John. He was half laughing. Her eyes followed his, down to the spot on his leg that he was looking at. Now she saw that there was a jagged tear in his trousers, and around the tear was a big splotch of blood.

Garnet heard herself gasp. She began to understand what that salty taste in her mouth had been. She hadn't known she was doing it, but she had bitten him savagely, like an animal. But for the fact that John's leg was nearly as hard as a tree-trunk, she would have taken out a chunk of flesh.

John was wiping off the blood on his leg with the torn piece of petticoat he had taken out of Florinda's hand. Garnet cried, "Oh, I'm so sorry!" But the men seemed more amused than anything else. Oliver held the water-bottle to her lips, saying, "Here, don't you want to rinse your mouth?"

She rinsed her mouth, and Oliver gave her a drink of water.

She tried to say again that she was sorry, but John only answered, "Why, it doesn't matter."

Oliver had brought a piece of clean cloth from one of the packs, and was tearing it up to make a bandage. He handed the strips to Texas.

"Now stretch out here again, ma'am," Texas was saying. "I'll cover this burn to keep out the dust."

Garnet lay down on her back. The pain in her arm was intense, and she winced and bit her lip as Texas bandaged the burn. Oliver poured some whiskey into a tin cup, thinned it with water, and gave it to her.

"Drink this, Garnet. It'll put you to sleep."

She felt so shaken that she took it gratefully. Between sips she looked up at John. "Thank you for helping me, John. I didn't mean to hurt you."

"You didn't hurt me. Drink the rest of that and go to sleep."

Garnet looked around for Florinda. But Florinda was not there any longer.

Texas spoke to John. "You'd better go wash that leg."

"Very well."

"And here," Texas added, handing him a strip of bandage, "tie this over it."

"It's not deep."

"You'd better not risk getting dust into it. Cover it up."

"All right, then, I will." Taking the cloth, John walked down to the stream.

As he passed the bushes on the bank, he saw Florinda. John stopped in astonishment.

Behind the rocks, Florinda was crumpled up on her knees, retching. She was bareheaded, and her hair lay in damp strings on her cheeks and forehead. As John caught sight of her she pulled off her gloves and pushed her sleeves up above her elbows. He saw her cup her hands and bring up water to cool her face. For the first time he saw the scars on her arms and hands.

John took a step forward.

She heard him, and started violently as she looked around. "Oh," she said faintly. "It's you again. What do you want now?"

John came nearer. He paused by her. "I want to ask your pardon," he said.

Florinda looked half angry and half puzzled. With the back of her hand she pushed her wet hair out of her eyes. "Pardon? For what?"

"For what I said to you a while ago," John answered. He glanced at her hands and her bare arms. "I didn't know," he went on, "that you had any reason to dread burns."

"Oh," said Florinda. She began slowly to wipe her hands on her skirt, and smiled bitterly. "The one flaw," she said, "on an otherwise perfect body."

"I've never noticed your hands till now," said John. "I thought you wore gloves because of the sun." He paused a moment, and added, "Forgive me, Florinda."

"Oh, forget it. I'm sorry I acted like this. I tried not to throw up. But I couldn't help it. I got away just in time. Don't tell anybody, will you?"

"Of course not."

Florinda put her scarred hands to her forehead, and a shiver she could not control ran through her. John knelt by her, taking a flask of whiskey from his pocket.

"Would this do any good?"

"No thanks. I don't use it."

"I know you don't, but sometimes it helps in a pinch."

"Not me, it doesn't. I've tried it."

She pushed her hands up through her hair. They heard a yelp of pain, from some wounded man who had not Garnet's shame about screaming when the iron went into his wound. Florinda shuddered at the sound of it. There was another gagging noise in her throat. John said,

"I think I can help that nausea. Lie down flat on your back. Not here, it's out of sight and you can't tell what might be prowling around. Come up farther, beyond the rocks."

He helped her to her feet, and led her farther along the stream, to an open place where she was in sight of the camp.

"Here are your gloves," said John. "I'll put them on the ground by you. Lie perfectly quiet. I'll be back directly."

She lay down on the grass obediently. John left her. In a few minutes he came back with a piece of salt meat in his hand. He put his arm under her shoulder and raised her up.

"Eat this. Eat it slowly. Get all the salt."

Florinda did as she was told. She ate the meat in small pieces, pausing after each one to be sure she could keep it down. When the meat was gone she lay down again. John waited, sitting by her. After several minutes she took a deep breath, and turned to him. "That is a help. How did you know about it?"

"I came to California on a clipper ship out of Boston, around Cape Horn. After a bout of seasickness the cook would feed us salt meat. You'll be thirsty, but don't drink water for a while."

Florinda lay quietly on the grass. John stayed with her, waiting until she felt better. At length Florinda asked,

"Can I have a drink now?"

"Think you can hold it?"

"Yes, I think so."

He uncorked the water-bottle that hung from his belt, and she took a drink. She smiled at him as she pulled down her sleeves.

"I'm sorry, John. A baby could have acted better."

"I doubt it," said John. "In fact, I'm pretty sure now that your standing by Garnet through that operation took a good deal of courage."

"It did. But I can't go to pieces like this every time something happens to remind me. I've got to get used to it."

There was a silence. Florinda took out her hairpins and began to put up her tousled hair. "How is Garnet now?" she asked after a while.

"She's probably asleep. Oliver gave her a good-sized drink of whiskey, and she's not used to it."

"I'll go sit by her. She'll feel pretty awful when she wakes up."

Florinda put on her gloves. She glanced over toward the mules, and back at him.

"John," she said, "why didn't you want Garnet to go to California?"

"I've told you before," said John, "that it's none of my business."

"Stop being like that for about ten minutes, can't you? Is there trouble ahead for her?"

"I'm afraid so."

"What sort of trouble, John?"

"If she wants you to know," said John, "she'll tell you."

"Oh, rats," said Florinda. "She doesn't know it herself. Whatever you said to scare her, Oliver must have smoothed it out. She's perfectly happy."

"Maybe she'll stay that way. Anyhow, I can't do anything and neither can you. I hope you'll keep on being her friend. There's nobody else she can count on."

Florinda gave him a crooked little smile. "I wonder what Oliver would think about that remark."

"I thought," John said shortly, "that Oliver had the convenient habit of not thinking about anything."

Florinda fingered the grass. "He's crazy about her, John."

"Yes, he is. So maybe she'll be all right."

"And you can't do anything, so you're not going to talk about it."

"Right. And you'd better not talk about it either. Mind your own business."

"I guess I've got to."

John stood up. "Why don't you go on back to camp? They've started cooking. A bowl of atole would do you good."

He gave her his hand, and she stood up too. "Are you coming?" she asked.

"Not yet. I've got to put this bandage over my leg."

Florinda walked back toward the camp. Garnet lay asleep on her blanket. When she had stopped at the fire for a bowl of atole Florinda went and sat by her. Mr. Penrose passed, carrying some leather thongs he had been mending. He waved at her, and she waved back at him brightly. "You all right?" he called.

"Sure, fine," Florinda returned. "I've always wanted to know what an Indian fight was like."

Mr. Penrose laughed, and carried his thongs off to the picket-ground.

Florinda glanced after him with a lopsided smile. If he thought she was a cross between a doll-baby and a goddess, it was no more than he should have thought after all the nonsense she had told him. When he had asked about the scars on her hands, Florinda had made up a touching story. She told him another girl in the theater, less beautiful and less applauded than herself, had gone wild with envy backstage and had thrown a lighted lamp at her, with the purpose of ruining her flawless face. But, Florinda said, she had knocked the lamp aside with her elbow and it had fallen back on the other girl, setting her costume ablaze. "And what could I do?" Florinda exclaimed. "I had to throw her down and roll her over on the floor to crush out the fire. No, she was hardly burned at all. But you see what it did to my hands."

Mr. Penrose thought she was noble beyond the common run of mortals.

Florinda good-naturedly despised him. She was planning to get rid of him as soon as she could. But first she had to get to California,

223

and find out how a girl could live in that strange place. Florinda moved into the shade and leaned back against the rock. She felt terribly tired.

A few minutes later Texas came over. He squatted on the ground near where Florinda sat by Garnet.

"She's still out, Miss Florinda?"

"Yes. Oliver dosed her pretty well."

"That's fine. Let her sleep as long as she can." Texas stroked Garnet's hair. "It's hard on her," he remarked.

Florinda glanced at the torn sleeve dangling from Garnet's arm, and the bandage near the shoulder. She wondered if Texas, like John, foresaw trouble for Garnet in California. But evidently he did not, for he said,

"Well, she's stood it fine, and we'll be there pretty soon. And she'll have all winter to enjoy herself."

"You think she'll have a good time this winter?" Florinda asked.

"No reason why she shouldn't. Oliver's brother is about the most disagreeable man in California, but I don't guess they'll stay on the rancho much. Oliver has lots of friends."

Florinda moved a little to get the sun out of her tired eyes. "How much farther is it, Texas?"

"Two-fifty, three hundred miles. Depending on the waterholes."

"Three hundred miles, say. At twenty miles a day, fifteen days."

"Mostly nights. We'll have to ride at night. The days get a hundred and twenty."

Florinda gave a shudder, but she made no comment. "What do we do when we get there?" she asked.

"Well, we camp for a week or two at Don Antonio Costilla's rancho. That's the first rancho on the other side of Cajón Pass."

"Is it nice? The rancho, I mean, not the pass."

Texas pulled his beard and grinned. "It sure is, Miss Florinda. Good food, good rest, nothing to do all day."

Florinda let a weary little sigh escape her. Texas raised his soft brown eyes and looked at her with sympathy. "Say, Miss Florinda, you don't look any too well. Think you can hold out two weeks more?"

Florinda smiled. "You mean you think I'm going to flop and die in the desert? Don't worry, Texas. I'm not. Nobody's going to put up my skull for a target and shoot bullets through my eyes."

Texas chuckled without embarrassment. "You're a sassy creature, Miss Florinda."

"So I've been told," Florinda said. She yawned. "I'm a sleepy creature too. Those Diggers woke me up too early this morning. Why don't you run along so I can get a nap?"

She stretched out on the blanket by Garnet. Instead of going away, Texas stayed there, looking down at her wistfully. Shading her eyes with her hand, Florinda spoke to him.

"Haven't you got anything better to do than stare at me, mister?"

"I was just thinking," he said slowly, "if I had your nerve, I'd be a better man than I am."

She smiled at him. "You're all right, Texas."

"I'm a drunken bum," Texas said bitterly. "I always was."

"No you're not. You're a very nice man who gets drunk sometimes."

"You don't ever touch it, do you?"

"Not any more."

"Why did you quit?"

"Dear me," said Florinda. "What vulgar curiosity."

"Right. Sorry." Texas pulled up a handful of dry grass. She said nothing. "Well, go on," he said after a moment. "Preach me a sermon."

Florinda laughed a little. "You know, Texas, I don't give a hoot about reforming people. Either I like them the way they are, or I don't like them. And I like you fine."

Texas looked down, pulling blades of grass to pieces. "You're a pretty good sort, Miss Florinda."

"Oh, be quiet. Let me go to sleep. You talk too much."

She put her arm over her eyes to shut out the light. A moment later she heard Texas walk away. Off at the picket-ground, she could hear the men chanting as they worked.

> Tain't no place for the law-abidin',
> 'Tain't no place for the peaky and pale,
> You gotta keep tough if you gonta keep ridin',
> Ridin' down the Jubilee Trail.

Florinda bit her heat-cracked lip. A hundred and twenty in the desert ahead. John had told her she couldn't stand it. But she had to stand it. Only two weeks more. The men in the picket-ground sang with a cheerful brutal energy.

> Strap that pack so it won't start slidin',
> Drag that mule by his god-damned tail,

You gotta keep busy if you gonta keep ridin',
Ridin' down the Jubilee Trail.

TWENTY-TWO

FROM THE ARCHILLETTE they rode down to the Mojave Desert.
It was a harsh and terrible land. When she got out of it, Garnet
remembered cliffs of rock, and miles of white sand, and clouds of
dust so thick that the mules stumbled blindly. She remembered
thirst like a red-hot poker in her throat; and her arm blazing with
pain, though Texas bandaged it gently and told her it was healing
well. She remembered Florinda, thin as a toothpick, riding night
after night in an exhausted silence. She remembered how the dust
rose and covered them till men and mules were white, with red
eyes, like a line of savage ghosts.

This was the last lap of the journey, and the worst. Oliver told
her they were nearly done. They would get through. They always
did. And ahead, there was Cajón Pass, and a creek among the rocks,
and then the rancho of Don Antonio Costilla.

They got through, and rode up the mountains into the pass.
The mules smelt water. Tired as they were, they began to run, and
ran till they came to the creek Oliver had promised. When they
reached the creek, mules and men alike fell down and sprawled in
the water, gasping at the miracle of wetness. Oliver put his arm
around Garnet and told her the desert was over. She would not be
thirsty again.

Garnet sighed and let go her tense muscles. Just then she saw
Florinda. Nobody had an arm around Florinda. She was sitting with
her shoes on her knees and her bare feet in the water, leaning
back against a rock where the spray came up and wet her face.
She was alone.

Garnet got up and went over to sit by her. Florinda glanced
around and smiled in astonishment. "Why Garnet, I thought you
were over there with Oliver."

"I was. But the men are all talking at once, and there are so many
of them, I thought you and I could be together. You were alone."

"I don't mind being alone, dear. I'm used to it."

She was so brave that Garnet could not leave her. They stayed

226

together for the rest of the day. After supper when they said good night Florinda brushed her cheek with a kiss, soft and gentle like the brush of a flower-petal.

After this the traders took their time. The way was rocky and hard, and the creek was thin, so that they still had to be careful about water. But at least they had enough. And then at last, on Monday, the third of November, they saw the rancho of Don Antonio Costilla.

They came around a mountain, and far ahead, in the midst of a vast brown landscape, stood a group of brown adobe houses. Garnet blinked when she saw them, with a vague feeling of surprise. It had been so long since she had seen a house that the group looked unreal behind the dusty haze. She heard one of the men give a shout. All the men took it up, shouting hoarsely in voices thickened with dust. They began to hurry their tired mules. Garnet turned her head to look at Florinda. They both smiled wonderingly, hurting their cracked lips, and Florinda said in a faint voice,

"Garnet—are we there? Is it over?"

"I do believe it is," said Garnet. She drew a long breath.

They rode on, faster. Garnet felt release all through her aching body. The dust blew up at her and she tried not to cough, and just then she heard more shouting voices. From the huddle of brown houses she saw a group of men riding toward the train. They were gay in coats of red or blue, or striped serapes blowing as they rode. Against the long brown land the bright colors looked very strange.

"People!" Garnet gasped. "Florinda—not Diggers! Civilized people!"

The shouting was all in Spanish and they were too tired to try to understand it. But they saw the men from the rancho greeting the men of the caravan, and passing bottles of wine and water. Oliver leaped off his mule and came running over to Garnet, his dusty bearded face aglow.

"Take this, Garnet," he said, and thrust a bottle of white wine into her hand.

The wine was cool and tangy in her throat. Garnet gave a little sob as she drank. Oliver was sore and tired, but he grinned at her in triumph.

"We're here," he said, saying it as though it was almost too much to be believed. "We did it again!"

All around her she heard the same words. "We did it again!"

227

Oliver helped her dismount. Beside her, Garnet saw Florinda holding a leather water-bottle in both hands. Florinda was drinking so fast that the water was spilling and making streaks in the dust on her chin. But it did not matter. They were in sight of a California rancho; they had plenty of water, water enough to spill. Garnet hugged the wine-bottle to her bosom, and looked around at the shaggy, tired, savage-looking men who had come with her over the trail. Standing there, she put her head down on the saddle of her gaunt little mare and began to laugh and to cry all at once, and she thought of Columbus when he saw the first green branch floating in the sea. She thought she knew now what heroes were like. They were not calm brave generals on white steeds. They were rude filthy sweating men who kept going till they got where they wanted to go.

"Wait for me," said Oliver. "I'll be right back."

Garnet nodded and he went off. Everybody around her was shouting and bustling and talking at once. Some of the men were dragging the packs from the stumbling mules. Others were sitting down on the ground, happily starting to get drunk. Garnet put her hand to her aching head and sighed with rapture. She looked around at the new world.

And then, slowly, her forehead crinkled in a frown. She looked through the dancing haze of heat and dust. She blinked, and rubbed her eyes to get the dust out of them, and looked again.

This was the end of the trail. This was California. But California was not a land of grass and flowers. It was a land of gaunt mountains staring down upon a scorched and dismal plain.

Garnet did not know just what she had expected. But all through the desert she had dreamed of flowers and tall proud trees and rushing water. She saw nothing of the sort. All around her was a land of gray and brown, scrubby and shabby and covered with dust. She saw low hills thick with dry wild oats. The oats blew in the wind like the waves of a dull brown sea. Here and there on the hills she saw cattle grazing, knee-deep in the brown grass. Farther off, the high slopes were thick with the mountain brush called chaparral. The chaparral was a dull gloomy green, grayed with dust. In the distance it looked like a growth of rough fur on the hills. In places it was thick, elsewhere she saw great bare patches, as though the hills were moth-eaten. Still farther away were more peaks, blue with distance. They looked like pieces of cardboard standing up against the sky.

The rancho buildings stood in an open place among the hills. There was a long low brown adobe house, and around it a village of smaller houses, set helter-skelter without any particular plan. Among the houses were some low dusty trees, and fields cut with ditches leading from a stringy little creek. But even the trees and fields were not a bright happy green. They were merely greenish. Everything—trees, houses, fields, hills, chaparral—looked sad and tired under the dust.

Maybe, Garnet thought, she was a bit dazed from that wine she had drunk so greedily. But she could see perfectly well. And she thought California was just plain ugly.

She saw Florinda turn her head. Their eyes met again.

"Florinda," Garnet said in a low voice, "what do you think of it?"

Florinda smiled. She shrugged her thin shoulder. "The whole damn landscape," she said, "looks like it ought to be sent to the laundry."

They did not say anything else.

Garnet saw Oliver returning. He put his arm around her shoulders and told her to come with him. Glancing back, she saw Florinda walking away with Mr. Penrose.

Oliver led Garnet to the big adobe house. As they walked, he told her this was the home of Don Antonio himself, and the hospitable señor had given them a room here for their own use. Garnet looked around with curiosity.

There were a great many horses grazing about the place, saddled and ready for use. She asked in alarm if they were going to ride somewhere else today. Oliver laughed and said no, but nobody on a California rancho ever walked anywhere. The horses were kept ready all day long. A lot of people were going about, men and women and children, all in the brightest sort of clothes. These were the serving-people, Oliver said.

"But there are so many of them!" she exclaimed in wonder. "What do they do?"

"I've never found out," Oliver answered, laughing again. "Except at the spring rodeos, when the cattle are branded and slaughtered. Here we are. Now you can rest."

Garnet sighed hopefully at the words. She hurt all over. They were following a Mexican woman, gay in a white blouse and red skirt, her two black pigtails tied with red ribbon. She opened a door and stood aside, curtsying as they went in. Garnet found herself in a little room with bright-figured calico curtains around the walls. It had a wall-bench and a table, and at one side was a window with wooden shutters. Near the window was a bed, a real bed with pillows and blankets. On the wall-bench was a blue pottery basin and a blue jug full of water.

Garnet smiled. It seemed so strange and wonderful to be inside a house again. Sinking down on the bed, she sighed happily at the feel of softness.

Oliver was dragging in a mule-pack holding her clothes. With a proud grin at her, he took an orange out of his pocket, cut a hole in the end of it and gave it to her.

Garnet caught her breath. "Can I have it all?" she asked.

"Of course. The trees are full of them."

She sucked the orange dry. It was the first fruit she had tasted in so long that the juice had a strange tang in her mouth. Forgetting how dusty she was, she sank back into the pillow. California was an ugly place, but she did not care. California was a place where you could get all the sleep you wanted, all the water you wanted, fresh food, clean clothes, a bed. For a few minutes she was conscious that Oliver was taking off her shoes and drawing a blanket over her. That was all she knew before she went to sleep.

When she woke up, the afternoon sun was slanting on the wall-curtains and the air was rich with the odor of roasting beef. Before she was well awake Garnet remembered the long monotony of mush on the desert. She felt her stomach giving little jumps of ecstasy. Oliver told her they would not have supper for about an hour yet. The girls could not know just when to expect the caravan, so they did not start cooking till they saw the men ride in. But meanwhile, there was plenty of soap and water.

They laughed and scrubbed and combed their hair. Oliver opened the pack he had dragged in, and they put on clothes they had not worn since they left Santa Fe. The folds were yellow with dust, for no matter how tight the packing was, there was no way to keep dust from drifting in. But they brushed the clothes, and Oliver said the girls would wash everything.

Garnet looked at herself in the mirror on the wall. She was brown as an autumn leaf, and her arms and legs felt almost as firm as wood. In spite of the heavy gloves she had worn, months of riding had left her hands rough and hard.

"Oliver," she said, "the men I used to dance with—I could break them in two!"

Oliver squeezed her strong waistline. "I think you could," he agreed. "Now wait a minute while I put on my shirt, and we'll go outside."

Garnet went to the window and pushed open the shutters. The wall, like the walls of the houses in Santa Fe, was about a yard thick. She rested her elbows on the sill and looked out.

The rancho was full of movement. The older women were cooking at outdoor ovens that looked like big bee-hives, while the girls carried bowls toward tables set up on the grass, around an angle of the house. The men from the trail were idling about, drinking and flirting while they waited for supper. The girls' bright clothes made splashes of color against the brown background of the hills. Over everything, the scent of supper was like a whiff of glory.

Just then, as she looked out of the window, Garnet caught sight of the handsomest man she had ever seen in her life.

He was nearly seven feet tall and he weighed close to three hundred pounds, and every ounce of him was hard and healthy. His hair was a rich reddish gold, blowing in ripples from his forehead; his eyes were dark blue, almost purple; his skin had the rosy fairness of a baby's skin, and though he had strong masculine features his expression was as sweet as that of a happy baby. His clothes were gorgeous: a suit of sky-blue satin trimmed with gold braid, boots with bright star-shaped spurs, and leather gloves embroidered in gold. In one hand he carried a black hat with a blue silk cord around the crown.

This magnificent giant was strolling about the rancho with John Ives. John had changed his trail-clothes for a red silk shirt and dark gray Mexican trousers, but his garments looked staid in contrast with such splendor; and though John was six feet two and tough as a mule, beside his friend he seemed almost small.

As they passed her window, about fifteen feet away, the giant turned his head and saw Garnet leaning on the sill. His face broke into a smile. It was a smile of innocent pleasure, so winning and ingenuous that Garnet smiled back, and as she smiled she felt as if she had made a new friend. His violet eyes rested on her an instant, then he turned and said something to John. Glancing at Garnet, John chuckled and touched his hat as they walked on.

"Oliver!" Garnet exclaimed. "Who is that man?"

Oliver, who had seen John and his companion over her shoulder, laughed as he answered, "That's John's pet barbarian."

"What do you mean?"

"He's a Russian. Haven't I mentioned him? He used to live at one of the Russian fur stations up north. Now he has a rancho down here."

"What's his name?"

"His last name is Karakozof. Let him tell you the rest himself, I can't say it." Oliver pulled her hair mischievously. "You'll meet him, you can't help it. He loves women the way a baby loves candy."

"But why did you call him a barbarian?"

"Because he is one. Likable fellow, but quite uncivilized. John sort of adopted him and taught him a few manners, but John's never been able to teach him to use a fork. Want to go out?"

Garnet nodded. She felt a thrill of anticipation. California was an ugly place, but it wasn't going to be dull.

Just beyond the door Oliver stopped to speak to a driver who wanted to know about piling up the packs. Garnet saw Florinda sitting on a bench built against the wall of the house. Florinda had brushed her hair and put on a fresh cotton dress. She was so thin that the dress fitted her loosely, and she looked very tired, but as she saw Garnet she held out her hand, smiling with determined brightness. She had put on black silk house-mitts with half-fingers, which she would not have to take off while she ate supper.

"Come sit down," Florinda invited.

Garnet sat by her. "How do you feel?"

"Oh, pretty well. Say, Garnet, did you see the handsome brute?"

"The—oh, you mean the Russian?"

"Is he a Russian? That great big beautiful creature in blue?"

"That's what Oliver said."

"Well, well, I never saw a Russian before. Do they all look like that?"

Garnet laughed. "How would I know? I never saw one before either."

"Anyway," said Florinda, "he's the most beautiful object I ever laid eyes on. I saw him just a minute ago. Mr. Penrose went off to get raddled on the local firewater, and I came and sat down here. And then I saw him with John, and he looked at me and smiled so sweetly, like a nice little boy. Who is this handsome brute, Garnet?"

Garnet told her what Oliver had said. Florinda puckered her lips doubtfully.

"Him a barbarian?" she objected. Her face lit as she saw the

Russian and John coming toward them. "Here he is again. I do believe he wants to meet us. And if he's a barbarian I'm a cross-eyed Eskimo."

John came over to them with the good-looking stranger. The Russian was grinning eagerly. John looked amused, and Garnet remembered what Oliver had told her about the Russian's liking for women. John said,

"Mrs. Hale, Miss Grove, may I present my friend? Mr. Karakozof."

The Russian bowed deeply. Speaking with care, as though not quite at home in the language, he said, "It is a stupendous pleasure, ladies."

Garnet said, "How do you do," and Florinda said, "Pleased to meet you, I'm sure." Florinda added, "What's your name again, mister?"

"My name, beautiful lady," said the Russian, "is Nikolai Grigorievitch Karakozof."

Florinda winced. "Honestly?"

"Why yes," he said with amiable innocence, and as though to help her he repeated it. "Nikolai Grigorievitch Karakozof."

"I can't say that," Florinda told him. "Can you say it, Garnet?" Garnet shook her head frankly. Florinda thought a moment, then a light broke over her face. "Would you mind," she asked him, "if we called you something else?"

"I would like very much," he said earnestly, "anything I was called by such charming ladies. So you will call me—?"

"The Handsome Brute," said Florinda.

He laughed joyfully. "The Handsome Brute," he agreed. "That is me."

"That's you. Do you like it?"

"Oh yes. I like it. And I like you. I like all two of you. It is very happy, meeting lovely Yankee ladies. I have seen some Yankee ladies. Up at Sutter's Fort, which is close to Fort Ross where I lived. But they were not lovely like you." He addressed Garnet. "You are married to Oliver."

"Yes, that's right," she answered.

"John told me. If I was Oliver I would be so happy. And you," he said to Florinda, smiling as though he had found her a most enchanting surprise, "you are like me. You are a unfertilized egg."

"Hell for breakfast," said Florinda.

The Handsome Brute glanced questioningly at John. "What does she say?"

"She doesn't understand your language," said John. Turning to Florinda, he explained, "Un huero—an unfertilized egg. That's what the Californios call anybody with light hair and blue eyes. Nikolai was very glad to see you, because you're another freak like himself."

"Oh sure, I get it," said Florinda. She smiled up at him in comradeship. "They stare at me too, Handsome Brute. We'll just have to sympathize with each other for being eggs."

"I sympathize with you," the Handsome Brute said gently. "You are tired."

"Well, naturally," said Florinda. "Did you ever cross that desert?"

"I am not a hero," said the Brute. "I am a very lazy man. I have never go east of Cajón Pass and I do not want to go."

"You're a smart man," said Florinda.

The Handsome Brute spoke to John. "Can we stay with the ladies till supper, John?"

"If they have no objection." ·

"Of course not," said Garnet. "Sit down, both of you."

The men sat down on the dry grass. Linking his big hands around his knees, the Handsome Brute looked up at Garnet and Florinda. "My English is so bad," he said with apology in his voice. "Forgive me if I do not talk to you right. I am learning better. John give me a book. I read the book all winter."

"What sort of book?" asked Garnet.

The Brute glanced at John. "Tell her, John. I do not know how."

"It's a collection of poetry," John explained. "It was the only book I had. There aren't many books in California."

"Thank you," said the Brute. He smiled shyly at Garnet and Florinda. "I will talk some more to you, if you please? You will teach me to talk better."

"Of course," said Garnet. "But you speak very well already. How long have you been speaking English?"

"I had a—how do I say, John? When I was a little boy?"

"A tutor."

"That is right. A tutor who talked English. But I was very little then. I forget the English. Up at Fort Ross, we talked Russian. We learned how to talk Spanish too, because we came down to buy supplies from the ranchos. But I did not talk any more English till I met John and he was teaching me again."

"Did you live a long time at Fort Ross?" Florinda asked.

"Oh yes. My father, he was in the army. The army of the Czar. When I was such a little boy, I had eight years, the Czar sent some army to look at the fur stations in America. There are many fur stations. From Fort Ross in California all up to Alaska. My mother was dead, and my father brought me to America with him."

"And your father stayed here?" she asked.

"No, my father died too. When we were at Fort Ross, he was very sick. The ship had to go back to Russia without him. Then after the ship was gone, my father died. So I lived at Fort Ross. I worked with the men. We got the furs, seal and sea-otter, and we farmed the land to raise food for the Russians in Alaska."

"But didn't any other ships come from Russia?"

"Oh yes, the ship comes once in three years or four, to get the furs. But they did not want to take home a little boy. And when I was grown, why should I go? I was happy at Fort Ross."

"And when did you come to live here?" Florinda asked.

He grinned up at her. "We worked too well. The fur was giving up—that is wrong, how do I say, John?"

"Giving out."

"That is right. Thank you. The fur was giving out. The men said they would leave Fort Ross and go to the stations in the north. There was more fur in the north. They sold everything to a man from Switzerland. He is named Sutter. He has Sutter's Fort on the American River. Our trappers went to Alaska, but I did not want to go to Alaska. I liked California. So I came down to Los Angeles and I got baptized again and they gave me a rancho. I raised cattle. The people laughed at me. The Yankees said I am a barbarian and the Californios said I am a unfertilized egg. And one day I was taking my hides to the store of Mr. Abbott in Los Angeles, and stacking the hides was John. I helped him stack the hides. John did not call me a barbarian or a unfertilized egg. John was a very seldom person. We got to be friends."

"I had just arrived here," said John, "and I was stumbling around in the Spanish language and having a hard time with it. Nikolai spoke Spanish like a native, so we agreed that if he'd teach me Spanish I'd teach him English. That's all."

He spoke casually. But the Handsome Brute was looking at him with affection, and Garnet thought she saw a deep friendship between them. It seemed odd for John to have a real friend. The Brute had called him a seldom person. He must mean *unusual*—

the two words would be easily confused by a foreigner. The Brute, brought up by half-civilized Siberian trappers, had felt awkward among the dark proud rancheros, and John had not made fun of him. She wished Oliver had not called him a barbarian. John went on,

"Unfortunately, Nikolai hasn't had as much chance to practice his new language as I've had to practice mine. I have to speak Spanish every day to everybody I meet, and he can only speak English to the Yankees."

"But I will learn," the Handsome Brute said gravely. "I like the Yankees."

A servant girl went over to a scrub-oak near them, and struck a gong that hung from one of its limbs. As the noise clanged over the rancho the men shouted, and John and the Handsome Brute scrambled to their feet.

"Supper!" announced the Handsome Brute. Exuberant at the prospect, he put both his enormous hands on Garnet's waist, picked her up like a doll, and swung her in the air over his head. She squealed with astonishment. "Behave yourself, Nikolai," said John, but he was laughing, and as the Brute set her down Garnet saw Oliver coming toward them, and Oliver was laughing too. While Garnet caught her breath Oliver greeted the Brute in Spanish. The Brute laughed and answered him. Oliver took Garnet's arm, and as they walked toward the tables she exclaimed,

"Does he often act like that?"

"Don't mind him," said Oliver. "He's as harmless as a child. And by the way, don't gasp when you see him eat."

The tables were set up outdoors, with backless benches on either side. The men were leaping over the benches, finding places with helter-skelter joy. Sighing with ecstasy, they began to gobble.

They ate beef and beans, corn and grapes and olives and oranges. They ate eggs, tortillas, loaves of dark brown bread, strange but delicious dishes made of cornmeal with peppers and onions. They drank chocolate in big thick cups, or bottles of red and white wine, or the fierce Mexican aguardiente. The beef was tough and gamy, for the cattle on the hills were quite wild. Nobody paid them any attention except when they were rounded up once a year. But the beef was good. Everything was good. The dishes were made of bright-colored earthenware. The knives were metal, but the forks and spoons were cut from horn. This made them surprisingly light in weight, but they were easy to handle.

At first, Garnet was eating with such gusto that she did not notice anybody else. But after a while, when she began to go more slowly, she saw the Handsome Brute sitting across the table from her. Though Oliver had warned her, she stared at him in amazement.

The Handsome Brute had taken off his gloves and turned up his blue satin cuffs. Around his neck he had tied a vast white kerchief. In his hands he held a chunk of beef six ribs thick, from which he was tearing the meat with his teeth.

With the beef he ate a loaf of brown bread and drank a bottle of red wine. Then he picked up a roasted chicken. Pulling off the wings and legs, he disposed of those first, then he took the carcass between his hands and ate the meat off in rows, as though it were corn on the cob. With the chicken he ate a bowl of beans and a bowl of cornmeal porridge, using a spoon which he grasped in his great fist like a spear. When he had finished the chicken and another bottle of wine, he began to peel oranges, piling the skin on top of the bones.

Though he used neither knife nor fork, he was very neat. But he ate and drank until he made even the hungry traders look dainty. He was not self-conscious about it. As he finished his third orange and helped himself to a handful of tortillas, he saw Garnet watching him. She felt ashamed of herself for staring, but the Brute was not abashed. He smiled upon her like a cherub.

"It is good," he said to her.

"Why—yes," said Garnet. She felt effete as she cut off a bit of the beef on her plate and picked it up with a fork. The other men were laughing at her surprise. The Brute went on eating.

At last a serving-girl brought him a bowl of water. The Brute smiled upon her winsomely and told her she was beautiful. He washed his hands, took the kerchief from around his neck to dry them, and put the kerchief back into his pocket. This done, he drained the last of the wine in his bottle—Garnet had lost count of how many bottles there had been—and grinned around the table at them all. He was very happy.

When they left the table the Brute walked off with John. Florinda was staring after his broad blue satin back.

"Say, Oliver," she said, "is that his regular performance?"

"Yes," Oliver assured her.

"That much," said Florinda, "and like that?"

"Always."

"I think he's wonderful," said Florinda.

237

She went over to join Penrose, who was lounging on the grass with several of the other men. Oliver went to make sure the packs were being taken care of, and Garnet started indoors.

At the door, she paused and looked around. The light was beginning to fade and the air was chilly. The men lay about in groups, passing bottles and talking about how good it was to be here at last. Now and then a dog barked, and the horses whinneyed from the grazing-ground. Over to the east was the range of mountains that the train had climbed over to get to California.

What a strange place it was, she thought, so remote and so hard to reach. Cut off on one side by the largest ocean on earth, and on the other by that barrier of desert and mountains, California lay between them unconquered and almost unknown. She wondered how long it would be before somebody would really subdue this wild gaunt countryside, and who would do it at last.

Oliver said they would rest here a week or ten days before going on. As the time went by, Garnet found that the rancho was a very interesting place. Don Antonio Costilla had a vast grant of land, and thousands of cattle grazing on his hills. His land had once been the property of a mission. When Mexico won its independence from Spain the mission lands were broken up, and for some years now the government had been granting them to private owners.

There were several springs in Don Antonio's mountains, sending down streams of water. The streams were thin now, for there had been no rain for six months, but they were still enough for a little irrigation. The ground beyond the irrigated patches was so dry that it was as hard as the adobe bricks of his house. Around the patches were a few trees. The sycamores were bare, but there were some evergreen scrub-oaks by the streams, and orange and lemon and olive trees, grown from sprigs brought over long ago from Spain. These were evergreens too, but their leaves were furry with dust.

Around the main dwelling were the storehouses, and the homes of the Mexican bosses who supervised the rancho. Farther out were the low thatched huts of the tame Diggers and half-breeds who did the menial work. The Diggers were wretched creatures, dressed in rags or sheepskins that sometimes hardly covered a decent minimum of their blackish skins. They had wild hair and heavy bellies and stupid beady eyes. Garnet had shivered apprehensively when she learned that there were Diggers on the rancho, but Oliver told her these tame Diggers were harmless.

The Diggers were not called slaves, because they were not bought and sold; and they were not bought and sold because they were not worth anything. There were more of them than anybody could use, and the general opinion was that any ranchero who would keep a Digger out of mischief was entitled to any work he could get out of him. They were incredibly stupid. They could take orders, if the orders were given in very simple language. None of them seemed able to learn more than a few hundred words in any language. They were not allowed near the main house, and Garnet was glad of it.

Around the homes of the white people, everything was gay and comfortable. The traders were given rooms indoors, while the drivers slept outside, their heads on their saddles. Penrose and Florinda had a room in one of the smaller buildings around the main house. The lines of caste in California were clear; and Penrose, who owned neither rancho nor cattle, was by no means as important a man as Oliver.

Don Antonio never thought of charging them anything. Food and lodging were free at any rancho in California, and a guest who offered to pay for hospitality would have insulted his host. The traders expressed their thanks by giving presents to Don Antonio— blankets from Santa Fe, or American trinkets for his wife and daughters, bought from the Missouri traders.

The serving-women of the rancho cooked and did laundry, but except at rodeo time the men had very little to do. They played guitars and sang, while the men from the trail danced with the serving-girls and made love to them, and Don Antonio rode about, laughing and saying his home was theirs as long as they would honor him by staying here. His wife appeared sometimes, a stout, handsome woman, riding in state with a silver-mounted bridle. When they saw her all the men sprang to their feet and bowed low. Don Antonio had four sons, who rode about on stallions which they managed with great skill. But the traders never saw the young girls of the family at all. There was a walled courtyard behind the main house, where Don Antonio's three daughters took the air, but they never appeared. In California, though married women went about freely, girls of aristocratic families were kept in seclusion. Garnet asked how they ever made up their minds about husbands. Oliver answered that they didn't. Their parents chose husbands for them. "Oh dear," Garnet said with a shiver, thinking that if this custom had prevailed in New York her parents would probably have chosen Henry Trellen.

After a week of nothing to do but eat and sleep, Garnet felt as well as she ever had. But Florinda was still haggard. The desert had cost her more than a week's rest could pay back. She insisted that she felt better. But she did not look like it.

Garnet's arm was still sore, but it did not bother her much. Texas kept an eye on it. "You'll have a scar, ma'am," he said to her one afternoon, when he stopped her after dinner to ask how she was. "But it's a scar to be proud of."

John passed them, as he walked over toward the field where the horses were grazing. He paused, and smiling a little, he said,

> "Then will he strip his sleeve, and show his scars,
> And say, 'These wounds I had on Crispin's Day.'"

"Who said that?" asked Garnet. "Shakespeare?"

"He said nearly everything," John answered.

Garnet smiled. John could tease her if he liked, but all the same, she was going to be proud of that scar when she got back to New York. She was glad she had been wounded in the arm, instead of some unmentionable spot that she could not boast about. Texas laughed in a friendly fashion. There was an odor of wine about Texas. Now that he had come to the end of the trail, he was no longer keeping away from the bottles. But all the men had been drinking. And anyway, she could never be afraid of anybody as nice as Texas.

John's eyes went over her smooth hair and her clean cotton dress, as though admiring the difference the week had made in her. John too looked different. He had shaved, and his face had the mark of the trail, half white and half dark. He had on a plaid shirt and coarse dun-colored trousers, faded from sun and scrubbing, but as always he had an air of cool distinction. The corners of his lips quivered provokingly as he said,

"I have a scar too."

"Yes, you told me Texas had to burn a wound of yours once."

"I didn't mean that one," said John. "I've still got the marks of your teeth in my leg."

Garnet bit her lip, embarrassed. Texas spoke sternly.

"She's a lady, John."

"But an intelligent lady," John answered. He turned and went on toward the horses. Texas patted her wrist.

"Don't you mind John, Miss Garnet. He knows better than to talk about his lower limbs to a lady. But John just don't like people, somehow."

Garnet looked after John's tall lean figure. "He's all right, Texas. But I don't understand him."

"Don't try to understand any of us, Miss Garnet. We're just a lot of lost souls."

Texas walked off too. Garnet felt a twinge of sadness as she watched him go.

She wondered who he was and why he had taken the trail. It was hard to guess his age. When she had first seen him in Santa Fe she had thought he was about thirty-five, but sometimes when he had been drinking he looked ten years older than that. Texas was of medium height and rather slightly built, but life on the trail had given him a muscular toughness. He looked better riding than he did walking, for he walked with a shambling gait, and he did not stand erect like a man proud to face the world. He did not think much about his appearance. Most of the men, once they reached a place where there were girls to admire them, took pains to look well. Texas had had his hair and beard trimmed when he arrived, but he dressed carelessly, and Garnet suspected that he would soon let himself get shaggy again. He might have been good-looking if he had cared about it. His hair and beard were a rich copper-brown, and his eyes were brown too, under coppery eyebrows. They were sweet, gentle eyes, lovable eyes, but his whole expression had a sad shyness. She thought it was like the look of a child who wanted people to like him but was not sure they would.

His hands were different. They were hard, rough hands with big joints, used to the labor of the trail, and they had no uncertainty. When he tended a wound Texas did it deftly, giving only the necessary minimum of pain. Garnet wondered where he had learned so much, and why he had brought his skill away out here.

Lost souls, she thought as she looked around. Lost souls banished to the desert and these somber hills. Not a part of this life, as Don Antonio was a part of it. Not a part of anything but the great loneliness. Garnet wondered how it would feel to stand in this baked land of exile, and remember your home, and know you could not go back.

She started toward the house. Everybody on the rancho went to sleep in the afternoon. Already the men were stretching out here and there in whatever shade they could find. The Handsome Brute was asleep by an orange tree. Garnet glanced at him thoughtfully. He could go back to Russia if he pleased, for the ships came out every few years to get furs. But he had left Russia so young that probably he would be as foreign there as he was in California. She wondered if he felt like an exile.

She went into her bedroom and took off her clothes. Oliver had not come in. Probably he was taking his nap outdoors, as he often did. She stretched out luxuriously on the bed and went to sleep.

When she awoke there was still a thread of sunlight between the shutters, but the air was chilly. She had found already that the midday warmth of California did not mean a thing. As soon as the sun got low there was a chill in the air, and by dark it felt almost like winter. Oliver said the climate was like this all the year round. The native Californios took it for granted, since they had never lived anywhere else. But the Yankees described the climate by saying California had four seasons every day.

Garnet put on a dress of dark plaid wool with a white linen collar. She wondered what Oliver was doing. He had not been indoors at all. When she had dressed, she went out to look for him.

The rancho had come to life. The men were working with their horses or idling on the grass. The girls were cooking at the outdoor ovens. There was a tempting smell of food in the air. "Good heavens," Garnet said, "I'm hungry again." She laughed at herself, reflecting that she had no business commenting on the Brute's appetite.

She did not see the Brute or John. Penrose was swapping jokes with Silky and a couple of other men, but Florinda was not with them. Garnet hoped Florinda was still resting. She looked around for Oliver, but it was several minutes before she saw him.

Oliver sat on the ground under a sycamore tree. With him was a man Garnet did not know. The stranger was dressed like a California ranchero, in a red coat and buff-colored trousers and high embossed boots. On his knee he held a wide-brimmed black felt hat with a black silk cord around the crown. Garnet started toward them.

She took a dozen steps, and stopped. The two men were absorbed in their conversation. In the pre-supper bustle around them, they had not noticed her approach. Garnet stood still. For now she was close enough to get a good look at the stranger, and she had a feeling that she had seen him before. Almost as soon as she had it, she knew why he seemed familiar. He looked like Oliver.

He looked like Oliver, and yet he was very different. He was smaller than Oliver and a good deal older. His hair was light brown and curly, like Oliver's. But he seemed to have too much of it, and it made his head look too big for his hard little body. His features were something like Oliver's, but Oliver's expression was jolly and boyish, while this man's face was pinched up like a walnut shell. There were lines across his forehead, and lines between his eyes, and lines from his nostrils to the corners of his mouth as though he had pressed them there by keeping his lips shut very tight. He gave her an impression of tightness all over. And though he was muscular and deeply sunburned, he somehow struck her as unhealthy, like slimy creeping things. Garnet knew it was wrong to blame a man for his size or his appearance. But all the same, she thought this man looked like a nasty little shrimp.

She knew who he was, and he made her feel scared. But she gave a quick grab for her common sense. It was foolish of her to be scared. He could not possibly do her any harm. She had better go up right now and meet him, and try to make him like her if she could.

She took another step forward.

Maybe her tread was harder than it had been before, or maybe her skirts swished on the dry grass just as there came a break in their conversation. At any rate, the two men glanced around. Oliver gave her a startled look. He had not expected to see her quite yet. Garnet saw, rather than heard, him say, "Here she is now."

The stranger looked at her. His gaze was not friendly. It was intent and hard. It made her feel as if she had blundered into a place where she had no right to be.

They got to their feet. Garnet saw that the newcomer was not as tall as Oliver. As he stood up, his fluffy head looked bigger than ever. He looked like a forked carrot with a sponge on top. She had an impulse to giggle, but she smothered it, and as she went up to them she made herself smile courteously. Oliver said, in a voice that sounded breathless, as though he were bringing a piece of bad news and hated to say it,

"Garnet, may I present my brother Charles?"

TWENTY-THREE

CHARLES BOWED to her formally. Garnet felt a chill go down her backbone. She had been trying to think Charles was ridiculous, but he was not. He was threatening and sinister. Barely moving his lips, Charles said, "Good afternoon, madam."

Then she saw his eyes. Charles' whole character was in his eyes, but you did not notice them at first, because they were deep-set, under thick light eyebrows that looked like two caterpillars on his forehead. Charles' eyes were darker than his hair, and they were always shadowed by the deep sockets and thick eyebrows. But they had a hard, piercing quality, calculating and utterly merciless. When Charles fixed his attention upon an object he fixed his eyes upon it too. He held them there, unwavering, till if you were the object he was looking at you felt as if he were drilling into your head, and you could not pull away from him. He drilled into your head and put his own ideas there. His eyes said, Do this, do it, do it; and if you did not fight for yourself every minute, one day you would find that you had obeyed him. If you were much with Charles your life was either a constant yielding or a constant battle, and unless your own will was very strong you would yield to him at last from sheer weariness.

As he bowed to Garnet and said "Good afternoon," his lips turned slightly inward, as though he had to hold back the words he wanted to say. Garnet knew he hated her for being here. She felt his dislike as though it made a wall against her. Charles was holding his hat in both hands, his fingers clenching it over the brim. She had a feeling that it was costing him a hard effort to keep up even the form of politeness. Her own muscles got stiff to match his. But she remembered how often her mother had told her there was no defense like a quiet good breeding. So, smiling as though she thought Oliver's brother had greeted her cordially, she answered,

"How do you do, Charles. I am glad to see you at last. Oliver has told me so much about you."

It was not necessary to tell Charles what Oliver had told her. She was glad he had prepared her not to expect a welcome. She thought Oliver would say something now, but he did not. He stood looking guilty, like a little boy caught stealing the jam. Garnet felt a flash of anger at him, but she was not going to let Charles know it. Charles said nothing either, but stood looking at her with a cold contempt, as though she were a piece of shoddy merchandise somebody had tried to sell him. Garnet tried again.

"I'm sure you're surprised to find Oliver married," she said. "But I hope we're going to be friends."

"I confess I was surprised," said Charles. His eyes were still fixed on her. His tight little mouth gave a twitch at the corner. "We will leave here tomorrow," he said, "for my rancho."

Garnet felt a stab of wrath. The land had been granted to Charles and Oliver jointly, so Charles had no right to say "my rancho." As Oliver's wife, she had a perfect right to live there. But she still tried to speak pleasantly.

"Tomorrow? I didn't know that."

"We will leave tomorrow," Charles repeated crisply. "We will start at sunrise."

Garnet felt her fists doubling up. She buried them in the folds of her skirt. But she remembered that she had a good way to defy him. Charles hated her, no doubt, because Oliver had just been telling him of his plan to go back to the States for good, instead of staying here to help Charles realize his ambitions. It would serve Charles right to be reminded of it again.

"I'll be ready," she said graciously. "But since Oliver and I are only staying here till next April, please don't disturb your household for our sake."

Charles' lips got even tighter than they already were. He said, "We shall see."

"I am looking forward to a very interesting visit," said Garnet. She smiled at him, and at Oliver.

But Oliver was not looking at her. He had not met her eyes since she and Charles had begun talking. He was watching Charles, and he was strained, even scared. Garnet had been holding herself so rigidly that her knees hurt. She could not stay here any longer, keeping up this battle with sharp little pieces of ice. So she said in a bright voice,

"But now, I'm sure that after being apart for so long, you and Oliver must have a lot to say to each other. So I'll leave you to exchange news."

At last Oliver glanced at her and said something. He was evidently glad she was going. "We'll see you later, then. At supper."

245

Charles bowed to her. Garnet turned and walked away. Her heart was pounding. She was furiously angry with Charles, but she was even more angry with Oliver. Why hadn't he taken her part? Was he really scared to speak in his brother's presence?

Reaching the tables, she chose a place where there was a tree between herself and Charles, and sat down on the bench. She felt all mixed up.

She tried to think back. Charles knew the caravan was due, so he had ridden here to meet Oliver. He had arrived this afternoon. Oliver had told him the news of his marriage and Charles was boiling with fury because of it. Charles had said they were leaving tomorrow morning. That must have been his own decision, for Oliver had said nothing to her about it. He had not even told her he was expecting Charles to meet him here. Oliver had not, in fact, said anything about Charles at all.

Why, now that she thought of it, this was very odd. On the trail she had been so occupied with the effort to keep going that she had hardly thought of Charles. But now she remembered that Oliver had not mentioned Charles' name to her since they left Santa Fe. It was as though he had wanted to forget there was any such person waiting for him at the end of the trail.

She tried to remember when Oliver had stopped speaking of Charles. It was—this was very strange—it was the day John had met him in Santa Fe. John had come by to see Oliver, saying something in Spanish which she had thought meant he had a letter, and then he said he had not brought a letter. Oliver had said so too.

Garnet frowned and thought hard. That same evening, when Oliver said she had misunderstood John about the letter, he had said something else. While they were having supper Oliver had said, "You know I'm not nearly good enough for you, don't you, Garnet? Because I'm not."

She had laughed at him then. But now she wondered why he had said that. She had not had time to think of it that evening. As soon as they left the table they had gone to the Fonda, where Florinda had let Silky recognize her, and so much had begun to happen that she had forgotten Oliver's words; and she had not noticed his sudden silence on the subject of Charles.

And now Oliver was looking scared and guilty and ashamed of himself. Garnet felt baffled. But she made a grim resolve. All right, she would start for the rancho tomorrow. She would be pleasant to Charles and try to make him like her. But if he wouldn't like her she wasn't going to worry about it because she and Oliver would be starting home in April anyway. And meanwhile, right now, she felt like having some cheerful conversation. She looked around, hoping to see Florinda among the groups lounging on the grass.

Florinda was not in sight. Garnet saw Penrose, sharing drinks with a trader who rejoiced in the nickname of Devilbug, but Florinda was not with them. Garnet remembered Oliver's telling her that Charles would not approve of her friendship with Florinda. Well, Charles could mind his own business. She certainly liked Florinda better than she liked him.

John and the Handsome Brute were walking together not far off. They saw her, and the Handsome Brute grinned with pleasure at the sight of her. They came toward the bench.

Evidently they had noticed her looking around, for the Handsome Brute said,

"You were looking for somebody? Am I too hopeful if I hope it was me?"

Garnet laughed up at him. After Charles, he was such a joy. "I was looking for Florinda," she answered. "Have you seen her?"

"Ah!" the Brute said gravely. "You did not know?"

"Know what?" Garnet exclaimed with concern.

The Brute glanced at John.

"Florinda is ill," said John.

"She's ill?" Garnet repeated. "But I thought she was feeling better!"

"She *said* she was feeling better," John returned. He went on. "She finally collapsed just after dinner." After an instant's pause he added, "I'm sorry. Florinda has plenty of nerve. But she's been living on it for a long time now."

"But what happened?" Garnet demanded anxiously.

John and the Brute sat down on the bench. "Florinda went to her room right after dinner," said John. "Later Penrose went in, and she was unconscious on the floor. Penrose was frightened when he couldn't rouse her, and came out looking for somebody who might help. He had been drinking a lot, and so had most of the others. Nikolai and I went in to see what we could do. We managed to bring her around, but she seemed to be in pretty bad shape. So we found Texas, threw a bucket of water over him, and brought him to her. He said he'd take care of her, and told the rest of us to let her alone."

"Where is she now?" Garnet asked.

"In her room. Texas is with her. He can help her if anybody can."

"But is he—John, is he drunk?" Garnet asked. She felt frightened and indignant as she looked over toward where Penrose was drinking in company with Devilbug.

John saw her glance, and met it with a faint cynical smile. But instead of commenting, he gave a direct answer to her question. "Texas is not too drunk to know what he's doing, if that's what you mean."

"Can I see Florinda?"

"I suppose so."

The Brute smiled gently. "You go to see her, Miss Garnet. She likes you. And she is so tired."

Garnet felt a pain in her throat. Florinda was so tired, but she had refused to say so until she gave out completely. And Penrose was a callous lout, and Texas was a drunkard, and there was nobody who really cared whether Florinda died of exhaustion or not. Well, Garnet thought fiercely, she cared. "I'm going to see her," she said. "Right now."

Before they could answer she started off, walking as fast as she could over the bumpy tufts of grass. As she hurried, she caught sight of Charles and Oliver, sitting on the ground where she had left them. Again they were too deep in conversation to notice her as she passed. Charles certainly did look silly. He was shriveled up like an old onion.

Florinda was living in a little adobe house that had four rooms built in a row, each room with an outside door of its own. Garnet had never been into Florinda's room, but she knew which one it was. She knocked at the door.

Texas opened it. Texas smelt like brandy and his eyes were red, but he smiled upon her as kindly as ever. "Why come in, Miss Garnet," he said.

He shut the door as she stepped inside. The shutters were closed, and for a moment she blinked in the dimness. As her eyes got used to it she saw that the room was small, but exquisitely neat, as any room Florinda lived in always was. It had a wall-bench, and there were two mule-packs in a corner, and at one side was a bed. There was no other furniture. Florinda lay on her back, without a pillow, under a blanket drawn up to her shoulders. She had on a clean white nightgown. Texas had rolled up some other blankets and placed them under her hips, so that her head and shoulders were lower than the rest of her body.

Her eyes were closed, but as Garnet took a step toward the bed Florinda opened her eyes and turned her head a little.

"Who is it?" she asked faintly.

"It's Miss Garnet," Texas told her.

"Oh," said Florinda. She spoke weakly. "It was nice of you to come in."

Garnet knelt by the bed and took Florinda's hand. She had not often held Florinda's hand without a glove on it, and she felt now how rough the scars were. Holding Florinda's hand was like holding a root.

"I just this minute heard you were sick," Garnet said. "How are you?"

"Texas says I'll be all right," murmured Florinda. Garnet glanced over her shoulder. Texas had sat down on the bench, and was fingering a bottle that stood there. Florinda must have looked at him too, for she said, "If you need a drink, Texas, go ahead. I don't mind." Texas lifted the bottle. Florinda managed to smile at Garnet. "This is a fine mess I made, isn't it?"

"Nobody can help getting sick!" Garnet exclaimed. "Don't talk if you don't feel like it."

"Oh, I can talk. I feel pretty well as long as I keep lying quiet. It's just when I try to move that I get dizzy. I've been having dizzy spells every now and then. I guess I just had one too many."

"Do you remember what happened?"

"Not very well. I felt pretty awful at dinner today. Things kept going around. I didn't want to make a fuss, so I came in and got my clothes off. I thought if I got a nap I'd feel better. Then it all started to spin again, and I guess I just folded up. I think John and the Brute came in, and then I was here on the bed and Texas was fixing those blankets so my head would be lower than the rest of me. It seemed awfully funny at first, like being upside down, but it did make me feel better. Texas has been so good to me. I don't think I'm talking very loud—if he can't hear me tell him I said so."

Garnet turned her head. "Florinda says you've been very good to her, Texas."

Texas smiled vaguely. She saw that the bottle in his hand was empty. He stood up unsteadily.

"Now that you're with her, Miss Garnet, I think I'll step out for some air. Back soon, Miss Florinda."

Florinda gave a weak little laugh as he went out. "He's gone for another bottle. Poor Texas."

"Poor Texas!" Garnet repeated contemptuously. "Can't he even stay sober now, when you need him so?"

"No, dearie, he can't." There was a trace of compassion in Florinda's tired voice. "People like him, when they start, they can't stop." Her voice trailed off. Garnet kept silent to give her time to rest. After a little while Florinda spoke again. "I feel like such a fool, Garnet. I did try to keep going. Honestly I did."

"I know you did. Stop trying to apologize."

"I guess I was an idiot to tackle that desert," Florinda murmured. "John told me I couldn't take it. By the time I was halfway here I knew I shouldn't have started. But then I couldn't go back."

There was a brief pause. Garnet asked, "What are you going to do now?"

"I don't know," said Florinda.

She said it quietly. Garnet thought of Penrose, outside drinking with the boys. Penrose had wanted a glittering beauty. He had no interest in an exhausted woman who could hardly speak above a whisper. He had been glad to turn Florinda over to Texas. And though Texas was kind, he was also drunk, and he was going to be drunker than this. Florinda was not expressing any resentment. Garnet wondered if it was possible that she did not feel any.

But I feel it, Garnet thought wrathfully. I'm not sick and I haven't got the disposition of an angel. She said aloud, "Is that wretch Penrose going to leave you here?"

Florinda gave a grim little laugh. "Why yes, dear, he's going on to Los Angeles. He said he had to, he knew I'd understand. I do, of course, I understand damn well."

"But what does he think you're going to do?"

"Don Antonio has plenty of room. I guess he'll let me stay here till I'm better."

"So Penrose is going to leave you alone in a foreign country, among strangers speaking a foreign language! Well, I'm going to do something about it."

"You're sweet, dearie, but I don't know what you can do."

"I don't either, but I'm going to do something. So don't worry. Just stay here."

"I've got to stay here, baby. I can't walk as far as the wall." Florinda's eyelids began to close again, as though she were too

250

tired to hold them open. Garnet stood up. "I'll get you some help," she said firmly.

She went out and closed the door. Standing still a minute, she looked around at the rancho. The girls were carrying dishes to the tables. The men were idling, drinking, swapping yarns. Was there one of them, she wondered, who would help Florinda now? They were rested, and eager to start selling their goods. Several of the traders had already left for Los Angeles. She heard the supper gong. The men began hurrying toward the tables.

Garnet went slowly to her own place. Oliver was already there, with Charles beside him. Charles bowed to her formally as she sat down. He sat on the far side of Oliver. Garnet sat by Oliver, and the Handsome Brute took his place across the table from them.

The Brute said, "You saw Miss Florinda?"

"Yes," said Garnet. "I think she's very ill."

Several of the other men remarked that they were sorry to hear Florinda was ill. But plainly, right now they were more interested in the roast beef than in anybody's troubles. Charles asked, "Who is Florinda?" and Devilbug answered, "An actress from New York. Penrose brought her along." Charles shrugged without interest, and gave a disgusted glance across the table at the Brute, who was eating a chunk of beef from his fingers.

Oliver was very attentive to Garnet, but she did not feel much like eating. The other men were talking about business. They asked Charles about the prices being offered this year at the trading posts in Los Angeles. Charles answered in terms of hides, as though hides were money. Garnet's attention drifted. She had other things to think about.

She wanted to ask Oliver why Charles detested her so, and she wanted to talk to him about Florinda. Oliver would know of some way to help.

When they reached their room she spoke of Florinda first, as they were leaving tomorrow morning and any plans they made would have to be made tonight. But to her dismay, Oliver refused to consider Florinda. Garnet tried to explain how ill she was, and how helpless in this strange country, but Oliver retorted,

"My dear Garnet, there's nothing I can do! I'm sorry she's sick, but I didn't bring her here."

"Oh Oliver, don't be so heartless!" she cried. "You know this country—isn't there anywhere she can go?"

"Nowhere that I know of. There aren't any charity homes in

California." Oliver was on his knees, hastily putting clothes into a pack for their journey. "Forget about Florinda, can't you?" he urged impatiently.

Garnet was sitting on the bed. The sight of Oliver packing reminded her that it was not Oliver, but Charles, who had decided when they would leave. She stood up.

"So you won't even try to help her. Is it because you think Charles wouldn't approve?"

Oliver turned around. "Garnet," he said to her, "can't you understand that I'm already in trouble up to my neck? I can't take on anybody else's worries. Now shut up and leave me alone."

He had never spoken to her so shortly before. "I won't shut up," Garnet snapped. "And I won't have my life run by that loathsome little autocrat. I know he hates me. But I'm not afraid of him. And you are."

Oliver got up from his knees and came toward her. "Please forgive me, Garnet," he said contritely. "I never talked to you like that before. I never will again."

She took a step away from him. "And I never talked to you like this before, Oliver, but I'm doing it now. I'm worried about Florinda, but that's not the main thing that's worrying me. It's you. Why did you say you were in trouble up to your neck?"

Oliver tried to speak soothingly. "Garnet, I told you Charles wasn't going to like my being married to you. Don't you remember?"

"Of course I remember. I'm sorry he doesn't like me, but I'm not breaking my heart about it. What I want to know is, what's the matter with you? Why didn't you say a word this afternoon when he was practically taking me to pieces? Why are you afraid of him?"

Oliver answered her earnestly. "Garnet, believe me. I love you. Charles is not going to come between us."

"I know you love me!" she exclaimed. "I've never doubted it for a minute. But what is this about Charles?"

"Garnet, listen." Oliver put his hands on her shoulders. "Charles is angry, as I told you he would be. He doesn't like the idea of my going back to live in the States. But I'm going, no matter what he says. I promised you and I'm not going to break my promise. Now will you please not ask me any more questions?"

"Is that all you can tell me?"

Oliver put his arms around her and held her close to him. "Yes, my dearest girl, it is. I love you, and that's the most important thing that ever happened to me. You're the first woman I've ever loved, and you're the last. I mean it."

He kissed her with a long eager tenderness. Garnet leaned against him and ran her fingers through his curly hair. Oliver was so strong and so lovable. At length she smiled up at him.

"All right, Oliver. If there are things that are none of my business, all right."

"Thank you, Garnet," he said. He looked very serious. "Do you know you're quite a wonderful woman?" he asked, and kissed her again.

When he released her, and returned to filling the pack, Garnet went to the door.

"I love you, Oliver," she said, "and I trust you. But there's something I've got to do. I'll be back in a few minutes."

"You're not going out?" he protested. "It's pitch dark."

"There's a lot of moonlight. I'm going to see if I can't get Florinda some help. Don't tell me not to, because I'm going anyway."

Evidently he could tell that she meant it, for he only shrugged as she went out.

Garnet hurried across the grass. The men were gathered here and there around outdoor fires. The moon was nearly full, and very bright. She heard Silky's voice exclaim,

"Why good evening, Mrs. Hale! Are you looking for somebody?"

Silky had sprung to his feet and was bowing with grandiose respect. He looked suave and elegant again, his mustache tilted and his hair carefully combed.

Garnet stopped. "Have you seen John Ives, Silky? Or his Russian friend?"

"John? Indeed, madam, I do not know where—"

"Over yonder moon-gazing," said one of the other men in the circle. "John, that is. The Russian's not with him."

He pointed, and Garnet saw John lying flat on his back, his hands clasped under his head, looking up at the sky. She thanked them and went toward John. They had not told her what the Handsome Brute was doing, but she guessed that he was somewhere with a girl. She had overheard several remarks about his success with girls.

John raised himself on his elbow as he heard her approach, and got to his feet.

"Did you want something of me, Garnet?"

"Yes," said Garnet. She stood a moment looking up at him.

253

In the shadows John's face was lean and stern. She could not have told that his eyes were green if she had not already known it, but it seemed to her that they were the coldest eyes she had ever seen. Garnet felt a tremor. But she had to speak. She said, "John, will you help Florinda?"

Though she could not see his expression very well, she was sure her request surprised him. "Help her?" he asked. "What do you want me to do?"

Garnet shivered. She had come out without a shawl, and the night air was cold. John asked,

"Has Charles treated you decently?"

"Charles? He's barely spoken to me."

John gave her a slow smile. "When he does, talk back to him."

"Oh John," she exclaimed impatiently, "I didn't come out here to discuss Charles!"

"That's right, you didn't. You were saying something about Florinda." He spoke tersely. "I'm sorry she's ill, Garnet. But I don't know what you want me to do. I'm not a doctor."

"I suppose," she retorted, "you're going to say it's none of your business."

"It isn't, you know," John answered coolly.

"I think it is," said Garnet.

John did not answer. He was holding an orange he had broken off a tree, and he tossed it up and caught it again.

Garnet struggled for words that would say what she wanted him to understand. "John," she pled, "Florinda had a reason for coming to California. I don't know what it was. She hasn't told me and I'm never going to ask her. Oh, please!" she said as he was about to answer. "I know what you're going to say. You want to ask, 'What has that got to do with me?' Well, I'll tell you."

John smiled down at her with amusement and a touch of admiration. "You're very determined when your mind's made up, aren't you?"

"Yes, I suppose I am. Are you going to listen to me?"

"I can't help it. Go ahead."

She spoke vehemently, though she kept her voice low. "John, I don't know why you came to California either. And I'm never going to ask you. I can mind my own business too. But let me tell you something. Minding your own business doesn't mean you have to treat other people like a lot of dead sticks. I think you and Florinda—and the others like you—the people who came out here

254

all alone—I think you ought to understand each other! Because—because, John, you do understand each other's loneliness!"

By this time John was not looking at her. He stood turning the orange over and over in his hands, as though he had never seen one before.

"But what do you want me to do about Florinda, Garnet?" he asked at length. "Marry her? I won't, and neither will I take her on, Penrose-fashion."

Garnet felt herself blushing. "I never thought of that!" she cried.

"I know you didn't. I beg your pardon."

"I just thought," said Garnet, "that maybe there was somewhere she could stay until she got well. Where people would be good to her."

For several seconds John was silent. He peeled a bit of the skin off the orange. Finally he asked,

"You think she'll take care of herself after that?"

"Oh John, you know she will! Florinda has always taken care of herself. She's never had anybody." Garnet went on eagerly. "I hope I'm not betraying a confidence. But I've got to make you understand. Her father deserted her mother, and her mother was a weak stupid whining fool. Florinda didn't tell me that last. But she told me enough for me to draw my own conclusions. Her mother spent her whole life weeping and wanting somebody else to take care of her."

"Not the sort of person you'd admire," John remarked with a trace of humor.

"No, you're mighty right. But Florinda has got sense and she's got courage, and she won't be a burden any longer than she has to be. Please give her a hand, John."

He smiled. "How eloquent you are. All right."

"You will?" she cried joyfully.

"Yes," said John, "because I'm too big a fool to say no. She's going to be a nuisance and I'm going to wish I hadn't promised. But set your mind at rest. I'll tuck her away somewhere."

"Oh, thank you!" she exclaimed. He did not answer, and she held out her hand. "Good night."

John took her hand. "Good night. And goodby."

Garnet was surprised at how sorry she was to hear him say it. She had grown to like John more than she had realized. The trail had made her admire strength more than gentleness. But he could be gentle too, she remembered, thinking of the time he had held

255

her when Texas put the iron into her wound. "John," she asked in a low voice, "when will I see you again?"

"Sometime this winter. I'm coming up to buy some cattle from Charles, to stock my rancho."

"I'll be glad to see you," she said.

"I'll be glad to see you too," said John. She withdrew her hand and was about to turn away when he added, "Don't forget what I told you."

"What?"

"If Charles annoys you, tell him to go to hell."

"Do you think I can?" she asked. She could not help feeling timorous when she thought of Charles.

"You?" said John. He gave a short laugh. But then he stood still a moment, looking at her intently, and for some reason she got the impression that he was about to tell her something else. But John dreaded getting mixed up in affairs that did not concern him. He shrugged, and said,

"I'm sorry you're going back next year, Garnet. This country was made for people like you."

He turned abruptly and walked off. Garnet made her way back to the house. She wondered if she had been right, or merely imagining things in the dark, when she got the impression that John had looked at her with sympathy just then, a real fellow-feeling so strong that it had almost made him break his rule of silence about other people's business.

TWENTY-FOUR

CHARLES AND OLIVER'S RANCHO lay to the northwest, at a distance of eight days' riding. As Garnet had made up her mind to defy Charles, she began when she got up that morning. She brushed her hair till it shone, and put on a dark green riding-dress that fitted tight above her waist and spread into a big rippling skirt. When she walked toward the line of horses she knew she had never looked better in her life.

The horses were magnificent. Oliver gave her a beautiful mare, and a saddle of tooled leather, polished till it gleamed like satin in the sun. As she mounted and took her place in the train,

Charles' serving-men watched her admiringly. The traders who had come out to see them off waved and called, "Good riding, Mrs. Hale!" Garnet waved back to them, promising to see them again when the caravan met next April. She still felt quivery at the thought of living with Charles till then, but she was resolved that nobody was going to know it.

Charles looked very grand, and also, she thought, he looked absurd. Astride his great stallion he seemed more shrunken than ever. His face reminded her of a withered apple, and the brilliant eyes were like two bright-headed pins. He had on a red satin coat and embroidered trousers, and his saddle was all aglow with silver bosses. Oliver was grand too, for Charles had brought him new clothes to replace those Oliver had worn out on the trail. Oliver's trousers were mustard-colored, with green and scarlet embroidery down the sides; his jacket was blue satin, and the buttons were made of gold coins from Peru. He had on a fine white shirt and a white silk sash with gold fringe, boots with spurs made like stars, and a wide black Mexican hat with blue silk tassels around the brim. There was a long line of pack-horses and saddle-horses; there were ten serving-men, who wore trousers of many shades, and brilliant striped serapes over their shoulders. They all set off in such richness of color and silver and thudding hoofs and tossing manes that they looked like a royal procession. Nobody would have guessed their train bore such a load of threatening emotions as Garnet knew it did.

They traveled in luxury. The horses were sleek and fresh, and the serving-men treated Garnet like a princess. Though they watched her foreign ways with curiosity, the men accepted her at once as the great lady of the rancho. As soon as the train stopped for a rest they spread blankets for her, and brought her water and wine, bowing with respect as they set down the jugs. They cooked excellent meals, beef spiced with chili, porridges of corn and beans, bowls of chocolate crunchy with flakes of a coarse brown sugar called panocha; and they spread the food before her with shy charming smiles, as though she were a goddess and they hoped she would be pleased with their offering.

The way led them through a wild country, cut with canyons and ringed about with mountains that looked like piles of crumpled dark velvet. At noon they stopped by streams lined with willows and nicotine bushes, and here and there a strong old live-oak that had been clutching for a hundred years at the crooked earth. A month ago Garnet would have liked the hills, and she would have liked the flattering feudal ways of California. But now, she was in no mood to like anything.

Charles hated her. She could see it when his eyes swept over her in her graceful riding-dress; he hated her for her health and her spirits and her proud way of carrying herself, and he hated her for being here. He rarely spoke to her. When he did, it was with a cold politeness that was like an insult.

However, she was not overly concerned about Charles. Charles alone could not hurt her. What did hurt her, more and more as the days passed, was Oliver's attitude toward both Charles and herself. He would not have confessed it for ten thousand cattle-hides, but Oliver was scared.

She tried to understand it. Oliver had lost his parents when he was a child. Ever since then he had obeyed Charles, and Charles was an overbearing tyrant. Away from Charles, Oliver had fallen in love with her and married her. But now Oliver was like a boy who for the first time had dared to disobey a domineering father. Garnet was amazed, and baffled, and contemptuously angry.

When they lay in their shelter at night—the only privacy they had—she tried to make him be frank with her. But all her insistence was not enough to get an answer. Oliver begged, "My dearest, don't mind Charles! I told you it would take him a while to get used to you."

"I don't mind Charles," Garnet retorted. "But I do mind you. You act as if I'm something you have to apologize for."

"Garnet," Oliver exclaimed with a weary desperation, "for God's sake quit pestering me!"

Then he would put his arms around her and beg her to forgive him for speaking harshly. He loved her, he loved her more than anything else on earth—wasn't that enough?

No, Garnet thought when she lay awake at night, it was not enough. He loved her, but he did not have the courage to trust her. She wanted love. But she did not want an adoring weakness.

She slept restlessly, and she knew Oliver did too, though in the mornings he always said he felt fine. She said she also felt fine, but she did not. She felt wretched. It was not the sort of discomfort she had felt on the trail. Here there was no thirst, no killing heat, no bowls of cold pinole gritty with sand. Here there was simply Charles' tense fury, and Oliver's dread before it, and her own disgust with Oliver. She had no appetite for the excellent meals, and ate them only for the sake of the servants who had worked so hard to please her.

One morning they rode through a mountain pass, and there below her Garnet saw the place where she was to live this winter. It was easy to understand why Charles had called it "my rancho." Nobody who knew the Hale brothers could have imagined that Oliver had ever had anything to do with it.

Charles had clamped his own ways upon his land. His vast property was as neat as a starched collar. You knew as soon as you looked at it that Charles was rich, not with a gay warm abundance like Don Antonio, but rich with an austerity that counted every hide and every bunch of grapes.

The main building was a large house of adobe painted white, with glass in the windows. In front of it Charles had built a reservoir with walls of stone, fed by two streams that came down from the mountains. Around the house were gardens and orchards and vineyards. They were planted in straight lines with irrigation channels between them, and no clumps of weeds to use up the hard-won water. At a respectful distance behind Charles' house were the homes of the workers, and the storehouses and workshops. These also stood in rows, like the streets of a prim little village. Garnet saw a great many men in the fields, and a great many cattle roaming on the slopes beyond. Oh yes, the rancho was rich; smugly, nastily rich. Every acre of it proclaimed Charles' contempt for the native ways. At her first glimpse of it, Garnet felt her stomach give a twitch of nausea. But then she felt like laughing, because as she looked at this priggery and then at the huge tumbled hills beyond it, she thought she had never seen anything so silly in her life.

Oh Oliver, she thought with exasperation, why can't you talk back to this pompous little despot? And what, she wondered as she looked again at the rancho, what in God's name is waiting for you here, to make you so afraid?

She did not know. They rode toward the rancho, and servants came out to take their horses. Charles spoke to them with cold authority, saying that the señora was the wife of Don Olivero and they were to see to her comfort. They were surprised, but they bowed to her politely. Charles told her she and Oliver would have a bedroom and a sitting-room for their own use. He said it as if he were speaking to a poor relation.

Life at the rancho went by schedule. There was a big American clock on a shelf in the dining-room, which struck the hours in a doleful singsong voice. If Garnet had needed any proof of Charles' skill at tyranny, she could have found it in the way he had made a troop of easy-going Mexicans obedient to this clock. Charles' serving-people were afraid of him. They went about silently, and even when Garnet tried to make friends with them they seemed afraid of her too.

Breakfast was at seven o'clock. Dinner was at twelve. After dinner you could go to sleep. Charles despised the custom; he looked upon it as another sign of the hopeless laziness of the native population, but not even Charles could make Mexicans work in the afternoon. Supper was at six.

After breakfast, Charles and Oliver went for long rides over the rancho and Garnet was left to amuse herself in any way she could. She went for walks, and mended her clothes, and she found a few books in the dining-room. The books were set prominently on a shelf, and she guessed that they had been put here to impress callers in this bookless land, for the leaves clung together as if they were never opened. There were three books in Spanish, and a dozen worn volumes in English that might have been stuck in to fill up space in packing-cases—essays by forgotten moralists, some old novels, and books of poetry with tattered pages. She read them, for lack of anything else to do.

Her rooms were neat and cheerless, with crisp wall-curtains and straight hard chairs. Oliver dumped a stack of ledgers and papers on the table in their sitting-room, saying he would go over them later when he heard from John. The papers made a big disorderly pile. Garnet was glad of it, for the rest of the house was so tidy that it looked as if it had been got ready for a funeral.

Except at meals, and sometimes in the evenings when Charles would follow them into their sitting-room and talk business with Oliver, she scarcely saw Charles at all. He and Oliver were always together. If they came in early from riding, they went into one of the rooms she had never entered, and talked and talked. Once, through a door ajar, she heard Oliver exclaim, "But what do you want me to *do*, Charles?" He sounded like a man in pain. She did not hear Charles' answer.

She tried to make Oliver tell her what they talked about all day. "Oh, about the rancho," said Oliver, "and what's been going on

260

since I left." He would not tell her anything else. He kept pretending there was nothing else to tell.

It seemed like a long time, though they had been at the rancho only two weeks when a native youth rode up with a letter to Oliver from John. Oliver knew him: his name was Pablo Gomez and he had often run errands for John before. Charles stood in the doorway, giving orders that Pablo's horse was to be cared for. Oliver smiled as he read the letter, and handed it to Garnet.

John had sent a brief note, hastily written from the rancho of Don Antonio. He said he was leaving at once for Los Angeles, and would write later about the disposal of their goods. Then there was a second paragraph, saying,

"Here is a message for Mrs. Hale. I have just heard that the clipper Silver Star, now in port at San Diego, is leaving shortly for Boston. Her captain, Mr. Mitchell, is in Los Angeles buying supplies. If Mrs. Hale wishes to write to her people, informing them of her safe arrival, tell her to send a letter by Pablo. I will give the letter to Captain Mitchell, who will mail it when he reaches Boston. The utmost haste is essential. The Silver Star has been delayed by need of repair, and is sailing as soon as possible in order to round Cape Horn while it is still summer in the Southern Hemisphere. She will reach Boston in June or July. I have ordered Pablo to wait one night only at your rancho. See that he stays no longer, or it will be too late."

John's handwriting was clear, without flourishes. As Garnet read it, her eyes tingled and she blinked quickly so Charles and Oliver would not notice. The letter held no news for Oliver. John had written solely to say to her that here was a chance for her to write home. Remembering John's cold green eyes and his disdain of the human race, Garnet almost burst into tears.

Charles leaned against the side of the doorway, absently snapping his riding-crop. "What does your friend say, Garnet?" he asked, and held out his hand for the letter.

Garnet glanced at Oliver. "It's addressed to you. Shall I give it to Charles?"

"Why of course," said Oliver, and he smiled at Charles. "Garnet's sense of honor is very delicate."

"So I observe," Charles said coldly.

Garnet handed Charles the letter. When he had read it, Charles struck the side of the door three times with the butt of his crop. To the boy who ran up, he said that a fresh horse was to be ready for Pablo at half-past six in the morning. He spoke to Garnet. "You may write your letter now," he said.

Garnet went into her sitting-room. The insolent fool, she thought. Granting his permission for her to write a letter, as though she had to ask him first. She shut the door, and when she heard how it banged behind her she laughed angrily. Nobody banged doors in Charles' house. She'd bang a door whenever she felt like it, she told herself as she pushed aside the ledgers on the table to make room for her pen and paper.

She picked up the pen and bit the top of the feather. There was so much she felt like saying. "Dear mother and father, I need you so. I'm bewildered and I don't know what to do. Oliver's brother hates me and takes pleasure in letting me know it, and Oliver has changed—he won't tell me anything and I don't understand him at all. Nobody speaks to me all day. If you were only here, if you could make Oliver talk to me—"

But no. She could not say that. Her parents were half a year's journey away and they could not help her. She must not say anything that would give them concern. By the time she saw them again all this muddle would be over somehow. She dipped her pen into the ink and wrote firmly. "Dear mother and father, By a fortunate chance there is a Boston clipper in port at San Diego and so I have an opportunity to send you news. We have just reached California after a hard but very interesting journey."—Don't tell them how hard it was or they'll be worried about your getting back next year.—"I wish I could tell you about it, but I am writing this in great haste so you will have to wait for details until I see you. Oliver and I are living on the rancho with his brother Charles. The place is very comfortable. I am in my usual good health, and so strong and sunburned you would hardly know me. Now I will tell you something about this country of California. The mountains are tremendous—"

She wrote on and on, biting her lip hard in her resolve to be cheerful. As she wrote, her eyes filled with tears so that she could hardly see the words. She put her head down on her arm, trying not to cry, but the tears slipped out in spite of her. By the time this letter reached New York, it would be a hot midsummer. People would be scattering to the mountains and the seashore. Mother and father would show the letter proudly to their friends. "Good heavens, Pauline, what an adventure that girl is having! Weren't you afraid to let her go?" "Why yes, of course I was, but I feel much better about it now. You can see how happy she is."

Father would put the letter into his pocket, and take it out as though by accident at the bank. "Oh by the way, we just had this note from my daughter in California. Must be quite an interesting country out there. She says—"

Oh, they were so good, so safe. And she had not appreciated them at all.

She finished the letter that night after supper. The next morning before breakfast she gave it to Pablo, and watched him ride off. She was not going to give Charles a chance to say he would like to read what she had written. The letter held only the barest mention of him, but she did not intend to have anybody poking into her correspondence.

The day passed like the other days. Garnet roamed about lonesomely, thinking of John and Florinda and Texas and her other friends of the trail, wondering what they were doing, missing them. In the evening, Oliver said he and Charles wanted to go over some business records, so they all three went into the sitting-room next door to her bedroom. Garnet sat on one of the straight-backed chairs while Oliver picked up a ledger from the table and began going over its entries with Charles.

In a few minutes the men were lost in talk. Oliver sat on the wall-bench, the ledger on his knees. Charles stood by the fireplace. The sticks were laid in the fireplace, but nobody seemed to think of lighting them, though the night air was sharp. Garnet's thoughts drifted. What an ugly room this was, with its white walls and stiff wall-curtains. The lamp threw big shadows over the floor. This was an American lamp, bought from one of the ships. It had a round shade with pink roses painted on it. Charles' house was such a mixture of California and New England that it would have looked out of place at either end of the continent. It was the most disagreeable house she had ever been in, and he was the most disagreeable—

The house jumped as though somebody had kicked it. The window-panes rattled, the table did a little dance, and a ledger fell to the floor with a shower of loose papers tumbling after it. The walls shivered and the whole room gave a curtsy. Garnet's chair leaped and threw her sideways on the floor. She gave a cry, catching herself with one hand as she fell.

It all happened at once. She was so frightened that for a moment her head spun. Then she realized that Oliver was kneeling by her, his arm around her shoulders.

"Garnet!" he was exclaiming. "You're not hurt, are you?"

Garnet blinked up at him. She was still giddy, and her skin was cold with fright. The walls looked steady now, but the papers on the floor were still rustling and the wall-curtains trembled as though in a wind. The lamp had fallen over, and Charles was setting it up again, using his handkerchief to mop up a splash of oil from the table. Garnet heard him exclaim with annoyance that the shade was cracked. From outside, she heard the horses screeching in fear. Oliver was saying,

"It's all right, Garnet. Don't be frightened."

He helped her to her feet. "What happened?" she gasped. "The whole house moved!"

"Don't be frightened," he said again. "It was just an earthquake."

"An earthquake!" she cried. Her voice was shrill with terror. She had read about earthquakes—houses falling down, people running madly from the horrors of sudden death. "Where do we go? What do we do?"

And then, with anger and amazement, she saw that Oliver was laughing at her. Charles, leaning against the wall, was regarding her with the resigned impatience of a man interrupted in his business by a bothersome brat.

"We don't go anywhere, Garnet," Oliver said with gentle amusement, as though soothing a child who was afraid of the dark. "We don't do anything. They happen all the time. You'll get used to them."

Garnet looked from Oliver to Charles and back to Oliver. She was too startled to say anything. Oliver went on,

"We're always having these little shocks. They very seldom do any damage."

"For pity's sake, Garnet," Charles said with tight-lipped exasperation, "it didn't hurt you!"

His arm still around Garnet, Oliver spoke to Charles tersely. "Oh let her alone, Charles. You were pretty surprised yourself when you felt your first one. Here, Garnet, this will settle your nerves."

He picked up a wine-bottle, which had luckily been corked so the contents had not spilled, and filled a cup for her.

Garnet took the cup, drawing a long resolute breath as she did so. She felt nauseated, and she felt like bursting into tears. But she reminded herself desperately that she must not, she must not show any weakness in front of Charles.

"I'm sorry I made a fuss," she said carefully. "But I never felt an earthquake before and I was frightened when it knocked me down. Next time I'll know better."

"There, that's fine," Oliver said heartily. "You're all right now, are you?"

"Yes," said Garnet, "I'm quite all right." She wanted to sit down and give her insides a chance to stop shaking. Glancing at the papers on the floor, she added, "You and Charles go on checking your lists. I'll pick up those papers and stack them on the table again."

"Fine," said Oliver. He added a few more reassuring phrases, and he and Charles went back to the list of goods. In a few minutes they were talking trade as though nothing had happened. The horses were still making a racket outside, and Garnet heard the voices of the men quieting them. She thought resentfully that the servants were paying more attention to the horses than her own husband was paying to her. She sat on the floor, setting the cup of wine beside her. Later, maybe, she could drink it, but not yet. Her stomach still felt as if it would revolt against anything she put into it.

So this was California. This was the fair country at the end of the trail. California was not only ugly, it was a place where the very earth hated you and tried to throw you off.

If I ever get out of here, Garnet said to herself, I'll never leave New York again. Once I get back to the trail I won't say a word about the heat or the dust or the thirst. All I want is to get out of California.

Charles and Oliver had their heads bent over the ledger, talking as though she made not the slightest difference. Garnet began to gather up the scattered sheets of paper. At least this gave her something to do with her shaking hands, and it gave her a chance to keep her face lowered, so they would not see how angry she was.

On the papers were lists of goods and prices, written mostly in Spanish. Garnet reached for another couple of sheets that had fallen farther off. She held them in her hand, breathing slowly to quiet her nerves. The two sheets in her hand were covered with writing. The words this time were English. She was not consciously reading, but as she looked down the words began to form themselves into sentences before her.

As she read, her spine stiffened and her hands grew damp. The muscles all over her body seemed to be tying up into knots.

For now at last she knew what they had tried to keep her from knowing. She knew why John had denied bringing a letter to Oliver in Santa Fe. She knew why John had been shocked to learn that Oliver was married, and why he had been still more shocked when she said Oliver was bringing her to California. She knew why Charles regarded her with such rage and loathing, and why Oliver had looked so guilty in Charles' presence. She knew why John's green eyes, when he told her goodby, had had in them that glow of sympathy.

T W E N T Y - F I V E

THE WRITING began in the middle of one sentence and ended in the middle of another.

". . . before, but now the news is good. You don't deserve it, Oliver, to be sure. You never had any sense about women and I daresay you never will, but this time your gallivanting has brought us the greatest piece of luck we ever had. Not even I myself had dared to plan for you to marry such an heiress as Carmelita Velasco.

"But now, of course, there's nothing Don Rafael wants so much as for you to marry his precious daughter. Everything is arranged. Don Rafael came here again today. Carmelita gave birth to a son in January. She is in good health, and her relatives up north do not think of doubting the story that you are already her husband. They believe the ceremony was performed in Don Rafael's private chapel before you left.

"Don Rafael and I have made careful plans. I will meet you at Don Antonio's, and we will go north together. You and Carmelita will be married privately in her aunt's chapel up there.

"Don Rafael is in great spirits. He has always wanted a grandson. The boy will be his heir, inheriting his entire rancho property—which will probably make us the greatest landowners in California.

"So, if the early part of this letter has troubled you, you can set your mind at ease. The only other person who knows the truth is John, and John never talks. I don't like him, but we can be sure . . ."

This was the end of the second page. Garnet sat rigidly, staring at the words in front of her.

For a while—she did not know how long—her mind felt as jumbled as the papers on the floor. She heard the men's voices, and the noise of the horses outside, but she did not quite hear them. Then, slowly, her head began to clear. She sat still, too stunned to move, but she knew what had happened.

This was the letter John had brought to Oliver. This was the letter he had said he did not have, as soon as he found out she was Oliver's wife. John knew that before Oliver left California last year he had been making love to the daughter of a great rancho family. He was bringing Oliver news that the girl had had a child, and her father had told his friends that Oliver was already married to her.

So this was what Oliver would not tell her. Oliver had let her come into this tangle, without warning. For it was a tangle, and serious. She remembered the look of concern on John's usually impassive face, that day in Santa Fe when he first heard her say Oliver was taking her all the way to California. John, she thought angrily. Oh no, he would not tell her either. John liked to mind his own business.

Garnet felt rage come up into her throat like a hot coal. She turned her head to look at Charles and Oliver. They sat side by side on the wall-bench. Charles was telling Oliver about the rancho business. Charles always managed Oliver's share of the California property as well as his own. And if Oliver had married Carmelita Velasco and acquired another vast estate, Charles would no doubt have managed that too. Oliver would have let him do it, just as Oliver had always let Charles take care of everything. No wonder Charles had been so furious when he found that Oliver had made an American marriage. For a year now, Charles had considered the Velasco land as practically his own. When she appeared, Charles had felt robbed of something that belonged to him.

And Oliver! Garnet doubled up her fists. The hot coal in her throat exploded and went all over her, tingling down into her toes and fingertips. Why hadn't Oliver been honest with her? Long ago, she had guessed that Oliver must have made conquests before they knew each other. But she had been thinking of casual encounters with girls like those the traders picked up in Santa Fe. This was different. Carmelita Velasco was a high-bred aristocrat.

267

Through the stamping of the horses outside and the voices of the men in the room, Garnet heard herself talking to Florinda.

"I know about things like that, Florinda! Now and then I've heard nice people talk about a girl who's been—well, they call it 'unfortunate.' A girl like that is disgraced."

Sitting there on the floor, Garnet felt her forehead crinkling in a frown, and her eyes pulling together as though she were trying to see in a bad light. All that stuff she had said to Florinda—it had sounded so serious then. Now it sounded silly. Maybe she ought to feel damply sentimental about poor Carmelita. But she did not. She simply thought Carmelita should have had better sense. She also thought Oliver should have had better sense. She did not feel compassionate at all. She just felt mad.

She picked up the two pages that had fallen out of Charles' letter, and scrambled to her feet.

"Oliver," she said harshly.

"Just a minute, dear," he said without lifting his eyes. "Are those the figures for this year's shipping only, Charles, or for—"

"Oliver!" she said again.

Charles glanced up impatiently. "We're counting, Garnet."

"I'm not talking to you," she retorted with a snap in her voice.

Her manners were usually so gentle that they both looked at her in astonishment. Handing the ledger to Charles, Oliver stood up. "What's the trouble, Garnet?" he asked affectionately. "If you're still scared of that earthquake—"

"I'm not scared," said Garnet. "But I'm so damn mad I could kill you." It was the first time she had ever said "damn." The word slipped out before she knew it and gave her a surprising sense of freedom, like the breaking of a tight belt. She held out the two pages in her hand. "Why did you tell me John had not brought you a letter in Santa Fe?"

Oliver snatched the papers from her hand and stared at them. "My God," he said in a low voice. "Where did you get this?"

She made a gesture toward the sheets scattered on the floor. Charles, who had also risen to his feet, glanced at the letter and shrugged as he recognized his own handwriting. "I thought you said you'd burnt that up," he remarked.

"I thought I had," said Oliver. "I don't know how these two sheets slipped out." Crumpling the sheets into a ball, he threw it at the fireplace. The ball missed and bounced on the floor.

"I told you," said Charles, "you couldn't keep it from her."

Oliver took a step forward. He put his hand on Garnet's shoulder. "Garnet, my darling," he said, "believe me. This has nothing to do with you and me."

Garnet felt suddenly tired. Her head had begun to ache. She drew her shoulder out from under his hand. "Please," she said, "let me alone for a while." Turning around, she put her hand on the latch of the bedroom door. Behind her she heard Charles say,

"Oliver meant no harm, Garnet." As she pushed open the door Charles added dryly, "He never does."

Garnet turned around. "I suppose you didn't mean any harm either," she said to Charles, "when all you thought of was that this was a fine chance for Oliver to get his hands on that girl's property. I think you're cheats and cowards, both of you."

She went into the bedroom and shut the door and sat on the edge of the bed, holding her head in her hands. The bedroom was dark. There was a candle on the table, but she had no way to light it, and the darkness made the place seem even colder than the other room had been. Garnet tried to think, but she was so shocked and confused and angry that her mind felt as shaky as the earth of California. Her thoughts went around as though she had no control over them. Maybe Oliver was really in love with this girl Carmelita.

After all, Garnet said to herself, without meaning to say it, I practically asked him to marry me. Maybe he's sorry now that he took me.

Could that be true? she wondered. Yes, it could be. Maybe Oliver was sorry for his impulsive marriage in New York. That letter had sounded as if Carmelita's fortune was a very big one. If Carmelita was so rich, and if Oliver was in love with her, maybe he wished now that he could be free to marry her. Maybe he would like a divorce.

Garnet started. She had never seen anybody who had been divorced. She knew only that divorces were shameful and scandalous. Nice people spoke of such things in undertones, when they had to speak of them at all. But being divorced, she thought now, would be better than spending the rest of her life with a husband who did not want her.

But even that might not do any good. The California natives were all Catholics. Garnet knew Catholic priests would not marry divorced people. Still, she and Oliver had been married in New York by a Presbyterian minister. Possibly they were not so strict about Protestant marriages. She did not know. She felt as if she did not know anything. Her head ached and she felt nauseated and her thoughts were all mixed up. Nothing was very clear, except that she was in a strange country eight months' journey from home, and there was not a soul to tell her what to do.

She heard the door open, and started up as Oliver came in. He was carrying a lighted candle. The shadows leaped around the room as he set the candle on the table and shut the door behind him.

"Garnet," he said, "I want to talk to you. There's a lot about this that needs to be explained."

There was, but Garnet wanted one answer first. "Are you in love with her?" she asked abruptly.

"In love with her!" Oliver repeated. He stopped, staring at Garnet with amazement. The shadows threw his features into high relief as he took a step nearer. "You are the only girl I ever loved in my life," he said. "How many times do I have to tell you that?"

Garnet gave a baffled shake of her head. "But Carmelita," she said. "Weren't you in love with her?"

Oliver picked up both her hands and held them in his. His hands were warm around her cold fingers. "Garnet," he said, "as God is my witness, I never saw that girl in my life until two weeks before I left California last year. I never thought of her again. The whole episode was about as important as drinking a glass of wine."

Garnet had a sense of relief. At least it was good to know she was wanted. She asked, "You didn't know she was going to have a baby?"

"Good Lord, no!" he exclaimed. "I tell you, I had forgotten she ever existed."

"When did you think about her again?"

"When John brought me that letter in Santa Fe."

Garnet jerked her hands out of his and stood up. She walked away from him, toward the wall-bench. "Why didn't you tell me about her then?" she demanded. "What made you say no when I asked if John had brought you a letter?"

"Because I didn't want to trouble you," Oliver answered sincerely. "I thought you'd never find out. There was no reason to tell you."

"What did you plan to do about it?" she asked.

"I thought I'd come on here and tell Charles I'd make any possible amends, but I couldn't marry that little goose because—thank God—I was already married to you. Her father could get her another husband. She's rich enough to marry any man from here to Mexico City. I expected Charles to be mad with me, but I didn't expect him to go into the black rage he's been in ever since we got here."

"And then—?" she began, and paused questioningly.

"And then I thought I'd take you home, and you'd never know anything about it. Garnet, don't you understand? I didn't want you to be troubled by anything."

Garnet sat down on the wall-bench. The pain was thumping in her head. Oliver had not wanted her to be troubled. Oliver seemed to have the childish notion that as long as everything could be made to look all right, then everything really was all right.

"I'm surprised you came here at all," she said with a touch of bitterness. "You could have gone back to New York from Santa Fe. I was so trustful and simple-minded, you could have made up any sort of story to explain why we weren't going on to California, and I'd have believed you. Why didn't you go back?"

"Frankly, my dear," Oliver said quietly, "I couldn't afford it. Everything I owned was here. The only way to get it was to come for it. Besides, it didn't seem fair to Charles to turn around without warning him."

Garnet smiled grimly at the flickering shadows. "I like that answer. It's honest. Oh Oliver, don't ever lie to me again."

Oliver struck the table with his hand. The candle trembled and the shadows danced violently on the walls. "Maybe I should have told you. But—I don't suppose you'll ever know how much I want your good opinion." He came over to the wall-bench where she sat. For a moment he stood looking down at her earnestly, then he dropped on his knees before her and put both his arms around her waist. "Garnet," he said, "loving you is the only right and beautiful thing that ever happened to me. You looked up to me. You thought I was ten thousand times better than I was. You trusted me and believed in me. I never had anything like that before. You'll never know how I've loved you for it. Now in God's name, don't take it away from me."

Garnet put both her hands to her head. It was like the gesture she had seen Florinda make on the trail, as though she thought her head would split open if she did not hold it together. She felt like that now; the pain was like a hammer beating on her temples. As she looked down at Oliver's face, raised to hers with such a pleading worship, suddenly she was sorry for him, for she knew he was speaking the truth now, more vehemently than he had ever spoken it before. She had looked up to him. She had had him all mixed up in her mind with the great strong challenge of the trail. Through the pounding in her head she heard what her father had said to her. "I'm wondering if you're in love with Oliver, or in love with California. Would you marry him if he only wanted to move into the house next door?"

She had not known what her father was asking her. Now, all of a sudden, she knew.

She remembered so many things together—how willing Oliver had been in New Orleans and Santa Fe to take her everywhere she wanted to go, whether it was proper or not; how he had agreed with her idea for getting Florinda out of town in a widow's costume; how ready he had always been to do anything she wanted him to do. She remembered how he had pleased her father with his business acumen, how he had pleased her mother by his gallant manners, how he had pleased herself by making fun of the proprieties that irked her so; and how the traders had liked him because the minute he got among them he was one of them. She had seen all this, and it had not occurred to her until this minute that no man would have had such a power of pleasing so many different persons if he had had any character of his own. She began to understand that with all his physical courage, in his mind Oliver was only a pleasant echo of other people. He would agree with anybody he happened to be with—herself, or Charles, or John, or anybody else who would spare him the trouble of doing his own thinking.

But he loved her, and so he was begging her to think well of him, because now his opinion of himself was an echo of her opinion of him. Unless she respected him, or pretended to, he could not respect himself. Garnet felt a stab of fright.

Why did they let me do this? she thought. I wasn't of age. They could have said no!

But at once a hard little voice in her mind answered her. That's right, Garnet. Blame your mother and father. Blame the Czar of Russia and the King of Spain. Blame everybody on the face of the earth but yourself. You wanted to have your own way, didn't you? So you married a man who will let you have it as long as you live. Oliver loves you, and what he means by this is that he'll be anything you want him to be. All right, this is what you've got, and you'd better start right now to put up with it.

She looked down at him, running her hands over his light brown curls. "I love you very much, Oliver," she said. "I'm terribly shocked. But I love you, and I'll never go back on you as long as I live."

Oliver's arms tightened around her and he dropped his head into her lap. "God bless you, Garnet," he whispered. She stroked his hair, and felt the strength in the arms around her, and thought how strange it was that a man of such bodily power should be so much like a child.

"Now tell me about this," she said. "Tell me everything."

"All right," said Oliver. "I'll tell you everything."

He sat on the floor, one arm across her lap, and held her hand in his as he talked.

He told her Don Rafael Velasco was a man of noble name and great riches. He was now in his seventies. Carmelita was his only child. Don Rafael's first wife had been crippled by a fall soon after their marriage, and though she had lived twenty years after that, she had had no children. His second wife had died young, leaving him this one daughter.

Don Rafael was so delighted to have a child at last that he petted Carmelita into a spoiled little brat. Carmelita had a duenna, an elderly aunt who idled about after her for the sake of appearances. But the old lady was a stupid soul, dozing half the time. Pampered and pretty, Carmelita was bored to distraction in the big house where she had absolutely nothing to do.

Oliver had arranged to buy some mules from Don Rafael for his trip eastward last year. Just before the caravan was to meet in Los Angeles, Oliver went up to the rancho to get the mules.

"I can't tell you just how it came about," said Oliver, "except that I was a Yankee and the California girls find the Yankees very exciting. We're so different from the native men. I suppose Carmelita thought she was having a thrilling adventure, outwitting that old fool of a duenna and slipping out into the courtyard to meet me under the crescent moon, all that sort of thing. But I never once thought of her after I drove off with the mules. I was a simpleton, of course. I should have known that a rich ranchero's daughter couldn't be forgotten so lightly. But I did forget her. And by the time Don Rafael came over here in a shaking rage and told Charles that Carmelita was going to have a baby, I was a thousand miles away."

"And that's all?" said Garnet.

"That, my dearest, is absolutely all. Except that Charles thought it was a piece of heaven falling on the Hale family. With no brothers or sisters, Carmelita is one of the greatest heiresses in California. Charles told Don Rafael I had been planning to marry her, I had talked of nothing else—of course it had been rash of me to anticipate the wedding day, but that could be taken care of. With Don Rafael's influence, he could easily persuade a priest to marry us privately and say nothing about the ceremony's being late. Don Rafael took Carmelita up north to her aunt. I knew nothing about all this, until John handed me that letter in Santa Fe."

"How did John know about it?"

"Charles told him. Charles wanted John to tell the other traders I was married to Carmelita, so they would be used to the idea before they saw me in Santa Fe. John declined, as Charles should have known he would. John said he had no objection to bringing me a letter, but he would not discuss my affairs behind my back."

"What did he say when he gave you the letter?" asked Garnet.

"Nothing. Except 'Charles sent you this.' When I read it I was nearly dumb with astonishment. The first thing I thought of—the only thing, in fact—was you. I told John to keep his mouth shut. He said, 'I always do,' or words to that effect, and he never referred to the subject again." Oliver looked up at her. "Garnet, if you'll forgive me, and forget about it, I swear before God Almighty that you'll never, never have another minute's concern because of me."

Garnet drew a long tired breath. Her head was still pounding so hard that it had taken all her strength to listen to what he was saying. Oliver wanted her to forget about it. Well, even if she could forget it, Carmelita never could, nor Carmelita's heartbroken father. She did not know where the blame ought to lie. From what she was learning about Oliver, she felt pretty sure Carmelita had pitched herself at his head. Maybe Carmelita had wanted what she had so nearly obtained, marriage with an exciting young Yankee. But anyway, the damage was done, and she herself could not undo it, and she was so tired that she ached in every corner of her body. Reaching desperately for the only refuge she knew, she said,

"We are going home."

"Yes," Oliver answered. He gave a wry little smile, adding, "Charles has been begging me to stay."

"What!" she cried in alarm. "Stay here? For how long?"

"For good. Charles is very fond of me, you know. I'm all he's got."

"I won't stay here," said Garnet. "We never meant to stay any longer than this winter."

"Yes, dear, I know it. I told him so."

After a moment Garnet said slowly, "So that's what you and Charles have been talking about all this time. He wants you to stay here, I want you to take me home. You've been sort of pulled apart by the two of us."

"It has felt like that," he admitted.

"No wonder Charles hates me," she said. "But I should think, after all this muddle, he'd be glad to get rid of me. I should think he'd be glad to get rid of us both."

Oliver stood up. He walked over to the window and raised the sash. Garnet shivered at the rush of cold air, and Oliver closed the window, answering as he did so.

"Charles says there's no proof that I had anything to do with Carmelita's child. She said I did, but that was when I was a long way off and couldn't answer. It would be easy for me to say it wasn't so. And Charles says it's foolish for me to be a middle-class businessman in New York when I could be pretty nearly a king in California. He says the Yankees are going to take over the whole place before long."

"How does he know?" Garnet asked shortly.

Oliver laughed a little, as though glad to be talking about something besides himself. "The Republic of Texas wants to be a state of the Union. That will almost certainly mean war between Mexico and the United States. And if there is war, we'll probably wind up owning California."

"Fiddlesticks," said Garnet. She stood up too, and walked over to him. "I don't care who owns California and you don't either. Charles is just one of the people who'd rather die than find out they can't manage everything and everybody around them. You're going to take me home."

"Yes, Garnet, I'll take you home," said Oliver. But he sighed faintly as he said it, as though he were already tired of being pulled apart between her and Charles, and she realized how thin his promise was. Thin enough to break any time Charles could think of a really strong argument against it. Every day, until she and Oliver were safely on the trail, she would have to do battle with Charles. Garnet said,

"Remember, Oliver. You've promised."

"Yes, dear, I've promised. I'll go to Los Angeles with Charles and deed my share of the rancho to him, and you and I will go back to New York. Don't you trust me?"

Garnet rested her head on his shoulder. She was so tired, and she felt so ill, that it was good to lean on him. The pains in her head were like explosions, breaking afresh with every beat of her heart. "Oliver," she murmured, "I've got to lie down. I'm sick. Too much has happened tonight. I can't talk about it any more."

He was all sympathy. "Of course. You've had a lot to stand and it's all my fault. I'll help you get to bed."

He was very tender with her. He helped her undress, and drew the covers about her warmly. When he lay down by her he took her in his arms, telling her again how much he loved her, and promising over and over that he would never let her be troubled about anything again.

Oliver went to sleep, but Garnet lay awake for a long time. The pain in her head got easier with the quiet, but her emotions were all in a hodgepodge. She felt angry and disappointed and guilty and scared. She was tired of new places and new people and new experiences. She yearned for something warm and familiar. Remembering the boisterous vitality of the trail, she ached to go back to it. Those bare dark mountains east of her were like a prison wall, holding her here till next spring. Next spring. It seemed a thousand years away. At last she fell asleep.

She woke suddenly, roused by a noise. Before she was fully awake she knew it was a noise she had heard before, but not for a long time, and it was startling to hear it again. She raised her head.

Oliver was still asleep. Garnet listened for an instant, then she sat up straight and gasped with delight.

It was raining. After those miles on the hard stony mountains, after those months of dust and sun, here in the scorched dingy land of California it was raining.

She could hear the rain, a great steady storm beating on the roof and the wall and the ground outside. Garnet sprang up and ran barefooted to the window and pushed up the sash. She could smell the rain. There were a hundred fresh odors of wet earth and trees. She could taste the dampness on her lips, and feel the suddenly changed texture of her nightgown. Somewhere in the house a lamp was still burning, for there was a faint glow from a window and she could even see the rain. It was like twisting curtains in the dark.

Shivering in the cold wet air, Garnet held out her hands to feel the drops falling on them, while she tried to realize the amazing fact that it really did rain in California. Just beyond the window she could see that the rain had torn up the earth to make creeks and runnels, and they were all bubbly as they ran along. Though the storm had not wakened Oliver, here and there among the outbuildings she heard the voices of serving-people who had been roused by it, and they all seemed to be laughing. You did want to laugh with sheer joy when you were feeling the wonder of the first rain.

Garnet tried to remember how long it had been since these people had seen any rain. Probably not since April or May; Oliver had told her it seldom rained after May. And now it was November—no, it must be December by this time. She had had so much to think about that she had not kept track of the days.

She took a step back from the window. For a moment she stood quite still, biting the joint of her left forefinger while she tried to think. All of a sudden it had flashed upon her that the calendar, in relation to herself, was all wrong.

She noticed that she felt very cold. The sleeves of her nightgown were wet, and the cold air was making her breasts hurt as though they had been struck. She said in a low voice, "I'm going to have a baby."

The knowledge came to her as clearly and suddenly as the rain had come. She wondered why she had not known it before. She had always been so healthy. Headaches had never bothered her, or this strange nausea that she had felt several times of late. She had thought it was her conflict with Charles that had been making her feel so unwell.

Shivering, she crept back into bed and drew up the covers. In the darkness she could just make out Oliver's head on the pillow. Shall I wake him now, and tell him, she thought, or shall I wait till morning? I wonder if he'll be glad.

But she caught herself with a sudden fright.

I can't tell him, she said.

It was quite plain. She must not tell Oliver. She must not tell anybody. If Charles found out she was going to have a baby, he would take instant advantage of Oliver's tenderness for her. He would persuade Oliver that she could not stand the journey back across the desert. And next year, Charles would tell him a tiny baby could not stand the journey. And so on and on, and she would be stranded here the rest of her life. Garnet clenched her fists. She *was* going home. But she felt her clenched hands get damp when she thought of the journey, which had been hard enough when she was in her usual health. Oh my God, she thought with a sense of panic, why did this have to happen to me *now*?

She should not have let it happen, she thought frantically. There must be some way to keep it from happening. Florinda must know about such things. She should have asked Florinda. Oh, why hadn't she had sense enough to ask Florinda while she had a chance?

She wondered if keeping silent would be enough. How soon did it begin to change your shape so much that you could not deny it?

She did not know. But she did know that she was going to deny it as long as she possibly could. Her baby would be born—she counted quickly—next August. The caravan would be somewhere on the prairie, not yet as far east as Independence. The baby would be born in a covered wagon. She did not care. The mountains and the desert and the buffalo wallows would be trivial annoyances compared to having to live here and spend her life fighting against Oliver's dependence on Charles. Nobody, nobody, nobody was going to make her stay in California.

T W E N T Y · S I X

FLORINDA WAS WRITING a letter. She had been writing it for several days now and she was nearly finished.

The month was February, and the air had a cool crystal sheen. Outside, the hills were glittering with the green and gold of wild mustard that had sprung up during the winter rains. The only flowers Florinda had ever noticed were those that came in florists' boxes, but she was aware that California had turned out to be a much pleasanter place than she had thought it was when she got here. She glanced at herself in the mirror on the wall.

The mirror hung where she could see it whenever she raised her eyes. She could not write very long at a time, writing was too much trouble, and between sentences it was agreeable to look up and see herself. She smiled with pleasure at her reflection. The fatigue of the trail was gone now, and her skin was glossy with health. Florinda gave a mischievous wink at the glass. "Not bad," she told herself. "Not bad at all. You're all right, my girl. Good as new."

When she had signed her name, she picked up her letter and read it over.

Dear Garnet, I take my pen in hand to tell you that I am doing fine. I will write some every day and as soon as I meet a Yankee who is going by Hales Rancho I will ask him to take you my letter. Well now let me see. I had better start from the last time you saw me at Don Antonios.

Well the day you left I was feeling pretty bad. Texas had been very sweet to me but Texas had gone to sleep on the floor smelling like the rag in a bartenders belt. Then John came in. He looked as glum as usuall. He said you had asked him to take me to a place where I would be comfortable. I said, I am sorry to be such a new-sance. He said, Well we wont argue about it now. He picked up Texas by the sholders and pitched him outside. Then he brot in a nice Mexican girl. He said he had to go to Los Angielies but the girl would look after me till he could come back.

The girl was very kind and cheerfull. She brot me things to eat and I tryed to eat them. Sometimes I would even get up and walk around a little bit. After some days John came back. He said, short and crisp, Do you feel able to get up and ride. I said, I guess so. He said, well if you are ready lets go.

So I got up and put on some clothes and packed my things, and we started. John was riding a horse and he had another horse for me and some more horses to carry the packs and three boys to wait on us. You know how John is, for all he said to me I might have been a blanket strapped to the horse, but that was alright with me. I did not feel like talking anyway. We kept going for severall days. At night we slept on the ground rolled up in blankets like on the trail. But there was plenty of water and the boys cooked beef and beans.

Well at last we came to Los Angielies. And my dear, tired and dredful as I felt I could not help laughing at it.

Los Angielies is the funniest little village I ever saw. There is a creek about a yard wide and by the creek are some houses. They look like square boxes made out of mud. There are not any streets. I mean the houses do not sit in rows, they are just sprinkled around like if you took a pepper shaker and shook out the grains and they stayed where they happened to fall. There are hundreds and hundreds of dogs. The dogs do not belong to anybody, they just run wild. They came rushing and barking and leaping up around the horses and they scared me half to death.

The people were all outdoors. Some of the women looked busy, cooking at those outdoor ovens or washing clothes in the creek. But the men were just sitting in the sun with their backs against the houses and their hats over their eyes. There were a lot of children playing about and some tame Diggers. The Diggers did not have on any clothes except a rag around the middle, and they had wooden yokes across their backs with a jar of water at each end. It seems they dip up the water from the creek and go about selling it.

There were some ox-carts and a lot of horses and they were all mixed up with the people and the dogs. It made hard riding becaus there are not any sidewalks and everrything is out among the houses together. And pretty soon we were all scratching becaus the dogs have fleas and as you know dear fleas are very acrobatick.

Well finaly we came to a bilding which John said was the store of Mr. Abbott. It is made of adoby like the rest of them but it has two stories and a wooden porch all around it. There was a pile of hides in a corner of the porch and oh my Lord did they stink. We went inside and there was a big counter and shelves full of things and people in there buying them. Behind the counter sat Mr. Abbott. He is a great big fat man with a shiny bald head and a little fringe of white hair around the back of it, and he has blue eyes and a jolly pink face. I stood leaning against the wall. I was too tired and miserable even to stand up strait and the fleas were hopping all over me.

John talked to Mr. Abbott and told him I was sick. Mr. Abbott was very nice. He said I could sleep that night in the loft over his store. He told a clerk to show me how to get upstairs. I climbed up a wooden staircase nearly as steep as a ladder, and then I went into a room and it had a bed. The bed had a hide instead of a mattress, and blankets on it. Some girls came up and they brot my pack and also jugs of water. So I washed off the fleas, and I lay down and slept all night.

The next morning we started riding again. We kept on riding for three or four days more. The country was all dead and dried up and dusty, and I kept on being dizzy and sick. John took care of me the best he could. I thanked him but as usuall he did not seem to care whether I said anything or not. He just made me keep going.

At last we got to a rancho. John said this rancho belonged to a Yankee whose name was Mr. Kerridge. He said Mr. Kerridge had been living in Calafornia for a long time and he was married to a native lady.

I was wondering what they would say when they saw me. I certainly did not look very fassinating. I was thin and scrawny and covered with dust and I was so tired I could hardly hold up my head.

I sort of stumbled off the horse and John took my arm and we went indoors. We went into a parlor with rugs on the floor and pretty calico curtains all around the walls.

Mr. Kerridge came right in. He was a tall lean man with gray hair and very ellegant Mexican clothes. He began saying polite things like Well well John, to what do we owe the honor of this visit. But John got right down to bisness. He told Mr. Kerridge he had brot him an American woman who had practicaly died on the desert and would Mr. Kerridge take care of her for awhile.

Mr. Kerridge told me to sit down on the wall-bench and I sat there drooping. He clapped his hands and a lot of servants came running in and they brot wine and chockolate. While the servants were clattering around I saw John spring to his feet and bow low. My eyes went after him and then I really started looking. John was kissing the hand of a lady. She was the lady of the house. Mrs. Kerridge.

Garnet my dear, her name was Donya Manuela and she wayed about three hundred pounds. She was the fattest lady I ever saw. She looked like a lot of pillows tied together. She was so fat you could hardly see her face. She had black eyes kind of bedded in the fat and a little round nose. Her face looked like a big potato with a little potato stuck on it. Her clothes were red and yellow and purple, swaying with fringe and jingling with beads and bracelets. I never saw anybody wear so many different things at the same time. When she moved she shook and trembled all over and the beads and bracelets sang a tune.

Well this remarkable specktacle had waddled in, and John was bending from the waist to kiss her hand. John and her husband spoke to her in Spannish and she looked at me. She was naturaly kind of astonished to see such a skinny dusty thing in her nice clean parlor. But after a minute she smiled at me and oh she did look so sweet and fat and kind.

They brot a big chair for her and she settled into it with much singing of bracelets and shaking of fringe and bobbling of fat. John picked up her fan and handed it to a servant girl. The girl stood there fanning her and Mr. Kerridge poured some wine for her and gave her some cakes. Then John began telling his story. He spoke in English first to Mr. Kerridge and they both translated to Donya Manuela. Of course Mr. Kerridge speaks Spannish but I could tell John was saying everrything in English first so I could understand the yarn he was spinning.

He told them I was a married lady who had started from the United States to Calafornia with my husband. But then he said we had some Digger trouble and my husband got killed in the fight. And now here I was, poor thing, worn out from the desert and dying of a broken heart. So he had brot me here hoping they would let me stay with them till I had got my strength back and mended my broken heart a little. I began to think, oh dear now I have started that widow bisness again, will I never get over that. But I did not care what he told them if only they would let me lie down somewhere and rest.

John talked very seriously but every now and then he gave me a glance out of the corner of his eye to make sure I was keeping up with what he said. Mr. Kerridge listened seriously too, but he glanced at me once in awhile and I do not think he beleived one single word of it. But then they translated to Donya Manuela, and she beleived it all. That dear lady, she kept shaking her head and making sweet little sounds of sympathy. I could not understand the things she was saying but I knew by her voice that they were sweet things.

And then she got up with a great pushing and heaving, and toddled over to sit on the bench by me. She put her big fat arms around me and took me on her lap and put my head down on her bosm just like I was a baby. It was like sinking away down into a soft warm featherbed. I was so tired I just sank. She stroked me and patted me and said soft little things to me, and oh I was so tired and she was so sweet, and I put my arms around her neck and kissed her.

Then Mr. Kerridge came over and he looked like he was about to burst out laughing. I said to him, I am sorry to be so much trouble to you. And he said, Oh do not think of that, my wife loves nothing so much as fussing over babies and she has not had a baby in four years. So now she will make a baby out of you.

Then Donya Manuela gave me a great big hug and she said something in Spannish to him and he helped me get off her lap, and they both began clapping their hands at a great rate. More servants came running in and also a great swarm of children of all ages, dancing around and pointing at me and asking questions. Donya Manuela gave one of the children a slap on the side of his jaw, and with her other hand she slapped a servant girl, all this time yelling orders in a voice fit to split the ceiling. They all started running around and falling over each other, doing useless things in a great hurry the way people do when the house is on fire, and Donya Manuela kept storming around the room in a frenzy, shouting orders, and anybody who got in her way got slapped. John and Mr. Kerridge fell back meekly and I stood still and listened to all this slapping and shouting and I hoped they knew what was going on becaus I certainly did not.

But evidently they got the idea. The next thing I knew they were hustling me down a long row of rooms and then I was in a bedroom and the girls had put me on the bed. Donya Manuela was taking off my clothes and shouting, and the girls were bringing her cakes and wine, and she was sipping and nibbling between shouts.

My dear, from the minute that woman got her hands on me I was perfectly and absolutely helpless. She took off my clothes and rolled me into the bed and covered me up and put pillows under me and fed me something with a spoon. She acted like I was about three months old. I beleive she really thought I was. I do not think she would have been surprised if I had wet my pants. Only by this time I did not have on any pants. I was stark naked and she was rubbing me all over with some kind of nice-smelling oil, talking all the time. I could not understand what she said, but I could tell she was pointing out to the girls how thin I was and showing them how my bones stuck out and scolding them like it was all their fault. Then she started feeding me some more. Finaly she put a nice soft robe on me and covered me up again.

And oh my dear, how I loved it. I was so tired setting my jaw and wondering if I could hold out one more day. I lay back limp as a rag doll and let her do anything she pleased. She fussed and waddled and jingled and shook, and some more girls came in with a bowl of meat broth.

I was about to bust already with so much food but she shoved more spoonfuls into me all the same. Just when I thought I was going to die of overfeeding, there was a noise at the door and questions in men's voices, and in came two beautiful young Calafornio men, wanting to have a look at the Yankee lady. Donya Manuela leaped and charged at them like a bull and slapped their faces till I thought their brains would rattle. They were her sons and though I was all muffled up in this robe she had put on me, she was raising cain with them for their lack of respect in daring to poke their heads in and try to see a lady in her bed. And my dear, those two grown men took the slaps and the scolding, and they appologized and got out, and Donya Manuela sat by me and stroked my forehead, just as soft and sweet as an angel. And I could not stand any more. I turned over and started to laugh.

So Donya Manuela ate some more cakes and drank some more wine, and she patted me and cuddled me till I went to sleep. I slept for hours and hours. When I woke up I felt ever so much better. Everything was soft and warm and lovely and I knew she was going to take care of me and oh I did love her so. It was morning but she had made the room dark. And there on a table by my bed was a snack consisting of a chunk of beef and a loaf of bread and two oranges and a bunch of grapes and a bowl of beans, just in case I felt the need of a little something to bild up my strength before breckfast.

Well Garnet, that was the beginning of the most remarkable period of my life. I never saw anything like this household.

Mr. Kerridge is tall and gray and dignified, but he has a kind of wicked humor sometimes when he looks at me. He married Donya Manuela when she was about fifteen and after that she had babies as fast as she could, and now she is not sorry about anything except that she is not having babies any more. Their house is always full of people. Everybody who travels anywhere near here stops for a night or mabie for longer. So there are all these visitors and the servants and these quantities of children, and they clatter around all day long and Donya Manuela bosses the whole concern. Mr. Kerridge calmly tends to his rancho while Donya Manuela goes rolling about the house like a bubble, banging her children around and shouting orders, and God help anybody who does not move fast enough. And then some child falls down and hurts his knee and she is all soft and sweet and gentle, cuddling him up and kissing the place to make it well, and then some other child comes in with his clothes muddy and she is up again slapping him for going out when she told him not to, and he says his big brother was only showing him a colt and she slaps his big brother and the racket starts all over again.

She has dozens of cooks and the food in this place is wonderful, I never saw so much or anything so good. Donya Manuela eats all day long and she figures anybody who is not constantly hungry must be sick.

Well you see, she knew I was sick. So she fed me and kissed me and sang me lullibies and then fed me some more. It was the first time anybody had ever treated me like a baby and I did not know how nice it was. But really I could not eat all the food she gave me.

I tryed my best becaus she was so sweet and also becaus I was afraid if I did not eat it like she told me I would get slapped. But she did not slap me when I could not eat any more, she just looked wor- reyed and scolded the girls becaus the food was not good enough and chased them off to cook something else that would tempt my failing appetite.

So pretty soon I felt fine. One day when she was not there I got out of bed and took off my nightie and looked at myself in the mirror and really Garnet I was just beautiful. You could not see my bones any more and the curves were all back in the right places and my hair was shiny and my skin was smooth. I wanted to stay up becaus I was afraid if I did not start moving around I would get even fatter from all that food Donya Manuela was giving me. And besides I wanted to see some people and be sociable. But Donya Manuela would not let me come into the parlor until I had some black dresses. She was very simpathetic and she said of course she understood that I must meet some gents so I could get myself a husband, but for a while I must wear black becaus I was a widow.

Well darling I had forgotten all about being a widow again. But she gathered some girls together and they started sewing me some things so I could go into mourning. Mr. Kerridge came in and saw me standing up meekly in the middle of the room being fitted with yards of dismal black stuff, and he caught my eye and I giggled, I could not help it, and he giggled back at me. Honestly Garnet that man is just as wonderful as his wife is, only in a different way.

So now I am all dressed up in black but I must say I look quite ravishing in it. Donya Manuela lets me come out and meet all the visitors that drop in, and she tells them a long sad story and looks around to see if I am impressing any of the gents enough to have him look like a follower of my late lamented.

Well dear writing this letter has taken me quite a long time. Mr. Kerridge has been cutting my pens for me. I never did much writing and I do not know how to make a feather into a pen. He does the cutting becaus Donya Manuela can do practically every- thing else but she never learned to read or write. Every now and then she and her family come in and watch me respectfully, quite impressed that I should have so much learning.

Well now it is another day and I have something else to tell you. I have had a great piece of luck.

I had been wondering what I was going to do now. Donya

Manuela has planned that I will get a husband soon but between you and me Garnet you know I am not the domestick type. And then day before yesterday who should turn up among the visitors but some Americans.

And my dear among them was John and also the Handsome Brute, and also of all people Silky Van Dorn. Oh I was so glad to see them. John is buying cattle for his rancho. He has got some from Mr. Kerridge and he says he is going down to Hales in a few days to get some more and he will take this letter to you. John told me he has named his rancho for the yellow poppies. I cannot spell the words becaus they are Spannish but it sounds like a lovely name. The Handsome Brute is handsomer than ever and he has fine clothes, how he does love to dress up, and he is so sweet and innocent, my dear I do like him.

But this is the great news. Silky was so surprised to see how I looked, he had got used to seeing me all tired and bony the way I was on the trail. He regarded me with great interest and twirled his mustash and bowed, very grand, and walked off to think and then he came back and told me what he had been thinking about.

Silky has quit the trail. It is such hard work and he has saved up a nice piece of capital so he can leave off. He has opened a gambling house and saloon in Los Angielies and he wants me to come down and work with him. He says I can serve drinks and sing for the customers. So I told him I thought it was a great idea, and I was ready to start working right away.

It will all be strictly bisness. So any time you come to Los Angielies, ask anybody for Silky's Place and I will be there.

Well I must stop writing now becaus John is leaving in the morning and I must give him this letter tonight. I do hope you are happy dearest and you will never know how greatfull I am for all you have done for me and I love you very much.

Your true frend,
Florinda Grove.

TWENTY-SEVEN

THE GOLDEN LIGHT swept over the mountains and filled the valley where Charles Hale's rancho lay. The sun was hot, but as soon as you reached the shade you felt cold. The air had a tingle; it was like the heat of sun and the sting of snowflakes together.

Garnet sat on the grass by an orange tree and leaned back on her hands. The light gave a glory even to the stiff lines of Charles' rancho. The orange trees were lacy with blossoms, and the fragrance of them was rich in the air. On the slopes the wild flowers grew in beds of blue and gold, and the distant peaks were white points of snow against the sky. It was so beautiful that she hurt with a pleasure almost like pain.

She heard the sound of horses' hoofs, and looking around she saw John. He had arrived at the rancho a week ago, bringing Florinda's letter. John sprang off his horse, tossing the bridle to the boy who had been riding with him. He stood looking out toward the mountains as though he too felt the pain of too much pleasure, and she wondered if he had ever looked at a woman as he was looking now at the wonder of the earth.

Then he saw her, and smiled as he said, "Good morning."

"Good morning," said Garnet. She added, "Where were you at breakfast time?"

"I rode out early to see some calves."

Garnet looked up at his green eyes and his cool aristocratic face. John was her friend; he had never said so, but she felt that he was. She had been so lonely during these past months, hiding the secret of her pregnancy with a frightened silence. She was glad he was here.

"John," she said, "I owe you an apology."

"Yes? For what?" John asked as he sat on the grass by her.

Garnet gestured toward the flowering hills. "You told me California was like this. And then when I got here last fall, I was dreadfully disappointed. I thought you had made it up."

John gathered a handful of the young wild oats and broke off the tops. "That was my fault. I always think of California like this, in the big spring. But if you were going to stay here," he went on, "in a year or two you'd find a surprising beauty about the dry season. It's such a foreign sort of beauty that we don't see it right away."

Well, she never would see it, Garnet thought, and she did not want to. In another month she would be on her way back to New York. Glancing at the yellow poppies blooming among the oats, she said,

"In Florinda's letter she said you had named your rancho for the poppies."

He nodded. "The Californios call the poppy the flor torosa, the sturdy flower. So I called my place El Rancho de la Flor Torosa. For short, Torosa."

There was a moment of silence. John looked away from her, toward the mountains.

"Where did you learn to love flowers so?" she asked. "I always liked them, but I never knew much about them."

"You grew up among bricks and stones," said John. "I lived on a plantation."

"But you notice everything," said Garnet. "The rocks and trees and mountains as well as the flowers. So many people don't see the earth at all."

John looked down. He pulled off another handful of the wild oats. "I had a rather lonely childhood," he said. "The earth was my friend. The growing things that changed every day, the rocks that never changed at all—I could count on them." He paused, and went on. "You can always count on the things of the earth. You know what to expect of them. Sometimes they are cruel, but it's a hard clean cruelty. They don't torture you with their own weakness."

Garnet felt her hand, like his, closing on the grass. John had not looked up at her as he spoke. She wondered if he had been thinking of Oliver with that last sentence. She asked,

"Is that why you don't like people? Because they torture you with their own weakness?"

"Yes," said John. "You can't count on people." He glanced up, and the corner of his mouth flickered with a grim little smile as he added, "I proved that to you, didn't I?"

"I don't understand you."

"I should have told you the truth about Carmelita Velasco," said John.

It was the first time he had ever spoken to her about Carmelita. But now that he had been a week on the rancho, of course he knew that she knew the story. Oliver had probably told him how the earthquake had shown her the letter. Oliver had not said so to her. Oliver did not tell her much about anything any more. He was keeping his promise to take her home, and had bought mules for the journey. But he had grown more and more silent under these months of Charles' cold resentful displeasure.

"I don't blame you for not telling me," Garnet answered. "It wasn't any of your business."

"No," said John. "It was not. But I am sorry you had to discover it in what must have been a shocking fashion."

Garnet picked up an orange blossom that had fallen on the ground, and crushed it in her hand. The petals were white and waxy. She felt guilty about Carmelita. She did not know why, but she did. Still looking down at the broken petals, she said in a low voice,

"I think I should have been angry if you had told me. I should have thought you were meddling in something that did not concern you."

"It did not concern me," said John, "and it still does not. But something else has happened," he went on steadily, "and I think you should know it, and I am going to tell you."

She started, and turned toward him. John had linked his hands around his knees. She noticed that his hands were long and slender. The skin was burned dark brown, and the hands looked very strong.

"I am going to tell you this now, myself," said John. He did not add "because Oliver won't," but she added it in her mind, and she was sure he was adding it in his. He went on. "If you resent my speaking, you have a right to say so. Carmelita is dead."

Garnet dropped the blossom. She felt half sick with guilt. "But I thought—she was quite well," she faltered.

"She was quite well," said John. "She was living up north with her aunt. She went riding, with her baby on her arm. She rode over a cliff. They are both dead."

Garnet put her fist to her lips. "Oh, John," she said from behind it, "do you mean—she did it on purpose? Because—because Oliver—is married to me?"

John answered as quietly as if he had been discussing the weather. "It would seem so. Of course, it might have been an accident. But California girls do not often have riding accidents. They learn to ride as soon as they learn to walk."

Garnet had shut her eyes and covered them with her hands. Tears slipped out between her fingers. "I'm sorry to be crying," she murmured. "I—I seem to cry so easily these days." She caught herself. She did cry more easily now, but she must not let John suspect there was any physical reason why she did. She wished she could put her head on a friendly shoulder and cry and cry. Everything was so tangled up. She did not know what emotions she ought to feel; all she did feel was confusion and a great loneliness.

John put a big red handkerchief into her hand. "I am not going to insult you by offering you pity, Garnet," he said. "You're too good for that. But I am sorry you have been caught in a situation you did not deserve."

She dried her tears. His voice was so steady and his words so direct that he calmed her spirit. Crumpling the red handkerchief in her lap, she raised her eyes to meet his. To her surprise she found that she could speak steadily too.

"When did you hear about this?" she asked.

"On the way down from Kerridge's. I stopped at Don Rafael's to ask for water. It's the most usual sort of request. Ordinarily any traveler can get food or water at any rancho he passes. Don Rafael's men let me water my horses at a creek, but they told me to leave at once and ride fast. Don Rafael has given orders that no American ever come on his land again. The men said he was half out of his mind. She was his only child."

Garnet folded the red handkerchief and creased it with her thumbnail. "Did you tell Oliver about this?" she asked after a while.

"Yes, I told him."

She bit her lip hard and gave her head a shake, as though that would shake her thoughts into place. "Oh John," she exclaimed, "what can I do?"

"Nothing but what you are doing, Garnet. Get Oliver away from here. He's very fond of you, and he never meant any harm to anybody in his life. But he has always taken orders from Charles. Once away from Charles, he'll make you a good husband."

John stood up. She thought she had never seen a man who gave her such a feeling of quiet strength. He said,

"Now I shall never refer to this matter again unless you tell me you want to talk about it. That's all." He gave her a brief smile as he turned away. "I have a great deal of respect for you, Garnet," he added.

He went toward the house. Garnet sat still. She bit the red handkerchief savagely, wondering how much more she could stand. Carmelita and her baby were dead, and poor old Don Rafael was half insane with grief. And she herself was going to have a baby, and she could not talk about it. Sometimes she felt so strange, and she could not ask if this was the way she ought to feel or if there was something wrong with her.

But she was going home. Oliver had deeded his share of the

rancho to Charles, and had spent a good part of the winter riding here and there to buy mules and supplies and merchandise. A few weeks more, and they would be on the trail. She would be on her way back to her mother and father, and all the strong dependable things of home.

She wondered if Oliver would tell her about Carmelita's death. No, he would not. He would think it would be easier on her not to know. What he would mean was that it would be easier on him if she did not know.

Garnet lifted her head and looked around at the blooming orange trees and the white peaks and the masses of flowers under the snowline. She understood why John loved the earth. The rocks and mountains did not fail you because they could not; even the desert was cruel by its own honest laws. The desert did not promise you roses and waterfalls and then give you rocks and sand. Only people did this. Only people like Oliver.

John was not like that. John reminded her of the desert: he offered nothing, but then suddenly he was like a rock guarding a spring. And the water was so much more precious than all the rivers of home, because when you found it you needed it so.

Oliver was tender and kind, as he always was, but as she had foreseen, he said nothing to her about Carmelita. As for Charles, he never spoke to her if he could help it. She was used to this by now. She kept to herself as much as she could. She went outdoors and walked among the flowers, or she spread her shawl on the grass and lay there, watching the changing lights on the mountains.

John came out sometimes and walked around the rancho with her. He never said anything about her personal affairs. But he showed her the plants: the little white creosote flowers, the wild nicotine with blooms like tiny trumpets of old gold, the deadly datura, from which the Diggers made a drug that drove them into frenzy and sometimes killed them. The datura was not blooming yet, but she would notice it later, he said, because it was so beautiful, great lavender flowers like morning-glories trailing over the ground. "Do you like new things to eat?" he asked her one morning, and when she said yes, he showed her how to cut the shoots of the young anise. The shoots were like little green ostrich plumes. John and Garnet brought the anise to one of the cooking-fires outdoors, and John asked the girl to give them a pot. They simmered the anise in hot water and ate it with sliced hard-boiled eggs. It had an odd taste, like licorice.

Garnet had not had much appetite. It was hard to eat with Charles' baleful eyes upon her, and Oliver's forced gaiety, and the long periods of silence. But she sat on the ground with John and ate all the anise and hard-boiled eggs, and scraped the dish.

"It's delicious," she exclaimed to him. "Why don't we use it at table?"

There was a glint of humor in John's green eyes. "I don't think," he answered, "that Charles would care to eat weeds. But since you like them, tomorrow we'll cut some of the wild mustard. It's very good."

He left her then. Garnet looked after him wistfully. She wished he were going back over the trail this year.

She gathered a handful of poppies and brought them to her room. When she had arranged them in a bowl she stood by the window, looking at the neat rancho buildings and the wild background of the mountains. The rancho was very busy. It was nearly time for dinner. After eating that big dish of anise, she didn't think she would want any dinner. It would be a good excuse for staying in her room.

Suddenly she heard a great commotion from around the other side of the house. The pass that led to the rancho was in front, where she could not see it from her window. She heard a stamping of horses, and a loud confusion of men's voices and the scream of a girl.

Garnet ran out, along the passage to the front door. Just in front of the door she stopped, pressing back against the house in fright.

Everybody had run outside. She saw Charles and Oliver and John, and a great crowd of the rancho people, and a lot of horses. Down from the pass several horsemen were rushing toward the house. They were riding furiously, and they all had guns, and there was something strange about them; for an instant she did not know what it was, and then she realized that instead of bright red and blue garments they all wore black. At their head was an old man. He wore no hat, and his white hair was streaming back from his swarthy forehead.

The old man had caught sight of Oliver. He turned his horse fiercely, holding the bridle with his left hand and his gun in his right. Garnet heard shouts, and another girl was screaming or maybe there were several of them. A serving-man began to pray aloud, and another man dropped on his knees and crossed himself. Children yelled as they ran out of the way of the rushing horses. Neither Charles nor Oliver was armed, nor John either, but John ran toward the white-haired man, calling to him. His words were Spanish, and Garnet was too terrified to try to understand them. Oliver had run forward too, though Charles had tried to hold him back.

The white-haired rider did not stop. Garnet saw his face, and it was a face terrible with grief and fury, and she knew he was Don Rafael. Nobody needed to tell her what he had come for. She felt sweat pouring out of her body. It all happened in a few seconds, but they were seconds stretched long and slow, so that although the horses were galloping she could see them pick up their hoofs and set them down again, very clearly, and it seemed to take a long time. Don Rafael lifted his gun. He shouted something to Oliver, and though she could not understand the words she knew they were terrible words. The gun cracked, and another gun cracked, and another, and the shots echoed against the hillsides. Oliver crumpled up in a slow horrible way, as she had seen Diggers crumple up at the Archillette.

Garnet heard a choking cry. She did not know she had given it until she found that she was running, stumbling over her skirts and over the tussocks of grass, and pushing the rancho people out of her way. The horsemen were galloping off as fast as they had come. Garnet ran to where Oliver lay in a dreadful huddle, and dropping on her knees she turned his body over. It had a horrid limpness in her hands. She saw a great red gash in his throat, and a red tear down his shirt, and streaks of blood. The blood was wet and warm as it covered her hands.

Her hands were wet and her fingers were dripping thickly. There was blood on her sleeves and blood down the front of her dress. She saw his face. She had seen dead men at the Archillette. Nobody needed to tell her this either.

This too had seemed to take a long time, though she had reached him only a second before the others. She felt a furious hand on her shoulder, grabbing her and flinging her back from Oliver, and as she looked up she saw Charles. He threw her away from him, to the ground.

As she struggled up to her knees she saw the huddle of scared screaming servants around her, and again she saw Charles. His strength had gone out of him. He had dropped across Oliver's body, and he lay there sobbing like a child.

Garnet felt a fierce heaving in the middle of herself. The people and the houses and the mountains began to swing around her. She found that she was running again, stumbling dizzily over the grass as she tried to get to her room so she could be away from all of them. She reached a corner of the house. The corner struck her as though it had come to meet her. The blow knocked her down to her knees and brought a rush of nausea so violent that she felt as if she were being torn to pieces.

At last, exhausted, she lay limply on the grass and could not get up. The landscape was a shimmering blur. She felt a wave of heat as though she had stepped into a kitchen with a roaring fire, then the heat was swept away by another wave of cold nausea. She doubled up and began to retch again.

"I can't stand any more," she thought desperately when the nausea had spent itself. "I can't stand any more."

But even then she knew there was a great deal more that she would have to stand. She was going to have a child, and Oliver was dead, and there was nobody to take her home. She had nowhere to live except in this hateful house with Charles.

She heard a lot of commotion—stamping horses, barking dogs, shrill shocked voices of men and women—but she heard it only as a jingling of sounds without sense. At length she tried again to stand up. But she was so giddy that the world spun around her. She dropped to the ground again, limp as an empty bag, and lay with her cheek on the grass while the ground teetered under her like a seesaw.

She did not know how long she lay there, gagging helplessly as the nausea kept surging through her, but at last she felt a hand on her arm. A voice close to her said, "Garnet! Garnet, can you hear me?"

Garnet could not answer for the squeezing in her throat, but she moved her eyes and saw John. He put his arm under her and picked her up and carried her into the house.

She had left the door of her room ajar when she ran out. Kicking the door open, John carried her in and laid her on the bed. This was all she knew. Everything turned black and silent.

TWENTY-EIGHT

SILKY'S PLACE SHONE through the rainy night. The rain fell into Los Angeles like big swinging ropes of water; the ropes lashed at the little square houses and made lakes of mud on the ground.

Most of the houses were dark, but at Silky's Place light streamed between the shutters. Two lanterns creaked from the roof of the porch, and two more shone over the front door. From inside, above the noise of the rain, sounded voices and the clink of money and the rattle of cups and bottles. On rainy nights Los Angeles was a gloomy town, and Silky's Place made a bright dry refuge.

It was a large building for Los Angeles, two stories high. The walls were made of adobe, but around all four sides there was a wooden porch with a roof one story high. Downstairs there were two rooms in front and two in back. In one of the front rooms was the bar, in the other the gambling tables. The two back rooms were a kitchen and a storeroom. In a little hall to the side of the kitchen was a steep staircase of unplaned boards. This led up to the loft, where there were bedrooms and more storerooms for the liquor supplies. The upstairs rooms were dark now, but the rooms downstairs were as bright as the hanging lamps could make them.

In the gambling room, Silky was in charge. He had two dealers, sleek young men from the Mexican port of Mazatlán. Silky walked about grandly, dressed and waxed with an elegance that did not lessen the warning look of the gun he wore at his belt. Silky's Place was orderly. Silky kept it that way.

In the saloon, Florinda was tending bar, assisted by a Mexican youth named José and a Chinese boy who washed the cups. The Chinese boy had a name, but as Florinda did not like it she called him Mickey. Mickey had a long queue dangling from the crown of his head. He wore a red Mexican jacket, gray trousers discarded by some Yankee, and a pair of soft felt house-slippers that he had bought at Mr. Abbott's store. Mickey worked deftly and usually in silence, but he understood Spanish very well and he was also picking up a good deal of English. He and Florinda were very good friends.

The bar was solidly built. Facing the door, it reached all the way across the room from wall to wall. To get from the back of the bar to the front of it, you had to go through two side doors, one behind and one in front of the bar; and the door in front of the bar was usually locked. Silky took no chance of anybody's getting to the liquor-shelves.

Florinda was wearing a dress of brown wool with yellow ribbons, and fingerless mitts of brown silk. She looked very charming, and she was very gay as she served her customers, but she also had a gun ready for use. Her gun was a Colt revolver that a Yankee trader had lost in the gambling room. Colts were so rare in California as to be almost priceless. Every now and then, when some of the boys bragged about their guns, Florinda smiled sweetly and asked them if they had noticed her Colt. "Wonderful invention," she said, stroking the Colt affectionately. "Fires five times without reloading. Practically impossible to get out here."

The boys knew that very well. The saloon was orderly too.

There were sixteen customers at the bar, ten of them Californios sipping the native wine, the rest Yankees drinking whiskey. Whiskey was hard to get in California, and expensive. Silky brought it from Yankee clippers, and from the occasional British ships that stopped at San Diego on their way to China.

The door opened, and two Yankees came in, shaking raindrops from their clothes. They were traders who had come with the train from Santa Fe last summer and were planning to start back with the spring caravan. Florinda met them as they came up to the bar. "What'll it be, gents?"

She had a bottle of American whiskey in her hand. They nodded and Mickey set two cups on the bar. "Nice weather we're having," Florinda remarked as she poured the drinks.

One of the traders, the one who was called Devilbug, said in a few well-chosen words what he thought of the weather. Florinda laughed at his language reproachfully.

"Why don't you save that for the trail, Devilbug? You might need it."

"If this keeps up we'll never get on the trail. Can't bring the mules down in this flood."

"It won't last long. Gent in here this afternoon said it had stopped raining above the Santa Susana Mountains. Anyway, it'll give you lots of grass."

"Grass no good if we can't get started," said Devilbug's companion. He was a tall blond fellow who was called Ticktock because of a large and noisy watch in which he took great pride. He fondled the watch as he added, "Still, though, it'll be a help if it's raining on the Mojave. Heard anybody say?"

"Fellow in here a couple of days ago said the cactus was blooming. That means rain, doesn't it? Imagine cactus blooming." Florinda gave a shrug that showed what she thought of the cactus.

Devilbug laughed. "You're not going to make the spring trip to see it?"

"Not me. I'm doing fine."

"Don't see your best customer," remarked Ticktock. "Texas. Where's he?"

"He's been here every day for a week. Silky and one of the boys sort of assisted him out this afternoon."

"Sozzled?"

"Utterly."

"He'll never start," said Ticktock, "if he doesn't sober up soon."

"Tie him on a mule," said Florinda. "He'll be all right." She turned to greet two sailors who had just leaned their elbows on the bar. "What'll it be, gents?"

One of the sailors pushed a coin toward her. "How much do I get for this?"

Florinda picked up the coin, rang it on the counter, and looked at it carefully. It was a French two-franc piece. "Thirty-six cents," she said.

"I mean, how much in whiskey?"

Glancing at the bottle, she made a mark on it with her thumb. "Down to there."

"That all? Damn cheat, this place."

"This liquor came around the Horn, boy. You know what a long way that is." She gave the two of them a friendly smile. "This your first time in California?"

"Yes, why?"

"Ever try aguardiente?"

"What's that?"

She took another bottle from the shelf. "Agua, water; ardiente, fiery. In short, firewater. Costs only one-tenth as much as the American stuff and gets you drunk twice as fast."

The two sailors grinned at each other and agreed to try it. "How much firewater do we get for that French money?"

"Want it all at once?"

"Sure, why not?"

Florinda took two larger cups from the shelf and filled them both. "There it is."

The sailors tasted the aguardiente and whistled. "Not bad."

"No, very good." She smiled at them brilliantly. Florinda tried to save the whiskey for the traders, who were her steady customers. She dropped the French coin into a box with a slit cover, which stood safely on a shelf behind the bar, and turned to greet a young Californio who had just come in. "¿Vino rojo? Sí, señor, pronto."

As she gave him his wine, the two sailors leaned over the bar. "What's your name, miss?"

"Florinda."

"How'd you get away out here?"

"Santa Claus brought me." Another man tapped his cup on the bar, and she went to wait on him. A moment later the sailors called her again.

"How much do we get for this?" one of them asked, handing her a Peruvian dollar.

"It's worth a hundred cents. Want it in aguardiente?"

"Sure, that's good stuff. Just keep pouring till you use up the dollar."

Florinda laughed and set the bottle on the bar. "For a dollar," she said, "you can pour it yourself." She turned to wait on several men who had come in from the gambling room. Silky, who had followed them, beckoned to her when she had poured their drinks. "How's it going?" he asked in an undertone.

"Fine."

"No trouble?"

"Not a bit. Those two brave mariners are putting down aguardiente like it was milk, but they're all right so far."

"Texas hasn't been in again, has he?"

"I don't imagine he can walk this far. But Texas never makes trouble, Silky."

"Well, let me know if you need any help," said Silky. He slipped back into the other room. The sailors were tapping again. "No, no," they protested when José approached them. "We want the lady. Nice Yankee lady. Miss Florinda, you come over here."

"Yes, gents, I'll be right there. Just getting a cloth to wipe up that splash of liquor."

The sailors felt fine. As she wiped up the splash on the bar they looked her over with hazy adoration and one of them mumbled in her ear. Smiling, Florinda shook her head.

"Sorry, fellow. Six doors west. Ask for Estelle." Devilbug was knocking on the counter, and she went back to the traders. "What'll it be this time, gents?"

"The same. How much credit have we got left?"

"I'll look it up. Wait a minute."

She took a ledger from the shelf and riffled the leaves. "Devilbug, six hides; Ticktock, three hides and a half. That's counting off the drinks you've just had." She jotted the scores on the two pages.

"That won't hold us till we leave," said Devilbug. "I'll bring you a credit paper from Abbott's tomorrow."

"Better bring a good big one. It's your last chance to cut capers between here and Santa Fe."

They laughed. Laughing back at them, Florinda turned to answer a knock from the other end of the counter, where some Californios wanted a bottle of wine. She set the bottle before them as the door opened again, letting in a gust of wind and rain.

Florinda glanced up and waved joyfully. "Well, I'll be a pink-eyed mackerel if it's not John Ives. How are you, Johnny?"

The other Americans called greetings. John did not answer. He came and leaned both elbows on the bar, resting his head on his hands. John's clothes were drenched, and spattered with mud. The rain was running out of his hair. He had not shaved for days, and his face was lined with fatigue. Behind him came his boy Pablo Gomez, who sat down on the floor in a corner. Pausing in front of John, Florinda exclaimed with concern,

"For pity's sake, Johnny, what's the matter? You look dead and dug up."

"I feel like it," John said wearily. He did not lift his head. "Give me a big drink. Whiskey. And a bottle of red wine for Pablo."

He threw some coins on the bar. Mickey put a cup in front of him and Florinda poured the whiskey. She took a Mexican dollar from the heap of coins, dropped it into the box with the slit cover, and pushed the rest of the money back toward him. John took the bottle of wine to Pablo and came back to the bar. Swallowing his own drink at a gulp, he pushed the cup toward her. Florinda filled it again. "How long have you been riding in this rain?" she asked him.

"I've been riding four days, but the rain only hit me two days ago. Fill it up again, will you?"

Florinda obeyed, picking up another coin from the heap, but she warned,

"Make this one last a little longer, Johnny, or you'll fall down. You're too tired to swallow it whole."

"I suppose you're right. Can you give me something to eat?"

"Of course. Stay here till I get a free minute. What's the trouble?"

"Tell you later. Let me catch my breath."

Florinda was called by another man and went to wait on him. The traders moved up to talk to John. John answered them briefly. He had come in from Hale's Rancho, he said. He had ridden hard, with little sleep. "I'm looking for Texas," said John. "Thought I'd find him here."

"He's in town," said Devilbug, "but Florinda says he's been drunk a week."

John swore, softly and skillfully. "I thought he'd be sobering up for the trail."

"No use while it's raining. I guess he'll start sobering next week."

"Next week?" John repeated angrily. "Next week?"

"What do you want with Texas?" asked Ticktock. "Somebody sick?"

"Mrs. Hale. She's dangerously ill. You remember her, don't you?"

"Why sure, nice girl. Too bad."

"John."

It was Florinda speaking. She had reached across the bar and caught his wrist.

"What did I hear you say about Garnet?" she asked sharply.

"Garnet's going to die if she doesn't get some help soon."

Florinda's lips tightened. "Stay where you are."

She turned around and caught Mickey's arm. "Take over, Mickey." Pointing to the side door, she said, "I go. Back soon."

Mickey smiled. "Yes, Miss Flinda."

A customer was knocking on the bar. Ignoring him, Florinda went through the side door at the end of the bar and came into the main room by the side door in front of it. With a firm grip, she took John's elbow. "Come with me. Through here."

John went out with her. The door opened into the little hall with the staircase. Locking the door after her, Florinda led him through the hall and into the kitchen. There was a fireplace here, with a pot hanging over a pile of glowing ashes. In front of the wall-bench was a long table on which were some dishes not yet washed.

"Sit down," said Florinda. John was so tired that he obeyed without question. Going to the fireplace, Florinda dished up a bowlful of beans from the pot, and brought it to him along with a plate of beef and some cold tortillas. She set the dishes in front of him and put a bottle of whiskey beside them. "There's liquor. But don't drink any more until you've eaten something. And don't try to talk either. You're so tired you're addled in the head."

John gave her a weary smile. He began to eat hungrily.

Florinda put a stick of wood on the fire. John's clothes began to steam. Bringing a square of cloth that might have been a towel or a dishrag, Florinda dried his hair and rubbed the splashes of mud off his stubbly cheeks. As he pushed back the empty bowl she sat on the bench by him and poured a stiff drink of whiskey into a cup. John smiled at her again as she pushed it toward him.

"You're very good, Florinda. Thank you."

"Feel better?"

"Much better."

"Now tell me what's happened to Garnet."

John's hand tightened around the yellow pottery cup she had set before him. "Garnet is going to have a baby," he said, "and she's just had a horrible shock."

"What's the matter with her?"

"Nausea. I never saw anything so violent, or so frightening. She vomited till she broke a blood vessel, then she started coughing up splashes of blood. She wasn't even doing that very much when I left, she was too weak."

Before he was done, Florinda had given a horrified exclamation. As he paused she said, "Tell me what happened, John. Start at the beginning."

John took a swallow of whiskey and told her the story, beginning with the letter that brought news of Carmelita's child. After one or two shocked words, Florinda heard him without interruption.

"When I carried her into the house," said John, "she fainted, and when I brought her around she babbled to me, hardly knowing what she was saying."

Florinda shut her eyes a minute, with a shiver. "What's Charles doing now?"

"He's shut up in his room, pacing. He did love Oliver, if you can call that damned clawing possessiveness by the name of love. Two days after Oliver was killed, when they were getting his body ready for burial, I went to Charles' room and told him I thought Garnet was going to die. He said, 'I hope she does,' and banged the door in my face. I left that day and rode to Los Angeles to look for Texas."

"Did you leave anybody with her?"

"A couple of native women. They're kindly souls, but they don't know what to do for her, any more than I do. And now Texas is swamped in liquor." John swore under his breath. He threw the cup across the room and it smashed on the wall.

"Here's another, Johnny. Break several if it makes you feel any better."

"That blasted rumhead. Why do they have to do it?"

"Oh John, they don't know why they have to do it! You wouldn't understand. You don't know what it's like." Florinda got up. She walked to the window, opening the shutters a trifle. "The rain's letting up," she said over her shoulder. "If you got a good night's sleep, could you start back to the rancho in the morning?"

"Of course. But what can I do when I get there?"

"I'll go with you."

"You? Do you know what to do for her?"

"Maybe." She turned around from the window, smiling at him in cool irony. "You're a bright boy, Johnny, and you've been around, but I don't think you know much about the New York slums. Women get shocked plenty down there. And I'll tell you something, bright boy. Half the shock is that awful feeling that nobody gives a damn what becomes of you."

"Then you'll take care of her?"

"I'll do my best." Florinda came back to where he sat. "Now come upstairs and I'll give you a place to sleep. We'll start as soon as you wake up in the morning."

She patted his whiskery cheek. The kitchen door opened and Silky came in.

"Say, Florinda, what are you doing away from the bar so long? Don't you know—why, how do you do, John. Come on back, Florinda."

"I'll be there as soon as I've shown John the way upstairs. He's staying here tonight."

"Hurry, won't you? José is mixing up the credit book and everybody's getting mad."

"Let her alone, Silky," said John.

He was sitting on the bench. Florinda stroked his damp hair. "Don't mind him, Silky, he's been drinking too much. I'll be there, and I'll sing 'em a nice bawdy song to get the house in good humor again."

Silky had put his hand on the door. "You'll be right out?"

302

"Certainly. But first I'd better tell you, I won't be here tomorrow. I've got to go away for a bit."

Silky turned around with a start. "What the hell are you talking about?" Silky's manners were not always elegant in private.

Florinda explained about Garnet. Silky was angry. He wanted to know how she expected him to run the bar and the gambling room all at once. John started to answer, but Florinda gave his shoulder a warning squeeze, so he let Silky rage.

"Sorry, Silky," Florinda said at last. "I wouldn't leave you for anything less than a matter of life and death. But that's what this is."

Silky scowled. He hesitated. He pulled one end of his mustache. "John, is that kid really very sick?"

"I'm hoping she'll still be alive when we get there," said John.

"Damn you to hell," said Silky. "Do you need anything?"

"Fresh horses," said John.

"You'll find those in the corral behind the house. Anything else?"

"I threw the saddlebags on the porch. Have somebody bring them in. And give Pablo something to eat and a place to sleep. Oh yes, I was to meet my friend here, the one Florinda calls the Handsome Brute. When he turns up, tell him where to find me."

"All right. I hope Mrs. Hale gets well. Florinda, if you ever do this to me again I'll kill you."

"Oh, fine. Then you'll have to look for another beautiful girl who speaks English and doesn't drink and never cheats the customers. Come on, John."

Florinda picked up a lamp. John followed her up the rickety stairs. As they reached the top he said,

"Silky behaved quite decently, for him. I have a pouch full of silver in one of the bags. Tell him I'll leave it to help make up the losses while you're away."

Florinda gave him a cynical smile. "Hell for breakfast, Johnny, if a man has one good impulse every ten years, can't you let him have it?"

"I don't know how long the impulse will last. But there's one universal language, and it's not music."

"Very smart of you, Johnny. This is my room. You can stay here."

She opened a door and went inside with the lamp. John stopped on the threshold. This was not the sort of room he had expected to find in Silky's Place.

It was a small room with rough adobe walls. But around the walls Florinda had hung curtains of blue checked gingham; and there were blue checked curtains over the window shutters, and a cover to match them on the bed. Several blue cushions were piled on the wall-bench. On the floor were black-and-white woolen rugs from Sante Fe. At one side was a rough wardrobe, painted white. There was a washstand with a bowl and pitcher and slop-jar, and a big mirror on the wall, and across a corner of the room was a blue gingham screen. The place was a little palace of bright clean comfort.

John looked around the room and down at his muddy clothes. "You didn't mean for me to sleep in here!"

"Why yes I did. There's nowhere else. We aren't used to having guests."

"But I'm crusted with dirt. I haven't washed for days. Where did you plan to stay?"

"I thought you could have the bed, since you're tuckered out. I can sleep on the floor. I've got plenty of blankets."

"I won't climb into that immaculate bed," said John. "I mean it."

"All right, I haven't got time to argue." Florinda was taking an armful of blankets from the top shelf of the wardrobe. "Go to sleep on the floor. I'll come in softly and won't wake you. There's soap and water on the washstand, and you'll find the other necessity of life behind the screen." She dropped the blankets on the bed. "Well, I've got to go now, and warble for those drunks downstairs. See you in the morning."

She went out before he could answer. The inside walls of the building were not thick, and John could hear the racket from the saloon below him. It did not bother him at all. He took off his boots and managed to stay awake long enough to wash his face and hands. This done, he put the blankets on the floor and rolled up.

When he woke he blinked a moment at the blue curtains, and then, remembering where he was, he turned over and stretched. The shutters were closed and the curtains drawn over them, but around the edges there were unmistakable gleams of light. Springing up, John went to open the window. The rain had stopped. The sun was out, and as usual when it was not raining, most of the population was outdoors. John saw women going down to the creek, and half-naked tame Diggers selling water. Here and there came a two-wheeled ox-cart loaded with hides. Remembering that

Florinda was still asleep, John shut the window against the noise.

He went over and looked down at the bed. Florinda slept on her side, without a pillow. Her bright hair was scattered on the sheet and her head lay in it as though in a nest. She had on a flannel nightgown buttoned up to her throat. The gown had long sleeves, and at the ends of the sleeves were deep ruffles that hid her hands almost down to the fingertips. So she was even vain about her nightgowns, John thought with a twinge of amused surprise, till he remembered that Florinda did not always sleep alone.

He did not want to wake her up until he had to. She had brought up an extra pail of water, which stood on the floor by the washstand. Filling the pitcher to replace the water he had used last night, John picked up the pail and went out softly.

The saloon was silent. Looking into the kitchen, John saw his saddlebags lying in a corner. He picked them up and made his toilet in the passage at the foot of the staircase. Shaved and dressed in fresh clothes, with a pair of dry boots from the bags, he felt well and hungry.

Behind the house, as Silky had said, was a corral with adobe walls, where several horses were nibbling at the oats that had sprung up during the winter rains. Going out by the gate of the corral, John found Pablo, who had struck up acquaintance with a neighbor woman and was now being served breakfast before her outdoor oven. John gave her some coppers for beans and a bowl of chocolate, and told Pablo to put their saddles on fresh horses from the corral. Taking another bowl of beans and one of chocolate, he went back upstairs to Florinda.

She was still asleep. Setting the bowls on the bench, he put his hand on her shoulder and shook her gently.

Florinda opened her eyes, gave him a blank stare for an instant, and sat up.

"Oh yes, it's you. Whoosh, it's cold!" She pulled the blankets up around her. "What time is it?"

"I don't know. I was so sleepy last night I forgot to wind my watch. But it's big daylight, and the sun's shining. Here's some breakfast."

Florinda gave her head a shake and rubbed her eyes. "Why John, you angel. Who gave it to you? Don't tell me Mickey is up so early."

"Mickey?"

"The China boy. He's a jewel and I love him dearly."

"I haven't seen Mickey. I got these from the woman who lives behind the corral."

"Oh yes, I know her. She's nice. Her name is Isabel and she does my laundry." Florinda began to sip the chocolate. "You run on down and tend to the horses and I'll get dressed. I've got a saddle, and I put some things into a saddlebag last night. You'll find it in the hall."

"You did all that? I didn't hear you."

"Brother, you were sleeping like you'd had a pipe of opium. A herd of oxen couldn't have waked you. Run on, Johnny, and I'll be right down."

She waved brightly to him as he went out.

"And don't look so glum, Johnny," she called. "We'll manage."

TWENTY-NINE

IT WAS LATE at night when they reached Hale's Rancho. The journey had taken them four days. Luckily the weather had been clear, though they had had to ride through fields of mud left by the rain.

The rancho was dark, but as they rode around the main house they could see lights from two windows. John told Florinda one of these was Charles' room, the other was Garnet's.

Florinda ignored Charles. "Garnet must be still alive if her room's lighted," she said. "Let's hurry, John."

John helped her off the horse, and told Pablo to bring in their packs. He opened the door of Garnet's room.

It was dimly lighted by a lamp on the wall-bench. A woman, sitting on the floor by the bed, looked up in surprise when she recognized John. He beckoned to her. "¿Cómo está la señora, Lolita?" he whispered.

Lolita shook her head sadly. John told her to get Florinda's packs and bring them into Garnet's sitting-room next door. As she went out, he turned back to Florinda.

Florinda had put her bonnet and shawl and gloves on the table, and was unstrapping her gun-belt as she looked down at the bed. Garnet lay on her back, a blanket drawn over her, and her hair in two untidy braids across the pillow. In the dim light her features were thin and sharp. Her lips were cracked with dryness, and her skin was flaky like old paper. She was not asleep, but her eyes were half closed in the semi-consciousness of exhaustion.

Florinda knelt by the bed. Garnet moved a little, and quivered into life.

Florinda slipped an arm around her. "It's me, Garnet. Florinda."

Garnet tried to turn a little toward her. Florinda said, "John brought me. We're going to stay with you till you get well."

Garnet sighed gratefully. She tried again to speak, but her tongue was so parched that the words were not clear. "Florinda—you're here—" Her voice trailed off.

"Now I'm going to make you comfortable," said Florinda, "so you can go to sleep. I'll stay right here by you."

Garnet moved her hand. With weak, unsteady little movements, she felt Florinda's hair and face. "Get me some water, John," Florinda said. "And a cloth."

Garnet murmured, "—I can't—drink water—comes back."

"You don't have to drink it. But your forehead is all hot. I'm going to bathe your face."

John poured some water into the basin on the washstand and set the basin on the table, with a towel beside it. Florinda rolled back her sleeves. The lamplight made deep shadows among her scars.

"I'll need a chair, John," she said.

He brought it to her. Florinda dipped the cloth into the water and wrung it out, and gently began to stroke Garnet's forehead. John waited for further instructions.

During their ride to the rancho he had come to admire Florinda a good deal. She had several traits that he liked. For one thing, she did not chatter. She rode by him in silence, interrupted only when she had to ask a question. And she knew how to take orders. She was eager to ride fast, but she had accepted his judgment about speed and rest, without argument. John's experience had been that people who had sense enough to take orders also had sense enough to give them, and he was ready to obey her now.

He watched her as she stroked Garnet's forehead with the damp cloth. It seemed like a long time. At last Florinda stood up and came over to him.

"She's asleep. A good natural sleep. Bring me some fresh water, John, and a spoon, and some kind of a clock."

John slipped out. He dipped a jug into the reservoir in front, and got the spoon from the dining room. Though he was trying to

307

walk softly, as he came back along the dark passage a door opened and Charles appeared. Charles was fully dressed. Evidently he was not sleeping much these nights.

"Who's prowling about?" Charles demanded. "Oh, John. I thought you'd gone back to your rancho." Charles was obviously none too glad that John had returned.

"I went to Los Angeles," said John. "I've brought a friend of Garnet's to nurse her."

"She's got two women taking care of her now," Charles returned in surprise. "Frankly, John, I don't like your dragging strangers into my house at this time."

Charles was making no effort to hold his voice down, and John saw now that in his haste to get the fresh water he had left Garnet's door open. Trying not to speak loud enough to wake her, he said,

"Charles, Garnet is very ill. I've brought an American woman, a friend of hers—"

"An American woman?" Charles repeated in a puzzled voice. "I don't know any American women in this part of the country."

"Her name is Florinda Grove. She came with us over the trail last summer."

"John!" Charles exclaimed. This time his voice was loud with angry disgust. "Is it possible you are referring to that woman Penrose dragged in from Santa Fe?"

"I wish you'd keep your voice down. You don't have to see Florinda or speak to her."

The passage was lit only by the faint glow from Garnet's room. John could not see the expression of Charles' face, but he could guess it. Charles made a great show of his own righteousness. Trying to keep his temper, John said,

"Let me get by, Charles. We can discuss this in the morning."

"There is no need to wait," said Charles. Planting himself in front of John, he continued. "I am aware that prostitutes follow the train to Los Angeles. I did not know that Oliver permitted his wife to scrape acquaintance with them. But this is not the trail. This is my house. I will not have a giggling harlot take up her residence here. Now where is that woman?"

"Here I am, Mr. Hale."

Florinda came out of Garnet's room. She closed the door behind her, making the passage almost pitch dark. She came toward them.

"John didn't mean to bring me here, Mr. Hale," she said. In the darkness her voice was low and urgent. "John came to Los Angeles to find Texas," she went on. "But Texas was drunk. So I came instead. Please let me stay. I won't make any trouble."

Charles stood still. He said icily,

"Mrs. Hale does not require your services."

"Oh yes she does, Mr. Hale. If you don't let me stay, she won't require anything but a coffin." Her voice was too low for Garnet to hear it beyond the closed door, but clear enough for Charles. "And there'll be two people in that coffin, you know, and one of them will be your brother's child. I think you loved your brother. This is all you've got left of him."

Charles made a wordless sound, deep in his throat. But he recovered himself quickly.

"I will thank you," he said, "not to discuss matters that do not concern you. And I will thank you to leave this house at daylight."

"Florinda is not leaving this house, Charles," said John, "until Garnet is out of danger."

"No, really, Mr. Hale, I'm not," Florinda said gently. "But I tell you what I'll do. I'll stay in those two rooms of Garnet's and not come out for any reason. John can bring my meals. I'll go back to Garnet's room now, and I won't come into the hall again till I'm leaving for good."

John asked, "Is that satisfactory, Charles?"

As he spoke John realized that he had his hand on his gun. He had not put it there consciously, but finding it there did not surprise him; he was quite capable of killing Charles if he tried to force Florinda out. Charles knew he was.

Charles said to Florinda, "Is that a promise?"

"Yes, sir."

"Very well. On that condition, you may stay." He spoke with self-conscious condescension.

As sweetly as before, Florinda said, "You are very good. I'll do my best. Good night, sir."

She turned and went back into the bedroom, closing the door silently behind her. John said,

"Very well, Charles. I'll do any necessary errands."

Without waiting for Charles to answer, John went back to the bedroom, shut the door and slipped the bolt. He set the jug of water on the table and went to Florinda. She stood breathing hard, her hands doubled up into fists, her lips trembling with fury.

John gave her a sardonic smile. "Go on and say it," he suggested.

Florinda shook her head. She glanced at the bed. Garnet had

been wakened by the voices. "I want to talk to you," Florinda said to John. Grabbing his hand, she drew him into the next room. In a fierce low voice she asked, "John, doesn't he want her to get well?"

"No."

"But I thought, when I reminded him about the baby—you said he loved Oliver."

"But it will be *her* baby, don't you understand? Charles would be glad to have her recover now, if he thought she'd die in childbirth and he could have Oliver's child to possess as he possessed Oliver. But if he can't own the child, he'd rather have it not born at all."

Florinda said it then. Her vocabulary was, as John had remarked before, magnificent.

He smiled grimly. "Feel better?"

"Not much. John, has that man ever had any trouble with his head?"

"I don't know whether it's his head or his heart, or just his liver. I only know he's like that."

There was a brief pause. Florinda pushed Charles out of her mind. "John," she said, "Garnet's in a dreadful state. We've got to work."

"Shall we go back to her now?"

"Yes. Be very quiet till I get her to sleep again."

They went back into the bedroom. Garnet stirred restlessly as they came in. Florinda sat by her and began to stroke her forehead. She moved her fingers lightly, across and across, and down Garnet's temples into her hair. Garnet was trying to talk.

"What—did he—call you?"

"He called me a giggling harlot, dear. Quite refined in his language. I don't believe he's been around much."

"Florinda, he—you—" A sob came up into Garnet's throat and choked her words. It made her cough. A drop of blood crept down from the corner of her mouth. Florinda wiped it off with the damp towel.

"Don't try to talk any more, Garnet. I don't mind what Charles says." Florinda's voice was low and soothing. "Poor fellow, I'm kind of sorry for him. I don't think he ever had any fun. Never had a girl sit on his knee and tell him how wonderful he was. Shut your eyes. Take a deep breath. You've got nothing to do but go to sleep. You can stay asleep as long as you want to. John's here, and I'm here, and we're not going to leave you."

She talked on and on, in a voice as soft as drifting feathers. At last Garnet relaxed and went to sleep again. Florinda came over to where John sat on the wall-bench.

"Let's give her a few minutes to get into really deep sleep," she whispered.

They waited. There was no sound but the occasional stamping of a horse outside. After a while Florinda whispered, "That clock?"

"Here." He handed her his watch.

"Put the lamp on the table so I can see the watch. Set up something between the light and her eyes."

She sat by Garnet again. Very carefully, she dipped the spoon into the water, let the water drip off it, and stroked Garnet's lips with the damp spoon. Garnet did not stir. Florinda watched the time for five minutes, then dampened the spoon again and drew it across Garnet's dry lips. After the third time, she beckoned to John. He came close, and stooped so she could whisper into his ear.

"You see what I'm doing?"

"Yes."

"We'll have to keep doing this every five minutes, all night, all day tomorrow, all tomorrow night. Except when she's awake. When she wakes up we'll have to stop, so she won't know we're doing anything. But she's so exhausted, she'll sleep most of the time. We'll keep her lips damp. After a while, she'll swallow a drop of water without knowing it, and it will stay down. Her stomach has got such jerks that it won't keep anything if she knows she's getting it."

John nodded. "Shall I take over?"

"No, I'd better do it first, because I know how. Have you got somewhere to sleep?"

"The next room, where they put our packs. But how about you?"

"I'll stay here. When I can't keep awake any longer, I'll call you. We'll take turns."

John agreed. Florinda wet the spoon again and stroked Garnet's lips. Garnet did not move.

John brought Florinda her packs, and told her she would be more comfortable if she put on some loose clothes. During the five-minute respites, Florinda put on a nightgown and a woolen robe she had brought with her. She took the pins out of her hair and shook it down. John found some blankets in the wardrobe and lay down to sleep on the floor of Garnet's sitting-room next door.

The dawn was breaking when Florinda woke him up.

"John, my hand is getting shaky. You'd better take my place."

He sat up. "How is she?"

"She woke up once. I talked to her and got her to sleep again. Come in and let me be sure you know how."

John went into the bedroom with her, and began to dampen Garnet's lips as he had seen Florinda do it.

"That's fine," she said when he had done it several times. "Every five minutes, no oftener."

"Very well. Now get some sleep."

Florinda went into the other room and lay down on the blankets he had left there.

Garnet kept having dreams. She dreamed about brooks, and ferns growing among the stones, beautiful ferns that dripped shining drops of water. She knelt down by the water to drink it, but it disappeared.

She dreamed about the desert. They were riding and the sun was hot. They came to a waterhole, but there was no water and the men had to dig. They waited and waited, and at last there was water, but when she held out her cup the water ran underground again and she was still thirsty. She was so thirsty that she woke up.

Waking up was harsh and painful. Her throat was fiery, her tongue was swollen, and her lips were cracked. As soon as she woke up she remembered the tragedy of Carmelita and the terrible way Oliver had died, and she remembered that she was going to have a baby. She felt a dazed panic as she wondered what was going to become of her.

She opened her eyes. John sat by her bed, dusty and unshaven as he had been on the trail. He had closed the shutters, but there was light enough to let her know it was daytime. She recalled then that he and Florinda had come to her in the middle of the night. It made her feel better to know they were there. Her lips felt slightly different too. It seemed to her that they were not as scaly as they had been. She tried to speak to him.

"Thank you—for coming back, John. Where's Florinda?"

"Don't try to talk," said John. "I'll turn you over, then I'll get Florinda."

He put his arms under her and lifted her, and turned her on her side to ease her cramped muscles. When he had drawn the blankets over her shoulders again he went into the next room, and a moment later Florinda came in. She was smothering a yawn.

"Were you—asleep?" asked Garnet. "I'm—sorry." It was hard to talk.

"Oh, I feel fine," said Florinda. She pulled the woolen robe around her, and pushing her hair back she fixed it in place with a pair of combs. "Now I'll get the bed straight."

She drew the covers down and rubbed Garnet all over with a cool damp cloth. She was deft and brisk, but very gentle. Garnet wished she could say how grateful she was.

After a while she went to sleep again. She woke up, and again she went to sleep. This happened several times. When she woke up Florinda or John was always there, but they did not bother her at all. The Mexican women had kept trying to give her spoonfuls of broth, which she could not keep down. John and Florinda did not make her swallow anything, but gradually her mouth began to feel less parched, and the cracks in her lips began to heal.

It was three o'clock in the morning. John was in the outer room, finishing a meal of beef and cold tortillas. They never brought any food into the bedroom lest the odor make Garnet sick again. He pushed back the plate and went in to tell Florinda he would take care of Garnet now.

In the lamplight Florinda's face was lined and tired, but as he came in she beckoned to him excitedly.

"John!" she whispered, and he bent over to hear her. "John, it's happening!"

"What's happening? Is she better?"

"Yes. Look."

She drained the spoon and passed it over Garnet's lips. As she did so, Garnet unconsciously moved her lips and passed her tongue over them to get the dampness.

"She's done that two or three times," Florinda said softly. "Now we can go on. We've got to be careful. Oh John, it's got to work! It's *got* to work."

She put out her left hand and he closed his own over it. They both held tight. The five minutes dragged. At last Florinda brought up the spoon again. This time she did not quite drain it. Tensely, holding her breath, she let a drop of water stay on Garnet's lower lip. Still asleep, Garnet put out her tongue and tasted it. John felt a shiver of suspense. His eyes met Florinda's.

"This is where it hurts," said Florinda. "You want to hurry. You *can't* hurry."

313

John knelt down and put his arm around her waist. Florinda rested her elbow on his shoulder. They watched, silently. Every five minutes, Florinda put another drop of water on Garnet's lips.

After a while John saw that her hand was trembling with fatigue. He took the spoon from her.

She yielded reluctantly. "Just a drop at a time," she whispered. "A tiny drop, Johnny."

She went into the other room and fell asleep. When she woke up John brought her beef and tortillas hot from the kitchen. Florinda had kept her bargain with Charles; she had not left the two rooms. John brought her water for washing, and she set the slop-jars outside the door so the servant girls could carry them away.

While Florinda was eating her breakfast John went to sit by Garnet. She opened her eyes.

Florinda had told him what to do when Garnet awoke, so now John leaned over the bed. "Garnet, you're a lot better. Do you understand me?"

She nodded, and looked at him questioningly.

"Now we want you to try something," said John. "You're very thirsty, aren't you?"

She nodded again.

"Florinda is going to give you a few drops of water. Just a tiny bit. Swallow it and keep very quiet."

With a frightened look, Garnet shook her head. "John, I can't!"

"Try, won't you?" he asked gently.

Garnet made an effort to smile at him. "All right. I'll try."

"Good." He heard the door open. "Here's Florinda now."

He put his arm under the pillow and raised her head. Florinda smiled down at Garnet, and put the spoon to her lips. Garnet swallowed. John laid her down again.

"Don't move, Garnet," said Florinda. "Take deep breaths. Very deep breaths."

Garnet obeyed, closing her eyes. Florinda held the watch in her hand.

This time she waited fifteen minutes.

"Now we'll try again, Garnet."

Garnet swallowed another teaspoonful of water. Again Florinda waited fifteen minutes. The water did not come back. Florinda said,

"Get yourself a nap, Johnny. I'm going to need you later."

When he woke up, that afternoon, Florinda told him trium-

314

phantly that Garnet had not gagged once. If she could take water she could take milk.

"Milk?" John repeated. He began to laugh. "In California?"

"Oh dear," said Florinda, "I forgot." She began to laugh too. There were thousands of cattle on the hills, but cattle in California meant beef and leather and tallow candles; few of the Californios ever used milk. "But can't you get some milk, John?" Florinda asked anxiously.

"Yes, I'll get it," said John. "It'll take a little time, that's all."

He went out. Acting on his orders, several of Charles' cow-hands mounted and set out to rope some of the wild cows on the hills. They dragged in six cows before they found one that had any milk. With no notion of what was going to be done to her, the cow kicked and bellowed in panic, while her calf leaped after her, fighting too. Amid a great howling and racket the men rolled the cow over and tied her legs together, two and two, then a man held her up at each end while a third man forced milk out of her udder. The cow bawled. The serving-people quit work and ran over to watch.

The men's efforts produced about a pint of milk. They untied the cow, and with yelps of relief she and her calf bounded back to the hills.

Florinda filled a cup with half milk and half water, and gave Garnet a spoonful every fifteen minutes. Garnet kept it down.

The next day she took the milk without any water to thin it, and in the afternoon Florinda said to John,

"She can try some meat broth now. You'll have to fix it, since I'm not allowed in the kitchen."

John obeyed her, and fed the broth to Garnet with a spoon. Garnet smiled at him as she finished it.

"John, I can't say much yet. But you've been very good to me."

He smiled back. "I've done nothing but take orders."

"Getting dark, Johnny," said Florinda. "Time for you to go to bed."

"What about yourself?" he asked, for Florinda had been getting very little sleep lately.

She went to the door of the room where they rested by turns, and beckoned to him. With the door shut so Garnet would not hear, she said,

"Let me sit up with her a while, John. Yes, I'm dreadfully tired. But I've got to see how her stomach takes the meat broth."

"You'll wake me as soon as it's safe to leave her?"

"Yes, and you can sit up the rest of the night."

He agreed, and lay down on the blankets. Florinda went back to the bedroom. She sat by the bed, now and then giving Garnet a sip of water. After a while Garnet fell asleep.

When she awoke it was deep night. There was a lamp on the table, but it was burning low, and they had made a screen of two empty jugs with a shawl hung over them to keep the light out of her eyes. Florinda sat by the table, but she had fallen asleep, her head on her arm.

Garnet wondered how long Florinda and John had been here. She was still very weak, but she was not nauseated any more, and she was not having those hideous dreams. She wondered if she was really going to get well, and how she was going to take care of herself if she did.

She moved restlessly. Florinda raised her head, blinking vaguely at the light and pushing back her tumbled hair. Then, remembering where she was, she sprang up and came to the bed.

"I'm here, Garnet."

"I'm all right," Garnet said. "I didn't mean to wake you up."

"I didn't mean to go to sleep, either. How do you feel?"

"Very well."

"No bumbles in the middle?"

Garnet shook her head.

"Fine. Here, take some milk. Drink it all, you need it."

As she gave back the cup, Garnet saw how weary Florinda looked. She held out her hand, and Florinda knelt by her.

Florinda dropped her head on the pillow. She was so sleepy that her eyes were closing again. "You don't look as if you've had any rest at all," said Garnet. "How long have you been here?"

"Four or five days, I'm not sure. I've lost track. But it doesn't matter." Florinda rubbed her eyes. "You're going to be all right, and you'll have your baby." She roused herself with an effort. "And I'll tell you something else," she added.

"Yes? What?"

"I can't get you back home," said Florinda, "but I can get you out of this house if you want to leave it. Would you like to come to Los Angeles with me?"

Garnet started. "You mean," she gasped incredulously, "you'd let me live with you? I don't have to stay here with Charles?"

"You're damn right you don't have to stay here. Do you want to come with me?"

"Do I want to! Oh, Florinda!"

"Then that's settled?" Florinda asked.

"Florinda, I can't tell you how I've wanted to get out of here. Oh, you are so good."

"Why no I'm not. It'll be fun having you there."

Garnet sighed happily. Then a doubt struck her, and she demurred, "But Florinda."

Florinda raised her head from the pillow. "What now, Garnet?"

"The baby."

"What about the baby? We'll take care of it."

"In a saloon?"

"Well, holy Christmas, you don't have to feed it whiskey. You'll have milk of your own. I'll show you how to take care of the baby."

"I'm glad you know how. I don't. In fact," Garnet confessed, tired of trying to be brave, "I'm scared about the whole thing."

"Of course you are, dear. But you've got no reason to be. I mean it, Garnet. It's not scary, it's wonderful. How long has it been now?"

"About four months."

"Pretty soon you'll feel the baby move. Just a tiny bit, like something quirking its finger. Then all of a sudden, the baby won't be an idea any more, it will be a person, and it's so surprising, and you'll love it. It will keep on moving, just those funny little quivers at first, but after a while you can feel it kicking, great big healthy kicks—"

"Doesn't it hurt?"

"Not a bit. It's thrilling. Oh Garnet, really it is, I'm not just talking to cheer you up. And then finally you see it—"

"That hurts dreadfully, doesn't it?"

"Why yes, but it won't hurt you too much because you're as tough as a pony. Once you've got the baby it doesn't seem to make any difference whether it hurt or not. The baby is so little, you can hardly believe anything alive could be so little, but it's got hands and feet and a face, such a queer screwed-up little face. Then they put it up to your bosom, and that's not like anything else on earth. I can't tell you, nobody can, but you'll find out. It's all so beautiful, and it's so right—"

"Florinda!"

Garnet had tried to raise herself on her elbow, but she was not strong enough. She lay staring incredulously at Florinda's blue eyes

317

and the shadows of fatigue under them, deepened by the faint light.

"Have you had a baby?" asked Garnet.

Florinda nodded.

"But you never said a word about it. Not till this minute."

"No. But I did have a baby. That's why I can help you take care of yours. I know what to do."

"But your baby!" said Garnet. She was so astonished that she had almost forgotten her own.

"A little girl. Do you want a little girl or a little boy?"

"I don't know. It doesn't matter. What happened to your little girl, Florinda?"

"She died. Your baby's not going to die. You're not going to find out what that's like, not if I have to crawl around the world on my knees." Florinda spoke with determination, but she was so drowsy that she let her head drop back on the pillow as though she could not hold it up any longer.

"Go to bed," Garnet began, but before she could say any more John came in, tousled from sleep, demanding,

"Why didn't you wake me up, Florinda?"

Florinda roused herself and stood up. "I meant to. But I went to sleep myself."

"How's Garnet?"

"Fine." Florinda picked up the water-jug. "Get some fresh water, will you, Johnny? And make some more broth like that, first thing in the morning."

John took the jug from her. "I'll be right back with this. You go on to sleep now, and sleep till you wake up."

Florinda nodded. But she waited by the bed until John had gone out, then she said to Garnet in a half-embarrassed undertone, "Say, Garnet, don't let out to John about all that babbling I did a minute ago. Or to anybody."

"You mean about your little girl?"

"Yes. I don't know what started me off. I guess I was so sleepy I didn't have right good sense."

"All right. I won't say anything about it."

"Thanks." Florinda bent and kissed Garnet's forehead quickly, and went out.

THIRTY

THREE DAYS LATER the Handsome Brute came riding up to the rancho. As usual, he rode in a great splendor of satin and fine leather, followed by retainers and a string of horses laden with packs. Charles went out to meet him. Charles despised the Brute as a stupid savage, but the Brute was a landowner, and neither his opinion nor his grief at Oliver's death could make Charles willing to omit the forms of courtesy customary among the landowners of California.

The Brute brought Garnet and Florinda silk shawls, Garnet's printed with red flowers and Florinda's with blue. Florinda put on her shawl at once, turning before the mirror to try various effects of draping. The Brute came over to the bedside. He patted Garnet's hair with his great hand.

"I am sorry about Oliver," he said gently.

"Thank you, Brute."

"But you are going to have a baby," said the Brute. "That is good."

Garnet smiled at him. In New York, a man who made such a remark to a lady would have been thought unpardonably ill-bred. But the Brute did not know this.

"You are not happy now," he went on, "because you are not strong and you feel helpless, and it is not happy to feel helpless. But you have strength inside. You will be happy."

She hoped he was right. Just now she did not feel strong or happy either.

Later that day, with a great effort, she managed to write a letter to her parents, telling them she could not come home. John said he would take the letter to Los Angeles and give it to Texas, who would give it to one of the Missouri traders in Santa Fe. Garnet sat up against a pile of pillows, and John brought her a tray that she could hold on her knees for a desk. He set the ink on a chair by her bed.

It was a very hard letter to write. She was so weak that the pen wobbled in her hand, and she had to move it very slowly lest the lines shake and tell them, in spite of her, that she had been ill.

She wrote that Oliver had died suddenly, but she did not tell them how; and she wrote that she was going to have a baby. The effort of pushing the pen was so great that it made her hands and forehead damp. Drying her hands on the sheet, she wrote, "My health, as always, is excellent. Oliver's brother is kindness itself, and I have a very pleasant home. Do not be concerned about me. With all my love, Garnet." The pen dropped out of her hand and rolled on the floor, and she fell back on the pillow, panting with fatigue. Tears crept out of her eyes and ran into the drops of sweat on her face. It seemed to her that this letter cut the last tie between herself and her home; she thought shipwrecked people must feel like this when they stood on the shore of some far lost island and watched their ship go down.

"Please read it, John," she murmured. "Is it fit to send?"

John took out his handkerchief and wiped the tears and the drops of sweat off her face. He picked up the letter.

"Why yes," he said quietly. "It's a very fine pack of lies. I'd better start for Los Angeles tomorrow—the train will be leaving any day now." He put the letter into his pocket and went to the door. "You have a great deal of courage, Garnet," he said over his shoulder.

When John went to Los Angeles, the Brute stayed to help Florinda take care of Garnet. "Charles will not make Florinda leave while I am here," the Brute said. "I could break Charles in two with my hands." He said it with such charming simplicity that Garnet could not help laughing.

The Brute was an excellent nurse. With his great strength he had great tenderness. He sat by Garnet's bed for hours at a time, talking to her. He did not speak of Oliver again. But he told her funny stories about the traders, and about the Yankee seamen who came up to Los Angeles in the hide-carts. Or he talked to her gently, letting her know he understood her loneliness in this strange country, since he had once been lonely here himself. Sometimes she laughed with him, sometimes she shed quiet tears, and he always seemed to know how she felt.

The Brute's English had improved since last fall. When she praised him for this, he said it was important for him to learn good English, because he thought there would be a lot more Yankees here pretty soon. To get Garnet's mind off her own troubles he told her what was going on.

He said the people of California did not like their present gov-

320

ernment. Their laws were made for them by a bunch of grandees down in Mexico City, and these gentlemen were being very stupid about California. "Like what John has told me about the British king George the Third," he said. "You have heard of him?"

Yes, Garnet said, she had heard of George the Third. Were the Mexican grandees really being as foolish as that?

Yes, the Brute answered, he thought they were. Mexico City was nearly two thousand miles from Los Angeles, but those men thought they knew more about California than the people who lived here. They made laws without bothering to learn the facts, and they sent up governors who had never laid eyes on California till they arrived to govern it. Some of the laws were so fantastic that nobody tried to enforce them. Others were petty rules that hampered trade and annoyed everybody.

Florinda, who sat on the wall-bench listening, laughed acidly as he spoke. "Oh dear, don't tell me about those rules!" she exclaimed with feeling. "Do you know it's against the law for us to bring in American whiskey? We get it, but we have to pay several fellows to look the other way."

That was the trouble with these laws, the Brute said. Nobody in California took them seriously. Each new one simply meant that a few more men made a living by taking bribes instead of by honest work. No wonder the people were tired of their rulers.

The Californios were peaceful folk, he continued, but they could be violent if they were exasperated enough. The last of the Mexican governors had been a man named Micheltorena. No doubt he was a well-meaning fellow. But the Mexican government, having promised him three hundred soldiers, had decided that this was a fine chance to thin out the jails of Mexico. The jailbirds arrived; they stole everything they could lay hands on, and were busy wrecking California when the citizens rebelled. Micheltorena had been chased back to Mexico with his flock, leaving the civil government to Pío Pico of Los Angeles and the military command to José Castro of Monterey.

Pico and Castro were always quarreling. Each one insisted he was above the other in authority. Neither of them would change his residence so they could get together on government affairs. If anything happened to upset the risky balance between them, said the Brute, somebody was going to get shot.

Garnet felt alarmed. She was about to go to Los Angeles with no protection but what her friends could give her, and they too were foreigners. "Oh Brute," she exclaimed, "don't tell me I'm going to get mixed up in a fight!"

The Brute smiled. "I do not think so," he said. "You see, up in Monterey is the Yankee consul, Mr. Larkin. It is said that Mr. Larkin has privately been asking some of the most important Californios what they would think of belonging to the United States instead of to Mexico. I have been told that many of them say they would be glad of it. The Californios like the Yankees, so I think your people will take this country some day."

Garnet wished they would. She did not care who owned California, but maybe if a lot of Americans came here they would set up some kind of safe transportation between Los Angeles and New York, and she could go home. She must have had a wistful look as she thought of it, for the Brute patted her shoulder.

"Would you like to try to walk a little bit?" he asked. "I will help you."

Garnet nodded, and he brought her a robe. She got up for a while every day now. When she did, the Brute walked up and down with her, supporting her with his great arm until she was able to walk alone.

But though she was stronger now, Garnet got tired and went to bed early. When she fell asleep the Brute and Florinda went into the other room, and he brought her a late supper from the kitchen. Florinda liked talking to him. Brought up by the trappers, and knowing only the simple ways of California, the Brute had an innocence of the world that struck her as appalling. He had never been inside a bank or a court of law, and his only knowledge of these and other institutions like them was what he had picked up from his American friends. But he had a great intuitive wisdom, and he was not civilized enough to be a hypocrite. "You are so astonishing, Brute," Florinda said to him. "When I hear you talk, I don't know whether to laugh or to cry."

"You will not cry," said the Brute. "You never cry." He gave her a thoughtful look across the candle. They sat by the table in Florinda's room. "Why do you never cry, Florinda?" he asked.

"You big ox, what have I got to cry about?"

"I do not know," said the Brute. "But it is not good to keep yourself all bottled up like you do."

"Oh, go eat hay," said Florinda.

But though she laughed at him, she talked to him more freely than she did to most people. One evening she told him about the

Norwegian sailor who had been her father. The Brute was shocked. Florinda told him cynically that if he had known as much about life as she did, he would not be so surprised. A lot of men were no good, and a lot of children grew up with nobody to love them.

"Nobody?" the Brute repeated. He considered, and then said, "But your mother. She loved you, didn't she?"

Florinda reflected a moment. "Not very much. Oh, she loved me in a way—I was all she had—but I looked so much like him. I can remember when I was a very little girl, sometimes she would grab me by the shoulders and stare at me, like she couldn't believe what she saw."

"Did that make you feel bad?" asked the Brute.

"Why yes, sometimes it did. I was sorry I had to be a child she didn't want instead of the man she wanted. It made me sort of ashamed to be so much like him when I couldn't be him."

The Brute thought this over. "Is that why you are always looking into mirrors?" he asked.

"I look into mirrors because I like what I see there, silly. What do you mean?"

"I mean," said the Brute, "your mother said you looked like your father, and she said he was a bad man. So you were ashamed of your looks. Then later when other people said you were beautiful, you were surprised and it made you so happy, and it still does."

Florinda puckered her lips. "I don't know. Maybe." Then she shrugged, laughing at him. "Well, no matter where I got my face, I like it," she said, and added as though he had overlooked something, "because I am rather beautiful, you know."

"Why yes," agreed the Brute, "you are very beautiful." He said it impersonally, as though commenting on a landscape. She laughed at him again.

A few evenings later, the Brute told her he wanted to go back to Russia. Some day soon, he said, he was going back on one of the Russian fur-ships.

"You mean you want to go back there to live?" she asked.

"I don't know," said the Brute. "Maybe I will not like it. But I want to see it again."

"It will be sort of strange, won't it?"

"It will be very strange. I left when I was eight years old. Now I am twenty-seven. That is a long time."

Florinda was drinking chocolate he had brought her from the kitchen. "Do you remember much about Russia?" she asked.

"Oh yes. I suppose there is much that I do not remember. But I remember the big snows, and our house in the country, and our house in St. Petersburg. And I remember my mother." In the flickering light his face was grave and happy, and his violet eyes had a soft faraway look.

Florinda smiled as she sat down her cup. "The way you say it, your mother must have been very nice."

"She was." The Brute smiled too.

"What was she like?"

"She was tall, and she had dark blue eyes and bright hair. I can remember her, when I was a very little boy, coming into my room to say good night. She and my father went to many parties, they were very gay, and there was a lot of snow outside all glowing in the light from the window. She would lean over my bed, and she wore white furs, and jewels in her hair, and she had a nice warm fragrance. When she kissed me good night I could feel the soft white fur on my cheeks."

"Oh Brute, it does sound lovely!" There was a note of wistfulness in Florinda's voice. "Tell me some more about her. When did she die?"

"When I was five years old."

"Was she always frail?"

"Frail? She was never sick in her life. She rode every horse that nobody else could ride, and she drove her own sleigh through the storms. She would come in with her cheeks all rosy and the snow-flakes on her clothes, and she would pick me up and hold me, she was very strong, and she would laugh and I would laugh too, because her clothes were so cold and when she hugged me her cheeks were so warm. What made you think she was frail?"

"You said she died young, that's all."

"She was killed riding a wild horse. None of the men could ride him, but she was sure she could. She had done it so often before. She sprang on his back, and they heard her laughing as he dashed off with her, and my father laughed too. He was sure she could ride the horse, she always could. But this time she could not. They heard her scream, and that was all. They found her where he had thrown her."

"Oh Brute, how terrible!"

"It was not terrible for her, Florinda. It was terrible for my father and for me, and for all of them who loved her. But not for her. It was what she wanted to do. We have got to die, that is not bad.

It is good to die doing what you want to do and not afraid. It would be bad to die afraid."

Florinda gave him a puzzled smile. "You didn't think up all that when you were five years old. Who told you?"

"My father."

"But you said it was dreadful for him. How could he feel that way?"

"He was good like her," said the Brute, "and full of courage. He took me on his knees and told me how strong and brave she had been, and he said I must be strong and brave like her. I loved my father very much, and he loved me. That is why he brought me to America with him."

"And then he died too, and left you away out here," Florinda said with sympathy. "Were you very lonesome, Brute?"

"At first I was. Such a little boy. But the trappers were kind to me. I liked Fort Ross. I like it here too, but I want to go back to Russia and see it. In Russia is so much that I like to remember."

There was a silence. The Brute said,

"Would you like to see something beautiful that belonged to my mother?"

"I'd love to. What is it?"

He unbuttoned the collar of his shirt, and drew out a long gold chain that he wore around his neck. "It is an ikon."

"A what?" asked Florinda.

"An ikon. A holy picture from the Eastern Orthodox Church."

"Is that the church they have in Russia?"

"Yes. Look," he said, slipping the chain over his head. Attached to it was a little case of blue velvet with gold clasps. Opening the case, the Brute showed her a picture painted on ivory and framed with pearls, and told her it represented the Biblical story of Abraham entertaining the Three Strangers. Florinda had never heard the story, and this was the first time she had ever seen the flat stylized sort of art used in the Eastern Church. She thought they might have got a better painter to do the job. But she was quite capable of appreciating the gold and pearls, and exclaimed admiringly when she saw them.

"Gee, Brute, it must be valuable!"

"I suppose so," said the Brute. "It is valuable to me, because it belonged to my mother, and to her mother before her. I have not much that belonged to my mother and father, because when we came to America my father brought only what we would need for the journey. But he would not have left this." Florinda turned the case in her hands, examining it with curiosity, and he added, "Do not tell anybody I carry my ikon."

"Oh no, I wouldn't. It might be stolen."

"That is not the reason. The reason is, if they knew in California that I still carried my ikon, I would have trouble. I had to be baptized again to get my rancho, you see."

Florinda frowned. "I do not see."

"You cannot own land in California unless you are a citizen of Mexico," he explained, "and you cannot be a citizen of Mexico unless you have been baptized by their church, which is Roman Catholic. The Californios do not make us go to church, but they must baptize us before they give us land. That is one of the laws they made in Mexico City. I think it is a foolish law."

"Do you mean," she asked in astonishment, "that if they knew you had this picture, they would take it away from you?"

"Oh yes," said the Brute. "And they might take away my rancho too."

"I don't know one church from another," said Florinda, "but I must say, I never heard anything so absurd in my life. Making trouble just because you've got a Russian picture. Here, Brute, take it back and hide it." She watched him as he put the chain back over his head and tucked the ikon inside his shirt. Impulsively she put her hand over his. "Brute," she said.

He smiled at her. "Yes?"

"You innocent angel, let me tell you something."

"Why yes. What?"

"Don't go around showing people that ikon," Florinda advised him. "Honestly, Brute, you mustn't. It was very stupid of you to show it to me."

"Was it? Why?"

"You dear overgrown baby," she said gently, "don't you know I could blackmail you?"

"What is blackmail?" asked the Brute.

"Oh you silly lamb," said Florinda. "It's like this. Suppose you were skinning your cattle at rodeo time. Suppose I rode in and said, 'There's a Yankee clipper in port with a lot of things for sale. Please give me a thousand hides to go shopping with.' Naturally you'd tell me to go home. But then I could say, 'All right, if you won't give me a thousand hides I'll go to Los Angeles and spread the word that you carry an ikon from the wrong church.' You'd have to give me the hides to make me keep my mouth shut. I could do that to you, couldn't I?"

The Brute gave her a glance of wise amusement. "You could, yes. But you won't."

"But you shouldn't trust me like that," Florinda urged. "It's not smart to trust everybody you meet. Why are you laughing at me?"

"Because I know more about some things than you do."

She flashed him a teasing glance. "What, for instance?"

"I know the people who can be trusted," he answered seriously. "Two people only in California have seen my ikon. John, and now you."

"Why Brute!" gasped Florinda. She stared up at him in astonishment.

"You would not either of you make trouble for me," said the Brute, "not if I had pearls as big as eggs."

Florinda looked down. "Thank you, Brute," she said softly.

"You are so much like John," said the Brute. "You have both a great rich goodness, but when somebody finds it out you are so ashamed you are almost angry."

"A great rich—oh Brute, don't talk like a half-wit." Florinda stood up. "Look here, it's time for you to go. I ought to be getting some sleep."

"Why do you make me leave all of a sudden?" asked the Brute. "Are you angry already?"

"Oh, talk sense," said Florinda.

He looked amused, but he objected no further. They said good night. The Brute had started out toward his own room when Florinda called him.

"Oh, by the way. Take these dishes, will you? I'm not allowed out."

He picked up the dishes. As he put his hand on the latch she spoke to him again.

"Brute."

"Yes?"

"You're a dear."

"Thank you," the Brute said smiling.

She kissed her hand to him as he closed the door.

John came back from Los Angeles full of news. The mule-train had left for Santa Fe, but Texas had not been able to go with it. Staggering out of Silky's Place one night, Texas had fallen into a mud-hole and twisted his knee. He was now flat on his back in Los Angeles. John had entrusted Garnet's letter to Devilbug.

Both the girls were distressed about Texas. "If I'd been there it wouldn't have happened," Florinda said indignantly. "I keep an eye on him, and when he's too drunk to walk I get one of the boys to help him home."

John told her Texas was being well treated. Señora Vargas, in whose home Texas stayed when he was in Los Angeles, was a motherly soul. John had been to see him, and Texas had given him a message for Garnet. He had asked when she was expecting her baby, and said he would be around to take care of her. He swore solemnly that he would be sober that week. She could count on him.

John also brought news of more public interest. There had been some disorder in the north, and rumors were thick. Sitting on the wall-bench in Garnet's room, John told them about it. The trouble had been started, he said, by a swaggering American army officer named John Charles Frémont.

John explained. Three years ago the United States government had sent a party of explorers under Frémont to survey a route to the Oregon Territory, north of California. Frémont had proved himself a first-class leader. So now the government had sent him back to Oregon to get more information for people who wanted to settle there.

But instead of going directly to Oregon this time, Frémont came into northern California to rest his men and buy supplies. That much was all right. But Frémont's men got themselves into trouble. There was an argument with a native ranchero about horse-stealing; and one of the men was accused of making improper advances to the daughter of another ranchero. The girl was a relative of Don José Castro, military commandant of California. Castro promptly ordered Frémont's party out of California.

Frémont did not obey. Instead, he moved his camp to a mountain called Gavilan Peak. Here he threw up some log breastworks and raised the American flag over them.

John shrugged with ironic humor as he told his story. "In short," he said, "Frémont seems to be one of the fellows who can do a great job as long as they're giving the orders, but who can't bear to mind anybody else. Castro had a perfect right to order him out if his men got disagreeable. Besides, this is Mexican territory, and Frémont has no business raising a flag here. So Castro threatened to shoot him off Gavilan Peak."

"Did they fight?" asked Florinda.

"No, but it's no fault of Frémont's that they didn't. Luckily for all of us, the United States consul, Mr. Larkin, is a mighty good man at his job. Larkin went to Castro and made official apologies. Then Larkin went to Frémont and persuaded him to pull down his flag and move north, toward Oregon."

"Then it's all over?" Garnet asked.

"Not quite," said John. "It looks as if Larkin doesn't quite trust Frémont to keep quiet. Larkin sent a message to the Pacific fleet of the United States, which is in port at Mazatlán on the west coast of Mexico. He asked that a ship be sent to California, to protect the Yankee traders in case Castro's men and Frémont's men should come to blows. So the sloop-of-war Portsmouth came up, and she's now in San Francisco Bay." John smiled wisely. "There she is, and rumors are flying around that she's going to stay."

"Say, wait a minute," said Florinda. "Do you mean somebody is going to start a war?"

"There's a good chance," John returned, "Frémont or no Frémont, that there may be a war any minute."

They started. "John, what do you mean?" exclaimed Garnet.

"The Republic of Texas," said John. "Possibly the state of Texas by now. All the Yankees seem to expect that Texas will be admitted to the Union, and that Mexico will go to war because of it."

"Oh good heavens," said Garnet. "John, if there is a war, what will we do?"

"I don't think we'll have to do anything. The Yankees in California have always got along well with the natives. If a few blustering fools like Frémont don't ruin our good reputation here, the Californios may be glad to wave good-by to Mexico."

"Then we won't get shot?" asked Florinda.

"Hardly."

"You relieve my mind considerably. Well, I'll let the heroes manage the war, if any. I've got to get back to my bar. When can we start, Johnny? Garnet's all right now."

John stood up. "Nikolai and I will ride with you to Los Angeles whenever you're ready." He chuckled. "I promised Silky I'd bring you back as soon as I could. He misses you."

Florinda smiled shrewdly. "Not me, Johnny. But the profits I bring in. Now Garnet, you rest and I'll pack your things. And I hope you never have to see Charles again as long as you live."

"I hope so too," said Garnet. She gave a long grateful sigh at the thought that now she would be rid of Charles forever.

THIRTY-ONE

CHARLES HAD NOT KNOWN Garnet was planning to go to Los Angeles. When she went into his study and told him, he was shocked and angry. He said he would not permit his brother's widow to live over a saloon. Garnet told him curtly that she had not asked his permission and was not asking it now.

For a moment Charles could not hide his astonishment. It was plain that he was not used to having anybody in his house who defied him. But he quickly recovered his usual contemptuous calm. "Very well," he said to her, "go to Los Angeles with that woman if you want to. I don't care what becomes of you."

"I'm glad of that," she retorted.

Charles did not seem to hear her. "I don't care what becomes of you," he repeated through his crooked teeth. "But I warn you, I am going to take a great deal of interest in what becomes of my brother's child."

"Oh let me alone, Charles!" Garnet said with exasperation as she stood up. She was no longer ill, but she felt heavy and uncomfortable and she was heartily tired of him.

"You are welcome to return here at any time," said Charles. He laughed disagreeably. "I think," he added, "that you will come back."

"No I won't," said Garnet. She went to her own room and banged the door.

The next morning the boys loaded the pack-horses, and by eight o'clock Garnet was on her way to Los Angeles.

As they turned through the pass, and the hills shut out the sight of the buildings behind them, Garnet drew a sigh of relief. She looked up at John, who was riding beside her.

"Oh dear, I feel better!" she exclaimed.

"I'm sure you do," John said with a dry chuckle. He added, "Silky's Place is no mansion. But at least there you'll be independent."

"I'll like it, whatever it is," she said. "And John," she went on.

She spoke earnestly. "Thank you for all you've done for me. I don't know any words that are strong enough to say it."

John brushed a shred of mesquite from his horse's mane. "Frankly, Garnet," he returned, "I'd rather you didn't say it at all."

As he spoke, he seemed to have the sternness that had chilled her the first time she saw him, as though he had become a stranger again. She said in surprise,

"But John, I want to thank you! You and Florinda probably saved my life. Why shouldn't I express my gratitude?"

"I just don't like the word, that's all," said John. He spoke tersely, stroking the mane of his horse, but then he raised his eyes with a smile of apology. "Forgive me. I don't mean to be as discourteous as I sound. But if I helped you get well, it was to please myself, because I liked you and wanted you to get well. You don't owe me anything."

Garnet heard him with a puzzled frown. "Does it embarrass you to be thanked?" she asked wonderingly.

"Yes," he acknowledged. "It makes me feel as if I had demanded it. And I hate people who demand it."

"People who demand it?" she repeated. "Who—I don't understand."

John's lips tightened and she saw the muscles knot in his lean jaws. For a moment he looked straight ahead at the fog veiling the russet hills ahead of them. Then he turned, and his green eyes met hers as he asked, "Have you ever been an object of charity, Garnet?"

Garnet felt her eyes stretch and her lips part, with astonishment and the beginning of a new comprehension of him. She shook her head. John said crisply,

"Well, I have."

Without giving her a chance to answer he hurried his horse and caught up with the Brute, who was riding a little way ahead.

"Turn south around the spur here," said John. "It's a little longer, but the fog on the north side is too thick."

After that he was busy with the train. When they stopped for the nooning he spread a blanket for Garnet, saying, "Here, get some rest while the boys are cooking the beans." Garnet started to say "Thank you," but caught herself and said "Very well." As she lay down she heard the fire crackling under the pots, and John's voice giving curt, competent orders. She wondered what he had meant when he said he had once been an object of charity. He looked like the last man on earth who would ever be willing to receive anything from anybody.

She felt her baby moving, and shook her head sadly. "You poor child," she said to the baby. "You're coming into such a complicated world. You've got such a lot to learn."

She did not try again to thank John, and he did not refer to this conversation. But he rode by her often, and showed her the strange beauty of the hills among which they were traveling. It was the end of May, the time of the high fog, and the days went by in a ghostly radiance. John told her May and June were the grayest months of the year, a period when there was no sun and no shadow, and almost no change of light between dawn and dark. The sky looked like a slate roof, so low that you felt as if you could almost reach up and touch it. There was very little fog on the ground. Sometimes you saw bits of it blowing around, like shreds of wet white muslin, but usually the earth was clear, and though the sky was so dark the earth was brilliant. The wild flowers loved the fog. The flowers glittered everywhere, blue lupin and yellow mustard and hazy purple sage, green plumes of anise curling through the oats, poppies in every shade from ivory to deep ruddy orange. The air was heavy with damp and the fragrance of sage. The damp stroked your skin, and got into your hair, and gathered on the flowers like a faint silver frost.

When they stopped for the noonings the Brute picked handfuls of blooms and brought them to Florinda and Garnet. Florinda had no special interest in flowers, as such; but she appreciated anything offered her by a masculine hand, and when he dropped the poppies and lupin into her lap she exclaimed at their beauty. Her admiration was brief, but quite sincere while it lasted. Garnet liked the flowers, and she liked the strange chilly light. But though she found the journey interesting she also found it very tiring. Riding a horse was harder now than it had been last year when she had had a straight figure. The others were very considerate. They took long noonings and rode slowly for her sake. But she was glad John was there to tell her about the countryside, for it kept her from thinking about how tired she was.

Here and there on the hillsides she saw a strange ugly growth, a vine that sprawled in dirty-yellow patches, greedily covering the bushes as far as it could reach. As they rode, she asked John about it.

"What is that yellowish vine that grows like cobwebs over the other plants?"

John looked up at the hills. "Wretched stuff, isn't it? They call it the love-vine."

"Love-vine," Garnet repeated. "That's an odd name for such an ugly thing. Or does it ever look better than it does now?"

"No, it's never pretty. It's a pest and a parasite. It climbs over the healthy bushes, clinging to them and smothering them. That's why it's called the love-vine."

"But who gave it such a name?" asked Garnet.

"I don't know," John said dryly.

She turned her head and looked him over. "John," she said.

"Yes?"

"I believe you think that's a very good name for it."

"I wasn't going to shock you by saying so," he returned smiling. "But don't try to make me be sentimental, Garnet."

"That's what you think of love?" she demanded.

"You don't?" he asked with a touch of amusement.

"No, I do not."

"I suppose I ought to admire your idealism. But I don't share it."

Garnet felt astonishment and a strange sort of sympathy. "I don't believe—anybody ever loved you," she said slowly.

He shrugged a lean shoulder. "Some people have said they did. Whatever it was they felt for me, it was something I was better off without."

He lapsed into silence. A moment later he rode away from her to help one of the boys manage a stubborn pack-horse.

Florinda was laughing at some story the Brute was telling her. Garnet rode behind them, thinking. John was right about some kinds of love. Charles had said he loved Oliver. Oliver had said he loved her. But all Charles had wanted to do for Oliver was cling to him until he had crushed the life out of him, like the love-vine; and Oliver—she still could not think very clearly about Oliver. It hurt her too much. But what Oliver had felt for her had not been what she meant when she thought of love.

But there was such a thing as *love*, she told herself defiantly. There was the love she had seen between her parents, strong and utterly dependable. And that was what she wanted. If I were sure somebody felt like that about me, thought Garnet, I could stand anything.

Later on they paused for the nooning. While they were resting on the grass after dinner Garnet pointed out the love-vine to Florinda and told her what John had said about it. "Do you believe he's right?" Garnet asked.

Glancing up at the tangled yellow patches, Florinda laughed a little. "I'm a strange one to ask, dearie. I've never been in love."

"Not at all?"

"Well, I liked them," Florinda said good-naturedly. "In fact, I've been quite fond of several gents in my time. But never so fond that I couldn't wave goodby quite cheerfully when it was over." She leaned back, supporting herself on her hands. "And if you're asking me," she added coolly, "that's enough."

"No it is not," Garnet said decidedly.

Florinda gave her a calm blue survey, up and down. "Yes it is enough, my sweet, and if you care to listen, I can tell you something about love."

"How can you? You've just told me you didn't know anything about it."

"Hell for breakfast," said Florinda, "I've never had smallpox either, but I know enough to know I don't want any." Her voice was clear and quiet as she went on. "Garnet, I've heard people babbling about love. And I've seen what it does to them. And it's a lot of twaddle, dearest, and the sooner you stop looking for it the sooner you'll stop being disappointed because you can't find it."

Garnet shook her head. Florinda took both Garnet's hands in hers. She had not put on her gloves since eating dinner, and her handclasp was rough.

"Please believe me, dear," she said.

Garnet shook her head again. "It's not true, Florinda. There are people who love each other all their lives, who stand by each other like two stone walls together! Don't you believe there were ever two people like that?"

"Oh, possibly. A pair of red-headed Indians in Peru."

"No," Garnet said vehemently. "I'm talking about my mother and father."

There was a pause. "All right," said Florinda. "I'm not going to say it can't happen. I never saw your mother. But if you'll excuse me for mentioning it, dearie, you never saw mine."

As though done with the subject, she stood up and said it was time for siesta and she'd get the blankets. She came back with the blankets in her arms.

"You don't need to move," she said to Garnet. "I'll fix yours and mine both."

Garnet smiled up at her. "Nobody who judged you by your talk would guess how thoughtful you are."

"This is different," said Florinda. "You're my friend and I like you. It's quite different."

She arranged the blankets to make two beds. Yawning, she took off her shoes, loosened her clothes at the waistline, and slipped into one of the beds. Garnet knew she needed her own nap too, but she did not feel sleepy. She sat watching John as he helped the boys picket the horses in a spot where the grass was thick. The Brute came over with a steaming cup of chocolate.

"This will make you warm inside and sleepy," he said.

She thanked him and took the cup. The Brute sat on the grass by her. After a moment he glanced over at Florinda, sound asleep, then looking back at Garnet he gave her his sweet innocent smile.

"They are very foolish people, Garnet," he said. "John and Florinda."

"You heard what they said to me?" she asked.

"Some of it. Don't blame them. They don't know any better."

"Then you do think they are wrong, don't you?" Garnet asked.

"Of course they are wrong. But you see, I think—" he hesitated.

"Tell me, Brute."

"Garnet, I don't know a great deal that you know. But I will tell you what I think about those two. I think they got hurt when they were so little they could not fight back."

For a little while Garnet was silent. She finished the chocolate and he took the cup. "You are a very wise man, Brute," she said.

"I don't know," said the Brute. "So many of the Yankees say I am a big fool, and I think they are big fools, and I don't know which of us is right. But I know you are a brave woman. When you have your baby you will not punish it for what it did not do."

"Oh no, Brute!"

He smiled. "Florinda's mother did that to her. I think somebody punished John too, but John has never told me. Now you must get your siesta."

She lay down obediently. The Brute pulled the blankets over her and tucked them in gently, like a woman soothing a child to sleep.

Since they rode so slowly, it took them ten days to make the trip to Los Angeles. But Garnet was worn out when they got there.

As she rode into the village she shivered with disgust. Los Angeles was the dirtiest town she had ever seen. It looked as if everybody threw the slops outdoors and nobody ever cleaned up anything. The wild dogs rooted in the garbage, the flies swarmed over it, the horses trod it into the earth. The air reeked with nasty odors. Here and there came an ox-cart loaded with hides, and they had a stench all their own. "Why do they smell like that?" she exclaimed to Florinda."

"Well, when the Diggers skin the animals, they don't bother to scrape all the flesh off the hides, and it rots." Florinda wrinkled her nose as she talked. "But they tell me this is nothing to San Diego. That's where they load the hides. The sailors say you can smell San Diego for miles out to sea."

Garnet put up one hand to scratch the back of her neck. Florinda gave her a smile.

"We're cleaner at Silky's," she said encouragingly. "You'll hardly ever feel them there."

Garnet felt goose-bumps running up her thighs, and her stomach felt queasy and for a moment she thought she was going to throw up. She put her fist to her mouth and bit on her leather glove, remembering the airy cleanliness of Union Square. She remembered Charles' rancho too. It had been a cheerless spot and she had not had a single pleasant day there, but it had been clean. She almost wished she had never left it. She swallowed hard, realizing bitterly that now her only home was a saloon in a dirty little village off at the end of the world; and wondering what sort of life she could make for her child in a place like this; and she thought she would give anything or do anything if only she could get out of here and go home. Half dizzy from the smells and the fleas and the yelping dogs, she looked around.

John and the Brute were riding ahead as guides. There were only about two hundred buildings in Los Angeles, but most of them were little brown cubes that looked just alike, and they were set so crazily that Garnet thought anybody who went twenty steps from home must get lost. The houses were roofed with tar, and though the tar looked solid enough now, evidently in hot weather it melted and ran down, for the sides of the houses were streaked with long black trickles. The spaces between the houses were overgrown with wild oats, brightened here and there with poppies, or blooms of datura trailing over the ground. Garnet saw a church, and several larger adobe houses which Florinda told her were the homes of well-to-do families, and a few big buildings which Florinda said were trading posts. Then after several more zigzags, they came to Silky's Place. John dismounted and helped Garnet off her horse.

The door of the saloon stood open, and she saw several men at the bar. Silky himself came hurrying out. He had on a red coat, and his mustache was curled and his hair glistened with pomade. He shouted joyfully to Florinda, and kissed Garnet's hand, saying it was an honor indeed to have her in his humble abode.

Garnet tried to answer politely. But she was aching all over, and the smells of liquor were pouring out of the saloon to mingle with the smells outside. Florinda put an arm around her.

"Leave her alone, Silky, she's not feeling any too good. John, Brute, go on up to the bar and get a drink. I'll take care of Garnet."

She helped Garnet up the stairs to the bedroom. Garnet sat down on the wall-bench, looking around with surprise at the neat furniture and fresh blue curtains. A moment later Florinda brought in a young native woman. This, Florinda said, was Isabel, who kept the room clean and did Florinda's sewing and laundry. She didn't speak English but she was very, very nice. Now if Garnet would just wait here a few minutes, Isabel would bring the packs so they could get out some clean clothes, and Florinda would go down to the kitchen and get a pail of hot water.

Left alone, Garnet went to the window and opened the shutters. The air and smells blew in together. She looked down, fairly shivering at the noise. Outside were the barking of dogs, shouts of ox-drivers, yells of children, calls of Diggers selling water; from inside the saloon she heard the voices, the clinks, the strumming of guitars and the tipsy songs. So this was Los Angeles. Garnet gave a little crooked smile. How different her life was from everything she had expected.

And yet, she told herself grimly, this is what I've got, because without knowing it, this is what I wanted.

Now that she saw it, she wondered why she had not seen it before. She had wanted freedom, and now she had freedom unlimited. Here in this mud village, far from every restraint that had ever been laid on her, she could do exactly as she pleased.

What a little girl she had been when she married Oliver! She had been so full of zest and curiosity, so eager to follow all those shining promises that did not exist anywhere except in her own head. She had thought freedom meant simply the chance to have her own way, with no need to take the consequences of having had it. Well, she knew better now. Life was not a lot of golden adventures that cost you nothing.

Resting her elbow on the sill of the window she looked back

at Florinda's neat, defiant little room. She thought of the first time she had talked to Florinda, when she had been amazed at the cheerful confidence with which Florinda had faced her future. Now she understood it. You developed that kind of courage because you had to. It was not a matter of noble ideals. It was a matter of self-defense. It was like getting over the desert—either you did or you didn't, and nobody cared very much but yourself.

The baby gave her a kick. Garnet clenched her fist on the window-sill. Out here in this half-savage land, there would be a lot that she could not give her child. But she could teach it what she had learned, and what Oliver had never learned: that no kindly providence was going to save you from the results of what you did, and that you had better be sure of your own strength because you could never be sure of anybody else's.

Among the oats growing against the wall of a house near by, Garnet saw a cluster of yellow poppies. She remembered that John had named his rancho for the poppies. La flor torosa, the sturdy flower. The poppies looked so delicate. You'd think they were frail hot-house flowers that couldn't stand a whiff of wind. But actually they were weeds that could stand anything. Garnet smiled at the bright golden cluster. "Torosa," she said aloud, and repeated it, "Torosa." She liked the word.

John and the Brute returned to their ranchos, and Garnet set about getting used to Los Angeles.

It was not easy. The noise broke her sleep so often that for the first few days she felt groggy all the time. The smells of hides and garbage were an endless insult to her nose. In spite of Isabel's cleaning, the fleas did manage to hop in now and then; and besides the fleas there were always the spiders. The spiders were mostly harmless, but they were a constant pest. They made nests of cobwebs on the window-sill, and hung festoons of them in the corners under the ceiling. During her first week in Los Angeles Garnet brushed down more cobwebs than she had ever seen in a year in New York.

But it could have been a great deal worse. At Silky's Place she had no sense of being unwanted as she had had in Charles' house. The Chinese boy Mickey smiled at her cordially, and Silky gave her grand bows whenever he saw her. As for Florinda, her affection was warm and solid, the sort of friendship that made no demands, but was simply there, like sunshine.

Texas came by, limping on a cane, for when he fell into the mud-hole his leg had been hurt worse than anybody had realized at the time. Leaning on the bar one morning, Texas repeated to Garnet what he had said to John: he knew all about delivering babies, had done it over and over, and the minute she needed him she was to send for him. Day or night, no trouble at all, no indeed, privilege to be of service. And meantime, he might just mention a few details about taking care of her health.

He knew what he was talking about, Florinda observed after he was gone. Florinda had never again spoken directly about having had a child. But Garnet thought she would have guessed it even if Florinda had never told her. Florinda had such a sympathetic understanding of the whole subject.

The town was so puzzling and so ugly, and Garnet felt so heavy on her legs, that she did not often go out. She spent most of her time in the kitchen or in the bedroom upstairs, making clothes for her baby from cloth Florinda had bought at Mr. Abbott's store. Isabel helped her cut them. Isabel also made over the black dresses Florinda had worn at Doña Manuela's, so Garnet could wear them. Florinda protested at Garnet's going into mourning, saying, "Black is not your color, I warn you." But Garnet would have felt almost indecent in anything but black, so Florinda yielded and got her last winter's dresses out of the wardrobe. Florinda never threw away anything that could be used again.

Called in to do the sewing, Isabel agreed with Garnet at once. Of course a widow must wear black, she said. She said it with an emphatic gravity that sent Florinda into spasms of mirth behind her back. Nobody had ever taught Florinda that traditions were sacred whether they meant anything or not. While she and Garnet ate supper that evening, Florinda explained what had made her laugh.

She said Isabel was a widow with three children. Her husband had been a drunken wretch, and one morning after a bout he was found lying face down in the creek. There was some talk about it in the village—some people said Isabel had pushed him in, and others said he fell in but she had not tried to help him out. But as his death was no loss to the community nobody inquired too closely.

This had happened four years ago, and Isabel had refused to get married again. She was young and handsome and she had had several good offers, but she had declined them all, saying firmly that she knew all she wanted to know about husbands. It had not been easy for her to make a living for her children, and when Florinda came to town they were welcome to each other. Isabel and Florinda agreed with each other heartily in the matter of husbands. Garnet heard them discussing the subject with an enthusiasm that made up for their difficulty with language. Men, said Florinda, were fine, but husbands—unable to think of a sufficiently strong Spanish word, she made a face and whistled. Isabel said she was quite right.

But Isabel had worn black for her husband, and she would have been scandalized if Garnet had not worn black for hers. Florinda laughed wonderingly at the idea. "I guess," she said, "I'll just never understand nice people."

She put on a fresh pair of mitts and went back to tend the bar.

Florinda was always busy. Her energy seemed endless. She worked ten or twelve hours a day, seven days a week, and never complained about it. As for the noise, the smells, the spiders, and the other nuisances, she bore them good-naturedly. In years of putting up with things she did not like, Florinda had developed a hard, cool cheerfulness that was like a shell around her.

"I admire you very much," Garnet said to her one night about two weeks after she came to Los Angeles. "And I envy you."

"For what?" asked Florinda, scrubbing her shoulders. When she came up from the bar she had brought a pail of warm water, and now she stood before the washstand giving herself a bath. It was an hour past midnight, and the street—if you could call it a street— was quiet. Florinda emptied the basin and filled it with clean water. "Come be an angel and wash my back," she said to Garnet, and as Garnet took the washcloth Florinda asked, "What did you mean by that remark?"

"I meant I admire the way you stand up to the business of living," said Garnet. "This place, for instance. You must hate it. But you never say so."

"Well, dear, it's not exactly what I was looking forward to when I was washing the cuspidors in Max Duren's saloon on Pearl Street. But I got out of that, and I'll get out of this, because I'm not the kind of girl who puts up forever with things she doesn't like." Florinda darted a bright blue glance over her shoulder. "And you aren't either, dearie."

Garnet smiled in agreement as she picked up the towel and dried Florinda's back. "No, I'm not going to stay in this wretched town without at least making a fight to get out. But meanwhile—Florinda, don't you ever just want to curl up and whine?"

"Sure, but what good would it do? And you aren't whining, are you?"

Garnet hung the towel on the rack and stretched out on the bed. Florinda scrubbed her legs.

"Look here, dearie," she went on. "This place is awful. But we aren't weeping about it. Not because we're high-minded, but because we're too smart to waste all the energy it would take." Glancing around again, she gave Garnet a wise smile. "And because, bad as Los Angeles is, we can think of two places worse. One of 'em's the New York state prison, and the other is any house occupied by Charles Hale. Right?"

Garnet laughed curtly. "Right."

Florinda began to wash her feet. Her way of doing it was to stand on her left leg while she lifted her right knee chest-high and put her right foot into the basin, then to stand on her right leg while she lifted the other. Years of dancing had kept her as supple as a baby. Watching her, Garnet sighed with envy.

"Do you think I'll ever be limber again?"

"Oh, sure," said Florinda. She smiled. "I know how you feel now, dearie—you can hardly put on your own shoes and you wonder if you'll ever be able to lace another corset. But it's amazing how you'll get right back into shape. And when you do, all this—" she made a wide gesture including Los Angeles and the country around it— "all this will be a lot easier than it is now." But Garnet was frowning and biting her lip, and Florinda asked, "Something else on your mind?"

"Yes. Something I've been wanting to ask you ever since I've been here."

"Go ahead." Florinda emptied the soiled water into the slop-jar, tucked her feet into slippers and put on her nightgown, and sat down on the wall-bench to brush her hair. Garnet looked down at the bed, stroking the nap of the blanket with her forefinger.

"Florinda, how much longer are you planning to have me stay in here with you?"

"Why, as long as you like."

"Couldn't you put a mattress for me in the storeroom? Silky must know I wouldn't drink up his liquor."

"But why do you want to stay in the storeroom?"

341

"You've been wonderful to me," said Garnet, "but I can't share your room indefinitely. You understand."

"I do not. Why shouldn't you share my room? You're not in my way."

"Oh, for heaven's sake don't pretend to be so stupid! I mean— I mean Silky!"

With a long startled stare, Florinda lowered her hairbrush to her knee. She began to laugh. "Oh, I'm a three-legged Indian," she said. "I've got a lump of dough where my head ought to be. Garnet, I'm so sorry. I didn't know that was worrying you. Darling, there's nothing like that between Silky and me."

Garnet sat up. "Oh Florinda, please forgive me!"

Florinda was still laughing. "It's my fault, I should have told you. I thought I had. Didn't I say it was strictly business?"

"Yes, but I didn't understand." Garnet felt an embarrassed warmth in her cheeks. "Am I getting red?"

"Wine-colored, and there's no reason why you should." Florinda went back to brushing her hair as she explained. "Most of the gents who come in here think that, but I didn't know you did too. I don't tell the gents any different, because all day long I get what you'd call improper suggestions, and it keeps matters simpler to let them think Silky would start shooting if I said yes. I don't mean I'm growing angel's wings, or anything like that. But here's how things really are." She spoke clearly. "Garnet, I'm not Silky's lady of the moment, and I don't work for him. I own half this place."

Garnet was astonished. "I never thought of that!"

"We rent this building from Mr. Abbott," said Florinda. "Silky was doing a nice little business here, but he wanted to enlarge. We talked it over when he came up to Mr. Kerridge's. I went shares with him. Understand?"

Garnet nodded.

"Now of course," Florinda went on smiling, "you're wondering where I got the capital and you're too polite to ask. So I'll tell you. Remember when I gave you my fare from New Orleans to St. Louis, I took the money out of a purse I had sewed to my corset?"

"Yes, I remember."

"Well, that was my bank. I thought I was fairly safe in New Orleans, but there was always the chance that I might have to make a quick getaway, just as I did. So I stitched a purse to every corset

I owned, and every morning when I got dressed I put my jewelry into it, and enough money to keep me going a while."

"You're very wise," Garnet said with admiration.

"Not always. But I learn as I go along. And one lesson I do know. Don't ever be without money. Money is the most important thing on earth."

Garnet smiled and frowned at the same time, considered, and shook her head. "No it's not, Florinda."

"What is, then?" asked Florinda.

"I don't know. That's one of the things I'm going to find out about living. But it's not money."

Florinda smiled sagely. Reaching along the wall-bench, she picked up Garnet's purse. It had lain there since this afternoon when Garnet had taken it out to pay Isabel for altering the black dresses. Florinda shifted the purse from one hand to the other, feeling how comfortably heavy it was. As she set it down she gave a significant look from Garnet to the purse and back again.

"Try doing without it sometime, dearie," she suggested.

Standing up, she stretched and yawned, as though to imply there was no more to be said on the subject.

THIRTY-TWO

THE MONTH OF JUNE was cool and misty and full of flowers. Then on the first of July the sun came out. After this the sun shone every day. It scorched the mountain brush to a hundred shades of purple and bronze, and made the grass crackle like paper underfoot.

Soon after the sun appeared, a trading party brought news of more disorder in the north. The men said Frémont had gone to Oregon as ordered, but he had come back to northern California almost at once. As soon as he got back trouble had started again.

Their story went like this. Don Mariano Guadalupe Vallejo, one of the richest men in California, lived on his rancho north of San Francisco Bay. One morning in June a group of thirty-three Yankees raided his home. They said they were a party of revolution, ready to take over the government, and they were here with the approval of Frémont.

They piled into Señor Vallejo's parlor, got drunk on his liquor, and called for pens and paper. Some of them could not write, and of those who could, several were not sober enough to do so. But the others drew up a document saying California was now a republic. This done, they made prisoners of Señor Vallejo and his family, as well as several other well-known men of that neighborhood. They marched their captives first to Frémont's camp and then to Sutter's Fort, where they locked them up. That afternoon, to clinch their conquest, they ran up a flag over Señor Vallejo's rancho.

A man named Todd made the flag. Some people said he made it out of a sheet and a woman's red flannel petticoat. Mr. Todd painted a red star in a corner of the sheet and drew a picture of a bear looking up at the star. Across the bottom he tacked a strip of red flannel, and above the strip he printed "California Republic." That is, he meant to print it that way, but he got confused and left the letter I out of the word Republic. He put it on later, above the C. The flag had about as much dignity as the rest of the day's performance.

Of the thirty-three men who raided Señor Vallejo's home, a few were village or rancho workers, but most of them had no permanent address and no known occupation. Twenty of the thirty-three had been in California less than eight months. Mr. Larkin, the American consul in Monterey, and Mr. Montgomery, captain of the American warship now in San Francisco Bay, condemned their behavior at once. The Yankee traders and rancheros heard the tale with dismay.

These Yankees were doing a good business and they wanted to go on doing it. True, they had long been hinting that any time California wished to be free of Mexico, they would be glad to help. But they wanted a friendly union. They did not want the Californios to get the idea that Yankees were hoodlums. In Silky's bar, the Yankee residents of Los Angeles talked angrily about the rumpus. They assured the Angelenos that they had nothing to do with those loafers up north, and that Frémont was going to get himself into rich trouble if he didn't go on back to Oregon.

Half amused and half annoyed, Silky and Florinda told Garnet about the conversations in the bar. Garnet felt exasperated. She was tired, she was within a few weeks of childbirth, and she thought she had put up with enough. "Do you mean," she demanded, "that we're going to get blamed for this, just because we're Americans too?"

344

Silky, who was checking the credit ledgers, pulled at his mustache a moment, and shook his head. Silky could be serious enough when he chose. "I don't think we need to be worried, Mrs. Hale. The Angelenos like us. Look how they come in here every evening to drink wine and play monte. They know men like me and Abbott and the rest of us, we don't have any truck with floaters like that crew."

Garnet felt better, and went back to her sewing. Silky resumed his checking of the profits. Business was good and Silky was in a cheerful mood. His satisfied expression as he added the figures reminded Garnet that she had not yet made any arrangement for paying her own expenses. She had told Florinda she wanted to, and Florinda had said, "You don't have to do that. Beef is so cheap here that all you can eat wouldn't come to a dollar a month." But Garnet still wanted to pay her share. Both Silky and Florinda were more interested in getting rich than in anything else, and Garnet was pretty sure that neither of them would persist in refusing good money. Besides, she was about to have a baby, and with Silky at least she suspected that regular cash payments might make the difference between a squalling brat and a sweet little cherub.

She decided she had better see Mr. Abbott now, and get this matter straightened out before her baby was born. When she went upstairs that evening, she looked at her figure in the glass. In New York, she would never have dreamed of going out where people could see her. But she had observed that in California women about to have children went about as usual and nobody took any notice of them. So she would go to see Mr. Abbott tomorrow, if Florinda would go with her to show her the way.

The thought of being responsible for her own property gave her a shaky feeling, for she knew so little about such things. At home her father had given her an allowance, and Oliver had always been generous. In New Orleans, whenever she said she was going shopping he would offer her a bill or two from his pocket. In Santa Fe he had given her a handful of Mexican coins before she had thought of asking for them. Since reaching California she had not spent any money at all except what she had given Isabel for altering the black dresses. She had offered to pay for the cloth Florinda bought for the baby's clothes, but Florinda had said, "Oh, that's paid for. I told Mr. Abbott to check it off in Oliver's credit book."

Florinda understood money. She had told Garnet how much to pay Isabel for the sewing, and she could explain the odd mixture of coins and hides and credit books used in California. When Florinda came up to their room that night, Garnet told her she wanted to see Mr. Abbott. Florinda nodded.

"Why sure, dear, I understand. It's confusing not to know how much you've got. I'll go with you tomorrow—José can take care of the bar, and I need some shoes anyway."

Garnet was sitting on the wall-bench before the window, looking out at the stars. She saw the Big Dipper, and remembered how her father had first shown it to her when she was a little girl. It gave her a wrench of homesickness. Looking at the stars, she said suddenly,

"I wish my child was not going to be a foreigner!"

Florinda was piling her laundry into a basket to be given to Isabel the next day. "It's a shame, Garnet," she said. "Having to stay here when you didn't mean to."

"I don't think I ever really thought about my own country before," said Garnet. "In New York, the Fourth of July was just a lot of fireworks and a fat man on a platform reading the Declaration of Independence. But out here, when the day went by and it was just another day—" She stopped. "I'm sorry! This won't do either of us any good."

"People do get back, you know," said Florinda.

"Yes, of course. Maybe I could get the captain of a clipper ship to take me as a passenger. Do those ships ever carry women?"

"Sometimes. Once in a while a captain brings his wife with him. If there's one woman along he might not mind having another. You'd be company for her."

"I'd pay him everything I had," said Garnet. After a pause she asked, "Would you go with me?"

"No, dearie," said Florinda.

So Garnet did not pursue the subject. But as she looked out at the stars and thought of home, she felt her eyes smarting with tears.

The next day they went to Mr. Abbott's. Garnet wore one of her black Mexican dresses, and Florinda showed her how to cover her head with the strip of black silk that the Californios called a rebozo. It was a glittering midsummer day. They went by paths trodden through the wild oats, winding this way and that among the houses. Dogs and children scampered around them, and here and there they stepped aside to let a horseman go by. The walk took them only ten minutes, but they turned so often that Garnet looked back more than once to make sure of the direction they were taking.

At the trading post a stack of hides lay on the porch in front. As she smelt them Garnet made a face.

"What would you have said in New York," she asked Florinda, "if somebody had told you where your slippers came from?"

"I guess I'd have said, 'Thank heaven I don't have to live there.' Well, you never know what's going to happen next. There's a step under these weeds, be careful. There, fine. That's Mr. Abbott, the fat man sitting behind the counter."

Mr. Abbott, round and bald and jovial, smiled broadly upon them as they came in.

"Well now, this is a treat. How do you do, Miss Florinda?"

"Healthy as a weed, thank you, sir. Let me make you acquainted with my friend Mrs. Oliver Hale. She wants to see you on a little matter of business."

Mr. Abbott did not look as if he ever moved any more than he had to. But out of respect for Garnet's black dress and her obvious state of health, he now pushed himself up out of his chair with a great puffing and heaving, gave her a big soft hand and told her how deeply he felt for her in the grief displayed by her widow's weeds. Drawing up a chair for her behind the counter, he invited her to sit down.

Garnet thanked him, went around the end of the counter, and took the chair. Solemnly clasping his hands over his paunch, Mr. Abbott told her Oliver had been a fine man, and he would be happy to do any service in his power for Oliver's widow.

Garnet did not want to discuss Oliver. Sensing this, Florinda interrupted Mr. Abbott to say she'd like to try on some shoes, please, if he had any nice ones. Why of course he had, Mr. Abbott exclaimed, some real stylish shoes from the best factory in Connecticut. He shouted for somebody to come wait on Miss Florinda, and two Yankee clerks appeared from the back room behind the counter. Florinda flashed her charm upon them, and they hurried to bring not only shoes but ribbons and dress-goods as well. Sitting on the wall-bench to slip off the shoes she was wearing, Florinda wanted to know if they thought she owned a rancho, that she could buy a thousand hides' worth of clothes all at once.

"There now, don't you go teasing me," Mr. Abbott boomed at her. "If everybody kept their credit on the books as good as you do I'd not have a care in the world. Collins! Bring some wine for Mrs. Hale, she looks a bit peaky. Well, yes, a cup for me too, don't mind if I do. Join us, Miss Florinda? Better reconsider, ma'am, nothing like a little wine for the stomach's sake, so says the Good Book itself."

Florinda thanked him but shook her head, admiring her foot in a black kid slipper with a silk rosette, and flirting with both clerks at once. While they talked, Garnet looked around at the trading post. The front and both side walls of the room had adobe wall-benches, and the counter faced the door so Mr. Abbott could greet his customers as they came in. At one end of the counter was a pile of old newspapers that had been wadded and stuffed into the chinks of the goods-boxes. Some of the pages were whole, others had been torn, but all had been smoothed out so the American customers could read them. Few of the papers were less than a year old, for they had come on ships around Cape Horn, but they brought the latest news to be had from the United States.

On the back wall of the room, behind the counter, were shelves piled with ledgers. The rancheros brought in their hides, got credit for them on the books, and took their credit papers to be exchanged for goods as they needed them. There was very little cash handled anywhere.

Behind this room was another, where the clerks had been working when Mr. Abbott bawled for their services. Evidently they had been unpacking a shipment of goods, for Garnet could see the open crates, and the pots and pans, mirrors and cloth and shoes that had come out of them. Young Mr. Collins, the clerk, set a bottle of red wine and two cups on the counter. Mr. Abbott poured a cupful of wine for Garnet and handed it to her with as much of a bow as a fat man could manage sitting down.

Mr. Abbott never hurried. Sipping his wine, he asked Garnet what she thought of that ruckus up north. Disgraceful, wasn't it? Bad for business. And how'd she like this fine summer weather? Hot days and cool nights, never got anything like this back in the States, no sirree they didn't. Another man dropped in, a stringy, lantern-jawed character in a red shirt and dusty black trousers. Mr. Abbott introduced him to Garnet as Mr. Bugs McLane. Garnet had heard of Mr. Bugs McLane, who was well known at Silky's: he did a thriving business in bringing whiskey and other contraband goods from the ships. Mr. McLane said he had come by to talk over some little things with Mr. Abbott, but he was in no hurry and could wait till Mrs. Hale was finished. Meanwhile, he had noticed a woman selling hot tamales yonder by the church. If Florinda had picked out the shoes she wanted, he would be mighty pleased if she would drop over there with him, and they could refresh themselves with a few tamales.

Florinda said she was positively suffering for want of hot tamales, and she'd be delighted to accept the invitation if Mr. Collins would put aside this pair of slippers for her. She and Mr. Bugs McLane went out arm in arm.

Mr. Abbott chatted a few minutes longer, but finally he got around to asking Garnet what was the business she wanted to see him about. Garnet said that since Mr. Abbott had acted as Oliver's banker, she had come to learn what Oliver had left on deposit.

Yes, yes, of course, said Mr. Abbott, and he told Mr. Collins to hand him down a ledger. As his pudgy fingers rustled the pages Mr. Abbott was pleasant and fatherly, and at the same time respectful, as became a merchant dealing with a rich woman.

Twenty minutes later Garnet thanked him and stood up. Mr. Abbott nodded to Mr. Collins, who sprang forward to take her arm and walk with her to the porch. A little distance away, Garnet saw Florinda and Mr. Bugs McLane and a group of natives, blissfully consuming hot tamales. "Will you tell Miss Grove I am ready to go now, Mr. Collins?" Garnet asked.

Being hatless, Mr. Collins touched his forehead and went off. Standing on the porch, Garnet held tight with one hand to a post that supported the roof. She could feel her baby moving. It gave her a sense of panic. Mr. Abbott had bowed her out with deference, and Mr. Collins was obeying her because he thought she was rich. They did not know what she had just found out, that she had almost nothing to live on.

The facts were clear. Mr. Abbott had told them to her affably, not knowing what he was telling her. Oliver had brought a lot of merchandise from Santa Fe last summer; John had placed it to Oliver's credit at the store; Mr. Abbott had sold it, and after deducting his own fee he had recorded the proceeds in Oliver's credit book. Everything was in order. But then, when she herself had insisted that Oliver leave California for good, he had withdrawn his credit. He had left only a few dollars for last-minute trifles.

What he had done with his credit, of course Mr. Abbott did not know. Probably he had contracted with rancheros for mules, with sea-captains for silk and coffee and spices to sell in Santa Fe. "No doubt," said Mr. Abbott, "you've already found these records at the rancho. I guess Mr. Charles Hale took charge of them, to keep them for you."

Garnet remembered Oliver's trips here and there in the weeks before he died. She had told him to leave nothing in California, because they were never coming back. Typically, Oliver had obeyed.

To be sure, Mr. Abbott continued, all the goods Oliver had bought could be put back on credit here. Mr. Charles Hale would know where they were. Any time she or Charles brought in the receipts, Mr. Abbott would be glad to put them to her account. And of course, the rancho itself had been granted to the Hale brothers jointly. Mr. Charles Hale would have her share of this year's hide sales, if he had not given it to her already. Any time she brought in the hide receipts, Mr. Abbott would put this sum too on the books.

The rancho, the rancho, Charles. As she stood on the porch, the words clanged in Garnet's mind. Mr. Abbott did not know that Oliver had deeded his share of the rancho to Charles. She had said, "Yes, yes, give it to him!"—not dreaming that land in California would ever have any value for her.

The credit Oliver had left at Mr. Abbott's, less what Florinda had spent for the baby's clothes, amounted to thirty-eight dollars. Mr. Abbott said he had transferred this to Mrs. Hale's name when Florinda told him she had come to live in town. It had hardly seemed necessary to ask her to come in and sign for so trifling a sum. Now that she was here, she would be good enough to sign the page. He was glad to have the account and it would be an honor to serve Mrs. Hale at any time. And if all this business about hides and credits confused her, well, she could leave everything to him. Ask any Yankee or any Angeleno, and they'd tell her that his reputation for square dealing was lily-white.

Garnet braced herself against the post because she felt as if she might fall down. Now she knew what Charles had meant when he told her, with sneering assurance, that she would come back to him. She had no way to make him give up Oliver's property. There were no lawyers in California, and she had been here long enough to know how few laws there were that anybody respected.

Around the store, the dogs barked and the children ran up and down. Men swapped stories and women cooked at the outdoor ovens. A two-wheeled cart full of hides creaked up to the store, the driver walking by the head of the ox, and his Digger servants began to stack the hides on Mr. Abbott's porch. Garnet could smell the hides. She could smell the Diggers too, and the dogs and the garbage in the street, and the hot tamales from the stand over there, and the beef and chili cooking at the outdoor fires. The smells made her sick, and her flesh crawled, or maybe that sensation meant fleas. For a moment the whole scene trembled as though she saw it from under water. Biting her lip savagely, she closed her eyes tight and opened them, several times, until her head cleared. She saw Florinda coming toward her with Mr. Collins and Mr. Bugs McLane.

Florinda was wiping her fingers on her handkerchief and slipping on her gloves over her half-mitts. As they reached the porch step, Mr. McLane and Mr. Collins bowed to Garnet, and Florinda thanked Mr. McLane for the hot tamales. "Now just wait a minute till I pick up my new shoes," she said to Garnet as the men went into the store. "Why Garnet, what's the trouble?" she exclaimed, as she noticed Garnet's face. "You look kind of green. Sick?"

"A little bit. I'll be all right in a minute."

"Maybe you should sit down for a while indoors."

"No, I'd rather go home," said Garnet. The word "home" sounded mocking as she said it. She had no home. She could live in the loft over the saloon, dependent on Florinda's kindness, or she could live with Charles, which meant Charles would take charge of her child so completely that the baby would grow up with no more sense of responsible self-reliance than Oliver had had.

"All right, dear," said Florinda, "we'll go right home and you can lie down." She stepped to the doorway of the store. "Oh, Mr. Collins! Mrs. Hale is feeling a bit faint. Could you leave the store long enough to help her get home?"

Mr. Collins came out at once and said certainly. He was an ambitious young Yankee with dreams of saving enough to go into the Santa Fe trade. Glad to be of service to one of his employer's rich customers, he took Garnet's arm respectfully while Florinda hurried inside. Garnet could hear her talking.

"Mr. Abbott, have you got some smelling salts or lavender water? Why yes, this will do. Put it on Mrs. Hale's account." She came out, carrying her shoes in one hand and a little blue jar in the other. "Here, Garnet, this is some nice fragrant stuff the ladies use here. It'll make you feel better. Sometimes this town makes me wish I didn't have any nose."

Garnet thanked her, trying not to sound ironic. Nice fragrant stuff, put it on Mrs. Hale's account. Florinda too thought she was rich.

Walking between Florinda and Mr. Collins, she got back to

351

Silky's Place. Mr. Collins bowed and told her it had been a pleasure to assist her. Garnet wondered how deferential he would have been if he had known she owned less than a hundred dollars. She and Florinda went into the saloon by the side door. Silky saw them and called to Florinda, "Couple of customers been asking for you."

"Be right there," she called back, slipping her hand under Garnet's elbow to help her up the stairs. At the bedroom door Garnet said,

"You can go down now. I feel better. I'm sorry I got dizzy just then."

"Oh rats, don't apologize. You can't help it. These last few weeks, the baby feels like it weighs ninety pounds."

She helped Garnet take off her dress and put on a robe, and told her to lie down. Garnet obeyed, and Florinda ran downstairs. A moment later Garnet heard the men at the bar asking where she had been. Garnet shrugged. When your business was to entertain people, as Florinda's was, you were never supposed to be tired or to have anything else to do. But Florinda had never had much consideration from other people, so she did not expect it.

That's my trouble, Garnet said to herself. All my life other people have taken care of me. Now that's over. I've got to take care of myself. And I've got to take care of my baby.

But what in the world, she wondered, was she going to do? It was all right to say you were willing to take care of yourself, but how did you go about it? When you found yourself in a mess like this, what did you *do?*

She could, of course, stay here and let Florinda support her. But even as she thought of it, she felt as though she were seeing the bitterness in John's green eyes and the knot of muscle at his jaw as he said, "Have you ever been an object of charity, Garnet?"

She was not going back to Charles. That was final.

She thought of her father. But he had not even received her letter saying Oliver was dead; he was still expecting her and Oliver to reach New York this fall. When he did get the letter, if he wanted to send her anything he would have to find a sea-captain about to sail for California and trust him to bring it to her. It might be two or three years before she could hear from home.

Garnet tried to figure how much she had. About fifty dollars in her purse; thirty-eight dollars at Mr. Abbott's, less the price of the jar of fragrant stuff Florinda had bought; the emeralds Florinda had left her in New Orleans, and the garnets for which she had been named. She had no idea what the jewels were worth.

At siesta time Florinda came in, took off her dress, lay down and fell asleep at once. She woke just before sunset. Garnet need not come down to supper, she said. Mickey would bring it up. She hurried back to work before Garnet could say she was not hungry.

A little while later a tap on the door signaled the arrival of Mickey. He carried a tray on which was a bowl of beans cooked with beef and chili, along with a pile of tortillas. When he had gone Garnet set the tray on the wall-bench, spreading a towel over it to keep out the spiders. Later, maybe, she would feel like eating something.

She glanced out of the window. The town basked in late afternoon light, and the air had an autumnal coolness. At the east side of the town she could see the creek overgrown with bushes of wild nicotine, and east of the creek was a mesa, like a hill with its top cut off. Beyond the mesa the ground rolled and tumbled, going higher and higher as it went, until at last, miles away, she could see the line of the great mountains. The westering sun fell on the mountains in a pattern of tawny lights and purple shadows and deep gray folds. Above the squalid little settlement the mountains looked strong and beautiful, like fortresses built for a race of giant kings.

Garnet turned around. As she did so she caught sight of her face in the glass. How healthy she looked, quite healthy enough to make a living if she only knew how. Since her illness her color had come back, and her complexion was as bright as ever. The sight of her black hair and rosy cheeks reminded her of the day she and Florinda had stood before the glass in New Orleans, when Florinda, enchanted by the contrast in their looks, had exclaimed, "I wish we could do a sister act."

Garnet started and moved nearer the glass. "We could," she said aloud. "We could work side by side at the bar."

The thought struck her like a blow. All the ladyism of her lifetime recoiled from it. A shiver ran over her as she heard a burst of drunken laughter from downstairs. "I can't!" she cried. But even as she said it she knew it wasn't so, because she could.

Garnet remembered how she had resented the barriers of gentility her parents had set up around her. She thought of how she used to wonder about the Jewel Box, and those gay places around City Hall Park, and those streets she had never been allowed to walk on. She remembered how much she had wanted to see the world as it was. As she remembered, she smiled with a grim understanding. Life let you have what you wanted. But life was like a storekeeper who put up a sign saying "Buy now, pay later," and tempted you into buying so much that you were in debt for years.

Her baby kicked as though in protest. Garnet put her hands over the place where it was. "I'm sorry," she said as though speaking to the baby. "But what do you want me to do? I can live on charity, or I can let Charles turn you into a human marshmallow, or I can work at the bar. I'll work at the bar."

All of a sudden, she had a sense of lightness. She felt better. She also felt hungry, so she took the towel off the tray and ate her supper.

"Oh Garnet," exclaimed Florinda, "you don't have to work at the bar!"

"I want to," Garnet repeated stubbornly.

"But darling, you won't like it."

"I don't expect to like it."

"Garnet, please, I don't need to be paid for having you stay with me. You can stay as long as you want to."

"I know I can," said Garnet. She sat on the bed, looking up at Florinda, who stood by the washstand pinching drops of grease that had fallen from the candle. "But I'm not going to have you supporting me."

There was a silence. Florinda pinched the candle out of shape. At length she turned around. "Garnet," she said, "you thought this up all by yourself."

"Why yes, of course."

"I didn't suggest it," said Florinda.

"Certainly not."

"In fact, I did everything I could to stop you."

"What are you getting at, Florinda?"

"Look me straight in the eye."

Garnet looked her straight in the eye.

"Well, glory hallelujah," said Florinda. "I sure do feel virtuous. I guess that's the first time in my whole life I honestly tried not to get something I wanted."

"Do you mean you can use me?"

"Garnet, I can use you like I could use money in the bank. Think of us! Two American girls—they'll come miles to see us!

354

Every Yankee in California, every sailor who lands at San Diego, why they'll flock up here if they have to walk."

She laughed joyously and chattered on.

"You'll wear red and I'll wear blue, or you'll wear pink and I'll wear green. We'll get some fancy pins for your hair—"

"I'm still in mourning," Garnet protested.

"Not in that saloon you won't be. Nobody's making you do this and if you do it you're going to do it right. About terms, you'll get a percentage, I'll talk that over with Silky. Oh, wait till I tell Silky! He'll faint with glee. When can you start?"

"I'm expecting the baby early in August. As soon as possible after that."

"I must tell him right away." Florinda ran to the door and opened it. "That Charles—he's a pig and a spider and a two-legged rat, but—" She banged the door and clattered down the stairs. "Silky! Silky! Come into the kitchen a minute. Right now, yes. I've got something *important* to tell you."

Garnet's baby was born one night not long before daybreak. True to his promise Texas had stayed sober and was there to help her. As soon as Florinda thought he was needed she scribbled a note and had Mickey take it to his lodging, and Texas came to the saloon as fast as a man with a lame leg could get there. He told Florinda to go on back to the bar. He'd take care of everything.

Florinda went downstairs, but she did not stay long. She poured a few drinks and exchanged a few gay remarks, and then told the bar-boys to take care of the customers. Promising to be back right away, she went up to Garnet's room again. By this time Garnet was in a good deal of pain. Florinda sat by her, watching as Garnet clamped her teeth on the blanket to keep from crying out. When she saw that the pain was passing, Florinda bent her head and spoke softly.

"Garnet, I've come to tell you something. Listen." She gently pushed a damp lock of hair off Garnet's forehead. "Don't fight the pains like that. You can't take it in silence, dear. I know what I'm talking about, remember?" She smiled. "Of course I understand what you're thinking. You're so modest, you can't bear to have those pinheads at the bar guess what's going on up here. Right?"

Garnet nodded. Florinda went on with assurance.

"Don't worry. They won't guess. I'm going to put on a show. I put on a right good show all by myself one night in Santa Fe and

355

I can do it again. I'm going to sing 'em every bawdy song I know. I'll sing at the top of my voice and they'll join in the choruses, and believe me, sweetheart, I know enough songs to keep 'em shouting till next Tuesday."

Garnet murmured, "Florinda, you—you make me laugh at the strangest times."

"Then you do get the idea? Fine. I'll go right down and start. And when the pains hit you, scream all you please. Nobody's going to hear. I can make more noise with my throat than you can with yours."

She dropped a kiss on Garnet's forehead and scampered downstairs again. They heard her lift her voice in song. In a minute or two, banging cups and shouts of laughter were providing the rest of the noise she had promised. She gave the men no explanation, except to tell them that tonight she felt fine and full of mischief and was just in the mood to have a show. As she did it so well, they were too much amused to think of asking questions. She kept it up until all of a sudden Texas opened the door, put his head in and called, "That's enough," and banged the door again. By this time Florinda was hoarse and tired and dripping with sweat. She finished the song she was singing, and said, "Good night, gents, the place is closed." They protested, but Silky came in from the gambling room to help her get them out. Silky knew what she had been doing, and approved. Wiping her face on her sleeve, Florinda went up to have a look at the baby.

Texas met her at the head of the stairs. "It's a boy," he said, "and he's got all his hands and feet the way he ought to have."

"How's Garnet?"

"Fine." Texas gave her a grin. "Say, you know some right juicy ditties, don't you?"

"Dear me," said Florinda. "Just think of you having such a delicate mind. If they shocked you, you shouldn't have listened."

"But the singing was a good idea," he assured her hastily. "I didn't mean to be criticizing."

Florinda smiled at him. She liked Texas, Texas with his shaggy brown hair and beard, and the fine network of red veins that years of too much drinking had laced across his nose, and the sweet, affectionate look of his brown eyes. "Sure, Texas," she said, "I understand. Go on down and get some beans. I'll stay with her."

Texas limped down the stairs, and Florinda went softly into the bedroom. Garnet had fallen asleep.

356

Garnet had never in her life been so glad to have anybody with her as she had been to have Texas that night. He took care of her with such a wise blending of authority and tenderness that though she had been frightened before he got there, after he got there she was not frightened at all. She never did know how he managed to give her such ease of mind. But by the time he had been with her ten minutes she trusted him completely. Texas could not make childbirth a light experience, but he did make her feel that everything was going to be all right, and everything was. When at last it was over and he brought her the baby, she turned her head and kissed his hard rough hand on the pillow beside her. "Thank you, Texas," she murmured. "I can't say it very well. But thank you."

Texas said, "Now then, now then, you know I was glad to help. You stood it mighty well, and he's a fine baby." He gave her head an affectionate pat, and told her he was going to let in some fresh air.

Garnet sighed happily as she felt the baby's fuzzy little head against her cheek. As Texas opened the shutters she saw that the sky behind the mountains was beginning to grow pale. There was a violet glow along the mountain edges, and the stars were like flakes of silver in the air above them. She had a drowsy sense that the world was lovely.

She dozed off again. When she opened her eyes the room had been put in order and Texas was not there. On the floor lay the mattress Florinda would sleep on. Florinda sat on the wall-bench by the window. The baby still lay beside Garnet, but evidently Florinda was going to move him, for she was arranging the basket they had got ready to use for his bed. The window at Florinda's side was open, and beyond her Garnet could see the reddening sky and the line of mountains against it.

There was a pad in the basket. Florinda put a little sheet over the pad and smoothed it and tucked it in, working with the sureness of one who had done this sort of thing many times before. Suddenly, as if struck by a familiarity she could not bear, she pushed the basket away from her, and put her elbow on the sill and rested her head on her hand. Garnet saw her beautiful profile, clear against the red sky. Florinda was not crying. But she sat quite still, like a person whose nerves were tight with pain. Garnet felt a great compassion. She was hardly strong enough to say anything, and she would not have said anything if she had been able to. Florinda had let her know, quite clearly, that she did not want to talk about the child she had lost. But Garnet turned her face toward her own tiny little warm baby, and her tears were running down his cheeks when she went to sleep again.

THIRTY-THREE

THE SALOON was very gay. Yankees were crowded at the bar, drinking toasts and clapping each other on the back. The few Angelenos in the room were half amused and half bewildered. They were used to Yankees, but they never would understand why even a great piece of news had to be celebrated with so much noise.

Florinda was out of breath. She had poured what seemed like ten thousand drinks, and every time she pushed a cup across the bar one of her exuberant countrymen would smack her with a kiss. She had received three proposals of marriage. She had also received several proposals that were not of marriage; to these she gave her usual retort.

"Six doors west. Ask for Estelle."

She wondered how Garnet was bearing this racket. Garnet's baby was only forty hours old, and though she had had a fairly easy delivery she ought to have a little peace. Florinda glanced around. Her assistant José was as breathless as she was, but he and Mickey could handle the trade for a few minutes. Mickey came in from the kitchen, his pigtail bobbing and his felt shoes flapping as he walked, and set a tray of clean cups on the counter. He was tired too, but he smiled at her brightly. Florinda spoke into his ear.

"Mickey, I go now. I want to see Miss Garnet."

Mickey nodded. "Yes, Miss Flinda."

Florinda told her customers she was leaving to eat a few beans and would be right back. Going through the kitchen, she ran upstairs.

Below her the saloon clattered merrily. She knocked on the bedroom door, but Texas did not hear her, so she opened the door a crack and called him.

He came out, carrying a candle. Texas no longer had to use a cane, but he limped. His right knee was almost stiff.

"How is she?" asked Florinda.

"All right. Can't sleep, of course, with so much rowdydow. What's it all about?"

"Big news," said Florinda. They went inside, and Texas set the candle on the washstand where the pitcher would shield Garnet's eyes from the light.

"Is that Florinda?" Garnet asked from the bed.

"Yes, it's me. I've got something exciting to tell you."

Florinda came and knelt by the bed. She took Garnet's hand in hers and spoke impressively. "Garnet, do you remember what you said about not wanting your baby to be a foreigner?"

Garnet nodded.

"He's not a foreigner," said Florinda.

Garnet glanced at Texas, who stood by the washstand, but he smiled and shook his head to show that he knew no more about it than she did.

Florinda spoke slowly, to make it clear. "Garnet, your little boy was born in the United States."

"The United States? What do you mean? This is Mexico."

"No it isn't. Not any more. The United States has taken California. It happened a month ago, only the news just got here tonight. An American ship sailed up to Monterey in July and raised the flag there."

Garnet heard her with a gasp. "You mean this is the war John was telling us about?"

"Yes, this is it. It seems the war has been going on for three or four months, but we never hear anything away out here. It's about the Republic of Texas."

"But what about California?" Garnet asked.

"Well dear, I guess the President figured if he could take Texas he could take California too, so the ships came and took it. Just like that. There wasn't a bit of trouble at Monterey. The sailors came ashore and raised the flag, and the band played Yankee Doodle, and the natives all seemed to like it. So then the Yankees raised another flag at Yerba Buena, that's the village on San Francisco Bay. Then they started south. And now a shipload of marines has landed at San Pedro and they are marching here."

"To Los Angeles?"

"Yes. And the fellows think there's an army on its way overland too."

"Miss Florinda," Texas said suddenly.

He had not moved from where he stood by the washstand. The candlelight flickered over his face, showing his eyes fixed on Florinda and a hard double line between his eyebrows.

359

"What was that you said about the army?" he asked in a low voice.

"The boys say it's probably marching overland from Fort Leavenworth. You must remember Fort Leavenworth, Garnet. It's on the Santa Fe Trail, just this side of the Missouri River. Do you know where Fort Leavenworth is, Texas?"

"What? Oh yes, yes, I know where that is." Texas spoke jerkily, looking down at the floor.

"And there's no trouble at all?" Garnet insisted. She did not know much about wars, but she had studied enough history at school to know that a change of flag was usually more difficult than this.

"Not a bit of trouble," said Florinda. "The Californios seem to think being in the United States is quite a good idea, and the Yankees are all yelling fit to bust their breeches."

Garnet drew a long breath. "An American army, coming to take California—why Florinda, it's wonderful!"

"Isn't it? I came up to tell you as soon as I could get away." Florinda scrambled to her feet. "I'll have to go back now. If you won't mind being alone for a few minutes, Texas can come down with me and I'll give him some beans." She put her hand on the door, but turned around laughing. "Oh, I almost forgot to tell you. Those men who raided Señor Vallejo's rancho, well it seems they've been enrolled under Frémont along with some other volunteers, and now they are known as Frémont's battalion and they are marching south in glory."

"You mean they're soldiers now?" Garnet exclaimed.

"Exactly. The fellows say if news of the war had been delayed a few weeks more, those raiders would have been chased out of the country. But coming when it did, now they think they started the conquest of California when they made that bear flag out of a sheet and a red flannel petticoat. And that," said Florinda, "is the difference between being a hero and a hoodlum."

"Please stop. You're making me laugh, and it hurts."

"Sorry. But it really is funny. Come down whenever you're ready, Texas. There's a pot of beans on the hearth-stove."

Florinda kissed her hand to them and shut the door. Garnet felt a warm rush of happiness. If she could not go back to her country, it was good to have her country come to her.

Texas still stood by the washstand. Thinking he might be waiting to give her some instructions, Garnet turned her head toward him. But Texas was not looking at her. He seemed to have forgotten she was there. He stood looking at the floor, restlessly moving his hand back and forth along the side of the wash-basin. The candle, standing where he had set it by the pitcher, shone up into his face.

As she looked at him, Garnet frowned and pushed her hand over her eyes. At first she thought she was not seeing him clearly. She was still weak, and it was easy to be mistaken about things. But after a moment she knew she was not mistaken about Texas. The candlelight shone full on his bearded face, and on the cheeks above his beard she saw the glint of tears.

The tears trickled down into his beard. Suddenly, as though remembering he was not alone, he turned on his good leg, and without saying anything he limped across the room and went out, shutting the door behind him. But he did not go down to the kitchen. Over the gay noise, Garnet heard him sit down on the top step of the staircase, his stiff leg bumping awkwardly as he did so.

She hoped he did not know she had seen his tears. Maybe later on when she did not feel so limp, she would understand them. But tonight she was baffled. Texas should have been happy at Florinda's news, like the other Americans, like herself. But he was not happy. The United States army was marching into California, and Texas was crying.

During the next few days Garnet learned more about the war. The Republic of Texas had won its freedom from Mexico ten years before. Texas had been settled by Americans, and the Texans wanted to join the United States. But though the leading countries of the world had recognized Texas as a nation, Mexico still looked on it as a rebellious province. If Texas joined the Union, the Mexicans said they would fight.

There were many Americans who did not think Texas was worth a war. This had been the main issue in the election of 1844, when James K. Polk and Henry Clay ran for President. Mr. Polk wanted the country to grow westward, war or no war. Mr. Clay thought the United States was big enough. Mr. Polk was elected, and Congress made Texas a state. After this came a few nervous months while each side waited for the other to shoot first. Then in April, 1846, the war began on the Texas border.

At this time the Pacific fleet of the United States was at Mazatlán on the west side of Mexico. Commodore John Drake Sloat, commander of the fleet, knew his country wanted not only Texas but California too. On hearing of the battles in eastern Mexico, Sloat sailed up to Monterey, capital of California. Here he raised the Stars and Stripes over the customhouse.

Señores Pico and Castro, the civil and military heads of California, had long been so busy quarreling with each other that they had not thought of anybody's coming in from outside to depose them both. Neither Pico nor Castro was in Monterey when Sloat got there. Nor was there anybody else in town who had authority to accept or refuse Sloat's demand for surrender. Neither, apparently, was there anybody who cared.

This happened on the seventh of July, 1846. Two days later Captain Montgomery of the sloop-of-war Portsmouth ran up the flag at Yerba Buena. Pico and Castro tried to raise an army of Californios to fight for Mexico. But it was too late. The Californios frankly had no love for Mexico. The American flags rippled from the flagpoles, the bands played American tunes in the village plazas, and Yankees and Californios alike seemed well content with this state of things.

On July 15 the USS Congress, commanded by Commodore Robert F. Stockton, reached Monterey. Since by this time northern California seemed to be well taken care of, Stockton sailed south to occupy Los Angeles. The marines were expected to march in any day.

If this was a conquest, it was the simplest one in history.

Texas was spending all his time at the saloon, taking care of Garnet and her baby. Even at night he did not go home, but slept on a blanket in the hall.

He did not go near the bar. Whether this was because he did not want to drink or because he did not want to discuss the war, Garnet could not tell. He never once mentioned the conquest of California. If anyone else spoke of it, he stood by silently.

Everybody else was delighted. Silky came up and kissed Garnet's hand and told her it filled him with pride to have a new Yankee born under his simple roof. Florinda dashed up as often as she could, to bring news of what was going on. In the street below the window Garnet could hear the Yankees laughing and congratulating each other all day. "You'd think they had done it themselves," Florinda said. "Even the ones who don't like to tell how they got here are pleased about it. I guess they figure the army has got something better to do than look up everybody's record and put 'em in jail for some little matter that happened three thousand miles back." She winked, and Garnet laughed, remembering New Orleans and the widow's veil. But Texas, who sat by the window, looking out toward the mountains, did not laugh.

Garnet thought a good deal about what she would name her baby. His father's name was the obvious choice, but she rejected it. Oliver had disillusioned her too deeply, and speaking his name in any connection still hurt her. She asked Florinda to make a suggestion. Florinda said she thought Leander was a grand-sounding name, and so was Murgatroyd.

Garnet thanked her, but said these were not exactly the sort of names she had in mind. After a moment's reflection, Florinda smiled with a sudden idea.

"Why don't you ask Texas to name him?" she said.

"Why Florinda," Garnet exclaimed, "I hadn't thought of that. Do you really believe he'd be pleased?"

"I think it would mean a lot to him," said Florinda. She paused thoughtfully, and added, "Texas has something on his mind, Garnet."

"So you've noticed that too."

Florinda nodded. "I don't know what it is. But he thinks so much of you, maybe if you sort of made a gesture toward him, letting him know you like him, it might make him feel better. Does that make sense?"

"Why yes, that makes plenty of sense," said Garnet. "I'll ask him today."

That afternoon, when Florinda had gone down to the bar, she asked Texas to help her choose a name.

Texas grinned proudly. He sat down on the wall-bench, clenching his eyebrows in thought. His stiff leg stuck out in front of him. He could bend the knee a little, but not enough to keep him from looking clumsy.

"Is there a man you especially admire?" Garnet asked. "A man with a fine strong character, the sort a boy would be proud to be named for?"

Texas stroked his beard. "Why yes ma'am, there is." He smiled at her shyly. "You might name him for Stephen Austin," he suggested.

"Stephen Austin?" she repeated doubtfully. "I don't think I know about him."

"The fellow who started the Republic of Texas," he explained. "Stephen Austin was a man with a lot of nerve, Miss Garnet. He got things done. His father had the first grant of land for settlement in Texas, but his father died, and it was Stephen Austin who brought in the first Americans. He was only twenty-six years old then. And later, he led the revolution that made Texas a free country."

There was such enthusiasm in his voice that Garnet asked, "Did you know him?"

"Yes ma'am, I knew him. I remember him from when I was a boy. He was a good friend of our folks. In fact," Texas added, unconsciously lifting his chin with the pride of it, "we went into Texas with him."

"Then you weren't born in Texas?" Garnet asked.

"Oh no ma'am. I was born in Mississippi. There weren't any Americans in Texas when I was born." He smiled, and his soft brown eyes had a wistful look as he added, "I was eleven years old when we went to Texas with Stephen Austin. He was a fine man, Miss Garnet, the sort of man a boy respected."

"That's the sort of man I meant," she said. "Thank you, Texas. The baby's name is Stephen. Stephen Hale."

"Well, well," said Texas. He looked at the basket, and held out his finger so Stephen's hand would curl around it. After a little silence he stood up awkwardly. "Er—Miss Garnet, I sure do thank you for letting me name him. It was quite an honor." He stuck his hands into his pockets, stood in the middle of the floor as though he did not know what to do next, and finally said he guessed it must be about time for beans. He'd better go down to the kitchen.

He opened the door, but on the threshold he paused and looked back at Garnet and the baby, and the look he gave them was so tender, and so sweet, and so wistful, that she hurt with seeing it. He closed the door, and Garnet remembered what he had said to her that day at Don Antonio's rancho. "Don't try to understand any of us. We're just a lot of lost souls."

She looked over at her tiny pink baby asleep in his basket. Stephen Hale, named for Stephen Austin. She wondered what had happened to Texas since the time he had been a boy following his hero.

Her eyes began to sting. Maybe it was foolish to shed tears for something that was over and done with, but she could not help it. She knew by now that in the matter of medical skill Texas was no amateur. He had delivered the baby and taught her to nurse him,

364

and during the past few days he had continued performing the most intimate services for her, and he was neither unsure nor self-conscious. He went about everything with the serenity of a man doing the work he was meant to do. Texas might have had a brilliant career, if only something had not gone wrong.

Garnet wondered what had gone wrong. She did not know. All she knew was that he was here without friends or family or even a name, a cripple now who would probably never ride the trail again. She wondered if his drinking bouts occurred when he could no longer bear the desperate loneliness of feeling that nobody cared what happened to him.

Well, she cared. She was never going to forget what his presence had meant to her the night Stephen was born. As long as she and Texas lived in the same world he was going to have a friend.

On the thirteenth of August, 1846, when Stephen was five days old, the Americans entered Los Angeles.

Texas made a nest of blankets on the wall-bench so Garnet could sit by the window and watch the men march in. There were United States marines; and the seamen led by Commodore Stockton; and Frémont's battalion, consisting of the army explorers who had come with him and the volunteers who had joined him in the north. They marched in with flags and music, while the Angelenos looked on, interested but slightly puzzled by the whole business, and the Yankees cheered and laughed and shouted a welcome. Here as elsewhere in California, nobody made any resistance. Pico and Castro had fled to Mexico. They had gone separately, for they had quarreled so long that not even a foreign invasion could make them get together.

Garnet felt goose-bumps run up and down her back as she watched the blue uniforms and the bright familiar flags that she had not seen for so long. Her hand on the baby's basket, she wondered if Stephen would ever love his country as much as she loved it. She shook her head. No, he would not love it that much, not unless some day he too found himself an exile.

The parade had gone by. Some of the onlookers hurried toward the plaza to watch the raising of the flag, others headed for the taverns to get refreshments after standing so long in the sun. From beneath her, Garnet could hear the rattle of jugs and cups and the sound of voices. The noise sounded blurry under the lilt of Yankee Doodle from the band in the plaza.

365

Her back had begun to ache. She turned her head, to tell Texas she would like to lie down now.

But Texas was not there. Garnet had been so much interested in the arrival of the Americans that she had not heard him go out. But now, through the music and the noise at the bar, she heard an uneven thumping step on the stairs. The steps crossed the little passage at the foot of the staircase, went past the kitchen, and on to the bar.

Garnet put her head down on her hand. She was so sorry for him. She did not understand why he had to get drunk today, but she felt that if she had understood it, she would have known all about his wrecked and wasted life.

The baby woke and started to cry. He was hungry and his diaper was wet, and for the first time Texas had forgotten him. Garnet changed the diaper, and took the baby into bed with her and gave him her breast. It was awkward to be doing all this without Texas to help her.

The whole town was full of hubbub. From the saloon below her, and the native wineshops, and Estelle's place down the street, and the street itself, Garnet could hear songs and laughter. Everybody seemed to be having fun. She wondered if Texas was having any fun.

The day began to fade. On the wall-curtains the light turned from gold to pink, from pink to blue, and then dwindled down to gray. The floor shivered from the merriment downstairs. Garnet yawned, and moved her position in bed. She was tired. She was also hungry, for she had had nothing to eat since before noon. Now and then Stephen woke up and cried, and she soothed him back to sleep. She began to have a hungry headache.

It was dark when Florinda finally brought her some supper. Florinda's hair was coming down, there were splashes of liquor on her dress, and one sleeve was partly torn out of its armhole. In one hand she carried a candle and in the other a bowl of beans.

"Darling, I'm so sorry," she said as she set down the candle and gave Garnet a towel to tuck under her chin. "You must be starved. Here, eat this. I'll take the baby, soon as I've washed my hands."

Garnet thanked her and began to eat. Catching sight of herself in the mirror, Florinda laughed and sighed together. "Whoops, how I do look. What with the army, the navy, and the marines, all clustered around me at once, it's a marvel I'm not torn to shreds. But they're fun, Garnet." She poured water into the basin and rolled

366

up her sleeves. "And also," she added, with a mischievous glance over her shoulder, "how they do spend money!"

"How long are they going to stay at the bar?" asked Garnet.

"I don't know. But I think the officers have set a time limit. I'll pour drinks as long as they'll pay for them. Oh, there's Mickey," she exclaimed as she heard a knock on the door and went to open it. Mickey handed her a tray. "He's brought some hot tea for both of us," said Florinda. "That Mickey, he's a tower of strength." She picked up Stephen, made him comfortable in his basket, and sat down on the wall-bench to pour the tea.

For a few moments they both sipped tea in silent enjoyment. Then Garnet asked about Texas.

Florinda shrugged, and answered with terse regret. Texas was drunk. He was very drunk. And he had been having a crying jag. He had sat on the floor in a corner, a bottle in his hand and tears running down his cheeks, until Florinda could stand it no longer. She had told two of the bar-boys to take him home. That was why Garnet's supper had been delayed: Florinda could not leave the bar until the boys came back. Yes, they had got him home safely. His landlady, Señora Vargas, had promised to take care of him. Texas paid her a good rent and she was used to his ways. Florinda begged Garnet not to lie there worrying about him. "Just be nice to him when he comes out of it," she said. She added, with a sad wisdom, that this was about as much as anybody could do for him, and Garnet had to agree that it probably was.

THIRTY-FOUR

BUT THE CONQUEST of Los Angeles did not prove to be as easy as they thought it was.

At first it looked simple. Commodore Stockton sent Frémont north to seek recruits among the Yankees there; and as Los Angeles was perfectly quiet, Stockton himself went to Yerba Buena, where the people had planned a celebration in his honor. He left Captain Gillespie of the Marine Corps in Los Angeles with a token garrison of about fifty marines.

Captain Gillespie could have asked advice of the Yankees who had been trading in Los Angeles for years. If he had done so, they would have told him that he need not expect the Angelenos to make any resistance to American rule. This was one of the least warlike neighborhoods on earth. Now and then wild Diggers raided an isolated dwelling and armed men went out to put them down. Sometimes two lads fought over a girl, or a man borrowed a saddle and forgot to bing it back. But these disputes could usually be settled by the alcalde, a local officer like a mayor.

There were no more than a thousand people who lived in the village all the year round. But it was a busy little place, the market for the southern ranchos, the end of the caravan trail from Santa Fe, and a center of supply for ships in the hide trade. Most of this business was in Yankee hands. Generally speaking, the native Angelenos went their way in a lazy good-humor. They had little to complain about. Fresh beef was so cheap that it was their staple food. There was no proverty. Most people did not even have locks on their doors. Life in Los Angeles consisted of a little work and a great deal of music, wine, and dancing, and the Angelenos took this as the natural state of things. The Yankees could have told Captain Gillespie—in fact, they did their best to tell him—that he had been set over a cheerful folk who would remain cheerful if only they were let alone.

But Gillespie did not ask advice and did not listen when they gave it. He began to issue orders that first astounded the people and then enraged them.

In this fun-loving town, Gillespie forbade social gatherings. He had private homes searched for firearms. He ordered that liquor be sold only when and where he gave permission. His countrymen warned him that guns were more necessary to California dignity than shoes. They told him the Californios would resent a curb on their red wine as much as the American colonists had resented the tax on tea. But he paid no heed. Gillespie was left in command on the last day of August; by the middle of September the people were muttering and turning their backs when an American passed them in the street. They went into the Yankee trading posts only when they had to. The native bar-boys stopped coming to work at Silky's.

As for Silky himself, he had not escaped interference. His gambling room was closed, and the saloon was allowed to stay open only from noon till six. As the Angelenos slept through half the afternoon, this order cut off a large slice of income. Silky and

Florinda were as angry as the Angelenos. But they obeyed, lest Gillespie lock up the place for good.

Garnet agreed that the captain was foolish. But she could not help being glad she was having a chance to get used to the bar by working in the daytime at first, instead of starting with those noisy evenings she used to hear from upstairs. She went to work as soon as she was well. During the bar-hours Isabel took care of Stephen. Isabel did not admire Gillespie, but Garnet and Florinda paid her well and Isabel said she would rather work for Yankees than get married.

Florinda had not exaggerated Garnet's value to the bar. The marines had been stationed at Mazatlán and they were used to Mexican girls, but two real live Americans were something else again. The boys spent as much time in Silky's Place as their captain would let them. They were a rowdy but good-natured bunch, and Garnet found her work less unpleasant than she had feared. But now and then she heard rumblings of rebellion that frightened her.

It was an afternoon late in September. From her place behind the bar, Garnet greeted two marines who had just come in. "May I serve you, gentlemen?" she asked.

They grinned at her with a yearning admiration. "You sure do look pretty today," said the marine named Bill.

"Mighty pretty," said the marine named Pete. "Them flowers on your dress, and your eyes—say, what color are your eyes?"

"Some people call them gray. Some say hazel. Don't you want to order? It's getting late."

The two marines agreed that they'd better order. "That bottled earthquake the Mexes drink," said Bill. "I never could say it."

"You mean aguardiente?"

"Gee, listen to her, rattling it off like a native. How does it go? Aggadenty?"

Garnet poured the drinks. "Why don't you just say Mexican brandy?" she asked smiling. "We'll understand."

"Now that's what I call a smart girl," Bill said to Pete. "She ain't a Mex, we ain't Mexes, how come we got to talk Mex? Talk United States, that's good enough for me. Say, Garnet."

"Yes?" she said. It still felt odd to have strange men call her by her first name, but she was getting used to it.

"You sure are pretty. Do you paint your cheeks?"

Garnet said she didn't. She wiped up some drops of liquor on

369

the bar and pretended not to hear their next few comments, which concerned her figure and not her face. When they asked her what she would be doing after the bar closed, she answered that she would be busy taking care of her baby. She tried not to make her reply too curt. But though she was doing her best, she had not yet acquired Florinda's ability to keep them at bay while at the same time keeping them in good-humor. A little farther along the bar, a group of marines bantered with Florinda.

". . . a girl like you, Florinda, away out here at the end of the world! How'd you get here anyway?"

"Why I've always been here. I was the first white child born in this settlement. No, that's not quite enough, you still owe me seven cents. Oh, now what a shame!" she sympathized as he spilt the liquor down the front of his coat.

"You jiggled my elbow!" he accused her.

"Well, you shouldn't have tried to pinch me. Behave yourself and you won't get into trouble. Yes, sergeant? Whiskey, yes sir, right away."

At Garnet's end of the bar, Texas stood leaning on his elbow. Texas was sober again. His spree had been a rather bad one, but Garnet pretended she did not know it. Texas had said he was sorry for leaving her that day—he had meant to have just a couple with the boys, didn't know how they happened to hit him so hard— but remembering Florinda's advice, Garnet had taken his apology lightly. "Why Texas, everybody was drinking too much that day. Isabel came up to wait on me, and anyway, I was up very soon afterward."

Though Texas had not been drinking lately, he often came and stood at the bar, watching Garnet like a bodyguard. She liked having him there. He asked her for a glass of water, and as she brought it he glanced along the bar and back at her, shaking his head.

"I hate to see you in here, Miss Garnet," he said.

"I'm all right, Texas. Really I am."

"Don't they bother you?"

"Not too much. I'm learning to handle them."

"Miss Garnet," said Texas, "I wish you were clean out of town. We're liable to have trouble. That damn fool Gillespie—"

"Please, Texas! Not here."

Nobody was allowed to talk about Gillespie at the bar. If any of the marines chose to defend their captain with their fists, that was all right with Silky, but he didn't want it happening in his saloon. The place was allowed to do business only on condition that it stayed orderly. Texas gave a shrug, but he ceased his comments. Mr. Bugs McLane came in with Mr. Collins, the clerk from Mr. Abbott's store. Garnet poured drinks for them, and professed to admire the marines' attempt to warble a Mexican song they had brought up from Mazatlán. Through the singing she heard a little sound from the kitchen.

"Stephen is awake," she said to Florinda. "I'll be back as soon as I can."

Florinda smiled and nodded, and Garnet went into the kitchen. The baby's basket stood on the wall-bench. Isabel had just picked him up. While Garnet sat down to nurse him, Isabel went to the fireplace and helped herself to beans from the pot on the hearth-stove.

Garnet pressed Stephen's soft little body to her bosom. She was so glad she had him. Sometimes, in spite of all she could do to keep cheerful, such a wave of loneliness swept over her that her heart felt as barren as the desert. Without her baby it would have been even worse. When Stephen had finished she cuddled him back into his basket, then went to the table to drink a cup of chocolate with Isabel. She and Florinda and Silky would eat their supper later, after they had closed the saloon. Garnet poured another cup of chocolate and took it out to Texas.

Silky was making an entry in the credit book and Florinda was pouring fresh drinks for Collins and McLane. As Garnet set the cup in front of Texas she heard a brush of elbows on the bar to her right, and turned her head. She started. Leaning on the bar, his hands clasped around a cup of whiskey, was Charles.

Charles was dressed in mourning. He had on a fine white shirt and a black coat and trousers, and he carried a tasseled black hat under his arm. Thrust under his belt were white leather gloves embroidered with black silk. He looked rich, but it was not possible for Charles to look imposing. His brown face had so many little lines that Garnet thought of a monkey she had once seen at Barnum's Museum. His small brown hands, linked around the cup, were hard and knuckly, and the veins stood out on the backs. As on the first time she had seen him, Garnet was reminded of something creeping and unhealthy. Then again, as on the first time she had seen him, she saw his eyes.

His eyes, brilliant and deep-set, were fixed on her. His look slid over her with a slimy contempt. She had never known anybody who could put as much contempt into a look as he could; she almost felt it, like a worm crawling over her body. As his eyes held her, she saw that the drink he was holding was not the first he had had this evening. She was surprised, for she had never known him to drink much. Without even a formal greeting, Charles said,

"I want to talk to you."

She did not want to talk to him, but she did not know how she could avoid it. "About what, Charles?" she asked.

"I should prefer," said Charles, glancing around the room in disgust, "that we have less company. Where can we go?"

"The bar closes at six," she answered. "After that I can take you into the kitchen."

The marine named Bill, by now somewhat the worse for aguardiente, sidled along the bar and gazed at Charles. "Hi there, pizen-face," he said.

Charles ignored him, but Texas put his hand on Bill's arm. "I wouldn't be disrespectful, son. The gentleman is a good friend of Captain Gillespie's."

Garnet had no idea whether or not this statement was true. But Bill subsided, leaning his head on his hand and grinning at nothing in particular. Charles finished his whiskey. As he set the cup on the bar his eyes came to rest on Florinda. At leisure for the moment, Florinda stood back from the bar. It was the first time Charles and Florinda had ever had a good look at each other. At the rancho their one conversation had taken place in the dark hall, and after that Florinda had kept out of his way, so that they had exchanged only a few passing glimpses. Now they looked each other over with mutual distaste.

Charles pushed his cup across the bar. "Fill this up," he said curtly.

Florinda took a bottle from the shelf, but she did not pour. "You haven't paid for the first one, Mr. Hale, and you've put no credit on the books."

With a curl of his lip Charles tossed her a Spanish doubloon, worth fifteen dollars. It was an obvious gesture of disdain to remind her that he could buy every bottle on the shelf if he wanted to. Garnet felt like throwing the money back into his face. She must have looked like it too, for as the coin rattled on the counter Texas laid a hand on her wrist, shaking his head. Garnet caught

372

her breath. But Florinda, with a coolness that Garnet envied, picked up the doubloon and pushed the bottle into Charles' hands.

"Take it all, Mr. Hale, and thank you. I'll write down the extra credit." She dropped the doubloon into the cash-box, opened the book, and on a fresh page she made a note of one gold doubloon less one bottle of whiskey, credit of Mr. Charles Hale.

Without comment, Charles poured a drink. Bill the marine drained the last of his aguardiente and grinned hazily at Garnet. "Who's the pizen-face?" he inquired.

"Be quiet, Bill," she said.

"Last round, gentlemen," Silky called.

There was a flurry of orders. Under cover of the final drinks Florinda whispered to Garnet, "If you want to take him back to the kitchen now, dearie, I'll clear up."

"No you won't. If he wants to talk to me he can wait till I'm ready. I'm not going to leave you to do the work."

"Six o'clock, gentlemen," said Silky.

Sometimes he had trouble getting them out, but this evening there was a sergeant present who did the job for him. Evidently the sergeant knew Charles was a person of importance, for he made no effort to have him leave with the others. Florinda came through the side doorway into the front half of the room and began fastening the shutters. Silky picked up the ledgers and cash-box to check the day's business, and Garnet piled the cups on a tray. Indicating the bottle in front of Charles, she said,

"I can put that on the shelf, marked with your name. Or do you want to keep it?"

"I'll keep it," he returned shortly, and picked it up. Garnet took the cups into the kitchen, came back and washed off the bar, and finally said, "You can come in here now, Charles."

They went into the kitchen. Silky already sat at the end of the table near the fireplace, and Mickey was bringing him his supper. Garnet told Isabel she could go. Charles stood looking down at the basket.

"So this," he said, "is Oliver's child." He drew down the covers. Stephen made a little sleepy protest at being disturbed, and Garnet put out her hand to cover him again. "I'm not hurting him," Charles said. He gazed at Stephen a moment, and nodded in satisfaction. "A fine healthy child," he said. Garnet rearranged the blankets. When she had tucked them in Charles said, "Come over here."

He led the way to the end of the table away from the end where Silky was. Garnet sat down on the bench, facing him. Florinda came over and asked,

"Can we give you some supper, Mr. Hale?"

"No," said Charles, "but you might bring me a cup."

She went to get it, and Charles gave a long look around the room. The shutters were closed, and there was no light but the fire and two candles on the table.

"So this," he said to Garnet, "is what you have chosen. And these are the friends you prefer."

"Charles," she demanded, "what do you want with me?"

Charles glanced contemptuously at Florinda, who was setting a cup before him. Florinda asked,

"Shall I leave you now, Garnet?"

Garnet thought she might as well get it over with. Charles was not drunk yet, but he was going to be if he kept on with that straight whiskey, and she wanted him to say what he had to say, and go. "Yes," she said to Florinda, "get your beans while they're hot."

Florinda went to the other end of the long table and sat by Silky. Garnet heard them talking to each other, and the soft padding of Mickey's shoes as he served them. Charles poured a drink. When he spoke to her, his manner seemed less stiff, as though he were trying to win her consent rather than command her obedience.

"Garnet," he said, "I came to get you out of this place."

"Thank you, Charles," she returned. "But I don't want to leave."

Charles shook his head. "I can't believe you want to stay here," he urged. "You—forgive the trite old word, but there's no other—you are a lady. Won't you come back to the rancho and live like one?"

She thought, It's no use explaining why I won't come back. He wouldn't understand. He wouldn't understand even if he hadn't touched that liquor. Aloud she said,

"I don't want to come back, Charles."

"Garnet, you can't go on working at that bar. Don't you hate it?"

She took a deep breath and made herself speak calmly. "I don't like it, Charles. But you must know why I'm working there." He said nothing, and she went on, "Oliver left thirty-eight dollars on deposit with Mr. Abbott."

Charles looked her over. In the flickering light she could see that his eyes were getting vague, the eyes of a man who had already drunk too much. But his voice was steady. "I am holding Oliver's property," he said, "in trust for Oliver's son. When the boy comes of age, I shall be glad to take him into partnership with me at the rancho."

"And in the meantime?" asked Garnet.

"In the meantime," he replied, "I shall administer the Hale property as I see fit."

"Do you think I'm too stupid to take care of his share of it?" she asked. She wondered why she had asked it. Charles had poured another drink, and he tossed it down before he answered.

"Do you think," he said, "that I'd trust you with Oliver's property after the evidence you have given of your tastes? And leave you free to bring up Oliver's child among rascals and prostitutes? I have better plans for that boy, if you haven't."

Garnet clenched her jaw. She was both tired and hungry, but at the moment she was not aware of being either. She was simply thinking that Charles was even more repellent drunk than sober. He did not stop drinking, but he did catch hold of his temper and make another effort to persuade her.

"Come back to the rancho, Garnet. You can live there in cleanliness, in comfort, in dignity. The boy will have his own dogs and horses, his own servants. His friends will be boys of the leading families, native and American."

Charles' tongue was getting thick. He was speaking slowly, separating his syllables with care. There's no use answering him, Garnet thought. But he's not going to get my child.

Charles continued, "There is going to be trouble in Los Angeles. The people are on the verge of revolt."

Garnet knew this. If she had had anywhere to take refuge except Charles' rancho, she would have gone gladly. But not there. If Charles ever got hold of Stephen he would never let him go.

Charles was watching her over the rim of his cup. His eyes wobbled as he tried to fix them on her face. What strange things liquor did to people's eyes. When he spoke again his words were thick.

"You, of course, can do as you please," he said. "But I want Oliver's child on the rancho. He has a right to a decent life."

"A decent life!" Garnet repeated scornfully. "Is that what you think you gave Oliver?" She did not know why she had said that. But she was so tired of his hate and contempt, and his passion for domineering. She was so tired of everything.

"You," said Charles, "can damn well shut up about Oliver."

His hand shook as he lifted the cup. Garnet heard Silky say something about checking the supplies for tomorrow. He went into the front room. Florinda got up too, and went to the door leading to the stairs. "Call me if you want me, Garnet," she said over her shoulder.

Charles paid no attention to her. He glared at Garnet, trying to focus his blurry eyes.

"Oliver was my brother. He was my brother, till you came." His voice was like the growl of an animal. "You! Telling him to go back to the States, telling him never to see me again. Getting in the way, keeping him from making a good marriage in California, driving him to his death." He pushed himself back from the table, and tried to stand up, holding to the table with both hands. As he glowered at her his lips pulled back from his teeth. Garnet drew away from him, startled and frightened by his look of malevolence. Charles laughed, bitterly and evilly. "You thought you had left me nothing at all of him, didn't you? But there is something left of Oliver. He had a child. I looked at his son just now. His son is strong and healthy, like Oliver. And you are trying to tell me you can keep that child away from me and make him grow up like a savage. You say— you—"

The whiskey had been gaining on him. Now it struck him like a club. Crumpling down on the bench he dropped his head on his arm.

Garnet sprang up. If she had thought before that Charles was no fit guardian for a child, now she knew he was not. How he hated her, she thought as she looked down at him, as crooked ugly creatures nearly always hated those who were straight and well. And if she let him, he would destroy Stephen's moral power as he had destroyed Oliver's, so that Stephen, like Oliver, would pay for his strength by being forever dependent on Charles' weakness. Cold with loathing, Garnet moved along the bench, away from Charles, to where Stephen lay asleep in his basket. She took up the baby and held him in her arms.

Charles had sunk into an ugly unconsciousness. She thought she would have killed him with the meat-knife before she would have let him take Stephen, and wreak vengeance again for his shriveled little body and his scorched little soul.

THIRTY-FIVE

GARNET HAD TAKEN Stephen upstairs to be out of sight in case Charles woke suddenly, and now she sat at the table finishing her supper. At first she had said she could not eat anything, but Florinda cut off a chunk of beef the size of her fist and put it on a plate with big spoonfuls of beans and cornmeal mush, saying, "There. A dish of wholesome food never hurt anybody." After the first few bites Garnet agreed with her. Food was a great restorer.

Hands on her hips, Florinda stood looking down at the sodden lump of Charles. With his arms sprawled over the table and his head down between them, Charles was snoring. His mouth was half open, showing the edges of his teeth; his face was wet, and a sourish smell of liquor hovered around him. Florinda gave him a poke, and when he made no response she shrugged.

"Temporarily dead," she commented. Puckering her lips, she glanced over at Garnet. "Now what," she inquired, "are we going to do with him?"

"Where is Mickey?" Garnet asked.

"Fast asleep on a blanket in the gambling room."

"And Silky?"

"Silky's gone a-courting."

Garnet nodded. She should have known that. Florinda's partnership with Silky remained strictly business, but there were several pretty native girls in Los Angeles who liked him and who were not troubled by the present strain on international relations. Now that the saloon had to close at sunset, Silky rarely spent an evening at home. Florinda continued,

"So you and I, all by our little selves, have got to dispose of this scrambled egg."

Garnet rested her chin on her fists, scowling. She was afraid of Charles, and she did not want him waking up under the same roof with Stephen. She and Florinda could have dragged him outside and thrown him down among the wild oats to sleep it off, but they did not dare to. Charles was no common drunk. He was a man of influence, and if he was not treated with respect he would be

377

likely to tell Captain Gillespie that Silky's Place was disorderly and ought to be closed for good.

"We'll have to take some blankets to the gambling room and put him in there," Garnet said at length. "And we'd better leave a note for Silky, so he'll know."

"I guess that's the best we can do," Florinda agreed reluctantly, glancing at Charles again. "He doesn't seem to be in any mad rush to leave. Well, you write the note to Silky and I'll wash these dishes."

She picked up the pot of hot water from the hearth-stove. Garnet tore a blank page from one of the ledgers, and took the pen and ink from the shelf. As she dipped the pen into the ink she heard footsteps on the side porch and the sound of men's voices beyond the door. She started and looked around.

"Sh!" whispered Florinda. "Be quiet and they'll think we're all asleep, and maybe they'll go away."

Her hands in the dishpan, she held the dishes lest they clink against each other. There was a knock on the door. "Garnet! Florinda!" called a voice outside. Charles squirmed uneasily but did not wake up. The men on the porch called again.

"Hell's blazes," said Florinda. "Garnet, my hands are all soapy—go speak to them through the crack of the door. Say we're not going to let them in and they may as well go on. If they're after the usual, send 'em to Estelle's."

Garnet had not yet developed enough nonchalance to direct customers to Estelle's house. But she went to the door, which was still rattling as the callers knocked on it. Her lips to the crack above the bolt, she said,

"I'm sorry, gentlemen, but this place is closed until noon tomorrow. Captain Gillespie's orders."

"Is that Garnet?" said one of the voices outside. "Let us in! This is John Ives."

"Oh good heavens!" Garnet exclaimed, laughing as another voice beyond the door went on,

"It is also me. Nikolai Grigorievitch Karakozof the Handsome Brute. It is also Pablo and Vicente and the horses and we are hungry. Let us in."

Her hands awkward with eagerness, Garnet pushed back the bolt. As the door opened John said, "Good evening," and the Handsome Brute picked her up and swung her around and hugged her in his enormous comforting arms. "Oh Brute," she said, "oh John, I'm so

378

glad to see you!" The Brute laughed with great lovable warmth, and kissed her on both cheeks before he set her down. Florinda, with the speed she had learned in years of quick-changes backstage, had already dried her hands and put on her mitts. Rushing to John and the Brute she flung an arm impartially about each of them and kissed them both. "Oh, you darlings!" she sighed. "You sweaty dusty revolting unshaven darlings, I do love you so!"

Garnet put the pot of beans on the hearth-stove to warm while Florinda got out the wine. A bottle in his fist, the Brute sat down on the floor. John went outside with drinks for the boys, and told them the beans would be dished up by the time they had unloaded the horses and put them into Silky's corral. Standing in the doorway so he could direct them if necessary, John beckoned to Garnet. As she came over to him he slipped off his leather gloves and took her hands in both of his, looking down at her intently. His face was coppery with sunburn, and three days' stubble was black on his jaw. In his dark face, his eyes looked green as absinthe.

"How are you, Garnet?" he asked her. "Please don't smile politely and say 'Very well, thank you.' I have a reason for wanting to know."

His hands were so hard and muscular that she felt as if they could have snapped her fingers like toothpicks. The gentleness of their touch was astonishing.

"I'm perfectly well, John," she answered. "I mean it," she insisted, for he was watching her anxiously. With a smile she added, "And I have the most beautiful little boy."

"Born—let me see—a month ago?"

"Six weeks tomorrow."

"That's better. You've had more time to get your strength back."

"John, what do you mean? Is something wrong?"

"There's plenty wrong, and you probably know it. I wanted to be sure you were strong enough to stand a journey. We've come to get you and Florinda out of Los Angeles before the town explodes."

"Oh John! Thank you!" Garnet exclaimed. Until he spoke, she had not let herself realize how uneasy she had been. John let go her hands and picked up the bottle Florinda had set on the wall-bench beside him, regarding it with disfavor when he saw it held only the ordinary red wine of California.

"Haven't you got any whiskey, Florinda?" he asked.

Florinda stood by the fireplace cutting meat from the joint. "Yes, brave laddie, but I can't afford to give it away."

"Florinda!" Garnet exclaimed in reproach. "Do you know what he's here for?"

But John, quietly amused, had already drawn a leather purse from his pocket and was taking out a paper. "It's all right, Garnet. Florinda and I understand each other perfectly. Here's a credit paper from Mr. Abbott's, Florinda. Give me a pen and I'll put a couple of hides on deposit with you." Florinda had laid down the meat-knife when they heard a snore from the shadow over by the far wall. "Who's that?" John asked in surprise.

Florinda glanced around. "If you mean the wet subject, that's Mr. Charles Hale."

"Oh," said John, nodding slowly. "But what's he doing here?"

"He came in and raised hell with Garnet. I haven't had time to hear the details, so you'll have to ask her. Meanwhile, you'll do us a great favor if you'll get him out of here."

"We'll get him out," John said crisply. "Give me a hand, Nikolai."

Hurriedly drinking the last of the wine in his bottle, the Brute scrambled to his feet. "I will help. What do you want us to do with him, Florinda?"

"Feed him to the pigs for all I care. And you'd better hurry, because Gillespie has clamped down a ten o'clock curfew and it must be nearly ten by now."

As soon as John took over, disposal of Charles became simple. John said when Charles came to Los Angeles he was usually the guest of a rich family named Escobar. Between them, John and the Brute got Charles on his feet and out of the house. The girls heard him mumbling as the fresh air began to revive him.

They gave supper to Pablo and Vicente, and told them they could unroll their blankets in the gambling room. But like most Californios, Pablo and Vicente had little use for houses except when it was raining. They went outdoors, and were asleep with their heads on their saddles when John and the Brute returned.

John said they had had no trouble with Charles. On reaching Señor Escobar's home they told the señor they had found Don Carlos Hale sitting on the ground with his back against a wall and his head in his hands, made ill, no doubt, by sour cornmeal or stale meat. Señor Escobar was not stupid enough to believe this, but he was gentlemanly enough to pretend he did. He told his servants to give every care to the unfortunate Don Carlos, and after an exchange of courteous remarks John and the Brute bowed themselves out and came back to the saloon.

While Garnet set out the beef and beans, John signed a credit paper and Florinda brought him a bottle of whiskey. John asked if they could be ready to leave Los Angeles the day after tomorrow.

"Why yes," said Garnet. "Of course."

The Brute, who was eating meat from a big bone he held in his fists, smiled at her across the bone. "I will help you take care of the baby. I like babies."

"Be careful not to smash him," Florinda warned. "He's not much bigger than your hand." She set another bottle of red wine by the Brute's elbow, and sat on the edge of the table, across from the wall-bench. "Say, John."

"Yes?"

"I gather I'm invited to this party."

"Certainly. We came to get both of you."

"Don't tell me you rode all the way down from your rancho just for our sakes."

"No, we didn't. We thought everything was quiet in Los Angeles. But since nobody knows what's happening east of the mountains, nobody knows how much merchandise the traders will bring from Santa Fe this year. So I rode over to Nikolai's place one day and suggested that we come to town now and put in our orders at the trading posts, in case there's not enough to go around. On the way here we heard about the situation, and we decided we'd better get you away."

"A very sweet thought, I'm sure," said Florinda. But she spoke doubtfully. "Look, Johnny. I've got quite an investment in this business. Are you advising me to leave it?"

"Yes I am," said John, "and I think Silky will have to leave it too." He went on to explain. "Stockton left only about fifty men in Los Angeles, and Gillespie has sent several of those to San Diego. Besides the garrison, there aren't twenty Americans in town. In spite of Gillespie's orders there are still hundreds of Californios in this district who have guns, and Gillespie seems to be doing his best to make them want to shoot."

"Yes, that's true," Florinda said reluctantly. "Well, I guess it's better to lose money than to get murdered."

Garnet heard a little cry from Stephen, and stood up. "I'll be down to help you clear the dishes," she said to Florinda.

The Brute, who was now eating a bowl of beans and chili, halted his spoon in mid-air and smiled at her. Like John, the Brute needed a shave, but instead of being dark with stubble his chin flashed with little gold sparkles. "I will wash the dishes," said the Brute.

"But you're our guest," she objected.

"I am a nice guest," said the Brute.

"Go on up to your baby," said John. "We didn't come to make work for you. See you in the morning."

"All right then, and thanks," said Garnet. She picked up a candle. "Good night."

"Good night," said John, and the Brute kissed his hand to her. As she reached the staircase she heard Florinda ask,

"Where are you planning to take us, John?"

"Kerridge's."

"Back to Doña Manuela! Why John, you darling! She won't mind?"

"She'll be delighted, if I know her," said John. Garnet, climbing the stairs, did not hear what else he said. She was feeling a twinge of surprise that it had not occurred to her to ask John where he was going to take them. Her confidence in him went very deep, she realized now, deeper than she had known.

When she had put Stephen to sleep again she tucked him back into his basket, and setting the candle in a corner out of the draft she opened the shutters. The air was cool after the hot day, and tangy with the scent of sage. Garnet sat on the wall-bench, her arms on the sill, and looked out at the mountains looming against the stars. She was glad to have a few minutes alone. She was desperately tired. She had not said so; she had made up her mind to do whatever she had to do and be gallant about it, but she was tired in body and spirit. Tonight, after that scene with Charles, she felt battered. But she could not rest. The day after tomorrow she would have to set out on another journey.

It seemed to her that she spent most of her life going from one place to another on a long trail that had no end. How good it would be to get somewhere. How good to say, "Now I can stop moving. Here is where I belong. Here I will have quietness, and safety, and peace."

She put her forehead down on her hands. Quietness and safety and peace—she wondered if there really were any such things. Certainly not here. Her life in California was like the land of California itself. California was a place where you could ride for days and not seem to be going anywhere, a place where the mountains had nothing beyond them but deserts and more mountains. In such a land as this, and in such a life as this, you could only set your jaw and keep going, trying to pretend you were going somewhere. You laughed bravely and poured drinks at the bar, you were gay even with your best friends like Florinda and Texas. You kept on and on, trying to hide from them and from yourself the dull gray truth that you did not know what was going to become of you, and that you were lonely and terribly scared.

From below her Garnet heard the buoyant voices of Florinda and the Brute, and the clatter of dishes as they put the kitchen in order. There was a thud of hoofs in the corral behind the house. She heard John in the corral, speaking to a restless horse. Over past the other side of the plaza, a dog bayed faintly.

There were footsteps on the ground under her window. John came out of the corral and around the side of the house, where she could see him in a shimmer of moonlight. The dry undergrowth cracked as he walked on it. The cactus made a lacework of shadows, and for a moment John paused among them, looking out toward the great black mountains. He had on the shirt and trousers in which he had been riding all day, but as her eyes followed his figure she thought she had never seen a man who had such a look of strong patrician grace. John had muscles like steel, and there was not a man on the trail who could work harder than he. But he moved with such rhythmic ease that wherever he was, indoors or out, he made every other man there look clumsy.

Garnet remembered the first time she had seen him, in Santa Fe. She thought of how he had stood back while Silky and Texas and Penrose made their tipsy compliments, and then with what quiet authority he had got them out when he thought they had been there long enough. He was always like that, among them but not one of them. The other men found him hard and stern and more than a trifle awesome. They respected him, they worked with him, and they let him alone. None of them, except possibly the Brute, had discovered the tenderness that lay under John's rocky shell. She might not have found it either, if she had not needed it so. But whenever she had needed it John had been there, as he was here now; and this was not the first time she had thought he was like shade and a well in the desert.

All of a sudden, Garnet had a feeling that time had stopped. There was no clock ticking, the earth had ceased to turn, the stars had paused on their way across the sky. Nothing was happening anywhere. The universe stood in a moment of silence.

Then the whole creation spoke. She did not know, she never did know, whether she said it aloud or whether every star and mountain and cactus-thorn said it for her. But the world within and without her said, "John," and she knew what it was she had been looking for since those far-off girlish days in New York.

This was where the trail had been leading her. From New York to New Orleans, from New Orleans to Santa Fe, across the desert and over the mountains to California, all the way she had been coming to find John. She loved him and she wanted him. There was nothing surprising about it. It was like opening a door and seeing for the first time something that had always been there.

It had always been there, but until now she had not known it. She had needed all those miles and all the events of them to make her know it. If she had met John two years ago in New York she would have thought him a strange sort of man, sinister and even frightening. This was what she had thought when she did meet him in Santa Fe. In those days she had wanted fun and freedom and a lover who would lead her into romantic adventures. Now she did not want any of that. She simply wanted John.

Below the window, John turned and went back into the house. Garnet watched him, smiling to herself. John had never said a word to suggest that he was in love with her. But he had certainly let her know that he took a lot of interest in her. She felt a warm rush of happiness.

From the foot of the staircase she heard Florinda's voice.

"Well, good night, fellows. See you tomorrow."

Garnet began to close the shutters. The country had a weird beauty in the moonlight. As she reached out she saw the moon, all lopsided, like a fat man with a toothache. She was so happy that she was laughing at the moon when Florinda came in.

Garnet thought Silky might object to their leaving the bar. But Florinda assured her that Silky would urge them to start at once, and this proved to be true. As Florinda had observed long ago, Silky did not want to be responsible for anybody but himself. While business was normal the girls had great value to him and the baby was not too much of a nuisance. But if there was going to be shooting, Silky was glad to have them all out of his way.

Silky himself did not intend to leave town unless he had to.

Like the other Yankees who had trading posts in Los Angeles, he wanted to stay by his stock. Before they parted, he and Florinda split their cash and made a list of the liquor on hand. They entrusted the list to Mr. Abbott. As long as they could both go over the books at any time, Silky and Florinda maintained a friendly partnership, but neither of them cared to tempt the other too far. John came over to watch as Florinda checked the last entries in the books.

"Are you always as careful as this?" he asked.

Florinda glanced at him over her shoulder, giving him a wise smile. "Johnny my boy, you can trust Silky with your life and you could trust him with your wife if you had one, but you cannot trust him with thirty cents."

John chuckled. "I should not like to try to cheat you," he said.

"He doesn't mean to, John. Silky likes me and he's slightly afraid of me. But he simply cannot do a straight job of arithmetic, and by a strange coincidence all his mistakes are in his own favor." She closed the book and stood up. "Well, this is the best I can do. Now I'll run up and pack my clothes."

The next day they left early and rode northeast, toward the rancho of Mr. Kerridge. John rode ahead to look out for the way, for there was always a chance that the tension might have broken somewhere. Pablo and Vicente led the pack-horses. The boys had worked for John and the Brute a long time, and as they had not lived in Los Angeles to feel Gillespie's tyranny, they had no resentment against the foreigners.

As they started out the Brute offered to carry Stephen. He put one hand under Stephen's head and picked him up expertly, put him into his basket and carried the basket on his saddle. John had provided a piece of black cloth to protect the baby's eyes from the sun, but except for this he had hardly noticed him. All babies that age looked just alike to John and it did not occur to him to pretend otherwise. Florinda said he had a heart of stone, but Garnet rather admired his honesty. She thought John would have sounded absurd trying to coo over a baby.

Three days after Garnet and Florinda left Los Angeles, Gillespie's troubles began. A group of unruly young fellows, led by a man named Varela, attacked the house where the American garrison made their headquarters. The Americans drove them off and arrested several men for taking part in the attack, but this was not the end.

Varela and his gang had been making trouble since long before Gillespie came to town. Ordinarily the better people would have had nothing to do with them. But Gillespie had made himself so unpopular that this time many of the leading citizens grabbed their guns in Varela's defense. By the next day, three hundred armed Californios had surrounded the headquarters, demanding that the Americans get out of town.

While Gillespie was under siege, the revolt spread to the nearby villages. The garrison of Santa Barbara was driven out and had to flee to the mountains, and the garrison of San Diego took refuge on a Yankee whaling ship. East of Los Angeles a hundred Californios made prisoners of twenty Yankees, most of them men of substance who had been living in California for years. These men were brought to Los Angeles, and their captors joined the force besieging Gillespie.

Though he had been inept as a civil governor, as a military man Gillespie was no fool. His men were outnumbered eight to one, their supplies were running low, and he knew they could not hold out long. But he managed to get a messenger out of the house, with orders to ride north to Yerba Buena and report the revolt to Commodore Stockton. Then he said he would quit Los Angeles if they would let him lead his men unharmed to San Pedro. The Californios agreed. Gillespie's forces marched to San Pedro, where they boarded a Yankee merchant ship they found in the harbor. There they waited for help from the north.

But Yerba Buena was four hundred miles away. By the time Stockton's men got from there to San Pedro—in October—the Americans had been driven out of every place they had held in the south. The Californios, who had gathered all the weapons they could lay hands on, were watching the harbors, and of the first marines who landed, seven were killed. By this time the whole south was in disorder. For safety's sake, the Yankee tradesmen had disappeared from Los Angeles. Most of them took refuge with friendly rancheros. Even Silky had found it wise to go, leaving his precious liquor-stock behind him.

Luckily, Garnet and Florinda had reached Kerridge's Rancho before they heard of the revolt in Los Angeles. Along with a number of other Americans, they spent the winter in cheerful comfort. The Americans were all welcome guests. Mr. Kerridge had Yankee blood and a long tradition of California hospitality. As for Doña Manuela, she ruled her own kingdom and she did not care who ran the government. Doña Manuela said all these riots were disgraceful. Yankees and Californios had always got along very well in her house and there was no reason why they should not get along elsewhere. If she were in Los Angeles right now she'd have the town quiet by sundown. Nobody in the house disagreed with her.

THIRTY-SIX

Doña Manuela was delighted to see Florinda again, though disappointed that she was not married yet. As for Garnet and Stephen, Doña Manuela gathered them into her arms and wept over them. The story of Carmelita had flown around the ranchos on the wings of gossip. As innocent victim of the tragedy, Garnet and her baby reached the depths of Doña Manuela's deep heart.

She led them to the room Florinda had stayed in last winter. With tears and kisses and loving pats, while her fat bosom bobbled and her bracelets jingled up and down, Doña Manuela told them her home was theirs. She also told them her heart bled for them in their sorrows, she would see to it that they met some worthy young men to console them, and dinner would be ready at once. The girls understood no more than half she said, but as the door banged and they heard her go off yelling for the cooks, they hugged each other in delight.

John and the Brute rested at Kerridge's only one night. They had to see to their own ranchos, and also they wanted to go up to Monterey and ask for news. Garnet and Florinda went out early in the morning to see them ride off.

The serving-boys were loading the packs. John and the Brute stood holding their horses' bridles.

"I'll come back to get you as soon as it's safe," John said to Garnet. "In the meantime I think you'll be happy here."

She thought, I'd be happier with you, wherever you're going. But she answered, "Of course I will. After that saloon in Los Angeles this is like paradise."

He smiled, glad she liked it. "You'll be comfortable, and I'm pretty sure you'll be safe. This rancho is off the main north-south trail, so it's not likely to be in anybody's line of march. But please, Garnet," he added gravely, "be careful."

"I will if you'll tell me how. What does 'be careful' include?"

"Don't go beyond the gardens alone. And when you ride, no matter who's with you, stay in sight of the main house. You can see it for miles from these hills, so I'm not denying you plenty of exercise. But there are horse-thieves about, taking advantage of the war, and I shouldn't like to have you run into them. You'll remember?"

Garnet promised. John's horse stamped, restless to be off. He turned to quiet it, and the Brute, who had been talking to Florinda, spoke to Garnet. "I'll be coming back through here soon. Do you want me to bring you something from Monterey?"

"I'd like some yarn, if you can get it," said Garnet. "Silk or wool, I don't care which, just so the colors are pretty. While I'm here I can crochet a shawl for Doña Manuela."

The Brute said he would look for the yarn. He and John sprang into their saddles, and the Brute glanced down at Florinda. They had ridden to the rancho through a hot sun, and she had a streak of sunburn on her forehead. The Brute told her to put some olive oil on the burn. While they were talking John said to Garnet, "I'll send you news as soon as I can. Meanwhile, don't worry."

"I won't. You don't know how glad I am to be here, John. I was more uneasy in Los Angeles than I was telling anybody, and I'm very gratef—"

"Please, Garnet!" he exclaimed. Then as though ashamed of himself, he laughed a little and added, "I'm sorry. I know I sound like a barbarian. But that word makes me wince like a scratch on a rusty stovepipe."

What an exasperating creature he was, she thought. "I forgot," she said. "I won't say it again."

"Try not to think it either, won't you? I don't need to be paid for doing what I want to do." His green eyes swept her up and down. "Goodby," he said.

For another instant his eyes held hers. Then, abruptly, he turned his horse. The Brute called goodby, and both men waved as they rode away, followed by their pack-horses and a troop of servants. Garnet stood watching the dust waving after them like a long yellowish feather in the sun. John had not touched her, not even to take her hand as he said goodby. He had spoken to her no lover's words. But just then, if she had ever seen such a thing, he had looked at her with a lover's eyes.

She heard the dwindling thud of horses' hoofs, swift and soft through the wild oats as the men rode away. Florinda said she was going indoors and take the Brute's advice about putting olive oil on her sunburn.

Garnet walked to a grove behind a wing of the house, where vines and trees offered a shady place to rest. She sat down on an adobe bench by an olive tree, thinking. John did find her desirable. She was sure of this. But she was not sure why he had not said so.

True, she had been a widow less than a year and her baby was only two months old. Back home, if a man had spoken ardent words to her so soon his haste would have been thought shocking. But she was sure John would not be deterred by any calendar of polite usage. If he loved her he would tell her so when it suited him. But he had not told her, and she wished she knew why.

Suddenly she wondered what John had been talking about when he said, while they were riding from Charles' rancho to Los Angeles, that he had once been an object of charity. Garnet looked down with a puzzled scowl. She had always thought "charity" meant bundles for the ragged poor. That was certainly not what John meant, not John with his high-bred manners and his cultured speech. But she wondered what he did mean.

How little she knew about him. Not that it mattered. She knew how important he was to her, and how much she wanted to be important to him. Garnet looked out toward the far toast-colored hills where she had watched John ride away, and hoped she could pretend to be patient until he came back.

Mr. Kerridge lived in a house with adobe walls and a roof made of red tiles. It was a long, low, sprawling house, with many wings. In front was a grove of sycamores and live-oaks, where horses ready saddled stood under the trees all day. On both sides were courtyards planted with vines and fruit-trees, and at the back, enclosed by a high wall, was the courtyard of the young girls. Men were not allowed to enter here, and the unmarried daughters of the house could not go beyond it unchaperoned. Married women could go anywhere they pleased.

This fall Mr. Kerridge was having more Yankee visitors than ever before. Now that they were sure California was about to become American territory, scores of men were coming down from Oregon.

389

Many of them found their way to Kerridge's, since they wanted advice from a Yankee long established in the country. Other men brought strings of horses, which they asked Mr. Kerridge to keep for them. Men of Frémont's battalion were roaming around, taking horses and leaving promises that some day the United States government would pay for them. The rancheros did not trust any such promises. Since Kerridge's was not on the main trail, they thought the horses would be safer here than on the ranchos near the coast.

The visitors usually meant to stay only a few days. But they rarely left so soon. They had not expected Mr. Kerridge to introduce them to two marriageable American women. The men prolonged their visits, and seldom left without having proposed marriage to at least one of the girls, usually both. Neither Garnet nor Florinda had a notion of marrying any of these eager strangers. But after the dirt and smells and spiders of Los Angeles it was very agreeable to stroll among the olive trees and be adored.

Altogether, Garnet and Florinda were having a gay holiday. Their days began at the first streak of dawn, when a girl brought hot chocolate to their bedside. When they were dressed they joined the others for long rides over the hills, and came in ravenous for the vast, magnificent meals. There was a mid-morning breakfast, and dinner was at noon. After dinner they all had a siesta. When they were dressed again they went into the courtyards, where girls were walking about with plates of wafers and pots of a hot drink called cha, brewed from native herbs and flavored with orange blossoms.

The first rain came in November. The earth turned green and the high peaks turned white, for what had been rain in the valleys had been snow in the mountains. Not long after the storm the Handsome Brute rode in from Monterey. To Garnet's disappointment, he rode alone. He brought her a note from John, clear and brief. John said he had found he could be useful to the American troops. He knew every pass, every trail, almost every gully in southern California, so they were using him as guide and interpreter. He would come to get her and Stephen and Florinda as soon as he thought it safe for them to travel, but he did not think this would be for some months yet.

The letter was so provokingly impersonal that Garnet's first impulse was to tear it to pieces. That stick of wood, she thought savagely. What could you do with a man like that? When every time you heard his name you felt like a volcano, and he wrote to you as if he had been writing to his aunt!

390

You couldn't do anything. Whatever John's feelings were, he kept them locked up. As Garnet thought of this, the storm within her began to subside. She remembered how John had stood by her when she needed him, and the way his eyes had held hers that last moment before he rode away. John did care for her, and it was foolish of her to doubt it.

She was sitting on the wall bench in the room she shared with Florinda. Laying the sheet of paper beside her, she began sorting the yarn the Brute had brought her to crochet a shawl for Doña Manuela. The yarn was beautiful: hanks of silk in many colors, which he had got from a Yankee clipper engaged in the China trade. Stephen woke and gabbled for somebody to come and pay attention to him. As Garnet picked him up Florinda came in, and Garnet glanced around to say, "There's John's letter. He says we'll have to stay here all winter."

It was time for siesta. Florinda began to take the pins out of her hair. "Well, if we've got to kill time this is a mighty pleasant place to do it." She put her hairpins in a pile beside the wash basin and unbuttoned her dress. "But I do wish," she went on, "that all these nice blockheads would quit asking me to marry them. I don't want any husband cluttering up my life. Tell me a ladylike way to refuse a gent, Garnet."

Garnet considered. "You can say you admire him, and you are honored by the evidence of his esteem. But you do not feel for him that peculiar preference which a woman should entertain for the man whose life she expects to share—"

"Hail Columbia, does it have to be that fancy? Well, write it down so I can memorize it." Florinda put on her nightgown. "All winter," she said with a shake of her head. "That means losing *lots* of money. I do hope Silky has managed to hide our whiskey somewhere. It was so awfully expensive."

With her face bent over Stephen, Garnet wondered doesn't Florinda ever think about anything but money? The baby had gone back to sleep, and she stood up to put him into his bed. Florinda turned to stroke Stephen's head, smiling down at him tenderly. As Garnet saw her scarred hand caressing the little rings of baby hair, her own conscience gave a twist. No wonder Florinda thought so highly of money. Why shouldn't she? That was all she had.

Later on, when they were up from their nap, a girl brought in a pile of clothes freshly laundered. Garnet was mending a dress of

Stephen's, so Florinda sat on the floor by the clothes chest to put them away. When she had finished she took her jewel box from the chest. After studying the ornaments inside it, she picked up a ring set with an enormous aquamarine.

"I think I'll give this to Doña Manuela when we leave," she said. "Pretty, isn't it?"

She tossed the ring into Garnet's lap. "What a gorgeous stone!" Garnet exclaimed.

"Seventy-five carats," Florinda said complacently.

Garnet turned the ring between her fingers, watching as the aquamarine caught the light in blue-green flashes. She wondered how long it had been since Florinda's hands had been as lovely as the rest of her, so she could wear rings. The hanks of silk yarn lay on the bench beside her. It made Garnet feel almost guilty to have them there, reminding her that while she could express her thanks to Doña Manuela with a gift of fine needlework, Florinda could not. But though this fact was evident, neither of them had ever spoken of it and they were not going to do so now. Garnet said,

"It's a beautiful ring, Florinda. She'll love it."

"If she can get it on," Florinda said laughing. "Her fingers are so very fat. But there must be somebody hereabouts who can make it larger." She smiled reminiscently as Garnet handed back the ring. "Quite a nice gent he was, the one who gave me this," she remarked.

"Did you like him very much?" Garnet asked.

"Why sure, I liked him fine," said Florinda. She put the ring back into the box. Closing the lid, she glanced over her shoulder. "Are you trying to ask me again if I've ever been in love?" she asked with a touch of humor.

"No. I know you never have."

"Darling, what makes you look so sober about it?"

"I was wishing you weren't such a cynic."

"I don't know what a cynic is," Florinda returned cheerfully. "However—" she hesitated, and her own face grew sober too. After she had thought about it, Florinda went on. "Garnet, I wish you didn't believe in so many rainbows. About love and marriage and all that."

"You don't think I ought to get married again?" Garnet asked. "Not ever?"

"Oh, it's all right to get married if you like the idea. But I mean— you ought not to expect so much." She spoke with conviction.

"I don't want to shock your dainty feelings, Garnet, but girls on my side of the park know quite a lot about girls on your side. We know about those vows of undying adoration you get, and we know what fools you are to believe them."

Garnet pressed her hand on the window-sill, feeling the rough earthy texture of the adobe under her fingers. "We're not always fools to believe them!" she retorted.

"Garnet, dear," Florinda pled, "I don't want you to get hurt again. And the only way not to get hurt is, don't give anybody a chance to hurt you. Don't ask for much, and then you won't be hurt when you don't get much. Can't you understand that?"

"I understand it. I don't believe it. I'll never accept any such patchwork as long as I live."

"Oh, hell and whiskers," said Florinda. "Let's go out and get a cup of cha."

Garnet wondered if Florinda was trying to warn her about men in general, or about John in particular. It did not matter. She did not need to be warned about men in general, because she wanted only one. And as for John, he would never make a promise to her, or to any man or woman on earth, unless he was ready to risk his life to keep it.

THIRTY-SEVEN

In that same month of November, Frémont decided to lead his battalion to Los Angeles. He had been ordered there a month before, when Stockton first got news of the revolt and went south himself, but Frémont had waited while his men gathered up horses and cattle from the ranchos. Now he set out from Monterey with five hundred men, several cannon, and a drove of animals.

But he had forgotten about the California seasons. When he was four days' march out of Monterey the rains began. The valleys turned into lakes of mud. The cannon bogged, the men got sick, the cattle died. Monterey and Los Angeles were three hundred miles apart, and the twisting mountain passes added more miles to the journey. It took Frémont two months to make the march to Los Angeles. By the time he got there the American flag was again flying over the plaza and American soldiers were guarding the streets.

The Army of the West, commanded by Brigadier-General Stephen W. Kearny, had reached California in December. They had marched overland from Fort Leavenworth on the Missouri River.

General Kearny was a graduate of West Point, a veteran of the War of 1812, and a seasoned officer of the frontier. After leading his men across two thousand miles of prairie and desert, Kearny was in no mood to wait for any dawdling heroes. He had come to fight, and fight he did, immediately. Learning that there were American troops in San Diego, Kearny sent them word that he was on his way. Captain Gillespie hurried to meet him with his small party of marines. Joining forces with Gillespie's men, Kearny met the Californios in battle at a Digger village called San Pascual, east of San Diego. After two days' fighting the Californios fled, though they had made the Americans pay dearly in both killed and wounded for their victory. In this battle Gillespie proved again that though he was a poor governor, he was no coward. He fought gallantly, and got a wound that nearly cost him his life.

Though General Kearny had also been wounded, he managed to get into his saddle the next day and lead his men to San Diego. Here they joined the forces under Commodore Stockton and set out for Los Angeles. After several skirmishes outside the town, the Americans entered Los Angeles on the tenth of January, 1847.

At Kerridge's Rancho, they did not hear the news till a month later. The winter storms were hard; the mountains were full of snow, and travelers were few. This winter especially, there was so much disorder in the land that most people who had homes were glad to stay in them.

For the rancheros, it was a time full of irritations. Even in Mr. Kerridge's well-guarded grazing lands there were thieves. Frémont's high-handed tactics had inspired a lot of scamps to gallop about the country stealing horses and anything else they could find, hoping Frémont would get the blame. The rancheros, both Yankees and Californios, were in a state of exasperation. Loudly they asked if the United States wasn't ever going to send an army to make California safe again for honest folk.

At Kerridge's, they heard a thousand rumors about the American army. But they got no real news until one bright morning in February, when the Handsome Brute, grand in a purple coat and gold satin breeches, came riding through the pass and told them the Yankees had entered Los Angeles. No, he said, he had not been down there. He had spent the past few months quite comfortably, seeing to his own rancho and John's. He had heard of the army from a couple of Yankee traders who had stopped at his place one night. The traders had left the next morning, and as he watched them go over the hills he had felt lonesome. The sun had been shining for two weeks, riding would be easy, and he thought he'd go over to Kerridge's Rancho and see his friends. So here he was.

He brought Doña Manuela a bead necklace, which she at once put on. In high good-humor she went jangling off toward the outdoor ovens, leaving the Brute in the courtyard with Garnet and Florinda and Mr. Kerridge. While the Brute emptied a bottle of wine he told them what he knew about events in the south.

The traders who had brought him the news, he said, were two of the fellows who went every year from Los Angeles to Santa Fe. The girls would remember them, Devilbug and Ticktock. Why yes, the mule-train had made the trip as usual. It had left last spring, while Garnet was ill at Charles' rancho, before anybody in California had heard of the war. The traders had not heard of it themselves until they got to the settlements around Santa Fe.

The war had not hindered their trade. General Kearny had taken Santa Fe with very little trouble. The governor of New Mexico, fat Armijo, had blustered with a great noise about how many Yankees he was going to kill, but as soon as the first Yankee in uniform had appeared on the horizon Armijo had run like a scared pig. He had taken everything that belonged to him and a good deal that did not, and as far as Devilbug and Ticktock could learn, nobody had shed any tears at losing him.

General Kearny had organized the province quickly and competently. The great sensation of the conquest came when the people found that goods brought from Missouri by the Santa Fe traders would be vastly cheaper than ever before. For now that New Mexico belonged to the United States, Armijo's customs duties were done with.

And now the army had reached Los Angeles. The Yankee residents were coming back, the town was open for trade again, and here as in Santa Fe there would be no more of those pestilential customs duties on American goods.

"Then we won't have to pay the boys to smuggle in whiskey for us!" Florinda exclaimed joyfully. "Did they tell you anything about Silky, Brute? Is the saloon open again?"

Yes, the saloon was open, said the Brute. Devilbug and Ticktock had been there, and Silky had said he hoped the girls would be back soon. Now that Los Angeles was full of Yankees, Garnet and Florinda would be more valuable than ever as barmaids.

"And Mickey?" Florinda asked.

The boys had seen Mickey too. But other details the Brute had asked about, they didn't remember. They had stayed in Los Angeles only long enough to put their goods on sale at the trading posts, then they had left to ride out to the rancho country. Spring was nearly here and they had to get mules for their next journey. Usually they contracted for mules early in the winter, but this year the war had prevented them, so now they had to make haste.

Sitting on the bench by the olive tree, Garnet looked down at the red surface of her wine. The Brute was telling Mr. Kerridge that mules would bring fine prices this year. What with fighting and thieves, the supply would be scarce. Mr. Kerridge and Florinda were both asking questions. Garnet was not asking any. The only question she wanted to ask was sticking in her throat.

Where is John? Silky and Mickey and mules—oh, who cares? Where is John?

She could not ask. Such timidity made her feel like an idiot, but all the same she could not. The little gray leaves of the olive tree rustled in a breath of wind.

"Say, Brute, what's John doing these days? Last time we heard was when you brought that letter to Garnet, saying he was going to be a guide through the gullies."

"John is in Los Angeles," said the Brute. "Devilbug and Ticktock saw him at Mr. Abbott's." The dining-gong clanged, and the Brute scrambled to his feet. "There! I am hungry."

"That's not news," said Florinda, "you always are. Say, listen a minute, you big glutton. Why doesn't John quit guiding the army and come guide us back to Los Angeles? If my bar is open I want to be there."

They had started toward the dining-hall. The Brute looked down from his great height and smiled upon all three of them.

"John said he would come back as soon as it was safe for you and Garnet to travel," he said to Florinda. "So that is what he will do."

So that is what he will do, Garnet echoed in her mind. How few men there were whose friends could speak of them with such unquestioning certainty. Involuntarily, she smiled as she took her place at the long table, and the Brute smiled back at her.

Ten days later John arrived at the rancho. It was a sunny afternoon, and when Garnet had dressed after her siesta she left Florinda trying a new coiffure while she took her workbasket and started outdoors. The shawl was nearly finished now. Doña Manuela, who loved things to wear only a little less than she loved things to eat, had been watching its progress with pleasure.

Their bedroom door opened on a corridor leading to the girls' courtyard, but Garnet and Florinda did not often go there. Florinda would as soon have thought to pass a pleasant hour in the desert as in a place where men were forbidden. While Garnet did not feel quite so strongly about the matter, she did not like to be isolated either; so as she came out of her room she went to a side door leading to an open courtyard.

Outdoors the air was crisp. The sky was so blue and the earth was so green that the few bare trees looked out of place. On the near slopes the chaparral grew thickly, and here and there the white buckthorn bushes were in bloom. Against the dark green of the chaparral the bushes looked like piles of soapsuds. Far away, the high peaks were white on the bright blue sky. Pausing a moment to look, Garnet heard men and horses at the front of the house, and among the sounds she heard John's voice. He was not shouting—she could not remember that she had ever heard him shout—but she had been waiting for his voice too long to mistake it now. Her basket on her arm, she caught up her skirts to free her footsteps as she hurried through the long winter grass. Nobody in California ever cut the grass, and after a rainstorm she really believed it grew an inch in a night. For some reason this seemed funny, and she was laughing at the idea of it when she saw John.

He had just dismounted, and his boys had not begun to unload the horses. Nobody knew yet that he was here, nobody but herself and one of Mr. Kerridge's men, a long weedy fellow who had been asleep by the front door and was now getting lazily to his feet, saying he would tell the family that the Señor Ives had come. Yawning, he ambled indoors. As John turned to speak to his boys he caught sight of Garnet. Breaking his sentence in the middle, he came with quick long strides to meet her.

John had on an old plaid woolen shirt and colorless trousers and heavy boots, and as usual after a journey his jaws were black with stubble. From head to foot he was spattered with mud. In his dark face his teeth were gleaming white and his eyes were like Florinda's aquamarine. He caught Garnet's hands in his.

"How good to see you, Garnet," John said. He spoke in a low voice.

"Oh, I'm so glad you're back!" Garnet exclaimed. As she said it she laughed a little, and wondered if John knew what she was laughing at. She was laughing at herself, at her utter inability to be shy and coy and make a man wonder if she cared for him. She did not know how, she never had known how, she was as clear as the sun on the mountains; but John looked surprised at her words.

"But didn't you know I was coming back? I sent you a letter by Nikolai. I told you I'd be here as soon as it was safe for you to travel."

"Oh yes, yes, I got your letter," she returned, and she was thinking, You exasperating fool, do you think I was afraid that you, of all men on earth, wouldn't keep a promise? Can't you see it's just that I'm tingling with joy and gladness at the sight of you? Oh, don't you love me, John?

But at least he was still holding her hands, with the hard firm pressure she knew so well, and he had not moved his eyes from her since he saw her first. He asked,

"How has it been for you here?"

She did her best to answer calmly. "Safe and comfortable, just as you said it would be."

She wished those boys were not so dutiful about tethering the horses. If they would only go away somewhere maybe John would kiss her. But the boys did not understand English; their presence need not keep him from saying he loved her. But he did not say it. Instead he asked, "No trouble here at all?"

"No trouble for me," Garnet answered. "Mr. Kerridge lost some horses, and some grain too, and hides. He can tell you how much. But what about you, John? What have you been doing?"

"Oh, carrying messages, and giving advice about weather and trails and where to get meat for the army. I suppose you've heard we're finally in Los Angeles?"

I could choke you for talking about the war, thought Garnet. She said, "Yes, but we don't know many details."

"I'll fill in the outlines. I've just come up from Los Angeles."

"Was it a hard ride?" she asked.

"Not too bad. A lot of mud, and cold pinole sometimes when we

398

couldn't find any dry wood for a fire." His lean cheeks creased humorously. "Remember cold pinole?"

She laughed and nodded, and John laughed too, intimately, as if their having shared cold mush on the desert made a sort of home-town link between them. The comradeship of his laughter brushed away the last shred of her reserve. She exclaimed,

"Oh John, I've missed you so!"

John's hands tightened on hers. His eyes were eager as he searched her face. She wondered how she could ever have thought John's eyes were cold. He said earnestly,

"Garnet, I've thought of you every day and night since I left you."

All winter Garnet had tried to tell herself that she did not need to hear this, because she was already sure he loved her. But the minute she heard it she knew all her self-assurance had been a singing in the dark, for her spirit leaped so joyously at his words. John went on,

"I've never had the thought of anybody so constantly with me. It was always as if you were just out of sight, in the next room or beyond the next turn of the trail. And when I got that far and you weren't there, I had such a strange sense of being alone—strange, I mean, because I've always preferred to be alone. But then of course, you're the only woman I ever gave a damn about."

As he spoke, she felt a wild glow of pleasure. And because she had not a shadow of subtlety in her, when he ceased speaking she said the first thing she wanted to say. "John, why did you wait so long to tell me this?"

He laughed silently. "Maybe it's because I'm a fool, Garnet. Tell me, I could have said it before, couldn't I? You did want me, didn't you?"

"Want you? Oh John! If you knew how—"

Behind her Garnet heard the voices of Mr. Kerridge and the Handsome Brute, calling a welcome to John as they hurried out of the house to meet him. John said under his breath, "Oh, damn all these nice people," as he let go of her hands and turned to greet his host. Mr. Kerridge was telling him that his room was waiting, and Doña Manuela was already calling the servants to bring him wine to drink and hot water to wash in. The men went in together, leaving Garnet resentful that Mr. Kerridge and the Brute could go with John to his room while she could not. But waves and waves of delight were breaking through her. John did want her. He was here with her at last, and she loved him.

John reappeared at supper, shaved and scrubbed, and dressed in a white shirt and black velveteen breeches laced up the sides with scarlet cords. After supper the adults of the household gathered in the parlor, where Mr. Kerridge had ordered the rare luxury of a fire. John was fresh from the scene of action and they had a lot of questions to ask.

The servants went about pouring wine and passing wafers. While the others discussed the war, Doña Manuela sipped and nibbled and dozed. Every now and then she roused herself with a start and shouted to one servant to bring more wood for the fire, to another servant to bring more wine, and to a third to brew some more cha for Doña Florinda—couldn't the fools ever get it through their thick heads that the white-headed Yankee lady did not take wine? And she would be grateful if her son Arturo would bring her that bottle of angélica, and she would be even more grateful if his wife Carlota would stop rustling her skirts so people could hear what Don Juan Ives was saying. Everybody scurried to obey her. Doña Manuela sipped the sweet angélica and dozed off again, and Mr. Kerridge, with a quiet chuckle, asked John to go on with his story.

John told them about the battle at San Pascual, the march to San Diego, and the fighting along the San Gabriel River before the American army entered Los Angeles. He told them about General Kearny, who never flaunted his authority but who always got things done. With a cynical humor, John told them about Frémont.

Shortly after the American army entered Los Angeles, Frémont's weary march had brought him to town with his battalion. Stockton had appointed Frémont civil governor. Both Stockton and Kearny had to leave Los Angeles, John explained, and go up to Monterey. Somebody had to be in Los Angeles to carry out their orders. But Frémont was showing no inclination to take orders from anybody, not even the general himself. Frémont had taken the biggest house in town for his residence, and was setting himself up as governor in fine style. John rather suspected that the boisterous gentleman was heading for trouble.

Since nobody in the family could understand English but Mr. Kerridge, John was speaking Spanish. At intervals he paused to make sure Garnet and Florinda were following him, and sometimes Florinda asked him to translate. Garnet did not interrupt him. She sat with her head bent over her crochet. The candlelight was hardly strong enough for such fine work, but she kept at it because it gave her something to look at besides John. Her eyes wanted to follow his every movement, in a way that would have betrayed what she was thinking as clearly as if she had spoken it aloud. But now and then she could not help looking up, and when she did John's eyes would catch hers, and hold them with a brief intensity that she could feel almost like a kiss.

John told them the name of the northern village Yerba Buena had been changed to San Francisco. Florinda nodded with approval. "San Francisco," she repeated. "That's easier to say."

John thought this was the reason the name had been changed. The village was growing fast; it now had close to four hundred people, nearly all of them Yankees, and they found the words Yerba Buena too much of a lip-twister. As the town stood at the edge of San Francisco Bay, the American alcalde had issued an order saying that hereafter the town was to have the same name as the bay.

John also told them that still more American soldiers had lately arrived. A battalion of Mormons had reached San Diego after an overland march, and they were going to garrison Los Angeles.

"Mormons?" Florinda repeated. "What are they?"

John explained to her in English. The Mormons were believers in a new religion, he said. They had been living mostly in Missouri and Illinois, but people of other faiths had come to dislike them violently, and last year about twenty thousand Mormons had been driven out of their homes. The elders of the church were now planning to take their people into the West, where they could set up their own community. On the outbreak of the war the Mormon leader Brigham Young had offered a battalion to President Polk. It was a canny move, John observed. Brigham Young wanted to prove the patriotism of the Mormons—whose enemies had been calling them anti-American—and also he wanted to have a lot of healthy young men in the West ready to join the Mormon colony after the war.

"How many of them are there?" Florinda asked.

"I'm not sure. Three or four hundred."

She gave a satisfied smile, evidently counting the value of so many new customers at the bar, but John, with an amused glance at her, shook his head.

"They don't drink," he said.

Florinda stared in dismay. "What's the matter with them?"

Garnet thought any other man would have made a bright remark about Florinda's not drinking either, but John seldom said the obvious. He answered,

"Their church forbids it. Oh, I suppose some of them drink, there

401

never was a church yet that could make all its members keep the rules, but generally they're a very sober lot. However, the bar doesn't need them. Silky is doing a thriving business."

"Then he must have saved the whiskey!" Florinda exclaimed.

John nodded, and Florinda listened jubilantly while he told her about it. As Silky and Florinda rented the saloon from Mr. Abbott, Silky had adroitly figured that Mr. Abbott would not like to see them go broke. So he had left the whiskey in Mr. Abbott's care. Mr. Abbott was married to a native woman and had three stalwart sons who were Angelenos by birth but who had a good share of their father's Yankee enterprise. These three sons had seen to it that the saloon stayed locked up. Mickey had continued to live there, sleeping under the roof of the back porch, while Isabel supplied him with beans.

"And where did Mr. Abbott go during the troubles?" Florinda asked.

John chuckled. Mr. Abbott had not been on a horse in twenty years and no war could make him get on one now. When the other Yankees fled from Los Angeles Mr. Abbott had merely retired to an upper room of his own house. He closed the shutters, settled his huge bulk into an armchair, and while his family told people he had left town Mr. Abbott passed a pleasant winter reading the old American newspapers that he generally kept stacked on the counter of his store. Florinda laughed too. Then with a glance at Garnet she said,

"Oh yes, something else we've been wondering about. What's become of our precious friend Charles?"

John asked the others to forgive him if he went on speaking English for a few minutes. There were some details Florinda had not understood. He said Charles had been very busy of late. Charles was a leading American ranchero and he had lost no time letting the American army know it. He had given the army considerable aid in the form of shelter and supplies, and shortly after they entered Los Angeles he had come there too, and had been bustling about importantly. "But he didn't stay in Los Angeles long after the occupation," John added. "He went north early in the year. Monterey, and probably San Francisco too."

"What's he doing up there?" Florinda asked.

"Oh, sniffing around," said John. "A man never can tell when he might run into a good thing, you know."

"Sure, I understand," agreed Florinda. "Well, I hope he stays out of our place. He makes me think óf an attic full of cobwebs."

Doña Manuela woke up again. This time she announced that it was time for bed. It was, in fact, past midnight, long after their usual bedtime, so the others were quite willing to obey her.

Garnet and Florinda went to their room. But Garnet wanted to be by herself a while and think about John. She said she had a headache from crocheting in the dim light—which was true—and would like to get some fresh air before she went to bed. Wrapping a shawl around her she went down the corridor to the door leading out to the girls' courtyard.

The court was chilly and rustling and very dark. There were stars overhead, but only a faint scrap of moon, and the trees had been planted thickly for daytime shade. Closing the door behind her, Garnet walked toward a group of lemon trees by the enclosing wall. The air was full of pungent odors, refreshing after the smoky parlor, and she liked the feel of the wind in her hair. On the wall the grape-vines were swishing like taffeta petticoats. Breaking a leaf off a lemon tree Garnet crushed it in her hand and drew in a long breath of fragrance. Her foot touched a bench in the velvet blackness under the tree and she sat down, leaning back and singing a little tune. Alone in the dark she had a sense of freedom and privacy. She hoped Florinda was falling asleep.

Suddenly, beside her on the wall she heard a rustling like a gust of wind. Over her head the branches shook with a soft clatter, and a man swung down from the tree to the grass. Garnet had sprung to her feet, but before she could move away she heard him whisper, "It's only me, Garnet—John."

She could see him only as a thicker blackness in the dark. For an instant she shivered at the risk he was running, for Doña Manuela's sons would not have hesitated to shoot at any male figure they saw prowling in the court that opened from their sisters' bedrooms. "John!" she gasped. "Do you know where this is?"

"Why yes," said John, "I've got no business being here." His voice was so low that she could barely hear him above the rattling leaves, but she thought she would have recognized that note of cool amusement anywhere in the world. "I was crossing the outer court," he went on, "when I heard somebody singing on this side of the wall. It could have been you, so I came close and listened. The words were English and the voice wasn't Florinda's, and I knew then it was you. So I scrambled over." He laughed under his breath.

"Most reprehensible. But I wanted so much to kiss you good night. Do you mind?"

He swept her into his arms and kissed her. For an instant Garnet was aware that the trees were murmuring around her and the wind was blowing John's hair down over her eyes, and then she was not aware of anything except that now at last John was holding her close to him and she loved him. She loved the strength and fire and gentleness of him, and she wanted him to belong to her completely and forever.

She had no idea of time. But all at once the hall door began to bang in the wind. None of the doors had locks, and the latches were so flimsy that if you were not careful to catch them properly the doors would blow open at the first breeze. Garnet started at the noise, but John said "Sh!" and she stood still, his arm around her and his hand holding her head against his shoulder as he kissed her hair. An instant later they heard the voice of one of the little girls, roused by the banging door. A light shone from the far end of the corridor, and Doña Manuela's voice called to the child that it was only the wind, and she was coming to shut the door herself.

John drew Garnet deeper into the blackness of the trees. His lips close to her ear, he whispered, "You aren't frightened, are you? She can't lock you out."

Garnet began to laugh silently. She was so happy she could not help it. She whispered to John, "What will Doña Manuela do if she sees us?"

"Something violent, no doubt," John said, and his words too were quivering with laughter. "But I don't think she'll see us. I can't even see you myself."

In the doorway appeared Doña Manuela's vast figure, vaster than ever in the shawl she had thrown over her nightgown. Behind her was a servant girl carrying a candle. Luckily John and Garnet were over in a far corner, but Doña Manuela had heard a movement. "¿Quién está ahí?" she demanded loudly.

"Answer her," John whispered. Garnet called back, giving her name and saying she had come out for some air.

Doña Manuela repeated her name sharply.

"Sí, señora," said Garnet.

She was still laughing, though at the same time she felt a twinge of apprehension lest Doña Manuela snatch the candle and come waddling out. She did not know what would happen if John should be found with her. Probably they would both be sent off in disgrace.

She would not have minded, if only she and John were sent together, but after Doña Manuela's kindness she would have been sorry to seem careless of the rules of her house. Fortunately, however, the wind was cold, and Doña Manuela had drunk a lot of angélica and was very sleepy. She shouted to Garnet again, ordering her to come to bed at once before the night air gave her a string of ailments Garnet had never heard of before. Garnet answered that she was coming right in. The little girl was calling again, and Doña Manuela, giving the servant a poke with her elbow, turned around and started for the child's room. "I must go now," Garnet whispered to John.

His arm tightened around her. The fingers of his other hand felt along the line of her temple and down her cheek. Garnet was thinking, I wish I could see his eyes. Right now, he is looking at me the way he looks at the hills when they are full of flowers.

"All right," John whispered reluctantly. "You must go now. When can we be together again?"

"Tomorrow."

"In the morning? Early?"

"As early as you please."

"As soon as it's light, then. In the outer courtyard. The olive grove toward the east." He kissed the edge of her eyebrow. "Good night, my dear."

With a great effort she made herself let him go. Throwing her shawl over her head so it would cast a shadow lest her face was betraying too much, she ran to the house. But to her relief Doña Manuela had gone to the child's bedside, and the hall was dark and empty.

In the doorway, Garnet paused to look back. The sturdy old lemon tree creaked as John caught a branch of it, swung himself up, and vaulted over the wall. Garnet blew a kiss into the darkness after him as she closed the door. This time she made sure the latch was tight. From one of the bedrooms came Doña Manuela's voice, sweet as a cradle song as she soothed her little girl back to sleep. Garnet felt her way along the hall to her room, where a line of light under the door showed that Florinda had left the candle burning to guide her.

Florinda was asleep. Garnet went to the glass and took the pins out of her hair. She smiled at her reflection. In the dim light her face seemed to have a radiance of its own. It was the first time she had ever genuinely thought she looked beautiful.

When the girl brought the early chocolate Garnet sprang up eagerly and opened the shutters to see the weather. The wind had died down, but a mist had gathered and the air was damp and cold. Florinda squealed, and Garnet closed the shutters again.

Florinda was sitting up in bed, sipping her chocolate and voicing her regular morning grumble about people who made you get up at this ungodly time of night. She always grumbled, but she always got up, for she liked the morning rides. However, she was in no such hurry to be out as Garnet was, and she was still yawning and stretching when Garnet left her. Garnet said over her shoulder that she would not ride this morning. She did not say why, though she thought Florinda probably guessed.

Carrying Stephen, she found his nurse Luisa having her chocolate in the outdoor kitchen. Garnet gave her the baby, and told her she was walking out to the olive grove.

She made her way among the trees. The night-fog was going, but it was not yet gone, and in the east she could see the purple hilltops rising here and there above the mist. They looked like plums in a bowl of cream. Around her the trees were bright with dampness. When she brushed them as she passed, the leaves tossed little showers at her cheeks. She could hear the birds twittering, and she could smell the fresh odors of the garden. The path turned, and she saw John.

He stood with one foot on an adobe bench and his elbow on his knee, watching a black-and-gold butterfly that had lit on a twig. As he heard the rustle of her skirts he turned his head, and with a quick eagerness he came to meet her. Lifting her hands he turned them over and kissed the palms, grinning at her across them as if he and she were sharing a delicious secret that nobody knew but themselves.

"I do like you, Garnet," he said. "Why didn't you keep me waiting till noon?"

"Noon?" she repeated laughing. "Because I couldn't wait that long to see you."

"That's why I like you," said John. "No coquetry and no pretenses. Come over here." He led her to the bench. She sat down, and John sat turned so as to face her, one leg across the other and his long brown hands laced around his knee. With a quiver of humor on his lips he asked, "Should I apologize for being so impulsive last night? I'm not at all sorry, you know."

"I'm not sorry either," said Garnet, and she laughed again as she thought, No coquetry, no pretenses, well, thank heaven he likes me this way, because it's the way I am. She said aloud, "Now at last I can ask you something. John, why did you take so long to come back? Why did you send me that frosty little note instead of coming with the Brute on your way down from Monterey?"

"You still don't know?" he asked with some surprise.

She shook her head.

"I was scared," John answered simply.

"Scared?" Garnet echoed. "You're not scared of anything!" Somewhere away back in her mind she heard, "Not anything he can shoot." For the moment she could not remember who had said that, and she wished the line had not pushed its way into her head. She pushed it back, exclaiming, "What were you scared of?"

"You," said John.

"Oh John! Oh my dear," she protested, and put her hands over his, which were still clasped around his knee. "Do you mean—you were scared I wouldn't have you?"

"No, I was scared you would. For the wrong reasons." He smiled a little. "Is that foolish?"

"I don't know," said Garnet. "I don't know what you're talking about."

"Then I'll tell you," said John. His green eyes were looking straight into hers, and he spoke with a smiling candor. "I wanted you more than I had ever wanted any other woman. I couldn't tell whether you wanted me that much or not. But I thought you might say you did."

He stood up abruptly, walked a few steps away from her, and turned around.

"There. That's out. Now tell me I'm a fool, and the louder you say it the happier I'll be. Understand?"

"I do not," said Garnet. "You're not as rich as all that, are you? If I didn't love you, what reason could I have for taking you?"

John answered with a terseness that was almost like anger. "Gratitude, damn you!"

For a moment she stared at him, her eyes wide and her mouth open, then she began to laugh at him. "Oh you fool. You dear incredible goose. John Ives, do you think I'd have you or any other man because I was grateful to him?"

"Then," he demanded, "what made you babble so much about it? Why in God's name did you keep talking as if you owed me a debt? As if you were expecting that any day I was going to ask for payment?"

"John," she said, "I swear to you, I never thought of any such thing."

"Well, I thought of it," he returned. "And I don't want to be a sense of duty to anybody. Least of all to you." He broke a couple of leaves off the tree. "So I went away and stayed away till you'd had time to know I wasn't going to demand anything. Then when I rode in yesterday—" He smiled at her frankly. "You were glad to see me, weren't you?"

"I was never so happy to see anybody in my life," said Garnet. "I had been wanting you every minute since you waved goodby. Didn't I look like it?"

"Yes," said John, "you looked like it. You were shining all over at the sight of me. And you couldn't have looked like that if you hadn't meant it." With a flicker of amusement he added, "Florinda, yes, she's very skillful at that sort of thing. But not you. So when I saw you yesterday I knew you were glad to see me."

Garnet leaned back against the trunk of the tree behind her and looked up at him, laughing happily. John stood with one hand on the limb of the tree and the other hand caught in his belt. It was a fine tooled leather belt with a silver buckle. He said,

"I don't know how to make beautiful speeches, Garnet. But as I told you yesterday, you are the only woman I ever gave a damn about. I should like very much to be married to you. Do you like me well enough for that?"

A flash of sun struck the buckle of his belt. The mist was lifting. The sun was sending long bright shafts between the mountains, and the dew was all a-glitter on the leaves. Garnet went to him, and stood looking up at his lean dark face and the astonishingly light eyes under the black lashes; and though he was smiling as his eyes met hers, she saw the bitter lines about his eyes and mouth, the same lines she had seen the first time she had met him. She thought that now at last she would find out what had put them there, and she would spend the rest of her life loving him and making him understand that the world did not have to be as hard as he had found it. She said, "John, I love you. You are the only man I have ever loved, and I will love you as long as I live."

John did not answer at once. She had thought that now he would put his arms around her again and give her a kiss that would not have to be interrupted by Doña Manuela's shouting. But he did not. He looked down at her, with a smile that was half surprised and half indulgent. Then after a moment he said, "I don't demand that either, Garnet. We're both grown up. So let's be honest. You know as well as I do that 'love' is a lot of moonshine."

THIRTY-EIGHT

As LONG AS SHE LIVED Garnet was going to remember the background of that morning in the olive grove. Years later something would happen to remind her, and all sorts of trifles would come back to her: the glitter of the dew, the lavender lights on the hills, the fresh odor of the grass her feet had crushed. She would see again John's sunburnt face, with his hair growing to a point on his forehead, his light green eyes under the black lashes, his faint smile and the bitter lines about his mouth. When she remembered that morning she would flinch, feeling again the shock she had felt when she found out that John too thought love was a lot of moonshine.

At first she did not believe him. She was sure he had not understood what she was saying. With an amazement that twisted her spirit like hot irons twisting her flesh, she found that John had understood her quite well. But he thought she had said it because she thought he wanted to hear it; and he was telling her that he did not expect any such sentimental promises. Lovers' vows, no matter how hot and sweet, would cool quickly in the fresh air of facts, so why make them at all? People with grown-up minds talked sense instead.

John was surprised that anybody as clear-headed as she was should have thought he wanted to hear such romantic words as "I will love you as long as I live." When she exclaimed that she meant it, he was still more surprised, because he had no notion of saying it back to her. John liked her immensely, he thought she was the most desirable woman he had ever known, but he was not going to promise her any deathless passion. He did not believe he was capable of such a thing, and he did not believe anybody else was capable of it either. "For God's sake, Garnet," he urged, "nobody can make promises like that! It will be so much simpler for both of us if we don't pretend we can."

Her astounded pain must have shown in her eyes, for he led her back to the bench and took her hands in his. "I didn't mean to hurt you, Garnet," he said.

He spoke sincerely, with a tenderness that surprised her. But it was not the tenderness of a man toward a beloved woman; it was more the gentleness of a man who had the hard task of telling a child that the world was not always gay and bright. He went on, "Garnet, I'm very fond of you. But all that talk about eternal adoration—it's nonsense, and you know it is."

"I don't know anything of the sort," she retorted. "When I said I loved you, I know I was not talking nonsense." She had tried to speak tersely. But she could not keep it up. She loved him and wanted him so much. "John," she pled, "don't you love me?"

John stood up. "Oh Garnet," he exclaimed, "what does that word mean?"

"You don't know?" she asked in a hurt wonder.

"No, Garnet, I don't. And I don't believe anybody else knows either. It hasn't got any meaning. Men 'love' their dogs and women 'love' pretty clothes and captains 'love' their ships and little girls 'love' their dolls and various other people 'love' music or hunting or the Swiss mountains. Then people say they 'love' each other."

"And you don't believe they mean it?"

"I don't believe they mean anything," John said.

"Oh John," she urged, "haven't you seen people who loved each other?"

He shrugged. "I've seen people who said they did. I've heard them talk about love. They call it a high and holy emotion. Then they use it to excuse every stupid revolting crime they want to commit. 'Because I love you, you must do everything I want you to do.' 'Because I love you, you belong to me like a lapdog.' 'Because I love you, I will bind you to me and possess you and make you wait on every whim of mine, and it's all for your own good, my dear boy, I know what you want better than you do, because I love you.'" John shook his head in disgust. "No, Garnet. I don't know what it is, but I've seen how it works. I don't want any."

He stood in a beam of sunlight. The sun struck him from the side, brightening that side of his face and body and leaving the other side in shadow. It seemed to her that John had always been like that, half of him clear and half in the dark. "I don't understand you," she said. "If you don't love me, what is all this? Are you still asking me to marry you?"

410

"Why of course," said John. He sat down by her again. "And God knows that's more than I ever said to any woman before."

Garnet felt as if she were groping her way through a fog. She said nothing, because she did not know what to say. John linked his hands between his knees, and looking down at them he added gravely,

"I'm sorry I shocked you so. I never had any tact in my life, but I never minded until now." He turned his head, smiling at her in a way that was penitent and somehow touching, and it almost made her shed tears. "Garnet," he said, "tell me what you want of me."

Garnet lowered her head, resting her chin on her clasped hands. It was so hard to put this into words. Love was something people ought to know by instinct, and not want to have explained to them bit by bit as though it were a recipe for making a pie. But she tried to tell him.

"I want you to love me," she said. "That means, I don't want to be just the only woman you ever gave a damn about! I want to be the heart, the center, the roots of you. I want to be more important to you than everything else on earth together because that's how important you are to me. And I want to know we'll always be that important to each other, no matter what we do or what happens to us." She gazed at him, pleading so hard that it seemed her heart was hurting in her chest. "Now, do you understand?"

John did not answer immediately. He looked down at the wild oats, and bent a cluster of green young spikes with his boot. Watching the bent grass spring up again, he spoke slowly.

"Garnet, I wish I could say yes."

"You still don't know what I mean?" she cried.

John went on as though she had not spoken. "I almost did say yes. But I didn't say it, because no matter how much you wanted to believe me, you couldn't have believed me very long. I simply haven't got any talent for pretending." He turned so as to face her squarely. "Garnet, I don't trust the future. I know the here and now, but I don't know anything else. That's why I can't understand all those easy promises. A man can promise that he will never beat this woman, or that he will do his best to give her food and shelter. Those things are possible. But I don't understand how he can swear that he'll feel certain emotions for the rest of his life. How can he know?"

The corner of Garnet's mouth gave a sardonic curl. She was remembering what Florinda had said to her about promises of love, and what she herself had thought that day: that John would never make a promise unless he was ready to risk his life to keep it. At least, she thought now, she had been right about that. John was not going to make her any promises. She asked,

"Then why do you want to marry me, John?"

He did not hesitate about answering this. "Because I want you so. You've got the kind of proud independent strength I admire, and I think you and I could have a very good time together."

"But if that's all you feel—suppose it doesn't last?"

"Suppose it doesn't," he said. "We'll have a very good time while it does last." He smiled at her. "Now do you understand that?"

All of a sudden she got mad. She had been shocked and hurt; at first the shock had been so great that it had dulled her feeling of how deep the hurt was. But now she felt it, and John's thin-lipped smile seemed to her to be mocking, as though he were making fun of her. She said deliberately, "I understand it. I think it's about as exciting as warm dishwater." She stood up, and John stood up too. Taking her elbow in his hard grip, he said,

"Garnet, the world is full of men who can talk the kind of trumpery you want to hear. You're too smart to want it. If you do insist on it, you'll deserve just what you'll get."

"And I'll get—what do you mean?"

"Disillusion," said John. "You've had that. It's no fun—remember?"

She winced, but he did not apologize. He continued,

"I lied to you once. That day in Santa Fe, when I told you I had no letter for Oliver. It was a sentimental effort to spare you. If I had been honest with you that day I would have spared you a good deal of worse suffering later on. Doesn't that prove anything to you?"

Garnet caught her breath. "Florinda gave me this same advice long ago," she retorted. "But I didn't expect it from you. Are you completely heartless, John?"

"I don't know whether I'm heartless or merely reasonable," said John. "But at least I'm honest. If it hurts you, it's probably because I'm the first honest man you've ever known."

"Oh shut up," said Garnet. She was blazing with anger. "I know what I want and I won't take less. You say you're honest! Fiddle-sticks. You're as hard as glass. You can't feel anything deeply so you laugh at people who can. It's so easy to say you despise something you can't understand. Like tone-deaf people who brag that they can't enjoy music and say that people who go to concerts are just putting on airs. I'm sorry I bothered you with my nonsense and I never will again."

She was so angry that she could not see him clearly. She was aware that his dark face was close to hers, and his hand was still tight on her elbow, and he was beginning to say something. But she did not want to hear him say any more. With a quick effort she wrenched herself free, and gathering up her skirts she began to run. She had been so sure of what she wanted, and so sure John had come back to give it to her. Now she felt rejected and humiliated, as if she had asked for pearls and he had tossed her a handful of sea-shells. She was angry with him, and even more angry with herself for having asked so frankly. She felt that she had left herself not a shred of pride or dignity. If he was laughing at her it was no more than she should have expected after such outrageous candor as hers.

She ran through the high grass, scraping her shoulders against the low-hanging limbs of the trees and feeling the twigs slap her cheeks and catch in her hair. The ground was rough, and the wild oats was nearly knee-high and thick as fur. She was so eager to get away from John that she did not notice how rough it was until her foot caught in a clump of grass and pitched her forward.

She was not hurt, for she had instinctively put her hands under her as she fell, so that she caught most of the shock on her arms. But it was a shock nevertheless, and for a moment she could not move. How idiotic she must look, she thought as she struggled to breathe again, and how ridiculous. She hoped violently that John had not seen her fall. Half dazed, she pushed herself up with both hands.

It was hard to get her breath. No part of her body was actually painful, but she had a shaken-up feeling all over and her elbows and the palms of her hands were stinging. She blinked to clear her eyes, and as she did so she saw John. He had knelt down beside her and was about to help her up. Garnet jerked back from him. At least he might have had the tact to pretend he had not seen her tumble down in this graceless fashion. But of course, John had no tact and he never pretended anything. He had just finished telling her so. She was still dizzy, but she could see his face bent over hers.

"Please listen to me!" he was saying. "You just told me something I'd never thought of before. Maybe I am tone-deaf about love. That could be so, because I know what you mean about music."

He was kneeling by her, supporting her with an arm under her

413

shoulders. For the moment she still had no voice to answer. John went on.

"I am tone-deaf, Garnet. Almost, that is. I can usually recognize a tune I've heard ten times, but more than that I can't do. You wouldn't blame me for that, would you? So if I was born without any talent for love, do you have to punish me for it?"

Garnet was catching the air in painful gasps. The jolt of her fall, added to the thunder in her mind, was making her tremble all over. "John, let me alone!" she exclaimed. "Stop laughing at me. Let me go."

"Oh you dear tormenting woman," said John, "don't you know if I had what you want I'd give it to you?"

Garnet barely heard him. Though it was still hard for her to move, she tried to scramble to her feet. Her movements were unsteady, and John took her elbows in his hands and raised her. Before she could pull away from him she heard him say, "Is this what you were running away from, Garnet?" and he put his arms around her and kissed her as she had never been kissed before.

At first she yielded in a breathless rapture. But then suddenly she realized that she was yielding. A wave of rage and shame swept down like a red curtain in front of her eyes. With all the strength she had she broke away from him, and she was so angry with herself that she slapped his face. It made her hand sting again. She rushed away from him as fast as she could, but by good luck or because she knew he was looking, this time she did not stumble. It was only a few seconds before she came out of the grove and heard her footsteps crunching on the flagstones of the court between the grove and the house.

She stopped abruptly, letting go her skirts, and glanced over her shoulder. John had not followed her. He was back there among the olive trees and she could not see him. She hoped she would never have to see him again.

She was glad to find that Florinda was not in their bedroom. Garnet dropped face down across the bed, feeling as limp as a boiled fish. A little while later she heard the gong sounding for the mid-morning breakfast, but she paid no attention. She felt as exhausted as if she had been riding a mountain trail all day.

Shortly before noon Florinda came in. She had been riding; her hair was windblown and her cheeks had a bright flush, and altogether she had such an air of well-being that Garnet would have liked to slap her too. Florinda took off her leather gloves, and dropping them on the wall-bench she came over to the bed and put her hand on Garnet's shoulder.

"Dear," she said gently, "I'm so sorry."

Startled, Garnet looked up. "How do you know?"

"I don't, not exactly. But he hurt you dreadfully, didn't he?"

Garnet's throat puckered and she could not answer. Florinda said, "Don't talk about it if you'd rather not. But's it pretty clear. You were so happy. You were all ready to be hurt."

Garnet gave her a crooked smile. Swallowing the pucker in her throat she said, "You tried to tell me, didn't you?"

"Yes."

"How did you know?"

"You're so gay and shining, Garnet. And John, he's like a house with the doors locked and the shades down." She gave Garnet a critical survey. "You've got grass-stains on your dress."

"I slipped and fell down."

"Lucky I came in. I figured you'd want to be let alone, so I stayed out as long as I could. But you've got to come to dinner. Want me to get out a clean dress for you?"

Garnet did not want to come to dinner, but Florinda insisted.

"If you go on missing meals," she warned darkly, "Doña Manuela will decide you're sick. And if Doña Manuela decides you're sick, heaven help you. Anyway, there's no danger of running into John today. I just saw him riding on the hills like seven ghosts were after him."

Garnet went to the dining-hall, and to her surprise she was able to eat when she got there. The food made her feel better, for she had had nothing all day but the cup of chocolate at dawn. After dinner she was sure she could not get a siesta, but to avoid being a nuisance she went to bed when Florinda did, and long habit made her fall asleep. When she woke up her mind was quieter. She was still hurt and bewildered, but at least she did not feel as if every nerve in her body was as tight as a violin-string.

During the siesta hour a hard rain had started, and the room was so cold that instead of getting dressed they curled up on the bed with blankets over their knees. As there was no glass in the window they had to keep the shutters closed, but they had plenty of candles. Florinda was stitching a fresh ruffle around the neck of a dress. She took exquisite care of her clothes, but she would not do her sewing anywhere but in the bedroom, for she could not sew with gloves on and the movements of needlework drew attention to her hands.

She had pried for no confidences. But by now Garnet felt like talking. While the rain fell outside, she told Florinda a good deal about what she and John had said to each other. Florinda listened with sympathy, but she was frankly baffled.

"But Garnet, he said he'd marry you! I was afraid he would want you just to be his lady-friend, and I knew that would shock you something awful. Are you sure he said he'd marry you?"

"He's willing to go through a ceremony. He quite evidently hasn't any respect for it."

Florinda sighed patiently. "None of them have, dear. The only difference is that John tells you the truth beforehand." For a moment she was silent, puzzling over Garnet's ways, then she said, "Garnet, I guess I'm simple-minded. But why won't you take him?"

Garnet tried to explain. "Because what he feels for me isn't big enough. He'd get tired of me."

"Well dear, you'd probably get tired of him too. I can't imagine being with one man day and night and not getting tired of him."

"I can," Garnet said stubbornly.

"I guess you've got more imagination than I have. Look, Garnet, let's think about the worst. Suppose you married John. And then suppose he did get tired of you. You could get a divorce. Back in New York I wouldn't be saying this. It's easier to bite your elbow than it is to get a divorce in New York. But here in California since the Americans came in, it's quite simple. Mr. Kerridge was talking about it the other day. The American alcaldes can grant divorces, and they are being very obliging about it."

Garnet pushed her fingers up through her hair. For a moment she was silent, listening to the rattle of the rain. The mere idea of divorce did not scandalize her as it had once. But she had built a dream-castle of a marriage enclosing a love that was strong and proud and above all, lasting. The idea of getting married with the expectation of getting tired of it seemed to her no more satisfying than one of Florinda's so-called love affairs. She lifted her head and shook back her hair.

"That's no good," she said. "Some women might find that kind of marriage better than nothing. But I wouldn't. If I knew he didn't really love me, I'd tremble with uncertainty. Every day I'd expect him to say, 'Well, good-by, this is all.' And one day he would say it, and where would I be then?"

416

Florinda shrugged. "Well, at least you'd be no worse off than you are now."

"Oh yes I would," snapped Garnet. "I'm so revoltingly healthy, I'd probably have a basketful of babies."

"I daresay I could help you there," said Florinda. "However, that's always a risk and you do have to think of it." She laid down her sewing and wrapped her arms about her knees. "I've got an idea. Why don't you tell John you want half of Torosa?"

Garnet gave a gasp. The idea was so startling that for a moment she could not answer. Florinda went on,

"Tell him you'll marry him, but first you want to be sure he's not going to leave you stranded with a lot of brats. Of course he'll swear he wouldn't, but promises are worth a dime a dozen."

That last line was like what John had said this morning. Garnet felt a creepy sensation at the back of her neck. Florinda continued,

"I don't know how big Torosa is, but it must be at least twenty thousand acres. Half of that is ten. Ten thousand acres isn't a vast holding for California, but it would be enough to make you independent, and if you left California you'd have a nice profit to take home."

Her arms rigid and her fists buried in the pillows behind her, Garnet was thinking, I wonder what John would say if he could hear her. I wonder if he would find this as sensible as she does.

Florinda went back to sewing the ruffle on her dress. She sighed dreamily. "Oh Garnet, what you can do with ten thousand acres! You know, the Californios are sweet and charming, but they're dreadfully lazy. Holy Christmas, with ten thousand acres and some Yankee ambition—"

Garnet began to laugh. Her laughter was harsh and tinny; as she heard it, it seemed to come out of her throat in clinking lumps of sound. Florinda stopped and turned her head with concern.

"Garnet, darling! What's the matter?"

Garnet managed to answer. "I was just thinking, I wish I didn't love him. I wish I'd never found out what it means to love a man. If I didn't love him I could ask him to pay me for marrying him. It would be so simple—I hope I can live with him agreeably, but if I can't, I can certainly live with ten thousand acres of good land. But I love him, Florinda!"

"But why should that stop you?"

"I don't want John's rancho. I want John."

"Oh, hell on toast," Florinda said with resignation.

"I know you don't understand. But I won't take a halfway marriage. I want what I want."

Florinda put her arm around Garnet's waist. "Garnet," she said gently, "by the time you've scuffled around as much as I have, you'll find that there are mighty few times when you get what you want. So take what you can get, and make it do."

Garnet shook her head. "I'll put up with anything else. I'll take what I can get, and make it do. But I won't take John if he doesn't love me."

Florinda sighed. "Well dear, you're beyond me. I think I'll quit."

For several seconds Garnet watched her, stitching away as though she had nothing on her mind but getting the new ruffle sewed on in time to wear the dress to supper. Garnet asked, "You'd take the land on those terms, wouldn't you?"

"My sweet, if I could get that much property, I'd take it on damn near any terms at all."

"Instead of love?"

"Love?" said Florinda. "Love? My grandma's left hind leg!"

The storm lasted only six hours, but it meant that John had to stay another week at Kerridge's. The rain turned the creeks into roaring torrents, and since there were no bridges it was impossible to cross. Garnet wished fervently that he would go away. Whenever she caught sight of him she thought how absurd she must have seemed when she lost her temper and fell down, and she was so embarrassed that she would have felt uncomfortable even if he had not noticed her. But John did notice her, and to her chagrin he did not seem embarrassed at all. At mealtimes when she saw him at the other end of the dining-hall, his eyes flickered over her as though she were a bit of overpriced merchandise and he thought it was time the price came down. She nearly choked with rage and could only hope Doña Manuela was too busy to notice how little she was eating.

Even Florinda was no help right now, for Florinda had a new crop of admirers. Three Californios and two Yankees, none of whom had ever seen her before, had taken refuge at Kerridge's during the storm, and like John they had to wait till the creeks went down. The Californios were enchanted by her coloring and the Yankees by her conversation, and Florinda was enchanted by having five brand-new men all at once. She did not have much time to consider Garnet's affairs. Anyway, she thought Garnet was being a goose to take this episode so seriously. Florinda's idea was that if one man vexed you there were always plenty of others.

Garnet was rather glad to have Florinda's mind occupied. They were not alone much except for the time they spent dressing and undressing. In these intervals Florinda was usually busy telling her Mr. Perkins had said this and Mr. Middleton had said that; and the Handsome Brute had approached her privately to say that the three new Californios were panting to see her with her hair down but were too polite to suggest it, so why didn't she offer to show it to them?—which of course she did, choosing a breezy spot in the courtyard so that her hair blew about her like a great big halo. And they were bewitched. She couldn't understand all they said but it was plain that they were utterly bewitched.

Garnet listened with a puzzled envy. I wish I could be like that, she said to herself. I wish I could get excited about a lot of men I never saw until three days ago and don't expect ever to see again. Is it because I was born different or because I was brought up to be different or merely because I am not a great beauty? She went to the glass and looked at her face. It did not have the exquisite structure of Florinda's nor such delicacy of line, but she was certainly not ugly. Men had always found her attractive. She was glad they did, but it had never occurred to her to try to fascinate every Tom, Dick, and Harry she met. She turned to look at Florinda, who was combing her front hair into little curls that would blow like floss-silk over her cheeks and temples. I simply was not meant to be a heartbreaker, thought Garnet. Love means too much to me.

It was afternoon and they were just up from their siesta. Florinda finished combing her hair, put on a dress decorated with the silver buttons Mr. Bartlett had given her in Santa Fe, and went out to rejoin her adorers. Garnet got dressed more slowly. She wanted to go outside too, but she wanted to be alone.

As she came out of the house she met a serving-girl carrying around wafers and a steaming pot of cha on a tray. Taking a cup of cha, Garnet walked a long way from the house, to a bench in a secluded corner where trees and bushes gave her a pleasant green privacy. As she sipped the cha she tried to think.

She wished to high heaven the creeks would go down so John could get away. Damn those mocking eyes of his and his hard jaw and his hard spirit, why did she want him to love her? There were plenty of other men.

Plenty of other men—that was what Florinda said, and it was true. Yes, yes, yes, she told herself vigorously as she watched a dot of sunlight that came through the tree and lay like a golden bead on the grass. Face it, Garnet. You can't make John love you. But if you've got the courage to do it, you can pull him up from your heart as you'd pull up a weed in a garden. And somehow, before always, you can go back to New York. You can bring up your little boy in a civilized place, and maybe after you get over the pain of this you can love a man who loves you. That's what you were born and bred for, that's what you want.

She felt lighter, and more at ease. Taking a sip of cha she got a whiff of its orange-blossom fragrance and thought how delicious it was. Then as she lowered the cup, she turned her head with a sensation of being looked at. About twenty feet away from her was a leafless fig tree, looking as gaunt and naked as all bare trees did here where so few trees lost their leaves in winter; and standing by it, leaning his back against a branch, was John.

He had come toward the tree with the silence he had learned in years of Indian-stalking. In one hand he was holding a small tattered book, the volume of verse he had lent the Brute to practice reading the English language. In his other hand he held a pencil with which he was marking some lines on the page. Evidently he knew the poem well, for he glanced at it only a second now and then, the rest of the time looking at her.

She did not want to see him or talk to him, and she was about to spring up and hurry away. But she had to get rid of the cup in her hand, and in the instant it took her to set it down John had reached her with his long swift strides. He was smiling a little. It was the same indulgent smile he had given her when he told her they could be honest about those impossible vows of love. Garnet felt all her disappointment rolling back over her and she was afraid she was going to have tears on her cheeks any minute, and she thought if he saw her shed tears now she would want to kill him for seeing them. But John paused by her only a second. Speaking hardly above a whisper he said, "My dear girl," and he bent over her and kissed the parting of her hair, so lightly that she barely felt it before he was gone, moving among the trees with his silent Indian-hunter steps. As he disappeared she saw that he had dropped a piece of paper into her lap, a page he had torn out of the tattered little book of verse. Garnet picked up the page. A ray of sun pointed a bright finger to the lines John had marked for her to read, lines

that a man named Andrew Marvell had written two hundred years
before to a lady who would not say yes to him.

> Had we but world enough, and time,
> This coyness, Lady, were no crime . . .

It was the first time anybody had ever accused her of being coy.
In spite of all she had said to him, was it possible that John thought
she was teasing him, like a schoolmiss who thought it was fun to
keep a man dangling while she made up her mind? Garnet trembled
with anger as her eyes followed the other lines he had checked for
her.

> But at my back I always hear
> Time's wingèd chariot hurrying near . . .
> The grave's a fine and private place,
> But none, I think, do there embrace.

Garnet crushed the page and threw it at the fig tree. If she could
have no peace in the courtyard she would go back to her rocm
and stay there. But in heaven's name, Garnet, she warned herself
as she picked up her skirts to go through the grass, don't run! Maybe
he's behind you, watching for you to fall down again.

Walking as sedately as her leaping nerves would let her, she
came out into an open part of the courtyard, where a path of
flagstones went through the wild oats. Without meaning to at all,
she stopped and looked back. There stood John, beside a tree behind her, the last tree before the path began. Garnet felt her face
get hot, and knew she was turning red. John's lips trembled with
humor as he spoke to her.

"I'm leaving early tomorrow. The trails should be dry enough
now."

"Goodby," said Garnet, because she had to say something.

"Nikolai will stay here," he went on, "to take you and Florinda
to Los Angeles whenever you are ready to go. Horses and supplies
and serving-men have been arranged for."

She had not thought of how she was going to get back to Los
Angeles. But evidently he had, and had taken care of it. Something
else to be grateful to him for—and she began to know what he meant
when he spoke of gratitude, for she felt a blast of resentment at
having to take a favor from him, and it was not a pretty emotion.
John was saying,

"I'm leaving tomorrow, but this is not goodby." He was speaking gravely now. Again with smooth quick steps he came to her. His hands on her shoulders, he asked, "Garnet, why won't you take me as I am? What's so wrong with me?"

Before her mind had consciously formed an answer she heard herself answering. "The other night when you kissed me in the dark, I thought, 'Now John is looking at me the way he looks at the flowers.' But you were not. You never have looked at me with such awe and discovery. And I'm not going to spend my life being jealous of a poppy-field!"

John was still holding her. "You needn't cringe from me like that," he said. "I'm not going to kiss you again till you ask me to."

If she gave a start he seemed not to notice it. He released her, and in another moment he was gone again among the trees. Garnet stood still, looking after him, and then without any will of her own she sat down on the cold flagstone path and covered her face with her hands and cried silently, the tears trickling between her fingers.

The Handsome Brute saw her there. The Brute had been flirting with the girl who was serving the cha, but when he started to walk across the courtyard with her he caught sight of Garnet. Breaking off in the middle of a compliment he hurried down the path, and knelt by Garnet and put his big arm around her and lifted her up and gave her a handkerchief to dry her eyes. It was a soft fine handkerchief, embroidered by one of the Brute's lady-friends. "Now you will come with me," said the Brute, and he led her back among the trees so nobody else would see her tears. Standing under a little scrub-oak, he put his arm around her and drew her head down to rest against him and patted her cheek with his great hand. How sweet he was, Garnet thought. He was like a dear little brother. It struck her as an odd comparison, for he was seven years older than she was and more than a foot taller, and he weighed at least a hundred pounds more than she did. But he was so good of heart and he had no sham about him. There were not many grown people like that. He was speaking to her in a low voice.

"Now you can cry all you please. And do not be ashamed. Everybody should cry sometimes."

Tears still trembling on her eyelashes, she looked up and smiled at him. "Brute, you are such a dear. Thank you." He smiled down at her, with such tender sympathy that she asked, "Brute, am I being a fool?"

"I don't know," said the Brute. "I am not wise and I cannot tell

422

you what to do. But I love you very much, and I love John very much, and I am sorry you are not happy."

"What has John told you about us, Brute?"

"Why Garnet, I don't know anything but what I have seen. John has never talked to me about you. He has never talked to anybody about you. John does not like to talk about anything that is important to him."

"Am I important to him, Brute?"

"Oh yes. That is why he resents you."

"Resents me?"

"He resents anybody who is important to him. He wants to be enough for himself. There are a lot of people like that. People are great fools, Garnet. All of us."

Tears came into her eyes again. From another pocket the Brute drew another handkerchief, embroidered in a different design by a different lady. He patted her eyelids gently. For a while they did not say anything more. He stood with his arm around her and she leaned against him, and slowly her tense nerves relaxed. At length she looked up into his beautiful violet eyes. "I feel better," she said. "Thank you, Brute."

"Now," said the Brute, "I will walk to the house with you, and you will go to your room and I will tell one of the girls to bring you some good light wine. You will sit down and drink it slowly, and by the time the gong rings you will be ready for supper. You will do that?"

"Yes, Brute."

He tucked her arm into the bend of his elbow, and they began to walk along the path as though they had nothing to do but enjoy the last sunshine of the day. When they reached the house the Brute bowed and kissed her hand, and Garnet went indoors.

She did feel better. But she was holding even harder than before to the resolution she had made in the garden.

She was going to get rid of her dream of John. If so brief an interview with him could leave her hurt and shaken like this, all to no purpose, she wanted him out of her heart. She was going to root him up, and she was going to take her baby and go home.

THIRTY-NINE

THEY REACHED Los Angeles the last week in March. The first piece of news they heard was that Charles Hale was married.

Texas told them about it the day after their arrival. He sat at the kitchen table with them, while Stephen played on the floor under the care of Isabel, and the Brute sat by the fireplace consuming beef, and Mickey padded about pouring tea for them all.

After being away for six months Garnet and Florinda expected to hear of some changes, but they gasped when Texas told them Charles was married. Garnet was glad of it. Now Charles would probably have children of his own and he would be less interested in trying to get Stephen.

They asked eagerly about the new Mrs. Hale. Was she young? Pretty? Rich? Was she a Yankee or a Californian? When had the wedding taken place, and where were she and Charles now?

As though he understood what Garnet was thinking, Texas glanced at Stephen and gave her arm a fatherly pat. Texas looked dreadful. His eyes were red, his beard was as wild as when he was crossing the desert, and his hands were unsteady. But his manner was as sweet and gentle as it had been when he took care of her the night Stephen was born. Garnet smiled at him, and Florinda said, "I'll get you some fresh tea, Texas. Go on about Charles, I'm listening."

Well, Texas told them, Charles had married a widow from his own city of Boston. The lady's name had been Mrs. Lydia Radney. She had come out with her husband on a Pacific trading voyage, and he had died on the high seas between Honolulu and San Francisco.

The late Mr. Radney had been half owner of a merchant brig, named the Lydia Belle in honor of the wives of her two owners. The brig had sailed from Boston. Mr. Radney had come along to keep an eye on the supercargo, the man in charge of selling the goods the brig had brought out and loading her with more goods to be sold in Boston. Usually the owner of a ship would hire a supercargo and trust him, but it seemed that Mr. Radney was the sort of man who didn't trust anybody.

Silky put in a word here. Silky had come into the kitchen for a brief rest from the bar, and now stood leaning against the wall, drinking a cup of tea. "I thought," said Silky, "it was *Mrs.* Radney who didn't trust anybody. Remember what that fellow Morrison told us, Texas?"

Florinda came back to the table with a cup of tea for Texas. In her other hand she carried a bottle of aguardiente. Without comment, she laced the tea with aguardiente as she set down the cup. "Who's Morrison?" she asked, taking her place on the wall-bench again.

"Morrison is the ship's steward," said Texas. He picked up his cup and began to brighten as he drank the hot tea laced with brandy. "The steward is the man in charge of the table," he continued. "But he's also the captain's personal servant, so he knows a lot about what goes on. What he said was, Mr. Radney had had lung fever back in Boston, and he never should have taken this voyage, but his wife made him."

"This is a very interesting story," the Brute said as he contemplated the joint of beef in his hand. "Tell us some more."

Prompting each other, Silky and Texas continued. Morrison the steward had dropped in here one rainy night and got drunk. He said that on this voyage the brig Lydia Belle had brought two ladies, the captain's wife and Mrs. Radney. From the first, the captain's wife had disliked Mrs. Radney. Morrison had heard the captain's wife say that Mr. Radney had not wanted to leave home in his poor state of health. But Lydia Radney had insisted on it, because she did not trust anybody else to drive the best bargains. When Mr. Radney died aboard ship, Morrison had heard the captain's wife say that Lydia had really caused her husband's death, since she had persuaded him to make this voyage. Why hadn't she urged him to stay at home so she could nurse him as a proper wife should? Some people, said the captain's wife, would do *anything* for money.

"Lydia sounds like a perfect match for Charles," Garnet said dryly. "Go on, Texas."

Mr. Radney had died some time last fall, Texas said. Then in January Charles went to San Francisco to get acquainted with the American officers there. When Charles reached San Francisco the brig was in port, with the bereaved Mrs. Radney on board. Charles went to the afflicted widow and offered his aid in straightening out her business affairs. No doubt they had quickly recognized each other as kindred souls, for about two months later they were married by the town alcalde.

The brig had brought them south and then had returned to San Francisco. It was on the trip south that the steward had come by Silky's Place and brought the story to the interested ears of Silky and Texas.

Silky set down his empty cup and started back to the bar. "Coming, Texas?" he asked.

Texas stood up. Well, yes, he said, he guessed he'd better be getting out to the bar too. Pausing by Garnet he put his hand on her shoulder. "I'm glad you're back, Miss Garnet," he said, "you and the little fellow." He grinned at Stephen. "I've been making him a present."

"Why, that's good of you. What sort of present?"

"A bed for him to sleep in. With sides, you know, so he can't fall out of it. I like to whittle a bit to pass the time."

"I do appreciate that, Texas," she said warmly. "I've been wondering about a safe bed for him, now that he can move around by himself."

"I'll bring it over soon as it's done," said Texas. He turned away, giving Stephen the sweet, wistful smile that always brought a pain to Garnet's throat. He limped to the door, his bad leg dragging heavily.

Florinda went to show Isabel some clothes that needed mending. Garnet still sat by the table, watching Stephen. She was thinking, not about Charles or Texas now, but about herself. Tomorrow she was going back to work in the saloon, and she had no right to speak a word of complaint because it was her own fault. She had left herself nothing else to do.

Well, that was all right, she reflected grimly. In payment for her work she would get her board and keep, and ten per cent of the profit on the liquor. She was going to spend as little as possible, so she could save enough to pay some sea-captain to take her and Stephen around the Horn to New York. For a moment she wondered if she could go home on the ship that had brought out Mrs. Radney, now Mrs. Charles Hale. But she abandoned the idea at once. She had no money yet to pay for the journey, and she was not going to ask favors, certainly not of those people. She did not need to. Being a barmaid was not a lofty occupation, but it did mean she was independent.

All of a sudden Garnet realized that John had never made any objection to her working at the bar. Florinda, glad as she was to have help, had at least voiced a protest. Texas had said not once but often, "I hate to see you in here." Charles had objected loudly. But John had never said a word about it. Even when he was asking her to marry him John had not mentioned the saloon.

He didn't love me, she thought, but at least he didn't affront me by hinting that if I married him I'd have an easier life than this. She smiled as she thought of it. That was a tribute to her integrity which until now she had not recognized. Thank you, John, she said in her mind, and caught herself sharply. Stop it, Garnet! If you don't, you'll want him so much that you'll fall right into his arms the next time you see him, and he'll treat you with that self-contained indifference of his, and break your heart into little pieces and step on them.

It was hard to stop thinking about John. On the way down from Kerridge's the valleys in their bright spring greening had reminded her every day of how much John loved all this, how much more than he loved her.

Well, he had gone back to Torosa and she was going to forget him. Tomorrow morning she would strap on her gun-belt and get back to work. Silky had given her a .34-caliber Colt revolving pistol, like Florinda's. He did not say how he had got it and Garnet thought it wise not to ask. Silky had told both the girls to wear their Colts all the time. Not that he expected any trouble. But seeing that the girls were armed had a wholesome effect on the customers.

Garnet glanced across the room, to where Florinda was telling Isabel about sewing some new buttons down the front of a dress. This dress had once been decorated with the silver buttons Mr. Bartlett had given her, but Florinda had cut them off and given them to Doña Manuela. For to Florinda's amazement, Doña Manuela had said she would rather have the silver buttons than the aquamarine ring. She had a lot of rings, but she did not have any buttons like these. Florinda was at first incredulous, for the giant aquamarine was worth so much more money than the buttons. She found it hard to understand that Doña Manuela, who had passed her whole life amid unlimited abundance, rarely thought of the money value of anything.

Florinda was telling Isabel to put the dress away until she had a chance to buy some new buttons at Mr. Abbott's, and meanwhile there was a basket of clothes on the back porch to be laundered.

Isabel went out to look them over. On the floor Stephen began to whimper, so Garnet took him upstairs for a nap. From the saloon, Silky called Mickey to come and wash off the bar.

Florinda and the Handsome Brute were left alone in the kitchen. The Handsome Brute had eaten all the meat off the joint he was holding. He put the bone into the fire and spoke to Florinda, who sat on the wall-bench arranging the articles in her workbasket.

"Please, may I have some wine?" he asked.

"Go ahead," she said tolerantly. "Don't you ever get enough of anything?"

"It takes a lot to keep up my strength," said the Brute. Bringing a bottle from the shelf, he sat down on the floor in front of her, his legs bent and one arm across his knees while he held the neck of the bottle in his other hand. He took a drink. "This is very good. I suppose you have not tried it."

Florinda was sticking the needles into the flannel leaves of her needle-case, in tidy rows according to size. "No," she said, "I haven't tried it."

"Why don't you ever take wine?" asked the Brute.

"Because it makes me act like a lunatic. And by the way, my little squashblossom. I don't like people who ask smart questions."

"Oh, but you like me," said the Brute.

"Really? You think so?"

"Why yes. In fact, you like me very much."

"Dear me," said Florinda, "it's nice to be satisfied." She folded her needle-case, tied the ribbon that kept it closed, and began sorting the spools of thread in her basket.

There was a flicker of mischief in the Brute's eyes. "Shall I tell you why you like me?" he asked.

"If you want to. I'm not what you might call dying of curiosity."

"You like me," the Brute said coolly, "because I have never told you how beautiful you were or asked you to spend a night with me."

For an instant Florinda was startled into silence. She stared at him, and the Brute took another drink.

"That's a fact, you know," he said. "Only I don't believe you ever thought of it yourself, did you?"

Florinda sighed as she might have sighed at an exasperating child. She was not angry; she rarely lost her temper, and anyway, it was almost impossible to be angry with anybody who looked so beguiling and so innocent.

"The only men you have any respect for," the Brute continued,

428

"are the men who do not make love to you. You are beautiful, of course," he went on smiling, "your eyes and your hair and your skin and the shape of you, and you can be fascinating when you want to be, which you usually do, and men adore you. You like that. But you do not like *them*."

Florinda gazed at him with wonder at his audacity. "Well, I'll be shot for a jackrabbit," she murmured.

The Brute smiled wisely. "Most of those men, you do not even remember their names. There are so many of them and they are so easy. But the men you like—I do not know who they were in New York, but in California they are John and Silky and me and Texas and Mr. Kerridge. Now that is true, isn't it?"

"I don't know, you big ape. I never thought about it, and I never saw anybody in my life who had such an absolute lack of manners. But go on. Tell me some more."

"You are interested?"

"Certainly. So few men ever tell me things I haven't heard before."

"But that is what I am explaining to you," said the Brute. "The men who tell you the same things you have heard so often, you have no respect for them. The men you respect are the men who have noticed that you are a particular person who is you. When you prefer such men as I am, it is like saying to us, thank you for noticing me. Not just my eyes and hair and figure, but me." He was looking up at her with an adorable candor. "Now that is true, isn't it?"

Florinda was laughing, half abashed and half amused. "I don't know, Brute, really I don't. I'll have to think about it."

"Of course it is true," said the Brute.

There was a pause. Florinda looked him up and down. After a while she shook her head with a musing disapproval. "I don't believe I'm quite comfortable around untutored savages," she said. "Nobody ever taught them anything so they have to go seeing for themselves, and they see too much."

The Brute chuckled softly.

"How big is your rancho?" asked Florinda.

"Nine leagues."

"Stop talking Mexican. How big in acres?"

"I don't know."

"You don't know anything, do you?"

"Not much," the Brute said meekly.

429

"Well, anyway, the rancho is big enough to hold you. It was very kind of you to bring us to Los Angeles, but we won't try to keep you from your work. Go on home."

"I am going in a few days. First I want to find out what ships have been in port at San Diego. I keep up with the ships, you know, so when a Russian fur-ship touches at this coast I can get on it and go back to St. Petersburg."

"Oh yes, I forgot, you told me you were going to Russia. That will be fine. You don't know when you'll start, do you?"

"Do you want me to go?"

"Well, you do get on my nerves," she returned with a sigh.

The Brute smiled complacently and returned to his bottle. Florinda said, "You look very cheerful too." He burst out laughing, so abruptly that he spilt some wine on the floor. She was referring to a remark he had made before they left Kerridge's. Mr. Kerridge had told Florinda he was going to miss her, one reason being that she had such a cheerful disposition and smiled so brightly at everybody. The Brute heard him, and after Mr. Kerridge had gone out of earshot the Brute turned to Florinda with a wicked grin, asking, "Are all civilized men as easy to fool as that?" When she demanded to know what nonsense he was talking now, the Brute replied, "You do not smile because you are cheerful. You smile because you have such beautiful teeth. If your teeth were crooked you would be much more solemn than you are."

Now, as he laughed and spilt his wine, she laughed too, but she ordered, "Wipe that up. We have spiders enough without putting out bait for them."

The Brute drew out one of his beautiful embroidered handkerchiefs and obeyed. Florinda stood up, taking her workbasket, and started toward the door leading to the stairs.

"Look, Brute, I can't sit here gabbling forever. I'm going back to work tending bar tomorrow, and I've got a lot to do today."

"Are you mad with me?" he asked with a grin.

"Oh, go to St. Petersburg," said Florinda.

Silky's Place was prospering vastly. It was the only saloon in town that was well supplied with whiskey. Few of the native wine-shops had any whiskey, for the Californios did not care for it. But before the war Silky and Florinda had bought all they could get from the smugglers, and thanks to Mr. Abbott, they still had their stock. With it, they had most of the Yankee trade.

Now that the girls were back at work the saloon was open twelve hours a day: from eight in the morning till noon, and again from four o'clock till midnight. Both Silky and Florinda regretted having to close in the afternoons, for it cut down the profits. But the army, having had one revolt, wanted to get the Californios into a friendly mood. Yankees who owned places of business were told to keep in tune with the local customs.

Since business was so good they decided to improve the saloon. They put wall-benches along both sides of the barroom, and a table in front of each bench. They also added some extra space at one side of the building. This meant they would have another store-room, and also another bedroom upstairs, so Garnet and Florinda could have two rooms instead of one. They joyfully set Isabel to work making new bedspreads and wall-curtains. For though they had not much leisure, it was refreshing to have pleasant rooms of their own to spend it in.

As John had told them, Los Angeles was teeming with Yankees. There were men of the regular army; Frémont was still here with the men who had marched with him from the north; and there was also the Mormon battalion under Colonel Philip St. George Cooke.

The Mormons were very well-behaved. This was partly because their religion enjoined a strict code of morals, and partly because Colonel Cooke kept them so busy that they had little time for mischief. He first set them to work getting rid of the wild dogs that swarmed over Los Angeles. He told them to catch and kill every dog that did not have an owner who would be responsible for it. This took several weeks, and when it was done the town was so much more agreeable that everybody asked why it had not been done long ago.

Having got rid of the dogs, Colonel Cooke told his men to clean up the town. They cleared the streets of garbage, whitewashed the houses, and cut down the weeds. Garnet and Florinda wished they would stay forever. Not all the Mormons were as good as their elders wanted them to be, but they were a very decent lot, and to the astonishment of both Garnet and Florinda, most of them actually did not drink. They gathered on the saloon porch, or they even came inside for the chance to talk to two real American girls, but they had been taught that liquor was an invention of Satan and they would not touch it.

Like most converts to a new religion they were devout to the point of fanaticism, but except when someone questioned their tenets they were very polite. Whenever Garnet or Florinda came out on the porch, bound on an errand, two or three Mormons would spring up from somewhere, bowing and asking for the honor of being escorts, "since you never can tell when some lowdown fellow might forget his raising, ma'am." The girls always accepted the bodyguard. The town now had so many more men than women that it was hardly safe to go out alone. Garnet thanked heaven for the Mormons, and Florinda, though she regretted the money they did not spend at the bar, had to agree that it was mighty nice to have all these sober men around.

The upper-class families of Los Angeles had made friends with the army officers soon after their arrival. The Yankees gave balls and dinners, and added a new gaiety to the life of the village. But the general run of the people did not like the Yankee soldiers.

To begin with, there were simply too many of them. They overran everything, they crowded the stores and saloons; and though Estelle's establishment was larger than it used to be and now had several rivals, still nice girls had to be carefully guarded. Besides, the Yankees had no respect for the native ways and were not tactful about saying so. The Yankees had been taught every day of their lives that there was no sin greater than laziness. In the United States the most scornful remark you could make about a man was to say, "He won't work." But the Angelenos had the old Spanish idea that work was a curse.

The Angelenos lived in mud shacks. Their streets were choked with weeds and rubbish. They had no schoolhouse. They had no wish to learn anything or to change anything. All day long they sat in the sun and talked and dozed and sipped red wine. The Yankees, fresh from the bustle of their own country, watched the Angelenos with a mystified contempt. Why, they demanded, why didn't the lazy fools *do* something?

The Angelenos, who saw no reason why they should do anything they did not have to, gazed with equal bafflement upon these men who could not keep still. The Yankees were always moving something or scrubbing something or trying to make something different from the way it was. The Angelenos thought they were a public nuisance.

Though Pico and Castro had long since fled the country, there was a legend going around that they would come back and chase out the foreigners. The children had a song about it, which they shouted at the Americans in the street. Garnet heard it for what seemed like the thousandth time, one April morning as she was coming back to the saloon from Mr. Abbott's, where she had been to buy flannel to make nightgowns for Stephen. She was walking between two escorts, a big red-headed Mormon named McConnell and a small dark Mormon named Dorkins. McConnell carried her parcel, while he and Dorkins each held one of her elbows, guiding her with earnest care.

"Here's a puddle, ma'am, now be just a wee mite careful," McConnell was saying, when a group of three or four youngsters in a doorway they had just passed, began to sing vehemently.

> Poco tiempo
> Viene Castro
> Con mucho gente—
> ¡Vamos americanos!

Grinning, the Mormons glanced back at the children. "I get the idea in a general way," McConnell said to Garnet, "but what does it mean?"

"Why, it means that pretty soon Castro is coming back with a big force, and when he does—scat, Americans!"

Dorkins wanted to know who Castro was. Garnet had begun to explain that he had formerly been the military commandant, when McConnell said,

"Why, it wasn't us they were singing at. It was them rich folks down the road on horseback. Say, they're grand, ain't they?"

Garnet glanced over her shoulder. Down the road, she saw a procession approaching. The riders were Charles Hale and a dozen retainers, mounted in their usual splendor. Garnet drew the soldiers to a standstill and felt her bosom get hot with a curious anger as she caught sight of the woman riding at his side. So this was the former Mrs. Lydia Radney, now Mrs. Hale. As the train came nearer Garnet watched her with a wrathful interest.

Lydia Hale was about thirty years old. At least as tall as her husband, perhaps a trifle taller, firm of shoulder and straight of spine, she sat her horse (thought Garnet, remembering the young ladies' academy) like a governess who had to set an example to her pupils. She was as colorless as a pencil sketch. Her clear pale skin had hardly a touch of pink even at the cheekbones; her hair was the grayish-brown that is neither dark nor light but the shade of a dead leaf; and her eyes were merely eyes, with no particular shade of their own. Even her riding-dress had no color: it was dark gray, with a line of white about the throat. But nevertheless, in a cold granite way, Lydia Hale was a handsome woman. Her features were finely cut, she had a good figure, and her dress was made of good material and well fitted. Her whole appearance was austere, and nothing about her suggested warmth or friendliness, but she was by no means ugly. And while she was certainly not a woman with a talent for gracious trifles, still in matters of importance she looked as if she would be quite capable of holding her own.

As they drew near and passed, Charles saw Garnet. He made no gesture of greeting. His eyes paused for an instant, and then he looked away, like a man carefully not seeing a poor relation. Mrs. Hale saw Garnet too. Charles must have told her who this stranger was, for though they had never seen each other before, Lydia's eyes swept her over with a cool, speculative curiosity (as though I were a savage with a ring in my nose, Garnet thought). Then the other woman's nostrils quivered and her lips curled faintly in contemptuous dismissal, and she too looked away.

Garnet felt anger rising and wrapping around her like a flame. At the moment she would have enjoyed using the Colt revolver at her belt. Her eyes narrowed as she watched the procession go by.

I should like to kill them, she thought fiercely. Taking Oliver's property from me and then sneering at me because I have to make a living tending bar. Damn that woman and her curling lip. Does she think I *like* having my child grow up in a saloon?

The brilliant line of riders turned around the corner of a building and went out of sight. Probably they were on their way to the home of Señor Escobar.

"Say, Miss Garnet," exclaimed McConnell's voice beside her, "don't you feel good? You look kind of feverish."

Garnet was not surprised. She certainly felt feverish. She said she had a raging headache, which she did. McConnell and Dorkins walked back to the saloon with her, and said goodby on the porch. Garnet went into the kitchen and told Mickey to make a pot of strong coffee. Sitting by the table she covered her face with her hands. "Please, God, let me go home," she whispered. "Please, please, get me out of this place!"

FORTY

BUT IN THE DAYS that followed, Garnet grew calmer. She did not like Charles any better than before. But her common sense told her that after the war American courts would be set up in California. When this happened, as the widow of a man who had owned property she could demand an accounting for her son.

How soon this would be she could not tell, as the war was not yet over. For the present she would have to stay at the bar. But with what she could earn, together with what Oliver had left, she could pay her passage home after the war. There would no doubt be something over, which her father could invest for her. She would have again the safe and pleasant life she used to have, and this time she would never, never let it go.

Down in a corner of her mind a little demon whispered, And John?

Be still, Garnet retorted. I'm going home.

She strapped on her gun-belt and went back to work.

Working at the bar was harder now than it had been last fall, for there were more customers and the hours were longer. Garnet did not like the airless room, full of the fumes of liquor and the smell of sweaty bodies; she did not like having men stroke her and pinch her and make indecent suggestions. Not all the men were like this, but sometimes she thought the respectful ones were even more exasperating. For they had a way of saying, "You ought not to be in a place like this, Miss Garnet." They said it reproachfully, as if they thought she was tending bar because she wanted to. Sometimes, late at night when she was short-tempered from weariness, she let a snappish reply escape her lips. But not often. One terse line from her, and instantly Florinda's eyes were sending a warning. As soon as the bar was closed and they were alone Florinda urged, "Garnet, please remember, they come in here to have fun. You and I are part of the fun. Any peevish old crone can pour liquor out of a bottle."

Garnet smiled ruefully. "I know. I'm sorry. If only my back didn't ache so at the end of the day I'd have a sweeter disposition."

"Yes, dearie," said Florinda. She was not impressed by backaches. She had laughed and flirted above too many of her own. "How much money have you got on deposit at Mr. Abbott's?" she asked.

"About two hundred dollars."

"Mighty good to have, isn't it? So smile at them, Garnet, and any time you feel like something that fell out of a garbage can, remember they're paying you for every smile."

During bar-hours Florinda was enchanting to the boys, and when closing time came she brushed them off like mosquitoes. If there had been one among them who had superlative charm, or one who could have offered her something like a really valuable bit of jewelry, she might not have been so cool. As it was, she was too busy to be interested. So she continued to occupy her pretty blue-curtained room all by herself.

But little by little, Garnet got used to the bar. She learned to say no in a quiet voice that clearly meant what it said, and she was no longer embarrassed by having to say it. She never did learn Florinda's skill at bright answers, and she never acquired Florinda's ability to listen with a look of fascination to yarns she had already heard forty times. But she did learn to stand up twelve hours a day without complaining about it, and talk cheerfully to the customers when she was so tired she thought her legs were going to buckle under her. She learned what a dollar meant in terms of time and aching muscles and screaming nerves, and this was one of the greatest surprises of her life.

Since the men at the bar discussed everything that went on, Garnet and Florinda were kept well abreast of events. Through the month of April there was more and more talk about Frémont and his dispute with General Kearny. Frémont was in Los Angeles and the general was in Monterey, but angry letters had been blistering the trail between them. Frémont was a brilliant leader. But he had to lead. He did not know how to obey.

General Kearny finally sent another officer, Colonel Richard B. Mason, to Los Angeles. Mason summoned Frémont to his headquarters to give an account of himself. Though Mason was a colonel and Frémont only a lieutenant-colonel, Frémont did not obey the summons till it had been issued three times. When at length he did go, the interview waxed so violent that Mason threatened to put him in irons. Frémont responded by challenging Mason to a duel.

By this time Mason was so angry that he was willing to fight.

For a while it looked as if the town was going to be treated to the spectacle of a United States army officer fighting a duel with a subordinate because the subordinate would not obey orders. Fortunately, General Kearny himself came to Los Angeles and saw to it that no such duel took place.

Frémont seemed to understand at last that he would have to accept the general's commands. He asked permission to join his own regiment, which was fighting in Mexico; or to lead his exploring party back to the United States. Kearny refused both requests. He told Frémont to come to Monterey and wait there for orders.

Opinions at the bar ran high. Frémont was an attractive fellow with a great gift for making friends, and many of the men could find good reasons for all he did. Some of them said General Kearny was so good that he was a mite too good, and did not realize that some people could not meet the strict standards he set for himself. Others, especially those who were used to regular army discipline, thought Kearny was right and Frémont deserved to face a court-martial. They prophesied that this was what he was going to get. But though the arguments were heated, there was very little trouble at the bar. Garnet and Florinda began to notice thankfully that nearly always, especially in the evenings, there were two or three officers present, drinking very little but keeping an eye on the men. Nothing was said about it. But they did prevent fights.

The late rains fell, the fogs blew in, the land broke into bloom. But this year Garnet hardly noticed it. She was working so hard that she could think of scarcely anything but what she was doing. She did remember John, but the image of him gave her such a sharp swift pain that she pushed it away with all her might. Sometimes she thought of Oliver, or Charles, or the desert journey, or the peace of home. But even these ideas were vague like something seen through a mist. Always she was saying aloud, "May I serve you, gentlemen?" and saying to herself, "Oh Lord, how my legs hurt!"

So she was astonished one afternoon when Charles walked up to the bar. It was a chilly white spring day, and the bar was full of men who had come to get something to warm them against the fog. Holding the door open, Charles stood in the doorway a moment, looking around. One of the men turned his head, shouting, "Hey you, shut the door!" One or two others joined him. Charles slid them a contemptuous glance. Before the men could say anything more, Florinda was turning an enticing glow upon them.

"Oh boys, there's something I've been meaning to ask you. Is

437

there any truth in these rumors that a regiment from New York is on its way here?"

As she had expected, all the men started to answer at once, and the resulting noise made it possible for Garnet to listen in some privacy to Charles. He had walked directly over to where Garnet stood. Placing his elbows on the bar, he fixed his eyes upon her in the fashion she knew so well. "How do you do, Garnet," he said.

"How do you do, Charles," said Garnet. Automatically, she started to add, "May I serve you?"—but checked herself. This was the first time Charles had spoken to her since that night last fall when he had got drunk. She did not know how much of that he remembered, but she did not want to remind him of it. If he wanted a drink he could ask for one.

He did not ask for one. He said, "I shall not detain you long. I only want to know if you have considered the offer I made you some time ago."

"An offer?" she repeated.

"The offer of a home at my rancho."

My rancho, she echoed angrily in her mind. She remembered how he had said it the first time he ever saw her. Keeping her voice low, she returned, "I prefer to live here, Charles."

Charles nodded. She wondered how long he could hold his eyes that way, fixed like two points. He said,

"I feared this would be your answer. I am powerless to improve your taste."

"You can't make me change my mind," said Garnet, "if that's what you mean. Is that all you wanted to say?"

"No, it is not," said Charles. He went on, "You have perhaps heard of my marriage?"

"Yes," said Garnet. She was thinking, I wish you were dead. Then you'd have to let me alone.

Charles continued, "If you do not want to make a home for my brother's child, my wife will be happy to care for him."

Your brother's child, Garnet's mind repeated furiously. Anybody hearing you would think I had stolen him. She clenched her fists, below the bar where he could not see them and thus guess what an effort her self-command was costing her. "Charles," she exclaimed, "why don't you stop this? Don't you know I'm not going to give my child to you?"

His eyes narrowed threateningly. They were like two bright pinheads. "I might remind you," said Charles, "that California is no

438

longer a Mexican outpost. If I should speak to my friends among the army officers, they might agree with me that a saloon is not a good place for a child. They might tell you to give that boy to me. Do you understand?"

Garnet understood, better than he thought she did. She was surprised that she had ever been so stupid as to think Charles' marriage would make her free of him. He also had realized that the establishment of American laws here would give her the chance to get Oliver's property for Stephen. But if Stephen was living on the rancho under Charles' guardianship, he would be legally getting the benefit of anything his father had left. And by the time Stephen was twenty-one, Charles would probably have drained all the character out of him so thoroughly that he would meekly take whatever he was given. Garnet was so angry she felt as if she had thorns in her throat.

"If you say one word to anybody in authority about taking Stephen away from me because I work at this bar," she said, in a voice that sounded like a rusty scrape, "I'll tell them why I work here. Any time they'll make you give me my husband's property I'll leave this saloon. In the meantime get out of here. And don't speak to me again, damn your slimy little soul."

Charles gave a short, disagreeable laugh.

"You had better listen to me, Garnet," he said, "before you make a fool of yourself. Right now, I am willing to give you a home as well as the child. Much more of your disgraceful conduct, and that offer will be withdrawn."

"Get out of here," she said between her teeth.

"You'll see me again, Garnet," he said. For a moment he stood where he was, his eyes drilling into her head as though to be sure he was leaving his closing words in her mind. Then he put on his hat and went out. From the other end of the bar Garnet heard Florinda's bright voice.

"Won't that be fun! Hundreds of men from New York—I wonder if I'll know many of them. Do go on. When will they get to Los Angeles?"

Frémont left Los Angeles on the twelfth of May, 1847. That same day, Los Angeles was occupied by the New York Regiment, under Colonel Jonathan Stevenson. The New Yorkers were seven or eight hundred young fellows, nearly all of them under twenty-five and many of them boys in their teens. They had been recruited last summer with the purpose of getting American settlers for California. The terms of their enlistment provided that they would serve as soldiers till the end of the war. At the end of the war they were to be mustered out in California, or in the nearest piece of United States territory.

After two months training at Governor's Island the volunteers left New York in September, 1846, on three transports convoyed by a sloop-of-war. They reached San Francisco in March, 1847. Most of them were sent to Los Angeles when Colonel Stevenson took command there in May. They were a fair sample of nearly all sorts—workers and lazybones, college men and men who could not read, mechanics, clerks, farmers, and boys who had never had a trade.

Garnet had hoped she would find somebody she knew among them. But she had had to choose her friends from a small and sheltered circle. As the New Yorkers dropped into Silky's Place during their first days in Los Angeles, she saw nobody she had ever seen before. But their talk was like a letter from home. Nearly all these lads had grown up in New York state or the states near by, and about half of them had spent their lives in New York city. They talked about Broadway and the Bowery Theater and Barnum's Museum, about ices at Niblo's Gardens on hot afternoons, and Sunday excursions to Weehawken for picnics on the dueling ground where Aaron Burr had shot Alexander Hamilton. As she listened to them, Garnet had a strange double reaction. Sometimes it seemed to her that she had left New York only yesterday. But sometimes everything they talked about seemed remote, far more remote than the calendar could make it. So much had happened to her in the past two years that she felt as if she had lived most of her life since that windy March day when she and Oliver had sailed out of New York harbor. Listening to these boys, she had an odd, dazed feeling of enormous time.

As for Florinda, though she found nobody among them that she remembered, she found a good many who remembered her. It had been four years since she had appeared on the stage in New York, so most of the younger fellows had never seen her. But many of the others had not only seen her but had adored her from a distance, and they were thrilled to see her again, especially close up across a bar. They knew why she had disappeared from New York, for the Selkirk scandal had been talked about everywhere. "You didn't really shoot that fellow, did you?" they asked.

440

"Certainly not," said Florinda. "Did you think I had?"

"Of course I didn't! Some people said you had, but I always stood up for you. Right from the very first."

"Did you really? Now that was mighty good of you," she exclaimed. She always said it as if she believed them, which she did not. But as she said privately to Garnet, it made no difference now.

"By dropping a few tactful questions," she went on, "I have found out what became of that precious Mr. Reese. He never was put on trial. But there was such a lot of unpleasant talk about him that he found it convenient to go live in Europe." She laughed to herself. She was enjoying this influx of New Yorkers.

At the end of May, when Garnet had been back in Los Angeles two months, John's errand-boy Pablo came into the saloon with a bow and a bright good morning, and handed her a note from John.

When she saw her name on the outside in John's handwriting, Garnet's heart began to pound so that she had to make an effort to speak even a few words of thanks to Pablo and offer him the customary courtesy of a bottle of wine. He said he would wait for an answer. Garnet went into the kitchen and sank down on the wall-bench.

Her heart was beating so hard that she felt as if an ox were kicking her in the chest. Angry with herself for being like this, and even more angry with John for being able to do it to her, she wondered if there was any humiliation worse than knowing you loved a man more than he loved you and knowing also that you did not have enough will-power to get over it. She wished she had the courage to tear his letter in half without reading it. But she had not.

John' note was short.

Dear Garnet,

I can live without you, but I don't enjoy it. I miss you. I want you very much. Have you relented at all? Will you have me? Say yes, and I'll come to Los Angeles to get you. Say no, and I'll probably come anyway.

John.

Garnet's first thought was that she had better wait awhile before writing an answer, but her second thought was that she had better write it now, while she was still so angry with him for making her heart cut up these absurd capers. If she let herself think about how much she wanted him she might lose what little sense she had left. She got the pen and ink from the shelf and wrote hastily.

Dear John,
   No. *Either you love me or you don't. I won't have any lukewarm milktoast kind of marriage and I won't have that kind of man. I am going home as soon as I can find a ship that will take me. Meanwhile I wish you would let me alone.*
                                                                    Garnet.

She went back to the bar and gave her reply to Pablo. He smiled and bowed and went off. Garnet set her jaw and began to dust the bottles, while Florinda chattered with a group of New Yorkers. Florinda did not ask what Pablo had wanted. Garnet thought she must have seen the exchange of notes, but as often before, she silently blessed Florinda for minding her own business.

Several days later, the Brute came in from San Diego. The Brute was enthusiastic, for he had heard there was a Russian fur-ship on the California coast. The ship was said to have put in at San Francisco to buy supplies before going up to the Russian settlements in Alaska. The Brute was on his way north to look for the ship and find out when she was going back to Russia.

The evening after he left, while Garnet and Florinda took a few minutes to have a cup of chocolate in the kitchen, they talked about him, wondering if he would like Russia well enough to want to stay there. They told each other they would miss him. "And we won't be the only ones," Florinda said. Garnet flinched, remembering that John was the Brute's best friend and would miss him even more than they would, but Florinda caught herself and went on hurriedly, "Everybody will miss him." She stood up. "Well, we'd better be getting back to work."

"Do you mind if I go upstairs first," Garnet asked, "and have a look at Stephen?"

Florinda said she didn't mind, and Garnet went upstairs gratefully. A look at Stephen, healthy and untroubled, could always cheer her spirit. In her room, Stephen was fast asleep in the little bed Texas had made for him. It was a stout wooden structure pegged at the joints, with a well-tanned piece of hide across the bottom to make a springy support for the mattress, and high sides to keep the baby from crawling out. This was the sort of bed children had on the most luxurious ranchos. Few babies in the village slept in such comfort, but Texas said the best was none too good

442

for the baby he had brought and named. Dear Texas, Garnet thought, and felt a tug of pain. Texas had been drinking heavily for several days. He was downstairs in the saloon now, sitting on a wall-bench with a bottle on the table in front of him, drinking steadily and silently, getting it over with.

She went back downstairs. In the saloon, they had had a minor disturbance. One of the New York volunteers had got into an argument with a native Angeleno. As neither of them knew more than ten words of the other's language, a quarrel would have been impossible except that they were not sober enough to realize it. Luckily two officers of the regiment were present. They had sent the American back to barracks with an escort, and the bar-boy José had gone home with the native opponent. When Garnet came in, everything was subsiding. Mickey was wiping off the bar. Florinda, having just poured aguardiente for some exuberant young gentlemen, was rearranging the bottles on the shelf. The two officers, Major Lyndon and Captain Brown, leaned on the bar with glasses in their hands.

They were chatting about the probable fate of Frémont, but Garnet noticed that they stood with their backs to the bar so they could keep their eyes on the room in case there should be a threat of more disorder. She glanced at the table where Texas was. Texas had gone to sleep, his head on his outstretched arm. The far corner where he sat was shadowy, but he lay so that his face was upward, toward the light. It looked like a very uncomfortable position. Garnet wished José would hurry back, so he could help Texas get home.

She could hear Major Lyndon and Captain Brown as they talked. They were saying that General Kearny had left Monterey, to make an overland march to Fort Leavenworth, and Colonel Mason was now governor of California. Frémont had been required to go to Fort Leavenworth with the general. Nearly all the men took it for granted that he was going to face a court-martial.

"How many men did the general take with him?" Captain Brown was asking.

"I'm not sure," said Major Lyndon. "But I know he took several who belonged to Frémont's exploring party."

"To testify?" asked Captain Brown.

"Looks like it."

Captain Brown shook his head regretfully.

The two officers had been to the bar often, but neither of them ever drank much. Major Lyndon was a thickset man with a grayish

443

beard and dark hair going gray at the temples. Captain Brown was younger, apparently not yet out of his thirties; a strong, muscular man of middle height. Though not especially good-looking, he had attractive dark eyes and good teeth and a generally pleasant manner. He had never spoken to Garnet except to give orders across the bar, and these were always brief and impersonal, but she thought she might have liked him. As she glanced in his direction, he lifted his hand in a gesture of good-by to a man who was going out, and said something about an appointment for tomorrow. The door closed behind the man who was leaving, and Captain Brown's hand stopped in mid-air. He stared across the room at something he had just caught sight of, near the door. Major Lyndon asked in astonishment,

"What's the matter, Brown? Seen a ghost?"

At the sound of his friend's voice Captain Brown gave a start. With a quick movement he reached to set his glass on the bar, without looking at it. The glass nearly fell off the edge. Garnet rescued it, but Captain Brown did not notice her. He was still staring at the far side of the room.

"Yes," he said in answer to Major Lyndon, "a ghost—just about that. Lyndon, look over there. In the shadows, dead drunk with his head on the table."

Garnet felt a shiver as though a rat had run down her spine. She might have known this would happen some day. Oh, poor Texas. Poor Texas, who thought he had left his past behind him.

Major Lyndon turned his head, his eyes following Captain Brown's. He gasped, and his voice was rough with shock as he said, "My God, Brown! It's not—it can't be—"

"Yes it is," said Captain Brown. "It's Ernest Conway."

The two men's eyes met. They shook their heads at each other, and looked back at Texas. Garnet looked at him too. She saw his unkempt hair and beard, his mouth half open, his shirt with splashes of liquor on it, his not very clean hand on the table; she saw the whole grimy clammy look of him, a man drunk and sodden and no good. Major Lyndon made a wordless sound of disgust. "So that's what became of him," he said after a moment. He gave a little shudder. "Damn it, Brown, I thought he was dead."

"I wish he was," said Captain Brown. "The most brilliant—oh good Lord, Lyndon, I could cry."

He did not sound disgusted or contemptuous. He sounded sorry. He sounded, Garnet thought, as if he felt about Texas the same way she did; as if he knew Texas did not want to be like this, because no man could want to be like this; as if he did not understand him, but he could be sorry for Texas without understanding him.

A merry freckled private was asking Garnet for a drink. She filled several orders, and declined one proposal of marriage and one of the other sort. At last José came back, and he got Texas out of the saloon.

The evening was nearly over and the crowd in the room was thinning. A good many of the men had to leave before midnight. Major Lyndon was gone. Captain Brown was half sitting, half leaning on the end of the table nearest the bar. He was gazing moodily at the place where Texas had sat, as though he could not get his thoughts away from what he had seen there. Another officer came in and told him he could go, saying he would himself keep an eye on the place till closing time. Thanking him, Captain Brown stood up. Before he could move toward the door Garnet spoke to him.

"Captain Brown," she said.

He looked around in surprise. "Did you call me?"

Garnet nodded, feeling a tremor at her own boldness. His knowledge of Texas was none of her business and she did not know how he would like her referring to it, but all the same she felt impelled to do so. "May I speak to you, Captain Brown?" she asked, trying not to sound as shy as she felt.

"Certainly," said Captain Brown. He spoke with the formality of a man who would never be rude to any woman unless she demanded it, but he came to the bar without enthusiasm. Garnet kept her voice low so as to attract no attention.

"Captain Brown, a little while ago you and Major Lyndon were talking to each other. I wasn't trying to listen, but I couldn't help hearing part of what you said."

Apparently her diffidence impressed him more than assurance would have done. "I'm sure it's all right," he said encouragingly. "We weren't discussing any military secrets. Go on."

She spoke with more confidence. "You recognized a man who was—asleep, over at that table there, by the door."

"Why yes, I did," said Captain Brown. He waited gravely for her to continue.

"I know this is no concern of mine," said Garnet, "but please tell me, is there anybody else who would know him?"

445

He considered. "I believe not. Major Lyndon and I happened to be at Fort Leavenworth the winter Conway was there." Captain Brown was evidently puzzled. "May I ask why you want to know?"

"Of course you may. It's like this. You're assuming that I know who he is. But I don't. Nobody here knows him. I'll explain."

"I wish you would," said Captain Brown.

"He came to California some years ago," Garnet went on. "He has never told anybody what his name is, or anything about himself. We know him simply as Texas."

"We knew him as Texas too," Captain Brown said smiling. "He was always talking about the Republic of Texas, telling us what a great country it was. But I didn't mean to interrupt you. Please go on."

"Everybody likes him," said Garnet. "But nobody has ever tried to find out who he is."

Captain Brown was listening with interest now. Garnet continued,

"You see, before the war with Mexico, several hundred men came to California from the United States and from other countries too. They came here for all sorts of reasons. But gradually, they worked out some rules of living. You might call it a sort of code. One of the rules was that they took a man as they found him. They never, never asked him what he had done at home. You might trust a man or you might not, but as long as he made no trouble you let him mind his own business. Do you understand how that was?"

"Why yes," said Captain Brown, "I think I do." He nodded thoughtfully.

"Now please," said Garnet, "let me tell you something about Texas. Have you got time to listen?"

Captain Brown was watching her intently as she talked. "I should like very much to hear it."

"Texas has a fault," said Garnet. "You know what it is. But believe me, that's the only fault he has. He's kind and generous and honorable. More than once he has been a friend to me when I needed help. That's why I'm asking you now, don't give Texas away. Whatever it is that he left behind him, let it stay there."

Captain Brown answered her with a quiet sincerity. "Thank you for telling me all this," he said. "I won't give him away."

"That's very good of you," said Garnet. "And you'll tell Major Lyndon?"

"I'll tell him what you've told me, yes," he returned. He reflected a moment, and asked, "Suppose Texas sees one of us?"

"Can't you pretend you don't recognize him?" she suggested. "After all, it must have been years since you saw him. That isn't asking too much, is it?"

Still watching her with a serious, rather baffled look, Captain Brown answered slowly, "No, that's not asking too much. I repeat, I'm very glad you told me."

"Thank you," said Garnet. Before she could say anything else there was a tap on the bar, and she saw Mr. Collins and Mr. Bugs McLane, who had dropped in for a nightcap. With an apology to Captain Brown, she turned to pour their drinks. When she looked around again Captain Brown was about to leave. He had put on his cap and was opening the door. Catching her eye, he tipped his cap to her, smiling. Garnet smiled back with a sense of refreshment. Though he was saying good night to a barmaid in Silky's Place, Captain Brown was saying it exactly as if he had been standing in the doorway of her mother's parlor.

That night she told Florinda about him. She and Florinda took turns washing each other's hair, and tonight it was Florinda's turn to get washed. When they had closed the bar they went up to Florinda's room. There was not much chance for conversation while the scrubbing was going on, but during the last rinsing they could talk. Florinda knelt on the floor in front of two buckets, one empty and one full of water. While she held her head down over the empty bucket, Garnet poured gourdfuls of water over her hair, holding the gourd in her right hand and with her left hand rubbing Florinda's head to dislodge any invisible specks of soap that might still be clinging to the roots of her hair. While she rinsed, Garnet told Florinda how much she liked Captain Brown.

Her head over the bucket, Florinda returned, "He likes you too. I saw the way he was looking at you while you talked. And he's a real gent, that's plain."

"I wish there were more like him," said Garnet.

"If there were, dear, Silky's Place would go bust for lack of trade. A few like him, fine; too many, no. Anyway, it doesn't hurt you to get to know all sorts." Florinda gave a chuckle. "All sorts of men, but the same idea in every head. Did you get many proposals tonight?"

"Several," said Garnet. "Both kinds."

447

"That nice young fellow O'Neal," said Florinda, "kept asking me to marry him, saying it over and over till it was like the chorus of a song, repeated with new additions every time."

"What did he say?" asked Garnet. Then she added, "That's the last of the water."

With a sigh of relief Florinda straightened her back and began rubbing her head with a towel. "Thanks, I'll wash yours tomorrow night. On the first few drinks he just asked me to marry him. As he got drunker he elaborated. Kept thinking up more and more details of wedded bliss. By midnight he had me all fixed up with a parlor rug and two children." She got up and sat on the wall-bench, fluffing her hair with the towel.

Garnet dried her hands and went to sit on the wall-bench. "Florinda," she said suddenly.

"Yes, dearie?" said Florinda from under a mask of hair.

"Why don't you get married?" asked Garnet.

"Who, me? Are you joking?"

"No, I'm not joking. Why don't you?"

"Because I don't want to," said Florinda. She was combing her hair carefully, pinching the waves into place with her hands. "What makes you think I need a husband?"

"Oh Florinda," Garnet exclaimed, "hasn't it occurred to you that we won't be young forever? Don't you want some stability in your life—something you can count on?"

"Certainly I do," said Florinda. "I'm putting it away in Mr. Abbott's safe."

"Money is a lot more important than I used to think it was," said Garnet. "But it won't buy everything."

"It'll buy anything I'm likely to want," Florinda said calmly. She went on combing her hair. "Garnet, my sweet," she continued, "you can get married all you please. But not me. I'm not going to work twelve hours a day in this groggery and then bring in a husband to drink up the stock." She shrugged. "Have you got one picked out for me?"

"Of course not. But you could take your choice of the New York Regiment, you know, and some of them are fine fellows. They expect to stay in California, they want to get married and have homes. And that *is* important, Florinda! Didn't you ever want a home of your own?"

"Yes, but I'd rather have it all to myself," said Florinda. While she talked she finished the rest of her bedtime washing and put on

448

her nightgown. "How often do I have to tell you this, Garnet? I know about husbands! I know about the gents who bought me champagne and sat up till sunrise telling me their wives didn't understand them. I know about the fine young bluebloods who married girls like you and then left 'em at home with the baby while they hovered around the stage door of the Jewel Box. Men are fun, dearie, and I adore them, but the minute you turn a man into a husband—no, thank you. I'm doing fine."

With a quick jerky movement of her head Florinda tossed her hair behind her shoulders. She began folding the dress and petticoats she had taken off.

Garnet watched her thoughtfully. "Why are you so bitter about it?" she asked after a pause.

Florinda went on folding her clothes. "Well, I'd better say it. The fact is, Garnet, I've tried marriage. I don't like it."

Garnet gave a gasp. "You've been married?" she exclaimed.

"Yes," said Florinda. She smiled a little. "Surprised?"

"Yes, but maybe I shouldn't be. You told me you'd had a child."

"My God," Florinda exclaimed with a start of horror, "he wasn't her father!" She shuddered. "If I'd had a child by that fungus," she said through her teeth, "I'd have thrown it down the well."

Garnet heard her in amazement. She was amazed not so much by the fact that Florinda had been married as by the look of her when she spoke of it. Florinda took the world as she found it, with an uncomplaining gallantry that Garnet had envied a thousand times. But now her beautiful eyes were narrowed to two slits and her mouth had an ugly curve as though it had been turned upside down. She had put her dress and petticoats on the wall-bench, and she was sitting by them, running her fingers along the edge of the bench as though the feel of adobe were new to her. In a thin, startled voice, Garnet exclaimed,

"How you hate him!"

Florinda's whole body looked stiff. She drew a deep breath as though trying to relax. "I think," she said slowly, "he's the only person I ever really hated in my life." Turning her head so as to look at Garnet more directly, she asked, "Did you ever hate anybody, Garnet?"

"Not like that," Garnet answered with conviction.

"Don't try it," said Florinda. "Don't find out what it does to you. Garnet, I like people. Some of them I don't like overmuch, but

449

I don't hate them. I don't lie awake all night shaking with hate of them. Did you ever do that?"

"No," said Garnet, "I never did." She felt young and inexperienced. This dreadfulness Florinda was remembering now was not like anything she had ever known.

"When you hate somebody," said Florinda, "it's like a torture inside of you. You think about him and you feel like your skin is rising up off your body. You feel like your hair is turning to hot wires on your head. And if you're married to him you're helpless. All you did was go down to City Hall and speak a dozen words and sign your name in a book, and you've put yourself in chains. You can't get away." Florinda stopped. After a moment she shook her head as though to clear it of what she was remembering. Some damp silvery tendrils of hair fell over her face. As she pushed them back she gave Garnet a small one-sided smile. "Well, I told you," she said.

Garnet wished she could somehow help to lessen the pain of what Florinda was remembering. "Florinda," she said gently, "he can't hurt you any more. Not away out here."

Florinda said nothing. She looked down, pulling out the ruffle on the sleeve of her nightgown.

"Where is he now?" Garnet asked.

"Dead," said Florinda. She did not look up.

"Oh," Garnet said softly.

"Quite safely dead," said Florinda.

Garnet started and put her hand to her lips. "I think—I understand," she said in a low voice.

"Yes, dear," Florinda replied quietly, "I think you do." Raising her eyes to meet Garnet's, she went on in a steady voice. "His name was William Cadwallader Mallory. I shot him on the night of the sixteenth of August, 1844, in the Alhambra Gambling Palace on Park Row."

She laced her fingers on her knee. The ruffles on her sleeve fell back, and her hands looked rough and crusty as the candlelight flickered over the scars.

"I didn't lie to you that day in New Orleans," she went on. "I told you I hadn't killed Selkirk. I hadn't. Everything I told you was true. But there were some things I didn't tell you." After a moment of silence she looked up again, half smiling as though she felt relieved to have said all this. "Like me any less than you did?" she asked.

"Of course not," Garnet exclaimed. "I don't like you any less. Did you think I would?"

Florinda regarded her thoughtfully. "Well, dear, I didn't know. Some people think murder is a rather serious crime."

Garnet spoke without hesitation. "Florinda, you are the kindest, most considerate, least resentful person I've ever known. If you killed a man it must have been because he deserved it. That's all."

Florinda shook her head slowly, with a look of wonder. "Garnet, I guess that's about the nicest thing anybody ever said to me in my whole life. Do you mean it?"

"Yes, I mean it. I usually mean what I say."

"Thank you, Garnet," said Florinda. "And thank you for the way you stood by me that day in New Orleans. I'm going to say something I've been wanting to say to you ever since then." She leaned sideways against the wall and began making little pleats in the blue gingham curtain. "Oliver didn't have your grace of heart, Garnet. I wouldn't have said so then, and I didn't know how to thank you without saying so. But—do you remember?—Oliver started probing. He wanted to know a lot that I didn't want to talk about. I suppose he had a right to ask questions. He didn't know me from Adam's grandmother and there I was wanting the two of you to keep me out of jail. But I couldn't have answered him, I simply could not have lived through it again. And somehow you understood it and you told him to let me alone. And I loved you for that, oh I did love you so much for it, and I've wanted to tell you so."

Garnet stood up. She went over to Florinda and knelt down, putting her own warm healthy hands over the ridgy knots of Florinda's. "It still hurts you to talk about it, doesn't it?" she asked.

"Yes, I guess it does," said Florinda. She looked down.

"Then don't talk about it. Don't tell me any more."

There was a silence. After a while Florinda stood up, felt her hair to see how nearly dry it was, and began to turn down her bedclothes. She spoke in her normal voice. "Well, dearie, I suppose you get the idea. I've had one husband, and now that I'm rid of him I'll be a lot of blue words if I want to try another."

"I understand," said Garnet, "and I can't blame you. No wonder you'd rather go on being a widow."

"A what?" said Florinda. She turned around. "Am I a widow? You mean all those black dresses—" For a moment she stared at Garnet with blank astonishment. Then she burst out laughing. "Oh, my uncle's carbuncle! Garnet, who on earth would have thought of that but you?"

Garnet had begun to laugh too. She was glad Florinda had such a gift for laughter when the tension got too strong. "You hadn't thought of that?" she asked.

"Garnet, I do declare to you that in all this time it never once entered my head. Well, well." Florinda threw back her head and stretched her neck, still chuckling. "That's the first time William Mallory ever gave me anything to laugh about," she said, with grimness under her mirth. "Garnet, you're wonderful. You always were."

FORTY-ONE

They did not see Texas the next day. But that evening Captain Brown came to the bar and told Garnet she could be at ease about Texas' wish to be nameless in California. Captain Brown said he had spoken to Major Lyndon, and the major had agreed that if Texas did not want his past talked about, no good could be done by talking about it.

Garnet thanked him, and went to serve several men who were waiting. When she had time to look around Captain Brown was still at the bar.

"What is your name?" he asked. "Ruby, Pearl, Opal—?"

"Garnet," she said.

"That's it. I knew it was some kind of jewel." His eyes crinkled in a pleasant sort of apology as he added, "As you can see, I haven't paid you much attention. That is, not until last night."

"Thank you for paying attention last night," she said, smiling back at him.

Captain Brown studied her face, with that same baffled expression he had had last night. At length he said,

"Do you mind if I tell you that you puzzle me considerably?"

"Why no," she returned, laughing a little. "I don't mind. But why do I puzzle you?"

"For one thing," said Captain Brown, "you remind me of somebody, and I can't think who it is. For another—I'm not asking any questions," he assured her. "But if I can ever be of service, won't you let me know?"

She heard him with surprise. "Why thank you," she said, "but I'm not sure I understand what that means."

"Then I'll tell you," he returned. He spoke with a simple friendly candor. "I don't want to meddle in what doesn't concern me. But it's obvious that you don't belong in here."

Garnet looked down at the counter. His manner of saying this was so different from the way men usually asked questions that she did not know how to answer him. He was not reproachful, and he was not starting off with the familiar "How'd a nice girl like you ever get in this God-forsaken hole?" Captain Brown was waiting for an answer. She said, without looking up,

"Why do you think I don't belong here?"

"Because of the way you talk," he answered promptly. "The habit of well-bred speech is as hard to break as the other kind." He paused, and then went on, "Now if I've said too much, forgive me. I don't know anything about you and I'm not going to try to find out anything. But I think you're in a tight spot, and I'd like to be your friend."

She raised her eyes. Because he had asked for no explanation and evidently did not expect one, this time she wanted to give it. She said,

"Thank you very much, Captain Brown. I came to California with my husband. But he died, and I can't go back alone. I'm working here to make a living. That's all."

He started to reply. But Garnet saw a group of privates, waiting with what patience they could muster for that pest of a captain to get through talking to the barmaid so they could get something to drink. "I'll have to leave you now," she said, and turned away from him to take their orders. When she had served them she saw that Captain Brown had not moved from his place at the bar.

Garnet brightened, and spoke to him. "Did you mean what you said a minute ago, Captain Brown?"

"Certainly I meant it."

"There is something you can do for me. I just thought of it. If I'm asking too much, tell me. But the army must be sending letters back to the States. Would it be possible for me to get a message to my people? I'd like to tell them I'm well and safe."

Captain Brown took a slip of paper and a pencil from his pocket. "I'll see what I can do. Where do they live?"

453

"New York. Mr. and Mrs. Horace Cameron."

"What!" He dropped his pencil on the bar. "Of course," he said, his words slow with astonishment, "of course. That's who it is you remind me of. Mr. Cameron."

Garnet started. "Where did you know my father?" she asked breathlessly.

"In New York. I saw him at the bank about a week before the regiment sailed. He showed me a letter from you. It must have been from you—are you Mrs. Hale?"

She nodded. Captain Brown went on.

"But he didn't know you had lost your husband. He was expecting to hear any day that you were back in the States. This was a letter you had written just after you reached California. You described the scenery, but—" he gave a little laugh of apology—"but of course you know what was in a letter you wrote yourself."

Garnet winced. How well she knew. That was the letter she had sent just after she reached Charles' rancho, when she was so determined not to let her parents know anything was wrong. The letter had reached New York last summer, and her father had done just what she had known he would do, he had taken the letter to the bank so he could show it to his friends. And naturally, since Captain Brown was coming to California, father would show it to him. "Since you're going out there, you might be interested in this letter from my daughter . . ."

The New York Regiment had sailed in September. It had not occurred to her father to ask Captain Brown to bring her a message, because he was expecting any day to get a letter from her, mailed in some town on the frontier, saying she was back from the trail and on her way home. But instead, after the regiment had left, he got that letter she had written just before she came to Los Angeles with Florinda and John. That was the letter saying Oliver was dead, and she was going to have a baby, and she could not come home.

"Mrs. Hale," Captain Brown said in a low voice.

Garnet started and looked up. "Forgive me. I'm afraid I was—" She bit her lip.

"Homesick?" he finished for her, with sympathy.

"Yes." She smiled. "Every now and then it catches hold of me and gives me a pinch. But please believe me," she added hastily, "I'm not unhappy here. It's just knowing I can't get away, feeling

454

remote and cut off, that's all. Tell me, did my father look well? Did he say anything about the rest of the family?"

"Your father looked well and cheerful. I'm sure the others were well too, since he said something about having to hurry home because he and Mrs. Cameron were having a dinner-party that evening. They would hardly have been having a party if anything had been wrong." Captain Brown picked up his pencil from the bar where it had fallen, and put it back into his pocket. "I'll inquire at once about getting a letter to them, and I'll let you know."

Mr. Collins and Mr. McLane came in for their nightcap. Captain Brown said good night, and Garnet went to wait on the others. At the door, Captain Brown caught her eye as he had last night, and lifted his hand in a friendly gesture of goodby. Again, Garnet felt a warmth of comradeship.

The army had put up a fort on a hill overlooking the plaza. Here the men celebrated the Fourth of July.

They began at sunrise, firing a federal salute as the flag was raised on the hill. The crack of the guns banged against the mountains, waking everybody who was not awake already. The Angelenos sighed and asked each other if the Yankees really had to make so much noise about all they did. At Silky's Place, where nobody ever got to sleep till long after midnight, the guns nearly jolted them out of bed.

Garnet sat up in fright. In the little bed Stephen was bawling. As she rubbed her eyes Garnet remembered that Colonel Stevenson had announced some days ago that the Fourth of July would be observed this way. With a yawn, she put on a wrapper and took Stephen down to the kitchen. There was some cold gruel left from last night. She was scraping this up from the pot for him when Mickey came in, his pigtail bobbing and his felt shoes flapping and his smile as tranquil as ever. Mickey set about making chocolate. He had no idea why the Yankees were firing guns. But Mickey had long since got used to the fact that Yankees did a lot of things he could not understand. He smiled at Garnet, and she smiled back at him. She had not had much sleep, but she was remembering how lonesome she had felt last year when the Fourth of July went by and it was just another day, and she thought it was worth it.

Florinda was less patriotic. Florinda had heard of the Declaration of Independence, but she was not sure what it was. As they drank the chocolate Garnet told her something about it. Florinda said it sounded very fine, but she still did not see why they had to get up at the bust of dawn to celebrate. She thought the middle of the day would do just as well. But of course she didn't know much about such things, and in the meantime where was the ink? Now that she was up this would be a good chance to check the accounts for the past week, before Silky squeezed himself a new coat out of her share of the profits.

Silky was already opening the bar. He told the girls to get ready for a busy day, for cheers made thirsty throats. At the new fort, the Declaration was to be read in both English and Spanish, in the presence of the troops and anybody else who cared to climb the hill and hear it. The structure was to be formally named Fort Moore, in honor of Captain Moore who had lost his life at the battle of San Pascual, when Kearny's men met the Californios last December. Later there were to be more ceremonies, more guns, and more cheering. Everybody would be in a gay mood and would want plenty to drink.

He was right. The day was blazing hot and the saloon was packed. By midnight Garnet and Florinda were so tired that their eyes were hazy. But they were aware that Captain Brown had been standing for some time at Garnet's end of the bar. He had stood quietly, always with a drink in front of him but taking his time about swallowing it. He said very little. But as long as he stayed there, the boys did not get too rowdy. When Silky and José were finally helping the last customers down the front step, Garnet gathered up the remnant of her strength and went over to him.

"Thank you for being here," she said.

"Don't try to talk," Captain Brown said smiling. "Get some rest."

He said good night then, and went out. Florinda, who was standing at the bar with her head sunk upon her hands, murmured appreciatively, "That's a real gent you've got there, Garnet."

Garnet agreed with her. She had grown very fond of Captain Brown. In the bluster of Los Angeles his quiet friendliness was as bracing as a breeze on a sultry day. His father, he told her, had for some years been doing business with the bank where Mr. Cameron worked. Mr. Brown was an importer of laces and other luxury goods from Europe. There had been two sons in the family, and the plan had been that the older son should go into business with his father, while the younger went into the army. Captain Brown, the younger son, had gone to West Point. But his brother had died, and Captain Brown had asked to be put on the army's inactive list so he could carry on the family business. He had been called back to duty at the outbreak of the war, but he expected to return to civilian life when the country no longer needed him.

He had arranged for Garnet to send a letter home, in a bag with some military dispatches being sent by way of Mexico. She could use only one sheet of paper, and the commanding officer had to read what she wrote. But at least it was a way of letting her parents know that Stephen had been safely born and she was in good health.

Later in July the Mormon battalion was mustered out. Some of the men re-enlisted, and the army sent them to San Diego. Here, with their customary energy, the Mormons went to work. They whitewashed houses, shod horses, made carts, and set up a bakery; and altogether they made themselves so useful that the people of San Diego sent a petition to Governor Mason asking him to use his influence to get the Mormons to stay in California for good. Most of the Mormons, however, shook their heads. They had been sent West to be ready for the new Mormon colony that Brigham Young was starting, and this was where they wanted to go.

The Mormons who did not re-enlist set out for the new colony at once. They filled their pockets with seeds of crops that grew in California and so were already adapted to conditions this side of the Great Divide. They came by the saloon to say goodby, and Garnet and Florinda wished them luck, though Florinda added admiringly that she didn't think they would need it.

Now and then Captain Brown came into the saloon when Texas was there. But Captain Brown always managed to look the other way, and Texas gave no sign of recognizing him. Texas was in good spirits these days. His main interest seemed to be Stephen. When Stephen had his first birthday Texas brought him a marvelous confection that his landlady Señora Vargas had made out of beaten egg-whites, sweetened with panocha and crisped in the oven; and now that Stephen was old enough to play with toys, Texas spent a lot of time making playthings for him—a rattle, a set of straw animals, a soft woolly ball that would not hurt him if he dropped it.

Texas was a great help to Garnet, telling her how to take care of Stephen and what to give him to eat. Isabel was a comfort, for Isabel had brought up three children of her own; but Texas was a doctor, and an American. He could understand—as Isabel could not—Garnet's tremors about feeding a baby in a land where she could not get milk for him to drink. Like most California mothers, Isabel thought of cow's milk merely as food for calves. She made Stephen a gruel of cornmeal and beans and squash and any other vegetables that happened to be available, all cooked together and strained. In a little while she was flavoring the gruel with beef-juice. Garnet was frightened, but Texas soothed her. California babies thrived on this fare, he said. To her relief and surprise, Stephen thrived on it too.

In September a wave of hot air blew in from the desert and they had the hottest weather Garnet and Florinda had felt since they came through Cajón Pass. The nights still had a harsh dusty coolness, but from sunrise to sunset the town trembled in a tawny glare. The heat felt heavy, and lay like a weight on their necks. But even so, such weather had its good points. As the men had come in during the fogs to drink something to warm them up, now they came in to drink something to cool them off, and the cash-box tinkled sweetly under Florinda's caressing hands.

During the heat wave Garnet caught sight of Mr. and Mrs. Charles Hale one morning, riding past the saloon in their usual splendor. She remarked that she thought anybody who had a chance to stay in the country during weather like this would have been glad to do so, but Silky set her right. Charles' rancho was east of Los Angeles, he reminded her. With every mile eastward you got farther from the sea and nearer the desert, and consequently the heat increased. So no wonder Charles had taken refuge in town.

It was also during this breathless September that Garnet had her first glimpse of Estelle, the woman who conducted the bawdyhouse six doors down from Silky's. Though Estelle's place of business was so near, Garnet had never seen her. She herself almost never left the saloon except in the morning, and at that time of day Estelle's house stood silent with the shutters closed. She had never seen Estelle in the saloon. The men who came to the bar sometimes had girls with them, but not often. As for Silky, though he frequently went a-courting he had never had any feminine visitors. Silky was careful to keep his business and personal interests apart. Garnet was astonished, therefore, one afternoon when she came down after the siesta, to find Silky talking to a woman who sat with him at the kitchen table.

Garnet had come down the stairs with Stephen in her arms. His gruel was keeping warm on the hearth-stove, ready for her to feed him before going to the bar for the afternoon. As she opened the door to the kitchen, she heard a woman speaking.

". . . it's a shame, Silky, I tell you it is, bad for business and everything. But I swear to God, it's so pitiful."

She had a jangly tin-spoon sort of voice, and her accent was like that of some of the bullwhackers on the Santa Fe Trail. There were so few women in Los Angeles who spoke English that Garnet gave a start of perplexity. If she had not had to feed the baby she would have gone away without interrupting them. But Stephen was hungry, and since she had already opened the door she thought if they were talking about private matters she would stay only long enough to get his pot of gruel and leave them. As she took a step across the threshold she heard Silky say,

"And you're sure you can't get him out?"

"I ain't got the heart, Silky!" the visitor pled. "I swear to God I ain't got the heart."

Then Silky caught sight of Garnet, coming into the room with her baby in her arms. He sprang to his feet and bowed to her, so low that his forehead nearly touched his knees. Garnet did not know what to make of him. Since he had grown used to seeing her every day Silky no longer thought it necessary to show off his highflown manners for her sake. But now he was twirling his mustache and speaking his absurd stagey lines, and while he said his piece Garnet got a good look at the stranger who sat by the table.

The woman did not look old. But she had the look of an object that had been roughly used, so that it had lost its freshness long before it had begun to wear out. And while no part of her was obviously dirty, she gave a general impression that she could have been improved by soap and water.

She had sagging bright pink cheeks, the same color as the big pink velvet rose that she wore tilted at one side of her head. Her hair was the color of a brass door-knob except where it was darker along the parting, and over her ears she wore bunches of curls that were a still brighter shade of brass. Her dress was silk, printed with large pink flowers. The heat of the day had put big rings of sweat in the armholes. The hem was dusty, and her slippers—black with pink rosettes—were dusty too. She wore a lot of ornaments: swinging gold earrings, a gold necklace, rings and bracelets on both hands, besides a leather gun-belt that was dingy from lack of polishing. The look of her made Garnet conscious of her own smooth hair and her crisp dress of green and white gingham, and she felt a twinge of distaste. But as Silky sprang to his feet the strange woman turned her head, smiling at Garnet and Stephen with a friendly curiosity. She had large brown eyes and a good-natured smile, and Garnet noticed with surprise that though she did look cheap and common and second-hand, she was in her own way an attractive person. As the two of them observed each other, Silky was speaking his lines.

"Ah, Mrs. Hale, what a pleasure it is to see you looking so well, like a rose sparkling with dew on a spring day! And the little one, so fine and strong, such a joy to his doting mother—"

"Glubble glubble," said Stephen. "Glubble bam." Stephen had smelt a whiff of his gruel on the hearth-stove, and he wanted it, and he wanted it now, and he wanted no nonsense beforehand. Screwing up his face he began to cry. At the same time he dug his hand into his mother's hair and drew out a lock, thereby destroying the neatness of the whole. The woman at the table said, "Ah, poor little fellow!" She smiled at him and waved cheerily. "He's all right," Garnet said, still not sure who the visitor was. "Just hungry, and cross because of it." At that instant she heard footsteps on the stairs. Florinda was coming down, intending to have a cup of chocolate in the kitchen as usual before opening the barroom for the afternoon trade.

Just over the threshold she stopped, her hand still on the door. Her eyes moved swiftly in surprise as she saw who was there. Florinda was wearing a clean calico dress printed in a design of tiny blue flowers on a gray background, with a little white collar at the neck. She had brushed her hair till it shone like eggshell satin, and her skin was glowing from having just been scrubbed with cold water. Even the leather holster at her belt had a well-rubbed sheen. Altogether she looked so fastidious that she made the hot room seem cooler the minute she came in. Garnet knew how much work it cost to keep clean in Los Angeles, because she had to make the same effort herself. She knew also that while Florinda's efforts were caused partly by self-respect, they were also prompted by the reward of good business. On these blistering days, when the men saw the fresh unwilted look of the girls at the bar they went out and told their friends that Silky's saloon was the coolest place in town. But all the same, Florinda did look exquisite and the other woman did not, and the thought flashed through Garnet's mind, That's the difference between a courtesan and a streetwalker. As she thought this, it dawned upon her that this caller must have come from that place nearby.

All this had gone through her head in an instant of time. Stephen was fussing tearfully for want of his afternoon meal; Florinda stood holding the door-latch with a hand in a neat fingerless mitt, gray to

460

match the gray background of her dress. She was exclaiming in a voice of reproach,

"Silky, you promised!"

Estelle glanced down, turning one of her rings around her finger. But she gave a shrug and glanced up again at Florinda, a faint touch of humor on her lips. She was not embarrassed, but Silky was. Having nothing to say, Silky took refuge in words.

"Indeed, Florinda, I regret profoundly that you or Mrs. Hale should be discommoded in any fashion! But this, I assure you with all my heart, this is an exigency, a most distressing imbroglio—"

"Is that so?" said Florinda. "Well, bless my soul."

Garnet bit back a wild impulse to giggle. Stephen was pulling at her hair again and she could not stop him, for she had to hold his feet lest he squirm down and kick the gun she was wearing. Florinda let go of the door-latch and put her hand on Garnet's elbow.

"Come outside with me, Garnet," she said. "Please."

Garnet was glad to comply, for Stephen had begun to feel very heavy. She went with Florinda back into the dark little hall where the staircase was. Florinda shut the door. Garnet sat down on a step, putting Stephen beside her and sighing with relief as she got the weight of him off her arms. Trying to make some order out of the wreckage of her hair, she asked, "Is that woman the Estelle I've heard about?"

"Yes," Florinda said shortly.

"What is she doing here?" asked Garnet. "I suppose I shouldn't be angry, or shocked either, but—"

"Maybe you aren't, but I am. He told me he wouldn't." Stephen was still fussing, so Florinda added, "Wait here and I'll bring his porridge. Also I'll find out what's going on. Silky's not going to speak plain English if you're in sight." She started to open the door, but paused and looked over her shoulder. "Garnet, what's an exi—exige—what is it?"

"An exigency? It means an emergency. A tight spot."

"And what's an imbroglio?"

Garnet was laughing. "That means a mix-up."

"Well, well," Florinda said respectfully. "I wonder how it feels to know so much." She opened the door. "I'll be right back."

She reappeared almost at once, bringing the pot and a spoon, and a towel to protect Garnet's dress. At sight of the spoon Stephen popped his mouth open like a baby bird. Florinda went back into the kitchen, and Garnet set about feeding him.

461

From beyond the closed door she could hear the other three—Florinda's low, carefully trained speech, the jangly tones of Estelle, and Silky's voice, which was deep and rather pleasant when he was talking naturally. They all had a good deal to say, but they did not sound angry.

Before long she heard Isabel come up on the porch. Garnet took Stephen outside and told Isabel to take care of him.

José had opened the saloon. Garnet would have liked a cup of chocolate before going to work, but she was pretty sure that she was not wanted in the kitchen right now. So when she had gone up to her room and combed her hair again, she went back through the stuffy little hallway and into the barroom by the side door. Several customers were there already. As she poured their drinks, one of the men asked her if she had ever been to New York, and without waiting for her to answer he began telling her all about it. In the midst of his description Florinda opened the door. The boys exclaimed and called to her. Florinda waved back brightly, saying, "I'll be there right away. Will you come here a minute, Garnet?"

Leaving José in charge, Garnet went back to the kitchen. Except for herself and Florinda the room was empty now. Florinda had put on a pot of coffee, and she filled cups for Garnet and herself. "Look, dearie," she began as she sat down. "Please don't be mad with Silky."

"I'm not mad with him," Garnet assured her.

"Promise?"

"Yes." Garnet began to laugh again. "Honestly, Florinda, I don't have to be treated as if I were made of glass!"

"Of course not, dear. But let me tell you how it is with Silky." She gave Garnet a look that was half humorous and half earnest. "You see, you're a—how do I say it?—you're a chaste woman."

Garnet listened, wondering what was going to come next.

"You're the first chaste woman," said Florinda, "that Silky has had around him since his mother died."

Garnet frowned slightly, puzzled as to how she should interpret all this. "When did his mother die?" she asked.

"When he was ten or twelve years old," said Florinda. She gave Garnet a confidential smile. "You know," she commented in an undertone, "I rather suspect Silky's family was kind of genteel. But they died and left no money, and there wasn't anybody to take care of him. And when a kid is turned loose on the town, you know how it is—no, I guess you don't."

462

"No," Garnet agreed, "I guess I don't."

"Well, anyway," Florinda went on, "Silky's mother was a good woman. And so are you. And of course too, you're a mother. And the sight of a sweet pure young woman with a baby in her arms, it does something to a man like Silky. I think it touches the last morsel of goodness he's got left in him. Because of course, dear, Silky is a thief and a liar and a scamp of every description. If I didn't keep watch on the books he'd cheat you out of half you earn here. But he respects you, Garnet, I mean really he does."

This was too complex for Garnet to grasp it all at once. She asked, "But what has this got to do with Estelle?"

"I know it seems mighty roundabout," said Florinda. "But I had to explain a little. Silky respects you, and when I brought you here he told me that neither Estelle nor any of her girls would come inside this building while you lived in it. That's why I was so surprised to see her today. I was mad besides."

"I'm not mad," said Garnet. "I'll tell him so if you want me to."

"I wish you would. Because really, she had to see him. Something had happened and she had to tell him about it."

"What was it? Or is it none of my business?"

"Yes, it's your business. It's—it's what I'm about to tell you." Florinda stopped and took a sip of coffee.

Garnet was alarmed. Florinda did not often speak jerkily. "I'm not going to make a scene," Garnet promised. "So go ahead and tell me. Is it bad?"

"Yes, dear. I'm so sorry. It's Texas."

For a moment Garnet could not say anything. She swallowed and made herself speak steadily. "What's happened to him?"

"He's had a fall," said Florinda. "A bad fall." She hesitated, then gave a shrug. "I don't know why I'm trying to say it so delicately. You're no such apple blossom as you used to be. Texas was down at Estelle's. The usual reason, I suppose, I don't know of any other reason to go there. He was drunk. Maybe he was too drunk to see where he was going, maybe he slipped because he was lame. He's dying. And Estelle—she knows it will hurt business, having a death in the house. But he's all broken to pieces and he's been in dreadful pain and delirious. He's easier now and in his right mind, but he can't stand to have anybody touch him. It would be like cutting him up with a blunt knife if they carried him out and put him into a cart and took him home, and she says she just can't do it."

"God bless her," said Garnet. She had thought she was going to speak vehemently, but she was so touched and so choked with pity that her voice came out in a thin little thread. "Florinda, we can get a message to Estelle, can't we?"

"Why yes, of course. What do you want to say?"

"Tell her I've got a little money saved up. If she'll let him stay there and die in peace, I'll help pay for the business she'll lose."

Florinda smiled. "All right. Mighty sweet of you."

Garnet rested her forehead on her hands. "Does he know he's dying, Florinda?"

"Oh yes. He's the one that told her. But she says anybody would know it to look at him."

There was a silence. Florinda finished her coffee. She fingered the handle of the cup.

"I guess you know how Texas feels about you," she said. "And he adores Stephen, I guess you know that too. When he was out of his head he talked to you all the time. Estelle said would I please tell you—here, have some more coffee."

Garnet heard her with a sense of pain. Poor Texas, dear Texas. Florinda refilled both their cups. Garnet asked,

"What did Estelle want you to tell me?"

Florinda smiled wryly. "Well dear, she said it would mean a frightful lot to Texas if you'd come and say good-by to him and bring the baby."

Garnet jerked up straight. "If I'd—you mean, Texas wants me to go there?"

"He didn't suggest it!" Florinda exclaimed. "Texas wouldn't dream of asking you to go inside a fancy house. Estelle thought it up. She said the way Texas talked to you and the baby when he was out of his head—she couldn't stand it, it made the tears pour down her cheeks." As though afraid she might have said too much, Florinda added quickly, "You don't have to go, Garnet. Silky didn't even want me to tell you."

Garnet looked down. Without raising her eyes she said, "Of course I'll go, Florinda."

"Would you really?" Florinda exclaimed.

"Why yes. If it would mean that much to him."

"Oh Garnet, I'm so glad. I'm so glad, Garnet!"

"Does she want me to come with her now?"

"Oh my Lord, no. Not in the late afternoon, there's too much going on. But early tomorrow morning. The place is quiet as a parsonage then."

Garnet twisted her handkerchief through her fingers. "Florinda, you're sure I'll be safe there, aren't you?"

"You'll be as safe," said Florinda, "as if you were locked up in the fort." She gave Garnet a one-sided smile. "Don't let Silky know I told you this. But the fact is, that establishment belongs to Silky. He wouldn't let—"

"Silky!"

"He doesn't want it known, so don't repeat it. I told you so you'd be sure nobody would bother you there. Silky and Estelle have been friends for years. They got acquainted in St. Louis when he was working the river-boats, and when he took the trail he brought her out here and set her up in business."

Garnet nodded slowly. Florinda gave her a knowing look.

"Now you're dying to ask," Florinda said with amusement, "if I have an investment in Estelle's outfit too. No, dearie, I haven't. I own half of this one, just as I told you before, and that's all. Is there anything else?"

Garnet shook her head. She could not help laughing at Florinda's shrewdness. "Tell Estelle," she said, "if somebody I can trust will walk over there with me, I'll bring Stephen to see Texas tomorrow morning. I'll be ready whenever she says."

"Silky will go with you, and he'll see to it that the house is empty of customers before you get there. Gee, Garnet, that's good of you. I'll tell him right away."

She went to call Silky from the gambling room. Garnet sat where she was. An odd little shiver ran up her back as though someone had touched her with an icicle. It was not that she was afraid to go to Estelle's. She was sure she ran no risk of the sort that would ordinarily have made her afraid to go inside any such house. But later she was to remember that shiver, and the vague disquiet that plagued her all evening and made her sleep restlessly that night. Remembering it, she wondered if there was any such thing as a hunch, or a forewarning, or anything that could have come out of the future to touch her with cold fingers and tell her not to go.

FORTY-TWO

"MISS GARNET," said Texas, "there's one or two little things I wish you'd tend to for me."

"Why of course, Texas," said Garnet. "What are they?"

Texas turned his head a little and smiled at her. She sat on the wall-bench at the head of his bed, while Stephen, curled up on the floor, was tearing up one of the straw animals Texas had made for him during the past summer. Texas held Garnet's hand in his as he spoke. His voice was weak, but the words were plain enough.

"I've got a few hides on deposit with Mr. Abbott. Tell him to pay up everything."

"Yes, Texas."

"And if there's any left over—" Texas smiled again as his eyes moved toward Stephen—"buy something for him."

"You're so good to him, Texas. But isn't there—isn't there anybody else?"

"No ma'am," said Texas. There was a pause. Texas stroked her hand. After a while he asked, "Miss Garnet, do you guess I could have a drink?"

"Why yes," said Garnet. "I'll pour it for you." She poured the drink from a bottle she had brought with her, and held Texas' head up so he could swallow. It was Florinda's best whiskey. Garnet had offered to pay for it, but Florinda had answered, "Not necessary, dear. Texas always keeps plenty of hides on the books."

Stephen toddled over and pulled at the not very clean blanket lying across Texas' broken body. Texas winced, though he tried to smile at the baby, and Garnet drew Stephen away. Stephen was tired and getting cross. She gave him some cold porridge from a pail she had brought, and at length Stephen curled up on his own blanket, which she had spread in a corner for him, and went to sleep.

Texas lay quietly. His bed had no sheets, but he had a pillow, and he seemed to be comfortable. The light was dim, for Garnet had closed the shutters; and though the sun was blazing outside, the thick adobe walls kept the room fairly cool. This was about all that could be said in its favor. Smells of garbage crept in through the cracks around the shutters, along with the other smells of hides and chili and unwashed Diggers that always hung over Los Angeles. By now Garnet was so used to the atmosphere that she did not often notice it. But here in this little cubbyhole at Estelle's the smells were thick and stale, as though they clung to the walls.

Besides the smells, the cracks let in streaks of sun. Garnet could see the dust in the air and the flaking whitewash on the walls; and over her head she saw tatters of cobweb dangling from the rafters.

466

The wall-curtains were faded at the folds and dingy at the hems. On the walls above the curtains hung two mirrors in gilt frames, and some pictures cut from old magazines that had filled up the chinks in M. Abbott's goods-boxes. The pictures were smudgy, and curling at the edges.

Garnet could hear ox-carts creaking and drivers shouting, men's talk and women's talk and the voices of children, and the rough drone of Digger water-sellers calling their trade. She did not often notice the noise either. But today she heard it, perhaps because the racket outside was in such contrast to the silence within. Estelle's girls were all asleep, and so, probably, was Estelle. Early this morning when Garnet had walked over here with Silky, Estelle had opened the door for them. Garnet had had only a glimpse of her. Silky, holding her elbow tight, had guided her straight through a dusky little passageway to this room. He had promised her that the house would be locked up until he himself came back to get her. Before leaving he had asked to see her Colt, to make sure it was ready for use. Nothing was going to happen, he assured her again, but a good Colt was a comforting thing to have. Silky did not approve of this visit.

Until she had actually entered the room where Texas lay, Garnet had not been sure that she was wise to come here. Her little cold shiver of yesterday had come back over and over during her wakeful night. But when she saw Texas, and the glow that broke over his face when she came in, her doubts went away. Maybe it was because she had not been sure before that Texas was really dying. But now she saw the green tinge of his face, the strange uncertainty of his eyes, the flutters of his hands, the limpness of the lower part of his body, which lay under the blanket like a bundle of weeds. Little as she knew about the look of coming death, she knew as though by some ancient instinct that this was not the look of life. With Stephen in her arms, she knelt on the dusty floor by the bed. For a moment Texas' hands fumbled on the blanket, then as he looked at them he got a better sense of direction. His hands moved toward her. He touched Stephen, and stroked Garnet's cheek with his hard dry fingers, whispering, "God bless you, Miss Garnet, God bless you."

Garnet had never sat with a person who was dying. Before leaving the saloon she had packed a basket, putting in the whiskey for Texas and the things that Stephen would need; and at the last minute she had put her Bible into the basket too. Now that Stephen was asleep, she picked up the Bible and asked bashfully, "Texas, would you like to have me read to you?"

Texas turned his head. Garnet had spoken shyly because she did not know whether or not he would welcome this. She did not know what his faith was, or even if he had any. But Texas smiled, murmuring, "You're very sweet, Miss Garnet." After a little silence he said, "You might read me the one about 'The Lord is my shepherd.' "

She read it to him. At first her voice was unsteady, for she was not used to reading aloud, and she was not at all used to a time like this. But she was glad he had asked for a psalm that she knew almost by heart, for it was easier to read than a less familiar passage would have been. When she had finished she saw that his eyes were closed, but after a moment he opened them, saying, "That's mighty pretty. Thank you." He was silent again, but after a little while he asked her, "Miss Garnet, do you reckon the Lord will have me?"

"Yes, Texas," she answered gently, "I'm sure He will."

Texas smiled a little. "You know," he said, "I think so too." He fumbled across the blanket again, feeling for her hand, and she slipped it into his. Texas said, "I don't mean I think I've been good or anything like that. I mean, I just think He'll have me anyway." He waited a moment to get his breath, and went on. "Before you got here, I had a sort of been talking to Him. I don't mean praying exactly. I wouldn't know how to make a real prayer. I mean I just *talked* to Him. And you know, I think it's all right."

She pressed his hand. "I think it's all right too, Texas."

Again there was a silence. Garnet wondered if there might not be something else he would like to have attended to on earth. When she had waited to let him rest, she asked if there was anybody he wanted her to write to. She thought Captain Brown would help her get a letter through. "Your mother, maybe?" she suggested.

"No ma'am, thank you. My mother died a long time ago."

"And you've no wife, Texas?"

"No ma'am, I've never been married. And my father's been gone since I was a little boy." Texas was silent a minute, then he went on. "My father died of a wound he got at Fort Bowyer. That was in 1814. I don't guess you were even born then."

"No, I was born in '26. I don't believe I know about Fort Bowyer."

"That was the fort guarding Mobile Bay," said Texas. "General Andrew Jackson was in command there, and the British attacked under Admiral Percy. But they didn't get inside Mobile. It was a good fight, and my father was a good soldier and he died like a hero."

So long a speech had made Texas tired. He tried to draw a deep breath, and winced at the pain of it. But after he had rested awhile he went on talking.

"So don't you bother about letters, Miss Garnet. I've got no family. Nor—friends either, I guess."

"You've got me, Texas," she said firmly.

"God bless your soul, Miss Garnet, I know it."

"And I'm not the only one," she told him with certainty. "Don't you remember all the lives you've saved on the desert?"

"Oh, I guess I've done a good turn now and then. But—" Texas' voice was very low. She had to bend her head to hear him. "But when a man thinks what he could have been. When I think what they expected of me. Stephen Austin himself putting his hand on my shoulder and saying, 'You'll be like your father, Ernest. It's boys like you who'll make Texas a great country.' And then to be no good."

He moved his head uneasily. But weak as he was, he wanted to talk.

"I never could let it alone," he said huskily. "I don't know why. The vows and the promises I made. And still I couldn't let it alone."

He went on, still talking in that low, husky voice. He said the men of his family had always been in the army. Ancestors of his had served in the colonial troops before the Revolution. Ever since he was born Texas had been meant for the army. When his father was killed at Fort Bowyer, Texas and his mother had gone to live with his uncle, his mother's brother. Texas was his mother's only child, and she had centered all her hopes in him. She was a venturesome soul, enthusiastic when her brother wanted to go pioneering with Stephen Austin. She wanted her son to be venturesome too, a hero like the rest of them.

It was a shame, said Texas, his being so no-count when he had so much to live up to. He was just not good enough.

They had given him every advantage. His mother had planned for him to go to West Point, but when he turned out to have such a turn for doctoring his uncle said West Point wasn't the place for him. Let the boy do what God meant him to do. Let him study medicine and surgery. Then he could go into the army. What was wrong with that? Army doctors were mighty useful.

But he couldn't let it alone. At first, they had called him a gay young blade. Then the older men began to warn him. He hadn't done anything serious. But if he didn't look out, one day it might get serious. And in the army, they warned him, it only needs to happen once.

And it happened, just as they had said it would. It happened when Texas was stationed at Fort Leavenworth.

He had been talking slowly, with long pauses between his lines. He stopped again here, and waited awhile to gather up his strength. But he wanted to finish his story. So at length he went on.

Well, one winter he was stationed at Fort Leavenworth. For months everything had been deadly dull. A small garrison, a remote outpost, a long hard winter. Life was a monotonous round: for the men, the same duties over and over; for the doctor, nothing but an occasional smashed finger or a cold in the head.

When you're on duty like that, what can you do with yourself? Mighty few books to read, you've run out of conversation long ago, you can't play cards all the time. And the weather is cold. If you take a few drinks to warm up, nobody thinks anything of it. Everybody has a drink now and then. If you take too many once in a while there's no harm done. It gives you a heavy head in the morning, but you've got nothing to do anyway.

But one night there was a sudden alarm. Indians were attacking the fort. The hard winter had lowered their food supplies and they wanted the stores of the white men.

The men sprang up from sleep and grabbed their guns. They were heavily outnumbered by the attackers, and in spite of the law forbidding white men to sell guns to the savages, these Indians were well armed.

Three men were injured early in the fight. Their wounds were not serious and the doctor should have been able to attend to them quickly. But the doctor's eyes were foggy and his hands fumbled. The doctor was drunk.

Texas told Garnet all about it.

The Indians had not taken the fort. But by sunrise, six men were dead and others were groaning in agony from wounds tended only by volunteers who had done the best they could in the doctor's place. Fourteen wounded men died later. Of course, some of them would have died anyway. But no matter what might or might not have happened, it was still true that when they had needed him the the doctor was drunk.

There was court-martial after that, and dishonorable discharge from the army.

"Miss Garnet," said Texas, "you're going to think I'm out of my mind when I say this. But I swear to you, ma'am, when it happened it was a kind of relief.

"It was like a man finally giving up a fight he had known all along he couldn't win. Nothing this bad could ever happen to me again.

"I had always known I wasn't good enough. I'd always had a feeling something would happen some day to give me away. And now it had happened. Of course it hurt. It hurt worse than I ever knew anything could hurt. But at least I didn't have to go on waiting for it. Things were easier on the trail. I felt kind of at home there. Nobody expected me to be any better than I was."

Texas was silent for a while, remembering. His tired brown eyes began to close. When he spoke again he seemed to be talking to himself. "Funny. Mighty funny. Who'd have thought the army would come to California?" He rested and got his breath. "It sure gave me a strange feeling, seeing the boys march in." Texas turned his head as though looking for her, and she bent nearer. He said, "Miss Garnet, you know something?"

"What, Texas?"

"There's a couple of men here who were at Fort Leavenworth that winter," Texas confided. "I don't think they know me, though. One of 'em's a friend of yours. Name of Roger Brown. Fine man. Trusty as daylight."

Texas closed his eyes again. But though he looked so tired he looked peaceful too.

After a while Stephen woke up. As he was rested now and wanted to play, Garnet played with him, keeping him as quiet as she could. Texas opened his eyes and lay watching them, smiling tenderly. At length when Stephen was content to sit on the floor with his straw animals, Garnet came back to the wall-bench.

"That's a fine little boy," Texas said. "Miss Garnet, you don't mind if I pretended he was part mine, do you?"

"I'm proud that you like him so much, Texas," she said. "I'll tell him when he's old enough to understand."

Stephen made his way to her and she held out her hand. He pulled himself up, and she put an arm around him. Leaning against her knee he prattled a lot of nonsense syllables, while Texas watched him lovingly.

Suddenly the door opened. There was so much noise outside that Garnet had not heard anybody come into the house. Her arm still around Stephen, she looked up, thinking this was Silky here to take her home and feeling some surprise that Silky, with all his fine manners, should have burst in without knocking. The door was near the foot of Texas' bed, facing the bench, so that as she raised her head she looked straight at the man who stood in the doorway. The man was not Silky. He was Charles.

Charles was speaking over his shoulder to someone Garnet could not see. "I was right," he was saying. "This is the room. He's in here."

"Looking for me?" Texas murmured.

Garnet had sprung to her feet, indignant that Charles should have come to annoy Texas now. She moved along the bedside to stand between them. "Texas is very ill, Charles," she said urgently. "Please don't disturb him."

Stephen was peeking out from behind her skirts. Charles said nothing. He bent as though to pick up the baby, and Stephen started back with a little cry. Garnet stroked his head, saying,

"Don't try to take him, Charles. He's not used to being handled by strangers." As she spoke Stephen held up his arms to her and she started to take him up herself. But as her hands touched the two sides of his body Charles snatched at him. Stephen cried out in fright. With an instinctive movement of defense Garnet grabbed him in both arms and stood holding him to her breast as tightly as her muscles would clamp on him, but as she took a step back from Charles she heard him say,

"It's no use, Garnet. You may as well give him to me. I've given you every chance and now I have done with you."

Garnet became aware of a lot of details at once—doors opening and feet scampering, and girls' voices shrill with fright, and a man's voice curtly ordering, "Stand back, sisters, and be quiet! This is serious."

Charles was saying, "I had hopes of changing you. But when you were found to be in this house, it was obvious that you were no fit guardian for a child."

Garnet gave a gasp of rage. Stephen was crying, half in fear and half in pain, for she was clutching him with such force that she was nearly breaking his bones. Behind her on the bed she heard Texas say, his voice full of fury in spite of his weakness, "You God-damned yellow-livered scoundrel."

Charles was cold and sure. Two points of light were reflected in his eyes. When he spoke again his voice was not loud but she heard him clearly, though Stephen was crying and Texas was swearing, his wrath made even more violent by his sense of helplessness, and in the hall Estelle's voice was shouting in Spanish to the girls. Charles was saying,

"The brig Lydia Belle is sailing shortly for Boston. My wife and I will go to Boston to wind up the affairs of Mrs. Hale's first husband. We are going to take my brother's son with us—"

"Are you out of your mind?" Garnet cried. Her whole body had begun to tremble with anger. Charles went right on past her words.

"—and leave him there to be sent to school, so he will grow up under good moral influences instead of the environment you prefer."

Garnet could hear Stephen and Texas and Estelle; from beyond the house she could hear the creak of carts and the lowing of oxen. But she heard Charles' words as though he were speaking against a background of silence. Rage was sharpening her eyes and ears, and giving a sense of rare strength to her muscles. Charles went on without a pause.

"We have no power to change you. But we can and will take that boy away from you."

"Oh no you will not," said Garnet. She was so angry that she had no sense of being afraid. She wondered how he had known she was here, but at the moment it did not matter. She was clutching her baby to her and speaking through clenched teeth. "You won't take him. Not if I have to tear your nasty little body to pieces. If you put your hands on my child—"

With a smile of contempt, Charles interrupted her. "Your temper is not pretty, Garnet. Nor will it do you any good. I am not acting on my own responsibility. I have an order from the colonel in command of Los Angeles, giving that child to me. Here it is. Do you see?"

He was holding out a paper. His eyes were fixed on her. They were like two hot needles boring into her forehead. She could almost feel the sizzling sensation. She could not move any farther back from him, for the backs of her legs were already pressing against the bed where Texas lay, and she could not get out of the room because Charles himself stood in the doorway. Behind her she heard Texas say something, she did not know what. A wave

473

of heat started at the back of her neck and went up into her head and swept down through her body. In her arms Stephen was still crying. Scared and half smothered by the fierce grip she was giving him, he began to kick at her, trying to get free. Garnet pushed her hand down to hold his surprisingly strong little legs. Her fingers touched the holster at her belt, and she felt the handle of her Colt revolver.

Instantly she knew what she was going to do. It was as simple as walking down a straight road in the sunlight. She saw Charles: the paper in his hand, his smile of sneering triumph, his eyebrows like two caterpillars above his terrible piercing eyes. She saw him take a step toward her and put his hands on Stephen to pull him away from her; she felt her own arm tighten savagely to hold Stephen to herself, she heard Stephen yell with fright and she felt his hard angry little kicks, and then, it seemed quite without any deliberate effort of her own, the pistol fired twice in her hand. There was an acrid smell in her nostrils, and in front of her Charles was crumpling up, slowly, and crumpling up with him were all his dreams of greatness. She stood staring at what she had done, and all she could think of in that first instant was that she was sorry she had made such a mess.

FORTY-THREE

TERRIFIED BY THE NOISE, Stephen was fighting her with all his might. Garnet stood half stunned, her left arm holding him and her right arm at her side, the revolver still in her hand. It seemed like a long time, though she knew later that it was only a fraction of a second before she felt Texas' hand take her wrist from behind and his other hand take the pistol out of her hand. At the moment she was only vaguely aware that he was doing it. She was watching, with fascinated horror, the thick slow stream of blood that was creeping toward her from the huddle on the floor.

At the same time the girls were screaming, and the men who had been keeping them quiet were exclaiming in loud shocked voices. There were sounds of feet hurrying this way. Garnet heard them, but she did not know she had heard them until the voices of two men burst out together, one saying, "Look, it's Mr. Hale!" and the other, "Who did this? Who did it, I say?"

She looked up. In front of her were two boys in the uniforms of army privates, one of them standing in the doorway and the other bent over the body of Charles. They were very young; the thought flashed through her head that they were too young to see things like this. Before she could pull her senses together she heard Texas say, more loudly than he had spoken all day, "I did it, boys."

That roused her. She wheeled around. "Texas!" she cried. "What are you saying?"

"Wish you'd—get her out of here, boys," Texas murmured. One of the privates was taking the pistol from him, and as Garnet started to protest again Texas added shakily, "She's about to—have hysterics. Make her—shut up."

"Shut up, lady," one of the boys said obediently. They both turned to keep out the people who were crowding around the door. There were girls in dingy wrappers, and Estelle with a shawl around her and her hair in crimping-pins, and half a dozen idlers who had been loafing in the neighborhood and had come running at the sound of the shots. Evidently the door had not been locked after Charles came in. They were all screeching and gasping and asking questions. The door opened inward, and the boys could not have closed it without dragging Charles' body aside, so they planted themselves on the threshold and locked their arms, shouting to the others to stay out of here. Under cover of the noise Garnet knelt by the bed and spoke to Texas.

"Don't try to say you did it!" she exclaimed. "I'll tell them—"

"No, please! Miss Garnet—" Texas' weak voice shook with eagerness—"Miss Garnet, let me do this."

"I can't, Texas!"

"I would have done it if I'd had the Colt," said Texas. "They can't—do anything to me. I won't—last long enough." He reached to fumble with Stephen's hair. "You—you take care of the little fellow."

From beyond the doorway Garnet heard Estelle giving orders. In her coarse rasping voice, changing from bad Spanish to bad English and back again, she was telling them to get out of the way of somebody who was coming in. Later Garnet was to remember Estelle's self-possession and admire it. Now she was hardly conscious of anything but what Texas was saying.

475

"When they ask you, tell them I did it," he whispered. He saw her clamp her teeth hard on her lip, still not wanting to obey him, and he added, "It would mean a lot to me. Miss Garnet, won't you please?"

"Yes," she whispered back. She pressed the baby's head down on her shoulder so he could not see the dreadful motionless thing that used to be Charles. "God reward you for this, Texas."

"Thank you, Miss Garnet," he said softly.

Garnet could not answer. She had killed Charles, and when she did it she had felt steady and unafraid; but now that she had done it she was feeling a wild reaction made of a hundred emotions all at war with one another. The only idea she could think of clearly was that if Texas was wrong, if he was not dying, she would not let him suffer for her sake. But if he was going to die he could take the blame, because the colonel had already issued an order giving Stephen to Charles, and if he found she had added murder to the list of her other sins he would never let her see Stephen again. She got up from the floor, her arms aching with the weight of the baby. Estelle's commands had been effective. The girls and the street-loafers alike were slinking back from the door, clearing the way for another man in a blue uniform. As he reached the doorway the two privates parted to let him into the room. The lines of light from the window fell on him, and Garnet gave a sob of thankfulness when she recognized Captain Brown.

She heard one of the privates say, "Yes sir, it's Mr. Hale. Yes sir, he's dead. Shot twice. He told us to wait by the front door and we didn't see nothing. But that sick man in the bed there, he says he did it. Here's his gun, sir."

Captain Brown came in. He did not seem surprised to see Garnet. Bowing to her as courteously as ever, he said, "How do you do, Mrs. Hale. If you will excuse me, I think I had better speak first to—this man." She felt a flash of gratitude to him for still pretending not to know Texas' name.

She had to step aside to make room for Captain Brown to get to the bedside. Her skirt brushed Charles' body. With a shudder she looked at it again. The body lay sprawled on the floor, face down. One hand was flung out toward her, and under the fingers was a paper still half folded. Garnet felt a spasm in her throat. That was the paper Charles had been holding out to her when she fired the gun, the colonel's order that she was to give Stephen up. Charles was dead, but the order might still be in force.

476

She looked around. Captain Brown had bent over Texas to hear what he was saying. The privates at the door were facing outward so they could keep back anybody who might want to come in. Nobody was noticing her. She stooped quickly and got the paper, crumpling it in her hand as she stood up. Before anybody had looked her way she slipped it inside her chemise. Stephen was crying miserably and her arms were nearly numb with holding him. Sinking down on the bench she tried to pet him so he would stop crying. Nearly as tired as she was, Stephen finally got quiet and let his head drop against her shoulder. Garnet heard Texas' voice. He was so weak now that he had to stop between every few words to rest.

"Should be—hanged no doubt. But if you want to—hang me— you'd better be—damn quick about it—see why—pull down the blanket."

Captain Brown drew down the blanket. As he did so he gave a start, and Garnet gasped in horror. The effort Texas had been making had caused one of his injuries to break open, and he lay in a splotch of blood that was slowly spreading over the mattress. "Get him a doctor!" Garnet burst out.

"Yes, yes, of course," said Captain Brown. "But first I need something to stop the bleeding." He looked around. There was no sheet on the bed. "Give me one of your petticoats," he said. "Quick—this is no time to be modest."

Garnet put Stephen on the floor. "All right. Stand in front of the baby so he won't see—that thing over there."

She drew up the skirt of her dress, took off her top petticoat, and handed it to Captain Brown. He bent over Texas again. She heard the cloth tearing.

"Can I help you?" she asked.

"No, I think this will hold till our doctor can get here from the barracks. I'll have one of the men go for him." He added, "And as soon as I give some necessary orders, Mrs. Hale, I will see you home." He went to the door and began speaking to the men.

Drawing Stephen close to her, Garnet knelt by the bed again and put her hand on Texas' forehead. His skin was clammy. As he felt the touch of her hand his eyelids fluttered, but he said nothing. It was as though he had used all his strength and now had none left. "I'll remember you, Texas," she said softly, "and love you, as long as I live. And I'll never, never let Stephen forget you."

Texas smiled a little, but he did not try to answer. She stroked his damp hair back from his forehead.

She could hear Captain Brown giving orders. To her surprise, there were now a dozen soldiers instead of only two. News of the shooting had got around quickly, and they had been sent to keep order. Captain Brown told them no one was to enter the building except the army doctor who had been sent for. Anything the sick man said was to be written down, and he appointed one soldier to sit by the bed for that purpose. He gave instructions to two others about disposal of Charles' body. Then at length he turned back to the room.

"I will see you home now, Mrs. Hale," he said.

"All right," said Garnet. He gave her his hand and she stood up, with Stephen in her arms.

He glanced around the room and took up the Bible from where it lay on the wall-bench. "Is this yours, Mrs. Hale?"

"Yes. But leave it for Texas if he wants it."

He glanced compassionately at the bed. Texas was lying with his eyes closed, his chest barely moving as he breathed. Captain Brown said in a low voice, "I don't think he's able to read. Shall we go now?"

Garnet agreed. She paused by the bed. "Goodby, Texas. Thank you for being such a good man."

He made no movement of response. She never knew whether he heard her or not.

His hand on her elbow, Captain Brown guided her through the doorway, along the hall where half a dozen girls with wide scared eyes watched her as she passed, and out by the door where she had entered this morning. Groups of stragglers stood around, staring at the house. On seeing Captain Brown's uniform they moved aside to let him and Garnet go by.

They walked side by side among the scattered adobe houses. Garnet's legs felt heavy. There was a bloodstain on the hem of her skirt where it had brushed Charles' body, and she was revoltingly conscious of it. Stephen felt as if he weighed a ton. The sun was beating on her head. She was panting as she walked, and she could feel the sweat trickling down her face and neck and legs. Clouds of dust blew up and settled stickily on her. Captain Brown asked, "Don't you want me to carry the baby, Mrs. Hale?"

Garnet shook her head. "Thank you, no. He's been frightened so much already—and he's—not used to you." Her breaths were so short that the words jerked out of her.

It seemed like a long walk through the heat, though actually it took them hardly ten minutes to reach the saloon. Captain Brown led her around to the side, and finding the kitchen door bolted he knocked and called out who he was. The door was opened by Mickey, smiling as engagingly as usual. Garnet heard Isabel's voice thanking heaven that the dear baby was safe. She rushed up to take him. Since he knew her, Stephen went to her willingly, and Garnet dropped her aching arms.

As Isabel took the baby, the door from the bar opened and Florinda rushed in. She held out her hand to shake the hand of Captain Brown.

"Captain," she said heartily, "you're a real gent. I always said so, ask Garnet if I didn't. Will you have a drink of whiskey on the house?"

This was the rarest compliment Florinda ever paid anybody, but Captain Brown said no. He had to go back to Estelle's and complete his inquiry into what had happened there.

Garnet only half heard them. Dazed with fatigue and reaction, she had sunk down on the wall-bench. Isabel was hugging Stephen and kissing him, to his great discomfort, but as long as he was safe Garnet was to tired to care whether he was comfortable or not. She thought she had never felt so used up.

After a brief conversation with Florinda, Captain Brown came over to where she sat.

"I shall come back later to get a statement from you, Mrs. Hale," he said.

"Yes," said Garnet. She made herself raise her eyes to his.

"Do not leave this building," said Captain Brown. "Do not go back to work at the bar until you have permission. Do not discuss today's events with anybody. These are orders, Mrs. Hale."

"Yes," she said. "I understand."

Captain Brown put his hand on her shoulder, looking into her eyes significantly. "Don't be nervous," he said. "You have nothing to be afraid of."

He crossed the room again and spoke to Florinda. Garnet sat where she was, staring at the opposite wall and not seeing it. Only one idea was clear in her mind, but this was bright as a flame. There was one more thing she had to do. She had to do it now, because she had a curious feeling that the strength was slipping out of her and if she did not do it now she never would. Captain Brown had said she had nothing to be afraid of, but he did not know about that piece of paper she had taken out of Charles' hand. She had to get rid of that. Charles was dead, but Lydia Hale might still want Stephen for the sake of keeping Stephen's property, and if that written order was still in existence Lydia might be able to take him. Garnet could feel the twist of paper scratching her skin between her breasts.

Captain Brown had gone. Garnet stood up and went to kneel before the hearth. On such a hot day nobody had tried to keep up the fire after the cooking was done, and there was nothing in the fireplace but a pile of ashes. She poked among them with a stick until she found a few that were glowing still. Taking out the paper, she dropped it carefully among them. The paper caught fire and made a flame like an arrowhead above the ashes.

Garnet watched it. As she saw the paper burn, it seemed to her that now things were all right. There was nothing else she had to do. She sat there on the floor by the hearth, watching the little arrowhead of flame leap and then fade. Watching it, she had the most delicious feeling of emptiness, as if her spirit had left her body and gone visiting.

Then all of a sudden she felt a firm arm across her shoulders, and a burning sensation on her tongue. Florinda's voice was saying, "Drink this. Drink it all."

Florinda was giving her a sharp strong brandy. Garnet swallowed it. Reluctantly she felt her strength coming back. "What happened?" she asked.

"You started turning green, dearie. Gave me quite a scare."

Garnet looked around toward the table. Isabel sat there with Stephen on her lap, feeding him spoonfuls of something out of a bowl. Stephen was gurgling happily.

Garnet looked down at her hands, linked in her lap. The fingers were as steady as they had been when she fired the gun at Charles. She was surprised at herself, because although she had killed Charles she did not feel any remorse at all. She only felt a great welcome sense that she was done with him.

Florinda still sat there beside her.

Garnet turned her head. Their eyes met. Florinda was smiling at her with a deep quiet understanding. Garnet asked, "Florinda, do you know—"

"Don't talk about it. I know Charles is dead, and Texas said he shot him. And Captain Brown told me you were not to talk about it at all. So be quiet."

Garnet reached out and gave Florinda's hand a squeeze. How good it was to have such a friend.

Later she found that Florinda had been an even better friend than she had known. It was not a lucky chance, but Florinda's doing, that Captain Brown had been there to take charge.

For though Florinda had approved of Garnet's going to sit with Texas, after Garnet had gone Florinda began to be worried about her. Silky had promised she would be safe; Estelle had promised to bolt the doors and let nobody in while Garnet was there; but Florinda was still not at ease. So while she was serving drinks to some officers of the New York Regiment, she remarked to them that she had a message for Captain Brown, an important message concerning Garnet. She put a good deal of urgency into that expert voice of hers, and it was not long before Captain Brown came to the bar to say he had heard she was looking for him. Florinda told him where Garnet had gone and why. Captain Brown, who was conservative in his ideas, was appalled. He wanted to go and make her leave Estelle's house at once. Florinda begged him not to interfere, but she asked him if he would please keep an eye on the place, just to make sure everything was all right. Captain Brown said he certainly would.

Florinda had not expected Charles to learn Garnet's whereabouts, though she thought later that maybe she should have. For in Los Angeles there was a group of professional gossips who made a living out of carrying tales. They had been started off by the American army. Eager to forestall another uprising like the one led by Varela last year, the Yankees had offered to pay for reports of anybody who was plotting insurrection. The town soon developed a class of idlers who strolled about keeping their ears open, and then went off to report any chance bit of talk that suggested dislike of the new people. The Yankees paid, and investigated; and the gossip-sellers thought they were assured of easy incomes for life.

But this sort of thing had been going on all summer and there was still no rebellion to justify it. The Yankee officers were getting tired of paying for rumors that came to nothing. The talebearers were having to look around for new sources of revenue. Among a people as talkative as the Angelenos, everybody knew something about everybody else. When Charles came to town he always brought servants with him, and though they kept quiet in his presence they talked freely elsewhere. It was pretty generally known in Los Angeles that Charles and Garnet were not friends. So, on this early morning, when one of the tattlers saw Garnet going into Estelle's, he ambled off to the back door of Señor Escobar's house. Here he found a servant of Señor Hale, and he sent word to Señor Hale that he had news. He told his news to Charles, got paid for it, and went off to a wineshop, happy in the feeling that though it was not yet nine o'clock in the morning he had already done a good day's work.

Charles at once went to see an officer of the army of occupation. He said a report had reached him that his sister-in-law had been seen going into the notorious house operated by this woman Estelle, and he wanted a military escort to go into the place with him, so if she was there he could get her out. Charles represented to the officer that Garnet very likely did not know what sort of place it was and had been lured there on some pretext. He had no trouble getting two soldiers assigned to him. He also had no trouble getting the door opened to him when the girls, waked from sleep, saw that the soldiers had guns and were in earnest.

Garnet heard all this from Captain Brown. The military authorities were making a full investigation of the episode, for Charles was too rich and prominent a man for his death to be dismissed without a study of what had brought it about. Captain Brown came to see her on the evening of that day. He had only a few minutes to spare, but he told her briefly that Texas had rallied sufficiently to repeat his statement that he had fired the gun. Captain Brown said he would state this in his official report.

"And Texas?" Garnet asked.

"Texas is not conscious, Mrs. Hale. The doctor does not expect him to live through the night."

She thanked him and he went out.

Garnet went to bed, but she could not sleep. She had forgotten what a racket came up from the bar, and looked wonderingly at Stephen, sound asleep in the crib Texas had made for him. At last she put a shawl around her and went and sat on the staircase. She was still there when Florinda finally closed the saloon and came upstairs.

Florinda paused on the stairs and smiled down at her. "Still feel like you're all tied up in a knot, dearie?"

Garnet nodded. "Florinda, you know about Charles, don't you?"

"Yes, dear."

"Does Silky?"

"No. Who would tell him?"

"Who told you?"

"Captain Brown. Not in so many words, but I got the idea."

"Tell me what happened here this morning."

Florinda set her candlestick on the floor and sat down by Garnet. "Well, I was at the bar with José when somebody ran in to say there'd been a shooting at Estelle's. Other fellows were coming in, saying this one and that one had been shot, but they finally agreed it was Charles Hale, and they were giggling at the idea of the noble Charles being caught dead in a place like that."

Florinda clasped her hands around her knees and went on.

"I was about to go for Silky and tell him he and I had to get you out of there, when the boys saw you pass with Captain Brown and I ran into the kitchen to meet you. You were sinking on the bench like a busted balloon. Captain Brown came over and talked to me in a quick whisper. He said, 'Take care of Mrs. Hale. See to it that she speaks to nobody till I come back.' He sure did sound like a boss giving orders. I told him I'd look out for you. I said, 'Did she kill Charles?' He gave me a look that went clean through me. He said, 'The man who calls himself Texas has confessed that he shot Charles Hale. Texas is dying.' And I said, 'Captain Brown, Texas is a great man. And so are you.' He gave my shoulder a grip that nearly broke my collar-bone and then he went striding out like a general about to win a war."

Garnet drew a long breath. Florinda put her arm around Garnet's waist.

"Feel better, dear?"

"Yes. I'm more loosened up."

"Good. Go on back to bed, and sleep as long as you can. I'll tell Isabel to slip in and get Stephen so you won't have to wake up."

Garnet went back to bed. She was so tired that at last she did fall asleep, and in spite of the street-noises she slept late.

The next day she heard that Texas was dead. She spent a long time curled up on the wall-bench in a corner of the kitchen, thinking about him. Her own emotions still surprised her. At home and at school, she had been taught what she ought to feel about the various experiences of life. She knew that when a dear friend died, she ought to be sorry. She ought to shed tears. But she was not sorry about Texas and she was not shedding any tears. She had felt

483

a great affection for him and she was going to miss him, but she did not think he had been happy in this world. Certainly he had shown no regret at leaving it. She hoped he had changed it for a better one. And she was not going to pretend any sorrow about him, any more than she was going to pretend any guilt about Charles. What she did feel was a deep gratitude to Texas for having spared her the consequences of Charles' death, and she hoped heaven would reward him since she could not.

For he had spared her, completely. As Captain Brown had been the first officer on the scene, he was put in charge of the investigation. Several days later he brought her a copy of his report. According to this, Mrs. Hale had gone to Estelle's house to wait upon a dying man who had been kind to her. Charles Hale, not knowing why she was there, had gone with two soldiers to get her. The soldiers, left on guard, had heard shots and had rushed in to see Charles on the floor, beyond help, and a Colt revolver in Texas' hand. When they asked who had shot Mr. Hale, Texas had replied without hesitation that he had. He had repeated this several times.

Garnet and Captain Brown sat on the wall-bench in the kitchen. They were alone, for he had said he wanted to question her in private. She read the report. When she had finished she was silent for some time. Captain Brown was waiting for her to speak. At length she asked,

"What do you want me to do now, Captain Brown?"

"I want you to sign a statement I have here. The men who heard Texas' confession have all said so in writing. This statement simply says you saw Texas shoot Mr. Hale, as he said he did."

Captain Brown laid the paper in front of her, and put a pen and bottle of ink by her hand. Garnet said,

"Your report doesn't give any reason why Texas shot him."

"I don't know why he shot him," said Captain Brown. "Texas was dying. Since nobody seems to know of any quarrel he had with Charles Hale, we can only assume that he was not in his right mind."

He was speaking to her as formally as if they were barely acquainted with each other. Throughout this affair he had been speaking to her like that. He added,

"Will you be good enough to sign this statement now, Mrs. Hale?"

Garnet picked up the pen. It was not a good pen. The quill had

484

been cut a long time ago, and since then the point had worn down till it was blunt and uneven. Looking at the worn point, she said,

"Captain Brown, hasn't it occurred to you to wonder if Texas was strong enough to lift that gun?"

Captain Brown took out his watch. "I'm sorry, Mrs. Hale, but I haven't time to discuss this any further. Will you please sign that paper and be done with it?"

She signed her name. The pen spluttered and sent out some drops of ink to speckle the paper.

"Thank you," said Captain Brown. He picked up the sheet of paper, decided to wait for it to dry, and laid it down again. As he did so he gave her a gentle sort of smile. "The investigation is closed, Mrs. Hale," he said.

Garnet looked straight at him. "Now do you want me to tell you what happened?" she asked.

"If you like. You don't have to." His smile had a flicker of humor, very different from his formal gravity of the past few days. "But first, now that I'm speaking unofficially, I'd like to tell you something."

"Yes?" said Garnet.

"I should advise you," said Captain Brown, "to lead an absolutely open life. You are the worst actress I ever saw."

He was so simple and strong. Garnet said,

"It's like a weight on me. I'll feel better if I talk to you."

"All right. Go ahead."

She told him about Charles and how he had tried to take Stephen for the sake of Stephen's inheritance. Finally she told him how Charles had come to her at Estelle's and had thrust that paper at her, and how she had shot him when he was trying to force Stephen out of her arms.

"I burnt the paper in the fireplace," said Garnet. "I thought my head was very clear, but now I don't think it was, because I didn't realize that Mrs. Charles Hale could probably get another order like that from Colonel Stevenson if she wanted it."

She had been speaking with determined calmness, but when she got this far a shudder ran over her nerves. Captain Brown put his hand over hers.

"I don't think you need to be distressed on that score, Mrs. Hale," he said.

"Don't I?" she exclaimed. "Why not?"

485

"Did you read what was written on that paper," he asked, "before you burnt it up?"

She shook her head.

He smiled at her reassuringly. "If you had read it, I think you would have found it was a receipt from a trading post, or something like that."

Garnet had started violently. "What? Do you mean—" Her voice choked with thankfulness.

"I am sure," he went on, "that Colonel Stevenson never issued any such order. In the first place I don't think he has the authority; in the second place, I know him well enough to say he wouldn't do it. Besides, when would he have written it? He didn't see Charles Hale that morning. The two privates who escorted Mr. Hale were assigned by a lieutenant named Fletcher."

Garnet let out a sigh. "Oh, thank you! I should have thought of that last myself. But I didn't."

"My dear girl," said Captain Brown, "after what you've been through, you're rather remarkable to be able to think at all."

Garnet's head dropped forward wearily till her chin touched her chest. She did not answer.

Captain Brown pressed her hand. "Charles Hale stuck a paper under your nose, counting on the fact that you would be too terrified to see what was written on it. Then by the time you found that Colonel Stevenson had issued no such order, Charles would have been on his way to Boston with your baby."

Garnet did not raise her head. She felt limp all over. She had done her best to be strong and calm. But it seemed to her that everything that had happened since she left New York had been something else to wear down her strength. And then she heard Captain Brown's voice, comforting and very gentle.

"Won't you let me take you home, Garnet?"

She never did know quite how it happened. But she found herself leaning against him with a quiet confidence. His arms were around her, and he kissed her lips and her eyes and the locks of hair on her temples, and he was saying,

"You've been as brave as ten armies, but you don't have to fight any more. Let me take care of you."

He said a good deal more than this, though she was too tired and too astonished to be sure of the separate words. But she did understand their meaning, and their meaning was dignity and security and peace. He was offering to give her back everything she had missed so desperately in these years of exile. And more than this, he was offering her a warm lasting love.

FORTY-FOUR

GARNET THOUGHT long and hard about Captain Brown.

She had asked him to give her time. Of course he would, Captain Brown agreed. He understood that she was in no state now to make up her mind about anything. But he begged her to remember that he had had time already to think about her, and he loved her very much.

She was not in love with him. She could not pretend to herself that she was. Garnet had never had any talent for believing what she knew was not so. But on that first day when he had asked her to marry him, she had thought of the old comparison of the storm-tossed sailor who saw a safe harbor at last. She had felt just like that.

As they talked to each other, that day and again and again in the days that followed, her sense of safety with him increased. He loved her, and what he felt was no boyish infatuation. He was thirty-five years old, and he was not light-minded. He was not an exciting man nor a brilliant man, but he was a good man. He was kind, he was generous, he had clear principles of right and wrong and he did his best to live up to them. And Garnet reflected that while these might not be romantic qualities, they were mighty fine traits to be sure of in the man who wanted you to live with him for the rest of your life. After tumbling around among so many nerve-racking uncertainties, she did so yearn for something firm and secure.

And he would give her, not only safety, but safety among the dear familiar things that she missed so much. New York was his home, as it was hers, and he meant to go back there when the war was over. He was a man of her own world. He knew a good many of the families she knew, they had the whole background of their lives in common. He told her frankly how she could expect to live as his wife. They would not be rich, but he could give her all the comforts and a good many of the luxuries of living. She would have a home like the one she had left; she would shop again at Stewart's and go to plays at the Park Theater and concerts at Castle Garden; she would have love and dignity and leisure, and uneventful peace.

She had plenty of time to think, for he had told her not to go back to the bar for a month. He thought it wise for her to stay out of the saloon until the talk about Charles' death had had time to quiet down. That was what he said. But she knew that in less than a month he hoped she would have promised to marry him, so he would have the right to tell her never to work at the bar again.

But the more she thought of Captain Brown, the more the mischievous imp of her spirit would make her think of John.

She thought of both men, and thought and thought, until she was worn out with thinking. Here was Roger Brown, who loved her, and there was John Ives, who said, "We're both grown up. So let's be honest. You know as well as I do that 'love' is a lot of moonshine."

But she did not love Roger Brown. She had found out what it meant to love a man. And she did love John. In spite of her conviction that he would get tired of her and break her heart if she gave him a chance, she loved him and she wanted him. It was worse because she did not know if he still wanted her. She had not heard from him since Pablo brought her that note from him four months ago, the note in answer to which she had angrily scribbled, "I won't have any lukewarm milktoast kind of marriage and I won't have that kind of man." Remembering her letter, she could not be surprised that she had not heard from him again. As she thought of it she let her sewing fall into her lap. She was in the kitchen, alone but for Stephen playing on the floor. She rested her arm on the table and put her head down into the bend of her elbow, whispering, "Oh God in heaven, Roger Brown does love me, and he can give me everything I want. Can't You please, please make me love him just a little?"

Later that day, during the time for siesta, she had a talk with Florinda. Florinda could not advise her and would not try. But she listened with sympathy. Garnet told her all the reasons why she wanted to marry Captain Brown and the one reason why she did not. Talking out the problem made it clearer to herself. She thought now that she would be wise to marry him. She had often heard people say that if there had to be a difference of affection between a husband and wife, it was better that the man feel the greater love at the start. A woman's life nearly always centered around her home and family, and if she had a devoted husband her love for him was sure to increase as time went on.

It seemed to Garnet that people were right when they said this. It would be romantic foolishness on her part not to take so fine a man while she had the chance.

In the evening she put on a fresh dress and took her sewing down to the kitchen. It was nearly time for supper. Mickey stirred up the fire and put on the beef and the pot of beans, and leaving them to cook he went to collect the used cups and glasses from the bar. Garnet gave Stephen his porridge and sat down to play with him until he got sleepy.

Mickey came in from the bar, carrying a tray. Setting it on the table, he came over to her, his hands tucked into his sleeves and his pigtail bobbing. "Miss Golnet."

She smiled back at him. "Yes, Mickey?"

Mickey beamed. "Miss Flinda say Blute."

"Blute?" Garnet repeated. "The Handsome Brute?" She dropped Stephen's hand and sprang up. "Did she say anything else, Mickey?"

Mickey smiled placidly. "She say damfool," he returned.

"Stephen, do be quiet," Garnet exclaimed. She caught herself and smiled at him remorsefully, patting his head. "Is the Brute here, Mickey?"

Mickey did not need to answer, for the door from the bar opened again and in walked the Handsome Brute, his coat covered with dust and his chin aglow with a stubble of bright golden beard. In his fist was a bottle of wine. Putting it on the table the Brute strode over to her, lifted her by the waist till her face was level with his, and kissed her cheek. "You are much too thin," he remarked as he set her down, "but I love you just the same."

Garnet had not thought about getting thin, but she realized that in the past few weeks she probably had. The Brute spoke to Stephen, gave him a toy bird made of bright-colored feathers, and returned his attention to Garnet.

"I am tired and thirsty and hungry," he announced. "I have ridden all the way from Santa Barbara. That is ninety miles. Have you got something to eat?"

"In a few minutes, it's on the fire now. Oh Brute, I'm so glad to see you! Here's your wine, drink it while the meat cooks."

The Brute went toward the fireplace. "I have brought you a

letter from John," he said over his shoulder, as calmly as though he were observing that it had been a warm day.

He was at the fireplace now, and had taken his knife out of its sheath. The beef was still nearly raw, a fact that troubled the Brute not at all. He cut off a chunk, whistled as it burnt his fingers, and wrapping one of his beautiful handkerchiefs around the end of the chunk, proceeded to tear off red pieces with his teeth. Garnet's knees had gone weak under her. Holding herself up with one hand on the table, she demanded,

"Brute, give me my letter!"

His mouth was too full for speech. With his left elbow, he made a gesture that she did not understand. She cried,

"You big lout, don't you ever think about anything but eating? Did you say you had a letter for me? Where is John?"

By this time the Brute could speak. "I am sorry, Garnet. I was so hungry I did not think. John is in Santa Barbara. He had a fall, riding."

"A fall? John rides like an Indian!"

"Yes, but the gully was too wide for the horse to jump. John was coming down here to punch you in the face."

"Brute, what are you talking about?"

The Brute was eating again. "He said he was coming to punch you in the face. It is in my left-hand pocket. Not your face, the letter. You get it out, my hands are all dripping with beef-juice."

He gestured with his elbow again and she began to rummage in his pocket. She found another handkerchief, and a bow of red ribbon from a girl's hair and a string of beads from her neck, and another knife in a case, and a package of salt, and two papers. One paper was a receipt for hides. The other was the one she wanted.

It was folded, and worn from being carried in the Brute's pocket with all his other trash. Garnet's hands shook as she unfolded it. The writing looked all strange and lop-sided. For a moment she thought her eyes were not focusing right, then she realized that what she was seeing was the fault of the letter itself. The words were printed, and they straggled all over the page like the exercise of a child just learning to write.

DAMN YOU WHAT DO YOU MEAN

BY CALLING ME

LUKEWARM MILKTOAST

WAIT TILL I GET MY STRENGTH BACK

ILL SHOW YOU

JOHN

Garnet dropped on the bench. Her breaths were short and fast as though she had been running. Her hands were shaky, and her eyes were not behaving themselves. Nothing outside her was clear. But within her it was all as plain and bright as noon. John wanted her. That was all she needed to know. She felt such a bubbling up of joy that she thought she had never known what it meant to be happy till now.

Then the things around her began to come back into their normal places and she could see and hear again. The Brute, having finished his beef, was scrubbing his face and hands at the basin on the shelf. Mickey was washing the cups. Stephen was pulling at her skirt, trying to get her to notice the new toy the Brute had brought him. She admired the bird, laughing at it so blithely that Stephen laughed too, as though a toy bird was the funniest thing on earth. Isabel came in with some mended clothes, and Garnet told her to play with him. The Brute, having dried his hands, stood back from the mirror and surveyed himself with disapproval.

"I do not look nice at all," he observed sadly. "I need a shave and a bath and some fresh clothes."

"Brute!" she ordered. "Come here at once."

He turned from the glass.

"Tell me about John," said Garnet. "Is he badly hurt? Why does he write like this?"

The Brute came and sat by her. "He wrote it with his left hand. His right arm is all bundled up and hanging in a sling."

"Go on! Is he hurt anywhere besides his arm?"

"His right leg is bundled up too. He hurt his hip and he cannot walk. Oh no, no, you must not turn white like that. He will be well." The Brute took up the bottle of wine he had set on the table when he came in. He poured some into a cup for her. "Drink this, and I will tell you all about him. They are taking care of him.

491

There is a good bone-setting man in Santa Barbara." The Brute smiled at her. "You must not be mad with him. Please do not be mad with him, Garnet."

Garnet caught her breath in a quick little sob. "But isn't he mad with me?"

"Oh yes," said the Brute. "But please understand him, Garnet," he begged, and he spoke as though they were two grown people who must understand and forgive a naughty child. "I know John, and you should know him too by now. John is so afraid of his own heart."

She whispered, "Brute, I don't understand him. But I love him so."

"I know you do," said the Brute.

He took the empty cup out of her hand. As he set it on the table, he said,

"You must go to him, because he cannot come here now. You will go to Santa Barbara with me?"

"Oh yes!"

"That is good," said the Brute.

"Did he tell you to bring me?" Garnet asked hopefully.

"No," said the Brute smiling, "but he would be very mad with me if I did not."

"Oh Brute," she exclaimed with an exasperated little laugh, "why did I have to fall in love with such a blockhead?"

"Why, I don't know," the Brute said gravely.

Garnet did not know there were tears on her cheeks until the Brute took out his handkerchief and wiped them away. She thought she had never known till now how much she wanted John. When she saw that piece of paper with his words shambling across it, a flame had leaped up within her that burnt up all her consciousness of anything else. She wanted John, and he wanted her. She was going to him, and she would not make any more demands of him. John could say he loved her, or he could omit saying it; he could promise her lifelong devotion or he could refuse to promise anything past tomorrow; either way it was all right. If she could have him now she would let the future take care of itself. In these lonely frightening months just past she had learned the value of Florinda's advice: Take what you can get and make it do.

She raised her head. "Brute, tell me what happened to him."

"I will tell you." He filled her cup again. "Take this. It is good for you."

"Yes, now go ahead."

"John sent you a letter by Pablo. I do not know what was in it. You gave Pablo an answer, but Pablo did not go back to the rancho right away. Pablo is most of the time a good boy, but this time he was not a good boy. He stopped on the way to visit some friends of his who had a beautiful daughter. This time the young lady looked more beautiful than ever so Pablo got married. They made a big fiesta for the wedding and Pablo stayed and feasted and drank wine. At last he brought his new wife up to Torosa, but it was a long time and John was mad. John thought you had not written to him at all."

"And when he read what I had written," said Garnet, "he was madder than ever."

"Yes. What did you write him? Something about a piece of toast, he said. I do not understand that."

"You don't need to understand it," she retorted. "Go on."

The Brute grinned and tilted his bottle. When Pablo finally brought John her note, he said, John had been about to go up to San Francisco. As she knew, John intended to be a rich man and was always finding new ways to make money. San Francisco now had nearly five hundred people, most of them Yankees, four-fifths of them under forty years old, and all of them prosperous. John was sure land around San Francisco was going to be valuable, and he had recently bought some. A certain gay-living ranchero of that district had died, leaving a lot of debts, and part of his land had been offered for sale to pay them. John had bought the property through an agent, and now he wanted to go up and look it over. He had been ready to leave when Pablo came home.

John read Garnet's letter. He put off his trip north and told his serving-boys they were going down to Los Angeles instead. This was during that bad September heat—surely Garnet remembered how hot it had been in September. Because of the heat John had kept near the coast, where there was more water and better grass for the horses.

"They were near Santa Barbara," said the Brute, "when John tried to jump a gully. He might have gone around it, but John was in a hurry. And he was mad and jumping the gully was a help to his temper. He was riding a fine stallion, but the gully was too wide. John had a bad fall. Pablo and his new wife took care of him the best they could while the other boys rode to Santa Barbara and got help from some good people John had visited before. Their name is Lorca. They brought a stretcher and carried John to Santa Barbara and got the man who sets bones."

"Were you there?"

"No, I did not know about it. I had been in San Francisco myself. That is where the Russian ship was in port. I got passage, but she will not sail till spring, so I came south to tell John he could have my cattle when I left. At Torosa they told me he had gone to Los Angeles by the coast way, so I thought I would come here too, and I could see him and you and Florinda besides. When I got as far as Santa Barbara I found he was at the house of Señor Lorca, so I went to see him and he was all bundled up in the bandages."

"How bad are his hurts, Brute?"

"Not bad enough to last. He will get well. John is such a fool, Garnet. I want to give him my cattle. He won't take them unless he can pay for them. He is so stupid."

"Yes, I know it. Brute, has he suffered very much?"

"He had some pain and fever at first, but no more fever now and not much pain as long as he will lie quiet. He hates to lie quiet."

"He hates to be helpless, I can well believe that. Oh Brute, that exasperating man, why didn't he write to me before?"

"He could not write. And maybe he did not want a stranger writing to you for him."

Garnet laughed shortly. "Oh, I know him. He didn't send me a message because no power on earth could make him say, 'I am sick and helpless and I need you.' He wouldn't have written to me even now, except that you were coming to Los Angeles and he knew you would tell me he'd been hurt."

"Do not ask me questions," the Brute said coolly, "when you know the answers already. When can you go to Santa Barbara?"

"Tomorrow. Isabel can take care of Stephen while I'm gone."

"I have brought two women to wait on you," said the Brute.

"Why Brute, how good of you!"

"Señora Lorca said I must bring some women. She said you must not travel with me except with some women too, because that would not be nice."

Garnet could not help laughing. "I'd trust you around the world, Brute."

"Thank you," said the Brute. "You would, but Señora Lorca would not. She says I am a wicked man. I should like some more wine. May I take it off the shelf?"

"Of course, go ahead."

He went to get the wine. Mickey crossed the room to the door opening into the barroom. She heard him say, "Miss Flinda, come to beans."

Florinda came in. Without pausing she came over to where Garnet sat, and stood before her, hands on hips.

"So," she said, "I suppose the Brute has told you about John."

"Why yes," said Garnet.

"I suppose you are going straight up to Santa Barbara to see him."

"I certainly am."

"Love must be a wonderful thing," said Florinda. Her lips quivered with mirth. "What about all I've heard you say," she continued, "to the effect that he'd get tired of you and grind your heart to powder?"

"I don't care what I've said," Garnet retorted. "I love him."

Florinda smothered a chuckle, and Garnet added, "Go on. Say what you're thinking."

"Well dear, it's plain that it doesn't make any difference what I think. But I think you and John are the two stubbornest people I know. I think in a year you will be throwing dishes at each other. And in spite of all the good advice I have given you and am going to give you, I think by that time you'll probably be the size and shape of a covered wagon. And I wonder what you'll do then. However—" She paused.

Garnet was laughing. Maybe all Florinda said was true, but right now she was so happy she did not care.

Florinda bent and kissed her forehead. "Go ahead and do as you please, Garnet. I'll be on your side cheering for you as long as I live."

"Thank you," Garnet returned sincerely. "I knew that, but it's good to hear you say it."

Mickey was heaping up the plates. The Brute had gone over to watch him with eager pleasure. But Florinda, paying no attention to supper, went across to the shelves on the wall. Taking down pen and ink and paper, she brought them to the end of the table where Garnet still sat. "Here, Garnet," she said.

"What's that for?"

"After beans," Florinda said quietly, "write a letter to Captain Brown."

Garnet caught her breath. "Oh Florinda!" she gasped. "I forgot about him!"

"I know you did," said Florinda. Her voice was low. "But you're not going off without leaving him a letter saying where you're going and why. You may be addled with love, my dear, but I'm not. And I won't let you be shabby to the finest man you ever had a chance to marry in your life."

Garnet was looking down. "I'll write to him," she said. "But—" She felt a swift panic, and raised her eyes abruptly. "But Florinda, what can I say to him?"

Florinda's big blue eyes swept her up and down with blank innocence. "Why, tell him you admire him, and you are honored by the evidence of his esteem. But you do not feel for him that peculiar preference which a woman should entertain for the man whose life she expects to share—"

"Oh, stop! Are you making fun of me?"

"I certainly am. That's what you told me to say, remember? I never had the nerve to talk such flapdoodle to any man. Now maybe you know why."

Garnet doubled her hands on her knees. "I'll write him a decent letter if it takes all night. Oh, I'm ashamed of myself."

"It's not that dreadful, dear. But you've got to be nice to him." Florinda glanced over her shoulder. "Come on. The beans are waiting, but the Brute's not."

The ride to Santa Barbara was easy and Garnet enjoyed it. The October days were crisp and jewel-clear. For the first three days they rode inland, behind the mountains. The landscape was noisy with dryness; the plants rustled and snapped at them as they rode. On the morning of the fourth day they went through a rocky pass that led them toward the coast, where the sea came crashing up against the mountains. The water splashed their clothes and threw spray into their faces and Garnet was glad when the coastline began to have an easier slope and they came near the bay of Santa Barbara.

Out in the bay she saw a merchant brig flying the American flag. When she saw it the old question popped into her mind, I wonder if that captain would take me home? But even as she thought it her heart gave a little skip. She was not going home. She was going to marry John and stay in California. Garnet laughed with astonishment. She was not homesick. Since the day she had first met Charles Hale and a shadow had come over her bright dream of California, this was the first time she had not felt like an exile.

They came into Santa Barbara and she looked around. Santa Barbara was built like Los Angeles: there was a plaza full of brown weeds, and a church, and adobe houses scattered at random. But Garnet thought it was a much better town. It stood by a beautiful crescent beach, and the air was fresh. There were hide-carts winding among the houses, and the oxen were followed by Diggers who had plainly never been washed in their lives. But there was a sea-breeze blowing the smells away. The people looked better too. Garnet saw several groups of Californios, handsomely dressed and mounted. She also noticed an unusual number of homes larger than the little cubes of one or two rooms where most people lived. Around these larger houses the weeds were cut down, and they had walled courtyards with trees. Compared to the average California village, Santa Barbara was a very pleasant place.

The train paused before one of these larger houses. This, the Brute told her, was the home of Señor Lorca, where John was staying. Pablo got off his horse and struck the butt of his whip on the courtyard gate. Both the house and the courtyard wall were newly whitewashed, and they had the spanking-fresh look of a little girl in a starched frock. On the wall were vines, and over the wall Garnet could see orange trees full of green oranges the size of walnuts. She felt embarrassed. John's hosts were nice people, no doubt about it, and she looked like a ragamuffin. Her hair was blown by the wind, her clothes were rumpled, splashes of sea-water had dried on her, and she was covered with dust. If Señor and Señora Lorca had ever traveled they would know she could not help it, but she looked like a ragamuffin all the same.

The gate opened to Pablo's knock. The Brute sprang off his horse and came over to take her hand as she dismounted. Garnet dropped her eyes, feeling as bashful as if he had read her thoughts and laughed at them. For she knew she did not care what the Lorca family thought of her looks. But she did not want John to see her like this. The last time he had seen her, under the trees at Kerridge's, she had been cross as an alley-cat but at least she had been fresh and crisp and her hair had been brushed. Servants were coming out to unload their horses. Garnet began to say, "Brute, do you think I can get washed up a little before—"

But the Brute did not hear her. He had led her into the courtyard. Down a flagged path came a gentleman who could be none other than Señor Lorca himself, splendid in a scarlet coat and a white silk shirt and blue trousers laced up the sides with gold cords. He bowed and kissed her hand, saying it was an honor indeed to receive her and everything in his humble home was hers. They went into the parlor, a long low room shining with whitewash and bright curtains. Here came the señora, stout and hospitable and gaily dressed.

Garnet summoned her best Spanish to thank them for her welcome, meanwhile yearning for soap and water. But they seemed to take travel-stains for granted. Señora Lorca was saying that ordinarily she would not have thought it right for a lady to go into the bedroom of a gentleman who was not yet her husband, but the poor Señor Ives could not come outside to meet her and besides the lady was a widow. So Señora Hale would please come this way.

Garnet followed her. She felt scared. She and John would have to greet each other in public, for not only was Señora Lorca going with her but a serving-girl was coming too. The girl opened the door of John's room. Señora Lorca gestured for Garnet to go in.

It was not a large room, but it was airy and sunny, with two windows looking into the courtyard. By one of the windows was a big bed, all dressed up with the fine embroidered sheets in which California housewives took such pride. And there in the bed, propped up on pillows, was John.

His swarthy face looked darker than ever against the pillows, and his green eyes had a wicked sparkle as he saw her. His right arm was in a sling, and so swathed in bandages that she could see only the tips of his fingers; and his right hip was bundled up too, for it made a big ungainly lump under the bedclothes. He had on a ruffled white shirt, the right sleeve cut out to give room for the sling. As she came in he grinned. He held out his left hand and took hers in a grip that hurt her, and he said, "Hi there, dirty-face."

"You wretch," said Garnet. "I can't help it if my face is dirty. She didn't give me any chance to wash it."

"Don't blame her. I've made her promise twenty times a day that she'd bring you in the minute you got here. I was never so mad with anybody in my life. Are you going to behave yourself?"

"Yes," said Garnet.

"Lukewarm milk toast!" said John. "If I had two good arms I'd beat you. Don't be scared of what she's hearing—she doesn't understand a word of it and she thinks I'm prattling sweet nothings into your ears. Thanks for coming, damn you."

Garnet began to laugh. The wall-bench was by the head of his bed. She sank down on it and laughed and laughed, and John laughed too; and the señora, happy that her guests were so happy, joined in their laughter.

John squeezed Garnet's hand. "Ask me to kiss you," he said.

"Why, stupid?"

"The last time I saw you, I told you I wouldn't kiss you again till you asked me. Remember?"

Garnet began to laugh again. "Please kiss me, John," she said. He kissed the hand he was holding. "That's the best I can do in front of an audience. You can go now and get washed, but you'll come back as soon as she'll let you?"

"Yes," said Garnet, "as soon as she'll let me." She stood up, and the beaming señora started for the door again, to show her the room where she would stay. Garnet wished manners did not require her to go. She did not care whether she got washed or not.

FORTY-FIVE

WHILE SHE WAS at Doña Manuela's, Garnet had learned the ways of a California home. She was careful to conduct herself as they thought she should, and in a few days she had won Señora Lorca's complete approval. So the señora made no objection to Garnet's spending nearly all her time in John's room, and kept no guard on their behavior. They were careful to have the door open all the time, but as nobody in the house understood English except the Brute they could talk as freely as they pleased.

They talked and talked. She would have him, then, John asked. Yes, said Garnet, she would have him, whenever he wanted her, and he need make no promises. Nobody could manage the future, she knew this now. "We'll be married," she said, "because I'm not going to have any affair like one of Florinda's—"

"My dearest girl," John said laughing, "when did I ever suggest any such thing? I know you wouldn't."

"—but what I was going to say," she went on, "is that if we can't make it last forever, then all right, we can't. I'm not going to think about that. I'm going to think about what you told me, the here and now. I tried to stop wanting you, John. It was no use."

"I tried too," John returned. He was speaking soberly. "I called you every kind of a fool I could think of. But I couldn't get rid of you. There was nothing to do but come down to Los Angeles and try again to get you. If I hadn't been in such a hurry I'd have paid more attention to that damned jump." He smiled at her wryly. "But of course I had to be in a hurry, so here you are and here I am and I can touch you, and we might as well be a thousand miles apart."

"How long before you'll be well? Does the man have any idea?"

"Oh yes. I'll be walking in another month. The arm will take longer than that. But I'll get over it all in time. I've got the constitution of an ox."

He grinned at her. John persisted in making light of his injuries. Señora Lorca told her he had suffered a good deal, and even allowing for her lavish Latin sympathy Garnet was sure he had. He probably still did. Every now and then when he made a careless movement she saw a flash of pain on his face, but he hated to admit it. John was ashamed of helplessness.

She found that he was not even willing to stay in this hospitable house until he got well. He was still planning to go to San Francisco. He had arranged for the trip with the captain of the brig she had seen in the bay. The brig had come to California for hides, and could not start back until she had forty thousand of them on board. When she had loaded all she could get at Santa Barbara she was going to sail up to San Francisco to get more from the northern ranchos. To Garnet's protests that he was not strong enough to travel, John retorted that he could get well on a ship as fast as he could on land. His serving-boys would carry him aboard and take care of him on the voyage, and no doubt he would be able to walk ashore. As soon as he had attended to his business he would come south again and they would be married. He might as well use these weeks of lameness to go to San Francisco, he said. He was certainly not going to marry her until he could stand upright.

Garnet guessed that he was going to make the trip not only because he wanted to see his new property. He also wanted to go because if he had to be crippled, it was easier for him to take help from servants who were paid to wait on him than from his friends. John could give so readily, but he could not bear to receive.

When she had been in Santa Barbara two weeks, she said it was time she went home. John agreed reluctantly. It was now early November, and while the rains did not often begin as soon as this, still you never could be sure. A storm could keep her here for weeks.

Garnet laughed when he said this. "Like that storm that kept you at Kerridge's last spring, when I did so want you to go away."

"I didn't mind that one," John said humorously. "I didn't want to go."

"Well, I wanted you to. I was so angry with you!"

"I was angry too, before I left. I thought at first I could make you see reason. But when I couldn't, I decided to clear out." John covered her hand with his. "You must know, Garnet," he said slowly, "that all last summer I disliked you heartily."

"Why?"

"Because I missed you so. I didn't want to miss anybody the way I missed you."

"I missed you the same way," she said. "Didn't I prove that by coming here the minute the Brute came for me?"

"I didn't want him to go for you," John said. He looked a little bit embarrassed. "I wanted to wait till I was on my feet again and could go myself. But—" He laughed at himself. "I might as well confess it. I was lying here worrying myself into a fever for fear some other man would get you. With American men swarming all over Los Angeles, you must have had hundreds of proposals."

"Why yes. But most of them I didn't pay any attention to."

"Most?" His hand tightened on her wrist.

Garnet felt a wild delight at his eagerness and the fear in his voice. She dropped her head on the pillow beside him as she said,

"Oh John, did you think I could go on like that forever? When the Brute came to Silky's I had practically made up my mind to marry a man of the New York Regiment."

Maybe she should have told him this before. She had told him everything else—about going to Estelle's, and about Charles, and Texas' saying he had fired the shots that killed Charles. But she had not told him about Captain Brown. Now he gave a start that jerked his bad hip and sent a shiver of pain across his face. She raised her head. John said, "What about him?"

"He's good, John," she said, and now that she had started the words poured out. "He's as solid as those rocks on the coast. He loves me. He was going to take me home and give me everything you wouldn't promise me and never will—love and peace and security and the feeling that I belonged somewhere. And I'm a fool not to take him. But the minute I saw that note from you I forgot him completely. I didn't think of him until Florinda told me it wouldn't be common decency to rush off to Santa Barbara without at least leaving him a letter saying why I had gone."

John's face had a puzzling expression—wisdom and gladness and a touch of guilt. He asked, "Did you write the letter?"

"Yes. It was the hardest letter I ever had to write. I started it a dozen times over. I was still trying to write it when they closed the saloon and Florinda came in and sat by me. She said, 'Stop trying to make pretty sentences. Just tell him the truth. Tell him there's a man you've been a fool about since long before the New York Regiment came to town, but you'd quarreled, and now you've made it up and he's been hurt by a fall from a horse—' "

"I never fell off a horse in my life," John snapped at her.

"Well, it amounts to that! A good rider would have had enough judgment to know how much of a jump his horse could take."

"If I hadn't been so addled from thinking about your foolishness I would have had more judgment."

He spoke as though it had been all her fault. Garnet trembled with pleasure that he could be so jealous of even an unsuccessful rival. "Well, go on," he said. "You wrote the letter?"

"Yes, finally. I told Captain Brown I liked him and admired him and I'd be grateful the rest of my life for what he had done for me—"

"Oh, gratitude again!" John said witheringly. "I suppose he's the sort who'd appreciate it. Then any time you didn't do exactly what he wanted he could wail, 'After all I've done for you, *this* is my reward!' "

"Oh, be still," she retorted. "If he hadn't pretended to believe Texas, I could have been hanged for murder. You don't think I should have felt any gratitude for that?"

"Certainly not. If he was hoping to take you home as his dearest conquest, why in hell should he want to see you hanged instead?"

"John Ives," she said, "there are times when I hate you."

"I know it, and I'd rather have a healthy hate than a lot of sickly meekness."

"I was not meek and he never expected any such thing. He loved me, John! He saved me then because he loved me."

John smiled at her with an affectionate amusement. "My dear girl, I'm not denying that he loved you. But I can't see that an attractive woman owes a man any debt of gratitude because he falls in love with her." Garnet burst out laughing in spite of herself, and John went on, "Now tell me the rest. You gave Florinda your letter?"

"Yes. It was very plain, and simple. I told him I couldn't marry him, but I hoped with all my heart he would find a woman as good as he deserved. Florinda sat there with me till I'd finished, and she read it. She said, 'That's right. I'll give it to him, and if he feels like talking I'll listen, and I'll do my best to make it right with him.' And oh John, how I loved her for it. You can't know."

"Yes I can." John said quietly. There was a simple respect in the way he spoke. "Florinda has a quality I admire very much. A gentle courtesy, a warm genuine consideration for other people. I haven't got it, but I know it when I see it."

There was a short silence. At length Garnet said,

"John, Florinda gave me a pair of emerald earrings. You won't mind my wearing them, will you?"

"Real emeralds?"

"Oh yes. Why?"

"I hate fake jewelry. But if they're real, why did you think I'd mind your wearing them?"

"Because you know how Florinda got her jewelry."

"Why yes. But I also know how she values it, and if she gave you a pair of earrings it must have been because she loved you very much."

Garnet smiled at him with admiration. "Now I want to ask you something else. Did you mind my working at the bar?"

"I admired your guts. Why did you think I'd mind?"

"My other friends thought it was dreadful."

"I don't imagine it was very pleasant. But how else could you have lived?"

"With Charles. Or I could have let Florinda support me. She was willing to."

John gave a long low contemptuous whistle. Garnet thought, All this time I've been trying to tell myself I didn't know why I loved him so. I love him because I never have to explain anything to him. His head isn't all befuddled with a lot of make-believe and what-will-people-say. It's true, what he said to me at Kerridge's— he's the only honest man I've ever known.

John took her hand in his, smiling. "Garnet, isn't it great to find out you don't need anybody?"

She shook her head firmly. "I won't ever find that out. I don't want to."

"You've already found it out," said John.

"I have not. I need you. I don't need you for the sake of beef and beans—I can earn those for myself as long as there are men to get drunk. But I need you, John."

"No you don't," John said with assurance, and he looked proud to be saying it. "That's why I'm so happy at the thought of having you. Anything you give me will be absolutely free, because you want to give it, not because you want something back. You've got independence of spirit. You won't have to be told a dozen times a day that you're wanted and appreciated."

"I hope not," she said smiling. "But how do you know I won't?"

John let go her hand and put his good left arm behind his head, to raise himself a little. He was regarding her with affection and a glint of mischief. He said, "You haven't even asked me, not once since you've been here, if I loved you."

Garnet set her teeth hard on her lip. Over and over, she had nearly bitten her tongue in half to keep from asking.

"And do you know," said John, "I believe I do."

"John!" she cried. She could not say any more. Hearing him speak sent a wave of delight breaking over her and flooding her with ecstasy. John went on,

"I didn't want to say it. I'm as bashful about saying it as any fool in the moonlight. I hate the word, because as I told you before it's been so kicked about that it's worn out, but I suppose there's no other word to use."

Garnet slipped to her knees beside the bed. "Don't stop, John!" she pled breathlessly. "Tell me some more."

John spoke slowly. "I've thought a lot about what it is I feel for you. It's not just wanting a woman because she's got an exciting body. I'm used to that. This is different. It's not merely that I want you more than I've ever wanted any other woman. It's *different*. I feel so right when you're with me and so lost and empty when you're not." He shook his head a little, as though the whole thing puzzled him, and asked, "Is that love, Garnet?"

He asked it like a boy asking a question about the big world. She stroked back his crisp dark hair and kissed him where the hair grew into a point on his forehead. "Yes, John," she said.

"And I can talk to you," said John. "I never could talk to anybody before. Just talk and talk about anything that comes into my head, with no feeling that you'll be bored or that you'll laugh at me."

"Be bored? Laugh at you? Oh John!"

"Is that love, Garnet?"

"Yes. John, don't you understand what I've tried to tell you?"

"I'm not sure," said John. "It's so new and I'm so astonished by it. Maybe it's everything you said it was. Maybe it's not. I don't know. Maybe it will last. Maybe I'll get over it and wonder what ever possessed me. But right now, right this minute, it's true. I can't tell you any more than that."

"That's enough," said Garnet. She laid her cheek against his. "That's all I wanted."

"It's not all you wanted. You wanted a lot of stuff about the next forty years."

"I don't any more. I told you I've decided to live one day at a time."

"I hope so," John said, "because that's the best I can do myself."

Garnet raised her head so she could look down at his face, the dark skin and green eyes and the harshly cut lines about his mouth. He was watching her with a tender teasing look. "John," she said, "why have you been so afraid of love? So apart from people?" He looked puzzled, and she asked, "Didn't anybody ever love you?"

He shook his head.

"I don't mean the way I love you," said Garnet. "But there must have been some people who cared about you."

"Why no," said John. He shrugged his good shoulder. "I'm afraid that sounds as if I were making a bid for sympathy. I don't mean to be."

Garnet had been kneeling by the bed. She moved back a little and sat on the floor, looking at him in a pained astonishment. "Not even your mother and father, John?"

"Oh, I suppose they did. But they died when I was a year old."

"And then what happened?"

"I told you I was an object of charity," John returned.

Garnet gave him a long look. She saw the tenseness about his eyes, and the hard set of his mouth; John was remembering, and what he was remembering was not pleasant. "John, my darling," she exclaimed, "what did they do to you? Did they beat you?"

"Certainly not. They gave me expensive clothes to wear and linen sheets to sleep on and a tutor to teach me Latin. Everybody said how kind they were and how grateful I ought to be. Grateful!"

John said the last word as though it were an ugly oath. Then he gave a one-sided smile as though ashamed of his own vehemence. He added,

"I suppose I'm being too hard on them. They never meant to be cruel. But they resented me so much they couldn't help themselves. You see, I was the shame of a fine old clan. The Ives family has been in Virginia since what amounts to the year one for Americans. They're very rich, and very proud. My uncle Augustus was typical of them. Augustus improved his plantation, he was a pillar of society, he married just as they had hoped. Aunt Edith was the perfect wife for him. She never did anything that was not utterly correct. Garnet, do you know that kind of woman?"

Garnet was reminded of the mother of Henry Trellen, that pompous young bore who had asked her to marry him just before she met Oliver. She remembered the description she had secretly given Mrs. Trellen long ago. Hearing what John said about his aunt Edith, she asked, "You mean she looked like a marble angel on a tombstone?"

"Exactly," John said with a tart amusement.

"Go on about the Ives family," said Garnet.

John continued. "Edith and Augustus had just the sort of life they wanted. The only flaw in their peace was Augustus' brother, John Richard. He was my father. From his youth on, John Richard was no good. He drank, he gambled, he spent his money on worthless women—"

"John!" she interrupted him sharply.

He turned with a look of surprise. "Don't you understand?"

"John, they didn't tell you all this about your father!"

"Why yes they did. How else would I have known?"

"But even if it was true, why tell you? You couldn't be blamed for it!"

"You think not?" he asked with a cold wisdom.

Garnet shivered at the thought of what they had done to him. John went on.

He told her John Richard Ives had finally run off and married a girl who worked in a milliner's shop. The Ives family never saw this girl, or wanted to. They knew nothing about her. But since they set so high a value on property and blue blood, it was plain to them that she must be a smart little baggage who had enticed John Richard Ives into marrying her because he had money and a fine old name. It was equally plain that John Richard was an even bigger fool than they had thought he was.

John Richard took a house in Norfolk, where he poured out money buying his wife every silly frippery he could think of. Among other things, he bought a pleasure boat so they could go sailing on the bay. They were out in the boat one day when there came a sudden storm. The boat was torn to pieces. A day or two later both their bodies were cast up by the tide.

At least the wastrel brother could now bring no more shame upon the family. Augustus might have sighed with relief, except for two appalling facts. The wastrel brother had left five thousand dollars' worth of debts. He had also left a son a year old.

Augustus and his wife Edith talked it over. There was a disagreeable duty before them. They told each other in grim righteousness that they were not people to shirk their duty. Augustus paid the debts. He and Edith took the baby into their home to grow up with their own children. Everybody told them how noble they were. Haloed with nobility, they put John through eighteen years of torture.

They never cuffed him about, or let him shiver for lack of coat or blanket. They merely *talked* to him. They explained to him, in the kindest way, how much they were doing for him. They told him he must be good, he must be grateful, and they sorrowfully said he was not good and he was not grateful. They told him he must not be like his parents, and they told him every day that he was just like them. Every childish fault of his was met with the gentle reproach, "Now that's how your father used to behave. You don't want to be like your father, do you, dear?" Rumpled hair and untidy clothes brought the advice that if he wanted people to forget his mother had been a common woman, he must not look common himself. And the general rebuke, the one he heard oftenest, from an aunt and uncle with pain in their voices, was, "After all we've done for you, *this* is our reward!"

When he was fourteen years old John ran away. They found him the next day and brought him back. They were surprised and hurt. They could not understand why a boy who had such a happy home should not appreciate it.

They sent him to the University of Virginia with his cousin, their own son. But John could not stand any more of their self-righteous favors. By this time he had made up his mind that he was going to repay his uncle and aunt every cent they had spent on him, and then he was going to make himself richer than they had ever been. He was never again going to be dependent on anybody in any way.

He quit the university, and with six dollars in his pocket he went to Boston. He went there for no reason except that it was a busy town where a man should be able to make a living. He had no equipment for making a living. He had studied Latin, philosophy, and Greek, but he had never learned carpentry or tailoring. He got jobs at unskilled labor. He hung around the wharfs, loaded cargo, carried baggage for travelers. He worked twelve or fourteen hours a day and lived in a tenement room. For the first time in his life he had a sense of independence.

He made no friends. He did not quarrel with his fellow-workers, but he did not know how to make friends. They thought he was a good laborer, but stuck-up. John was held back from them by a dread of intimacy. He had a compulsion to pay for everything he received, and he was afraid that if he got close to anybody he would somehow get under obligation.

He unloaded ships bringing hides from California. The sailors told him about the big ranchos, and said an American could get a land-grant there. It sounded like a place where a shrewd fellow could get rich. John found a job as assistant to the supercargo of a ship going around the Horn. When he got to California, he made his way up to Los Angeles and asked Mr. Abbott for work.

As always, he worked hard and talked little. He made no friends except the Brute, and this was the Brute's doing more than his own. John found it very pleasant to have a friend. It did not enter his head that he had been starving for human affection. He knew only that he liked the big Russian very much, and he was surprised at how much the big Russian liked him.

But he never talked to the Brute about himself. He hated people who complained. His aunt Edith's attacks of refined self-pity had given him a dread of whining. Until this very day, when he finally told Garnet about it, he had never spoken of his childhood to a living soul.

He had kept silent about it for so long that telling of it now was not easy. He talked in brief sentences, speaking in a monotone that Garnet found more moving than any passionate speech. He did not tell her a great deal, but she heard more than he said. Between his sentences she heard the secret sobs of a little boy who could not understand why nobody wanted him, and behind his quiet voice she guessed the shell of indifference he had put on to protect himself from ever being hurt like that again. She knelt by him and put her arms around him and told him she loved him. It was all she could do, and as she felt his good left arm go around her and hold her as close to him as he could, she knew it was enough.

FORTY-SIX

GARNET WENT BACK to Los Angeles with the Brute. He stayed only a day or two before returning to Santa Barbara, but he came back soon, bringing another note crookedly printed by John's left hand. John said he was taking the ship to San Francisco, but would come south again as soon as he could and they would be married.

Garnet had gone back to work at the bar. Florinda had said it was not necessary, but Garnet could see how much she was needed. The traders were back from Santa Fe, and the saloon was full all day.

Garnet was glad to see the traders. She had not seen them last winter, for when the train came in she and Florinda had been at Doña Manuela's. But she was somewhat dismayed to find that Mr. Penrose was back with the others. She had nearly forgotten him. But here he was, again gazing eagerly upon Florinda. Garnet thought Florinda would have at least a few sharp words to say to him, reminding him that he had left her half dead at Don Antonio's. But to Garnet's surprise, Florinda regarded him with indifference. If he spoke to her she said carelessly, "Oh run along, do. Can't you see I'm busy?"

She really felt no resentment toward him. Florinda had not taken the trail because of any love for Mr. Penrose. She had wanted to come to California and she had needed an escort. He was not the only man in the train who would have been glad to have her. She had chosen him because he was thick-headed enough not to give her any trouble. Penrose was a successful trader, and one reason for his success was his lubberly insensitiveness. He could work a mule to death or kick a dying Indian out of his way, without any feeling in the matter. Florinda knew this. She was too clear in her thinking to feel any wrath toward him simply because he had behaved as he might have been expected to behave. Right now he was a bit of a nuisance, but no more.

Garnet admired her coolness. Florinda had had a long hard battle, and it had taught her not to expect too much of the human race. Garnet envied such wisdom, because she knew very well that she did not have it.

She did not, for instance, feel indifferent about Mrs. Charles Hale. She felt for her a guilty dislike. Though she found it impossible to believe any woman could have married Charles for love of him, though she knew that Mr. Radney's fortune and Charles' together had made Lydia Hale an immensely rich woman, still the fact remained that she herself had fired the gun. Lydia did not know this, but it was still true. Garnet was glad when she heard that Lydia had sailed for Boston on the brig of which she was now half owner. She had left the rancho in charge of a Yankee she had brought down from the north, promising that she would attend to her property in Boston and come back to California on the brig's next voyage. That seemed to Garnet an excellent arrangement. By the time Lydia got back she herself would have been long married to John. She was never going to try to get any of the Hale property. Leaving it in Lydia's hands seemed like making some compensation for having shot Lydia's husband. Her conscience was not quite clear on any of it, but it was the best she could do.

For several days she wondered what had become of Captain Brown. Other officers came to the bar as often as ever, but Captain Brown did not. Florinda did not speak of him and Garnet was pretty sure she would not until she was asked. So one evening when they were alone she asked what he was doing.

"He's in town," said Florinda. "Probably will be here till the New York Regiment is mustered out. But you won't see him if he can help it. He asked me to let him know when you got back, so I did."

"I suppose he hates every bone in my body," said Garnet.

"No," Florinda said quietly, "I don't think so. He and I had a couple of long talks. I told him how things were."

"What did you tell him?"

"I told him you had been just about to marry him. But I said, 'Captain Brown, she was no more in love with you than she was in love with General Kearny. She'd have made you a good wife as they go. But she'd have been unfaithful to you in her mind every night of her life.' "

"You said that to him?"

"I did, my dear, because that's the truth, isn't it? I'm a very good liar, as you know, but there are times when I tell the truth. I believe he was a bit shocked at my mentioning such things, but he got the idea. He's badly hurt, but he'll get over it. He told me to tell you he hoped he wouldn't have to see you again, because he thought it would be easier on you both if he didn't. That's all."

Garnet went over to her and kissed the top of her head. "Thank you, Florinda," she said.

"Did I do right?"

"You did it better than anybody else could have. Thank you."

A week after her return to Los Angeles, Mr. Abbott wrote Garnet a note about Texas. He told her Texas had said to him, several times, that if anything should happen to him he wanted his little property to be given to Mrs. Hale and her baby. There was nothing about this in writing, but Texas had no natural heirs and Mr. Abbott thought he ought to follow his wishes. After everything Texas owed had been paid up, there was about a thousand dollars in hides and merchandise on deposit. If Mrs. Hale would call at the store to sign a receipt, he would put this to her account.

Garnet felt rich. In a town where living was so cheap, a thousand dollars was a fortune. She told Mr. Abbott to give a hundred dollars to Señora Vargas, Texas' landlady, to reward her for taking care of him so many times when he was drunk. Señora Vargas, who had never had this much money at one time in her life, bought a red shawl and a pair of red shoes and invited her friends to a party at which, also for the first time, she got drunk herself.

Garnet told Florinda she wanted to keep her promise of helping to pay Estelle for the business she had lost by letting Texas die at her house. The episode had cost a good deal, for Estelle's place had been closed for several days while the army investigated Charles' death. Garnet asked Florinda how much she should give her.

Florinda considered, and said, "Would two hundred be all right?"

"Yes, that's all right. How do I give it to her? Would it shock Mr. Abbott if I told him to assign two hundred dollars' worth of my credit to Estelle?"

"He would die of insulted modesty, dear. Have it assigned to me, and I'll transfer it to Silky. Since Silky and I own the saloon jointly Mr. Abbott will think nothing of that. I'll tell Silky you gave it to me, and what it's for. I won't mention that I told you he had any connection with Estelle's business, but I will personally stand over him while he writes the paper giving Estelle her share."

Garnet agreed. Silky never mentioned the assignment to her. But she noticed that he treated her with a special deference thereafter, urging her to sit in the most comfortable place and cutting off the choicest pieces of meat for her. He even once or twice patted Stephen's head as he passed. People who parted with money when they did not have to were beyond Silky's understanding. But though he could not comprehend such behavior, he gave it an awed respect.

Garnet had hoped for a quiet winter in which she could catch her breath. She felt mentally and emotionally spent and she yearned for the time when she and John could finally go up to his rancho. At Torosa there were the great billowing hills of wild oats, and the miles of poppies, and the mountains against the sky. There were the distances and the great solitudes. After these crowded years, Garnet felt there was nothing her tired spirit needed so much as being at Torosa, with John.

But if she was destined to have peace at Torosa, she was not destined to have it in Los Angeles. Fate seemed to have determined that Los Angeles should not be a quiet town. Not long after Garnet came back there was an accidental explosion at the soldiers' guardhouse. Several men were killed, and the townspeople were thrown into a panic. After this there were the usual December storms; there was Christmas, when business was so brisk that Garnet and Florinda nearly dropped of exhaustion; there were a few days of calm, and then the same kind of celebration for New Year's; and then there was an earthquake.

The earthquake came one night in January. Garnet and Florinda were both at the bar with José. The bar was full of men. Florinda was listening to four or five of them at once. Ticktock was showing her the large noisy watch that had given him his name, telling her how old it was and how accurate and how valuable, and how many battles it had been through, and how it had been his good luck charm and as long as he had it he felt safe and sound. Ticktock's friend Devilbug was telling her about a Digger fight they had had on the way. Several of the New York boys were telling her about a storm they had run into on their way around the Horn. Florinda, as usual, was flirting with them all and at the same time pouring their drinks and keeping up with what they paid her. The light from the hanging lamps, so garish on most people, was tossing lovely shadows over her and making a nimbus about her head.

José was taking care of a group of very young New Yorkers who were awed by the sophistication of the traders, too awed to elbow their way into the group around Florinda. Garnet, at the other end of the bar, was pouring drinks for two New York officers. Other men sat at the tables, their drinks before them. In front of the bar, drinking red wine and enjoying himself, was the Handsome Brute.

The Brute grinned at Garnet. "It is nice and warm in here," he said. "It is cold outside."

The two officers glanced at him and smiled tolerantly. Like most other people, they regarded the Brute as a cheerful barbarian. They thought a man of his size looked so absurd in his embroidered satins that they could never take him seriously. One of the officers picked up his glass, found it empty, and said, "Will you fill this for me, Garnet? Whiskey."

Garnet turned to get the bottle from the shelf. As she put out her hand the bottle came forward to meet her. The floor jerked, the bar itself rose up and hit her in the ribs, her feet went out from under her and she sat down on the floor with a bump so hard that it made her teeth hit. Three bottles crashed at her side, splashing her with wine and aguardiente. The bottle of whiskey fell into her lap and then fell off and went rolling around. Behind her she heard the cash-box fall and the coins go jingling about the floor. At the same time she heard what sounded like a hundred other bumps and crashes as the men at the bar were knocked down, and what sounded like a hundred male voices yelling in a shock of frightened profanity. She heard the Brute shouting to them, "You need not be so scared, it happens often like this," and she heard Florinda exclaim, "If the earth wiggles one more time I'm going to live in a tree!"

Garnet put her hands to her head. Everything seemed to be falling down and she was so scared she was dizzy. Later she thought if she lived through ten thousand of these temblors she would still be scared out of her wits by every one. Right now she was thinking that her bottom was probably a large purple patch and she would not be able to sit down again for a week. She painfully struggled up and held to the bar, which now seemed to be miraculously firm in the tumbling world.

Cups and glasses rolled among splashes of liquor on the floor. The men were picking themselves up, many of them sucking fingers cut by broken glass. The Brute had evidently made his speech while he was down flat, for he was just now getting up too. There was a tear down the front of his blue coat. Devilbug and Ticktock were holding a New Yorker who did not look more than sixteen and who was so terrified he could not stand on his own legs. They were shaking him and telling him he'd better get used to these things. José was rescuing some bottles that had fallen but not broken. On the floor behind the bar Florinda was raking up the spilt money. Most of the New Yorkers, as soon as they could get to their feet, were rushing outdoors. They were voicing their fright in outlandish phrases, which they would repeat with elaborations when they told their grandchildren about their youth, until the temblor of 1848 would come to sound like the rain of fire that fell on the town of Pompeii.

The house was standing still again. The jolt had come and gone like a blow from a fist. The Brute leaned over the bar and caught Garnet's hands.

"You are all right? You are not hurt?"

"No, no," she said breathlessly. "I'm not hurt."

"And you, Florinda?"

Florinda was getting up, the cash-box hugged to her bosom. "I don't know whether I'm hurt or not. No time yet to find out." She put the cash-box carefully on the shelf where it belonged.

Outdoors there was a vast lot of yelling and running about. Garnet was not the only person in Los Angeles who would never get used to these shakes. The door behind the bar opened and Silky put his head in.

"You'd better lock up," he called. Every hoodlum in town is going to be on the loose."

Behind him Garnet heard Stephen, bawling his little throat to pieces. She ran past Silky and into the kitchen. Stephen had been knocked down, like everybody else, and Isabel was just now getting to him, for the supper had spilt into the fire and she had been helping Mickey sweep back the hot ashes that had fallen from the fireplace. Garnet rushed past her and took Stephen into her arms. He was bumped but not otherwise hurt. Carrying him, she went back toward the bar to see what else was happening there.

Silky was on his way to clear up the gambling room. As Garnet came to the door behind the bar with Stephen, Florinda asked, "He's all right?"

"Yes, he's all right," said Garnet. "Just scared like the rest of us."

She leaned against the side of the doorway, petting and quieting him. The Brute was still standing in front of the bar, but the other customers were gone. José was closing the front door as Silky had ordered. Florinda had pulled off her liquor-soaked mitts and was drying her hands on her skirt. A bottle of wine, which had been

514

jolted to the edge of the shelf, fell off and smashed to pieces at her feet. "Damn," she said. "We'll be all day tomorrow cleaning up this place."

Then something else happened. Garnet was always amazed to see how very slowly things seemed to happen in a moment of stress. They had all forgotten the two lamps that hung from the beams over the bar. The lamps had always been there; Silky had bought them when he first opened the saloon, so the barroom would not have to be lit by candles that any drunken man might turn over. The lamps hung to the beams by metal brackets, and in the past few minutes' confusion nobody had looked up to see that one of the brackets had broken loose. Nobody thought of them till this very instant, when the lamp slid off the bracket and came down, in what seemed to Garnet to be a journey so long and slow that it might have been a mile from the ceiling to the floor behind the bar. The lamp fell close to where Florinda stood and crashed with a silvery shiver at her feet. The flame ran like a dancer over the top of the oil and touched the hem of her skirt and caught the cloth. The fire began to climb up the side of her dress.

Florinda did not move. She stared at the flame in a paralysis of horror. Her eyes were as blank as two blue china eggs. Florinda who had never in the sight of any of them lost her gallant self-command, lost it now. Her mouth opened, the lips pulling up and down from her teeth. Her scarred hands fluttered like two spiders in the air. Out of her mouth came a scream that ripped through the house and brought Silky running from the gambling room and made Mickey drop an earthenware pot and shatter it to pieces on the kitchen floor.

It had all happened in an instant. It was so sudden that José, locking the door, heard the crash of the lamp and Florinda's scream at the same time. He wheeled about, but not seeing the flame behind the bar, he could not tell what had happened. He rushed across the room. But before he could get there, before Silky could reach the door and before Garnet, with Stephen in her arms, could move at all, the Brute had leaped over the bar. His great strength carried him over as lightly as a child leaping over a fence. He caught Florinda's skirt in both hands and ripped it off her, bringing her petticoats with it and leaving her standing in her white drawers and the top half of her dress. He stamped on the flame, and by the time Silky appeared to ask what all the noise was about, the fire was gone.

Florinda was holding herself up with both hands on the bar behind her, staring down at her scorched petticoats on the floor. She was trembling all over. Her face was a dead sort of white. The top of her dress, in shreds where the Brute had torn her skirt and bodice apart, dangled around her waist. The ruffles of her drawers stood out stiffly below her knees, and the light glanced on her silk stockings and her frivolous black kid slippers with silk lacings. She was fighting for self-control. In a faint breathless voice she said,

"Thank you— God I'm a fool to yell like that about nothing— somebody get me something to put on."

Garnet had already made a movement toward her, but the Brute put out his hand.

"Let her alone. I will take care of her."

He picked her up like a baby. Florinda made no resistance. The Brute said,

"Get out of the door, Silky. Garnet, put that child down. He is not hurt and if Isabel will stop weeping she can hold him until you go upstairs and bring Florinda a blanket."

They stood aside and let him carry Florinda into the kitchen and put her on the wall-bench. Isabel was weeping, as the Brute had said, though nobody else had noticed it. Garnet thrust Stephen into her arms and ran upstairs.

When she came down with the blanket Florinda was sitting on the bench, laughing at herself.

"I'm so sorry, dear people. It gave me such a turn in the head, that lamp falling practically on me just when I thought everything was over. Oh Garnet, thanks for the blanket. Cover me up, do. A girl can't be too careful."

Her laughter was tinny and unreal. The Brute knew it. He took the blanket from Garnet and tucked it around Florinda gently. But Silky did not know it. Silky thought Florinda's scream was merely hysterical fear, and he was surprised that anybody as calm as she usually was should have gone to pieces like that. He was bringing her the first remedy that occurred to him, a stiff drink of brandy. Florinda took the cup from him, saying, "Why thanks, Silky," then as she brought it to her lips and her nose got a whiff of alcohol she exclaimed, "Oh my God, no," and pushed the cup into the Brute's hand. But she caught herself, and smiled, saying, "Silky, how often do I have to tell you I can't handle that stuff?"

Garnet started out to the back porch to see if the water-barrel was still standing, so she could bring Florinda a harmless drink. But

Mickey had managed to rescue a kettle half full of water that had been keeping hot on the hearth-stove. Now he was quietly making a cup of tea. The water was not quite boiling, but it did give off a cheerful steam as he poured it out. He came over to Florinda and held out the cup. She took it, saying, "Bless you, Mickey," and Mickey nodded serenely.

Stephen, on Isabel's kindly lap, was no longer frightened and had gone to sleep. Garnet went over and sat on the bench by Florinda. As she sat down she winced. She had been right about the purple patch on her bottom.

With Garnet on one side of her and the Brute on the other, Florinda smiled at them both in turn. She drank the tea, and gave the cup back to Mickey with the remark that she didn't believe she'd wait for him to cook up another supper. The chance for a real night's sleep was too good to be missed. If they weren't going to open the bar again she thought she'd go to bed now, so she could come down early tomorrow and help clean up the mess. Garnet took Florinda's hand in hers, and Florinda pressed her hand affectionately.

And then, as she pressed Florinda's rough scarred hand in return, Garnet had a flash of insight. She did not know how it came or why. She remembered the day at the Archillette when Texas had put the red-hot iron into her arm. She remembered looking up, dazed with pain, and seeing Florinda's face above hers, green-tinged and dripping with sweat as though the pain had been Florinda's and not her own.

She had made up her mind long ago that she was never going to try to find out what had put those scars on Florinda's hands. But now it seemed to her that the reason for them was lying just over the edge of her mind. She was about to see it, as though she were riding down a road and was about to see something that lay just beyond her present vision. She could not help seeing it, because it was there.

FORTY-SEVEN

The Brute came back to the saloon through the dark spaces among the houses. He had gone out to see what the earthquake had done, but he had found very little damage. These squat little adobe structures were admirably built to stand the jerks of the earth.

But the people were not as firm as the houses they lived in. Some of them had gone to church to pray for peace and quiet. Some of them were looking for their children, who had run out of doors and were now lost among the tall dark weeds. There was the regular crop of rowdies on the lookout, and as always in times of shock, there were some people who were rambling around and who could not to save their lives have told why.

The army was doing its best to restore order. Sentinels had been posted, to prevent looting and help frightened people get back home. The Brute had been stopped several times to answer questions. But his appearance was so striking that most of the men recognized him. They knew he was a harmless blockhead, so when he said mildly that he had been out to look for news and was now going back to Silky's Place to protect the ladies there, they grinned and let him pass.

The Brute knocked on the kitchen door of the saloon. Mickey let him in. Mickey said Miss Golnet and Miss Flinda had gone up to their rooms. The Brute told him to go to bed, and said he would tiptoe upstairs and make sure they were not frightened any more.

Taking a candle, the Brute went into the little hallway and climbed the stairs softly. He had never been up here before, but he knew the girls' rooms were on this side of the loft. Looking around, he saw two closed doors. Everything was silent, but under one door was a line of light.

The Brute went to the door of the dark room and gave a gentle knock. There was no answer. Setting his candle on the floor he opened the door silently. This room, as he had guessed, was Garnet's. She was in bed asleep. In his crib Stephen was asleep too, covered up cozily against the sharp night air. The Brute closed the door as silently as he had opened it, and picking up his candle he knocked on the door of the lighted room.

From inside he heard a startled movement. Florinda's voice called, "Who is it?"

"It is me," he said. "Nikolai Grigorievitch Karakozof the Handsome Brute."

"Oh, rats," Florinda said ungraciously. She opened the door, but stood in the opening so he could not go past her. She had undressed and put on a woolen robe over her nightgown, but she had not gone to bed. Behind her he could see the bed, the blue gingham cover not yet turned down. She was regarding him with surprise and annoyance. In an undertone that would not disturb Garnet she demanded, "Now what do you want?"

"I want to see if you are all right."

"I'm quite all right, thank you," Florinda said tersely. "Go on home."

"I do not think you are quite all right," said the Brute. "So I think I will stay with you a while."

Florinda's blue eyes flickered up and down him. "My little daffodil," she said shortly, "I don't need a nurse. Why don't you go away and let me sleep?"

"Because you are not sleeping," the Brute answered. She said nothing, and he went on. "Garnet is asleep. She is easy in her mind. But you are not easy in your mind. When a person's nerves get tight in a knot, it is not good to be all by yourself."

"You bubble-witted ape," said Florinda. But she gave him a faint, affectionate little smile.

"It is cold up here," said the Brute. "So I think we will go down to the kitchen, and we will stay there till you get warm."

Florinda hesitated. But the room *was* cold, and the Brute picked up her candle firmly and handed it to her. She yielded. They went down to the kitchen. Florinda sat on the wall-bench while the Brute stirred up the ashes in the fireplace and put on some wood. When the flame leaped up Florinda started and looked down, avoiding the sight of it. The Brute came over to her and put his big hand on her shoulder.

"Florinda," he said gently.

She did not look up.

The Brute spoke to her earnestly. "Florinda, you do not have to tell me why you went into a panic tonight. But I think it will be better if you do. It is not good to keep something boxed up inside you and try to pretend it is not there."

Florinda shivered like a paper in the wind. The Brute's steady voice was almost ruthless.

"You will have to see your hands," he said, "as long as you live."

Florinda caught her breath.

"Your gloves will hide the scars from other people," said the Brute, "but they will never hide the scars from you."

"Oh, damn you," she said. "Damn you." She jerked her shoulder out from his grasp, and still looking down she said, "All right. I'll tell you. It was my child. My little girl. Her name was Arabella."

The Brute started. He had not known she had ever had a child.

"That's why I went into a panic," said Florinda. She spoke shortly, almost angrily. "When the fire caught my dress, just for a minute I saw it again. Like it was happening right there. That's why I screamed. Is that what you wanted to know?"

The Brute did not answer at once. When he did, his voice was low and full of compassion.

"No wonder you screamed. No wonder you cannot bear to think of it. An accident like that."

Florinda doubled her fists into knots on her lap. "It wasn't an accident," she said through her teeth. "Brute, it wasn't an accident. She was murdered."

The Brute took both her hands in his, and held them. After a moment Florinda looked up at him, and he thought her eyes had a pitiful bewilderment, like the eyes of a child who has suffered a great deal of pain. He sat down by her on the bench.

"She was murdered by a drunken beast," said Florinda. "I had married him because he said he would help me take care of her. I wanted somebody to help me take care of her. I was making lots of money at the Jewel Box, but I got worried for fear of what might become of Arabella if I should die, or if I should have a fall like my mother. I couldn't bear to think of her living in tenements with broken windows like I did, or having to go to work when she was eight years old. Her father didn't take any interest in her, he'd never even seen her. I didn't expect him to. He was a gent, very rich. He knew I'd had the baby and he was quite generous about it, he gave me money to take me through the time when I'd have to be out of the show. But his family was very high-toned and his mother would have raised Cain if she'd found out he'd been carrying on with an actress. I knew if anything happened to me I couldn't count on him.

"So I got married, to a man named William Cadwallader Mallory. He pretended to be so nice and so fond of Arabella. But he married me because he was mad for liquor and gambling, and his family had disowned him and he was desperate for money. And I had money in the bank and I was blazing with jewels, and he knew if he could get me down in front of a judge and marry me it would all belong to him. I didn't know that, I never thought of it, that's the kind of fool I was."

Florinda was talking fast and jerkily, getting her hidden hurt into words after years of not being able to do so. The Brute did not interrupt her. She went on.

"I couldn't get a divorce and I couldn't get away from him. I quit the show and tried to hide, but no matter where I went he found me, and he was always drunk and wanting money. Then at last he was arrested with some other fellows for street fighting and the judge put them in jail. I thought I could leave town while he was in jail and he'd never find me again. I got ready to take a boat. One afternoon I was ironing clothes. I had made up a big fire to heat the irons. Arabella was scampering around, she was nearly two years old then and meddling with everything. I put her in a chair with her dolls, and I tied her to the chair with a belt so she couldn't climb out and handle the hot irons. My things were all over the room, half packed, and my jewelry was in a box on the table. I was singing while I ironed, and Arabella tried to sing too, and I looked around and laughed at her and she laughed back, and she was so beautiful, and then the door opened and there stood William Mallory."

Florinda pulled in her breath with a sound like a rattle.

"The governor had let him out of jail. He had been drinking but he was not blind drunk. He tried to get the box of jewelry and I grabbed it and cried out that he was not going to have it because it belonged to my child. He said, 'To hell with your bastard,' and he kicked over her chair and sprang at me to get the box. I heard Arabella scream but he had me pinned to the wall and he was in front of me so for a minute I couldn't see her. I dropped the box on the floor and struck at him with both fists, and then I saw over his shoulder what he had done. He had knocked her into the fire. I had tied her into that chair and she couldn't get out. He had knocked the chair into the fire and there in front of me was my child roasting alive."

Florinda's voice choked in her throat again. Otherwise she did not move.

"I turned into a tiger. I knocked that man flat on the floor and ran to get my baby. The chair was burning like firewood. I got her free of it. She was blazing all over. I threw her on the floor and rolled her over in the rug to crush out the fire. I don't know whether I screamed or not. All I know is how I kept trying to beat the fire out of her pitiful little body, and how the room was full of the smell of burning flesh. And then all of a sudden I realized everything was quiet. She was dead. The jewelry was there, scattered on the floor, and Mallory was gone."

The Brute had listened to her in silence. But now he said, "Mallory saw what he had done. He got out before you had a chance to kill him."

"Yes. But I knew I was going to kill him. At first I couldn't, because I couldn't use my hands. But that was all I thought of, to be able to use my hands again so I could kill Mallory. I got a doctor and I did everything he told me. I moved my fingers no matter how much it hurt to do it. I worked and worked on my hands so I could kill Mallory. As soon as the burns had healed enough, I bought a gun and learned to use it. I went about with the gun under my shawl, looking for him. I found him in a gambling palace. I walked up to the roulette table and I didn't care who saw me. He saw me, and he tried to run, but I didn't give him time. I whipped out my gun and blew the top of his head off.

"I got out and they didn't catch me, because it was night and pouring rain and you couldn't see a yard ahead of you. But I had trouble anyway. At that same roulette table there were two rich gents named Reese and Selkirk, and they had been having an awful quarrel because Reese had been having an affair with Selkirk's wife, and they both had guns. When I shot Mallory, Reese did some split-second thinking and put a bullet into Selkirk before the smoke from my shot had cleared into the air. Then he told the police I had shot both men. And nobody cared about a drunken bum like Mallory, but Selkirk was murder at the top of town. I had to get away. My friends from the show came through like a ton of bricks, and they got me on a boat."

There was a silence. At length Florinda stirred and pushed back her loose pale hair.

The Brute said, "This is the first time you have told that story since you left New York, isn't it?"

She nodded. "It was like you said, all boxed up inside of me. I couldn't tell it. But somehow it got easier while I was talking."

"I thought it would." There was another pause, then the Brute said, "Your little girl's father never knew what had happened to her?"

"Why yes," said Florinda, "he did. A girl in the show went to him and told him. After I got on the boat he came to see me.

"It was all very surprising. I never heard anybody talk the way he talked. He had never paid any attention to Arabella, had never even laid eyes on her, but now that she had died like that his conscience blew up inside him. He walked up and down, he called himself

522

names, he said he was no good and never would be. I had to comfort him just as if he was the one in trouble instead of me.

"Brute, he told me all sorts of strange things that night. He said I was the only girl he'd ever cared for, he never would have let me go except that his mother had found out about me and had threatened to cut him off without a dollar if he ever saw me again, and he had never earned a dollar and didn't know how. He was scared to death of his mother. He said there was a girl she had picked out for him to marry. He supposed he would marry her. Maybe she'd be the making of him. And I tell you, Brute, I sat there listening to him and I never felt so sorry for anybody in my life. Heaven knows I was never in love with him, he was just another rich boy to me and if it hadn't been for Arabella I'd have forgotten about him. But I pitied him so much you might call it a kind of affection."

Florinda shook her head in wonder at the strange way things went in the world. She lifted her hands and looked at them. The Brute had never seen her look at her hands so candidly, turning them over and over as if she was no longer trying to hide them from herself as well as from other people. After a while she said,

"Brute, you asked me once why I never took wine. Remember?"

"Why yes. Do you want to tell me?"

She nodded. "You see, it was a long way from New York to New Orleans and I had plenty of time to think. I wondered why all this had happened to me. I wondered why I didn't see through Mallory before I married him. And then I figured it out. I had met him at a party, and always when we were together he was very sociable and he would order champagne, or something elegant to drink. And a couple of drinks always sets me floating through a wonderful world. I see everybody the way I want to see them, good and amusing and kind. And then I haven't got any self-defense. Even a tiny little bit of liquor does things to my head. There are some people like that. I'd heard of them but I hadn't known I was one of them. But there on the boat to New Orleans I realized I *was* one of them, and it all worked back to where if I'd never had a drink I would never have married Mallory and Arabella would not have died like that. I don't know why I didn't jump off the boat. I quit liquor, but it wasn't easy. That's why I'm so sorry for people like Texas. I know they can't help it." She smiled compassionately. "Well, I guess that's all."

There was a long silence between them. Florinda moved back and leaned against the wall, stretching her arms above her head. She turned to the Brute, smiling at him gratefully, and he saw her rub her eyes and smother a yawn. "Now you're sleepy, aren't you?" he asked.

"Yes. And oh, Brute, I feel better. Thank you."

He got up from the bench. "You go upstairs now and go to bed. I'll slip out and see how things are, then I'll come back and see how you are, then I'll go to sleep here in the kitchen."

"All right. Bless you."

"Will you throw me down some blankets?" he asked.

"Yes, come on."

She went upstairs, and the Brute waited at the foot of the staircase till she came out of her room with the blankets. She tossed them down to him. The Brute went back through the kitchen and outdoors. In the sky was a faint streak of dawn. The town was silent. The Brute came back inside, bolted the door, and tiptoed up the stairs again.

He tapped on Florinda's door, but got no answer, and he opened the door silently. In the faint light he could see that she had gone to sleep. He went in and looked at her. She had pushed her hair up from the back of her head, and it was spread out under her like a fan. She was breathing deeply, and her face had a look of peace. The Brute bent over and touched her hair, and then, very softly, he kissed her on the forehead.

FORTY-EIGHT

GARNET WAITED and waited for John to come back from San Francisco.

At first she was merely puzzled as to why he should stay so long, then she grew apprehensive. She knew he had reached San Francisco safely, because she had heard from him. General Kearny had established a military courier service for the garrisons between San Francisco and San Diego. Since there were no mails, the couriers sometimes carried letters for citizens, and John had taken advantage of this to write to her.

Like all John's letters, this one was brief. He said the voyage north had been a stormy one, and the ship had taken twenty days to go from Santa Barbara to San Francisco. But they had had no real trouble. His boys had taken good care of him and his injuries were greatly improved. He could walk now, and as she could see, he could also write. He was leaving in a few days to see his new property, then he would come south again and they would be married.

But January went by, and February, and March, and John did not arrive.

Garnet was not usually given to inventing fears. But she thought of a hundred things that might have happened to him. Or was it possible that he did not want to come back? When she thought of this Garnet's heart gave an angry flutter. No, that was not possible. Not with John. After all he had said to her, he was not changing now. But even if he were, John would not have run away. If he did not want her he would say so.

But then why didn't he come back?

She would have found it a comfort to talk to the Brute, but he had left Los Angeles shortly after the earthquake. The long voyage to Russia required a lot of preparation.

Florinda reminded Garnet how hard it was to travel in winter. San Francisco was four hundred miles away; the rains up north were heavier than they were here, and the mountains were full of snow. John might have decided to wait for easier weather.

Garnet exclaimed, "That could be true of anybody else I know. But not John. If John wanted to get here, he would get here. You know John."

"Yes," said Florinda. "Yes, I know John."

For a moment Garnet did not answer. It was late at night, and they were both in Florinda's room. Florinda sat on the floor arranging the chest where she kept her jewelry and her best clothes. Garnet watched her as she put her jewel-case into a corner and folded a silk shawl on top of it. Garnet said, "I believe you still don't want me to marry him."

Florinda looked up. "Why no, Garnet, that's not true. I think you ought to marry John because you'll be miserable the rest of your life if you don't."

"But you don't think much of it, do you?"

"Garnet, dearest," Florinda said slowly, "I don't want to meddle with your business. But John and I are so much alike. We've both lived alone in a sense that you never have, and that's a hard habit to break. I just wonder if he can give himself up to anybody."

Garnet thought this over. She asked, "Is that why he's staying away so long? Because he's not used to having anybody worry about him, and he doesn't realize I'm doing it now?"

"Yes, I think it is. John is tending to some business of his own, and he hasn't thought about you pacing the floor in suspense down here. When he does turn up, he's going to say, 'But what were you worried about? I told you I'd be here, and here I am.'"

"Do you think he's always going to be like this?"

"I can't tell," answered Florinda. "But anybody who's so used to going his own way, he'll find it hard to change. And you won't like that. You can give half and a little more, but you won't be a piece of jelly."

"John wouldn't want me," Garnet retorted, "if I were a piece of jelly!"

"No," said Florinda, "he wouldn't want you if you were, but he's liable to punch you in the nose because you're not."

They did not discuss the matter any further. But when Garnet got up to go to her own room, Florinda smiled and said, "Maybe I'm wrong about John, dear. I hope I am."

The next morning they walked over to Mr. Abbott's to get some cloth for spring dresses. It was a dazzling day, and the anise and the little mustard flowers danced against their skirts as they walked. Florinda remarked that on the way back they might pick some leaves for dinner, and Garnet felt a tug of mingled tenderness and wrath, remembering how John had first showed her how to cook these wild plants.

They went into Mr. Abbott's. He greeted them heartily and called for Mr. Collins to come show the ladies those fine calicoes he'd been saving for them. While Mr. Collins unrolled bolts of cloth, Mr. Abbott asked them if they'd heard the news. He was always full of news. Some soldiers had been loafing around here earlier today, and they had told him about poor Colonel Frémont. Too bad. He'd always kind of liked Frémont, Mr. Abbott said. The boys had told him Frémont had been court-martialed. Charges were mutiny and disobedience. Found guilty and dismissed from the service. But President Polk had—er, how did they put it?— he had approved the sentence but remitted the dismissal. Probably the President wanted to show appreciation for Frémont's fine work as an explorer. Still, it was too bad. Mr. Abbott shook his head sadly.

Garnet was sorry for Frémont, but at the moment she could not be much concerned about any problems but her own. She asked

526

Mr. Abbott if there had been any news from San Francisco. Mr. Abbott ran his hand over his bald head and reflected. Not much had come through of late, he murmured, bad time of year, you know. But he did not like admitting there was no news when he was asked for it, so he began talking about San Francisco. Fine town, he said. Regular American town. Growing fast. Men coming in from Oregon and everywhere. They had hotels and newspapers, and they were even building a schoolhouse for the young ones. Plenty of young ones. Four men to every woman in town, so you could be mighty sure there weren't any old maids, and the population would be growing even without any help from Oregon. Mr. Abbott chuckled at his own wit. Garnet laughed too, but this was not the sort of news she was looking for.

Mr. Abbott slapped his fat hands on the counter. "Well bless my soul," he exclaimed cordially. "Come right in, sir!" Garnet and Florinda turned around, and there was the Handsome Brute.

When she saw the Brute Garnet's heart leaped, for he might have news of John. But for the first few minutes she had no chance to ask him. Everybody was greeting him at once, Mr. Abbott and Florinda and Mr. Collins and a native ranchero who had come in to talk about the hide trade. The Handsome Brute said he had ridden in last night to say good-by to his friends in Los Angeles, for he was going north in a few days to take his ship. He had been so covered with mud that he was ashamed to be seen, so he had gone straight to the home of his friend Señor Cereceda, where he often stayed when he was in town. Here he had cleaned up and got a night's sleep, and the first thing this morning he had gone by the saloon. José had told him the ladies could be found at Mr. Abbott's, so here he was. And they both grew more beautiful every day, didn't Mr. Abbott agree with him?

To be sure he did, and Mr. Abbott called for wine and Mr. Collins passed the cups around. As always, Mr. Abbott scolded Florinda for declining, but she laughed and said she was sorry but wine always gave her indigestion. The others drank a toast to the Brute's health and happiness and a good voyage to St. Petersburg. Under cover of the welcoming voices, the Brute spoke to Garnet. "Where is John?" he asked.

Garnet felt as if a lump of dough had taken form in her throat and was dropping slowly down through her windpipe. "I don't know where he is, Brute," she said. "I thought you could tell me."

The Brute shook his head in surprise. "No, I have not seen him.

527

I have been up on my rancho. On the way here I went by Torosa, but they have not heard from him there, so I thought he was in Los Angeles getting married to you. You have had no letter?"

"No, except one I had last January, saying he had reached San Francisco."

The Brute looked perplexed, but he smiled at her encouragingly. "It is hard to travel so far in the rainy season," he said.

Garnet did not answer. She was tired of hearing that. Here it was the first of April, and she could not believe weather alone would hold John away so long. Not if he wanted to get through.

In a quick gesture of sympathy Florinda slipped her hand into Garnet's, and changed the subject by asking the Brute about the preparations he had had to make before taking the ship. The Brute said he had engaged an overseer for his rancho, a smart Yankee who had come down from Oregon. The day of the great Mexican land-grants was over, and the men newly arrived were eager to get work on the ranchos already established. The Brute had brought some papers to Los Angeles to be put in the care of the American alcalde, Mr. Foster. These were orders that his land was to go to John, if he himself had not returned from Russia in ten years from now.

"Ten years!" they all gasped together.

The Brute smiled and shrugged. The Russian Czar did not send a ship to California every year, he reminded them, not by any means. And once a ship started, the voyage took a long time. At least a year, maybe a year and a half.

"How far do you have to go to get from here to St. Petersburg?" asked Florinda.

"Maybe ten thousand miles," said the Brute. "Maybe more, maybe less, I am not sure."

Florinda gave a long wondering whistle. "How do you get there, Brute?" she asked.

"We go around the Horn. Then up through the Atlantic Ocean and into the North Sea and then the Baltic Sea."

"Where are they?"

"Why, I don't know," the Brute said innocently. "That is what the captain told me. I suppose I sailed through those same seas on the way here, but I didn't know the names of them."

"But won't you die of scurvy?" she exclaimed.

"I don't think so. I got here without dying of scurvy."

"But really, Brute, aren't you afraid you—" She stopped.

528

He laughed at her. "That I won't get there? Of course that is possible. But I got here once."

"You're mighty calm about it," she said admiringly.

"I have wanted to do this for a long time. I would not be happy if I did not see Russia again. So what is the use of being frightened?" He smiled around at them all, and spoke to Florinda again. "Now I must go to see Mr. Foster, but if you should invite me to supper I would come."

"You're invited," said Florinda.

The Brute waved his hat to them as he went out. Florinda turned back to the counter. "Now about this calico, Mr. Collins. I like the blue flower print, and the white with the little green sprigs. Have you got some big white buttons?"

Garnet bought some calico too, but her mind was not on it. She was thinking about John. She was also thinking about how much she was going to miss the Brute. She wondered if he would like St. Petersburg.

That night their supper was half gay and half wistful. They were all thinking about how few more times they would be together like this. When Garnet and Florinda finally went upstairs, Florinda said,

"Garnet, I think that big savage is the dearest, kindest man I ever knew. If they aren't good to him in St. Petersburg—" She stopped with a shrug. If they were not good to him in St. Petersburg there was nothing she could do about it.

Isabel had carried up a pile of Garnet's laundry. While Garnet was putting away the clothes she found a petticoat that belonged to Florinda, and took it to Florinda's room. Florinda was sitting on the floor in front of her chest, turning over the ornaments in her jewel-case. As Garnet came in she said,

"I was just about to call you. Look, Garnet, would you like to have this?"

Garnet sat by her on the floor. Florinda was holding out the ring with the great aquamarine.

"Why I couldn't, Florinda!" Garnet exclaimed.

"Oh, take it. I wish you would. It's quite pretty."

"It's much too pretty. And too valuable."

Florinda tilted her shoulder carelessly. "I'm not giving you a fortune, dearie. Aquamarines aren't very precious stones. Besides, I don't value it."

She tossed the ring into Garnet's lap. Garnet picked it up. The candlelight stroked the blue-green surface of the aquamarine and struck glitters from the depths of it. Maybe it was not very valuable, but it was costly enough for her not to want Florinda to toss it into her lap like this. A guilty idea struck her, and she exclaimed, "Florinda, do you think I'm mad because of what you said about John last night? Because I'm not. I hope I'm not silly enough to be mad with you for speaking your opinion when I ask for it."

"Oh, of course, I know that. But I was already planning to give you this ring. I don't want it. I tried to give it to Doña Manuela, you remember, but she said she'd rather have the silver buttons. Don't you like it?"

"It's lovely," said Garnet. "But I still wish you'd keep it."

"I've got no use for it," Florinda insisted.

"You don't have to wear it on your hand," Garnet urged, turning the ring again to watch it catch the light. "You can have it re-set. As a pendant to a necklace, for instance. You've got a lovely throat."

Florinda did not answer. Still turning the stone. Garnet became aware of the silence. She looked up. Florinda sat watching her intently. There was a faint smile of astonishment on her lips. As she saw the smile, Garnet realized what she had said. Her own thoughts on herself and John, she had tripped over the resolution she had made in the hotel room in New Orleans, the resolution that she would never say a word about Florinda's scars. She felt a hot wave of color creep over her cheeks as Florinda said,

"Garnet, do you know, in all the time we've been together, that's the first hint you've ever given that there was anything wrong with my hands?"

Garnet dropped her eyes. "I didn't mean to now," she said faintly.

"Why Garnet, it's all right," Florinda said. "Don't blush like that."

But Garnet could not look up. "Please forgive me," she said. "I won't talk about it again."

"But Garnet, I tell you it's all right! Look at me, dear."

Garnet raised her eyes. Florinda was smiling fondly.

"If you had asked about my hands that day in New Orleans," said Florinda, "I couldn't have answered. It was so new and I was still having a fight to keep going in spite of it. I expected you to ask me when I took off my dress, and I was going to say I had stumbled into the fireplace. But you didn't ask. I knew right then what I thought of you. I knew you were great. I couldn't say it.

I couldn't talk about my hands and what they meant. But I can now."

Garnet shook her head. "You don't have to, Florinda."

"But I want to, Garnet. You see, one night I had a long talk with the Brute. I've felt better ever since. It's sort of like I've got my mind swept clean. And you're my best friend and I don't want any more silence between us."

"You don't have to tell me," Garnet said in a low voice. "I mean—I think I know."

"You know? But how?"

"I guessed it. That night after the earthquake. I think it was your little girl."

Florinda nodded. She did not wince or shiver. She could endure a mention of it now. Garnet went on.

"You couldn't talk about your baby, and you couldn't talk about your hands. You couldn't stand the smell and sound of burning flesh that day at the Archillette. Then that night when your dress caught fire and you screamed, everything seemed to fall into place."

Florinda had listened with a tender surprise. "You've known for three months, and you never said a word."

"No, and I was never going to. I didn't know you felt any easier about it."

"You dear," said Florinda. For a little while neither of them said anything else. Florinda lifted her hands and turned them over, looking at them. "They aren't as bad as they used to be, are they? Not so red. But they'll always be pretty awful."

"You manage very well with them. Your mitts are very becoming."

"Oh, I manage. Sometimes the fellows catch sight of my hands and ask about them. I give all sorts of silly answers." She moved her fingers. "Some things I can't do. I can close my fists, see?—but I can't spread my hands out wide. I couldn't reach an octave on the piano, and I couldn't move my fingers fast enough to play a guitar, and as you've noticed, I can't do fine sewing. But still, I get along."

She was speaking calmly, more calmly than Garnet had thought she would ever speak about her hands. Still looking at them, Florinda said,

"I'm glad you know. I think now I can bear to say sometimes, 'Garnet, help me with this, I'm so clumsy about it.' I couldn't possibly say that before."

She turned to look at Garnet again.

"Well, that's over," she said. "Now I can be honest about this." She reached to pick up the aquamarine ring. "Garnet, I'm never going to wear this, either as a ring or a pendant, and I'll tell you why. This is one of the presents my little girl's father gave me."

"Oh!" Garnet said with understanding. "I don't blame you."

"He gave me a lot of things," Florinda continued. "He was rich and generous. If she hadn't been born, I'd have thought no more of his presents than I think of any of these others. But after she died, whenever I looked at anything he'd given me, I just couldn't wear it. So I sold them in New Orleans. The jeweler wouldn't give me what this was worth, and I thought I'd sell it later when I got a chance. But then I came out here. So if you want this ring, you can have it, and don't get the notion that you're depriving me of anything."

Garnet thought she would take the ring if Florinda insisted, but she did not think she would ever want to wear it either. Florinda looked down at the ring, smiling reminiscently.

"He was a nice fellow," she said. "Terribly amusing. He had a wit like a firecracker. I wonder what became of him." She raised her head with a sudden thought. "Why, Garnet."

"Yes? What?"

"You could find out for me, couldn't you?"

"Find out what became of him? But how could I?"

"You could ask. With all these New Yorkers in town, there might be somebody who knows him. I didn't want to ask about him myself—you see, he was ashamed of the whole business, and besides he was about to be married and I wouldn't want any of these boys to be going back to New York and embarrassing him. But he belonged in your social set. You could have known him. Maybe you did. You could say, 'By the way, there's an old friend of mine—' couldn't you?"

"Why yes, I could," said Garnet. "Strange to think I might have known one of your admirers in those days. Who was he?"

Florinda handed her the ring. "Here, take it. He was highest society from Bleecker Street. His name was Henry Trellen."

Garnet dropped the ring. It fell on the floor with a tinkling clatter. Florinda said,

"Why, you did know him, didn't you?"

"Yes," said Garnet. For a moment she could not say anything else. Henry Trellen, that pompous bore—and Florinda had just said he had a wit like a firecracker. Henry Trellen, walking down Broadway with her when she said she had never been to the Jewel Box, and stiffly answering, "I am sure, Miss Cameron, that the type of entertainment presented at the Jewel Box would neither amuse nor instruct you." Henry Trellen, and Florinda! In a hoarse choked voice she gasped, "Florinda, when did you know Henry Trellen?"

"When I was at the Jewel Box. The last time I saw him was the night before I left New York. He told me—why Garnet!" Florinda broke off with a start.

"Yes, yes," said Garnet. "When was that? Just when did you leave New York?"

Florinda's eyes were wide and amazed. Her voice too had a strange sound. "In August '44. He told me his mother had picked out a girl for him to marry. Garnet, did he ask you to marry him?"

"Yes. In September of that same year. Just before I met Oliver. He told you his mother had picked out a girl?"

"Yes, he said she was a nice girl and maybe she'd be the making of him."

"He was talking about me."

Florinda spoke unevenly, as if she was having to get her thoughts in order before she could put them into words. "I don't know why I'm so surprised. There were mighty few people in New York Mrs. Trellen thought were as good as she was. And among those few there couldn't have been very many marriageable girls. You had a proper family, you had been to a proper school, you were young and pretty and refined—she thought a girl like you could get him away from girls like me."

"And all he was doing was minding his mamma!" said Garnet. "That fool. I might have known it."

"But—Garnet!" Florinda exclaimed.

"What now?"

"Did you know he was the heir to all that money?" asked Florinda. She spoke with the awe she always felt before great riches.

"Why yes, everybody knew that. He was the greatest catch in New York."

"And still you had sense enough to turn him down?"

"It didn't take any sense to turn him down. He bored me stiff."

"He bored you? But Garnet, he wasn't like that! He was one of the most amusing men in town."

"Maybe around you he was. Maybe he felt at ease with you. But with me—with girls like me—" Garnet could not say any more.

She wanted to laugh, and she could not. She also wanted to cry, and she could not; and she did not know why she wanted to do either one. They sat there on the floor, staring at each other.

Thinking back, Garnet could see everything so clearly. Henry could not feel at ease with girls like her because he preferred girls like Florinda. He was always afraid she might somehow suspect his taste, and then maybe his mother would suspect it, that mother who looked like a marble angel. But evidently his mother had found out anyway, because she had made him give up Florinda. She had chosen the flowerlike Miss Garnet Cameron, and Henry had meekly obeyed her. Garnet thought of Henry, having said goodby to Florinda, writing that very formal letter in which he had laid his heart, hand, and fortune at her feet.

Florinda was thinking about him too. She thought about the pitiful sight of Henry when she told him what had happened to that child he had never seen. She remembered how he had said he was no good and never would be, but his mother had picked out a nice girl for him to marry and he supposed he would have to do it. She thought how sorry she had felt for him then. She had also felt sorry for that nice girl, who would be so dazzled by the Trellen fortune that she would not realize she was marrying a man who had no guts.

Florinda still felt sorry for Henry. Poor Henry, who had never deliberately set out to do evil, but who had not had the courage to do either evil or good. Poor Henry, who would go through life spending money he had not earned, and getting very little pleasure from it. Florinda had no objection to men's spending money they had not earned, especially if they spent it on her; but she thought if they were going to have any fun they had better make up their minds what they wanted and use their money to get it. Still, while she had no respect for Henry, she had a great deal of respect for Henry's wealth, and the fact that Garnet had not been dazzled by it made her feel an admiration that for a while left her speechless.

"Garnet," she said at length, "how old were you then? When Henry asked you to marry him?"

"Eighteen. Nearly nineteen. Why?"

"And you were that smart at that age! Garnet, I'd like to tell you something. I'll never speak another word about not being sure you ought to marry John. You're smart enough to do anything you want to."

Garnet smothered a giggle and said, "Thank you." Florinda took up the aquamarine ring.

"Now what shall we do with this?" she asked. "Do you want it?"

"No, I don't want it," Garnet said decidedly.

"Let's keep it then," said Florinda, "and some day we'll give it to somebody we both like."

That seemed like a good arrangement, so Garnet agreed.

She did not have much trouble finding a New Yorker who had heard of Henry Trellen. The Trellen name was so well known that after a day or two of dropping carefully careless questions at the bar she found a young sergeant who could answer them. He had not known Henry Trellen personally—"Gee, Garnet, I never got about in society like that," he said laughing—but he had an uncle who had done some business with the Trellen interests. Garnet asked if Henry still lived in New York. "Oh sure," said the sergeant. "In one of those great big old houses on Bleecker Street." She asked if he was married. No, not when the sergeant left home. She asked what he was doing now. "Why, he's not doing anything that I ever heard of," the sergeant returned. "He doesn't need to."

Garnet told Florinda, who smiled derisively and brushed off her hands as though whisking dust from them. "About what I expected," Florinda said. "Well, that's something else rubbed out of my past."

That evening the Brute came in. He told them this would be his last evening at the bar. Tomorrow morning he was going to set out for San Francisco to board his ship.

Until she thought of his actually being gone, Garnet had not realized how fond she had grown of this big Russian with his great insight and his simple heart. "You can't wait here for John?" she asked wistfully.

The Brute shook his head with regret. "I cannot wait for anything, Garnet. If I do not go now, the ship will sail without me."

When they had closed the saloon the Brute came into the kitchen with them. While Mickey was bringing Garnet and Florinda their late cups of chocolate, the Brute opened a bundle and took out goodby presents. There was a bead necklace for Isabel and some embroidered leather gloves for Silky, both of which Florinda said she would keep till tomorrow, as Isabel had gone home and Silky had departed on some errand of his own. There was a wooden horse on wheels for Stephen, which he also would not see till morning as he was asleep upstairs. There were slippers for Mickey, which he put on at once, and for Garnet and Florinda there were gold pins to fasten their collars. "Not too fancy to wear every day," said the Brute. "I wanted to give you something you could wear often, so you would think of me often." He reached across the table and took a hand of each of them, squeezing their hands in his big fists.

"Garnet! Mickey! Florinda!" came a shout from beyond the door. "Let me in, somebody!"

Garnet had sprung to her feet at the first sound of her name. The gold pin clattered on the table, but she did not hear it. Florinda rescued the pin as she and the Brute too sprang up. They knew the voice as well as Garnet did. John was back from San Francisco.

The Brute put a restraining hand on Florinda's elbow. "Garnet will let him in," he said.

Garnet was already at the door, pushing back the bolts. The door swung inward, and there was John, John bristly with beard and splashed with mud, his boys Pablo and Vicente behind him, and his horses just visible in the dark outside. He swept Garnet into his arms. The Brute and Florinda looked at each other, and Florinda said,

"I guess we should clear out and leave them alone."

"Don't be so foolish," the Brute retorted. "Put on some supper. John will kiss her for two minutes and then he will start saying he has had nothing all day but cold pinole."

"You have such low instincts," said Florinda, "but I guess you're right. Mickey, let's get ready to feed that crew."

John and Garnet were coming toward them. Garnet's face was red where his beard had nearly scratched her skin off, and she was wiping tears from her eyes. John had his arm around her. He was grinning with such frank joy as neither Florinda nor the Brute had ever known him to show before. He shook hands with the Brute and kissed Florinda, and she squealed that kissing him was like kissing a hairbrush. John demanded,

"Can you feed us?"

Florinda glanced at the Brute and they both burst out laughing. The Brute said he would help get the supper ready, and Florinda went to get wine for the boys and a bottle of whiskey for John. "It's on the house," she said as she put the bottle before him. "Not that you deserve it, you pig. Now I'll give a hand with the beans. You and Garnet sit here and look at each other." She went off toward the fireplace, leaving them at the table together.

Garnet was still almost too choked up to speak. Except for gasping, "Oh John, where in the world have you been?"—she had said nothing since she saw him. Now, as she sat with his left arm around her waist while with his right hand he picked up the bottle to pour the whiskey, she thought it would not matter if neither of them said anything for hours. John was back, and she had never seen him look as happy as he did at the sight of her. But they could not be silent for long. John squeezed her waist, saying, "God, I'm glad to see you," and she said, "You're really all right now, aren't you? Your right hand is quite steady on that bottle."

"I've never been so all right in my life," said John. "Or so tired, or so muddy and unshaven, or so damn happy. And I never saw you look so beautiful."

He lifted the yellow pottery cup and drank to her, and she saw in his eyes that she did look beautiful to him, though she knew that right now she would not have looked beautiful to anybody else. She knew how she always was at the end of a day's work, her hair in strings and her dress rumpled and splatterings of liquor making her smell as if somebody had wiped up the bar with her. But it did not matter, not now. She asked him, "John, have I spent my last day at the bar?"

He laughed and squeezed her waist again. "You're mighty right you have. Tomorrow morning I'm going over to see the alcalde and ask him how soon he can marry us. And after that—" he grinned at her— "Garnet, I have such news!"

She had never known John to talk with so much excitement. "It must be good news," she said, "or you wouldn't look like that."

"Oh yes, good. Tremendous. Earth-shaking. I'll tell you all about it. Give me a few minutes to catch my breath." As he poured another drink of whiskey he asked, "Why did Florinda call me a pig and say I didn't deserve this?"

"Because you are a pig and you don't deserve it," Garnet retorted. "John, what made you take so long to come back?"

John's green eyes were sparkling with mischief. "I couldn't get here any sooner. Nothing but you would have brought me here now."

"Why didn't you send me a letter?"

"I've been where I couldn't. That's the great news, Garnet, but it'll take more than a minute to tell it. So let me rest and get

537

something to eat. I've been in the saddle since dawn. When I tell you, you'll forgive me."

"She'd forgive you," said Florinda's voice nearby, "if you told her you had killed six Diggers and eaten them. But that doesn't change the fact that we've all been having the vapors on your account. Speaking of eating, you can start."

She set a dish of beans in front of him. The Brute was calling the boys, who had been taking care of the horses outside. He told them to come in and get supper, and he would finish unloading the packs and would put the horses into the corral. Pablo and Vicente sat down on the floor joyfully and began to gobble. John was so hungry that he was gobbling too, without waiting to talk any more.

But at last both he and the boys had had enough. Pablo and Vicente rolled up in their blankets on the porch. Garnet told Mickey to go to sleep too. John apologized for being so hungry that he had even forgotten to wash his hands before eating, but said he would like to do so now. He and the Brute went out to get some water from the barrel on the back porch, and while John scrubbed, Garnet and Florinda washed the dishes. Florinda said, "It does me good to look at you and John. He's really wild about you, Garnet."

Garnet laughed. John was wild about her, she could see that. Also she was glad to see how much Florinda liked him. Garnet had observed long before now that the measure of Florinda's real liking for any man was the degree of her impoliteness toward him. When Florinda told a man he was a dim-witted damn fool, it was a term of comradeship. Garnet remembered that in all Florinda's association with Bartlett and Penrose, she had never heard her speak to either of them without putting Mr. in front of his name.

At length, when John and the Brute had come in, Florinda set out coffee and wine and whiskey on the table. She said affably,

"Johnny, you can be frank with the Brute and me. I heard you tell Garnet you had some news. If it's just for her, say so and we'll leave."

"No, it's for all of you," said John. "Come and sit down. I've got something to show you."

They gathered at the table. John reached into his pocket and brought out a bundle wrapped in a red handkerchief. He untied the handkerchief and showed them a small leather bag closed with a drawstring, the sort of bag men often used for carrying tobacco.

"Now what," said Florinda, "is so exciting about that?"

With a grin, John handed the little bag to Garnet. As she took it she gave a start. "Why, how heavy it is!" she exclaimed.

John did not enlighten her. He watched her with interest. Garnet squeezed the bag. It yielded to her fingers, for though there was something in it, the contents were not packed solid. The bag felt as if it were loosely filled with sand. But no sand was as heavy as this. She looked up at John questioningly.

John was in a mood to be dramatic. It was not like him. He was standing now, as though he were about to make a speech, and this was not like him either. His stubbled face was aglow with something resembling mischief, but it was not quite mischief. It was triumph and expectancy. He looked, she thought, like an adoring father on Christmas morning, about to show his children some present so wonderful that they could never have dreamed of having it for their very own. Still questioning, she started to undo the leather drawstring of the bag, but John said,

"No, no—let the others handle it first."

Garnet gave the bag to the Brute, who exclaimed, "Why, it *is* heavy!" as though he had not believed it could be as heavy as she had said. He too felt the bag, and looked up at John, puzzled by John's unusual behavior. Florinda said,

"Let me feel it. What's so remarkable about it? Hell for breakfast, it weighs a ton!"

Still grinning, John held out his hand for the bag and she gave it to him. He drew toward him a dish that stood on the table. Loosening the drawstring, he emptied the bag into the dish. Whatever was in the bag, it tumbled into the dish with a clatter like rain on the roof. The three of them bent forward to look at it. But they were still puzzled, for what they saw was something new and baffling.

The stuff lay there in a pile: tiny grains and flakes, and some bigger grains like gravel. The pile was flickering in the lamplight. Some bits of it were dull, as though they were dirty, but most of them were bright enough to catch the light. As John moved his fingers through it, like a child playing with sand on the seashore, the pile rattled on the dish with a faint ringing sound. Garnet put her fingers into it too, and stirred it up; the Brute picked up a few grains and examined them; and Florinda, who had put on her mitts again after washing the dishes, took them off now and rubbed the grains between her fingertips. Suddenly she gave an unbelieving little laugh, and said,

"Why John, if it wasn't so impossible, I'd think—" She stopped, because what she thought was so plainly impossible. The Brute said,

"John, I must be up early tomorrow to get away. Stop being mysterious."

Garnet said, "John, for heaven's sake, what is it?"

John smiled at them all. "It's what Florinda thinks it is," he answered.

"But what do you think, Florinda?" Garnet demanded, and John laughed and said,

"Florinda always did understand my mental processes better than either of you others, because my head is so much like her own. Tell them what it is, Florinda."

Florinda was still pinching the little grains between her fingers. She lifted amazed, awestruck eyes, and said bashfully, as though she was afraid of being laughed at,

"Why—if it wasn't so absolutely idiotic—I'd think these—I'd think they were tiny little specks of gold."

"Gold?" repeated Garnet and the Brute.

"Gold," said John.

FORTY-NINE

WHEN THEY HAD EXCLAIMED, and examined the gold-dust again, and asked him where it came from and what he was going to do with it, they finally settled back and gave John a chance to answer. John sat down too. He looked around at them, and said slowly,

"Listen, all of you. You know me pretty well. Has any of you ever, once, known me to go off into a bluster of excitement over anything? Have you known me to get rattled and tell an exaggerated yarn?"

They shook their heads.

"All right," said John. "Then you'll believe me now. What I'm saying is true, but it's almost past belief. It's so astounding that most people in San Francisco still don't believe it. They are hearing this story and laughing at it. A few men have gone to see for themselves, as I did. But the sane and sensible citizens who are making good livings as carpenters and printers and storekeepers, they are still shaking their heads and saying isn't it ridiculous the nonsense some folks will swallow whole. But I went to see, and I saw it, and I came back here to get Garnet and take her up to see it for herself."

His earnestness was impressive. They were listening, straining forward, hardly moving. John went on.

"In that wild country where I've been, you can see flakes of gold shining in the creek-beds. You can dip up a handful of sand, and there are grains of gold like these, shining all through the sand. There are veins of gold in the rocks. You can chip it out with a knife. There are little lumps of gold lying on the ground among the grass and pebbles. And that country—" he paused an instant, looking around at their wide incredulous eyes, at their lips trembling with unspoken protests— "that country doesn't belong to anybody. The gold has been there since the world was made, and until right now nobody has ever seen it but a few Diggers who didn't know what it was and had no use for it. It's there, waiting for any of us to go there and get it."

He stopped, but nobody said anything. Generally, Garnet and Florinda and the Brute were not silent people. But this tale was almost stunning. They had nothing to say.

So John continued.

"Tomorrow I'm going to see the alcalde to ask him how soon he can marry Garnet and me. Then we'll load our horses and go up there. It won't be easy living this summer, but it won't be too bad—we'll stop on the way to get a tent and supplies, and by the time we get there the rains ought to be over. We'll go right up and start before the word gets around, because it will get around and more and more people will come to believe it. By midsummer the gold-fields will be full. But we'll get there early, and before the rains start again we'll be rich." He reached for Garnet's hand and pressed it happily. "We'll be rich!" he repeated.

And then suddenly, Garnet found that something was happening to her. For the first few minutes she had been like the others, too startled to be aware of anything except a dazed surprise. But now she was beginning to feel again. And what she felt was a lump of cold fear down in the middle of her. She did not know why it was. But until she could understand it better she did not want John to know about it, so when he gave her hand a hard happy pressure, she returned it and asked,

"But how—who—what made them find this place?"

541

"I'll tell you about that too," John said. With his familiar cool chuckle, he added, "It's a story with a moral."

"Yes, tell us!" Florinda said eagerly. It was plain that Florinda was not disturbed by the news. She was hearing John with a joyous wonder, as though the world was good and every line he spoke made it better.

"You know where Sutter's Fort is, Nikolai," said John, and he explained to the girls, "Part of Sutter's land is the old Russian Fort Ross, where Nikolai used to live. Sutter is a Swiss, a naturalized Californian. He has built up a big enterprise—vast land-holdings, ten or twelve thousand head of cattle and even more sheep, thousands of horses and mules and hogs, and a farm where they say he raised about twenty thousand bushels of wheat last year. Besides all this he has a tannery and a flour-mill and the Lord knows what else. He employs a lot of American laborers, and he has several hundred tame Diggers and other Indians who are slaves of his in all but name. There are several smaller ranchos near his, mostly owned by Americans, and a number of stores on his property where the people of that district do their trading.

"Sutter uses a lot of lumber, and he needed a sawmill. The best place thereabouts for a sawmill was on a stream called the American River, in a part of the country that didn't belong to him. But it didn't belong to anybody else either, unless we count the wild Diggers who roam around there sometimes catching grasshoppers for dinner. Sutter sent out some laborers to build the sawmill, eight or ten white men and about a dozen tame Diggers, and they got to work.

"The men had dug a ditch for the tailrace of the sawmill, and had turned a flow of water into the ditch to deepen it."

"What's a tailrace?" asked Garnet.

"The mill was to be operated by water power," John explained. "The main flow of water that turns the wheel of a sawmill is called the millrace. The part of the millrace below the wheel, where the spent water runs off, is called the tailrace."

She nodded. "I see. So the men had dug a ditch for the tailrace, and had turned water into it to make it deeper."

"That's right. They left the water to run all night and work for them while they were asleep. In the morning the boss of the gang, a man named Marshall, walked down there to see how much work the water had done during the night. The sun was coming up, and Marshall saw something shiny under the water at the bottom of the

542

ditch. Maybe he thought one of the workmen had dropped a coin from his pocket, or a watch-fob. Maybe he didn't think anything. But he reached in and picked it up."

"And it was *gold*," said Florinda. She hardly spoke the line; she breathed it out reverently, in a voice that was almost a whisper. Garnet was not so thrilled. She was puzzled at herself. She did not know what she was afraid of. But she did not want John to guess that she was afraid of anything he was saying, so she asked, "When did this happen, John?"

"One day last January. I wish I'd been there."

"I wish I had too," said Florinda. She sighed happily, as though the air were full of perfume. The Brute said,

"You told us the story had a moral, John. What's the moral?"

John answered with amusement. "I couldn't help thinking of it when I saw all that gold lying around. You all know who the first white men were who came into this country. The Spanish conquistadores. They came looking for gold. Oh the dreams they had and the yarns they believed, palaces full of treasure, the seven golden cities of Cíbola, the people who lived in castles with golden towers, all there waiting to be plundered. Those Spanish lords were great gentlemen. They would never have humbled their spirits with work. A gentleman who had worked could never hold up his head again. The only right and proper way for them to get gold was to murder the people who had already worked for it and to steal what they had. They rode up here. But they couldn't find the golden cities. They couldn't find anything to steal. So they went home and said this was a worthless country nobody would want." John laughed again. "And all the time, everything they believed was true. There was gold enough here to fit their most fantastic dreams. Here it was, more gold than those thieving killers had ever seen in one place in their lives, and they never found it. But the first men who ever in the history of the world went up there to do a plain ordinary job of work, they found it."

John laughed, and Florinda laughed merrily, and Garnet laughed too, for this at least was something she could understand. The Brute laughed softly and said,

"Only an American would have thought of that."

Florinda demanded. "But it's true, isn't it? It's true, and it's right."

"Oh yes," said the Brute, "it's true and it's right, just as you said.

543

But—" he spoke gravely. "But I am not sure this gold is altogether good."

"Why not?" Florinda asked quickly.

"Because, if there is so much, gold will be cheap. It is not good to have something you have valued all your life turn out to be cheap. People do not behave well when that happens. They feel like somebody has not been fair to them."

"You're right there," John agreed. "Up near the gold-fields, gold is already getting cheap. It's worth sixteen dollars an ounce in Washington, but at the stores on Sutter's property they'll give you only eight dollars' worth of goods for an ounce of gold-dust. As for what that's going to do to the men, I don't know."

"I don't know either," said the Brute, "but I do not think it will be good. But maybe," he added, "there is not so much as you think."

"Do you want to come and see for yourself?" John asked smiling.

The Brute shook his head. "Oh no. I want to go to St. Petersburg. I do not need a lot of gold. What would I do with it?"

Florinda laughed at him. "Brute," she said, "you great big halfwit, I adore you."

But then she fell silent. John and the Brute and Garnet talked about the gold. John told them more about how the news had come into San Francisco—how Marshall took some gold and showed it to Sutter, and Sutter wanted it kept secret, but when the laborers began chipping flakes of gold out of the rocks with their knives they could not resist telling. They told a man who had been sent up to the sawmill to bring them provisions, and this man gathered a gold-supply of his own. When he got back to Sutter's property he went by a store and bought a drink and offered gold-dust in payment for it. The storekeeper did not know what the stuff was and refused to take it, but this started people talking, and three men employed at Sutter's flour-mill remarked that they felt tired of work and thought they'd go up to the woods and hunt deer. They brought back no venison, but they did bring back bags of gold. And now a good many men were setting out—quietly, almost stealthily, for they did not like to be made fun of. They were buying picks and shovels in San Francisco, besides beef and flour and blankets and other camping supplies. So far, John said, most of these gold-seekers were men with nothing much else to do. Men with good jobs or farms were not leaving them yet. But they would be leaving soon. The gold was there. Still Florinda said nothing, and at length the Brute turned to her, asking,

"What is your trouble, Florinda? You are so quiet."

Florinda roused herself with a start. She poured a cup of coffee, and smiled. "I've got some important thoughts."

"Can you tell us?" asked John.

"Why yes," said Florinda, "I'll tell you." She was serious. "Johnny," she said, "I'm interested in all this. You really believe that before the end of summer this gold-country will be full of men, all digging."

"Yes," said John, "I'm sure of that. What are you thinking?"

"I'm thinking of going north," said Florinda.

Garnet started, though she thought at once that she should not have done so. This tale was so exactly to Florinda's taste. John was not surprised, but he was doubtful.

"It's a hard country, Florinda," he warned her. "And a hard journey to get there."

"Yes, Johnny. But don't be worried. I'm not going to tag along on your honeymoon. It may be a hard journey, but I can get there. And as for its being a hard country, who said I was going to the gold-fields?" She smiled calmly. "There's a village up there. Rustling bustling American town, I hear. San Francisco. It kind of sounds like it was meant for me."

Garnet and the Brute were listening with curiosity. John was interested too. He asked, "What are you going to do there?"

"Well, bright boy, it's now the month of April. It's still liable to rain any day. But this is California. By June there won't be any more rain. That country will be full of men digging for gold. There aren't any houses for them to live in, but they won't need houses. You're going to get a tent for you and Garnet, but that's just because you're civilized people who want some civilized privacy. You won't really need it, because you're going to have perfect weather, and I imagine most of those gold-hunters won't bother with tents. Right?"

John nodded, laughing, and Garnet exclaimed as she had often done before,

"Florinda, what *have* you got in your head now?"

Florinda answered coolly, "What I have got in my head, dearie, is the month of November. Maybe December. It's going to rain, all of a sudden. It's going to drown those golden rocks and turn those inch-deep golden creeks into howling torrents. And those gold-hunters are going to come running to shelter. They'll come to town, where they can find roofs, and fires, and some good warming drinks of whiskey. They'll come laden with little bags of gold like this one. And I think, my pretty chickens—" she nodded sagely—"I think there are other ways of getting gold besides digging for it. I always knew I wasn't going to spend my life in any backwoods village like Los Angeles. I think I see my future before me. I think your friend Florinda is going up north, and she's going to open up a saloon in San Francisco."

Garnet began to laugh. She always did when Florinda decided to be completely frank. Florinda viewed the world with such clearness that to Garnet, with all her own dreams and her hopeful demands on life, it had to bring either tears or laughter. The Brute and John were laughing too. Florinda went on.

"I think what John says about that country is true. It's fabulous, and I wouldn't believe any other man on earth. But if John told me there was a two-headed mermaid on the back porch I'd believe him, because he hasn't got enough imagination to make it up. If John tells me there's gold lying around all over the place, I know it's true. And I think I'll go get it. And so, Johnny, when the rains hit the gold-fields, when you have to come into San Francisco, just ask anybody you meet to direct you to the best saloon in town."

John was listening to her with a teasing admiration. He asked, "Why are you so sure it will be the best saloon in town?"

Florinda had an olympic calm. "Because I'll be running it," she said. With a smile of challenge, she glanced around the room and back at them. "Whenever I run anything, it's the best in town. Look at this place, for instance."

"I thought," John suggested, "that Silky ran this place."

Florinda laughed under her breath. "That's what he thinks too. Quaint, isn't it? One of the secrets of my success in life."

They talked about Florinda's plan. John approved of it. There were several saloons in San Francisco already, but this was no reason why Florinda should not start another one, and he agreed with her that hers would be the best in town. Garnet wished she had Florinda's serene confidence in her own destiny. She wished she could have a little while alone with John, to talk about this gold business and get herself straightened out. But the night was moving toward morning; John had been in the saddle for more than twelve hours that day, and in the middle of a sentence she realized that he had fallen asleep, his head on his arm. Florinda sprang up.

"Oh, the poor fellow! Brute, we're a couple of insects. We haven't let these two darlings have a minute alone and they must have a thousand things to say to each other. Garnet, John can have my room. I'll get my nightie and stay with you for what's left of the night. See if you can get him waked up enough to walk upstairs."

The Brute promised to return in the morning to say a last goodby to them. Florinda walked out with him. Garnet hated to wake up John. He looked so tired that she wished she could leave him as he was to sleep. But now that the fire had died down the room was already chilly, and when the Brute had opened the door she had seen that a fog was rising. By daylight John would be miserably cold.

She spoke to him and shook his shoulder gently. John opened his eyes and saw her. He put his arm around her and drew her close to him and went back to sleep. Garnet let herself rest against him. Being there, like that, with John asleep and his arm around her, gave her such a sense of rightness and peace. It was good to have an occasional minute of peace, because she had had so little of it. And now she was about to go out on a new adventure.

She started up. This was why she had not been glad to hear the news of gold.

Peace—she had dreamed of it so longingly. She had looked forward to it, the remoteness of John's rancho, the great flowering solitudes, the long, long time when she would be safe and quiet because nothing was going to happen to her. But she was not going to have it. John wanted her to start with him on a new trail. It had not entered his head that she might not want to do it.

Florinda came in, and together they woke up John. He was surprised that he had fallen asleep, and laughed and said he was sorry, but even as he said it they could see that he was no more than half awake. Florinda held the door open for him, a candle in her hand so he could see his way upstairs, and John was not too sleepy to kiss Garnet and whisper, "Good night, sweetheart." Oh, he did love her, she thought. Then why couldn't he see that she didn't want to take that new trail?

In her room, she and Florinda moved about softly so as not to wake Stephen. Garnet wondered what she was going to do with a child in that crazy country up there. While they were getting undressed they said nothing, except that Florinda remarked that they had mighty little sleep ahead of them if they were going to be up to say goodby to the Brute in the morning. After they had gone to bed they lay silent for a few minutes, then Florinda raised herself on her elbow.

"Garnet," she said in a low voice, "are you worried about something?"

"How did you know?" Garnet asked.

"You look like it. When I came in after the Brute left, you were staring at John like you didn't know him and wondered what he was doing there. And you were so happy before. Can I help?"

"Maybe you can," Garnet said impulsively. "At least it might be a help if I talked. Aren't you sleepy?"

"Yes, but make it short and I'll listen."

Garnet told her what she had been thinking. "I've been so yearning for peace and rest," she finished. "Now there's no chance for it. Oh Florinda, I do love him so much—but why does he think I want to go up to that wild country?"

Florinda did not answer at once. Garnet turned her head inquiringly. She could hardly see her in the dark, but now she realized that Florinda was laughing.

"What's so funny?" Garnet demanded.

"You," said Florinda. "Garnet, John doesn't just think you want to go up to the gold-fields. He knows you want to go."

"I do not!" Garnet exclaimed.

"Garnet," said Florinda, "I love you, but sometimes you're so ridiculous. Peace and rest! You don't want peace and rest any more than you want to live on milk."

Garnet scowled at the darkness. Florinda didn't know what she was talking about—but still, Garnet had a curious feeling that she had heard this before, somewhere. Florinda sat up in bed. Because of Stephen she kept her voice down, but she spoke with an amused assurance.

"Garnet, you silly woman, haven't you noticed that people in this world get exactly what they look for? Everybody lives by a pattern. The same things happen over and over to the same people. So they must make the patterns they live by. They say they don't want this or that, but they keep on getting it, time after time, while other people get something else. And you don't want a quiet life, my dear."

Oh yes I do, thought Garnet—but what she says does make sense, somehow. Where have I heard this before? Aloud she asked, "How do you know I don't want a quiet life?"

"Because," Florinda said with conviction, "you've turned down every chance you ever had to get one. Why didn't you marry a nice man in New York and live like your friends? I don't mean Henry, but he wasn't the only man in town. What made you pick me up in New Orleans and go to all that risk and trouble about me? It was very sweet of you, but I bet most young ladies with your training wouldn't have done it. What made you come to work at the bar? Sure, I understand, you didn't want me supporting you and I admire you for that, but if you'd really wanted peace and quiet you'd have stayed out of my saloon. Why didn't you go back to live with Charles when he wanted you to? You'd have been safe there. When we were at Doña Manuela's you had several chances to marry men who wanted to settle down and raise a family, and very nice men some of them were, but you turned them down without thinking twice about it. You could have stayed there too, you know, instead of coming back to the bar. If you'd told Doña Manuela you wanted to live with her until you met a man you felt like marrying, she'd have been glad to have you."

"I never thought of that!" Garnet said faintly.

"I never did either till this minute," said Florinda, "but what I mean is that if you'd really believed peace and quiet were the most important things on earth you would have thought of it. Why didn't you marry Captain Brown?" Florinda began to laugh again. "Garnet, you know damn well why you want John. You want him because he's exciting. You want him because you never know what he's going to do tomorrow. You want excitement and you want adventures, and if John told you all about that gold-country and then said you would never get a chance to see it, but would have to stay at home doing embroidery—holy Christmas, what's the matter with you now? Are you crying?"

"No," said Garnet, "I'm laughing."

She held the blanket to her lips to keep her laughter quiet. But she could not help laughing. Florinda was so right, so bluntly and wisely right, and now Garnet remembered where she had heard this before. Her father had said it to her that day in New York when he had told her she could marry Oliver and go to California. He had told her why he was letting her do it. He had reminded her of her people, those adventurers who would not stay at home and behave themselves as the right-thinking folk of their day had thought they should. They had gone smashing into the wilderness, they had had their own way, they had made her and they had made her country.

And now she had their blood and their zest, and she wanted the same thing they had wanted, the danger and challenge of a n world.

And she had thought she wanted to go back to Union Squa She had thought she wanted the monotony of days when she wou always know what was going to happen. What a fool she had bee She did not want peace and she did not want a husband who wou give it to her. She wanted John, because with John the tomorro would always be unknown, and life would always have a beckonir thrill.

Florinda had lain down again. Garnet whispered,

"Florinda, are you asleep?"

"No, but I will be in a minute if you'll keep still."

"I just wanted to tell you, you're quite right. I do want to go t the gold-fields."

"Fine," said Florinda. "I'll see you in San Francisco."

FIFTY

THE SUN WAS BREAKING through the morning fog, and the Brute was ready to go. His train stood before the saloon, pack-horses and saddle-horses, looked after by serving-men whose serapes were like spots of colored light against the fog. At the head of the line was the Brute's big stallion, his saddle and bridle bright with silver. The horses stamped, and knots of townspeople stood gazing at the splendid cavalcade. The men chattered and adjusted the packs and flirted with the girls who had come out to see them off. The men were going to ride with the Brute to San Francisco, and he had told them that when he had taken his ship they could have both horses and saddles, so they would come back as splendidly as they had left.

The saloon was not open for business. Florinda had declared that it was not going to open until the Brute was out of sight. She made so few demands of her own that Silky had thought it wise not to object to this one. Silky himself had come down to accept the gloves the Brute had brought him last night, and after wishing him a prosperous voyage and a safe landing he had gone to Mr. Abbott's to check a shipment of whiskey.

The Brute was in the kitchen, with John and Florinda and Garnet. The girls both wore the gold pins he had given them. They were all hazy-eyed from lack of sleep, but Mickey had appeared without any orders to do so, and had put large pots of coffee before them. "That dear Mickey," Florinda said as they drank the coffee. "I hope he'll come to San Francisco with me."

"Do you think Silky will come with you too?" asked the Brute.

"I rather hope so, though I could do without him easier than without Mickey. But when Silky hears this tale of gold, I can't imagine his not wanting to get some."

But their conversation straggled. There was so little they could say. They loved the Brute and hated to part with him, but they could not find fault with his wish to see his own country and his own people again. They were all wondering if he would ever come back.

John was saying very little. He seldom said much about anything he felt deeply. But he was parting with his best friend, and Garnet and Florinda knew it was not easy.

After a while John and the Brute left the girls to finish their coffee, while they strolled over and stood by the door to the barroom, talking in low voices. They smiled gravely at each other, and the Brute put his hand on John's shoulder and gave it a hard friendly grip. Garnet and Florinda turned their eyes away, and Florinda poured more coffee, saying, "Gee, I'm going to miss that big lug."

In a few minutes the Brute came back to the table. He told them he would have to say goodby now. They sprang up. Garnet felt a lump in her throat and was glad of her sex. If she felt like crying she did not need to be asmamed to do so. She wondered if Florinda was going to shed tears too. But no, Florinda never did shed tears. Right now, she was smiling and saying, as though the Brute were going no farther away than San Diego,

"Well, a good journey, Brute, and good luck."

The Brute thanked her. He turned to Garnet.

"Will you kiss me goodby, Garnet?" he asked.

Garnet threw her arms around his neck. The Brute gave her a squeeze that took her breath away, and she kissed him, and the tears came tumbling down her cheeks. Still holding one arm around her, the Brute took out his handkerchief and wiped her eyes, saying,

"It makes me very happy that you think enough of me to cry at my going. I do not like to leave you. But I am happy to know that you and John are so happy. I will love you and think about you always."

Garnet told him she loved him too, and she begged him to come back if he could. When he released her she put her own handkerchief to her eyes, for her tears were still coming. John took her arm and drew her aside, toward the fireplace.

"Let's wait here," he said in an undertone.

"Aren't we going to walk out with him, to see him off?"

"Yes, but not quite yet. He said he wanted a minute to say something to Florinda."

Garnet glanced over her shoulder. The Brute and Florinda were about to go into the empty barroom. He had opened the door for her, and she was giving him a glance of puzzled questioning. Evidently she had not expected that he would want to say goodby to her in private. Garnet asked,

"What does he want to tell her, John?"

"I've no idea," John returned. He was poking the fire abstractedly. "I'm going to miss him, Garnet," he said.

"Yes, I know you are," she answered gently. "More than any of the rest of us."

"He's the finest man I ever knew," said John. Setting down the poker, he put his arm around her waist and drew her to him. "I'm glad I've got you," he said. "As soon as Nikolai is out of sight, I'll walk over to the alcalde's office."

"Don't you want to go a little way with the Brute?"

John shook his head. "No. Stretching out partings is like stretching out pain. I'd rather say goodby once and have it over with." He took a pencil and a piece of paper from his pocket. "So right now, instead of standing here getting wistful, let's attend to something important. The alcalde will probably want some information about you. Date and place of birth, citizenship of parents, and all that."

"Tenth of January, 1826," said Garnet. "New York city. Both my parents were born in the United States."

"Now about your first marriage. I suppose he'll want that too."

John was writing briskly. How wise he was, Garnet thought. Don't stand around yearning. Get busy. She glanced toward the barroom door again. The door was closed.

Florinda went into the barroom with the Brute. They stood together behind the bar, there where she had stood for so many hundred hours, serving drinks to so many hundred men. The room had a strange look when it was empty like this, with thin lines of sunlight coming in by the cracks between the shutters and the street-noises a muffled hum outside. It was all different. Garnet would never work here with her any more, and she herself would not be here much longer because she was going up to San Francisco.

Everything was changing. Well, there was no use feeling sad about it. Everything was always changing. How dull the world would be if it didn't change. The Brute was going to Russia. He had told her long ago that he was going, but she had never more than half believed him until now. Russia was such a vague, distant place, it was hard to think of anybody she knew as actually being there. He would never come to the bar again, to light up the dingy room with his shining good-will and the flash of his embroidered satins. Of course, if he came back to California, he could always find her in San Francisco. But maybe he would never come back. Oh, hell for breakfast, thought Florinda, now I'm getting sentimental. I've said goodby to lots of people before. Keep looking ahead, that's the only way. It's like I've always said, you never know what's coming next and it might be fun. It usually is. Let's get this over with.

She turned to the Brute with astonishment, for she had just realized that they had been standing here for several minutes and neither of them had said anything. The Brute stood with his elbow on the bar, looking down at her with his familiar smile of gentle affection. Florinda felt herself in danger of getting sentimental again when she thought that this might well be the last time she would ever see it. She noticed, almost with surprise, how big he was, and how very good-looking with his violet eyes and his bright golden hair and the clear-cut strength of his features. Women would go absolutely dizzy about him in St. Petersburg.

It was odd to be alone with him again. Since the night she had told about Arabella, they had had very little chance to talk to each other. The next day she had found a moment to thank him for listening, but he had left town soon afterward, and in these past few days since his return he had had very little leisure. Even last night when she had walked out with him to give Garnet a few minutes with John, he had asked her only if her mind was more at ease now, and she had said yes; and he had picked up her hand and kissed it lightly and said he would see her tomorrow. Now, as she looked up at him and he still said nothing, she began to feel self-conscious. That was rare for her. She gave a puzzled little laugh, and said to him,

"What is it, Brute? What are you thinking?"

"I am thinking about you," the Brute said. "I am thinking how lovely you are, and I am hoping that some day you will be as happy as you deserve to be."

A small frown flickered on Florinda's forehead, but she smoothed it out as she said, "Why, probably I am now. Because I'm not unhappy, you know."

"You are not unhappy," said the Brute, "but you are not as happy as I want you to be. You have had a very deep hurt. I do not mean to talk about that again. But I wanted to tell you, now that you have courage to bear it, and not just hide it and look away from it, the hurt will get easier. It will not ever quite heal. But you can live with it."

"Yes, Brute," she answered in a low voice. "I can live with it. You helped me there."

"I do not think so. I think you have helped yourself. You have a great deal of strength. I shall be happy remembering you. I shall remember you always."

For a moment Florinda said nothing. Then she asked, her voice almost a whisper, "Brute, will I ever see you again?"

"I don't know. It is so far, and I have no idea what it will be like when I get there. So I don't know."

"Then—I think I'll tell you something," said Florinda.

He smiled. "What do you want to tell me?"

"I like you very much," said Florinda.

"Thank you," said the Brute.

"I'm not used to talking like this to men," she went on, "and I feel kind of foolish to be doing it now. But I like you a lot, Brute. People are always saying, 'It's been good to know you.' I've said it myself often, and usually it doesn't mean a thing. But this time I mean it. It's been good to know you."

"Thank you," the Brute said again, earnestly. "That is the greatest compliment I have ever had."

"Oh, shut up. Don't say things like that to me."

"Why not?"

"Because it makes me feel like such a fool to hear it."

"I don't feel like a fool to say it. It's true. I am glad you like me so much, because I like you so much. Do you know why I wanted to see you by yourself?"

Florinda shook her head.

"Because I have brought you a present," said the Brute.

"A present? But you gave me a present last night. This gold pin— see, I'm wearing it now."

"Yes, I see. But this is another present. Here it is."

From the pocket of his jacket he took something wrapped in a blue silk scarf. It was not a large bundle, not nearly as large as his fist, but it was so wrapped in the scarf that she could not tell what it was. She exclaimed, "Why Brute, thank you," and held out her hand for it, but he shook his head.

"Not yet. First I want you to promise me something."

"Why yes, of course. What?"

"You will not open it till I have gone."

"But why, Brute?"

"Because I don't want you to."

"How can I thank you for it when I don't know what it is?"

"You don't have to thank me for it."

"All right, I promise. But I'm trembling with curiosity. When can I look at it?"

"Later this morning. When you are sure I am out of sight."

"Is it a secret? Or can I show it to other people?"

"You can show it to anybody you please. But until after I have gone, you will not pinch it or squeeze it or rattle it or try to find out what it is."

"I promise," said Florinda.

He put the package into her hands. She held it before her, looking down in perplexity at the blue silk wrapping, then she looked up again.

"Well, as I said, I can't thank you properly because I don't know what I'm thanking you for. But I'll tell you this much. Whatever it is, I'll take mighty fine care of it. I'll look at it often, and I'll—oh you big lout, I'll remember you." She looked down at the package again. "And—Brute," she said hesitantly.

"Yes?"

"I'm not asking what this is. But whatever it is—tell me—" She stopped again.

"Tell you what?"

"Why are you giving it to me?"

The Brute smiled tenderly. "Because you are a very good woman," he said.

"Oh Brute, do stop it. You said that once before. It's just as absurd now as it was then."

"It was not absurd then, and it is not absurd now. You are a very good woman. You don't know it, but I do." He smiled at her incredulous face. "You are the only person on earth I would give this to. And now, I must go."

She said reluctantly, "Yes, I suppose you must. Brute, I hope you're going to be very happy there."

"Will you kiss me goodby, Florinda?" he asked.

"Why of course," she said, and took a step toward him, then as he started to put his arms around her she drew back abruptly and stood away from him, with both hands holding the little blue package to her bosom. "Brute—I'd rather not."

"Why not?" he asked in surprise.

"Because—don't laugh at me."

"I've never laughed at you," said the Brute. "I never will. But why won't you kiss me?"

"Because—oh, don't you understand?—I've kissed so many men. You're different. I mean—when I kiss a man, it doesn't mean anything. It means something when I don't. Oh, maybe that doesn't make sense. But you're different, that's all. I'd rather not."

"I understand," said the Brute. He added in a low voice, "Thank you, Florinda. Thank you very, very much." He paused a moment, and when she said nothing else, he held out his hand. "Goodby, Florinda."

She put her hand into his. "Goodby, Brute."

He opened the door and stood aside for her to go through. John and Garnet were waiting in the kitchen.

They all walked out to the front to see the Brute ride off. Florinda and Garnet stood back a little, to let John walk to the Brute's horse with him. Garnet noticed that Florinda was carrying something blue in her hand; it looked like a very large handkerchief crumpled up with something inside it, but Garnet did not think much about it. She was thinking about the Brute and how sorry she was that he was leaving them. John and the Brute paused beside the horse, and Florinda said to Garnet,

"Have you said anything to John about that panic you got into last night?"

"No, and I'm not going to."

"You do want to go up there, don't you?"

"Yes," said Garnet. "If I didn't go, I'd miss it the rest of my life."

The Brute turned and shouted an order to his men. Garnet started. "Oh Florinda, he's leaving!" she exclaimed. Her voice caught, and she felt her eyes stinging again. "How silly of me. He's doing what he wants to do."

"Yes," said Florinda. "He's a smart man."

She spoke tersely, and Garnet gave her a puzzled look. "Aren't you sorry he's going?"

"Not as sorry as you are," Florinda answered. She gave a humorous shrug.

"I thought you liked him very much," Garnet said.

Florinda did not answer at once. She watched the serving-men scramble to mount their horses. As she heard the last orders of departure she turned to Garnet again.

"I like him better than any other man I know, Garnet," she said. "But he got in my way. I know what I want and I like to be let alone to live as I please. And he got in my way. He's the only man I ever met that I couldn't fool at least once in a while. I'll be more comfortable with him in St. Petersburg. That's all."

The Brute called to them and waved his hat. He was grinning cheerfully. They called and waved back. The train started with a clatter of hoofs and a lordly cloud of dust. John came back and stood beside them, tucking Garnet's hand into the bend of his elbow. They said nothing as they watched. The fog was gone now, and the sun was shining. They could see a long way. The Brute's train thudded off through the spaces between the squat little houses. At last all they could see was the dust, and then that drifted down and they could see no more sign of him. The Brute was off to St. Petersburg.

Garnet walked back into the kitchen. Without waiting for any re-livings of their farewell to the Brute, John had gone to see the alcalde. While he and Garnet were talking about it, Florinda had come indoors, and Garnet expected to find her in the kitchen. But she was not there. Nobody was there but Mickey, who was washing cups they had used this morning. From the back porch, Garnet could hear Stephen's voice as he played while Isabel sat on the step sewing. She saw the wooden horse the Brute had left for him, and picked it up.

Mickey had finished drying the cups, so she gave him the horse and told him to take it out and give it to Stephen to play with. Mickey smiled and nodded and went out to the porch.

Garnet stood uncertainly in the middle of the room. Its emptiness gave her a hollow feeling. She wondered where Florinda was.

Probably Florinda had gone upstairs to her room. She had not had much sleep last night, and she would want to get a little rest before she opened the bar. José was not here yet, and Silky had not come in from Mr. Abbott's. Or maybe Florinda, like John, wanted to set briskly about her next task so she would not think about the Brute. Maybe she had gone in to open the bar herself. If Florinda was opening the bar, Garnet thought she would go in and help. She too felt the need of something to do. She crossed the kitchen and opened the door to the barroom.

The room was still dim. The front door was locked and the shutters were closed. Florinda stood at the bar, as if ready to serve drinks, but she was not getting anything in order for the day. She was looking at something she held in her hands, and beside her, crumpled on the bar, was the kerchief of blue silk Garnet had seen her carrying when she went out to wave goodby to the Brute. As Florinda heard the door open she turned sharply.

"Who's that?" she demanded, but seeing Garnet she said in a less indignant voice, "Oh, it's you."

Garnet was startled by the expression of her face. Florinda's eyes had an angry look, and her mouth was angry too, the lower lip pushed forward defiantly. "Am I interrupting you?" Garnet asked in astonishment. "Do you want me to go?"

"No, come in. I need to turn loose on somebody. That damn fool. That idiot savage. Look what he gave me!"

Wonderingly, Garnet took the object Florinda thrust at her. She turned it over with a puzzled attention, for she had never seen anything like it and did not know what it was. Florinda had given her a little case of worn blue velvet, open to show a stiff, formalized picture of people with halos on their heads. The picture was in a gold frame set with pearls. The halos suggested that it was a religious picture of some kind, and apparently the Brute had given it to Florinda, but this was all Garnet could guess about it. She asked, "What is it, Florinda?"

"It's an ikon. His mother's ikon. That addle-pated ass! He gave me his mother's ikon!"

"What is an ikon?" Garnet asked in bewilderment.

"It's a picture from the Russian church. But that's not the point. He knows I don't know anything about churches. The point is, this belonged to his mother. He thinks more of his ikon than he does of his own precious neck. He wouldn't have sold this if he was starving. So why in hell's blazes did he have to give it to me?"

Garnet did not answer. There was no answer she knew how to give. They had been through a lot together, but this was the first time she had ever seen Florinda lose her temper.

But Florinda had lost her temper now. "Is he really gone?" she was demanding. "You're sure he's gone?"

"Yes, yes," Garnet said breathlessly. "He's gone."

"Good for him that he is. I'd like to throw this in his silly face. That bumbling fool. Is anybody in the kitchen?"

"No."

"Good. I need more room to get mad in. That rattlebrain. Giving me his mother's ikon!"

Florinda caught up the blue scarf and strode through the doorway. Garnet followed her. The kitchen did not offer much room to get mad in, for the table took up most of the floor-space, but Florinda was wrathfully pacing about what space there was, the blue scarf dangling from her arm and the ikon in her hand.

"That booby," she said. "That stupid pig. What the hell am I going to do with this? His mother's ikon! I'd like to crack his thick skull. Him going off to Russia so I can't tell him what I think of him. Wheedling me into promising I'd take care of it. I'd like to wring his neck. That buzzard. Damn his—"

Her voice broke. To Garnet's utter amazement, a rush of tears came to Florinda's eyes and rolled down her cheeks. She sobbed into the blue scarf. "That big lumbering ox," she choked. "That pinhead. Doing a crazy act like this."

Garnet was not at all sure what this was about. But she went to Florinda and put an arm around her so Florinda could cry on her shoulder. Florinda jerked back indignantly.

"Don't you get sentimental with me. I never felt like such a fool in my life. He wanted to make me feel like this. He wanted to make me cry. That's why he gave it to me. So I'd feel like a fool and act like one. That half-witted baboon. I wish I could knock his face in." But in spite of her rage the tears kept pouring down her cheeks. She wiped them off with the blue scarf.

Garnet said wonderingly, "I never saw you cry before."

"No, and you never will again. He told me once long ago I ought to cry sometimes. Now he left me this to make me do it. That big luggerhead. I'd like to kick him." She scrubbed her eyes with the scarf, and blew her nose on it. "Garnet," she demanded shortly, "how far is it to St. Petersburg?"

"I don't know. He guessed about ten thousand miles, remember?"

559

"Ten thousand miles. I wish it was ten million. I hope he drowns. I hope he gets caught by pirates and has to walk the plank. I hope he falls overboard and the whales eat him. I hope he gets scurvy and his teeth fall out. That pig. That crocodile. That God-damned fool. He told me he gave me this because I was a good woman. Hell for breakfast. Why does he talk such flapdoodle? If I've been good since I've been in Los Angeles it's merely because there's not a man here I'd look at twice and he knows it as well as I do. Just let this benighted country blossom out with a middling-pleasant gent who's really rich, and you'll see how good I'll be." She scrubbed her eyes again. "If there's a man like that around I'll be so good I'll have him spinning in his tracks. I've done it often enough before and I can do it again. That Russian imbecile. Giving me his mother's ikon. I hope he gets the smallpox."

They heard a sound of footsteps outside, and Florinda started violently. "My God, is that Silky coming in? Don't let him see me with my eyes red like this! Come upstairs."

She dashed out. Garnet heard her running up the rickety staircase. Silky came in. He said to Garnet that he had seen the Brute's train riding out of town, so now he was going to open up. José would be here any minute. "Where's Florinda?" he asked.

"She went to her room."

"Run up and tell her—" Silky began, and caught himself. He had just remembered that Garnet was no longer working for him. Garnet was about to be married to John, and while Silky had not yet heard anything about John's prospect of gathering bagfuls of gold up north, still Silky knew John was a prosperous ranchero. He smiled and bowed. "If it is quite convenient, Mrs. Hale, will you have the kindness to tell Florinda we're opening the bar?"

"Yes, I'll tell her," said Garnet. But she was sure Florinda was in no mood to come down yet, so she added, "I think Florinda would like to change her dress before she comes down. We threw on our clothes in such a hurry this morning."

"Indeed yes, certainly. There is no hurry, none at all. And Mrs. Hale. May I take this opportunity of wishing you all joy in your approaching marriage?"

"Thank you, Silky," said Garnet. Before he had a chance to get lost in a wilderness of words, she hurried toward the stairs and ran up. Florinda's door was closed. Garnet knocked.

"Is that Garnet?" Florinda called. "Come in."

Garnet went in. Florinda was sitting on the bed, gazing down at the ikon in her hand. Her eyes were still red, but she was not crying any more.

"Silky told me to tell you he's opening the bar," said Garnet.

Florinda did not raise her eyes. "Silky can go sit on a tack," she said. "I'm thinking. Garnet."

"Yes, dear."

"You won't tell anybody I stood up there bawling like a kid with the colic, will you?"

"You know I won't."

"And don't tell anybody the Brute left me this thing. I'd feel too silly to show my face in public again."

"I won't tell."

"That jingle-brained yokel," said Florinda. She was still looking down at the ikon. "That goose with a lump of dough in his head. And Garnet."

"Yes, Florinda," said Garnet. She went and sat by Florinda on the bed.

"You know I don't mean any of those things I said, don't you? About hoping he'd drown or get eaten by whales."

"Yes, dear, I know it."

"I don't hope any such thing. That simpleton. I could choke him. I hope he gets to Russia with no trouble at all and I hope he finds a woman who's good enough for him. No, he can't do that, there's not a woman on earth good enough for him. But I hope he finds one who'll spend her whole life trying to be. That donkey. Giving me his mother's ikon and making me cry. I could smash his nose."

Garnet did not answer. She did not think Florinda wanted her to. Florinda was looking so intently at the ikon that she seemed only half aware of having anybody there to hear what she was saying. But she had not quite forgotten Garnet's presence, for after a moment she put her hand over Garnet's and held it, as though glad to have her. There was a brief silence. Then suddenly, as though struck by a surprising idea, Florinda sat up straight.

"Garnet, run along, will you?"

"Yes, of course I will," said Garnet. She stood up.

Florinda caught her hand again and pressed it, looking up to smile at her. "You were a dear to stand by me just now. But I'd like to be by myself a minute."

Garnet bent and dropped a kiss on her head. She went out.

At the sound of the door closing, Florinda started. She waited a moment, listening, until she heard Garnet go into her own room and shut that door too. Florinda looked around, with a furtive attention, as though afraid there might be somebody else observing her. Laying the ikon beside her on the bed, she got up and went to the door. The door had a bolt, but she did not often use it. She had put it there in case some drunken fool got up here from the rooms downstairs, but the doors downstairs were so carefully locked that this had never happened. Nobody slept at this side of the loft but herself and Garnet, and she had never till now had any reason to want to lock Garnet out. But now she pushed at the bolt. It was stiff from disuse. Florinda struggled with it till she had got it over.

She waited a moment, making sure Garnet had not heard her moving the bolt and was not coming back to ask if something was the matter. She wanted to be sure she was alone.

Florinda had felt a mystifying impulse; she did not know what to make of it, but she knew she did not want to be caught in the middle of any such embarrassing performance. She looked around again. There was certainly nobody else in the room, but the window-shutters were open and she hurried to close them. It was not likely that anybody could see up here from the street, and the nearby houses had only one floor, but still she felt more private with the shutters closed.

She took care that they were tight, and dropped the latch across them. Standing in the middle of the floor, she tried to think what she ought to do now.

Florinda had only a sketchy notion of how to go about saying a prayer. Feeling very awkward, she went over and knelt by the bed. She folded her hands one on top of the other. Since she did not know what she was supposed to say, she said what she was thinking.

"Dear God,

I know I am going about this badly, but I apologize, and I hope You understand that I'm doing the best I can. Please don't let anything happen to him. Please let him get there safe and sound. And when he gets there please let everybody be nice to him and let him be happy.

"Now as to whether or not I want him to come back, I honestly don't know. He said even if he did come back it might not be for ten years and in ten years I'll be thirty-six years old and only You know what I'll look like by that time. Anyway, even if I'm still beautiful ten years from now, I just don't know if I want him back or not. So I guess I'll leave that up to You. But whatever he does, please let him be happy doing it. Please let him be happy always, as long as he lives.

"Yours respectfully, Florinda Grove.

"Amen."

Garnet sat on the wall-bench in her room, looking out at the ox-carts and the people idling in the sun and the water-sellers strolling about with yokes over their shoulders. Above the voices and the creaks of the carts she heard what she could always hear through any other kind of noise, Stephen babbling as he played on the back porch.

She looked out at Los Angeles. What an ugly, rackety, smelly town it was. This was the end of the Jubilee Trail. You left the States, wherever you were, you came to Independence and you took the trail to Santa Fe. You left Santa Fe, and you took the Jubilee Trail to Los Angeles. You left Los Angeles, and you took another trail to—where? She did not know. The end of every trail was the start of another; you never knew where you were going, but you had to go all the same. All you did know was that you were not a little girl any more. You would never again take a new trail with that same blissful confidence that the going would be easy and your happiness would be safe.

Oh, how hard it is, she thought, that we must give that up! That fair blundering business of being young, that gay incompetent way of living before we know how to live, that plunging into the trail full of joy because we don't know enough to be scared. Just take a look at Los Angeles, this huddle of brown boxes under this ma-jestic sweep of mountains—take a look at it, Garnet, and finally own up to yourself that you love it. You love it because you lived so fully and richly here. Yes you did, even when you thought you hated it and were trying so hard to get away. We always hate the school-room where we learn hard lessons. But then we love it, because that's the school that taught us all we know, and gave us all the strength we have. I wasn't fit for the Jubilee Trail when I took it. I wonder if I'm any more fit for the new one. I don't know.

All I know is that I am older, so much older, than I was when I took the trail before. Older by so much more than time. Older by three thousand miles and so many, many thousand hours of being scared and lonesome. I'm not lonesome any more. I've got John. But I'm still scared. That's because I've learned so much. When you are young, you are not scared; when you are older, you are scared and you know you'll be scared as long as you live.

Among the people and the ox-carts, she saw John. He was coming back from the alcalde's office, to tell her when they could be married. Garnet raised herself eagerly and knelt on the wall-bench. Leaning out between the shutters, she called to him.

"John!" she cried. "John!"

He heard her, and paused. For a moment he looked around, not sure where her voice was coming from. She called again.

"John!"

He looked up then, and saw her in the window. A light broke over his face. He waved at her, and she waved back. "Tomorrow!" he called. He beckoned her to come down.

She nodded, and hurried away from the window. As she ran down the stairs to meet him she felt little tingles of happiness running all over her skin. Tomorrow she would be married, and then she would start the new trail to the gold-fields. She wondered what was waiting for her there.